To:
Oins + Hazel
Thank you for your frien

Ken Sinclair.

THE NOWHERE MEN 2

Ken Sinclair

MINERVA PRESS

LONDON

MIAMI   RIO DE JANEIRO   DELHI

THE NOWHERE MEN 2
Copyright © Ken Sinclair 2001

ISBN 0 75411 670 0

First Published 2001 by
MINERVA PRESS
315–317 Regent Street
London W1B 2HS

Printed in Great Britain for Minerva Press

THE NOWHERE MEN 2

By the Same Author

The Nowhere Men
ISBN 1 85756 268 2

Preface

The Nowhere Men 2 is a sequel. As *The Nowhere Men* was a story with a message, warning of corruption and the need for vigilance on the part of one particular police force, the sequel progresses that vigilance and expands its theme into a European possibility with a dash of American help.

The world is ever decreasing in size; with electronic communications enabling monetary transfers worldwide almost instantly, with the availability of weaponry of all descriptions readily available to the corrupt, and with drugs, which are used as currency in the hands of organisations worldwide, the world needs to be vigilant.

The Nowhere Men 2 is a further warning of a possible scenario which could be used by the corrupt in the suppression of freedom of the individual.

Chapter One

The startled expression on Gregor Tashimov's face still showed; the face of Nadine Dashnikov must have still been burnt into his mind as his dead body was lifted onto the stretcher to make its last journey. The normal hard, stern face had been surprised at last. The drama which had taken place over the past hour was over, the curtain was falling and things would soon return to normal – at least, those were the optimistic thoughts of Klaus Mennen and Deiter as they held hands, shoulders pressed together, both staring empty-eyed at the end of the play which had taken place in their apartment. Their fear for each other – that the dead man had forced them to live through the stealth and vengefulness of Nadine begging Tashimov not to die until she had told him her story, their witnessing the subsequent cold-blooded murder of Nadine and then the message the man with the ringed hand had left with them to pass on to the whole world, that The Nowhere Men will always be there fighting for total control of all corruption throughout the world – was obvious. A message which both Klaus and Deiter had just finished relaying to the police as they had been chillingly instructed to do.

Klaus and Deiter's eyes moved in sequence to follow Tashimov's body as it was lifted from the floor and passed them on the stretcher, leaving their apartment for the morgue. The silence surrounding them was a relief. Or was it? The emptiness of their apartment after all that had happened emphasised the fear which had passed between them when their lives had been under threat – a fear they both hoped they would never experience again and that along with the evil which had encroached upon their lives, it had been contained forever.

The tightening of Klaus's fingers around Deiter's had brought back a spark of life into Deiter's eyes. A new life with no more lies, fear or distrust between them. Deiter slowly allowed the warmth inside him to spread over his handsome face as his body moved closer to *his* Klaus. The embrace they now enjoyed together was their first as true lovers. True love which had now fully grown between them from a very sordid beginning – a beginning which Dieter had been coerced into by his pimp. Forced by the hidden threats engineered by Tashimov to ensure that Dieter, a vain, conceited queer, had been forced into easy submission by the promise of money. The sort of money which would allow him to strut around, ever the peacock, in front of his less handsome friends. But now, as his self-loathing welled up and spilled over, bringing tears back into his eyes once again, he realised the man standing beside him was the only one he could ever love, and be loved by, despite the intense feelings of revulsion Dieter had previously had for Klaus with his spotty skin, bad breath and his being overweight. Klaus had forgiven Dieter his betrayal and proved his love for him by standing up to Tashimov, offering his own life to save Dieter's – Dieter, the conceited 'I'm better than anyone else' strutting peacock!

They turned to look out onto the dark, empty street below. The flare of a lighted match and a cigarette lit, the only thing to be seen. Deiter whispered playfully in Klaus's ear, 'Lovers in a doorway stopping for a smoke!' Klaus pulled Deiter tightly to him, happiness glowing on his face. Klaus, who had worshipped Deiter from a distance for such a long while, knew now he had conquered and that both their lives were full to overflowing. The deceit and betrayal had been a hurdle in their past but it was in their past, and now there was only the future.

The glow of the lighted match revealed the large, red-stoned ring on the hand in the doorway. The drawing of breath through the cigarette held in the steady hand, increased the intensity of red from the ring's stone. The suddenness of the light (from the match) being blown out, sent a slight shudder of fear through their entwined bodies. Klaus raised his arm and drew the curtain across the window, shutting out all the bad things in the world.

The train passed through the underlit station, eerie shadows were made as it continued its journey through sudden patches of light and dark along the length of the platform. The train carried on its rhythmic dance as it swayed and clattered over junctions in the track. The black overcoated man sitting motionless in the window seat was difficult for anyone entering the underlit carriage to see. The spill-light which entered from the station lights passed across his body only, missing the face and head which was pressed back into the seat's headrest. The silence of the scene was intense. So intense that even the normal rattle of the rickety old train was unheard. The train passed out of the station into the naked, black countryside. A virgin bareness stretching endlessly away, relinquishing not one single light from anything that might be hidden in the vast depths of Mother Russia.

There was the soft, brush-like sound as a packet of cigarettes was removed from a pocket, the muffled click as the packet was opened, then the delay before the cigarette was taken out followed by the stopping of time whilst the final decision to light up was taken. The flare from the match as the sulphur spluttered, then burst into flame, in conjunction with the cupped hands which instinctively came up to protect the now steady flame, revealed the ringed hand as it proceeded upwards to the waiting cigarette, where the draw of the flame exposed a cleft chin. A puff from the full lips blew the light away, leaving the carriage darkened again as the face of the man with the ringed hand stared out into the corridor.

Fear passed through his eyes as the military officer stopped at the carriage door. A quickening heartbeat seized the seated man at the thought of being caught by anyone before he was able to get back to his own people and explain the reason for the disaster which Tashimov had caused the Organisatiya. Explain also how he, Marshall Polenkovich of the Russian Army, will exonerate himself with his new plan, how he will fulfil the goal of world domination as set out by his masters long ago. The quickening heartbeat rose to fill his throat. The fear of capture would force him to kill anyone who dared to stand in his way and delay him even more. His hand went slowly to his coat pocket and gripped the flick knife. The fear of killing another man ran through his mind. Not fear of the actual killing, but the delay the killing would cause him in ensuring his tracks were covered. A delay he could ill afford in his haste to reach his masters on the Central Committee.

The officer standing in the doorway was undecided whether to enter the carriage or not, but then a voice along the corridor called out and finally he moved away from the doorway to join his friend, allowing the anxious Marshall to relax once more – until the next time he came across an unknown uniformed soldier.

The strain of over two weeks on the run showed heavily in his face as he rested his head back into the headrest. His lips moved in silent prayer. The two thousand mile journey from Hamburg to Krivog Rog in the Ukraine via Budapest had been long and tedious, giving him plenty of time to think about Tashimov's ruined plan. A plan which, he felt, had been brave and adventurous with a high probability of success. A plan which Tashimov had masterminded and sold to the Organisatiya with the support of General Nabialev, and which could have brought together the purchasing power of the Arab and Far Eastern world for the surplus arms that abounded all over Russia since Glasnost, along with opening up a dollar cash surplus by introducing a constant supply of easily acquired drugs into the American Mafia's network on a long-term basis. An exciting plan, but one which unfortunately had been allowed to move away into the private enterprise sector, as opposed to keeping it within the old ways, with everything working through the military regime of the old Russia. Marshall Polenkovich wanted those old days back. He wanted military control to return to the 'select few'. As he replayed his intentions in his mind, he relaxed his body and allowed his eyes to close for the first time in days.

Lanov and Mogatin only escaped the chaos of the dockyard through a skilful game of hide and seek throughout the chase. Carefully, they had planned for the unthinkable, but remembering what Tashimov had said – that failure would bring his personal retribution on each and everyone who failed him – they felt that to protect themselves with an escape route to Hamburg's docks and from there into obscurity, would be prudent. Between them they had decided they would separate and meet up again at a designated point each day at a prearranged time, until they could eventually meet over the Portuguese border in the relative safety of the Douro mountains. Their thinking for the elaborate scheme was to lay down a complicated network of false trails to make Tashimov's job in pursuit as difficult as possible. Having worked with Tashimov on numerous occasions in the past, they were fully aware how ruthless he was and that his threats were certainly not idle ones. Tashimov, they both knew, although he played his game as a loner, would certainly have kept in touch with every criminal he knew and his ruthless reputation would soon bring out an underworld of international criminals in support of his quest for information about both Lanov's and Mogatin's movements. Tashimov's vengeance took a long time to satisfy and the only release for the victim was death. Lanov and Mogatin feared no man, but Tashimov was the devil.

The hazardous journey throughout Europe, avoiding a sophisticated network of cooperating police forces from country to country, the constant worry and anxiety of being caught by the police or worse still, by Tashimov – after three weeks, the exhaustion showed in their faces. Ironically, this would have been considerably lessened had they known of Tashimov's death!

Joachim Baldin sat dejected alongside the unhooked telephone in his home, staring into space. The success and the total respect of his Organisatiya brethren had been all he really wanted, but once again because of one man's conceit, he was back at the bottom of the heap.

'Tashimov!' That one single word carried all the hate he felt. The deep loathing of a man driven by the want of power. Power which in his wisdom, Joachim Baldin knew, could and often did, bring sudden death to those who obtained it. All he had wanted was respect and a good living whilst he earned it. But now he was defeated and hounded by every one of his boys to whom he had promised so much on behalf of Tashimov. He had been hounded day and night on the telephone and at his house if he dared show his face or turn on a light. He was in purgatory and it should have been heaven, but for one stupid man's ambitions! He allowed himself to wallow in his self-pity, murmuring to himself, 'None of my beautiful boys will ever trust me again, even if I could regain control of such a handsome bunch!' The thought of his little empire in ruins brought the anger welling up from deep inside him. He could not stop himself from screaming, 'You bastard, Tashimov!' as he sank back in his chair, mentally and physically worn and exhausted. Life, which should have been so good for him, with the promise of selling his 'boys' into what would have been an exclusive, continuous international sex party, had crumbled. Now his life was in danger and the little empire of sex and pornography he had so diligently masterminded in Hamburg had ceased to exist, all because of that one man, Tashimov, who bore all of Baldin's hate.

He lumbered to his feet, tiredly stretching his arms above his head and shaking the life back into his body, then gazed into the darkened mirror. Moving closer to see his drawn features, he swore an oath to himself, 'Tashimov, when the Organisatiya come to Hamburg for the story I, Joachim Baldin, will betray you. I will lie to save my own soul!' The venom in his voice frightened him. A look of fear registered over his mirrored reflection, just before he furtively looked around his dark room, staring into the darkest corners to make certain that no one was there to overhear him swear this oath. He might still think and speak with bravado, but what if Tashimov had arranged for his friends to close the book that he could not close himself? 'Oh, Joachim Baldin, why did you get so easily led, you stupid fool?' the selfish anguish in his soul screamed out through his clenched teeth.

Chapter Two

The light, airy apartment of Officer Katerina Mayer, newly appointed to Ulbrecht's group of detectives, was alive with music and her lilting voice emanated from the bathroom. With a dancing flurry, she entered the lounge-cum-dining room, dressed somewhat out of character. The pressed-to-perfection uniform had gone now that she was one of Ulbrecht's team and when appointed to an investigation, she was allowed to wear civilian clothes which was, on this occasion, jeans and a roll-neck jumper with a chiffon scarf tied loosely around her neck. Katerina Mayer was supremely happy with her new status in life and with the kindness and help that the whole of Ulbrecht's team had shown her since her appointment.

When Commander Roth had finished debriefing her, unbeknownst to her, Chief Inspector Ernst Ulbrecht, her boss and mentor on the Nowhere Men case, had put in a request for her permanent transfer to his team, emphasising that her fluency in Russian, and the contacts she had made during her time in the Records Department would be invaluable, considering the number of Russians flooding into Europe from all directions. Commander Roth had initially refused the request but Ulbrecht's persistence and that of some of the other members of Ulbrecht's team had eventually persuaded him to capitulate to their requests.

Today, Mayer was on her first case with Inspector Willi Koslowski, a senior member of Ulbrecht's permanent staff and one of the first people she met on that fateful day when she had been first introduced to Chief Inspector Ulbrecht and the excitement of real-life crime investigation. Glancing in the mirror, she flicked her now slightly shorter hairstyle, paused for a moment, and deciding she was happy with what she saw, playfully pulled a funny face at her own reflection. Grabbing her reefer jacket, throwing it over her shoulder and holding it by the loop, she strode purposefully out of the apartment, confident and ready for any event that she might encounter.

The wind and rain lashed across the bleak cemetery. There were faint murmurings of the preacher's voice who was standing with the unpolished box and the gravedigger beside him, trying to make some sort of a service for this departing soul being committed to a pauper's grave. A man he had never known, but whom the police had established to have been a Russian. A man who, as far as the preacher could tell, had no relatives or friends and the only people to see him into his final resting place would be himself and the bent old gravedigger.

The words drifted slowly on: '…this man, Gregor Tashimov. Holy Father, we know him to be a criminal and that he met an untimely, violent death, but we pray you will accept him into your house and give him the same chance as you would give to all of us. May he be accepted into your house…' The wind rose at this point and whatever the preacher was about to say was inaudible to Ernst Ulbrecht's ears.

Standing there alone, hidden away from the graveside, Ulbrecht had been waiting for hours to make certain of being at the cemetery before time, as these town council burials often had no schedule. Ulbrecht had felt it important to attend, in case anyone interesting should show up at Tashimov's burial. He wanted to make absolutely sure that every last criminal who had caused so much havoc in his beloved Hamburg was accounted for, by double-checking at the last stage. Ernst had spoken with the American law agencies; the Russian and Arab legal organisations were convinced that everyone involved with the 'Nowhere Men' case was now known to Ulbrecht and his team. Most were being held for further investigation and those not being held by any police force were still being hunted down.

The cold was creeping into every bone and muscle, but he did not dare move for fear of giving himself away. He was worried he would not be able to endure another possible thirty minutes of silently waiting, but he was determined to stay put until the coffin was actually interred. It would help Ernst to clear his mind if no one turned up to say goodbye to Tashimov and that in all probability, all the scum had fled his town.

A smile of relief crossed his face as he picked up on the words 'Dust to dust…' faintly drifting towards him on the wind. Only a little while longer to wait, he thought. The same wind which had brought the words sailing to his ears forced a slight shudder through his cold, tired body. Was it only the cold that forced this involuntary movement, or was it one of Ernst's famous hunches that caused it? Was it fear that what had just been accepted by the Hamburgian Burgermeisters as a victory against international crime, was in fact a prelude to a more far-reaching Russian Organisatiya and, the already notorious, Mafiosa? The anguish racing around in Ernst's brain forced his eyelids shut, as if he was praying on behalf of the whole world that his dreadful fears would never be allowed to be inflicted on what he still believed could be a fine, clean, healthy and peaceful world.

Jocelyn Latimer's office was quietly efficient. His presence in it as his tall, broad-shouldered figure stood staring out of the window through the Venetian blinds, showed that it fitted his personality. As he turned to take his seat behind his tidy desk, a little agitation showed in his face and he swiftly slapped down the piece of paper he had been holding in his hand.

For years he had been interested – in an unofficial way – in all things European. So much so, that since his son and daughter had grown up and left the family nest, he had taken five or six European newspapers each Sunday, to fill up his time no longer spent ten-pin bowling or attending some prom concert. The fun things in life had gone. Liz, his wife, was now the problem with her nagging about his leaving all those papers everywhere and the collection of newspaper cuttings in his den especially, which he insisted should never be moved. All the years of living together had brought a roundness to them both however, and cross words were soon forgotten. As he sat down at his desk, he looked at the picture of his wife and children propped up there. His eyes softened as he whispered, 'I love you,' to the picture.

Relaxing in his high-backed chair, he closed his eyes and let the noises around him, along with those from outside his own little box, wash into his subconscious. The click of the second hand on his government-issue wall clock moved, pushing time forward; the muffled telephones ringing distantly in other people's offices; the occasional swish as someone passed through the airlocked doors, either allowing them passage from their own section through to another (providing their plastic card carried the right information), or allowing them back into their own little boxes after their brief escape. Jocelyn allowed a wry smile to run over his face as he remembered his early days at Langley, when the majority of staff stationed at HQ knew each other, allowing the exchange of ideas and information to be discussed freely amongst themselves, but now security itself had security forced upon it. Over the years, Jocelyn had wondered and often poked fun about the point that there they were, trying to protect the nation's security with the sectioning off of the HQ's offices by an ever-increasing number of airlocks!

As he pulled himself back from his brief lapse into reverie, he spoke to the family photograph on his desk, 'Why do we have so much bull? It worked so much better when we were "hands on" investigators. The left hand always seemed to know what the right hand was doing in those days!'

With a sigh, his hand moved forward, his fingers flicking the corner of the memo in front of him as he slowly pulled himself forward and lifted it into a reading position.

MEMO

To: SI Jocelyn Latimer, CIA Langley
From: L H Longworth, Chief of Station

Hamburg police have requested background reasons for Nadine Dashnikov (deceased) to have been operational in Hamburg without sanction from either the police or government departments. The request is signed by Commander Roth. He also asks that all communication on this matter be forwarded to a Chief Inspector Ulbrecht, who is in charge of the investigation into some drugs case during which the body of this alleged CIA operative was found.

Comment: My view is that the case is probably too big for them to handle by themselves. Give them all the help you can, but don't spend too long on it.

LH Longworth,
Chief of Station

Having now read the memo for the fourth time, Latimer pushed it away and relaxed back in his chair. A few seconds passed as he wrangled with his options. Should he go direct to this guy Ulbrecht, or go through channels via overseas operations here at Langley?

Decision made, he reached out and grabbed the telephone, punching in three numbers while the phone was still travelling towards his ear. One ring, two rings, the third was just about to start when the voice of his long-suffering secretary, Louise Norris, answered it.

'Yes, Joc?' she asked.

'Can you come in here, Louise; I've got some things for you to do.'

'Sure, give me a second, and I'll be right in.'

Louise lowered the phone and just heard Jocelyn's courteous, 'Thank you,' as the receiver met the cradle. Louise had got used to calling him 'Joc' now. When she had asked him all those years ago when he joined the Agency, why it was 'Joc' and not 'Josh' or 'Joss', his reply had been unequivocal. 'I don't like Jocelyn, Josh or Joss, or any other damn thing. Joc will have to do!'

As Louise entered his office, Joc half rose from his chair in acknowledgement of her presence as he usually did, along with the wave of his hand offering her a seat with his usual words, 'Sit down please, Louise.' Despite all the times she had heard him say it, the 'please Louise' rhyming as it did, had never grated on her nerves, although she and the other secretaries often laughed at his idiosyncrasies and wondered what would happen if he forgot his lines or – heaven forbid – he had to cope with a new secretary!

'Louise, you obviously saw the memo from the German police in Hamburg?'

'Yes, Joc. I couldn't understand why it hadn't been directed into the Foreign section.'

'Me too. However, I've decided I'm going to deal with it direct. Can you discreetly get me the direct line number for Chief Inspector Ulbrecht in Hamburg and sniff around for anything you can find out on this Dashnikov woman? But don't go snooping around the Foreign section yet, go to the training school – follow up any personal leads you can get hold of.'

'Do you want me to set up the normal file, with names and numbers on the flyleaf as usual?'

'Yes, if you would. You can do the normal forms as well, but I'd prefer it done my way... hold on to all copies and check with me before you circulate any information.'

'Okay. Will you speak to Germany now, or do you want to wait until we can phone on the cheap rate after 6 p.m.?' she asked him cheekily.

Joc smiled and jibed back, 'You get the background as soon as possible and we'll hold a union meeting about that when the time comes, okay?'

The phone rang on his direct line so Louise got up to leave the room.

'Latimer here.'

'Joc, it's Brian. Have you got a minute for a chat?'

'Sure, what can I do for you?'

'You've had a memo... about Hamburg? Well, we feel it should have been ours to deal with. What do you think?'

'Well, I didn't think about it at the time but since you've asked, it is addressed to me personally and maybe, Brian, you ought to put in your own request about this to the Chief?'

'It might not be politic to do that, Joc, but if you were to involve us, I'm sure it would work out fine.'

'Like a pig's bloody ear it would! You guys over there are so bloody mysterious and secretive, you disappear up your own asses!'

'That's not fair, Joc. We didn't write the policy for foreign affairs in the first place, but we never stop being shot down by every bloody politician and every other division within the CIA!'

'You should have stayed out in the field... you were a good cop.'

'Ouch! That's below the belt, Joc, and you know the reasons

why I came inside – Ruth would have left me if I hadn't got a nine-to-five job!'

'Bullshit! It was your gallivanting when you were away; never phoning home or being there when anyone phoned you!'

'Okay, okay, we've known each other for too long for me to use that ploy. Are you going to let us in on this job or not?'

'No way! You've already got me thinking that there's maybe a skeleton or two here that you guys want to stay hid! No, it's my case, if there is one at all, so if you've got something to hide you'd better bury it deep!'

'Is that your final word on the matter, Joc?'

'Bloody hell, Brian, how plain do I have to speak to you people? Are you thick or something? The only way you will get this case from me is by some official route!'

'Okay, Joc, you know there is something, even if you're just guessing at the moment. Can I just say as a friend, watch your back on this one. It's "international" in a big way, and a lot of the big guys' feathers have been ruffled. Joc, I'm sorry, but I had to ask…'

'Don't worry about it, Brian… and… thank you.'

Joc's brow was deeply furrowed as he placed the receiver back in the cradle. Experience warned him there was turmoil ahead. Having thought, sitting silently for a few moments, he decisively grabbed the phone again and punched out the three digits to reach his station boss.

Chapter Three

Commander Roth of the city of Hamburg police department was surrounded by reporters from all the media outlets. The hustle and bustle which had been constantly surrounding him since the reports of the 'Nowhere Men' case had hit the media was something that he personally loathed, but he suffered all of the jostling his body had been subjected to because, in the end, it was getting good publicity for his police force: publicity richly deserved – which also made things easier when budget time came around again. And after all, he really did feel that the press must be given every bit of information, providing of course that it did not affect national security!

Roth had habitually used press conferences as a method of keeping information flowing out, not only to the media and the town council to whom he was answerable, but more importantly, to the good people of Hamburg who read or listened to the reports and thought about the problems which could befall them were it not for the city's police force: the detectives, the patrolmen, traffic controllers and the administration staff, who had served them well and would continue to do so. Today's press call was set up at the request of the bosses of all the journalists standing before him as a 'question and answer session' with no holds barred. The press barons had pressurised the police force into what was about to happen now. A pressure which had to be given in to, but at the same time, Commander Roth appreciated it must not be allowed to jeopardise his own officers. The press must not be given the opportunity to make idols out of them.

The eventual silence which Roth had patiently waited for was interrupted only by the last-minute mutterings which inevitably occurred between the sound men and their cameramen. Finally, even that could delay the proceedings no more, and the first question came immediately after Roth had finished his opening words of welcome. 'Harald, sir... London, *The Times*. You have always protected long-term policies since you have held office. Do you feel that any other town or city could benefit from its adoption?'

'Yes, it has proven successful here, so I can see no reason why it should not work elsewhere.'

'Harald again, sir. Is your method something that you would be prepared to publish, to help others?'

'Only if it were published in *The Times*!' Roth answered jokingly, as a good-humoured titter ran through the audience.

'Sir... Leiterman, *Frankfurter*. Your methods have been acclaimed throughout Germany and I'm sure you and your men are glowing with pride, having caused such a scar on this corrupt organisation's attempts to flood us with drugs and violence, but how much did you overspend your budget by to pull in the increased resources?'

'Each episode concerning crime either affecting or potentially affecting this city, will not increase the overall tax paid per person throughout the country by any more than two Deutschmarks per year. A small amount to pay, but although the tax is paid annually over the two years that it has been levied by the government, we have only approached the City Fathers on two occasions for an increase in funding over and above our annual allowance, for all divisions of policing. The very supportive attitude of our city's council and their belief in my men, is the key factor in our success.'

'Thank you, sir. May I ask – does it increase the administration staff?'

'No. All senior police officers are the administrators. They know which way their investigations are twisting and turning and it is their requests for financial or material support that go to the council, through me. Sometimes it is not always possible to get all of the people at council together by telephone and I am left being the arbiter. It is sometimes difficult for me, but no one person in any division would make an unnecessary request, hence we have had only two occasions when we have had to address the fund.'

'Pitman, *New York Times*, sir. Is there any truth in the rumours that you are requesting the help of the CIA?'

Without hesitation, Roth glided on, unruffled by the remark.

'Mr Pitman, crime is an international business, I can assure you. So, in our considered opinion, if at any time during one of our investigations needs must, we will contact every single force around the world. This does not mean, however, that we are signalling for help, but that we are seeking information which may help us to either close our files or extend our investigations or, alternatively, should any foreign force request information from us, we will obviously reciprocate. It is in all of our interests to be international.'

The silence held for a moment, Roth's forthright delivery stunning some, and leaving others confused.

Pitman raised his hand again and Roth nodded his head at him giving permission for him to speak. Pitman lowered his arm and looked at Roth with a twinkle in his eye.

'So the answer to my previous question is "No", sir?'

'I think you could say that, Mr Pitman!'

The laughter rippled across the room with some guffaws and some wry smiles but there was an underlying suspense to the occasion, waiting for something. This was soon shattered as Pitman raised his hand for a third time and spoke. 'What will happen if the CIA don't cooperate, sir?'

Commander Roth knew and respected the journalistic skills of Mr Pitman of the *New York Times* and he also knew that Pitman must have a very good reason for his dogged questioning. Roth decided now was not the time to give Pitman's teasing question the dignity of an answer. It would be untimely to mention that contact had been made with the CIA, especially as the CIA were, in his eyes, and in those of his senior officers, working in the city of Hamburg without official permission and in fact, had been doing so for some considerable time prior to the 'Nowhere Men' escapade. A political stance at this time would be wrong, Roth knew that whatever he said would most likely be totally misconstrued.

The audience sat transfixed, not knowing what to expect, each of them waiting for someone else to speak. Taking the initiative, Roth closed down the session. 'Well, gentlemen, and ladies, if you have nothing further for me, I'll get back to my champagne and cigars…' The joke was enjoyed by all, except perhaps Pitman, and titters ran through the audience with a few handclaps as well, as they all packed up and prepared to leave. All of the press contingency knew that Pitman had caught Roth unawares with his line of questioning and more importantly, that if left alone, Roth would give them a fuller press conference next time. The only niggling worry for the European press was whether Pitman had any advantage over them!

Chapter Four

The inactivity after such an important operation was making Chief Inspector Ernst Ulbrecht nervous. All of the pieces of the jigsaw, barring three, had been sorted out during his own investigations but it was criminal records in the Eastern Bloc and the Arab world which were causing him the most anxiety at this moment. Why had nothing shown up from Russian Intelligence about Mogatin and Lanov? They both had criminal records, that much was known, and they were closely associated with Tashimov. Ernst had guessed that Russia would be their normal homing point and Russian border controls were still the strictest, so why had nothing been heard of them? But there again, Ernst mused, what if they had tried their escape through Europe? He had alerted Interpol just in case and had informed a few of his personal police chief friends, but no information had been forthcoming from them over the past three days. This late confirmation of both Lanov's and Mogatin's connection with Tashimov had happened only days prior to Ernst's team 'springing the trap' at the dockside, but their escape should have been covered more efficiently. Ernst knew key players like Lanov and Mogatin would have vital information which could potentially prevent further crimes being committed, but worse still, having escaped the net, they could start their own crime wave!

The most infuriating piece of the jigsaw was this 'ringed-hand man'. To date, no one had been able to identify him, nor had anyone anywhere reported a ring looking anything like the description Klaus and Deiter had given him. The waiting was always the most telling part for Ernst. He had withdrawn within himself, obviously unhappy. Normally so much rested on his 'hunches', but now it seemed, nothing would fall into place. Considering all that had been achieved, the fact that three ringleaders were currently unaccounted for would, by anyone else, be reluctantly accepted. Hadn't his group of detectives just stopped the largest consignment of drugs and arms and possibly the largest link-up between the Russian Organisatiya, the American Mafia and the fundamentalists in the Arab world? It had been a successful operation, but Ernst feared that one of the missing three may have been the mastermind behind the scam, and the connections within the network he could be forced to divulge needed to be exposed to the world's law enforcement agencies, found and stopped: just in case any one of them took the initiative and managed to set yet another destructive plan into action. The turmoil in Ernst's head would not let him rest. He must find all three of the missing links...

Ernst also felt that the 'ringed-hand man' was the most important. With a sadness in him, Ernst sat at his desk, his mind racing over the past actions he had taken. Had he missed anything? Had the 'ringed-hand man' been recognised anywhere before the final act had been played out in Klaus and Deiter's flat? Think, Ernst, think! His thoughts kept drumming inside his head. It seemed that a man everyone was afraid of and who investigations had proven, was the controller, if not the designer, of an elaborate plan to move ten billion dollars' worth of arms to the Arabs from an overstocked arsenal of weapons in Russia, using heroin freely gained in Afghanistan and opening a route into the American Mafia. All this making it impossible that this bloody mysterious 'ringed-hand man' had not been seen by anyone! Ernst thumped his desk. Lanov and Mogatin were the key to obtaining the 'ringed-hand man's' identity. Lanov and Mogatin were close to Tashimov, they must have seen him, even if they didn't know his name, they must be able to provide a physical description, surely? Realising that it could only be a matter of time before a sighting of Lanov or Mogatin would be reported, Ernst became a little more relaxed and settled back into his old comfortable chair.

The ringing of the phone on his desk quickly broke his inactivity which was transformed into the swiftness of his moving body with his arm and hand thrusting smoothly forward like the stroke of a synchronised swimmer. His mind was praying this would be the big break. His level voice entered the mouthpiece. 'Ulbrecht here.' A clearly American voice came back into Ernst's ear.

'Joc Latimer here. Say, do you speak English?'

'A little. How can I help?'

'Your Commander has sent a request to my Head of Station asking for information on one Nadine Dashnikov?'

'Yes, Mr Latimer, I believe he did. I hope you have some good information for me?'

'Herr Ulbrecht, only you can be the judge of that.'

'Mr Latimer, any information we can get from you will be information we have not had before, and hopefully it will help finish off our jigsaw puzzle.'

'Well, I haven't got much to tell you yet, other than to confirm she was a bona fide agent of the US government. She was of Russian origin and had been well educated. It also appears that she was on special assignment through our Foreign Services division, and your request has sent a few ripples through our Foreign division's corridors for some reason I haven't been able to figure out yet.'

'Well, Mr Latimer, to have the confirmation she was a US agent helps a little, but we were obviously hoping for a little more information than just that!'

'I'm sorry, Herr Ulbrecht, but that's it at the moment. The reason for my call was to ask if there was any specific information you might be looking for.'

'In fact, there is. Off the record, I don't give a damn about all of the political mish-mash that's behind this enquiry. I'm a policeman with some loose ends and I won't sleep at nights until they're tied up!'

'I know the feeling. I was in the field for twenty-five years before they put me behind a desk, but the feelings have never gone away.'

'Well, I'm pleased I'm talking to a real policeman and not some administrator in a dusty office who hasn't got a clue!'

'Oh, you have those sort of people too?'

The candid honesty broke the ice between them and they both had a little chuckle, then Ulbrecht continued, 'We probably have more than anyone else, it seems to me!'

'I know what you mean! In fact there are so many here, my imagination allows me to think there must be some special breeding farm for them somewhere nearby!'

'You sound just like the kind of man I want to talk to – my name is Ernst…'

'Thanks, Ernst, my name is Joc. Joc is short for Jocelyn, which I don't like.'

'Okay, Joc it is. Look, my problem is that we have managed to stop a large operation smuggling drugs and military weapons through the port of Hamburg. I have most of the people involved contained, but three of them, to my knowledge, are running free. Two of these have been identified and will no doubt turn up in our dragnet eventually, but it is the other one I consider to be the most important. He has never been identified properly and all we have to go on is that he wears a very unusual ring on his right hand. We know your girl Dashnikov definitely saw him, in fact she was killed by him, which gives your department the "need to know" factor, but the burning question is, did she meet the "ringed-hand man" in the US? Is he known to her family there? Is he listed anywhere in your criminal records?'

'Okay, I get the picture. You sound quite anxious, Ernst. Look, can you fax me what you've got direct to me on my private line? I'll let my secretary know I'm expecting it so that it doesn't go running around the building to some administration area. I'll get the wheels turning in the meantime with what I've got already.'

'Thank you, Joc. I'll get what I can to you right away and any supplementary stuff I can get will come separately. Thank you again… and don't let the jokers get you down!'

'I won't! I treat them as a joke! Anyway, they're all so career-minded it does them good to be strung along now and again! Listen, my direct line is (323) 202-3163 and the fax number is (323) 202-7788. You've got that on tape I suppose, so I won't bother to repeat it, right?'

'You too? I suppose perhaps the bureaucrats have got more control than we think they have!'

'But it's a great game teasing them!'

'Yes, I think we both agree on that, Joc! Thank you for your call; it's been most enjoyable.'

'Bye, Ernst, I'll be in touch!'

Both men replaced their receivers with confident smiles on

their faces, feeling more secure now they each knew they were dealing with 'dyed-in-the-wool' policemen and that they would support each other, even if the systems of management got in the way.

Ernst rested back in his chair for a brief moment. Quickly regaining his old momentum, he snatched his favourite yellow-paged note pad and wrote:

Mr Joc Latimer, Fax No. (323) 202-7788

Dear Joc, Thank you for your call – full report regarding our mystery 'ringed-hand man' will be sent tomorrow, for your personal attention. The ring is a square ruby set in a heavy scrolled surround, worn on his right index finger. Two witnesses support this information.

Thank you for making contact,

Ernst Ulbrecht,
Chief Inspector of Police

In block capitals, Ernst wrote a note to his secretary:

DISPATCH THIS IMMEDIATELY. LET ME CHECK THE DOCUMENTS I HAVE PROMISED AND ANY OTHER DOCUMENTS I MAY REQUEST TO BE SENT. ALL DOCUMENTS SENT WILL BE MY RESPONSIBILITY.

ERNST

The smart western-style-suited Army Marshall, Yute Polenkovich strode purposefully along the long echoing corridor. His whole being, although in civilian clothes, was militaristic in smartness and attitude. His eyes were set forward, never once veering to either side of the corridor – the room he was aiming for was familiar to him, having travelled that route many times before. Ten more paces, begin to move over, right, three more paces, hand on door handle and enter without knocking. Don't acknowledge anyone until the door is shut behind you, square up your body to the table with the five men facing, speak first, speak calmly, don't fluff it! This was the entrance he must make before the committee and it had been rehearsed in his mind dozens upon dozens of times; on trains, buses and simply walking across his zigzagging route through Europe, making certain his escape was undetected and that upon his next arrival from within the depths of Mother Russia, his identity would still be unknown to all but a few. The two thousand mile journey had given him time to formulate his plan to escape any blame for Tashimov's blunder, along with a proposal for a longer-term corruption of the West. His belief that communism and military rule should control the world by any means available, had now become his dream.

He filled his chest with the corridor's stale air, allowing, for a few seconds, an arrogant smile to creep over his face. He knew that his escape from Hamburg had not been traced and that confusion reigned throughout law enforcement agencies in Europe. The click of the lock sinking into its buttress, the whisper of leather shoes on woollen carpet then, as he turned to face the table, his first word, 'Gentlemen...' was out of his mouth and he was moving confidently forward. His performance so far was going to plan. His ring finger crossed over the other superstitiously as he halted before his comrades.

'I will not make excuses, but I will say that I never supported the disaster we have just suffered; you were all witness to that. I have a new proposal for you, utilising Tashimov's basic principle which I never objected to, but, two facets must change. Firstly, the time span must be extended, leaving fewer chances for error and eliminating the anxieties that get-rich programmes place upon all concerned. Secondly, everything should be controlled militarily with only the minimum of entrepreneurial people involved.'

His speech finished abruptly and he felt he had not lost the advantage he had so continually rehearsed for. He waited in the silence for the reaction of the men sat before him. His unknown fear was that his previous position of power and trust might have been usurped in his absence. The silence lingered until Chairman Malinovitch, without looking at his other colleagues, stared squarely into Polenkovich's unflinching eyes, saying, 'Explain yourself further, Comrade Polenkovich.' The slight movement of Polenkovich's fingers as they uncurled, went unnoticed by the panel before him.

Immediately, Polenkovich began explaining that the weakness of Tashimov's plan had been not entirely due to the plan itself, but as he had already mentioned in his opening statement, with the speed with which such an operation had been set up and executed. He emphasised Tashimov's use of people outside the normal military (although all the people he had selected had been accepted by the peers sitting in front of him) – they were into their own private enterprises in a foreign country and only respected Tashimov through fear.

'In brief,' he told them, 'they had gone soft and the timescale placed upon Tashimov gave no time to bring them to heel. The military discipline was not there, which made the whole operation vulnerable as has been proven. It should have been controlled by military officers of proven loyalty to the military high command.' He was referring to the accepted loyalty all selected men had to earn slowly, with a step-by-step indoctrination into a position of trust commencing at local level, then through districts, overseas postings, until eventually they earned the introduction to this very select committee Polenkovich now stood proudly in front of.

He paused for a moment to clear his throat. 'Comrades, military precision has always been the key to all of the controlled acts of deceit we have committed on the Russian people. The deceit of letting them think it was their politicians having to struggle against the oppression of the Western world which caused their misery and not the strength of their military commanders forcing the politicians into believing that to hold all of the rest of the world's aggressors from the borders of Mother Russia, that they – the military, would have to be given more and more money to enable them to keep the threat at bay. By paying our scientists, mathematicians, aircraft and rocket designers very little and forcing them to believe their work would fulfil the hope of the Russian people, allowing them a slightly larger apartment, or perhaps catering to any little foible they might have had, vast sums of capital built up. The high command quickly realised that this vast amount of capital was becoming an embarrassment, hence this much-respected body, which sits before me today, came into being. But now, with Europe becoming secure and the West accepting Glasnost, we are confronted with another dilemma: to be sure of our success, we must have dollars, pounds sterling and Deutschmarks. Currencies which are useable in the world of commerce. I propose we have the means of doing this with the plan I am now proposing and at the same time, of forcing a form of communism slowly on its way, to erode (as in the old days), religion and freedom through the Eastern and Western worlds.' Polenkovich paused. The attention of his audience assured him that he was winning over his 'friends'. Again, Polenkovich started speaking, slowly. 'Tashimov's plan was an excellent one in the first issue of obtaining dollar resources for the Organisatiya, but he was pushed too hard for the plan to succeed. My intention is to plan slowly and use our existing records of Russians who have defected or married foreign nationals, who are in the military or have military connections in Germany, France and Spain. We have to search our records for English speakers who are bilingual with French or German, are young and if possible, are already serving officers in the French, German or Spanish armies. Our aim, after our own selection and motivation of those selected, is to position them in Eurocorps, which is an organised collective defence corps, with high ideals of peacekeeping and humanitarianism. A fast-moving force with a command structure in the three countries mentioned, with further anticipated inclusions such as the likes of Luxembourg and Belgium in the near future. Gentlemen, if we can infiltrate this corps, its ideals could be motivated in our favour...'

The initial surprise around the table was obvious. The Chairman stood up, quickly followed by the rest. Resting his clenched fists firmly on the table, he stared coldly into Polenkovich's face. 'You have brought us something that could possibly be to our advantage. You will be informed of our decision in due course.' The Chairman lifted his hands quickly from the table and, placing them firmly in each other behind his back, turned and left the room, the rest of the committee following silently behind him.

Polenkovich was left on his own to endure the silence. His own thoughts were of his fear that he had given away too much of his plan and that he might not be left with a position in it for himself! Gathering his thoughts, he bowed to the empty table and whispered softly to himself, 'The next meeting will be either to announce my plan's approval or... my death!'

The Records Offices of the KGB, the Army, Navy and Air forces went from being quiet and silent as usual, to noisy and industrious. The orders coming in from who knows where, made work a little more exciting for the computer operators and researchers. In fact, it was just like it was before Glasnost. Everybody working, following one line, part of a plan – a plan bigger than any one of them could understand. However, total understanding of your work was not a necessary ingredient. The fear of becoming a fatal statistic, like the stories that you hear about, happened to other people and won't happen to you if you just kindly do the job as directed. Don't think about it, just do it to the satisfaction of your immediate boss and never think of anything other than leaving the office at six o'clock sharp.

The memo sent to all the supervisors throughout the vast network of the Records Offices with their secret files, had conveyed the same instruction, which was to find every Russian in Russian military service before the age of twenty-five who had French or English as a second language, preferably with transport and communications experience, as well as any ex-servicemen whose children had joined the military, either in Russia or any other European force, which could include Poles, Czechs, Slavs and so on. The qualification for both groups was to be the same. A separate memo sent under a different security category was sent to a few more senior officials; they were asked to perform a different task. On receipt of information received from the general search, they were to cross-match every single one who had had special training in espionage. With the older groups, they should establish whether any of them or their children were 'sleepers' waiting to be awakened into the service of Mother Russia.

The initial surge of information flooded in; it seemed to those who were cataloguing, that the sixteen hours a day they were already working was just not enough. There was only one way: three shifts a day would have to be introduced and as many staff as necessary would have to be provided. The orders mysteriously kept coming. The orders for the more senior officials with a more intricate task granted unlimited expenditure and manpower. Marshall Polenkovich's plan had been approved and the Organisatiya was stimulating its own selfish needs which, as always, would be to the Russian peoples' expense and detriment. Only the accepted few would reap the rewards.

Chapter Five

Joc Latimer's office had become more active since his call to his new German colleague, Ernst Ulbrecht. The pace had increased at least fourfold, driven by Joc's inquisitive mind with the foresight that if what he was doing at that moment kept European crime off the American doorstep, he was doing his job as a guardian of the peace. Louise and the other staff in the various offices around were not surprised at the activity emanating from Joc's direction, or that they themselves appeared to be finding new energy. They found it hard to believe when five o'clock arrived each day; it seemed far too early for them to have achieved their workload for the day.

Entering Joc's office for the umpteenth time that day, Louise was amazed at the untidiness, but happy to be part of it all. She attempted to speak to the top half of the head sat buried at the desk. 'Joc, your friend Brian from Foreign has been on again. He's not so rude now, but he has a threatening manner that is a little worrying. He feels you are making too many waves far too quickly and that he is riding in the middle of a political tornado.'

'Don't let him get through to me, Louise. He is the one person that could slow us down. He's been a friend a long time, but until we get everything here gathered up for our German friend, he is going to have to weather the storm alone.'

'I won't plug in your direct line just yet, then.'

'No, not until he has checked out of the building at least… let's hope he's still too mean to use a public call box!'

'Okay, but it worries me that our German friend can't get through to you either, that's all.'

'Yes, but he knows my position and will only phone at the agreed times or he'll ring your number and I'll call him back.'

'All right, but we're getting bored with Brian hassling us and those other stupid idiots from Foreign! Why are you standing up against them anyway?' The directness of the question stopped Joc in his tracks for a moment, then he pushed himself away from his desk and rested his aching back into the softness of his chair. Looking at Louise he smiled, stalling for time to formulate his answer and then said gently, 'You certainly have a right to know, I suppose. I'm sorry, I should have discussed it with you before now, but here goes. After I read Ulbrecht's dossier and the case history – one of the most audacious plans to turn the Western world, as we have grown to accept it, upside down. And frankly, it was a frightening revelation to have found out about it, but also to think that those daft idiots over at Foreign division put an agent in the field "just to gather information" without any prearrangement with the Hamburg authorities is damn stupidity itself. And when they realise their agent has taken revenge by murdering a third country's citizen, the proverbial is going to hit the fan and a lot of people are going to get sprayed.'

'But how come you've got involved in this?'

'At first, I was just obeying orders, but Ernst is my kind of cop. He plays his hunches and twists and turns whichever way he has to, to get his own way. And as you know, my favourite hobby is European news reports so for some time now, my dumb brain has been telling me things are beginning to happen all over Europe and it should be carefully monitored by all police forces, especially by us here in the USA. We have a longstanding European immigration policy which could repeat the trend started in the thirties and forties of planting sleepers, then activating them when needed. It happened with at least two of our imported Germans and Russians, not to mention the Corsicans and Greeks.'

'Hold on, Joc, you can't sort out the problems of the whole bloody world!'

'No, but maybe I can help solve another crime and stop ever-smarter criminals from walking all over us… or at the very least, slow them down!'

Louise sensed her boss was getting tense and angry just talking about it. His deep-rooted patriotism and pride in protecting his country was being attacked and like his new-found German friend, he would fight back with any means available to him. Slowly, Louise whispered Joc's name and, getting his attention again, she asked him, 'Tea or coffee?' Joc could just manage a smile at being brought back down to earth from his hobby horse before answering. Louise stopped in the office doorway, turned back around and said with all sincerity, 'Joc, you're right, forget those idiots over at Foreign and let's get the bad guys!'

Joc enjoyed the spontaneity of Louise's wisecrack and welcomed the momentary relief from the grind of sifting through all of the information. He also enjoyed the freedom of expounding his theories and fears in the knowledge that all his orations never went any further than Louise's trusted ears.

Moments later, Joc's reverie was broken once again by Louise's sudden re-entry into his office. 'Joc, I've just had Ernst on the phone… he seems to be in a bit of a "hurry up" mood!'

'Okay, I'll plug in my phone and call him right back.'

Louise left Joc to relay the message to Ernst and give Joc a few minutes to sort out plugging the phone back in. More likely than not, she knew she would need to go back in a minute or two and do it herself with Joc looking embarrassedly at her offering excuses such as, 'Sorry… I've left my glasses somewhere…' or, 'Why are all these sockets tucked into the corners like this? My hands are too big to fiddle with this!'

'Ernst? Is that you?'

'Ja! A piece of important information about Nadine Dashnikov as we know her, has come my way.' Ernst paused for a few moments to gather his thoughts into his faltering English before dropping his bombshell. 'She had connections with the Mafia in the States.' Again, Ernst paused before continuing. 'Whether it was a connection that your people made for her, or a real one, I can't say for sure yet, but a definite connection there certainly was. In my view, I think it was your people's connection, searching for a possible Mafia link that some source or other had turned up. But if she was working on her own, we may have a double agent or even a third country involved. What do you think?'

'Thanks for that bombshell, Ernst! Well, nothing is showing up at this end pointing to anything like that, but it may give me the opportunity to force the Foreign Desk's hand. They are still withholding information but confronted with something like this, they will have to own up if they planted her in the first place. Or, then again, "Did they know she was a double agent?" might be a good opening question!'

'I think I would play it that way, Joc. Good luck! Let me know what happens.'

The phone went silent but it was less than a second before Joc's fingers were punching out the digits. One ring... two rings... three rings. 'Come on, you bloody toad, answer your phone!'

With the sound of a breathless, 'Hello?' on the fourth ring, Joc crashed in before the voice could continue.

'Brian! Did you know about this bloody Nadine person being a possible double agent?'

'Officially, the answer is no, but we are trying to sort out this end, I can assure you. There are an awful lot of red faces and denials around here, that's for sure.'

'But what do you think?'

'Personally, I'm in the "No, she was not, camp". Purely and simply, when we heard about the Russians sneaking around the docks in Europe, we had no real evidence anything was going down, just a gut instinct that we should keep an eye on things, so we found Nadine through Records and went for her. The "red faces and denial" brigade are covering their asses just in case we found her a little too quickly or conveniently for comfort.'

'That's your honest opinion, Brian?'

'Yes. I know the damage that could be caused and how exposed policing could be if I'm wrong, but "No" is my vote.'

'Okay, Brian, thanks. Sorry about blocking your calls, by the way...'

'Only to be expected, Joc! But then again, you can always phone me!'

'Thanks, I will.'

'Don't make it so long next time. I'm being pushed into a corner and it's "Don't use the phone" time!'

'I understand. Thanks again.' After a short pause, Joc added, 'friend' and sincerely hoped he had managed to say the word 'friend' before his friend had put his phone down.

Joc pushed his phone away from him and reached for his scratchpad, drawing out in a family tree style all the people who had been in touch, with the date and time neatly written underneath, with any other notes which he felt relevant. Grabbing the phone again, he dialled Ulbrecht. The ringing phone was promptly answered. 'Ulbrecht here.'

Whimsically, Joc replied, 'Latimer here.' Both men smiled to themselves at each end of the transatlantic phone link, knowing their senses of humour were coming together.

'Ernst…' Joc continued, 'my man in Foreign tells me he personally gives a "no way" vote to the double agent theory, but he did say some of his executive team are rather red-faced and denying any involvement in the matter. He is quite clear in his own mind that we planted her direct into a situation we had a gut feeling about and wanted to keep an eye on, and he feels maybe he is the one being set up as the fall guy for overstepping his authority. I trust him, Ernst.'

'Good enough for me, Joc. I'll run along with the theory that she was only your girl.'

'Okay, I'm happy with that, but if I find out anything to change that opinion, I'll be in touch.'

'Thanks. I hope we'll get to meet one day…'

'Me too. By the way, any news on Lanov and Mogatin?'

'Nothing definite. A few possible sightings, but nothing confirmed as yet. And before you ask, the "ringed-hand man" has disappeared without trace.'

'You'll find him, given time.'

'Thanks. My only worry is, will it be too late to stop another onslaught of mayhem and corruption?'

'Mmm… Well, I'll keep trucking away this end… keep your fingers crossed something turns up soon. 'Bye for now.'

'Thanks again, Joc. As you say, "'Bye for now".'

Chapter Six

At the Russian Records Office, senior officials were sorting out the endless number of possible families, and sons and daughters of families, who had direct or indirect military connections. They were astounded at the number of families who fitted the criteria, but even more astounded at how many of them were Russian émigrés serving in many different armies, including the Foreign Legion. The constant demands from the Secretariat had been very annoying, but as civil servants in a new 'free will, free speech' society, they had no option but to stand by their new government's demands and acquire and catalogue all the information as instructed.

Igor Tatlanovich stood fidgeting by the side of the outdated photocopier, having already rerun several pages due to poor reproduction. He frequently looked at his cheap digital watch as if it would hold back time for him to be able to complete his task and be ready with the first lists of possible candidates for when the courier arrived. The orders placed upon his desk in the dead of night said 'without fail' and 'tomorrow at the same time, another courier will arrive to collect'. The panic he felt reminded him of the old days but then, as he had often said, 'Russians had a purpose and must protect themselves against the capitalist enemy constantly knocking at the door.' But now, all his skill and pride was being used to help Mother Russia move forward in competition with the rest of the world and the new equipment which had been promised yet again, would make things easier in the future. The last page passed through the copier and Igor checked it quickly for clarity. Before picking up his pile of papers, he swiftly crossed himself. This new freedom in Russia had revived his religious beliefs, but he often wondered what would be taken away…

Hurrying along the empty marble-floored and high-ceilinged corridor, he took another furtive glance at his watch; thirty seconds left to get to the glass-domed reception area. He had to hurry.

Marshall Yute Polenkovich was back, silently waiting in the room in which he had first of all pleaded for his life and made his excuses, blaming Tashimov. His judges sat stern-faced, opposite him. A wave of anxiety surged through his body but he must not give anything away – the slightest weakness will work against him. This meeting has been called by the Chairman of the Judges to assess whether all of the research that had been demanded by them will unearth a valid reason to continue with Marshall Polenkovich's plan for the long-term corruption of first Europe and then the world. Polenkovich could hear his heart pounding – surely they could too. Why am I like this? I've had a good life, better than many others… why am I so anxious? Death is death – I came to terms with that long ago, and yet here I am, sweating about the next big plan, the true value of which will come to fruition long after my own natural death and that of the others here in this room!

The question and answer game running through his head, slowly stopped racing as his ears picked up the sound of footsteps in the corridor outside pounding louder and louder as they neared the door and then stopped. Three short knocks on the door elicited the command 'Enter' from the Chairman of the Judges. The brown foolscap envelope was handed directly to him by the courier, who saluted before his dismissal. The envelope was duly opened and the lists circulated to each panel member. The Chairman raised his eyes to glance at Polenkovich's expression before starting to read. The silence fell again and with it, a cold sweat broke out on Polenkovich's back and the palm of his hands.

Igor Tatlanovich returned to his dingy office in the basement of the vast Kremlin building. He took out the file marked 'Russians Abroad – Civilians and Military'. He opened the cover and on the one loose piece of paper inside had been written in his own neat handwriting: 'Search commenced… 19.5.96'. The second entry, which he began to write neatly underneath, read 'First list supplied… 20.7.96. No copies filed'. He underlined each entry in red before lifting the page closer to his eyes to reread what he had written and then picking up a pencil he wrote 'Report not read, as ordered' and then he signed it, 'Igor Tatlanovich'.

The Chairman put down the file and looked coldly in Polenkovich's direction. 'It would seem more people absconded from Russia than we were led to believe, which may, on reflection, give you the chance you want to progress your plan further. You will leave now. We will contact you when we have discussed this information.' His index finger tapped lightly on the list still held in his hand. 'Thank you for attending this meeting.'

The curt dismissal as if he were some junior officer rankled, but there was no way he would dare disobey – at least his impending death sentence had been extended. When they sanctioned his plan – and he was confident they would – he hoped he would never be subservient to anyone again. After all, was he not a Marshall in the great, fearless army of Russia? He left the room, saluting his superiors before leaving and as he shut the door behind him and walked along the cold corridor, he wanted to shout at the top of his voice at the sheer relief he felt at getting at least this temporary reprieve. The more they talk, he thought to himself, the more likely it would become clearer to them that his plan was the only way forward to secure and protect the Organisatiya into the future.

Once Polenkovich had left, the panel relaxed and moved their chairs around so they could see one another more easily. The Chairman addressed the others. 'I think Polenkovich's plan is worth pursuing, particularly since, by the look of the information we have so far, we have many more people out there than certainly I had expected, and moreover, many of these people are military trained in the specific areas we would require. If we do sanction the military infiltration by any of our own officers, we must be doubly sure about our selection and that we have no weak links. Plus, as it is Polenkovich's idea, I feel he should be allowed to carry the responsibility of the final selection.'

The meaning was clear. Should Polenkovich make the wrong decision and the cards come tumbling down around his ears, the Chairman and his fellow colleagues would find it easier to extricate themselves without any attachment of blame. The rest of the panel accepted the Chairman's recommendations without question as he knew they would, so he rose from his chair and invited them to partake of the sumptuous feast of champagne, vodka, and of course, beluga caviar amongst other treats, laid out for their pleasure in the adjoining room.

There was an atmosphere of controlled urgency in Ulbrecht's office. This was quite normal in the circumstances, due to his frustration when the information he so desperately wanted would not come through, no matter how much pressure he placed on his detectives. He was taking the failure to find Lanov and Mogatin as a personal slight. He felt he should have placed more importance on finding them straight away. What had he been thinking of? Why had he not considered these two elusive Russians his first priority? He punched his fist into his open palm in a rage, muttering to himself, 'You're getting old, Ernst; now you'll just have to be patient. All this time being wasted, it's your own silly fault. You'll just have to sit through it and hope it doesn't go on for too much longer.'

Inspector Willi Koslowski got up from his desk, staring across the tops of the other detectives' heads as he approached the ever open door of his long-time colleague and friend, Ernst Ulbrecht. Willi knew how much anguish was in Ernst's mind and knew also what Ernst was putting himself through, having watched his friend carry out this same ritual many times before: pacing the office floor, punching his fist and most of all, the mumbling as he mentally chastised himself.

Willi couldn't help but poke his head around the door to say, 'Good morning, Chief, how's it all going?'

Ernst's head jerked upwards at the sound, stopping his murmuring in mid-sentence, then he replied with a welcoming smile on his face, 'Willi! Do come in; sit down!'

'Well, just for a minute. I've got a car coming in a few minutes, and I must clear up my desk before I go.'

'Are you still on that messy murder?'

'Yes, but it's mostly just the paperwork I've got to sort out now we've got the killer. There's just one more interview I've got to do with someone who I might just charge with aiding and abetting.'

'Well, at least you know where your men are!'

'What do you mean, Ernst?'

'Lanov and Mogatin are still on the run. I should have paid more attention to them as soon as we rousted them at the docks and I would know where they were now!'

'Ernst, you can't put yourself down for that! You can't anticipate everything! God knows how you do it anyway, all those little grains of information you tie together, your gut instinct, and next thing we know you've built it into the biggest crime bust in the history of policing! Don't punish yourself because you've got a couple of loose ends!'

'If you say so, Willi. But Lanov, Mogatin and the "ringed-hand man" are out there somewhere and heaven knows what they're going to be getting up to next!'

'I suppose anything could be turned into a potential disaster if we let our imaginations run riot.'

'But this one is different, Willi. I feel it. I'm sure there's got to be a follow up. It won't stop here. They lost billions of dollars and a hell of a lot of face in front of the Arabs who also lost their money, and the Americans with their possible Mafia connections… they won't forgive and forget, that's for sure.'

'Yes, you're probably right to be wary, but don't let it tear you apart. By the way,' he said with a cheeky grin, 'if it does all start up again, don't forget me for the controller's job, will you?'

Ernst smiled and reached for the back of his neck, giving it a rub as he answered, 'No of course I won't, Willi… in fact, I promise you'll be the first to know!'

'Great! Now I've got to go. Will I see you later on in the bar?'

'Yes, I'll drop in for a quick drink. See you then.'

There was a vagueness in his voice and with the rubbing of the back of his neck, Willi knew the signs. Somewhere in that great brain of Ernst's something was brewing away. With a final, 'See you!', Willi Koslowski left his friend to continue mulling over whatever problem it was that he foresaw. He doubted that no matter how long he, or any of the other members of Ulbrecht's team carried on performing their duties as police officers, they would never have Ulbrecht's natural instinct and foresight.

The piercing ring of the telephone on his desk cut through Ulbrecht's thoughts. Maybe it's time for that breakthrough that had been eluding them all week, he thought to himself, as he stretched forward to grab the receiver. 'Ulbrecht here.'

'Ernst… it's Commander Roth. Have you got a few minutes? I'll come down to your office if you like?'

'No, sir, I'll come to you. I'm all right for time, and it'll do me good to stretch my legs.' Ernst put down the telephone and lifted his weary body out of his chair. He made for the lift, passing through the large open-plan office where a few of his detectives were at their desks. He acknowledged those he had not yet seen that morning and they responded with their overwhelming respect for this strongly principled man they were proud to work for.

He listened to the purring of the lift as it rose to his floor, the clunk as it stopped and the shush as the cold steel doors opened for him, inviting him into the empty neon-lit passenger area with its mirrors on the walls. He walked in and pressed the button to the top floor, feeling very self-conscious having to confront his reflection, and after two or three furtive glances, he playfully stuck his tongue out and then blew a deflating raspberry at himself.

Commander Roth's office was plush and modern, located on the top of the newly built extension to police headquarters. A square room with very solid, heavy, and square furniture. There were pictures of his family growing up and of himself with them, his young attractive wife, all in expensively decorated, square picture frames, dotted around on the square furniture. The outer reception area was similar in style with the same heavy square furniture, but with the Commander's diplomas and awards regimentally aligned along each wall. The only concession here was the modern workstation with its computer system and up-to-the-minute fax machine-cum-printer-cum-photocopier along with its modem and telephone system, topped off with an incongruous bunch of colourful flowers in a tall, rounded vase which provided a little relief from all the square-boxed technology. Ernst knew he would be offered coffee and Roth knew Ernst would refuse it, as he always did, along with the proffered cigarette, to which Ernst would respond, 'Not just now, thanks.' The one solitary piece of paper on Roth's desk would not be touched, and the conversation would begin with Roth saying, 'Well, Ernst, it was good of you to come. How are things with you?' Ernst's reply might vary slightly, from good, bad, okay, or annoying to boring, and the next question would be the one which would indicate the real reason for Roth requesting the meeting.

'Ernst, these bloody Americans seem to be trying to politic themselves out of acknowledging that Nadine Dashnikov ever existed. What's your opinion? And how's it going with your man Latimer?'

'If she didn't belong to the Americans, we have at least two witnesses we can call on to corroborate that while she was desperately trying to keep Tashimov alive, she admitted to Deiter and Klaus that she was lucky to be working for the CIA and it will be difficult for the Americans to deny that. With regards to Latimer, he's of the old school and rather than going to charm school, he's already got their Foreign section at Langley running for cover. He has a personal friend in that section who apparently is taking a lot of flack because of this. Both of them are of the opinion that she was assigned by the CIA and that no one senior will own up, but they don't think she was a double agent.'

'Fine, keep me posted on that.'

'Yes, I will. Anything else, sir?'

'Any news about your missing Russians?'

'No, not yet, sir. We must get a break soon; three people can't hide out for ever. I just refuse to accept that it's possible to disappear for good.'

'I don't know how much longer I can give you on this, Ernst. It's beginning to get the bigwigs angry, but I'll hold off as long as I can, I promise you that much.'

'I know you will, sir.'

'Off the record, Ernst, I think they are all a load of ungrateful bastards. You've done your utmost to protect the city, you've exposed the heavy Organisatiya presence in Europe and stopped Hamburg from becoming a laughing stock all around the world… they will not understand what a laughing stock we almost became! Now all they can think of is the success we had, but they won't get it into their thick skulls that it could happen again, whether it's here in Hamburg or somewhere else; it is still important to world security to follow up even the narrowest of leads.'

'Thank you. I am grateful you at least appreciate the potential gravity of the situation, sir. Any extra time you can get for me I will be grateful for – you know that.'

'Ernst, on the basis of years of friendship and trust, I will do my utmost to get you all the time you need.'

Their business done, both men sat content in each other's company, feeling relieved they had got things off their chests and as usual, Roth changed the subject by enquiring sincerely about Ernst's wife and family. They chatted easily, indulging themselves in family matters, discussing their respective children and grandchildren for some while, catching up on each other's news, until Ernst was once more itching to get back to his work, knowing time was of the essence.

Walking back towards the lift, Ernst felt a little more cheery, his depression and frustration having lifted momentarily at least. He pressed the button and waited, listening for the purring, then the chunk–shush, as the doors opened, revealing the reflective void once more. Stepping in swiftly, he anxiously waited for the doors to close so that he could poke out his tongue once more and blow a raspberry for his own amusement as he travelled between floors.

In the complete silence of his apartment, Marshall Yute Polenkovich stood to attention in front of the long mirror, fully dressed in his uniform. The medals and jewel-encrusted stars gave the impression of a man who had served his country faithfully and without question, during his thirty-three years of military service. Rising through the ranks of commissioned officers reasonably quickly to Colonel, it had taken seventeen years for him to attain the rank of Marshall, to which he so desperately aspired. Seventeen years – during which, he had been forced to make a command decision against his own General. A decision which as a Field Army Colonel, he had had no choice but to accept.

Polenkovich did not realise that in those days long past, you could steal goods whatever they were, but only from the stores that were officially 'state' shipments. The mistake his General had made was to steal a case of wine from the privately-run military system that ran in parallel with the 'state' shipments. Yute saw a crime being committed by his General, witnessed him pilfering for his own personal use, but still Yute's loyalty would not allow him to denounce his fellow officer until, one day, he was approached by a KGB Major who promised him introductions which would help him with his promotion prospects and would speed up the process to obtain a travel visa for his wife so that she could go to America to have the eye operation she needed to prevent her from losing her sight. Yute grabbed the opportunity. His ego was boosted by the Major's flattery and the glowing reports which he knew were in the hands of senior officers in Moscow. All Yute had to do to gain their respect, was to speak out publicly about his General's misdemeanours. The offer of help to save his beautiful wife's eyesight for such a small betrayal seemed only right to his tormented mind. Wasn't his General a protector of the peoples of Russia like himself? Shouldn't he suffer a public reprimand as had happened many times in the past. The betrayal of the General was easy for him in those days, having no concept at all of the power and deception that prevailed. The reprimand would be a few lines written on his personal military record – which no doubt would never be looked at again!

It was not until a few years later that he had met the General's widow and learnt about the punishment handed out to him after his transfer to Moscow. He had been tortured and after suffering long and hard at their hands, he had been shot; his body dumped in some desolate alley like a beaten dog. They refused to believe he had only ever misappropriated one solitary case of wine! Yute Polenkovich had received his promotions over the years without realising or even considering that he had been the one to sign the death warrant of his own General. With hindsight, he knew he had been tested before being allowed to enter the inner circle of the Organisatiya, a test which he had passed, but at such cost to others, many, many, others over the years.

Pulling back from the mirror, reflecting his image in profile, his hand reached up to the wide-ribboned, jewel-encrusted star. He touched it gently and with reverence. As he did so, one word passed his lips: 'Hungary.' His body stiffened slightly as he recollected the carnage which he and his men had left behind, but his body relaxed again when he justified it with the thought that it was all for Mother Russia. Now he knew differently. The incident had been decided upon by the powers that be somewhere behind closed doors, having concluded that either not enough weaponry had been bought and sold or, alternatively, that if they invaded at that particular point in time, they could put up their price for oil! But when Yute was awarded his star, he still faithfully believed it had all been for the cause of Mother Russia as had been drummed into him from all military quarters – a soldier's duty is to protect his country's boundaries and the people within it.

His wry smile reflected back at him as, slowly, his mouth twisted into an expression of rage. A rage that he had been fighting within himself for many years but which had been carefully suppressed and must remain so, as his desires and vanities had now become more important to him than the creed he once believed in, that the suffering Russia was enduring would eventually turn itself into Lenin's utopian dream. Turning away from the mirror now, his face showing a momentary expression of shame, he angrily opened his shirt collar and tore open his jacket before throwing himself onto the padded sofa. Through clenched teeth he told himself emphatically, 'Yute, you have no time for remorse, you have a world to conquer!' Then after a second or two, he added softly, 'For yourself and your friends!' He sat there motionless while the emotion drained away. He told himself he must never allow himself to give quarter to his real feelings – sympathy and the voice of reason must be drilled out of his mind.

The buzz of the doorbell brought him instantly alert as he got up to walk towards the door, not forgetting to retrieve his revolver from the table in the hallway as he went. He stopped before the door and asked, 'Who's there?' as his fingers tightened around the trigger.

'Courier, sir. I have a package for Marshall Polenkovich.' The relief showed on Yute's face. He swiftly opened the door, still cautious, to see a uniformed private on the doorstep. The soldier saluted and smartly handed him a large envelope, then taking one step backwards, he saluted again before clumsily fumbling for his receipt pad. 'Will you sign here please… sir?' he asked once he had found it. Yute waited patiently while the flustered private calmed down enough to hold the book steady for him to sign.

Yute allowed himself a smile as he closed the door and walked back to his sitting room, envelope in hand, remembering that he was once a private himself. Steeling himself for the task in hand, he took his golden eagle-handled paper knife from his desk drawer and opened the envelope with some trepidation as he struggled to keep his anxiety under control. What if they've decided to veto my plan? he was thinking. He withdrew the single sheet of paper and stared at it. The message was simple, brief and to the point and bore five signatures at the bottom:

> The committee has reviewed your planned venture and decided to give our support in this instance. We shall issue instructions that your task shall not be impeded.

The signatures which followed read like a military *Who's Who*. Yute's eyes travelled down the page to the bottom, where he read 'No copy to file'.

He relaxed now, settling back in his chair, exultant at the committee's decision and relieved that he would live to see another day. Now he could exert his own pressures to speed things up. Now he would learn more about the real power within Russia's dark corridors, where fear and torment automatically spread out like tentacles. Now, those same corridors would be his to walk in without fear. His self-satisfied mood found his fingers twiddling with the unique ring on his hand. After several minutes of idly allowing himself to wallow in his good fortune, Yute reached forward and stretched both hands under the table, removing the white foolscap envelope which had been taped there. Placing it squarely on the desk, he read aloud the printed address on the flap, 'Eurocorps, Press and Public Relations Department', and then, in his best English accent, he read aloud the handwritten address on the front: 'Percival Thomason, The Gables, Wickham Bottom, Somerset, England' – the address of a very dear friend and a close supporter of the communist cause whom he had befriended whilst on Embassy duty in England, a friend who would apply for documents which Yute might find of interest, all of which would be done without pay of any kind, just purely to further the cause of Russia and the dream of creating utopia.

The document itself was not of any significance. The information contained nothing which could not have been found in any newspaper or by knocking on a few doors. But his plan, the plan he was saving his neck with and giving himself a new lease of life with, had been formulated in his agile mind from this document sent to Percival Thomason and given to Yute when they had last met. The simplicity of his plan was to infiltrate the Eurocorps' structure with Organisatiya-controlled citizens coerced into robotic Russians as in the not too distant past. They would be coerced using all manner of deception or bribery, anything to infiltrate the Eurocorps' structure which Yute's plan demanded. Their ignorance of what they would be doing to the stability of the world's economies and to world peace, they would never know. Yute would make certain that there would be no mistakes this time!

Slowly, Marshall Polenkovich walked over to the long mirror, doing up his jacket buttons and then his military collar, before standing to attention and saluting himself.

Chapter Seven

Joc Latimer had reluctantly said 'yes' to meeting Brian from Foreign division. Brian Fullerton had been pestering Joc's office for days now – even after putting his 'no's my vote' on Nadine Dashnikov. Walking briskly, his head slightly bent against the chill wind, Joc was unhappy he had succumbed to this meeting with Brian, but he had said yes out of sympathy, knowing his friend of many years was taking a lot of flack and was badly in need of someone to talk to. Running through Joc's mind was the conversation he knew they would have. 'Joc, you could throw me a few crumbs of information to at least keep these wolves at bay!' 'Truly, Joc, I won't let them crowd you,' and 'You've got all of the cards in the deck, don't play them so close to your chest!'

The neon sign from Chester's Bar blinked on and off about two hundred yards ahead of him and Joc increased his pace to get out of the wind. He reached to pull open the bar door as he muttered to himself under his breath, 'Thank goodness I phoned Liz and told her I won't be too late. I'll make sure I'm only here about an hour or so...' The warmth of Chester's Bar after the chill of the street was very welcome as Joc slid out of his top coat and folded it neatly before draping it over his arm and walking across to the bar where he had expected to see Brian already waiting, but instead all he could see was one glass on its own, with no one to keep it company. Joc sat on the stool next to it after hanging up his coat on a nearby coat stand. He ordered his favourite whisky sour and leisurely sucked the powder away prior to sipping any of the warming liquid. Brian's return from the men's room was as sharp as the bite of the sour whisky to the back of Joc's throat.

'Joc! Thanks for coming. It's been a long time since we've had a social drink together – in fact, I've just phoned my beloved and told her I could well be late home!'

'Good for you, Brian, but I've already phoned Liz and promised I wouldn't be too late.'

'You're such a spoil sport, Joc! Liz can live without you for one night.'

'She's done that many times over the years, but we are all getting older and I need my regulation eight hours' sleep, even if you don't!'

'Well, even that would give us five hours of drinking, even allowing for travelling time to get back home!'

'Not for me, Brian. By the way you're pumping, you must have had a couple already!'

'You're so right, old buddy, you're damned right! But tonight, we are not going to talk whys, we are going to enjoy ourselves and reminisce.'

'For an hour or so, Brian, that's great, but you may not last the course.'

'We'll see about that now. These drinks are on me, just to say thanks for coming and being my friend.'

'Okay, okay, let's get on with it, I'm empty right now!'

'Sure thing, Joc. Mister Barman sir, will you please purvey two large drinks here, and each time these glasses become empty, keep filling them up.'

The barman looked mildly amused and replied, 'You're the boss, sir; you'll have to live with yourself in the morning.'

'He's right, Brian. It's no fun when all the working parts of your brain are clogged up and your body is as sick as hell. Just ease up and we can have a good laugh about old times – it will be good for both of us.'

'Okay, Joc. You're both right of course.' Brian squirmed a little on his stool and then, as a passing shot to the barman, said, 'Mister Barman sir, when I do order another drink, you won't keep me waiting too long for it, will ya?' He winked broadly at the barman and both he and Joc smiled broadly in response to his wisecrack, then Joc accepted how incorrigible his friend could be and allowed his smile to turn into a laugh. Eventually even Brian's face cracked into a laugh too.

'When was it you got lucky and joined the Foreign section Brian?'

'Oh, back in nineteen eighty-five. Don't you remember? You had just come up from the south. You'd been on that drugs thing that had kept you away from the delicious Liz, and my eternally hard-done-by wife Sandra was away seeing her mother, so I gave Liz a call and asked her out to dinner. When we got back, you were about to explode because you had no idea where Liz was, and you'd phoned everyone you could think of, and all the time she was with little old me, of all people!' The teasing in Brian's voice was obvious.

'Well, how would you have felt! I'd phoned earlier and left a message for Liz on the answer machine, raced my guts out and bent a few rules to get home and after all that, she was out with a lug like you! It was enough to give anyone apoplexy when you two walked in through the door together!'

'I was sorry then, and I'm still sorry now, my friend, but you know very well there was nothing in it between Liz and me.'

'Yes I do now and in fact I believed you both shortly after you had left that night.'

'It was and still is friendship between Liz and me, Joc. We both love you too much.'

'Thanks, I know how it is. This business we're going through at the moment is hurting too. Why the hell did Longworth send me that bloody memo? It's got to be that someone somewhere has dropped a bloody clanger and someone else has got to clear up the mess!'

'Joc, you don't need to ask the question you know, you've got the answer to it. I think initially, you were a little flattered at being asked to talk to the German police, but now you've realised you're maybe involved in some sort of cover up, and in true fashion, you're putting your head down into the wind and to hell with anyone who gets in your way.'

'But you haven't got the whole picture. What this German did over in Hamburg was to cut the legs away from under one of the largest currency, drugs and arms heists the world has ever known. However, it seems he believes there are three important pieces of his jigsaw missing.'

'Hold on a minute, Joc, don't get too excited; we're here to have a good old nag and a laugh, remember?'

'Yes, I remember, but like our German friend, I'm not getting the information I'm asking for fast enough or researched thoroughly and coherently enough for me to take any immediate action, hence, I'm heavily into your office because someone is playing bloody tricks with the system!'

'Calm down, Joc! Have another drink! Look, you've always said that I was a good field man. I can't be active, but if we just jazz around with whatever's ailing you, maybe we can find some of these missing pieces.'

'You're great, Brian, and in the past we could have worked together, but with all the bloody protectionism by everyone with a little bit of power, it's slowly destroying all that we, and possibly now only me, believe in!'

'Christ, mate! That's a bit below the bloody belt, isn't it? I've never ever felt any different towards my job since the day I joined!'

'Bullshit! Sitting in ivory towers, building more ivory towers isn't police work and nothing you can say will convince me it is! Why don't you get real?'

'Okay, we do things differently now. We are in the sort of government department which often has to lick arse...' Joc laughed out loud. 'It isn't funny believe you me!' Brian continued. 'Bloody party after party in strange capital cities and towns throughout the world, fighting off those who are looking for a handout, the sorting out of the corrupt bastards who would take just about anything that was given them and turn it into personal gain, the audacity of those bastards who you very well know are turning their countries inside out to get their own personal multimillion dollar accounts in Swiss banks! Yes, my bloody life's been wonderful, but like you, Joc, I believe totally in the system we have and yes, I also believe there's some arse that needs kicking in my own division, and any other division that is working without a functional front wheel to their bike!'

The analogy Brian had used tickled them both and their smiles cracked wide open with laughter at the thought of it until slowly they settled down to take long sips of their drinks. Joc looked into Brian's eyes and asked with interest, 'What would you say was your worst moment at one of these functions that you can remember?'

'Oh, that's easy... our Embassy in Istanbul. Lots of fun, music, belly-dancers and a few males as queer as a nine-dollar bill... "Turkish delights" we used to call them! Then one of the wives – I think it was the wife of the French Naval Attaché, got so bloody fed up with their preening and ostriching around, she stripped off, completely stark naked, and began to show them what a real woman's all about! It caused considerable embarrassment, I can tell you! We had to write letters of apology to three Turkish department heads where these "Turkish delights" worked and then there was a rather irate request from high up in the Turkish government to the French Embassy, that they exert greater control over the abuse of alcohol by their Embassy staff's wives, followed by a request to the French Ambassador asking would he please forward his lists for invitations to the American Independence Day Ball!'

'Bloody funny, but where does all this verbal argy-bargy get you?'

'Precisely nowhere, other than to hold a little piece of the overall patchwork of diplomatic doorways open, should you need some quick consultations from any part of the world. It's a big club with very, very few skilful players fighting against the tell-tale Johnnies and the bullies, just as we did in school, only it's a much bigger pitch we're playing on now!'

'I still reckon you should have stayed where you were, in the field with me.'

'Don't you see, you big oaf? If I hadn't been trained in self-control and observance I would never have made anything of this job!'

'Okay, tell me what you've observed of any real significance, then?'

'Honestly, there have been many things which have helped the Embassies I've been at, to get information back in time to help a major discussion back at the Pentagon and even the White House!'

'Okay, big shot, tell me one.'

'All right. In Frankfurt, Germany we were invited to one of

our Air Force bases. It happens sometimes that a top brass takes it into his head to reciprocate or show off whatever the reason, anyway, they are generally good bashes to be at. The regimental band, female officers all dolled up in their finery, and not overly restricted either (some of them are not averse to showing out a bit, you know, exposing a little more flesh than usual), the guys flitting around from one to another of them, booze flowing as if from a tap; and we, the Embassy boys, get to know and learn a lot from the troops lower down the ranks than we are used to dealing with.'

'Get on with it, Brian! The angles you guys work don't tell me anything I don't already know, you know.'

'Okay, okay, straight to the story then. Five Russians were invited – all thought to be medium-weight military officers, nothing higher than a Major. Well, they were enjoying themselves possibly even a little more than we were. One bright spark had been playing up to one of our women and after a few too many drinks, started trying to get the girl outside. You can imagine the scene, Joc. Well, the girl wasn't giving in. He was getting drunker by the minute, so much so the girl decided enough was enough, and walked away. This Russian guy races after her, shouting, "Come on, you American whore, you come fuck with a good Russian boy, and when we finish, I tell you secrets about Berlin Wall!" I tell you, Joc, the whole place was stunned into complete silence until another Russian appeared from nowhere, shouted at him rapidly in Russian and believe me, the drunk sobered up instantly, he came to attention like a ramrod, took his dressing down and as if rehearsed, two of his mates fell in beside him and they marched off. Two days later, the Wall came tumbling down. We'd got the news in advance, but it was no use to us unfortunately, if it had been a few weeks or maybe even a few more days before, the breakout from the East could have been more controlled and far fewer bandits and subversives would have got through to the West. That was our Embassy's opinion, in actual fact.'

'Did the Russian guy who gave the drunk the dressing down leave?'

'Strangely enough, no, he just seemed to fade into the crowd.

In fact, it was his rapid disappearing act that made me rather curious about him. I caught sight of him a few moments later and I watched as he mingled for a while until he got to the Camp Commander. He was clearly apologising for his comrades' behaviour, which the Camp Commander accepted with good grace, but then when the Russian stood back to salute, I couldn't help noticing this magnificent ring he had on his index finger.

'He had what?'

'A ring. Stylish, expensive and highly unusual with scrolled gold work and an unforgettable ruby. I can't remember off the top of my head exactly, but he turned out to be some Colonel in the fast lane. CIA must have his name I'm sure... Bolanskovitch... Solanskovitch... or something like that. You know what these Russian names are like to try and remember. Anyway, I reported the incident to our security boss when I got back to the Embassy. A few days later they told me he was a full-blown Colonel and he was shooting up in the fast lane, but that's about all I know.'

Joc stood up and beamed delightedly at his friend, saying, 'You little darling... you absolute bloody darling! You might just have given me the help I need to sort out one of my German friend's problems. I don't know whether to kiss you or buy you a drink!'

'Cut it out, Joc, I'll settle for the drink!'

Chapter Eight

The bright autumn sunlight threw long speckled shadows across the pavement as Yute Polenkovich walked purposefully through the tree-lined streets on his way to meet Igor Tatlanovich, a meeting which the committee had sent instructions by courier for him to attend. The buildings towered above him, turning the streets he was passing through into vast canyons. In the shadowy gloom of Yute's imaginary canyon, his eyes were only too aware of the fact that all the buildings had seen better days and were in desperate need of having their heavy, solid stonework cleaned. He had decided to walk rather than use the car with driver which had automatically been allocated for his personal use. He had chosen to walk the wide tree-lined streets rather than furtively scuffle along the narrow dingy alleyways he could have selected so he had a better chance of spotting anyone who might just have been detailed to follow him. His plan for the day was to meet with his new 'friend' Igor, and to build up some kind of trust with the man. Having arranged the meeting on the telephone, they would undoubtedly know where he was going and although Yute didn't particularly mind them knowing this time, at some point he was going to have to arrange to meet Igor in secret.

Igor was a clerical-looking sort of person, pencils stuck into the top pocket of his jacket along with his fountain pen which had seen better days. His hair having had its morning combing, had become a little loose and untidy and the three buttons on his cheap suit jacket were all done up in a misguided attempt to give his weak, untoned body some shape. He stood shifting his body weight from foot to foot, waiting. Having not done any military service in any capacity because of his horribly flat feet, he would rather have the opportunity to have stories to tell about barrack-room life or overseas service like many of his colleagues in the Military Records department, but most of all, he wished he had actually been part of some of the brave escapades they got up to in the military – the sort of things that he read about in the newspapers almost every day of his life – but his blasted feet had not given him the chance to be a hero. He stamped his foot on the ground to vent his frustration. It didn't help, but the stamping made him feel militaristic. He was just about to stamp his foot again when a voice enquired, 'Comrade Igor Tatlanovich? Are you Igor Tatlanovich?'

'Y-y-yes, sir, I am.' The hesitancy in Igor's voice amused Yute. Igor continued the introduction having recovered his composure.

'It was very kind of you to phone me and arrange this meeting. I'll lead the way to my little office if you like, then we can talk as long as you want to and I can make you some tea. If you'd like anything else, I'm sure I could send out for it?'

Yute said nothing in reply but fell in beside this man who, with the help of his department, was rapidly securing all the information Yute needed to move his plan forward. It occurred to Yute that should this man ever realise his full potential and get a little power-hungry, he could cause havoc within the system. He was thinking to himself that these blasted people are always like this, flat and boring, when Igor's voice came washing through: '…basement, of course we could have taken the lift, but it's as broad as it's long and we would still have the length of this corridor to walk. Of course, coming this way, we have a flight of stairs to go down, but I feel it is good exercise for me and besides waiting for the lift can take up a lot of valuable time, so walking is often far quicker.'

'I'm sure you are quite right, Igor Tatlanovich, and we must save all the time we can to help Mother Russia.'

'Exactly my feelings. I preach that message to all of the staff below me at every opportunity I get.'

'I'm sure you do, Igor, I'm sure you do.' The bored monotone of Yute's voice was unmistakable and he quickly changed the subject. 'We seem to be quite honest and open with each other, which will help considerably in collating all the information you are gathering for Mother Russia. Do you mind if I call you Igor?'

Igor was quite taken aback that such a high-ranking official was offering his friendship while they simply worked together, and he was very flattered as he shyly replied, 'That is most kind of you, sir. Please do – call me Igor, it will be an honour!'

Yute shuddered inside, cringing at the subservience of this ingratiating human being, but managed to respond, 'Well, you must call me Yute.'

Igor's face came over all aglow. It was enough to brighten even the most dimly-lit corridor and he seemed to puff up with pride and gain in confidence by the minute as he walked by the side of his new friend. 'Yute.' The word sounded good to him. 'It is only a few more paces and we will turn left. My office is then at the end, not far now.'

'Good, Igor. Then we can go deeper into the lives of the people I have selected from the first list you have supplied, and I hope you have received permission for me to have access to a further list? Maybe you have something for me today, Igor?'

'Yes, there will be a further list for you to select from; it should be ready by noon.'

'Good. And thank you,' responded Yute politely.

Igor had never been treated with so much respect and consideration in his entire career. It must be true that great people are kind and courteous after all, he thought to himself. 'Here we are at last, Yute. Please sit down. Would you like some tea?'

'No thank you, Igor. I have been travelling a lot recently and I arrived home late last night, so I had breakfast late this morning. Please, if you don't mind, may we get on with the list I have brought you and do a more detailed analysis?'

'Of course, we will make a start straight away. Let me have your list.'

'If you don't mind, I would like to just give you the names verbally, one at a time. My notes are often personal to the history of the person concerned and I do not wish to influence any analysis that you may offer.'

'Oh I see.' Then, taking a bit more of a liberty with his new-found confidence than he would usually dare, he added, 'It will be better to have my own unbiased opinion, no doubt.'

Yute ignored the comment and immediately got down to business. 'The first name is Peter Donaldson of Toronto, Canada. Formerly Sonetolsky. We need to follow the career of the son. Emphasise that we need to know everything about him. Nothing must be missed out. Secondly, Rupert Helfmann, Stuttgart, Germany. He is a young Russian who changed his name when he broke through the Wall – he was a good loyal Russian, but we need more information on him and a way of getting him back to Mother Russia. Thirdly, Igor Inevskia, Moscow. He is old now, but he has three sons all of whom have had military training, especially in languages, which we need. Everything must be covered on all three sons and a full investigation of the mother and sister, as well as the father, in fact, everything on the whole family.' To soften the demand in his voice, he added, 'I'm sure you understand all the reasons why, Igor?'

It was clear from the puzzled expression on Igor's face that he had only had the simplest of briefings from whoever his puppeteer was, and it was obvious to Yute that he would have to keep a tight control over all of the information forthcoming from this pitiful man – Yute would have to vet everything. 'That won't be too much for a first task will it, Igor?'

'No, not at all, Yute. With you working closely with us, it will short-circuit the chain of events that we had to go through to get a first analysis for you to see!'

Yute couldn't believe his luck that this down-trodden glorified clerk had just offered him open house and full selection before anyone else saw anything. 'That will be most appreciated, Igor. It will help Mother Russia's cause enormously, thank you.'

By way of interruption, there was a light tap on the half-open door which made both men look up to stare at the spotty, dishevelled, adolescent boy standing in the doorway. He was holding out a brown envelope ready for someone to relieve him of it and since Yute was closest to the door, he took it and passed it on to Igor. Yute guessed the envelope contained about twenty pages. The boy sniffed, not knowing whether he was dismissed or not.

'Young man, have you anything for me to sign?' asked Igor as he looked up from the envelope. The boy sniffed again before saying, 'They didn't give me anything, sir.'

'Very well, then you may leave.' The boy slouched away and as soon as he was out of earshot, Igor started. 'Do you see what I have to work with? The appalling staff they send me these days…

untrained, unintelligent and unwashed…' Igor's voice trailed off, stopping briefly for a moment to search for a reaction on Yute's face. Seeing what he believed to be sympathy, he continued, 'After countless times of me telling them I will not allow documents to roam around the building unaccounted for…' Igor wanted to say more to his new friend, but decided it was better not to.

'It must be an enormous problem for you, Igor. Does it happen all that often?'

'Too damn often! It's scandalous – the wrong type of staff are recruited these days.' Igor looked dolefully at Yute and with a slight shrug of his shoulders coupled with a heavy sigh, he relaxed back into his chair once more.

Yute agreed with Igor that bad habits were also creeping into the military (Yute would have agreed with anything Igor said just to shut him up) then he asked Igor, seeing the contents of the freshly delivered envelope contained lists of names, each with a short précis alongside, 'If I were to take those lists with me, Igor, I could get on with my analysis while you get on with my first selection. It would speed up the process of helping Mother Russia if we both work on it simultaneously.'

Igor agreed enthusiastically and stood up excitedly from behind his desk, handing the envelope with its contents to Yute. Seizing the opportunity of taking his leave, Yute thanked Igor for all his assistance and added, 'I will start work on these straight away, so shall we meet at the same time tomorrow? If we arrange it now, it will save another phone call.'

'That would be fine, Yute. I'll be looking forward to it and don't bother with breakfast tomorrow, I shall have a little something ready for you here…'

Yute was finding these pleasantries rather a strain, but managed to keep up the pretence by responding, 'Great! I'll be here. Don't bother to see me out. I'm certain I know the way.' And with a wave of his ringed hand, he was gone.

Igor sat back down at his desk and reached for a file. He entered the following notes: 'Meeting with Marshall Yute Polenkovich commenced 1100 hours, completed 1215 hours, 23.7.96'. Turning the page over, he wrote his report of the meeting, adding: 'Passed envelope containing lists unseen by myself. Copy held in Research Office as ordered.'

Chapter Nine

Joc and Brian were still sitting in Chester's Bar – the smoke-filled alcove they had been languishing in, had suddenly become an office. With the startling news of the 'ringed-hand man', both men realised intuitively that this coincidence could well be the breakthrough Chief Inspector Ulbrecht desperately needed. Joc had obviously been very excited by Brian's information concerning the 'ringed-hand man', and now, in all fairness to Brian, he felt he had to tell him about the dossier sent over by Ernst Ulbrecht. He emphasised to Brian that his information may just be coincidental, particularly in view of the fact Brian had remembered seeing a ring on a Russian officer's finger, at a drinks party some years earlier. Brian was triumphant when he realised he had stumbled onto something so important to Joc's investigation and he teased him.

'Well, Joc, we always were a good team – I just knew you couldn't crack this one without me!'

'We were good together old buddy, but now you're in that soft job over at Foreign, you're in the wrong place!' retorted Joc in buoyant mood now.

'Don't rub it in, Joc. Anyway, you know where I am if you need me, okay?'

'Well… to save me an hour's work, can you remember the date the incident occurred?'

'Oh yes… 19 August '89, at 2221 precisely,' Brian joked.

'Did you report the incident the same evening or was it the next day?' pursued Joc, ignoring Brian's flippant remark.

'The security boss at that time had already heard of the incident before we got home, presumably from others who had been at the party but had arrived home before us. Whatever the exact time he wrote on his report, he definitely knew about the incident by about 0130 hours on 20 August from me.'

'Thanks, Brian. Well, it's been good having these few drinks, but it's time for a working cop like me to canter back to the office and start the ball rolling, tracking down that report, and to give my miserably depressed German friend a little warning to hopefully anticipate some good news!'

'Come off it, Joc, you're not leaving me after all I've done for you!'

'You're damn right I am! The way you've been laying into that booze over the past couple of hours you'll soon be in no fit state to get yourself home to your cherished Sandra. Oh, and give her Liz's and my love as well as your own.'

'I might just do that, old buddy. Come on then, let's get a cab. I'll give you a lift back to your office and make certain you get there safely... and then I'll slip round to your house to see Liz!' The playful expression on Brian's face as he said that caused an immediate outburst of laughter from both Joc and Brian as well as the barman who had been hovering nearby and had overheard the tail end of the banter. Joc slapped his old friend on the back and shouted in his ear, 'You're bloody incorrigible!'

Brian laughed again before throwing two twenty-dollar bills on the table and rather flamboyantly calling out to the barman, 'My good barkeeper... I trust you will find these bills more than enough to cover our beverages and that it may even allow you enough to partake of our good fortune yourself!'

Joc grabbed his buddy around the shoulders and dragged him towards the exit.

Joc glanced at his watch as he strode along the neon-lit, shadowless corridor. 8 p.m. already! he thought to himself... I'll just get on to Records and have the file sent up, phone Ernst in Hamburg and get out of here by nine. He reached for the outer office door handle and pushed the door wide, allowing a shaft of light to help him find his way through to his own office. As he opened his office door, the light overspilt straight onto his desk. He sat himself down slowly, allowing the events of the past couple of hours to run through his mind for the umpteenth time, then leant over to his desk light to turn it on, while simultaneously picking up the phone. The purr of the phone as he got a line seemed loud, being isolated in the vast, silent building. Joc shrugged his shoulders thinking, Does it get louder at night? He laughed at himself as he thought, Joc Latimer, you're getting as daft as everyone else around here! Smiling, he punched out the four-digit number for the Record Office in the hope there would be someone still there at this time of night to take his call and put him ahead of the game when the rest of his staff got in tomorrow morning. Five times, six times, the phone had rung. 'I'll give it to twenty,' he said to the invisible man sitting in front of his desk. 'Twenty, twenty-one… it seems a waste of time to have sat here this long. We'll go to fifty, shall we?' he spoke over the phone to his invisible man, but before he got an agreement, the earpiece burst into life.

'Sullivan, Records… You guys are working late!'

Joc was quite flustered for a moment but managed to stutter out, 'Y-yes… we've got a bit of a panic on.'

'How can I help? But first can I have your name, division, type of request, authority, and a case or any other reference number?'

Joc hurried over the details and for good measure gave his fax number and phone number, adding with his tongue in cheek, 'I'll give you my fax so that if at any time the office is unattended, you can still get the information through to me.'

'Okay, Mr Latimer, we'll see what we can do and get back to you.'

'Thank you, Mr—' Before Joc could get the Records clerk to repeat his name, the phone went dead. I'm pretty sure you said Sullivan – let's write your name down before I forget.

Now Joc reached for his German file and finding the phone number he wanted, he dialled out. On the third ring of the phone, Joc heard, 'Ulbrecht heir?'

'Latimer heir!' Joc responded playfully.

'You must be working late to call me at this time of day.'

'Well, I'm in the office still and yes, it's late because I've been having a few drinks with Brian, my friend in the Foreign section – reminiscing and so on, when he suddenly mentioned an incident just before the Berlin Wall came down, concerning a group of Russians who had been invited to a US Air Base for drinks. The base was in Frankfurt and the incident was reported to security when Brian got back to the Embassy. I'm having our records searched right now for the report.' Joc paused for a moment before continuing, 'My friend Brian saw what I believe could well be the "ringed-hand man" as described in your dossier – when you compare the artist's impression you sent with Brian's verbal description, it sounds to me there's a good chance it's the same Russian. If it is, at least we should get a name, even if we don't get much background information on him. Unfortunately, Brian could not remember the name, it's a while ago now, but please be patient with us… we'll come up with something!'

'Joc, I know we're not in a panic about this, but if you could get a lead for us sooner rather than later, that would be wonderful.'

'Ernst, you can rely on it!… Now, I'm off home to my wife and maybe watch a little TV!'

'Enjoy your evening and thanks again – your news has given me hope!'

The phone went dead. Did Joc hear a stifled sob in Ernst's throat?

Yute had made his first report back two weeks ago, at the Committee's request, and still his selection of the infiltrators he wished to use had not been approved. He had been warned the decision would not be taken hurriedly, as they had every intention to double, or even triple-check, the findings in his report. Meanwhile, he had been told to continue working with Igor Tatlanovich; searching even deeper than this initial selection of twenty-five names.

Yute had wanted to keep the selection to just twenty personnel, which he personally had felt sufficient for stage one, bearing in mind it would take at least six months to put them in place, and that in reality, a whole year would be better, but the panel were pushing for a greater number of infiltrations and the first compromise was an extra five. Yute's appeal to stay with his original plan was met with outright dismissal and although no threat was voiced, it was presented on the premise that it would suit the Committee, who support the wishes of the Council, to extend the encroachment of Eurocorps troop movements and administration in all three countries of the present Eurocorps alliance, before the coordination became too set between this newly formed tri-national group. As quickly as possible was the order of the day.

Yute had been away to reconnoitre the bases in Sigmarrengen in Germany, Saive in Belgium, Baden-Baden, 1st Division Bindee Française, Cordoba in Spain, Mülheim, Brigade Franco-Allemagne, Strasbourg, Achern and Speyer, even anticipating the expected location of the Spanish Armoured Division at Burgos. A journey the panel deemed it necessary for him to make. Yute had no option but to comply with their orders to him, but he personally felt the panel were flitting from one direction to another instead of completing things in sequence, as he had initially set out in his submission document. Yute could still see that sequence of events now, in his mind's eye:

1. Research possible candidates in the current Russian forces.
2. Research all past military service personnel living abroad.
3. All ex-military personnel up to the age of fifty, with children currently in the military.
4. Military personnel or their descendants who were trained in supply, transport and communications will be of particular interest.
5. Ex-military personnel living with, or married to non-Russians and personnel of military background from any of the ex-Russian satellite countries.
6. English and French speakers to be advanced to the top of each list for selection.
7. Children of ex-Russians who fled from Russia for any reason will be of special interest.

Polenkovich asserted his seven-part plan would allow them to arrive at a selection of intelligent soldiers and commissioned ranks. The research would confirm or deny the probability of a successful infiltration of Eurocorps' administration and command structure.

Yute felt his journeying around Europe was a waste of time at this particular moment, although useful for future reference. The prime reason for the failure of Tashimov's plan was that it had been put in place too quickly and had been operated by ill-disciplined disciples of Russia. Yute was only too aware that he was walking along the same path of Tashimov's disaster!

Waiting, just waiting. Yute found it infuriating. He was quite happy and patient when he was in control of the game, but having checked that the panel had not made any decision and that Igor was in his rabbit-hutch and had nothing for him to check through, he was left to just wait. He cursed as he jumped up from his chair and paced the room, angry with the situation, angry with the indecision all around him, and angry his original plan was being extended far too quickly. Grabbing his hat, he stormed towards the door but the doorbell rang before he reached it. He stopped sharply; it was second nature to reach for his hand gun on the hall table, then wait three seconds, listening, before responding, 'Who's there?'

Yute's face was a picture of surprise when the answer came back, 'Courier, sir!'

He momentarily dropped his guard in his excitement. This must be the new list of names from Igor, he thought. Snatching for the lock, his fingers were about to turn the catch when his built-in discipline took over. He stepped back from the door, taking a position behind the wall, out of the line of fire from any would-be assailant. 'Just a moment, who is it you want?'

'The envelope is addressed to Marshall T Polenkovich.'

Yute opened the door immediately the courier had finished speaking. He signed the proffered notebook and dismissed the courier quickly. As he closed the door behind him, he chuckled to himself, 'Next time I'll be Marshall U Polenkovich!' The light-hearted mood of a moment ago faded as he sat at the table opening the large brown envelope, flicking through the pages containing another one hundred names. There was no option but to obey the panel's wishes so he started immediately going through the long laborious process of selecting his initial candidates. Then, it would start again: returning the list to Igor for further selection, then the waiting, then the presentation to the panel and then more waiting. With a heavy heart, he sighed and carried on with his task.

At his desk, Igor Tatlanovich wrote: 'Selection sent to Marshall

T Polenkovich 23.8.96'. Turning the page as before, he wrote in pencil, 'One copy held in Records'.

Ernst sat smiling behind his desk in the knowledge that there was at last a glimmer of hope, thanks to his new friend, Joc, and somehow the 'cat that got the cream smile would not go away'. Was it an omen that his tenacity allied with the technical resources of the Americans' worldwide, information-gathering network meant he was going to be successful in at least identifying the 'ringed-hand' mystery man by name? That chance piece of news was electric. That first moment when he had heard of the possibility of a breakthrough had almost brought tears of happiness and relief from the tension which had built up within him, but today, although he was happy, his lightening mind was already pacing out a plan of action ready to implement it when they had the wherewithal to track down the 'ringed-hand man'. Was he a controller? Was he the designer of all that havoc at the docks? Or was he just a contract killer, or an independent trader? Was he Organisatiya? The questions kept flickering through Ernst's mind. Dozens of questions which would all need to be answered in the cause of justice for the crimes committed in his beautiful city of Hamburg. He also had a feeling of dread – what if this unknown man was given even more power? – what revenge could he wreak on Hamburg or anywhere else for that matter?

His phone suddenly ringing snapped Ernst out of his thoughts and his face returned to its normal, relaxed expression.

'Ulbrecht heir?' The telephone earpiece relayed some information which was immediately acknowledged by Ernst with a curt, 'Will you keep me informed?' and with a tilt of his head he then added, 'Thank you,' and placed the receiver down. His thoughts were just about to return to the torment of finding his three missing perpetrators, when officer Katerina Mayer walked past his open office door. Ernst rose quickly from his chair and strode to the doorway calling after her. 'Investigator Mayer! May I have a word with you please?'

'Yes, sir, of course.'

'Are you very busy with that case you're on?'

'It's mostly all cleared up, sir, just a few points I would like to ponder over, but Inspector Koslowski thinks I should go back into uniform at the end of next week.'

'Have you enjoyed your time working with us?'

'Oh, every minute, sir!' Mayer responded enthusiastically.

'Well, we'll see what we can do for you a little later on.'

'Thank you, sir.'

'It was Records you came from before I stole you away, wasn't it?'

'Yes, sir. Clever of you to remember…'

'No, not really. I'm at the age when I remember silly trivial things like that and then forget what day it is!'

'I can't believe that, sir!'

Ernst laughed; he liked Officer Mayer. 'Thank you. Anyway, back to the point… your colleagues in Records – do you still keep in touch with them?'

'Oh yes, sir. They're a great bunch; it's rather nice to have friends in the workplace.'

'It is indeed. Well, thank you for sparing the time to talk to me – I mustn't hold you up any more.'

'Thank you, sir. It has been nice to talk to you again. Goodbye, sir.'

'Goodbye, Mayer, and thank you again.'

Mayer could not help notice that just as she turned to walk away, a quizzical look crossed his face. As she walked out of his hearing, checking all around her first of all, she allowed herself to quietly mutter, 'That crafty old fox has got something on his mind, and whatever it is, I hope it will involve me!'

Ernst went to sit down at his desk muttering to himself, 'Must tell Koslowski to keep her here in the Investigations section. I'm sure when Joc Latimer phones, Investigator Mayer will be of great use – especially with her connections with the Russians; her fluency in the language will be a great advantage.' Ernst reached for his phone again, this time dialling Inspector Willi Koslowski's number. The phone was answered promptly but Willi's habit of mimicking Ernst's own style of answering went completely over Ernst's head.

'Koslowski heir?'

'Willi, can I ask a favour of you?'

'Of course, Ernst. If I can do anything, I will.'

'I know. I would like to try and keep Mayer on our team for a bit longer, if I can get away with it.'

'We discussed this a few weeks back, Chief, and the end of next week is as far as I can make the budget stretch.'

'I know, but something is moving with the Yanks and with her Records' experience, her fluency in Russian, and the little extra clout with her new trainee rank, she could push whatever information we may need through a little faster.'

'I know how worried you are about the missing three, but it all comes down to money!'

'Go with me on this, Willi; I'll find the money from somewhere.'

'Okay, Ernst. I want to keep her on the team anyway – she's a great asset, we all know that.'

'Thanks, Willi. She doesn't need to know yet, and if I don't get anything from the Yanks by the end of the week, let her go back. I can always start begging the Commander to get her back again, but it's just another bit of red tape and bullshit to have to go through, plus the Commander is always at conferences and things these days. It could take ages for me to even get an appointment with him.'

Willi jokingly said, 'He did look great on TV last night... I've never seen him in a dinner jacket before!'

Ernst cut in abruptly. 'He deserves all the recognition he's getting from the public and the bureaucrats. Don't forget he could have lost everything if we hadn't been successful; he gambled on using the Army, the Navy, the Air Force and they practically turned the docks into a war zone and he's still supporting our costs while we try to find our missing Russians!'

'Hold on, Ernst! I'm not having a go at him, he's a good, strong man, for sure.'

'I know, Willi, I just don't want to let anyone forget all the support he's given us.'

'Okay, okay, but shouldn't you remember you did a bit towards it too?'

'Possibly... but I only had the policing of it to worry about; he had the whole bloody city council.'

'If that's how you want it.'

'You know I do. Just keep Mayer on, okay?... I'll cover it somehow.'

'Consider it done, boss. Anytime, you know that. You'll phone me by the end of the week?'

'Yes I will. Thanks, Willi, bye for now.'

As he placed the receiver down, Ernst rubbed the back of his neck with his cupped hand. He found it very soothing, but he knew that the hunch he had had at the start of the drugs, arms and bullion scam they had just smashed, was not yet resolved. His famous hunches always started with a tingling on the back of his neck and the comfort of massaging his neck with his cupped hand always seemed to make things happen. His immediate response to his ringing phone was a quick and positive, 'Ulbrecht heir!'

'Joc here, Ernst.' His clear, nasal accent grabbed Ernst's attention straight away. 'I'm feeding you information just as soon as it comes in. We know the "ringed-hand man" was military. Well, first reports indicate he was Army and at the time he had the rank of full Colonel, but he could be anything now. Sorry, we've got no more than that at the moment.'

'Thanks, Joc. At least if your indications are right about him being Army, it cuts out the other two services. When do you think you can confirm that?'

'As soon as I know, you will; hopefully with a name as well. Brian is furious with himself that he can't remember the Russian's name. He's made all sorts of permutations of Igors and Ivans galore, but as Brian is unsure, and rather than setting you off in six or more directions at once, I think it's better to wait a little longer. Brian will extract the file we need as he has promised, but his position within his own department is... how shall we say... a little restricted at the moment. I've called the file up as well, but I think I'm being obstructed somewhere along the line.'

'You're probably right, Joc. I'm just eager to get on with it.'

'I know, my friend, but I promise, when I know, you'll know.'

'Well, thanks again, Joc. Bye for now.'

The brevity that was loosely known as conversation between two talented police officers had taken over, along with the trust and respect which had been built up over the past few question and answer sessions. At opposite sides of the world, both men leant back in their chairs to reflect on progress.

Chapter Ten

Yute sat in his apartment staring at the lists of names selected for deeper analysis by Igor Tatlanovich and his team. It had taken only a few days, days which he had spent wrangling over and over in his mind their potential as officers who would take orders under any conditions, as issued by their unknown superiors, along with the personality of each candidate and an ability to work side by side with other officers of Eurocorps.

Now, gathering up all his lists of profiles, he left for his prearranged meeting with Igor. The last thing to be placed into his briefcase was a bottle of whisky, a present for this poor, boring civil servant, in the hope that in future he would put a lot more pressure on his staff than he seemed to have been doing so far.

His cautious exit into the street from the walkdown steps gave Yute a good opportunity to scan the whole street for the position of the surveillance man allocated to him. He took out a cigarette. Having spotted him, Yute had made a habit of walking over towards him, allowing him to pick up a position behind his back. Yute wanted the man to be comfortable and by using the same tactics on every journey he made, he hoped that his tail would always expect the same of him and be lulled into a false sense of security, in preparation for the one important opportunity when Yute might want to get away unobserved. It was a precaution Yute felt he must take in the event of anything going wrong with his plan, particularly since his plan was being moved up in pace and dimension by the Committee. His cigarette was lit, the taking of the smoke into his lungs had been enjoyed, there was a short wait before the slow exhaling began, and on a mental count of three, he took his first step into the street. The game began again.

At Igor Tatlanovich's office building, instead of Igor himself waiting at the main entrance hall, there stood a thin weasel-like man who approached him, asking very politely for him to kindly follow him to Comrade Tatlanovich's office. Falling into step behind the whippet-thin man, it did not go unnoticed by Yute that his boring little civil servant, Igor, was showing off a little bit by not coming to meet him himself. In the same cubby hole of an office sat Igor, his pencil sliding over the paper in front of him, leaving no marks whatever. The pretence was obvious to Yute, and Igor, who was playing his own part, did not feel comfortable in the deception he was acting out. There was a deliberate pause before Igor rose up from his wooden chair and fawned over Marshall Polenkovich standing before him. It sent warning bells ringing in Yute's head.

'May I apologise, Comrade Marshall, for not meeting you personally. The pressure of work, you know. I do hope you will forgive me?'

The treacle oozing from every pore of this man was far too much, and not his normal, humble manner at all. The 'I know something you don't know…' impression heckled Yute's brain, but he couldn't yet figure out what, or why. 'I must play the game' was the only message his instincts could give him.

'No apology necessary, Igor; we are all working for the same cause, aren't we?'

'We most certainly are, Yute!'

Igor's insistence on using his first name set more alarm bells ringing. 'I'm afraid my new lists will increase your work load even more,' Yute continued.

'It was to be expected,' Igor immediately responded.

'I suppose so. Out of the one hundred and fifty names, I have added a further fifteen to my list, making seventy in all.' Stopping for a moment, Yute asked, 'Unless you have more coming through your system, I think we have enough candidates to start this project.'

'The pressure of work has kept me from checking what progress is being made, but you will be informed later,' Igor said, leaving a short pause before adding, '…after I have checked with my staff.' Those words just tumbled from his mouth, telling Yute that somehow, somewhere, this insignificant little bloody wimp was taking instructions behind his back.

Quickly and responsively, Yute changed the path of the

conversation. 'Igor, I hope you don't mind, but I've brought you a little present.'

'That is most kind of you, Yute, most kind.' Taking the bottle and admiring the label, he read: 'Glenmorangie Malt Whisky'. Looking straight into Yute's face, he said very sincerely, 'Oh, what a surprise! Thank you so much.'

Yute knew from Igor's reaction that he had not realised his mistake in saying, 'You will be informed later,' which had given him away a few moments ago.

'It is my pleasure, Igor. Without you, where would any of us uncontrolled, over-ambitious military types be? It's you people that hold us all together for Mother Russia.'

'We do help, more than we are given credit for, I think, but one day, no doubt we will be rewarded.'

'I'm sure you will be, Igor, I'm sure of it!'

In an uncharacteristic display of humour, Igor responded, 'Let's hope I won't be too old to enjoy it!'

Yute laughed along with Igor's little joke, but his brain was already working out ways to make certain that Igor was not going to enjoy anything for very much longer.

'Igor, in half an hour I have another meeting to attend. Would you mind if I left you with my list? My notations on each one make it quite obvious which of those I want further information on and you know the qualifications we are looking for as well as I do.'

'Well, thank you for your trust in me, Yute. I will certainly do as you ask. In fact, I have another meeting shortly myself, so if we break now, it will give me time to start the procedures moving on your latest list.'

'Okay, it suits us both well then. I'll say goodbye for now. You will contact me with your results as soon as possible?'

'As soon as possible. Yes, my friend, I certainly will.'

'Good. Goodbye then. I'll see myself out, don't worry about me.'

Igor responded a little curtly, 'I won't.' Then, as an after-thought, he added, 'Thank you again for my present.'

Yute wasted no time leaving the building; he wanted time to think. Time to work out what this bloody civil servant was up to.

Or was he under different orders entirely? The polluted air of the Moscow street at least felt purer than the air he had been inhaling in Igor's dungeon. He lit a cigarette and inhaled deeply, giving him time to pick out his tail, and the game began all over again.

Chapter Eleven

The phone was ringing in Ernst Ulbrecht's empty office. The direct line had no answer machine attached to it, and at the other end, Joc Latimer was talking into the unresponsive phone pleading with it. 'Oh, come on, Ernst old buddy! Have I got news for you... please answer this phone!... Please, come on, don't play possum at a time like this! Okay then, if you don't answer after five more rings, I'm going home and you can wait until tomorrow. One... two... three... four... five... Well, sorry old buddy, bye bye for now.' Joc placed the receiver back in its cradle and sat for a few moments collecting his thoughts before getting up to leave the office.

Meanwhile, Ernst raced into his office just as the last ring cut out. 'Damn it! That had to be Joc, I'll bet!' He snatched the phone and dialled the thirteen digits which seemed to take forever. Finally the last digit registered and there was an anxious pause while the call connected. Had Joc left his office? One ring... two... 'Hello, Joc Latimer...

'Sorry to trouble you, Joc, it's Ernst. Were you just trying to get hold of me?'

'Yes! Well done for guessing it was me – I have some great news for you. We are sure now that we have the right name: Yute Polenkovich. Our records show him as a General, but Intelligence think he may now be a Brigade Marshall, so you've got a big one to reel in!'

'Thank you so much! If you get any more information on him you will let me know, won't you?'

'You can bet on it. Now, try and get some sleep tonight and you can start working on it in earnest tomorrow!' Joc giggled at his own little pun, which Ernst obviously didn't understand.

'Well,' Ernst said slowly, a little confused, 'thanks again, Joc. Goodbye for now.'

The phone clicked off in Joc's ear and he had another little giggle at his own joke, '...start work in earnest!'

The relief at finding out a name for the most important one of his missing trio produced a jubilant, self-satisfied look on Ernst's face, but the self-satisfaction disappeared as he picked up the phone again and dialled Willi Koslowski's number.

'Koslowski heir!'

'Willi, it's Ernst. We've got a name for the missing "ringed-hand man"! It's been fully corroborated, the CIA seem certain they've got the right one. Would you believe, Willi, he could be an Army Brigade Marshall?'

'Christ, Ernst! That's going to be some hard nut to crack.'

'It depends, I think, on whether he's gone back into military work alone, in which case, a few of our men scattered around should make him fairly easy to keep an eye on and then we can serve a warrant whenever he crosses our borders. Should he be – as we both suspect – Organisatiya, then it could prove more difficult.'

'You'll have to wait to find out.'

'Yes, Willi, but I've waited this long and I'm not going to rock the boat and watch them scurry underground again. You're going to be the first to know his name – it's Yute Polenkovich. Obviously I will respect your decision on who you tell about this, but I hope you will be discreet. We must not let anything get out to the press, otherwise we'll have no chance to follow up and put the bugger to rest.'

'You have my word, but maybe you should call a meeting of everyone who was involved with the case and tell them yourself – they deserve to know. If the name did leak out, it could lower your prestige amongst them – they all worked hard for you, Ernst, and they're always totally trusting, as you well know.'

'Yes, you're right. Will you call them all together for me? Make it for about 1700 hours tomorrow in my office?'

'I'll do my best. I'll confirm it with you when I've spoken to them all. Will that be all, Ernst?'

'Yes thanks. I'll hear from you tomorrow then?'

'Yes, boss, as I said.' As Willi hung up the phone, he thought to himself that his somewhat eccentric boss must be on another planet, going by the distracted tone of his voice and in asking the same thing twice.

The panel sitting in judgement over Yute Polenkovich's plan were united in agreement with the overall concept, but there was a heated discussion over the selection of a controller. Names had been mentioned, then discarded. Although there were many suitable candidates for consideration, the problem was that Polenkovich was recognised as one of their most experienced men. One point which had been made by the Chairman in Yute's favour, was that had it not been for the misfortune which had befallen him in Hamburg, Marshall Yute Polenkovich would by now have been a member of this, or some other similar panel elsewhere in Russia. The Chairman spoke openly of Yute's past successes and emphasised his quality of accepting the risk of death and of being prepared to carry out death sentences on others – something which had never been a problem for this man. 'The quiet control this man exerts is well known to all of us…' he said. The prime mover against the Chairman's recommendation argued that Yute had escaped what should have been the severest penalty after his failure in Hamburg, and recommended restitution be taken instead, basing his opposition to the plan on the sole fact that it was selfishly motivated and brought before them with no set timescale and most of all, that it was simply a way for Yute to ensure he died in his bed of old age.

'Gentlemen!' the Chairman called them to order. 'We must take a vote. The matter has been fully discussed and Central Council permission has been granted for us to make this decision and then pass on our recommendation. To date, after weeks of deliberation, only one other name apart from Marshall Polenkovich's has been under consideration. May I suggest we put it to the vote now?' There were murmurs and rumblings around the table as each man took a small piece of plain paper in turn.

'Gentlemen, please write down your candidate's name.' The ensuing silence was only broken by the scratching of pen on paper and the rustle as each piece of paper was then folded before being placed in the large banner-red bowl in the centre of the table.

'Thank you, gentlemen. Will you pass the bowl along please?'

Taking the bowl as it reached him and making certain that neither of his hands went anywhere near the neck of the bowl, he stood up and, pulling back his cuffs, he placed his hand in, in full view of the panel members and pulled out between his fingertips one piece of paper, from which he read out loud the name written on it. 'Polenkovich,' he said. Placing the piece of paper on the table to his right, he proceeded to take another. 'Lesnovitch.' Placing the piece of paper to his left, he took another.

'Lesnovitch.' Placing the paper to his left, he took another. 'Lesnovitch.' He placed the paper on his left, and took another from the bowl. 'Polenkovich.' Placing the paper on his right, he took another. 'Polenkovich.' Placing the paper on the right, he continued, 'We have a draw, gentlemen, leaving me to cast the deciding vote. I vote Polenkovich, a decision you will not be surprised at since I have supported him and his plan throughout all of our recent meetings.'

A binding silence held them, all of them realising the enormity of the decision just made. A decision which would have to be forwarded for Central Council approval, looking as though they had all been unanimously in favour of Polenkovich since only the result of the vote would be forwarded. The Chairman sat down, his drawn face now showing the stress he had been hiding – the stress of the directive from Central Council that Polenkovich must win the vote. Rapping his knuckles on the table he invited, 'May I suggest we adjourn to the next room for refreshments? We will have to be back in an hour to review Polenkovich's strategy and training programme – I set the meeting with him yesterday.'

As the group moved towards the dining room, the furtive looks exchanged between them pushed them apart. Those who had voted for Polenkovich as ordered, were not in the mood to let it be known in case Polenkovich's plan should fail; the allegedly 'secret' voting paper had a habit of being used against the considered culprits. Democracy in Russia, despite 'perestroika', did not exist in real terms for the Russian people and each committee member leaving the room at this very moment knew that committee work, such as they had been administering over the past few weeks, was a sham. A sham that generally only lasted until the first vodka, when their shame lifted and allowed them to forget, until the next time their minds would be tormented into making a decision, only to be forgotten when the next vodka came. Their own payment for living.

Chapter Twelve

Cold winds were accompanying the squally showers across Eurocorps Command HQ's Strasbourg parade ground, where four countries' troops had been assembled to parade before their Commander-in-Chief, whose sole purpose on this dreadful day was to promote goodwill and *esprit de corps* amongst his newly formed European Command, strengthening European defence within the North Atlantic Alliance. The parade had been intended to be a colourful affair with French, German, Belgian and Spanish flags flying, gently swirling over their respective troops, led by the United Europe flag. The Commander was to stand proudly as his troops marched past at the very first parade of the now four nations group. The Parade Marshall had all of his men on parade, the bands positioned, all mustered thirty minutes before the C-in-C's arrival.

The seasoned troops, buffeted by the wind and made uncomfortable by the rain, were standing at ease. The command of 'Stand easy!' was bellowed across the parade ground, allowing them to move their bodies but not their feet. The moans whispered between each trooper were the same from all four nations assembled.

'Why the bloody hell are we standing here in weather like this?'

'I bet the C-in-C will be late!'

'He won't be getting wet in his bleedin' car, will he?'

'Bet yer when he gets a bit closer to us and sees how bad the weather is, he'll call it off and we'll get moved to the drill hall!'

'You're probably right, mate; even if he has got a batman to clean all of his kit, I'll bet he don't like getting wet!'

'He's human, then!' came a quip from the rank at the rear. A subdued titter had just started to run through the ranks when the word 'Parade!' bellowed across the square. 'Parade – stand at ease!' was the next command, followed by 'Parade – attention!' In unison, there was a loud crack as left feet hit the ground, bringing the moaning to an abrupt end.

The dais steps were hurriedly approached and the Adjutant announced for the benefit of all assembled, that the parade would be dismissed and reformed in the drill hall by command of the C-in-C. It was as much as the troops could do to contain their laughter until after the final command of 'Parade dismiss!' rang in their ears.

In the warmth of the Officers' Mess, after the hurried review of his command and his address in two languages, the C-in-C is charming and convivial with all he meets, his gin and tonic is constantly replenished as he walks around repeating the same words to each group of soldiers who seemed to be clustering together and not mixing with other nationalities.

'It's a shame we couldn't have a parade, but a bit unfair on the men to have to stand there getting soaked. Good idea to bring them inside though. You officers must encourage your men to mix with the other nationals, you know, otherwise it won't all come together, will it? Oh, I see you are all French! That won't do, will it?' Another sip of his drink and on to the next group…

The guard at the main gate had been stood down until the warning came from the Officers' Mess that the C-in-C was leaving when it would be their turn to stand out in the appalling conditions for at least five minutes before the expected, fleeting moment of their C-in-C passing through the gate. Meanwhile, they were all standing around in their wet clothes in the hot guard room, steaming.

Daniel Tomlevski stood sheltered from the rain watching from a barrack-room door. He was happy his application to join this unique European Corps had been accepted. It was a corps of many nations which would come to the defence of one another, for the first time in the history of Europe – working to unite and defend, had got to be better than fighting each other, Daniel mused. He had taken his commission as his father had done before him, at Sandhurst.

His father had been a refugee from Poland, having escaped the German invasion of World War Two; his fear was not the likely persecution for being a Jew, but more for being a Russian. Having gotten to England, his determination to fight the European oppressors took him almost straight from the quayside to enlistment in the British Army. Speaking little English at the time, he was refused, but the invasion of Poland took place shortly after he had managed to get a good grounding in English. Working in cafés, markets and on building sites – never once did he forget he was learning English to fight the oppressors of Europe. Presenting himself for acceptance again at the same enlistment centre, the Sergeant who had rejected him the first time, remembered him and complimented him on his English. He recommended to his superiors that he should be used in some way, helping to sort out the large influx of Poles, 'which was making things very difficult in the communications department, sir'. For Daniel's father, things moved rapidly from then on. He was inducted into the army, organising pockets of his countrymen across England, Scotland and Wales into camps, with their own officers. He became well known for his command of English throughout the railway network of England, Scotland and Wales, along bus routes and across London and other principal cities, so much so, that when porters or conductors saw him, followed by his flock of lively, unruly Poles, they held the bus or train to enable him to count them on and off the transport. Daniel's father respected the authority's wishes that he should continue with his liaison work, but his father really wanted to be in the fighting.

Daniel was born in England in nineteen sixty, the son of Jacob Tomlevski and his young English wife. As he stood looking out over the Eurocorps parade ground, he remembered the happiness it had brought his father when Daniel showed him his confirmation of an interview for a position within Eurocorps. Daniel remembered the stories his father told him of the chaos and degradation the Nazis put the Polish people through. Daniel had always liked the way his father called them 'his people' and in the early part of World War Two all his father's work was in getting 'his people' from one place to another, guiding them day and night to join units being formed by Poles in the Air Force and the army. In fact, didn't his father tell him how he became so well known to bus conductors and all manner of railway and underground railway staff that he had been known by the British as 'Jack, the Pied Piper of Poles'? A title he revelled in. Thankfully, the British authorities eventually allowed him to become a soldier with his now fluent English and with his shoulder flashes 'Poland', he soon found his way to Sandhurst and took the shortened wartime course, passing out with honour to become Lieutenant Jacob Tomlevski of the Polish Armed Forces in England. Hadn't his father told him so often that the turmoils besetting Europe because of Adolf Hitler's greed were horrendous? But when the hostilities ended and Hitler was beaten, even greater horrors confronted the world when the concentration camps were opened up. How millions upon millions of records had been burnt by the Germans – the constant movement of displaced people of this European tragedy, a continent which his father insisted has really always needed a full European government body or even an army to maintain peace.

Daniel had pulled himself upright, stretching his cupped hands as far down his back as possible, pulling his shoulders back and showing his Polish Army shoulder flashes prominently. Having stretched his body, Daniel reflected on his father's good work with all the refugees and his humanity; an inner kindness that was always there waiting for someone to come and suck from his father's strength. Daniel's father may not have received very much in return; in fact, only one promotion did he get prior to leaving the army, but Daniel had learnt a lot from his father and he knew from a very early age he was going to be a soldier and help oppressed people just as his father had continued to do even after leaving the services. Daniel remembered the conversations he had with his father and especially one particular time when his father was deliberating on the constant flow of refugees from Yugoslavia, Hungary and Africa to countries all over the world, but his driving passion in life was that no one should be allowed to live in a chasm of fear. Daniel's own dream was to bring the humane use of communication and new technology in the world to help further speed up his father's work. Today was Daniel's big day; the interview to join Eurocorps. Transferring from the British Army into the Polish Army, he had helped with Poland's restructuring after a period of political unrest, when he had met and then married Nicole, a beautiful young university student in Paris. Daniel was serving at the Polish Consulate, negotiating exchange schemes for French and Polish officers, where men would interchange their skills and all aspects of their military training. Marrying Nicole, with the love they clearly shared for each other, took over their lives. To everyone, their devotion to one another was openly apparent and the natural sympathies they shared for all oppressed peoples was a great bond between them. Daniel, being married to a French woman and now speaking fluent French, as well as English and his father's native tongue, decided that with his new-found trilingual skills, his French/English dual nationality through marriage, plus his own application for Polish nationality having been granted, that Eurocorps would be the right place for him to be, to protect the people of Europe and the rest of the world, as per Eurocorps' charter.

Glancing down at his watch, he read the time. Ten minutes to three. Ten minutes to walk the long corridor, walk up two flights of stairs, the short corridor to the office of the Adjutant of Eurocorps HQ, Strasbourg. Standing at ease directly in front of the door, Daniel clutched his military records and the special request for service with the 'Corps, listing his reasons for joining Eurocorps and requesting a transfer into the French Army as a right.

Ernst Ulbrecht's office had become more active; the usual pulse of things had increased by twenty per cent. His command over the information he was receiving was being monitored by him and then redirected to where he considered it would do the most good. Suddenly, Ernst threw himself back into his chair and his hand reached for the back of his neck. The gentle rubbing soothed him, although he was unaware he had been doing it most of the time. His mind was struggling with some small point – a time had come for a definite decision and commitment. Slowly reaching for the phone, he dialled the numbers. The ringing tone took over the rhythm of his mind; five, six, seven... 'Koslowski heir!' a breathless voice answered.

'Willi... Ernst. You remember what we talked about last time?

Well, can we talk again, with Mayer this time, when you are both free?'

'Mayer's out right now, she shouldn't be more than an hour shall we just come up when she gets back?'

'Yes please, Willi, I'll be around the office somewhere!'

'See you later then, Ernst.' No sooner were the words out of Willi's mouth, than the phone went dead immediately. Usually, the reason for Willi's habitual abruptness in hanging up the phone was his dislike for the annoying thing, but this time was different. He had worked with Ernst so often, he instinctively knew something had been decided and that both he and Mayer were going to be closely involved in it – a cranky old cop and a young woman trainee detective in the making. What was Ernst up to this time?

Mayer walked back into the squad room and finding the note left on her desk telling her to see Inspector Koslowski the moment she got back, put a frown on her face as she read it.

Searching out Koslowski proved more difficult than she had thought. Everywhere she was directed to, it seemed he had just left. From the cells below, to Personnel on the fifth floor, she followed him around the building. Then at last, her enquiry was answered with, 'He said he was going back to his office…' Mayer ran back down the stairs to save time waiting for the lift and pushing open the second floor door in haste, a sudden bump lurched Inspector Koslowski into the arms of Commander Roth, who had been exchanging pleasantries. Mayer apologised profusely, saluting, completely flustered by being so clumsy; she came to attention, regained her equilibrium and asked Inspector Koslowski directly, 'You wished to see me, sir?'

Willi could hardly stop laughing, but managed to say, 'Yes, Mayer. Wait in my office, I will be there shortly.'

Mayer answered abruptly, 'Yes, sir.' Her swift about turn after 'windmill-saluting' everything that came into view was the last thing she managed before she half-ran away down the corridor. The embarrassment of it all put a blush onto her pretty face.

Commander Roth and Willi Koslowski chuckled to one another and Koslowski commented, 'Wouldn't it be great to be that energetic?'

Commander Roth considered the comment carefully before answering, 'I don't think I ever was, Willi…'

'I might have been, I can't remember for sure, but I do know that whatever I did never looked as good as that!'

'I'll bet you never used the stairs if you were anything like me, Willi.'

'We have an excuse, sir. The lift was a new invention as far as government buildings were concerned in our day, and the novelty has never worn off!'

'You may be right, Willi.' Roth answered jokingly, adding, 'Did we have more or less heart attacks in those days?'

'A point to ponder, sir. Well, if we have finished our conversation, sir, I do need to get along to see Ernst.'

'Of course, you get along then, and give Ernst my regards.'

Both men went their separate ways, parting just as casually as they had met, no saluting or subservient 'after you' type of gestures. Entering his screened-off office, Koslowski found Mayer standing in front of his desk. 'Please sit down, Mayer. Now, how available are you?'

'I'm just clearing up loose ends, sir.'

'Have you got time right now to join me in a meeting?'

'Well yes, sir, I need to make a couple of phone calls first, but then there would be no problem.'

'Good. Go do them then.'

'Sir… sir, may I ask what the meeting's about?'

'It's with Chief Superintendent Ulbrecht and I don't know exactly what it's about myself, but we have been asked to be there together.'

'I'll be back as soon as I can, sir. Say ten minutes?'

'Fine. I'll tell Chief Superintendent Ulbrecht we'll be along then.'

Mayer's anxieties were racing through her mind as she was making her phone calls. Although her conversations were coherent and precise, the warmth of her voice was missing. She was distracted. Exactly nine and a half minutes later, she stood before Willi Koslowski's desk once more.

Entering the always-open door of Chief Superintendent Ulbrecht's office was, in Mayer's eyes, an honour. The respect she felt for this large, cuddly man after only working with him for that one brief spell, had given her a new insight into crime prevention. Prevention by anticipation – which she had never been taught at Police Training College.

'Please sit down, both of you,' Ulbrecht requested as they entered the doorway, while he finished off signing some letters which needed to be got out in the post by his secretary who was standing there patiently, smiling apologies to both Willi and Mayer from time to time. Finally, the closing of the book for signatures brought the secretary's hand swiftly down to remove it, and in silence, she left the office. 'Sorry to keep you waiting, this blasted paperwork is horrendous, and she is an absolute tyrant when it comes to keeping me up to date with it!'

Willi looked up and groaned, 'Don't tell me about it, it's so bad now I'm thinking of writing to the bloody environmentalists asking for a ban on the use of paper.'

Ernst smiled and joked, 'Don't do that, Willi. If you got your request granted, some silly sod would ban everything and we'd have nothing to wipe our arses on!'

Willi laughed out loud at Ernst's joke, but Mayer was unsure how to react, and just smiled.

'I apologise for my rudeness, Policewoman Mayer. Sometimes my brain is working faster than my tongue and I revert to colloquial Hamburgian speech.'

'I understand, sir. There is logic in what you say; if no new supplies of paper were let into the system we would run out of recycled paper also, so it wouldn't take long for your predicted situation to become a reality.'

Once again, as on previous occasions, both men were stunned by Mayer's sharp analysis and delivery. Ernst smiled a 'Thank you, Policewoman Mayer' smile, smiled again, and quickly got down to business.

'Willi, the meeting you were going to arrange for the whole team – I've decided against it. I hope you will understand.'

'I think I do, Ernst,' replied Willi.

Nodding his thanks to Willi, Ernst turned to speak to Mayer. 'A few days ago, Mayer, Inspector Koslowski and I had a discussion about you.' Ulbrecht waited for a moment before continuing. 'We were discussing ways of keeping you on your training programme with us and I, with Inspector Koslowski's permission, wish to ask you to stay with us a little longer. Your experience in the Records Section, your personal connections with your Russian counterparts and your fluency in the Russian language are all assets we need to retain. In brief, we have an assignment for you. You will recall, when we counted up the number of bad guys after the first case you worked on with us, we had a shortfall of three persons for certain, possibly more. Well, we now have all three of their names and we need you to find out every scrap of information you can, on one of them in particular. You will, until otherwise told, bring all your findings personally to me, and no one else. You are sworn to secrecy, so you will be treading a very lonely path. Will you accept the assignment?'

'Of course, sir,' Mayer replied without hesitation and the directness in her voice left no one in any doubt.

Ernst turned to Willi. 'Would you leave us now, Willi? You know the name of the man we are about to discuss, but I need to talk of specific details with Officer Mayer. Have you told anyone in the group about our little bit of success?'

'No, luckily I had decided it was probably better not to – which also seems to be your decision now!'

'That's good. If you could withhold the name from everyone, it will be better for Mayer in the long run.'

'If that is your wish, Ernst, but what about Commander Roth?'

'He will have to wait, along with the rest of the group for the time being,' answered Ernst decisively.

'You're the boss, Ernst. Shall I go now?'

'Please,' replied Ernst, 'and thank you.'

'Good luck, Mayer…' Willi shouted over his shoulder as he left his boss's office and strode out into the corridor.

'Mayer, I realise you are young and inexperienced. This responsibility I am placing on your shoulders is a heavy burden, but in my opinion you are more than worthy of my trust.' Making the conversation a little lighter, he added, 'After all, I'm only asking you to track down one man!' They both laughed, helping the butterflies of expectancy in Mayer's stomach to settle a little. Ernst took up the conversation again. 'You remember at the end of the dockyards affair, we lost three men. Lanov and Mogatin we already knew the names of, but the third one we could never put a name to. Well, the CIA picked up on one of our reports with a request for an explanation as to why Miss Dashnikov was working on our patch. With a bit of luck, a few bits and pieces of information have come together…' Pausing for a moment, Ernst watched for Mayer's reaction, but she sat before him silently, soaking up his words like a sponge. Ernst continued, 'And more by sheer fluke than anything, the "ringed-hand man" now has a name. You will be looking for Yute Polenkovich and I want you to help clip his wings!'

'Can I ask, sir, why is this so shrouded in secrecy?'

'Just as an added precaution, Mayer. A precaution which I hope will prove unnecessary, but until we get further into the picture, we need to move with stealth. If nothing else, I want the "ringed-hand man" for killing on my territory. Mayer was very aware of the venom in Ernst's voice as he almost spat out the words 'killing on my territory'. She was also aware his strong feelings were not for vengeance, but for justice.

'When do you want me to start, sir?'

'Now, Mayer. Now!'

'Okay, sir. Where do I sit? I will need a little space,' she said as she looked helplessly around the Chief Superintendent's office, every surface covered with files and paperwork.

'I'll clear out a corner over there, will that be okay?'

'Yes, sir, but what about phones?'

'You're too practical! I'll organise facilities and see what they've got. I'll let you know through Koslowski. Thank you, Mayer.'

Although she had witnessed many of his 'well, that's finished now' lines from her Chief, it was seconds before it sank in and she floated out of the office obediently.

Ernst rang for his secretary and she was soon in his office.

'Helena, Katerina Mayer will be working with us, trying to expand on the information Joc Latimer has been sending us, so could you please make sure she has copies of everything, including telephone tapes, under "confidential" cover, please?'

'She is with us, then?' said Helena, knowing that her foxy-when-necessary boss was bending the rules a little, by taking Mayer on.

'Of course she is!' replied Ernst.

There was nothing more to be said. With a warm smile, unseen by Ernst who had already got his head down into his paperwork, Helena left quietly to start her task.

The door opened in front of Daniel Tomlevski automatically. He came to attention and waited to be ordered into the Adjutant's office. He was a little disconcerted as the Adjutant himself stood before him and ushered him in with just a wave of the hand. Unused to this informal attitude, it took Daniel a little while to respond, but the few seconds' delay did not seem to worry Major A A Roche as he walked in front of Daniel to his chair, behind his overfull and disorganised desk.

'Sit down, my boy.' The strong voice of the Major filled the room.

'Thank you, sir.' Daniel's voice seemed weak by comparison, as the Major sat down in his own chair. 'Your application to join Eurocorps is going to give us a little difficulty...' The French accent from the north of the country made the words he was saying lilt like a song around the room. Daniel took 'a little difficulty' to mean that they were at least going to consider his application. The relief must have shown on his face.

'That seems to please you somehow?'

'Well, yes sir. If I assume correctly, "a little difficulty" means that I will not be automatically turned down and that dependent on this interview, my screening will proceed.'

'Your assumption is correct. You have qualifications which would serve our Corps well, we believe. Your British Military Academy Commission would be accepted as amongst the best in the world.' The Major pondered for a few moments, and staring straight into Daniel's face like a lion leaping at his prey, he suddenly leant forwards, placing both forearms and hands firmly onto the desk, as his forceful voice shot a question. 'What are your political beliefs?'

'I have none in particular, really...' answered Daniel, a little hesitantly.

'You sit there and tell me that after all that happened to your family, with your father being exiled from his beloved Poland at the onset of the German invasion because of his Russian birth, the hardships in crossing Europe, and then the hardships and the menial work that confronted him in England, you sit there and you say "none in particular"?... You are either an angel or a fool!'

'No, sir. Nor am I a Jew!'

'Don't try to be smart with me. I see no defence in your answer to my question!'

'Sir, as a Jew, my father who had carried his Jewish faith proudly all his life, taught me that to try to live in harmony with my friends and neighbours was a good way to live. My view is that my father was right. My faith is my own and I respect other faiths. I have sometimes had to defend this point in arguments, but at no time have I preached what I consider to be "the true faith" to anyone and the inevitable mix of politics has never been spoken of. If my life depended on having a political allegiance, I would probably claim for myself the utopia of liberalism – you don't have to say "yes" too often, and the opportunity to say "no" rarely occurs.' The sincerity apparent in Daniel's voice delayed the Major's next question slightly, but when it came, its implications surprised and stunned Daniel.

'Your wife was a member of the French National Front whilst at college?'

'Yes, I am aware of that. I assure you that it was a phase that the group she was attending college with, all went through. None of these people now believe in anything radical.'

'That seems to concur with our investigations. How does your wife feel about this application and possible loss of seniority?'

'We have discussed it and she would like very much to feel she is becoming more European in every way.'

'Good. Do you feel she would be a good asset socially for your career?'

'She is independent in her views, but yes, she would certainly support me. As an asset, she is fluent in four languages and is interested like myself for similar reasons, to work towards a united Europe.'

'Those reasons are?'

The suddenness of the question stunned Daniel at first, but he quickly recovered his composure and replied, 'Her family are proud Parisians and twice within three decades have lost family to the fight against tyranny by a European neighbour.'

'Well answered.' The pause that followed put Daniel's mind in a whirl. What will be the next question? he thought. The surprise on Daniel's face must have been obvious when the question eventually came. 'Throughout your life you have always been successful at sport. If you could only select one, what would it be?'

'That is easy for me to answer, sir. Golf.'

'Why?'

'The fresh air, playing different courses, meeting different people, and the constant changing scenery, plus my wife and I can play together, alone, or with friends.'

'Do you often include your wife in your private social life?'

'Whenever she wishes… I invariably ask her!'

'Good.'

The interview gradually took on a lighter and lighter attitude as time passed, each question seemingly got further and further away from anything military. The time drifted by quickly and sneaking a glance at his wristwatch, Daniel noticed that forty-five minutes had whizzed by. Noticing Daniel's furtive look at his watch, the Major quickly stood up from his desk and reaching across it, offered his hand in farewell. The unexpectedness of the Major's abrupt movement forced Daniel to rise and take the proffered hand. The ending to the interview had slightly confused him, but his discipline brought him to attention before daring to ask, 'Will there be another interview, sir?'

A look of instant relief formed on Daniel's face when he heard the words, 'I expect there will be…' floating into his ears.

He managed to force out a staccato, 'Thank you, sir,' as he automatically saluted, about-turned, and marched out of the Major's office.

Marshall Polenkovich fingered through the papers before him, happy with himself that his selection of the candidates listed was generally more political than the first list he had submitted to the panel. Political and disciplined; the first criteria he had set for himself to commence his task of infesting Eurocorps with 'his people', who would take over all the traffic movement and communication. The turn of the door handle was just audible as the panel filed through the door at the far end of the room. Gathering his papers swiftly into a neat pile, he set them square to the table edge, prior to standing up as the panel filed past him on the opposite side of the table. Yute looked at them one by one as they passed his set-to-attention eyes, their solemn faces giving nothing away. Silently they sat down and with a nod of the Chairman's head, permission was given for Yute to sit.

'Good morning, Comrade Marshall.' The steady, vibrant voice of the Chairman dispersed the silence.

'Good morning, Comrade Chairman, and members of the panel,' replied Yute. A rustle of papers in front of the Chairman interrupted the proceedings momentarily before he continued, 'All of these people on this list are approved by us, and we feel all of them should be used along with the others previously selected, if at all possible.'

The Chairman's statement was not welcomed by Yute, but he had anticipated this might be the panel's view. His reply started slowly and deliberately. 'Your requests are duly noted, Comrades, but may I again express my fears that if we infiltrate the ranks of Eurocorps with too many people too quickly, without slowly consolidating, performing a few trial runs and dispersing our wares through Eurocorps' existing infrastructure first, it is my opinion that we would have too many people in position making us vulnerable to discovery.'

The Chairman's vibrant voice cut through the air sharply. 'Your wishes are overruled by this panel, Comrade Marshall. Our names on today's list have been marked with our approval and will be used alongside the others already approved.'

'Comrade Chairman, I wish my concern to be duly noted by this panel.'

The strength of the delivery of these words caused a slight hesitation before the Chairman's response. 'The panel hears your objection. You will keep us informed when your training commences.'

The panel rose as one before Yute's eyes. He could not allow them to leave without one last plea. 'Comrade Chairman, panel… I request that you reconsider your order. You accepted my explanation over the Hamburg affair, moving too fast with a mixture of outside enforcers and organisers was the cause of our failure in Hamburg. I ask you, why should we risk the same mistake happening again? Consolidate Eurocorps first, let them slowly build their connections into NATO and build the American system. We *must* consolidate Eurocorps first before we expand further.'

'You will carry out the wishes of this panel. You seem to have adopted the attitude that you and you alone can make this plan work. The reports from Comrade Tatlanovich of your emphatic attitude in your search gave him the impression that you are reaching too high in your expectancy.' The Chairman realised too late that he had given away the name of his informant and hurriedly continued in an attempt to cover up, but his flustering over his mistake was creating more embarrassment in front of his colleagues on the panel, let alone Yute. He finally pulled himself together and categorically announced, 'You *will* at all times follow this panel's instruction without hesitation!' Then the Chairman, followed by the panel, walked immediately from the room.

Yute stood silently watching them go through the large door, with the name of Comrade Igor Tatlanovich still ringing in his ears as the door closed. Yute allowed himself to murmur through clenched teeth, 'Igor, I *will* find out what else you have been saying…'

The concentration on Investigator Mayer's face was obvious to all of her colleagues who happened to pass her desk. Colleagues she neither observed nor acknowledged as they passed by. Over the past few days the piles of faxes and copies of documents from both German and Russian Records Offices had grown rapidly. The sorting and logging of information gleaned from them was the reason for her all-absorbing concentration.

Chapter Thirteen

Igor Tatlanovich was lounging in his only armchair in his sparsely furnished flat, which was poorly lit, with very little ornamentation or pictures adorning the plain walls. Yet tonight, the apartment was alive with Western music playing on his old tape player. A new tape which obviously pleased him, from his new-found friends in high places. Though it was obvious he was enjoying himself, the clicking of his fingers in time to the tape, the spontaneous raising of his forearm and thrusting his finger high in the air in time with the crescendo of the music as it played, all was not entirely happy with Igor. His other new friend, Yute, was coming to visit him in his dingy little flat. Igor had mumbled to himself, 'I'm sure Yute will understand that although I am a section head of department, it gives me no rating as his military rank would. I've cleaned and cleaned, managed to borrow larger light bulbs to put in my lights – which does help to cheer the place up a little, but with my pay structure and ranking in the Records Office, it's the best I can expect at the moment.'

Igor stood up and moved over to the solitary picture in the room, a picture taken long before his mother's death. Lightly lifting the picture from the shelf, he kissed the face and whispered the word 'Mother' before placing it back on the shelf in the exact position from whence it came. Staring into his mother's face, he whispered, 'If you still love me, Mother, and can help in any way to make Yute trust me more and more and gain me more reward from my work, please do, Mother, please…'

Igor's hand was just about to lovingly touch his mother's face, when the knock on the door interrupted him. Quickly brushing the line of his jacket down, and adjusting the top button of his poor quality Russian suit, he moved swiftly to the door.

'Yute, welcome to my little apartment…' Igor gave a slight bow as Yute entered, and Yute taking the initiative responded sympathetically.

'I am sure, in view of your new assignment, your accommodation will improve…'

Humbly, Igor replied, 'It would be nice to have just a little more room, and I would like it to be brighter!'

'I'm sure your new-found friends will look out for you. Personally, I think you have made it very homely and I'm sure I will enjoy your invitation to supper. In fact I have taken the liberty of bringing some vodka, to make sure we do!'

'Oh thank you, Yute! You are most generous!'

'Nonsense!' Yute replied. 'The work you have been doing for me has, I'm sure, been far in excess of anything you have been asked to do before.'

'You are right, as always, but as a civil servant of many years' standing, many such unexpected things have happened before – as complicated as this task… possibly not, but there have been some peculiar requests over the years.'

'Has there been anything at all similar to the request that I and my superiors are making of you?'

'Oh no, up until this point, we have only ever searched for one or two people at most, normally from the advantage of them having had some kind of record. No, nothing like yours has ever happened before. Your request is unique – remember we are not only finding the right person, but it seems to me we are also searching the family background as far back as four generations, where possible. Research like that is very exacting and unusual work. No, Yute, your task is unique, but it will be worthwhile, I'm sure.'

The sickness in Yute's stomach every time he had to be with this man was rising again, but he knew he had to be pleasant to him a little longer. The snide way Igor always managed to make you feel personally guilty for his inadequacies – 'my little apartment…' '…will be worthwhile, I'm sure' – constantly in a whinging, pleading way. The pause between the two of them hung heavily in the air, Yute being the first with eventual comment.

'Igor, I am sure things will work out well for you and your future.' Then, in a desperate attempt to change the subject, he said, 'That's a beautiful picture over there, is it your mother?'

'Kind of you to ask, Yute… yes it is. I miss her terribly, but her death was a long time ago now.'

'A pity… and she looks so young in the photograph.'

'Just forty-two years old,' Igor replied.

'Life can be cruel sometimes, but let's not let it upset our evening together…' Turning swiftly away from the picture, he continued briskly, 'May I sit down?'

Slightly flustered by the abruptness of Yute's tone, Igor answered, 'Oh, please Yute, forgive me for not asking you to sit down before now. Please forgive my bad manners… please, take the armchair.'

Yute took the armchair at Igor's request. More blasted fawning, Yute thought. Why couldn't he have just said, 'Please sit down'?

Igor crossed the room to the table in the corner and removed the cloth which he had placed over the food laid out there. Turning to Yute with a sickly smile all over his face, he remarked, 'I'll uncover the food now and you can help yourself when you are ready.' Then he added, 'We don't want any formality here, do we? May I suggest a drink first… would you prefer whisky or vodka?'

Yute's eyes lifted as the words from Igor ran through his thoughts as another 'hard luck, I wish I had more, but life's not good to me' line. Shaking the thoughts from his mind, he said, 'I would prefer our national drink please, Igor.' Knowing that it, the bottle of whisky, had been opened, Igor would have less profit or none at all when the whisky went on the black market to be sold.

Igor smarmily replied, 'I feel very nationalistic this evening too, I'll have the same.' In lighter vein now, Igor started again. 'You have certainly kept my people very busy and as I understand it from the grapevine, many a senior person above me has been under pressure as well.'

'Igor, I'm surprised at you! You know these things happen. I do something, someone above me does something, when he does something, someone above him does something… it's the fleas on the backs of fleas syndrome.' The flippant way in which Yute said his piece, forced a little giggle from Igor. And Yute, seeing that Igor was amused, joined in laughing and Igor's giggle could not be held back any longer.

Through his laughter, Yute managed to say, 'Igor, you know it's true, it always happens!' Nodding in agreement, the volume of Igor's laugh rose. Once things had calmed down a little, knowing Igor was probably the happiest he had been for many a year, Yute asked him, 'Why don't we do this again? We both seem to get on so well, and we may be able to help each other along the way. I have access to a dacha… you could come with me for a weekend, what do you think?' The thought of being around this slimy person for a weekend brought on Yute's nausea, but in his mind, it had to happen this way.

Igor in his surprise at the invitation was speechless for a few moments. 'That would be very nice, Yute, it would be a really special treat for me.'

'Well, it will happen as soon as we get rid of all of this paper-work and get a little further towards solving our little problems.'

'Yes, there will not be much time until we finish our work, I agree.'

'You must promise me one thing, Igor, which I will have to make a condition of our sojourn. You must never tell anyone that we are close friends or that we will be in a controlled dacha for the weekend… I'm sure you understand why?'

'Of course I do, it would not do for the military and civil servants to be mixing.' With a sigh, Igor added, 'Glasnost hasn't really improved things much.'

'Give Glasnost time, Igor. We military people are finding changes in staff ranks which we consider to be better already.'

'I'm pleased. Maybe they will improve for us soon,' Igor said, adding mournfully, 'I don't know how much longer the photo-copier will last!'

Yute wanted to do nothing else but laugh at the worries of this pathetic little man, but managing to stop himself from laughing out loud, he said, 'Cheer up Igor, things will be fine. Now, may I have a little of your food and perhaps we could both have another drink?'

Both men stood up and moved to the table in comfortable silence. Igor poured another drink for each of them and Yute returned to his chair first, waiting for Igor to reach his seat and sit down before saying, 'What distribution do your lists have, Igor?'

'Very little, Yute. Why?'

'No reason really, I was just interested. In the military everything is in triplicate, then the next stage is in triplicate, and so on!'

'It's pretty much the same with us, but dealing with so many state departments they sometimes send special directives for us to follow.'

'That must make things more difficult for you?'

'Not difficult, it just means that after doing things our normal way, we read their directive again and make the necessary additions or deletions.' He added glibly, 'It's so simple even I can understand it!'

Yute detected the effects of the vodka beginning to take a hold of Igor. 'You make it sound so easy, but I'm sure it must be more difficult than that.'

'No, it isn't, Yute... well, maybe sometimes... do you know, sometimes we have the normal directives and then a mysterious phone call which will alter things slightly. These ones we tend to call the "dodgy ones" down in my basement, because it has been known especially in the old days, that if the "dodgy ones" were not attended to swiftly and also "to the letter" of the mystery voice's instructions, a civil servant would go "poof" and disappear. A few days later, a directive would arrive to say that person had been transferred.' Igor paused and looked blankly into Yute's eyes, adding, 'We, below stairs, often wondered where they were transferred to.'

'I hope my little exercise hasn't brought you any such phone call,' Yute stated lightly.

Igor's hesitant reply of 'No...' left Yute with a doubt in his mind. Perhaps the fluff Yute had detected in the Chairman's briefing a short while ago had mistakenly referred to someone other than Igor? he thought. It was not until Igor added, 'You are not one of our mysteries, Yute my friend... you have my full respect.' It was then that Yute knew Igor was the man with the direct line to his Chairman. The small amount of alcohol it had taken to make Igor talk had both surprised and worried Yute. What if Igor, this new sick-making friend, told anyone about this evening or of the dacha rendezvous? It was at that precise moment that Yute decided Igor's next list would finish their contact.

'Igor, it's getting a little late for me. Would you mind if I left? I have to do a little more work before I go to bed and we are in a pleasant mood now. It would be nicer to finish when we feel pleasantly relaxed rather than carry on drinking for too long and let the conversation become boring.'

Igor's heavy eyelids opened and closed again. 'I'm sure you are right, my friend. I'm sure you're right… Let me just say thank you for coming, it's been… friendly.'

'It has, and thank you. Don't forget, we will do it again soon, as promised but remember, it's just between us – it's better for both of us if we keep it secret.'

Igor nodded. 'I'll see you out, Yute.'

'Please, don't worry, my friend, there's no need.'

Before Igor could get up off his chair, Yute had risen and was at the door already. 'Stay there and relax, Igor, we will be in touch again very soon. Goodnight, and thank you again.' The words were spoken as he reached the other side of the door, just before he pulled it shut.

Igor sat slumped in his chair until he heard Yute's footsteps retreating along the passageway. He rose swiftly, walking over to the door, locking it and then throwing his back against the door, he said delightedly, 'We did have a dodgy phone call, Marshall Yute Polenkovich, and there is only one other piece of paper in existence about you, and I know who's got it!'

Chapter Fourteen

Ernst was at his desk looking over at Officer Mayer, his mind going back many years to when his beautiful wife and he were as young as Mayer was now. Sometimes Mayer reminded him of how his still-beautiful wife had worked so hard when she was working for the force, and how little mannerisms were so similar between them. I must invite Mayer to dinner one evening. I'm certain we would both enjoy having youngsters around again, he thought. I wonder if Mayer has a boyfriend she might like to bring along? The thoughts kept rushing through his mind. What if I didn't like the boyfriend?

Mayer sat upright in her chair, moving each and every paper to her – she didn't slouch. Reading intently, she then placed them on one of several piles which were building up neatly all around the desk. Pulling another towards her from the pile of unread reports, she then placed it squarely in front of her; she slowly leant back, still engrossed with what she was reading until, having rested her back for a few seconds, her body came forward and reached to one of the piles furthest away from her. Lifting the whole pile with one hand, she leant against the back of her chair and thumbing through the pile, she stopped occasionally to refresh her memory. Suddenly she turned her head towards Ulbrecht, who was caught unawares and was embarrassed to be found staring. Officer Mayer, however, was oblivious to Ulbrecht's embarrassment and calmly asked, 'Sir, could I speak to you for a moment?'

'Certainly, Mayer, what is it?'

'This may be something, sir.' She picked up the three pages which had raised her interest and walked around the desk to Ulbrecht's side. Placing the three pages down side by side, she pointed out, 'Each of these reports has been accredited to Afghanistan and are all around the same date.' Moving slightly away from Ernst's side, she looked down into his upturned face and continued, 'These reports are interesting. The three names

that we know of are here, Lanov, Mogatin and here, Tashimov.'
She pointed to one of the three pages. 'It shows, I think, they all
knew each other before Hamburg and, sir, I suggest they may
have met and worked together before Afghanistan. May I have
permission to extend my requests for any entry of these three
names reported anywhere in the European or Russian area to be
reported to us even if only one name turns up and is not
corroborated by either of the other two?'

'Good idea, Mayer. Yes, you may extend your research. May I
suggest that it may not only be reports coming in from outside
Russia that should interest us. Why not use that direct line you
have with Moscow. You never know what may turn up.'

'Thank you, sir. I did actually think of that, but I thought
maybe we might be letting our Russian friends know too much.'

'You could be right, Mayer, but I think taking that chance at
this moment could be of help to us.'

'I'm not so sure, sir, but thank you for the opportunity.'

Leaning across Ulbrecht, she picked up her pages, stood to
attention for a moment, and returned to her desk. Ulbrecht
picked up his phone and dialled Willi's number. The ring had
hardly begun when Willi picked it up. 'Koslowski heir,' came up
the line to Ulbrecht's ear.

'Willi...' Ernst said. 'Can we have a little talk?'

'Yes, when? Whenever you like suits me.'

'Let's make it now then!'

'Okay, I'll be along right away... It's about Mayer, isn't it?'
Willi said, cheekily.

Ernst, surprised at Willi's guesswork, replied, 'You wait and
see... everyone's trying to play detective around here! See you in a
minute.'

No sooner, it seemed, had the words left Ernst's mouth than
Willi's happy face was standing in the doorway to Ernst's office.
'Come straight in, Willi. Yes, your guess was right... Now, keep
your voice down, she is not to hear this conversation.'

'You're doing the talking, Ernst!'

Ernst continued in his strong, quieter voice, opening his
remarks with, 'Thank you, Willi, for going along with me with
regards to Mayer and the financial strain it has caused, but it has

been proven to be worthwhile. She has found historic links between Tashimov, Lanov and Mogatin in Afghanistan and is now investigating further directly with her Moscow contacts. I feel sure somehow Tashimov worked for our Marshall Polenkovich in the past. It needs confirming by as many sources as we can bring to bear. I'm going to ask the Yanks, but I'm hoping we can solve it through our people.'

Willi just sat waiting. He knew Ernst had more to say, that the events which were buzzing around in his head would eventually come out, and what he planned to do would soon follow.

'You see, Willi, my office is not the place for Mayer to work in from now on; it's going to become far too busy and she will need files and an internal and an external phone line, plus a computer and all kinds of things like that. I think we need another office to enable her to work more efficiently.'

The pause in Ernst's voice, with the strain of speaking clearly and quietly, seemed to show the possibility of another reason. Willi interrupted him teasingly, 'Is that the only reason, Ernst?'

'What do you mean, Willi?'

'Are you not finding the beautiful Mayer too much of a temptation?'

'I should be so lucky to have the time!'

'Time you can always make, Ernst. I think you're like me… past it!'

'Probably, Willi, but neither you nor I are ever going to find out.'

'True.'

'Can you get me an office sorted then, please, now you've had your little bit of fun?'

'I'll fix it as quick as I can.'

'Thanks, Willi.'

As Willi was about to leave the office, he couldn't resist raising his voice, with every intent of embarrassing Ernst with having to explain himself to Mayer. 'So, you want to get rid of Policewoman Mayer then, Ernst?' Then Willi accelerated from the room.

Joc Latimer sat silently in his office, a little perturbed that he had not heard from Ernst Ulbrecht. He twiddled his thumbs, willing the time away, until it was time to meet Brian from Foreign. Joc was accepting his friendship back again into the personal, comfortable state that it was before the numerous affairs which Brian had kept from his wife, but not from Joc. When he remembered the past, Joc still found it hard to forgive the excuses Brian had made to his wife and most of all, the covering up Joc had had to do every time his wife moaned about Brian always being away on business, the lies he had told to protect Brian, to try to stop his wife from enquiring any further. But now it was different. Now it seemed Brian was really trying to save his marriage, and both his own and Brian's wife seemed to be content, or at least, more content with the stories Brian was now releasing – stories Joc knew to be true – and could happily endorse them to his wife, who in turn confirmed them to Brian's wife. Joc was a lot happier for them both and for his own situation, but he did worry that Brian could be made the scapegoat for the Foreign Department's cock-up.

Joc's thumbs still twisted around one another. Joc in his silent room, uttered to himself softly, 'Why hasn't Foreign, or my own sources, come up with any other names? Surely there must have been some connection with others.' Reaching for his phone, he buzzed Louise, his secretary. As she entered his office, Joc's thumbs were still twisting around each other.

Light-heartedly, she said, 'Is that all you have to do, Joc?'

'No, I've finished playing now, look!' He stopped twiddling and continued, 'The thumbs have done their work. Take a memo, please, Louise.' The short pause allowed Louise to sit down, open her notepad and get ready with her pencil.

'To Foreign and all CIA Embassy Personnel, worldwide. Russian Army Marshall Yutc Polenkovich has been identified on behalf of Hamburg's Chief of Police, Ernst Ulbrecht. The undersigned requests any person having made personal contact with the Russian or any of his contacts, to notify this office. It is known Polenkovich served in Afghanistan – he must have had contact with others. We believe one to have been Gregor Tashimov, now deceased, rank of Colonel. Louise, emphasise this next sentence, please. *Both these men must have had contact with others*. Any information, no matter how insignificant it may seem, would be appreciated. This request has been authorised by Chief of Station, L H Longworth. Sign it off as usual please, Louise. Can you get it out today, do you think?'

'I'll have a go, Joc. It seems important to you, so I'll try all the harder.'

'Don't jazz about, get on with your job and don't forget today is a good day. Tomorrow may be too late. By the way, you know I don't like asking favours, but please, just this once?'

Louise was almost out of the door, but couldn't resist turning back just in time to see her boss's cheeky grin and the over-played wink of his right eye.

Klaus and Dieter are sitting in their flat, the soft lighting surrounding them displayed to full advantage, the refurbishment they had completed together since the terrible murder which had happened just a few short months ago. They had both decided the flat was where they should stay, as it was there Dieter had found the love and protection he had always wanted – protection which could have cost Klaus his life. But now the mood was happy and light-hearted as they teased and taunted each other, they wrestled with the problem as to which clothes they should pack for their holiday in Portugal, or as Dieter kept teasing Klaus, 'Maybe we should buy everything when we get there so we can be bang up to date with local fashion!'

Klaus had become younger looking and more adventurous in his dress, but he still lacked the exuberance of his partner, so the practical thoughts going through his mind were that what was fashionable in Portugal in August, would probably be a total waste in Hamburg, any month of the year! Looking up into Dieter's eyes, Klaus said, 'Dieter, we have so many summer clothes, why don't we take everything? We could buy any additional things we might need when we are there, what do you think?'

'Yes I suppose you're right, Klaus; besides it will be less expensive!'

'I wasn't thinking of that, Dieter, I think you're teasing me about being mean again.'

Dieter smiled warmly and pulled him close. 'I was teasing,

liebling, you mean everything to me now. I promise we will have a wonderful time.'

Daniel Tomlevski sat in the corner seat as the rickety suburban train jerked and shuddered, taking him back to Nicole. He was happy after two days of having had time to talk to friends – one army friend in particular, Captain James Butterfield. They had spent a long time analysing Daniel's interview and James had convinced Daniel that he would have no problem during his next, or any subsequent interviews that he might have to attend. After leaving Eurocorps HQ, he had phoned Nicole, who was normally warm and encouraging about anything that would help further Daniel's career but Daniel felt her voice was a little flat on the telephone. When Daniel asked her if there was anything wrong, he still remembered her reply. 'Of course not, silly. I'm just a little tired so I will go to bed and dream of you. And you must remember, when you are out with your friend, to be good!' Daniel ran Nicole's reply through his mind, searching for an explanation. She said the right words, but somehow it didn't sound quite true. She really wanted him to come straight home from his interview, but they had both agreed since his old friend was stationed on the way back from his interview, it would be a good opportunity to catch up with Butterfield especially, and as Daniel himself had put it, 'any other scallywag' who might be around. His unhappiness showed on his face as it became impossible to satisfy himself that there was nothing wrong. But, it would not be long before he was leaping from the train and running home to their little house and then all would be well between them.

Yute Polenkovich, sitting in a downtown restaurant, waited for his least favourite person to arrive. Igor was not late, but the irritating characteristics of Igor's personality left a lot to be desired in Yute's book. Today was a special day; it was Igor's birthday. Yute had initially felt that the urgency Igor had shown in the first days of the information-gathering exercise, had been second-to-none and his 'review and recall' system was almost spontaneous. But now that Yute knew his Chairman had found an inroad to Igor's weaknesses and could organise greater rewards for Igor than Yute himself could, things had become lackadaisical. Tonight is the night, Yute felt, that Igor was going to be pushed back into line. It was too soon to get rid of Igor for good. That will happen at the promised weekend at the dacha. Today will be a game of words, innuendo and suggestion designed to leave Igor unsure of his ground in the greedy game he is playing. Yute will enjoy confusing this inconsequential office servant who thinks he is on a parity with him within the echelons of power. Yute raised his hand slightly and smiled, as through the window he saw Igor hurrying towards him. The game will begin in a few more minutes.

Ernst Ulbrecht's office was unusually quiet, although people on the other side of the glass partition were going about their business as usual and the door was wide open as always. The movements and time seemed to be in slow motion as his own inactivity caused his eyelids to droop across his still lively eyes. Shaking himself, he got up from his chair and started restlessly pacing across his office floor. Waiting for information had always been the worst part of any investigation as far as Ernst was concerned. 'Come on, you Yanks, come on, you Russkies… information – as quick as you can, please,' he muttered, rubbing his hands together in front of himself.

'Please… as many times as it takes!' Ernst's pacing continued.

Mogatin stood outside the classically pillared archway which housed the ornate gates of the Palace Hotel, staring along the tree-lined drive. Even though Mogatin had become less formal in his dress during his travels, the Hawaiian-style orange and white patterned shirt, despite helping him look like a tourist, was a little too flamboyant for the majority of people passing by him. In fact, a lot of heads turned for a second look after they had passed him by. Mogatin never heard the sniggers and assumed every second glance they made indicated envy on their part.

Lanov, who had been happily watching his friend from a taxi rank across the street, smiled at his antics. Crossing the road swiftly to avoid the traffic, he jumped onto the kerb, knocking into Mogatin. Contact was made. Neither of them showed any back-slapping comradeship, but spent endless time in what looked like 'apologising' to any other observer, but actually, that was the time they needed to arrange their next rendezvous which would be somewhere more discreet.

Klaus, who was carrying two suitcases and a travel bag, burst into the hustle and bustle of Hamburg airport, closely followed by Dieter who was carrying his own travel bag. 'Come on, Dieter, it's desk twenty-four. This way!'

'Klaus, why don't we get a trolley?' asked Dieter, unhurriedly.

'This is quicker. By the time we look for a trolley, we could be at the check-in desk with fewer people in front of us… you'll see!'

Dieter asked cheekily, 'Does that mean we'll get to Portugal quicker?'

Klaus, who was just a little stressed out, looked disdainfully at his beautiful boyfriend and once again, one of those frequent thoughts passed through his head: Why is it, and how is it, someone can look so beautiful and sometimes be so stupid?

Major A A Roche's office looked a brighter, more homely place to Lieutenant Tomlevski. This was his second interview. He had been recalled after only one week and was sitting quietly waiting for Major Roche while he finished off a 'flush' of paperwork. Daniel paid little attention to the occasional glances Roche seemed to give him at the end of each page that he read, before placing his initial on each page in the box provided. Daniel watched as the pile of papers got smaller and he was pleased eventually, when the last one was revealed. Roche flashed his initials, then his signature in full on the last page, confirming that the total number of pages had been read.

Looking across at Daniel, Major Roche smiled warmly and said, 'Sorry to have kept you waiting – you know that the Army, any army, really runs on the paperwork… had to be done. Now, let's get on. The summary reports returned by the officers and men you have served with have all been very favourable. In fact, I will go so far as to say that when the next Eurocorps' entry board sit, your name will be on top of the list and will have my own recommendation with it.'

The relief and happiness beamed all over Daniel's face and momentarily lost for words, he managed a brief, 'Thank you, sir!'

Roche continued. 'I'm pleased for you and I'm sure you will be much happier when you finally join us.' Major Roche sat silently for a moment and leant back in his chair. Then, staring hard at Daniel, he asked sharply, 'Your wife and her family were communists, I believe?'

Daniel was slightly disturbed by that bold statement, but replied, 'Whilst at college, my wife had National Front leanings and possibly her parents did too. But you said "communists". Communism was never mentioned to me and I am sure that it is untrue. They have always been a close family, very patriotic, but I cannot accept that they are communists. In my opinion, their lifestyle, attitudes and religious beliefs would make your statement unbelievable.'

'Well, I can prove they were, which is what I said in the first place. Your defence of them bares out what we have since found out,' replied Roche.

Looking hard for any further signs of distress on Daniel's face, he continued, 'Paris at the end of World War Two was rife with communist activity and your wife's parents were active, as were many others. Your own wife was enrolled when she was just five years old.' Roche paused for a short moment, then added with laughter in his voice, 'She possibly didn't even realise she was a member!'

Daniel looked coldly back into the Major's eyes. 'I am sorry, but I do not see this as a laughing matter. I shall question them all when I get back.'

'There's really no need. We have done all the checking we need to do. You would probably only create a hornets' nest in your personal relationships with them. I'd forget it if I were you!' Deliberately breaking off the subject, Roche then asked, 'When do you think all of your paperwork will be organised so that you will be able to join us? I mean all of it – transfers out of the Polish Army into the French Army, citizenships, and so on?'

'I asked my CO and he thinks it will take about a month from the receipt of the notification of my acceptance by Eurocorps.'

'Good, let's say about six weeks after acceptance, then.'

'Daniel smiled and replied, 'That should give the system enough time!'

Roche answered wryly, 'Maybe,' and smiled back.

Both men sat for a few moments in silence, until Major Roche suddenly lifted himself out of his chair saying, 'Well, young man, I think that's all. We'll be in touch very soon, I expect.' Daniel was rather dismayed at the abrupt dismissal he unexpectedly received and got up and left the room almost in a trance, forgetting to say thank you or even salute. Once outside the office, he stood in silence and at attention, full of pride. The deep breaths he was taking in through his nose calmed his excitement just enough to prevent him screaming for joy, which he thought even his dear Nicole could probably have heard.

In Major Roche's office a muted telephone conversation was taking place. The Major was giving his full endorsement over the phone. The voice at the other end of the phone asked, 'Sir, do we continue with our background investigation on him or not?'

'Do you really see any point? We both agree the indiscretion was in the past, so unless you have any "sixth-sense" type feelings, I am prepared to accept it was all in the past and leave it at that.'

'I have no "sixth-sense" type feelings, as you put it, sir. My investigations so far have shown nothing disturbing, but I must point out that my investigations are not complete.'

'That surely must be the case on practically all of your investigations? What with the mixture of nationalities from broken governments across the whole of Europe, yours is an intolerable task, as well as being thankless. In my view, Daniel Tomlevski is worthy on merit alone, to be allowed entry into Eurocorps.'

'I fully understand, sir. He has good grades in everything military, but it's not him we are worried about, it's his wife's family.'

'I respect your concern, but do you think any further investigation would reveal anything more than we have right now? Bearing in mind we agreed at the start of this conversation and in our preliminary meeting, that the indiscretion of joining the communist party back then was an indiscretion that virtually the whole of France, Italy, the Netherlands, and even Germany itself for a period of at least thirty-five years, was guilty of sliding in and out of, that as well as other obscure and unbelievable things after World War Two.'

'I suppose you're right, sir.'

'In this case. I feel fairly confident.'

'All right, sir. I will close the file and forward it to you.'

'Thank you. Will you despatch it ASAP?'

'Today, sir, I love to get rid of the paperwork off my desk.'

'Well done.'

'Thank you, sir,' echoed softly around the office as the phone swiftly left the Major's ear and was laid to rest in its cradle.

Joc Latimer sat at home reading the European Sunday papers alongside his own country's East and West Coast papers. Whenever Joc was scanning the press for international news items, as he called it, the lounge looked more like a waste paper yard than a home. Liz looked in occasionally, shook her head then walked away, but her habit of doing this every twenty minutes or so, helped her to plan when to start cooking lunch; when Joc had all the papers tidied up into neat piles was the clue for her to start – her 'knowing her man' smile would spread across her pretty face. The next move would be Joc reading through once again the passages which had caught his eye on his 'scanning raid'. Then, should an article be of interest, it would be marked, placed over the arm of his chair and any which did not live up to his expectations on this second read-through, would be placed neatly on the pile for disposal. This exercise completed, Joc would stand up, stretch himself, walk across the lounge to Liz's needlework box, take out the scissors, come back to his chair, cut out the articles marked in the various papers, return the scissors to the needlework box, then go into his den and collect countless matching transparent folders, each of which had a label with a country marked on it. Each new clipping would be placed in its respective folder, the scrap of information contained therein already having been logged in Joc's mind.

The same routine had continued just so, since the last of their children had left home. A scene which Liz had witnessed countless times, but she would not change a minute of it; it was her time as well. Into the garden, clearing out a cupboard, phoning Mother and the kids, it was comfortable not boring, it was 'nice'; different from the worry and excitement of keeping up with Joc when he had been 'in the field', life was slower but still interesting with Joc, sometimes even exciting. Except for Sunday mornings, there was always something going on whenever he was around. Liz liked it comfortable and respected Joc's view that 'the biggest crime wave to hit the West will come from the East – mark my words!'

But now the small pile of papers was being picked up from the floor to be marked and cut up, then placed into their transparent folders. This is the time to start lunch – in about half an hour's time, Joc will become a nuisance around the house and nothing will get done.

Looking up, Joc saw his wife's smiling face. 'Hi, love. I'll be about half an hour… okay for you?'

Liz's smile broadened and she walked away towards the kitchen. Joc called out to her. 'I thought we might drop over and see the kids and your mum after lunch, what do you think?' Again, there was no answer, but Joc would mention it again over lunch.

As Joc placed clip after clip away, it seemed to him that lunch would most likely be on time and that he would see the kids and his mother-in-law after all. The very last clipping was now getting filed into the 'Turkish file' which had become a little higgledy-piggledy over the years and just needed straightening up a little. The smallest clipping in the file had been forced into the bottom corner and one corner of it was folded over. Joc murmured to himself, 'Come on, little fella,' as his hand lifted the creased clipping out. 'We can't have you folded up and unreadable, can we?' Flattening out the clipping, the by-line jumped off the page and hit him squarely:

MORE RUSSIANS IN INDIA

The two Russians apprehended by Kashmiri police were today almost confronted by a third Russian, claiming to be a Russian

Embassy official from Delhi and demanding the release of the two Russians already under arrest. However, as he refused to verify his identity satisfactorily to the Kashmiri police authorities, he was refused any contact with the two men in custody.

Checking for the date of the article which he always wrote in ballpoint pen, Joc muttered to himself, 'The dates are a little too early to fit anything we have learnt so far, but I'll tell Ernst and get our Embassy to see if they can get any names to fit this story.'

Placing the solitary clipping on the side table next to his armchair, he called out, 'Liz, how long for lunch?'

'A few more minutes… why?'

'Oh, I just thought I'd make a phone call, but it can wait.'

'Do it now, then we won't get held up before we leave to see the kids.'

'Okay.'

'Who are you phoning anyway?'

'Ernst, in Hamburg. Something just showed up in my clippings which may have a bearing… I just thought he'd like to know.'

'Joc, it's Sunday!'

'I know, but I'm travelling around most of tomorrow, and I hate that damn mobile… long distance calls cost a fortune.'

'Go on then, but don't be long!'

'Okay.' He reached for the phone as he pulled out his wallet from his back pocket. Ernst's home number stood out fresh and neat on the little card which Louise had typed out for him, complete with area code. The numbers clicked in, one after the other. After the last click, it seemed that the phone did not actually ring, but Ernst's 'Ulbrecht heir!' soon brought Joc's brain into gear.

'Joc here, sorry to trouble you at home, Ernst, but something has just jogged my memory.'

'It's good to hear your voice anytime, Joc. What is it that jogged your memory?'

Joc explained about his interest very briefly and that he had reread the old clipping. 'I thought', continued Joc, 'that if my Embassy guys in India could get the names of all three Russians, it might just fit our little puzzle.'

'It would be even more use and prove a longer association with Tashimov, if their names happened to be Lanov and Mogatin and, of course, if we widen our area of investigation we hopefully might further our knowledge of the way they work!'

'There are no names mentioned in the clipping, but my guys will find out who they were and what they were up to…'

'Thanks, Joc, every little helps. I suppose you must be just about to have lunch?'

'Absolutely, then it's off to see the kids and the wife's mother!'

'I've just done something similar… it's hell being a policeman, Joc.'

'Liz, my wife, says it's hell being a policeman's wife… Anyway, goodbye for now; if and when I get anything, I'll phone you.'

'Me too, Joc. Thanks a lot.'

Both phones were placed back in their resting places and they both felt warm and cheered by their friendship.

Chapter Fifteen

Although Daniel was anxiously awaiting the envelope from Eurocorps HQ Strasbourg, it still surprised him when the Mess Steward delivered it as he sat reading a volume of Military History. Two weeks had passed since his interview and it pleased him that he had not had to wait a month as they had told him, but his nervousness showed as his index finger tumbled to make an entry under the well-sealed flap. Panic struck him... a reply this quick must mean I've been rejected. The flap was finally torn through and his index finger and thumb gingerly slid out the single sheet from the envelope. Opening the first of the two folds of the page, he read, 'Eurocorps Movement Order'. The sigh of relief and tears of joy disturbed no one in the empty library.

Klaus and Dieter were sitting side by side facing the sun, outside a small roadside café, silently gazing at nothing, nothing that was of any importance, anyway. They had found contentment in their own world together. Klaus was slouching a little in his chair with his straw hat tilted forward, when Dieter's hand suddenly gripped his forearm. A grip which, as his fingers locked, cried out 'Protect me!' Klaus pushed his hat back on his head as he swiftly tried to rise from his chair, only to be pulled back down again by Dieter.

'What are you doing, Dieter?' he said quietly but angrily through his teeth in an attempt not to cause any disturbance to anyone else sitting nearby.

'Be quiet, Klaus, look!' directed Dieter, pointing irritatedly.

'At what?'

'That man in blue!'

'What about him?'

'Klaus, can't you see?'

'See what?'

'Look again, what do you see?'

As the blue-clad man moved further away, Klaus began to settle back to his daydreaming once more.

'That man meant nothing to you, Klaus?' Dieter's voice was breaking up and he was struggling to hold back a little tear. The panic he felt now came tumbling excitedly from his mouth. 'That man was the man with the ring... I'm willing to swear on my life that the ring on the hand I just saw, was the one worn by the man in our apartment... the man who pointed the gun at us, the one who warned us of danger from the "Nowhere Men", the men who are never seen, the men who lurk in the shadows and spread violence and corruption all around the world.'

'Dieter, my darling, calm yourself! I'll go after him and if I can find him, I'll follow him.'

'I'll come too.'

'No, the two of us will be conspicuous; it's better for just one of us to go after him. You stay here... I'll be back.'

'Be careful, Klaus. Please be careful,' floated towards Klaus's ears as he hurried away.

Starting off in the general direction of the man in blue, his mind was flooding with scrambled thoughts. Was it blue jeans and a blue denim shirt? What do we do if we find out where he is staying? The police will have to be told! He was wearing brown shoes with blue jeans. Are the Portuguese police good enough? Was his hair long or short? The thoughts racing around his head did not impair his vigilance as he stealthily moved forward. Gott! There is a main square ahead, crowds of people, must quicken my pace. There he is, hold back, Klaus, you mustn't be seen. Why has he stopped at a bakery? He's going in. That was quick; two long loaves. Why is he hurrying? He moves much faster than me. If he goes any faster, I'll have to run to keep up. He's running! I'll never catch him! He's going for that tram... I'll never catch up... what number tram was it?

Coming to a sudden stop, Klaus wiped the perspiration from his face. Turning back the way he had come, he felt dejected and was not looking forward to telling Dieter that he had lost the man in blue.

Ernst Ulbrecht was surprised when he picked up the phone to be confronted with, 'Inspector Ulbrecht, it's Klaus Mennen here, I hope you still remember Dieter and myself?'

'My dear Mennen, of course I do, it's nice to hear from you…'

'Thank you. Dieter and I are on holiday in Portugal at the moment and he swears he saw that terrible ring on that horrible man's hand, here just over an hour ago.'

'Please go on, Herr Mennen. If you like to give me your number, I will call you back.' Ernst was waving to anyone who would take notice of him to come and record the call. With relief as someone responded, Ernst saw one of his staff lift the receiver and push the record button.

'That's all right, Herr Ulbrecht, I'll carry on talking.'

'Well, if you don't mind paying for the call, Herr Mennen, who am I to insist the government pays?' Ernst felt guilty for sounding so glib, but thought it might help relax Klaus Mennen. 'What actually happened, Klaus?'

'Well, Dieter and I were sitting outside a small pavement café…' Klaus continued his story in full, even down to his losing the man in blue.

'That's a very thorough report! Could I ask you to go to our Embassy in Lisbon or perhaps to a Consulate near you, where I can arrange for a policeman to take a statement from you?'

'Anything to get this man captured and stop giving Dieter heart attacks!'

'Would you be able to do that today, sometime?'

'This afternoon will be fine. Lisbon's okay with us. You will want a statement from Dieter won't you… he saw the man first.'

'Yes please, Klaus.' Sensing Klaus's distress, he added, 'I wish I could be there to take the statement from you myself.'

'That would have been nice… thank you.'

Ernst was quite surprised when the phone went abruptly dead in his ear.

The surprise of the abrupt end to the phone call still showed on his face when Willi Koslowski looked into his office. So much so, Willi could not resist remarking, 'Are you set in stone, Ernst?'

Blinking himself back into the real world, Ernst finally responded, 'That was the damnedest thing, Willi…' shaking the phone before he placed it back down. 'That phone call was from

Klaus Mennen. He and Dieter are on holiday in Portugal and he says Dieter saw the "ringed-hand man"... our Yute Polenkovich. Klaus pursued him, but lost him in the crowd; he thinks he possibly got onto a tram, but Klaus didn't get the tram number. Send a description and anything useful to security at the Lisbon Embassy. Put in a brief summary of the case so they will be *au fait* with the importance of Klaus and Dieter when they get to the Embassy. I want security to understand they are to treat this as real police work and not to be as haphazard about it as they would a lost passport or a handbag!'

'Right away, Ernst.'

'Please, Willi, even if the Embassy boys are going to be upset about doing their jobs properly, the biggest worry is to pick up the trail again and finance some field officers from here.'

'What about your American friend – he might help.'

Without acknowledging Willi's remark, Ernst's hand darted to the phone, and before the phone reached his ear, his excited fingers punched out the numbers. Willi knew now was the time to leave; waving his fingers as 'goodbye' in Ernst's eyeline, he left the office. One ring, two rings, three rings, then click. 'Hello, Joc Latimer...'

With as much humour as he could muster, Ernst replied, 'Ulbrecht heir!'

Joc laughed a little. 'Great to hear from you, Ernst. Is there anything I can do?'

'Possibly, Joc. We have just had a reported sighting of Polenkovich in Portugal!'

'Great news! Tell me more.'

'The luckiest, but possibly the best witness we could ever have, if ever we get to court – it was Dieter and of course Klaus is there too, and would you believe, Klaus gave chase!'

'That's a lucky break, and if it all comes together, you will be able to close the book.'

'I really hope that will be the case, Joc, but until all of my instincts are satisfied, I won't let go.'

'I know you won't, Ernst. Anyway, I'm sorry to be rude, but how can I help? You just caught me on my way to a Bureau "pep talk". You know what they're like – if you turn up late, you're made to feel like a naughty school boy.'

'Yes, I know, we seem to be getting too many of those these days. Anyway, to the point, Joc. Is there any way your boys in Portugal could spread themselves around to support the men I'm sending down there?'

'That's a tricky one – bloody diplomats and their security units are like prima donnas. There are some good policemen among them, but when I ask, I'm sure they'll scream, "I have no appropriation for that, you know our budgets have been cut to the bone!" Anyway, let me see if I have any friends on board over there. I'll do my best.'

'I know you will, and thanks, Joc.'

'Be in touch as soon as I can, Ernst.'

'Thanks again, Joc.'

Ernst entered Commissioner Roth's office, happy in the knowledge that this time he was there asking for money for a good reason and Ernst was sure his friend would not have to crawl on his belly to the town fathers for money this time. Commissioner Roth spoke first. 'Ernst, what a surprise! Klaus and Dieter seeing the famous ring.'

'Not both of them, sir, it was only Dieter. Klaus went off in hot pursuit on Dieter's word. In a way, I'm pleased he didn't catch up with our Russian friend and I certainly hope Klaus wasn't spotted by him. If he was, it will warn Polenkovich and he will go to ground, or worst of all, run back home very swiftly and seek sanctuary with the Organisatiya.'

'Don't think the worst, Ernst. On hearing the rumours in the corridors and reading your report, I phoned one of my colleagues in Portugal… you see, not all of the conventions we attend are a complete waste of time. Manuel Vargas, Chief Inspector of Police there, has offered a link-up with your men when they arrive and all the necessary freedom you need to run around in a strange country.'

'You know me too well! You expected me to request we send some of our men, didn't you? I must admit this time I was expecting you to grudgingly authorise my request after giving me some opposition, but to throw me in Vargas, plus support, is just fantastic!'

Well, all of the various European police forces and security forces will eventually all work together automatically in the future, but at the moment, we have to sometimes use the old boy network to get things cracking.'

'I hope you don't mind, sir, but I've spoken to Joc Latimer – he said he will do what he can. Do you think that Vargas's boys would extend their offer to the Americans? After all it was them that found out the name of the "ringed-hand man" and they have been very helpful throughout. I felt it only right that Joc should know we have a lead in Portugal and a request for any help from his security down there seemed only natural to me.'

Ernst's hurried speech did not leave any room for Roth to interrupt; instead, he sat looking into the pleading eyes of his friend while a smile began to break over his face. Roth rubbed his hands together and said, 'This could be an intriguing exercise, Ernst. I'll speak to Vargas's boys as you requested.'

Ernst stood up, offering his hand to Commander Roth. 'Thank you, sir. They say two heads are better than one, perhaps three will be even more so!'

'Nicole!' Daniel's voice was harsh. 'Why are you like this? Suddenly you have become remote and petulant... nothing I do is right for you these days. We have always discussed everything, but if your mood doesn't improve very quickly, I shall insist that you see a doctor.'

'We will see about that! It's my body and I shall do what I like with it!'

'So there is something wrong?'

'I never said that!'

'Stop playing with me please, Nicole. This is not like us!'

'Well it may well be in the future!'

'I sincerely hope not. I love you now as I have always loved you, but I don't know if it will be strong enough to live out the rest of our lives in the anguish you are creating.'

'Why don't you go back to playing soldiers... That's all you're good for, anyway!'

124

'Stop it, Nicole!' The anger within him echoed in his throat.

'No! You stop it! Being a soldier isn't everything, you know!'

Daniel moved forward, his brain trying desperately to understand, but his body moved forward instinctively to strike out. Nicole recoiled, her arms rose up to protect her face. Daniel froze, his arm, as if struck by lightening, motionless in mid-air. He stared down at his wife with momentary hate, as she fell backwards onto the sofa. In disgust with himself, Daniel left their small lounge, slamming the door with all his might.

Chief Inspector Manuel Vargas was expecting more activity for his men and expecting to reap some wider recognition from his international crime fighters had he not balanced in his mind the additional cost to his budget. Commander Roth had explained to him about the tying up of the loose ends of one of the largest crimes the world's police forces had ever seen, and that it was felt by him and Chief Inspector Ulbrecht that with the additional effort from Vargas's own men allowing the courtesy of giving a few of Roth's men the liberty to work freely in Portugal, that it would not (now that a confirmed sighting had been made of this Russian) take very long before the file could be closed.

Vargas slammed his fist angrily down on his polished, uncluttered desk. Through his teeth, he forced the words, 'Bloody Americans!' Thumping the desk again, his anger allowed one more exclamation through his clenched teeth. 'Why wasn't I, Manuel Vargas, the Chief of Police, not told the Americans were involved?' Annoyed, Vargas reached for the phone and brusquely asked his secretary for head of security at the US Embassy. His fingers tapped on his desk as he sat and waited.

'Hello, Jim Lomax here, US Embassy security. How may we help?'

Bluntly, Vargas replied, 'Your people seem to be very active chasing Russians… why?'

'Oh, that, sir. It's not really official, sir. I'm sorry, it all started out with me doing a favour for an old classmate of mine. His exact words to me were, "Could you put a couple or so men out and ask a favour of any contacts you have about a Russian wanted by the Hamburg police." I must apologise, sir, every time you try to do someone a favour, it somehow takes over your normal routine. My guys will be told to cool it, sir. Will that satisfy you?'

'Not quite. You may carry on with what you are doing, but I do want a request in writing from your Ambassador.'

'I feel sure that could be arranged, sir, but all of a sudden it won't just be a favour for a friend, it will be official and could raise one hell of a storm for my friend at Langley who just wanted a helping hand for his German counterpart, if you see what I mean. Surely, sir, we don't have to be so rigid with the rules?' The pause in the conversation allowed Lomax to add, 'Would you accept a full report with a personal apology from me?'

'I don't think that will be necessary, your explanation will suffice. We must always keep our favourable options open, we never know when we may need a favour ourselves.' Vargas's chest swelled visibly as he became more and more magnanimous. He continued talking into the phone. 'May I suggest you phone my office from time to time to relay anything that you feel *we* should know. That is the same arrangement I have with the Germans. I feel sure that someone at your end could manage that at least a couple of times a week.' The sarcasm in Vargas's voice did not go unnoticed.

'I'm sure that could be arranged, sir. I will see that it starts from tomorrow. Thank you for your understanding – starting tomorrow, then!'

'Until tomorrow, Mr Lomax!'

After finishing the call, Lomax rested back in his chair with a wry smile stretching across his face. He murmured to himself, 'The crafty old fox, he's going to get both ours and the Germans' information handed to him on a plate and he doesn't have to give anything his boys find out to anyone!' After a short pause, he added, 'That's what he would like, I'd bet on it!'

Ernst Ulbrecht, for the last few days, had been walking around the offices grinning like a Cheshire cat. Everything had been going so well. The report that the 'ringed-hand man' was in Portugal, the courtesy which had been extended by the Portuguese, his men settling in nicely with them, and Joc Latimer's promise of seeing if he could pull a favour from the US Embassy in Lisbon. He was feeling good about the assurance that the game of hide and seek would not last very much longer. The sudden ring of his telephone brought Ernst back into the real world. As he snatched the phone up, he was ready for work, the relaxed contentment he had allowed himself disappeared immediately.

'Ulbrecht heir…'

'Latimer here!'

'Joc! Glad to hear from you. Good news I hope?'

'No, not really, just a bit of forward thinking.'

'What's that?'

'Well, the head of security in Lisbon is an old buddy, Jim Lomax by name. A few minutes ago, he had a phone call from a Chief of Police called Manuel Vargas, who rapped his knuckles for working his patch without our Ambassador obtaining permission first!'

'Joc, I'm sorry about that. Give this man my apologies, please.'

'There's no need for that. He's a great guy, he's dealt with many of these sorts of situations before.'

'Well, thank him anyway. Has he found out anything yet?'

'No, not really, but he felt this Vargas might not be fully straight up and down in his dealings. He has a hunch that Vargas may be collecting his own information and not feeding it through.'

'Interesting, Joc. What gave him that impression though?'

'Instinct mainly, that and the way he waded in and intimated that he wanted a written application from the Ambassador, then turned into Mr Nice Guy when Lomax explained this was all a favour for a friend. Vargas then said there was no need for written reports, but a couple of phoned reports each week would do.'

'On a hunch, your Lomax thinks like this?'

'Yes, and also when he became suspicious, he started asking around and found out Vargas is asking questions of all the Russians registered in Portugal!'

'He's what?'

'Jim thinks either Vargas is trying to solve the case on his own, or he's writing a bigger part for himself, or he's a bloody stupid policeman. His opinion is split between all three theories, but one thing's for certain, he's making a lot of waves down there amongst the Russian community which could easily make your man disappear again.'

'He's right, Joc, what a stupid man this Vargas must be.'

'You can say that again. Anyway, will you deal with it, Ernst?'

'Most certainly, Joc. Thank you… and thank Jim.'

'Be in touch if and when we get anything; bye.'

Ernst said his goodbye as his fingers reached for the cradle to get another line. With the phone still to his ear, he dialled Commander Roth's number. The metallic ring of the newly installed phone system was answered on its third ring.

'Roth.'

'Sorry to dial you direct, it's Ernst Ulbrecht here.'

'That's all right, Ernst. I know you would never dial me direct without a very good reason.'

'Thank you, sir. I have just had Joc Latimer on the phone. Vargas has found out about the Yanks helping us on his own…'

Ernst continued to tell the story and as he finished, Roth broke in, saying, 'Stupid bloody idiot!'

Ernst continued, 'Would you contact him, please. The politics you will have to work out for yourself, but with all the Russian community in Portugal being stopped and questioned it's going to make our man run for the hills and cause a lot of extra legwork. If Mr Vargas is only playing to get onto the world's stage, I think he is going the wrong way about it, sir.'

'You're right, Ernst. I will see what I can do to slow him down. Sorry I didn't get on to Vargas quicker about your American friend.'

'I know, sir, but thank you and goodbye.' As the conversation ended, Roth chuckled to himself at his wily old friend's remarks.

'Daniel Tomlevski Lt, Eurocorps' – the varnished plate with his name in black letters pleased him, as he stood back admiring it as the fresh paint caught the low autumn sun shining on it. His colleagues who passed him in the corridor knew how proud he was; they all had the same feelings and emotions the first time they had seen their names beside the unique 'Eurocorps' crest. The jibes came thick and fast from his new friends. 'You'll have an extra duty in the morning, Lieutenant… cleaning it!' 'You won't think so much of it when you've been here a week!' 'The door's pretty... wait 'til you see the furniture!' Daniel smiled back warmly and shook every hand. He felt at home as did everyone in this new young army. They all shared the same dream of unity and the additional selection process had made them all feel special. As he reached for his office door handle, the phone inside began to ring.

Since Dieter had seen the 'ringed-hand man', both he and Klaus had reported to the German Embassy as requested by Ernst. Their world of freedom and romance, had just seemed to fall apart. They both asked themselves what had they done to make the 'ringed-hand man' come to Portugal? Had he changed his mind and decided to kill them both anyway? Where was the life they had planned to live whilst they were on holiday; the museums, the walks, the dinners, romantic boat trips under equally romantic lit bridges? Everything was for their own pleasure, but now, the warning hanging heavily, that they should not leave the hotel in case they were seen, made them miserable and furtive. The old fears and threats from Hamburg had returned. Their love for each other was being tested again.

Mayer tapped lightly on the doorframe of Ernst's office door. The door was open, as always. As soon as the tap was acknowledged, she said, 'Lanov and Mogatin are confirmed as working with Tashimov in several theatres of operation where special talents like persuasion, blackmail and brute force were needed. Marshall Polenkovich, we feel sure, knew all three men. The connection being another General called Nabialev, who was found shot dead in his apartment before Tashimov arrived in Hamburg. My Russian contacts feel that Nabialev died in mysterious circumstances, even for an unsolved Russian crime.'

'Well done, Mayer! Please keep me informed if you come up with anything else.'

'Yes, sir.'

Ernst looked at her as she seemed to come to attention before moving away. Lifting up his phone, he dialled the digits slowly. One ring, two rings, three... impatiently he mumbled into the mouthpiece, 'Oh come on, Joc. Please be there.' The pulse of ring number four was just starting in his ear, when he heard the snatch of the phone as it was lifted from the cradle.

'Joc Latimer.' His strong voice sounded a little breathless.

'Ernst here... you sound as if you have been running.'

'Not far short of running, although I'd use the word "spinning" – you know, Ernst, like a top?'

'Yes, Joc, we have situations here that make us spin too.'

'I'm sure. I'm pleased you have rung me though. Lomax has been on from Portugal – it seems they are not being impeded on the streets of Lisbon anymore. In fact, it's all lovey dovey. Some of our guys have actually been given lifts by the Portuguese – whoever your fairy godfather is, he waves a pretty fierce wand!'

'It's my Commander – he said he had a friend from some convention or other.'

'Well, it's helping our boys down there. Thank him for us next time you see him. Is there anything we can do for you, Ernst?'

'Yes, we have two more names that are becoming important to us, Dimitri Lanov and Mogatin – we only have a surname for him – both are known to have worked alongside our dead Russian, Tashimov. All three are confirmed as operating in central Russia, Afghanistan and Central Africa is a strong possibility also. Lanov and Mogatin were sighted in Hamburg during our troubles and a new name in the game is General Nabialev, now deceased. We know Tashimov was connected in some way with Nabialev; Lanov and Mogatin seem to tie in, so anything you can give us on these names could help significantly.'

'That's quite a mouthful, Ernst. Of course we will help where we can. Will you fax me all you want me to see – the correct spellings of these Russian names would help.'

'It will be done, Joc. Thank you again.'

'Think nothing of it, Ernst. I don't want the blighters over here, but I'm sorry you're on the battleground.'

'Europe's used to that, Joc. Thanks again. The fax will be on its way in minutes. Bye.'

The legwork searching for the 'ringed-hand man' was endless. The Portuguese police using normal beat patrols and detective divisions with their knowledge of the underworld and all their informants, the German Embassy security men coupled with the detectives sent from Hamburg, plus the small support from the American Embassy security, were all getting tired. Although only a few days since the sighting of the 'ringed-hand man' and his identification as Marshall Yute Polenkovich, the frustration of not picking up one single lead was slowing the initial pace of the investigation down.

Jim Lomax sat impatiently, drumming his fingers on his desk. The few people sprinkled around the large, open-plan office gave way to their impatience in different ways. Phones rang intermittently and were answered sluggishly. The pace was slow, boring, with a feeling of 'couldn't care less' attitude.

Walking from his desk, Jim tried to raise morale, not that there was much he could do, other than make comments like, 'Lionel, I know it's boring, but think how lucky you are sitting here with the air conditioning on and your mates are walking the sweaty path.' 'Joe, cheer up! Just think… you could be stuck in traffic in a car with no air conditioning.' 'Keep it going, fellas, just think there's another day tomorrow!'

Walking back to his own desk, as he passed by one of the unattended phones, it rang out to be answered. Grabbing at the phone before the second ring had started and with the handset still travelling to his ear, he barked, 'Lomax…'

'Jim!' came the reply. 'I've got our guy! He's talking to another guy… they look Russian definitely… well, central European, anyway. I'll stay with our guy, but a couple more guys over here could give us three bites of the cherry.'

'Bert.' The operative calling was Bert Rawlinson. 'Have they just met? Have they been together long? Does it look as if they are set for a fairly long talk? Where are you now – at your allocated station?'

'Yes, no, yes and yes to your questions!'

'Smart arse! The cavalry is on its way.'

As the rest of the office staff started gathering around their excited boss, their lethargy immediately began to ebb away, all of them hoping to get some of the action.

In the short time it had taken Lomax's men to cross from their desks, his fingers had dialled out two sets of numbers on his handset and moved two of his closest players into position alongside Bert Rawlinson.

Jim was elated. Grabbing the phone, he dialled his old friend, Joc Latimer. The news was important and must surely help. When Joc received Jim Lomax's call, the information excited him and he related his recent call with Ernst Ulbrecht, giving Jim the surnames of Lanov and Mogatin only.

'I don't have the correct spellings for these names, Jim, but I should have them any time and I'll fax them through to you. It seems the Germans have made a three-way connection through a Russian who bought it called Tashimov, during the big Hamburg operation. If they are right about these two, your men have got our third man meeting with them.'

'Hope they are; it ties up nice and neat, except for the fact I haven't got the resources to send my guys on a European tour!'

'Jim, I know that Ernst appreciates that. Can I suggest you extract from Vargas the German team's names and make the responsibility theirs? I'll speak to Hamburg.'

'Fine, Joc. I'll carry on for as long as I can, you know that, but the Ambassador's looking over my shoulder quite a bit.'

'I understand, Jim. Get hold of the Germans… I'll push German HQ. Good work, Jim. I owe you one. Thanks a lot.'

The next few minutes were taken up phoning Ernst about the connection Jim had made and advising him he had given the names of Lanov and Mogatin as information, plus telling them to make contact with Ernst's boys in Portugal. No sooner was the phone back in the cradle than it was winging its way back to his ear and his fingers were racing to dial out numbers.

'Brian Fullerton,' came the swift response.

'Joc, Brian. About our Russians. We seem to have found Yute Polenkovich. Jim Lomax's team from the Embassy has found him plus some more possible Russians all on a favour.'

'That's great. Joc, you said "Russians"… I only know of one so far, but I have the feeling you're going to tell me more…'

'Well yes. The Germans have come up with two more names that are connected to Polenkovich's past, and I was wondering if any of your past reports might by some miracle, carry any one of their names?' Without waiting for a reply, Joc continued. 'Have you got a pen handy?'

'I suppose so, Joc, but I'm still being looked at and it's difficult to move things!'

'I understand, Brian, but I really feel it's important to help the Germans as much as we can. Please do what you can.'

'You know I will, but things take a little longer these days.'

'Thanks, I know what you mean. The names are...' Joc paused for Brian to pick up his pen, 'Dimitri Lanov and Mogatin – we have no Christian name for the second man. Do what you can, old buddy.'

'I will be in touch. By the way, Sandra sends her love to you both and says we ought to have dinner together sometime.'

'I'll speak to Liz and get her to set it up with Sandra.'

'Thanks. Look forward to it. Bye for now.'

'Bye, Brian, thanks again.'

Chapter Sixteen

As Daniel Tomlevski turned into the driveway, fear struck into his heart. The house stood in darkness. His mind raced. *Did she say she was going to be late or going out? No, I'm sure she didn't* say *either*, he answered himself. It's not Wednesday, her night for aerobics? You know it isn't, you bloody fool! You've been writing Friday all day! *My God!* his mind raced. *She's had an accident! Fallen downstairs, it could be anything! You bloody fool! Get in there!*

Leaving the car unlocked, he covered the ground to the front door at a run, searching for the keys as he went. The initial fear of disaster had left him. As he put the key in the lock, his military training took over. His fear must not be allowed to turn into panic. If she is hurt, he must be calm and loving. Entering the small hallway, he switched on the light. No one lying at the foot of the stairs... The spread of the light into the lounge gave just enough light to see the sobbing, upright figure of his darling Nicole. Racing to her side, gazing at her tear-swollen face, he said, 'You poor love, what have you done?'

Through great sobs, Nicole blurted out, 'It's not me they want, it's you!'

'Who wants me, dear?'

'I don't know!' The sobs were getting deeper, shaking her whole body.

'I don't understand.'

'You never do! You trudge on, seeing only good in the world.'

'I thought we both felt the same way – we discussed it thoroughly on many occasions and we agreed in principle on what I thought were our hopes for a better world.'

'Well you're wrong, I want nothing to do with it!' The sobs and tears became more intense.

'What on earth has made you change your views, Nicole? So much effort on both our parts would be wasted. You know, without you my life will be meaningless.'

Brutally, Nicole screamed at him. 'Your life will be meaningless? Your life? What about my father's life, my mother's life… my life… our life?' The torment within her exploded viciously as she pulled Daniel to her. 'I'm sorry, I'm sorry… It's those men's fault!'

'My love, it's all right.' His voice was muffled as he tried to speak with his head squeezed against her heaving breasts. 'When you calm down a little, I'll pour us a drink and we can talk for as long as you wish.'

'There's not much to talk about, really.' The sobs were easing a little now. The comfort of Daniel's head held tightly to her breasts gave her courage. 'Yes, Daniel, it is necessary that we talk. I hope I haven't left it too late already.' Her voice was getting back to normal. The tear-stained face and congested nose would take a little longer.

'Nicole, let me up. I can't hold my breath for much longer!'

Slowly her arms released him. Her hands came to each side of his face. Lovingly she kissed him gently and pulled him back against her body. 'I'm sorry, it's not you I'm fighting, it's them.'

'Who are "they"?'

The enquiring whisper, as if in a confessional, gave warmth and comfort to her and quizzically, she replied, 'I don't really know.'

'Nicole, don't you think you ought to start at the beginning – you're confusing me.'

'I was sitting having coffee, looking out at the people in the square, thinking of you. Nothing else, just you. These two large men sat abruptly down at my table. The smaller of the two asked me if my name was Madame Daniel Tomlevski. Naturally, I replied that I was. Without further ado, they told me that you had been accepted by Eurocorps. I told them we had not had any confirmation to that effect. They said, "You can believe us, but do not tell your husband yet." Naturally, I asked why, and their reply was straight and to the point. "Because we want him to do some things for us." They stood up and as they were about to leave, they said the next time we would meet, we would talk about my father.'

'Nicole, when was this?'

'About ten days before you told me you had been accepted by Eurocorps.'

'How did they know? They must have been investigators for the corps or some security people. But how does your father come into it?'

'About three days after this first meeting, I was walking in the park. They approached me and made me sit down with them on a park bench. They weren't rough with me, dear, but somehow I knew I had no choice but to do as they said. They started talking about the weather of all things, and how the car was running, you know, absolute trivia really, but then they went for the jugular and came straight out with it. Apparently my father had lived a double life during the war and he was not the good resistance fighter that he was cracked up to be. When I refused to believe them, they told me the communist records on my father can prove otherwise.'

'So they were communists, or at least, Russian?'

'I can only assume so. They warned me not to repeat any of this conversation to you, but I could talk to my father as much as I wished.'

'You poor darling. This has been tormenting you all this time?'

'Yes, it was a torment, they were so menacing...'

'Don't worry, my love, I'll get our security people informed and they will sort it out.'

'No you mustn't! They gave me a special message for you – that your father, while he was working for the British, was far from being as clean as the driven snow and that when you have spoken to him, you ought to have a chat with them!'

'What the hell are they on about? I'll meet them anytime and they can tell me their lies!'

'Hadn't you better speak to your father first, Daniel?'

'I really don't see the reason for doing so. If we bow to their wishes, we will be at their mercy forever. No. I'll be blowed if I will embarrass my father! Nicole, did you speak to your father about this?'

'I phoned him and told him what had happened and then he just changed the subject after he realised what I was saying, wanting to know what you wanted for your birthday! When I got back to asking him if there was anything I should know in view of your new position with Eurocorps, it felt like he was trying to hide something from me.'

'What about your mother? Have you spoken to her about it?'

'Yes I did. I've been so worried I felt I had to go behind Father's back, but Mother, in true fashion, exclaimed that my father was always wandering off, ever since they were first married and she used her favourite remark, "I don't know where he is or what he's doing half the time!" That seemed to be the end of it as far as Mother was concerned.'

'Do you think there is any truth in it?'

'No, I definitely do not. What about the implication about your own father?'

The acerbic manner Nicole delivered the defence and accusation in her last sentence jarred Daniel terribly, but as Nicole had almost calmed down, he held back the words that sprung to his mind after the sarcasm of her last remark: *my father I can assure you, will have no blemishes on his character*! To say the words would only start an argument. Instead, now, he thought to himself, was the time to organise visits to see their respective families.

'Dad, we have a little problem that Nicole and I would like to talk about with you.'

'Anytime you like, son,' replied his father affectionately. He added, 'Anything wrong?'

'I shouldn't think so, Dad. Shall we say about six o'clock? Then we will have time to drop in on Nicole's parents on the way to you – their phone's on the blink again.'

'Okay, son, any time you like. It's no problem, just come.'

'Okay, Dad, thanks. About six o'clock then.'

Nicole who had been standing with her arms around Daniel's middle with her head resting on his chest, asked, 'Did he sound normal, Daniel?'

'How do you mean "normal"?'

'You know!'

'No, I don't know, silly. He probably thinks we're going to announce there's a baby on the way!'

'Don't tease me, Daniel. You didn't think you were a little

overassertive when you asked him if we could have a talk with him?'

'No, I don't think he could have guessed anything from me. Anyway, make those puffy old eyes up and let's start getting ready to see your family first.'

The journey to Nicole's parents' house was a silent one. Each of them rode along with a deep sadness in their hearts, tormented that they both felt let down by their parents, and whether the accusations made by the Russians could be true – their own lives would be destroyed and they would have been living a lie. As Daniel turned the car into Nicole's parents' road, the oppressive silence was broken by a deep sigh from Nicole. Daniel placed his hand on hers for comfort. Nicole's father was working in the garden and looked up with delight when he recognised the car as it turned into the driveway. His smile dropped from his face when the customary wave from his daughter was not forthcoming and the tautness of Daniel's face muscles set his mind worrying.

There was no, 'Sorry to drop in on you at such short notice… hope you don't mind?'; no reply to his, 'Wonderful to see you, come in, Mother will be surprised…' The three of them, as they went through the motions of greeting each other, were like a group of stone statues. Even the excitement of Nicole's mother, as she came to greet them in the hallway, dropped away to silence. The walking into the lounge, the sitting down, the offer of tea or coffee did not overcome the oppression that had followed Daniel and Nicole from their own home and was now infesting the once happy home of Nicole's childhood.

Nicole's mother was the first to speak. 'What terrible thing has happened to you both? What can your father and I do to help?'

'Help? It isn't help we need. If the questions we have to ask are confirmed by Father, all we will need is a big hole to bury ourselves in!'

The anger in Nicole's voice was still echoing around the room when her father asked brusquely, 'What am I supposed to have done?'

Daniel, trying to ease the situation, cut in. 'Please forgive us, Mrs Claris! Nicole is very upset. Let me tell you what has happened. With regards to what you have allegedly done, we have not been told specifically, it has only been implied.' Daniel paused briefly, watching the surprised expressions on his in-laws' faces. 'Nicole was accosted and told that they have got a dossier on you, Father. They would be willing to use the information it contains to force me into collaborating with them in some way, through Eurocorps. You must forgive us both for approaching you in this way, but you must understand it is important that I at least know the facts before I go to Military Security.'

Nicole interrupted angrily, 'Don't lay all the blame at my father's doorstep, don't forget they implied your father was no angel as well!'

'I was coming to that... I personally think that there is nothing at all to worry about and our security boys will sort it out, but as you must understand I... we, must both know, if there was anything in your and my own father's past, which could affect my new appointment and all of our lives in the future.'

Nicole's father stood up and moved over to the fireplace, reaching for his pipe. 'I can think of nothing in any file on me that could hurt either of you. You know that I was once, long ago, in the communist party, along with Mother – Nicole automatically became involved. Both you and your military know that.'

'That's true, Father, you have always been completely open on that point.' Responding to Nicole, he asked, 'These people who accosted you, who did they say they were from?'

'They didn't, Father. They were quite menacing and were crowding me. Everything was implied but only the ultimate goal was actually stated. They want Daniel to do something for them.'

'These people, what nationality were they? European? American?'

'I think they were Russians, Father. They didn't exactly leave me a business card of course, they just said they will be in touch again.'

The fear that momentarily crossed Nicole's father's eyes at the mention of the word 'Russians' went unnoticed.

Nicole's mother asked quietly, 'Daniel, what do you think they may want you to do for them, or, to put it another way, what could you possibly do for them?' Her thoughtful quiet voice pulled them together, their conversation became more fluid, less brittle.

'Mrs Claris, I really don't know! My work pattern has not yet been set by Eurocorps. It is likely with my previous record that I will be in communications, transports, that sort of thing. Weaponry has not been my training, intelligence I've never been involved in by any stretch of the imagination, so, on the surface, I can see no obvious reason for their or anyone else's interest in me!'

'Fine, well, that's well answered, but what could they possibly have on your family to use against you?' asked Mrs Claris.

'You know my father, his only aim all his life has been basically to help everyone and his war was so long ago now, the whole system has changed. Should these people be after anything to do with weapons, a bow and arrow would confuse my father!' added Daniel.

Nicole's father interrupted his wife, who was just about to ask a further question. 'Your father and myself have often talked about the damn war and apart from translating, as he has often said, his job was shepherding people around, getting them billeted, sometimes locating brothers and sisters who had arrived in England – hardly anything sensitive in his background, I should have thought.'

'Nicole and I are happier now, Mr Claris. We both feel terrible about having to drag up the past, but you both know how our lives are involved in the unity of Europe. Nicole has been very distressed, as have I, but we feel better having had this conversation and your reassurance. It will be even better after we run over to Lunéville to see my parents and talk to them. I'm convinced that I can just report to Major Roche, my adjutant, and that will be the end of that.'

Nicole's mother asked, 'Is it necessary for you to confront your father with this, Daniel? You know he hasn't been all that well. In fact your mother and I had a long talk on the phone only this morning, and it seems he is going through a bad bout of bronchitis and is feeling very sorry for himself at the moment.'

'My mother never mentioned that to me yesterday. But Nicole and I did agree we would confront our families face to face, so I think it is only fair that my father is approached as well.'

Nicole's father promptly interrupted. 'Well, after all of the conversations I've had with your father, I personally, and I'm sure Mother here would have no objections, if you gave visiting your parents a miss. It seems pointless to aggravate him if he is so unwell.'

'He didn't sound so bad when I told him we were coming over.'

'Well, it's up to you to decide, but it could be a strain on him, as we both feel there is nothing to ask about and it's quite a long journey, so why don't you phone him and tell him you'll see him when he's feeling more up to it?'

'It is a fair old journey, and it would be nice not to have to go, I admit,' said Daniel.

Nicole took Daniel's hand lovingly. 'Come on now, let's go back home. Just think, you lucky man, you can help me with those curtains! We can phone your parents when we get home.'

'Or we could stop off at a nice cosy bar and have a few drinks!'

'We could, or we could just go home!'

Chapter Seventeen

Yute Polenkovich had not been aware of Klaus and Dieter sitting at the Plaza bar, nor the bungled attempt to follow him. Yute had been attentive to everything around him and the clumsiness of Klaus's pursuit caught his eye but was then rejected. No one, other than in Hollywood movies, could be so bad... but the one thing he never saw, was Klaus's face.

The tracking down of Lanov and Mogatin to Portugal had taken time and had used up a few favours along the way but now he had made the initial contact with them. He knew that the Council, who had made no objections to his request for a few days' vacation prior to the initiation of the great project they were about to embark upon, would have placed a good team together from the Ukraine, to watch his every move. A good team who would be almost invisible, but who would monitor his moves and contacts.

Yute's plans for meeting Lanov and Mogatin were accordingly elaborate, and Lanov's and Mogatin's skills at being invisible and knowing his own, along with his elaborate plans and the warning he had emphasised to Lanov and Mogatin, would keep all three of them on their mettle when they journeyed to a meeting. To this end, he had surveyed dozens of escape routes for himself and had advised Lanov and Mogatin during their earlier brief meeting to do the same. He had given them a list of telephone kiosk numbers with the times and places to be ready to receive his calls placed from another call box, plus the one emergency number he could be reached at every other day at six in the evening. He instinctively knew that both Lanov and Mogatin were anxious to be accepted by the Organisatiya again after their period out in the cold. Today, Yute, Lanov and Mogatin were to meet, an important one for all of them. They all felt that information should be exchanged between them without further delay.

Yute's approach to Hotel Splendide was clear. Just one knuckle tap on the door of Room 204, and it was swiftly opened by Lanov. Mogatin's large frame rose out of the chair and he offered his hand to Yute; it was accepted warmly. Lanov, after closing the door, followed down the short corridor to the lounge before he could welcome this man of mystery.

'What I am proposing is Tashimov's old plan, with a few strong differences.' Yute paused for a moment to watch the unemotional faces. 'Tashimov's plan of selling arms in bulk for US dollars and the dollars being paid by the US Mafia for our freely-acquired heroin was a good one, but it was a hurried operation, rushed along by the greed of some of our councillors. My plan differs in many ways, but what is on offer to the Organisatiya – and I emphasise it has been accepted by them – is a long-term plan, to be run only by proven professionals like yourselves to control the many pieces of the puzzle which will be spread initially through the whole of Europe.' After clearing his throat, Yute continued, 'The three elements coming together as Tashimov originally wanted, were the correct elements but the timescale forced upon him to set in motion and execute the plan was insufficient – that we all knew but the crux of its downfall, was the lunacy of using local Organisatiya without adequate supervision. It should have been men like ourselves, without someone breathing down our necks telling us we must not be too hard on our local brothers. We will control this operation – the likes of us. We will be the puppeteers, pulling strings with disciplined soldiers of all ranks and nationalities. The only thing we will have to do is make certain that the people we indoctrinate are frightened enough by the fear of their past indiscretions, or those of their families, being exposed. The people we will hold in the palm of our hands will be key members of a very elite band of men. They will have freedom of movement, control of their own communications and transport systems; air, road and sea. All these people will be obtained by the Committee, but finally approved by me before being put in place.'

The explanation had held Lanov's and Mogatin's attention. Yute took another sip of water before he announced his tagline, 'Gentlemen, we are selecting these men and women to be our "flag carriers" in Europe. Comrades, we are going to infiltrate the echelons of Eurocorps!'

There was a stony silence in the room after Yute's speech. The atmosphere could have been cut with a knife. Neither of the men knew what to say, so Yute struck in again. 'Gentlemen, when we have these men and women in place, they will need looking after. Who could do this better than you?'

Mogatin's deep voice answered with a question. 'Where is Tashimov in this?'

Surprised by the question, Yute asked, 'You don't know?'

'Know what?' replied Mogatin.

'He's dead,' answered Yute.

'When?' asked Lanov.

'He never got out of Hamburg. I thought you knew that. There were an awful lot of people running frantically around in Russia. I thought everyone must have felt the draught they caused as they went running by!'

Mogatin's deep voice cut in, 'We didn't go back to Russia!' The words came out of this man like a disappointed schoolboy.

'Why didn't you make your way straight back like the few of your group who remained did?'

'Because Tashimov promised us a lingering death if anything went wrong with his plan!' responded Lanov.

'I understand,' said Yute quietly. After waiting for a few moments for any other responses from either of them, he asked, 'Where have you been then?'

'Southern Germany, into France, Belgium, Denmark, Norway, a package flight to the Algarve, then up here to get lost in the crowds. We had intended to go across Spain then a boat to Italy to make some contact with people we know and some we just know of.'

'You would never have made it.' Yute's voice sounded sinister. 'Just think. I found you without having any real difficulty and given a world full of people and just one needing to be found, Tashimov was the best I've ever known!'

Mogatin jumped up from his seat. 'We know all of Tashimov's methods! How do you think we've managed to survive this long?

It's because we're so good at anticipating what he would have done.'

'You've forgotten one thing – he wasn't even there!' The viciousness in Yute's voice deflated both men. Yute sat silently with both the men waiting for any whisper of an explanation, but both he and they knew it would have been a different story had Tashimov been in pursuit. The seconds passed, no one willing to admit defeat in the chase. Yute not wishing to tease, suddenly asked again, 'Who could do this better than you? You haven't answered my question.'

Lanov got up from his seat and went across the room to Mogatin. Leaning his head nearer to Mogatin's ear, he whispered something. Their heads moved to hear each other's reply. Yute watched as the charade of discussing whether they came back into the bosom of Russia or go into crime on their own after all.

Boredom with the two men in front of him and the game they were playing, forced the issue. Yute could hold back no longer. 'Gentlemen…' That hard, throaty word stopped their whispers. 'I have decided I want you to continue on my team. Not only me, but you have my word the Council has agreed also. So with your first loyalty to me, shall we shake hands and prepare ourselves for the journey back to Russia?' Yute stood up, offering his hand. 'Shall we seal our new allegiance to each other?'

Lanov and Mogatin both knew the only alternative, having already been told the outline of Yute's new plan meant death in itself. Both Lanov and Mogatin's handshakes were firm.

Chapter Eighteen

Daniel sat in his office unable to concentrate on his work. The dilemma was whether he should mention the incident to Major Roche or not. He believed his own father's account of his life with all his heart. He had heard them all his life. There could be nothing to reproach his father with. The sincerity of Nicole's father's denial the evening before had convinced him there could be nothing in his past either which could cause problems with his chosen career. Anyway, hadn't he been thoroughly screened by security? The communist bit was well known and the mere fact of his being on this chair, in this office, in this HQ was proof that nothing untoward had been uncovered about his background.

Slowly, the clouds had lifted, and his thoughts gradually turned to the task of the allocation of supplies in an emergency situation to an imaginary island off the African coast. Major Roche need not be told.

Joe Lomax was happy with everything happening around him. There seemed to be no hassle from anywhere within his world. Even the help he had been giving his pal, Joc Latimer at dear old Langley, had not put him off schedule. Even Chief Inspector of Police, Manuel Vargas hadn't been quite so smarmy or deceitful, but the light tap on his door somehow had a warning about it. Not one to run away from any situation, he spontaneously reacted, 'Come in!'

Paul Isaac entered, his face looking as if it needed another shave. Joe had often thought this poor guy must have to shave between kisses, his bristles grew so fast. His hair, which was jet black and well-groomed, was the envy of most of the guys around the station.

'Can I have a few words, Joe?' his strong voice asked.

'Of course, Paul, come in, take a seat.'

'Thanks. I've got a little problem I want to bounce off you.'

'Go on.'

'Well, yesterday, as you know, three of us went over to that shindig at the Russians'. It was impossible not to notice the level of activity which was far more than any of us had ever seen before. It also seemed to be spread throughout the whole building. You know the sort of thing: phones ringing on all floors, doors opening and closing all over the place. Later on after a few vodkas, I got chatting to one of the "Ivans" and asked why there was so much activity. His reply was, "Oh, it's nothing. Mother Russia has misplaced another General or someone who has been naughty." He said "General"… I'm sure of it. He covered up with the "or someone". Anyway, you know the scenario. I pursued it through the next hour or so and finally got the name… it's the guy we're following. If we are looking for him on behalf of the Germans, and half of the police forces across Europe from time to time have been involved because he's a bloody Russian, why are they looking for him?'

'That's a bloody good question, Paul; are you meeting your "Ivan" again?'

'He was too drunk at the end of it all to ask anything, let alone remember!'

'Good. Have you got a name?'

'Sure. You know how they are these days, trying to be westernised and modern – I came back with his business card,' replied Paul.

'I think you ought to phone him, don't you, Paul?'

'That's what I thought you'd say. You don't want them to know that we know where he is?'

'No, I wouldn't think so, Paul. We don't know the full depth of Langley's intentions and the Germans originated the whole thing. Just poke around. Keep me informed though please, Paul.'

'Sure, Joe, I'll get on and get me another Seltzer before I phone…'

After that conversation with Paul, Joe had wanted to phone Joc at Langley, but he knew only half the story was often worse than no story at all. He felt guilty not phoning Joc straightaway, but he would phone Langley when Paul had dug a bit deeper and was happy in his own mind that the drunk 'Ivan' was not a plant. He resigned himself to getting on with a pile of paperwork which had been building up on his desk due to his lack of enthusiasm in dealing with it.

The following morning, Joe was still half-heartedly dealing with his paperwork in between taking phone calls when there was another knock on the door.

'Come in!' When the door opened, the dishevelled, unshaven face of Paul Isaac appeared. Joe couldn't believe his eyes.

'Paul, for Christ's sake, what has happened to you?' Jokingly, he added, 'Take a bed!'

'Thanks, Joe, I need it,' he said in a croaky voice and smiling weakly. 'It was a rough night with the Russkies. In fact, I've only been back an hour, just enough time to write up my report. It's being logged-in at the moment, it should be with you shortly. I told them this report may catch up with some very serious stuff from the past.'

'In what way, Paul?'

'Well, my "Ivan", who by the way, is an "Ivan" – Ivan Kapustin, to be exact, was getting very, very drunk and very melancholy. First it was the "my beautiful Russia" routine, then it was his mother and father, then his sister who married the wrong man, even down to his boyhood dog. The interest started when he began mouthing lyrical about all the stations he had been at over his ten short years in the service.'

'What rank is he, Paul? I suppose he is military?'

'Strange that, he claims no military connection, straight from the Moscow police, after completing criminology and psychology courses, with honours. It seems the new regime and Glasnost has helped him by removing a lot of the deadwood military and his hope is to bring some dignity back into the Russian diplomatic service!'

'Sounds like a nice guy. Is he talking through his ass?'

'Possibly, but at the moment he wants very much to be friends. Tomorrow could be another day, but at the moment I think he's talking to us because he wants to, and there are no strings.'

'Great... I'll accept that!' Joe enthused. 'So, where are we now?'

'During his reminiscing, he bumbled on about the wasted effort his unit has to commit to useless work put out to their embassies worldwide, stuff like this Yute Polenkovich. It seems it isn't only local stations get informed, it's everybody, which wastes manpower and doubles the workload in every embassy and consulate, because even if there is no news in their area, they have to reply daily to Moscow. I think I agree with him on that point! Anyway, about three years ago, when he was very much the "new boy", he was at the Paris Embassy when a hue and cry went up for two men – Lanov and Mogatin. They were needed back in Moscow urgently. Evidently, the Paris unit turned itself inside out and one officer got shot in mysterious circumstances by the French police. The two guys who were being tracked down were, in fact, in India.'

'What are you saying, Paul?'

'Well, these guys were sent to Afghanistan direct (not even via Russia) to meet and be assigned to Gregor Tashimov, who was working for our General, Yute Polenkovich. Maybe these two guys talking to the General are the same two guys?'

'Christ, Paul! Feed into the library anything you might think relevant. I'll speak to Joc right now to push things along his end. Paul, before you get some sleep, could you chase your paperwork for me? Well done, thanks.'

Paul signalled yes he would and don't mention it, in one very tired nod.

Joc Latimer was sitting at his desk; his agitation was being dispersed by the drumming of his fingers on the desk, the pulling on his ear lobes, and the pacing around his desk. Waiting in his job was a normal part of things. His agitation was not because of that, but because he knew the information he had was very important and could save a lot of people, throughout Europe at least, working unnecessarily. He followed his first instincts when Joe phoned him, asking him to stretch the resources he had even further and not to let any of the three Russians they had linked together, get out of their sight. He knew Ernst Ulbrecht would have done exactly the same as he was doing now, but it would be nice to have some confirmation. The finger drumming continued, while he waited for Ernst to return his call.

Daniel Tomlevski had arrived home, to find it looking empty. The remaining light before the early dusk had not worried him as he walked across the short gravel path to the front door. Nicole was sitting inside watching the twilight through the French doors across the lawn and hedgerows behind the house. She loved standing, waiting for the coming of darkness to engulf her. On the few occasions they had watched together, they had enjoyed a lingering kiss before Nicole happily went off to prepare supper. But tonight she was not there. Again, his mind raced through her schedule – tonight was not committed for anything other than themselves.

The headlights of Nicole's car turned into the driveway making shadows as they passed across the hedgerow. Daniel raced to the front door, anxious to hold her in his arms and find out why she was so late home. Opening the front door wide and stepping out onto the little porch, Daniel could not help but immediately notice the second car pulling up. Selfishly, Daniel felt that he was going to have to share Nicole with some of her stupid girlfriends, even if it would only be for a short time. Walking towards Nicole, who was still sitting in her car, anguish fell upon him. Nicole just sat there, her sobbing making the car rock, her tearful face full of sorrow. Snatching at the car door to open it, Daniel did not even notice the two men getting out of the car behind.

'Nicole, what has happened to you?' Getting no reply from the shocked face of his wife, he carried on speaking. 'Nicole, just sit there for a few moments longer. Let me speak to your friends, they will tell me what has happened.' As he turned away from her, the whole world went black…

The ache in his head as he slowly fought to bring his world back into focus. The sharp searing pain cutting down his brow ending up as needles pricking into his eyeballs followed by the cooling relief as the cold flannel was placed on his head with the ice-cold water trickling down his temples, which felt wonderful. The relief was soothing and his flickering eyelids allowed out-of-focus images to dance. There was no panic in him, just the cold effort of trying to get his mind to work and his sight and strength back so he could help Nicole. Nicole's name was firmly in place in his mind. He silently mouthed her name as his dry tongue searched to get moisture and with his eyes slowly gaining focus, there suddenly appeared a clear vision of the swollen tear-stained face sitting before him.

Strong hands on his shoulders forced him back down into the chair. His second attempt to rise was no more successful. The applied strength was holding him in a vice-like grip without too much effort from his assailants, Daniel thought. He must be a big fellow; he will come around in front of me, then I'll attack. His still muddled brain was struggling to find escape from the grip on his shoulders, but refused to let him see the large man standing behind his wife, holding her shoulders as she sat opposite him.

'Mr Tomlevski, may I suggest you sit still until your head clears, then we – my friend behind you and me – shall have a little talk.'

The voice that Daniel was hearing, was deep, assertive and with a good accent. Daniel opened his mouth to speak, but only meaningless sounds came out. The voice behind him said, 'Please make yourself comfortable, we can wait for you to rejoin us.' That voice was softer, even 'tinny' compared with the previous voice, but somehow there was menace. The sarcasm in the voice was an immediate annoyance to Daniel, which gave him enough energy to make another attempt at standing up, until the strength of his keeper's hands tightened. The deep voice cut in. 'We have all the time in the world, Mr Tomlevski, as long as it takes to give you our message. Of course, you must understand what we are going to tell you and of course, we must make certain that you will do as you are told.'

The tinny voice added, 'We like to talk, Mr Tomlevski, but we can be physical to get our message into your head, understand me, tovarich?'

'Yes, comrade, and we can also play with his pretty wife, but I'm sure Mr Tomlevski is well aware of his plight now. Is your head feeling better, Mr Tomlevski?'

'Yes it is. I don't know what you expect we or I might have done, but you are totally mistaken!'

The tinny voice behind him answered. 'Oh, Mr Tomlevski, we don't think for one moment you or your dear wife have done anything. In fact we know that other than the usual misguided political mistakes and pranks at college, you are totally flawless!'

'Well, if that's the case, what the hell are you doing here?'

The deep voice cut in. 'Shall we say that it's the sins of your fathers that will, after so many years, pay Mother Russia what she wants? Don't look so shocked. By the way, may we call you Daniel? It's better than all the formality, don't you think?'

'I've never really thought about formality as you call it, but it is normally only friends that call me by my Christian name, so in your case, Mr Tomlevski will do!'

I can assure you we will be friends, Daniel, so I'll take the liberty of calling you Daniel,' the deep voice replied.

Before Daniel could answer, the tinny voice said, 'You will *both* be our friends, Daniel, or you will *both* be dead!'

On the word 'dead' Nicole's head rose off her chest and she screamed, 'No! Daniel, don't let them do anything, please, Daniel, please!'

The deep voice whispered, 'Why don't you do as she says, Daniel?' The tinny voice added, 'Yes, why not please the lady… Daniel?' with increasing sarcasm.

'It would not be so difficult to understand if you explained what you want. Maybe I would not find it difficult to accept whatever you ask for.' Daniel's mind was racing, playing for time, hoping that someone might call at the house, or the phone would ring, so that he could scream very loudly.

The tinny voice interrupted Daniel's unclear thoughts. 'Oh, Mr Daniel, you are so kind, trying to be polite to us. We like to be around nice people. In fact, my friend and I were only saying in the car as we were following your wife back here, that it would be nice to be dealing with good people for a change!'

The oozing sarcasm enraged Daniel and as he struggled to get up, he yelled, 'You bastard! Stop patronising me… why don't you get on with whatever you think you have got to do!'

'Now, now,' the deep voice cut in. 'We haven't come to do

anything, other than talk. That little blow to your head was just to let you know we could do other things if necessary. Now, can I suggest we all sit around quietly? My friend and I have something to tell you both which I feel sure you will not be pleased to hear, but you can be sure that we have a solution which will benefit everybody, even yourselves.'

'Please get on with explaining to us what our parents are supposed to have done! We have already spoken to my parents, and my father reiterated his past to us, and both my husband and myself believe him.' The hurried reply and having to cope with her sobs had left Nicole almost breathless.

'Your father, when he was in Paris, sold his friends out to the Gestapo during World War Two. His whole life was controlled by the Communist Party and all the names, places and most of the dates of the acts were reported back by his commissar, Henri Duvalier. Your father was a great enthusiast for making his superiors' lives easier for them. In fact, we know he settled a few personal grievances along the way. The tinny voice seemed to get stronger as the brutal accusations came to a close.

'Nicole, my love…' whispered Daniel. 'Don't let them destroy your father like this. Proof is what they must give us, proof which will be impossible to provide. It will only be hearsay… our word against theirs… and who will believe them?… No one! Let them prove it. Come on… you big men, frightening ladies and attacking men from behind… prove what you say!'

The panic in Daniel's voice could be detected, he was sure of that, but he hoped these two villains would think it was defiance.

The tinny voice laughed. 'You fool, Daniel! Do you think we would come here without proof? I can assure you all of the facts are in France, readily available. Now let us take a moment to discuss your father… your illustrious father.' The snide sarcasm was becoming nauseous. Daniel tried to free himself from his captor's grip, but the fingers tightened again, this time with more pressure. 'Your father, the man who was respected by everyone he met, in his work as a rehabilitation officer for Polish forces in England, was a thief! He stole money from the people he was transporting around, stole from the British government, he stole from the people of Britain who had offered him a helping hand in putting up his Polish transients by not paying them the money the government had allowed for their keep and often on rail or buses he would underpay, by declaring less on his handwritten list than he was actually moving, relying on the kindness or the stupidity of the British, never to check. It became so very easy for him in the end, the frequency of his journeys, especially across London with the air-raids causing confusion, was such that the conductors and ticket-collectors were only too pleased to accept your father's word.'

'Lies! My father would never, ever cheat!'

'You would be surprised, Daniel, at what both of your fathers really did do,' said the tinny voice.

'Prove it! Just prove one occasion, then I might listen to you!' said Daniel loudly.

'We thought you might need convincing, so we brought these.' Reaching into his breast pocket, the deeper-voiced man produced photocopies of two original pieces of paper and started to read the first.

I, Henri Claude Duvalier, on the 12th day of December, 1949, on request and without force or bribery, do declare that Edwarde Charles Claris of the 31st Communist Cell, Rue de Brasil, Paris, did submit names to the Gestapo during the occupation of Paris. The entries in the Cell records will confirm most of these dates. Edwarde Claris, betrayed, on no less than three occasions, innocent civilians, and the Land Registers between January 1942 and August 1943 show that three properties were transferred to M Edwarde Claris:

Property Names: Duravel, 9 Rue de Segur, Paris.
                  Le Tour Blanche, Fontainebleau.
                  Les Fleurs, 32 Rue Tuileiles, Paris.

I declare that 'Le Tour Blanche' is the home of M Claris and his family to this day. The betrayal of his comrades to the Gestapo led to nine deaths and seven others severely injured. All entries are confirmed in my own handwriting in the above mentioned Cell records. I declare that Edwarde Charles Claris is a traitor to France.

Signed this day, 12 December, 1949,
Henri Claude Duvalier.

154

Daniel's eyes swept across the page, his face draining of colour as he read. His sullen face looked up from the paper to Nicole, his eyes conveying the disaster confronting them both. Turning the page, Daniel's eyes fell to the paper to read a further declaration from M Duvalier, which read:

On this day, 14 May 1999, I, Henri Claude Duvalier, have been shown the photocopy attached and I confirm its authenticity as a true copy of the declaration I made on 12 December 1949, denouncing Edwarde Charles Claris.

Signed

Henri Claude Duvalier,
Solicitor-at-Law, (Retired)

The tinny-voiced man saw the anguish on Daniel's face and could not resist a jibe. 'You can see, Daniel dear, that only this week we have had the accusation against your dear wife's father verified as being true, and the man is more than willing to see justice done to Monsieur Claris, even at this late stage in his life. The other confirmations which we have obtained from dozens of men who had contact with your father during those days will be shown to you as soon as we receive copies from Russia… In fact, not only from men, but a few ladies, also! You never know, Daniel, we may find out that there are some step-brothers or step-sisters floating around!'

'You pig! How dare you bring my wife's family into disrepute like this! She married me, her family isn't the one you need to blackmail! When you have your evidence from Russia about my father and if I feel it is damning enough, you will not need to tarnish her father's reputation.' Daniel's voice wavered slightly when he realised what he was saying was a committal of himself when the evidence against his father arrived.

'Tinny voice' cut into the racing thoughts rushing through Daniel's mind. 'Stop your floundering! You know we will use both of your families!' Daniel's mind seemed to freeze. The torment and fear struck home. Daniel's fingers struck out at the papers held in his trembling hand. Gazing into Nicole's eyes, the distraught face surrounding her normally beautiful eyes told him that she could not stand for much more of this persecution. In tenderness and defeat, Daniel whispered, 'The proof is here, my love. I feel there is little doubt.' As the words left his lips, his whole body collapsed in shame as the feeling that *there is nothing that can be done*, washed over him.

Chapter Nineteen

The warm sun played down onto the little fountain in the hacienda-style garden, one of Yute's favourite places. He had discovered it a short while ago, the high walls with their manicured trees and shrubs caressing the white painted walls, and the changing, deep shadows as the sun passed across the sky gave Yute dark corners to hide in. The square had but one entrance, in the centre of the south wall. Yute felt safe. The few tables which circled the fountain and those which were in the archways surrounding the square, could be seen at all times as he sat at his table on the north side. The sun danced on the fountain spouts. Yute was content as he waited for Lanov and Mogatin. He had arrived early to enable himself to get the position he wanted, so that neither he nor his two friends could be overheard or recognised.

Mogatin appeared suddenly in the entrance and swiftly covered the ground to the table. The warm handshake before they both sat down together confirmed to each other they had not been followed. Pleasantries over, Yute attracted the attention of one of the waiters and ordered a fresh pot of coffee with two more cups and saucers.

'Well, my friend, everything has been going well for you since we last met? Lanov and yourself have come to a decision, I hope.'

'I would prefer it if Lanov were here when we discuss the matter.' Mogatin's stony face gave nothing away.

'As you wish. Have you been sightseeing? Lisbon is a beautiful city.'

'We have, but separately. We agreed we would only meet at specific times after we left you. It was our intention, after the good news you brought us about Tashimov, to travel together, but old habits die hard. The constant checking if you are being followed is also easier if you are on your own.'

'You're right, of course!'

The coffee arrived and the waiter poured the black steaming liquid into one of the cups and offered Yute a refill, who gave a nod of his head.

Mogatin and Yute sat in silence, enjoying their coffee. The minutes turned to quarter-hours, then half-hours. Finally, Yute could not resist asking, in a jovial manner, if Mogatin had in fact confirmed the meeting with Lanov. Mogatin's stern face showed his contempt at the suggestion. Neither of them smiled. A further ten minutes passed before Mogatin whispered that Lanov had arrived.

Joe Lomax listened. His phone hadn't stopped ringing for the last ten minutes, call after call, but now after having had the news confirmed by his own people, Manuel Vargas had his undivided attention.

'So you see, my dear Lomax, I feel that these three men, who are now linked to one another here in Portugal and also in Afghanistan and, although not proven yet, in Germany too, should be arrested and questioned by my men.'

'Please, Manuel... please don't do that. I feel, and I'm sure you do too, that what is happening here is only a small part of a much bigger picture. It is the general feeling as you well know, that the crimes in Hamburg were... a rehearsal for bigger things, even if we are not certain of what exactly. Surely you agree they should be allowed to circulate under our combined surveillance. I think you should give us twenty-four hours at least, to get the opinions of our colleagues together. After all, what have you got to lose? Your men are well in control of our three Russian friends.'

Vargas, at the other end of the phone was following every word. His chest filled with pride as he listened. Spontaneously he replied, 'Yes, I agree with you, we should string our Russians along a little more. In twenty-four hours then, we will strike.'

The phone went dead in Joe's ear as Vargas terminated the call.

Joe screamed into the phone, 'You pompous, no good, vain, bloody peacock of a man!' The words said, Joe hurried to get another line and dialled Joc Latimer, telling him the whole story of the Vargas incident.

'What do they do over there to get a Chief of Police? Stick a pin in a telephone book?'

'You could be right, I suppose, but personally, I think it's good old-fashioned nepotism, but it's bloody dangerous when connected to international policing!' said Joe.

'Don't you think you can talk him into extending the time limit?' asked Joc.

'It's impossible to judge, but give me yours and Ernst's view and I'll try to get him out to dinner and push anything you give me.'

'Thanks, Joe. I'll speak to Ernst and get back to you. It's a shame we aren't legal over there, it would help if we could rattle a few cages.'

'You mean from the US point of view?'

'Yes, we've got contacts everywhere and it would be great to bring them in when these Russian guys leave you; we could all be cut right out of the pack: French, Belgians, Spanish, Portuguese… all of us!'

'It would be great to follow things through, but I don't think you have got a chance in hell of swinging it, Joc.'

'Perhaps you're right, but what if they allow me leave of absence to do my own thing with Ernst? I'm sure I know the system well enough to get the back-up I'd need.'

'You'd be drawing in an awful lot of favours, Joc. If it blows up in your face, you wouldn't be going any further. Think about your pension, old buddy!'

'Ease it off, Joe. I'm not that old!'

'Have it your way, buddy, but at least talk it over with your wife.'

'Wouldn't dream of doing anything else, Joe. Thanks a lot, I'll be in touch.'

'Don't mention it. Look after yourself, Joc.'

Ernst Ulbrecht answered his phone. 'Ulbrecht heir!'

Joc replied in his playful way, 'Latimer here!'

'Good to hear from you, Joc. I hope you have good news for me?'

'Not really, my friend... this stupid Vargas person wants to run in and start arresting people!'

'Why, Joc? He should be letting them run.'

'I know that, Joe Lomax knows that he should, along with his and your own team, but he's giving Joe Lomax twenty-four hours before he starts moving in on the three Russians.'

'*Our* three Russians, Joc. I'll have to speak to my Commander to see if he can get some control over Vargas. I'll come back to you very soon.'

'Thanks, Ernst. I'll await your call.'

No sooner had the phone gone dead than Ernst was dialling the direct line to his friend, Commander Roth.

Yute sat stern-faced, listening to the discussion taking place between Lanov and Mogatin. He could see their point of view with regards to their future within the new Russia on whether or not they should freelance now that the threat of Tashimov's personal hounding of them had been removed. They could work in Spain, Portugal; in fact, anywhere in Europe for themselves. A freedom which they felt would be a relief from the political minefield they had always worked in up to now.

Yute interrupted Mogatin, whom he felt sure was going to continue the discussion in the same vein. 'You men have been trained in the special requirements of Mother Russia. She still has the same needs. The same men who were in control before Glasnost, are back in control. The silent core is back. Now, don't you see, we will have the whole pitch to play on. Your talents will be more widely used and your rewards will be beyond the dreams of avarice!'

Mogatin looked at Lanov then both turned to face Yute and in unison, said, 'Okay, we are in, but only if you are our controller.'

'When the Council finally gives me the go-ahead and the first names come into our new, slower way of working, then I and only I, will have control, and only I will be answerable to the Council. Only professionals will be used to give me the support I will need to fulfil this vast plan. On my life, this will be so... Now, have you any further questions?'

Lanov muttered a polite, 'No.'

Mogatin confirmed his allegiance to Yute with a 'No', but asked, 'When do you want us to start working for you? We are beginning to run out of money…'

'I understand that,' replied Yute. 'I will get funds made available the moment we reach Russia. In US dollars, of course.'

All three men laughed quietly and then, having fulfilled their intentions, dispersed stealthily into the fading sunlight.

'Joe, an update for you.' The covered-in roadside telephone box made the handset sticky in Paul's hand. 'They left the hacienda place – they seemed pleased with themselves, then each went their separate ways. We are with them. Saw the Portuguese following, but haven't spotted the Krauts yet… Why are we all doing the same job, Joe?'

'It won't be for much longer. It really is daft, Paul, but you must remember, we are doing it unofficially, don't forget. Even after giving permission to the German team, the Portuguese seem to feel they have to check up on them. It's all a bit of a joke really.'

'It isn't in this bloody telephone box, they should be called sweat boxes! Gotta go, Joe, he's on the move again… Be in touch!' The phone went dead.

As he placed the receiver down, Joe muttered to himself, 'Take it easy, Paul. Good luck!'

Major Roche's office door opened following a soft knock, and his brusque voice answered, 'Come in!' catching Daniel by surprise. Although he did want to see the Adjutant, he was secretly hoping there would be no reply to his knock. At the sight of Daniel, Major Roche politely half rose from his chair saying, 'Come in my dear boy, sit down. Anything I can do?'

Gingerly, the words left Daniel's mouth. 'Well sir… no, not really.'

Seeing that something was obviously on Daniel's mind, Major Roche carried on light-heartedly, 'Well, that's good. Shall we have tea? A nice convivial chat? How about that? I have been lax, you know – I actually should have called you in for a chat before now, you know the sort of thing… have you settled in, are the group helping you to find your feet, any mysteries about Eurocorps you want answers to?'

'Well no, sir. The group has been most helpful. I'm reasonably settled and I feel sure the mysteries will unravel themselves, if there are any mysteries – as I go along.'

'I'm sure there are mysteries, Daniel, and I'm sure we will make many more as we grow and expand. By the way, what did you want to see me for?'

The pointedness of the unexpected question made Daniel flinch and twist in his chair. His mind raced. 'Well, sir, it was a small thing.' Come on brain, give my mouth an answer... 'It's... well, I see you don't have an entertainments officer listed and I well, my wife and I, would like to have the opportunity of designing a programme.'

The hesitancy in Daniel's voice worried Major Roche. What did he really want? he thought. The Major replied, 'Oh, good for you! We haven't appointed one yet, and you, my dear boy, have just left yourself open to take on the task. What do you think about that?'

Daniel felt a little more comfortable. Maybe the hesitancy really hadn't been noticed. 'Well, sir, thank you. Although we have no experience, we will certainly do our best.'

'Very good! I'll speak to the Colonel and get his approval. I'm sure there won't be any objection from him, but I must ask him, you do understand?'

'Of course, sir. I'll wait for you to inform me.' The usual strength in Daniel's voice was missing, as if he was distracted by something else.

'I look forward to seeing you again soon. Would you close the door on your way out, please? Thanks for our little chat, Daniel.' The chameleon in the Major's character had broken through and Daniel was left in no doubt that he had been dismissed.

On hearing the door close behind Daniel, Major Roche pushed himself away from his desk. Whenever he had a problem, it was necessary for him to pace the floor. The question was: was Daniel reaching out for help?

On leaving Major Roche's office, Daniel hung his head in remorse for not having enough guts to own up to the dilemma he and Nicole were going through. Why could he not stand up to the consequences as both of them had discussed late into the night before? Their discussion had been in whispers as they held each other tightly in the darkness of their bed. Daniel's father's crimes were considered trivial and after all this time it would be too much to expect any real enquiry to consider any real investigation. The worst thing, they both felt, was that his father would be branded as a Polish 'scallywag' and possibly fined, or at worst, have a minimal jail sentence imposed. Terms which he felt sure his father would gladly endure if it enabled his son to stay in the service of uniting Europe. Nicole's father's was a rather different accusation. Sending people to their deaths, with signed affidavits to corroborate the accusations, was a long way from the petty stealing Daniel's father had been accused of. Nicole, as was to be expected, defended her father, insisting he would only have done what he was accused of, if he was ordered to and that in all probability, he was inveigled into a web, in much the same way as they were being blackmailed now.

The hours had passed as they held each other close, the warmth of their bodies generating the strength they would need to accept the consequences that any trial might bring to their parents and the inevitable loss of Daniel's commission. Their arms tightened around each other at the terrifying thoughts and inevitable consequences.

Nicole had pulled away suddenly. There was determination in her voice as she looked into his eyes which made her more appealing than he had ever found her. Softening his embrace, he moistened his lips to kiss the tear-stained, swollen face. 'Daniel, don't. Tomorrow you must go to the Adjutant and report this blackmail to him. If they try to dismiss you, we will fight them in any court or tribunal in Europe. We cannot be expected to pay for the sins of our fathers – as we have already agreed. We must make the rest of the army acknowledge it too.'

'Nicole, I would not expect you to submit your parents to this. It's all too long ago, they are not getting any younger and I think the strain could kill them.'

'Don't you think I've thought of that? Although I love them dearly, why should I allow them to destroy our lives? We can win in the courts, I'm sure. We're supposedly Europeans, we've never done a thing wrong since we became adults, we want to work for peace and harmony… they must let us!' The gush of tears turned her rebellious speech into nothing. She only knew that what was in her heart was ruling her head. The tender kisses on her lips had slowly calmed her and her slender arms pulled Daniel to her.

They both lay on their backs, silently staring at the ceiling, their hands locked together. 'Nicole,' said the quiet, enquiring voice of Daniel. 'Are you still awake?'

'Hmmmm.'

'You know we can't do what you suggest, don't you? We could never live with ourselves if we did.'

Nicole lifted up her body and twisted onto her elbow to stare into Daniel's face. 'Yes we can,' she replied. 'We will stick together, you and I and all our families, no matter what happens. My mind is made up and as it will affect my family in a far greater way than yours, I say you should see your Major, tell him everything and ask for some kind of help.'

'Nicole, it doesn't work like that. It will open up a can of worms so quickly, we won't even have time to draw breath.'

'Daniel, it doesn't matter! We can't live in the shadows for the rest of our lives. You know that is what it would mean, don't you?'

'Of course I do, but we would be strong enough together to continue our fight, you know we would.'

'It's one hell of a gamble… it could go badly wrong.'

'If it does, it does. We would still have each other.'

Those words hung heavily around his ears as he went on his weary way back to his own office. The anger within him began to rise again at his own inadequacy, even after the agreement he had made with Nicole in the privacy of their bedroom and the promise he had sworn to fulfil at the earliest opportunity; he had failed the moment he had stepped into the Adjutant's office. Throwing his weight back against his own office door, his whole body screamed out: why did I let the moment pass? And then to himself, he admitted he could not gamble Nicole's safety.

Chapter Twenty

Police Chief Manuel Vargas smiled broadly when his secretary announced that Commander Roth of the Hamburg police would like to speak to him. Holding the phone slightly away from his ear as if it were a hand mirror, he squared his body, straightened his tie, swallowed, and then replied, 'Please put Commander Roth on the line, my dear,' the sickly smile still stretching across his face.

'Yes, Manuel...' her voice indicating the intimacy between them.

Vargas coughed lightly, placing his fingertips up to his mouth, straightened his tie again, then measuring his grin, said, 'My dear Roth, how are you? Your weather up there is not as good as it is here in Portugal you know. You must come and visit us again soon... What can I do for you?'

'Thank you for asking, I am well, thank you. I'm sure Portugal has far more sun than we in the north could ever expect and I would like to visit you again sometime, but meanwhile, I have more important things I feel sure you can help us with.' Roth did not want their conversation to go on and on as it normally did.

'What is the problem, my friend? Anything I can do... I am obliged to help.'

'That's most kind, Manuel... well, I don't want you to arrest those three Russians.'

The smile left Manuel Vargas's face instantly. 'But Roth, they are here in my country! It is my right to do so – if I feel it is the right thing to do.'

'Think, Manuel, of the bigger picture. We had a major crime committed here in Hamburg, we have been tracking these people for a long time and, with the help of the Americans, have confirmed the identities of these three men. My Chief Inspector asks for your tolerance. Let them run.'

'But we have given so much, we want some kudos out of this affair.'

'My dear friend, even if it is five years from now, we, as a united European operation, would obviously mention everyone involved with the case.'

Grudgingly, Manuel offered a very sulky reply. 'I suppose it would be better to let them run. After a short pause, he added, 'Of course, if they commit any crime on Portuguese soil, I will have no alternative but to arrest them.'

'I am sure they will be good boys and will do nothing wrong, unless they are provoked.'

Flustered now, Manuel replied, 'My men will only obey my orders and I shall reaffirm my orders right away, that they are only to watch them.'

'Thank you, Manuel. I think we are meeting in Madrid in three weeks' time… Look forward to seeing you then.'

'Madrid? What for?'

'The conference on transference of criminals throughout Europe. It will become an important matter. We hope we will be setting our guidelines and possibly setting up a committee. You will be there, won't you?'

'Well yes, my secretary must have forgotten to remind me about it.'

'Well, chase it up! It could be lost in channels and you'll never get your invitation.'

'No, it will be this secretary's fault, I'm sure. She is so protective of me, she's keeping everything from me until the last moment!'

'I hope you're right, today is the last day for the applications to be in.'

Manuel's face dropped further into his chest before he answered, 'I'm sure it has been sent off already, but I will check, thank you.'

'Thank you for your understanding in this Russian matter. See you in Madrid.'

'Yes, of course. Bye.' The abrupt manner in which Vargas terminated their conversation immediately confirmed to Commander Roth that Senor Vargas had not been told of the Madrid conference at all, and that possibly someone else might be taking the ride instead. If he had been in Vargas's office, his suspicions would have been confirmed.

The brief, signed note from Commander Roth arrived on Ernst's desk within ten minutes of the completion of Roth's telephone call, advising Ernst that Vargas would not interfere with the Russians unless they broke the law (which was underlined), and that Vargas was willing to let them run. Ernst read the note with delight and immediately snatched the phone to read his note over to Joc, who in turn would inform Joe Lomax in Portugal. Ernst rested back in his chair for a few minutes to reflect in the happenings of the past few days. Everything was going well, the only worry was the slowness of the information being obtained from within Russia. Lifting the phone, he dialled Mayer's number. Two rings, then it was answered. 'Mayer heir!'

Ernst smiled to himself. Was his 'Ulbrecht heir!' becoming so catchy? 'Hello, Mayer, Ernst Ulbrecht. When you have a few moments, could you possibly come up to my office?'

'Certainly, sir, now if you like.'

'Yes, if you can, thank you.'

It seemed that no sooner had he replaced the receiver, than Mayer was in the office. 'Thank you for coming so quickly, Mayer.'

'No bother, sir. I could do with stretching my legs at the moment, I'm being held up by our Russian friends.'

'In fact, that's exactly what I want to talk to you about. The corroboration you have obtained from your contacts has been wonderfully helpful, but a thought has just crossed my mind. When you are speaking to them, would you ask for the case histories as well as the confirmations? A thought struck me that in the histories, there could be more names mentioned, and also maybe we could work out the method or methods that are used during these operations. It could be useful, don't you think, Mayer?'

'Yes, sir, I do. I only wish I had thought of it.'

Ernst smiled at her enthusiasm and replied, 'Don't rush, Mayer, you'll make it, I'm sure.'

'Thank you, sir. Will that be all?'

'Yes, thank you, Mayer. Anything you get that you think might be of interest, please let me know…'

Mayer came to attention, it seemed, without moving and left Ernst alone with his thoughts.

The closed telephone booth in the little post office at Chantilly was full with the hulks of two men – Daniel and Nicole's persecutors. Having dialled from a street phone box half an hour previously, they found it necessary to find a public telephone box where they could speak freely, away from the hindrance of noise. The tinny-voiced man with his hand over the mouthpiece, whispered, 'He's taking a long time answering, considering he's expecting our call.'

'Give it time. You know he likes to play games with everyone, it makes him feel more important than he is.'

'Don't be stupid,' interrupted tinny voice. 'Don't underestimate him. He is the Chairman of the Council now, not the "pleb" we both thought he was when we met him in the East. He's come a long way.' The click in his ear grabbed his attention immediately. 'Sir, you wanted us to report direct to you.'

'Identify yourself properly!'

'S19 requests permission to speak. I am accompanied by L24. We are calling from a public phone in Chantilly, so there will be no trace.'

'My regards to you both from NC1. The last call you made, what time and what place was it made from?'

'10 a.m. Paris time, from the Gare du Nord.'

'You may deliver your message,' came the stern response.

'Sir, L24 and I have achieved the total breakdown of Daniel and Nicole Tomlevski. They will be very manageable, we can promise you – although we have still not received the copies of the reports as promised on Daniel's father.'

'Don't worry about them, you will receive them.'

'Thank you. We will stay around quietly until we hear from you again.'

'Yes, take the sequence of phone numbers you have, from tomorrow, use the list from the bottom to the top at the times stated for that day. Until then, NC1 signing off.'

No sooner were the words out of his mouth than the phone went dead in S19's ear.

Looking at the phone in his hand, he said, 'Do you know, NC1, our mastermind of the National Committee, is a bloody stupid "pleb" – always was, and always will be, I'm sure… having said that, I will deny it at all costs!' He playfully slapped L24 on the shoulder as he squeezed out of the booth. 'Come, my friend, now we have fulfilled our duty for today and our two little sparrows are frightened to death by two nasty birds of prey like us. Let's go and play for a little while.'

Major Roche and his pretty wife were walking around town. Out of uniform, he always chose to dress in cavalry twill trousers, a Harris tweed jacket with obligatory leather-patched elbows, checked shirt with an open neck, and a cravat. His wife usually wore a figure-hugging dress in summer time, with a light woolly cardigan either draped around her shoulders, or loosely held in the hand that was not locked into her husband's arm. Their bodies moved with ease after twenty years of marriage. They knew what each other would wish to see in the parade of shops or in the country houses they liked to visit. They both felt comfortable when they were together, they needed few words between them at any time – a unique balance of their minds and an awareness of each other's views and physical needs made for total contentment.

Today was, however, a little different. Diedra had felt the anxiety growing as she walked with her husband. Thoughts kept going through her mind. If there is another woman, what shall I do? Although she felt confident when they were alone together in the sanctuary of their bedroom, her insecurity was taking over now. As they walked side by side, she knew she was safe with the man she had loved since the moment they first met all those years ago, but why was she now allowing this obsession to take hold within her? There, there – there it is again – a little fidget in André's arm, a tightening and then a release of muscle tension. Diedra stopped walking, pulling hard on André's elbow.

'Now this walk is not working for either of us, neither has the last twenty-four hours. What is troubling you? Let's talk. Yes, right now in the middle of the street! Now, André… whatever is troubling you, spit it out!'

'Shhh, Diedra! Don't make a scene, old thing. Let's have coffee over there and then, yes, we will talk.'

'Fine!' The petulance in her voice could not be hidden. 'Fine,' she repeated, then added, 'It's about time too!'

Finding a table outside, away from the crowded café entrance area, they sat expectantly, facing one another, she expecting André to make an admission of his guilt, and he expecting an explanation or maybe an apology.

André looked into Diedra's eyes only to see emptiness. The insecurity he saw in her face disturbed him. He wanted to reach out and pull her to him, but it wasn't quite the right thing to do in public, he decided. 'Diedra…' Her name was spoken tenderly. 'What is it that's worrying you? Is it something I've done, or not done?'

'Nothing is worrying me, but I'm sure your little secret is worrying the hell out of you!'

'I don't understand, what secret for God's sake?'

The impatience in his voice surprised Diedra. He had never been impatient with her before… he must have another woman! He is trying to be kind to me and deny it. No, he won't get away with that. Before she could stop herself, the words came tumbling from her trembling lips. 'You've found another woman, haven't you, after all this time!'

'What the hell do you mean?'

'What do I mean? What do *you* mean, is more like the question! For twenty years, I've done everything for you… borne your children, sat alone endless days and nights whilst you played soldiers, now you have found a newer model. Well, you're welcome to her!' The tell-tale tears started to flood into her eyes, the thickening in her throat as the channels dried up – she didn't want their love to end. Let him forget her and her own verbal rejection of him… Why on earth did she say those words to him… Why won't he fight back, or at least deny it?

'Diedra, I don't understand what you are saying, and what's more, I cannot understand how or why you have such a crazy notion. There is no one but you in my life, or ever will be as far as

I am concerned. In fact, I do not want any further discussion on this subject ever again!'

'André, do you swear that there is no one else?'

'Of course!'

'Well, why are you so edgy? When you are with me, you seem to be so far away from me. These past twenty-four hours have been murder for me!'

'I'm sorry, love, I had no idea I was bringing my work home with me, sorry.'

'You don't normally let the army out of the barracks, which is one thing I've always admired in you, but André, don't you think if you are beginning to bring your work home, and we end up having many more conversations like this, don't you think it would be better to retire before it changes us?'

'Don't be silly, old thing, this isn't my personal problem... it's one of the new people who've just joined the Corps, a Lieutenant Daniel Tomlevski. He wants to talk to me, I know he does, I can feel it, but he just won't come out and ask to see me. You know I would see him either socially or through other channels as every other serving soldier in the Corps knows... I just can't understand why he won't come and see me!'

'You poor dear. Here I am throwing a wobbly, making things even more tiresome for you... Will you forgive me?'

'Of course I will. If you prove to me that the words, "you've found a newer model" were just said in haste.'

'Please forgive me for my stupidity. It was purely a defensive remark. I don't know how I can prove it to you, but I'll certainly think about it.' The teasing fluttering of her eyelashes caused them both to smile at each other as their hands met and their fingers entwined across the pure white linen tablecloth.

'It was my fault, I shouldn't let my imagination run away with me...'

'What things are you imagining for this Lieutenant Tomlevski?'

'Oh, I don't know really, it's varied from mother-in-law trouble to debts, to an unwanted pregnancy, even the possibility of an affair in their young married lives causing anguish between them. He was only accepted by the Corps in the last month and has only been in camp ten days of that time, so it's difficult to read him or their problems, he's still so new to my command.'

'It's probably something trivial. Perhaps he just wants a father and son talk about his career possibilities.'

'I hope that's all it is, but I've a feeling it's worse than that.'

'The waiter's coming… café au lait, my lord?'

'Please.' The waiter courteously took the order and left them still holding hands.

'So, what do you think you ought to do about Tomlevski?'

'That's really my problem. You see, I feel I ought to make a report to the Provost's department and at least get a surveillance team on both of them for a few weeks at least.'

'You what? That's an awful step to have to take! It could ruin his career. Has he any special qualifications which would make him vulnerable?'

'No, not at all, communications and transport, and there are hundreds at the moment with those qualifications, and we expect, with Spain integrating into the Corps soon, there will be hundreds more.'

'What's made you have this feeling about him?'

'He came into my office one day, acting rather furtively and I felt sure he needed to talk. He looked really tired and as if he had been up all night, but he waffled on about nothing. I felt sure he really wanted to open up, but he fluffed around and eventually asked if we had an entertainments officer, as he felt he and his wife could help in that area. I mean, Diedra, no one volunteers for the job of entertainments officer, do they?'

'No, I suppose you're right, but it doesn't seem enough of a suspicion to approach the Provost's office just yet.'

'I suppose you're right, my dear. Let's try and forget the Tomlevskis and enjoy our coffee before the walk back home.'

'And…?'

'Just you wait and see!' Their hands tightened in each other's simultaneously. The slow walk home, the silence between them, their body language saying everything to each other. Their dream world was in slow-motion, even placing their key into their front door didn't allow their experienced emotions to quicken. The twilight was enveloping them as they lay side by side, their union having confirmed that neither of them had anything to fear. The bond that had always been there was still there and any silliness which had tormented them was now completely behind them, forever. The stillness enveloped them until their searching hands touched. The slow turn towards each other, the gentle kiss, their arms encircling, the force of energy as their bodies engulfed each other… The twilight slipped into night. The spell of their minds' slow-motion world continued.

'André, would you like one egg or two?'

'I don't think I'll have time to eat, dear.'

'But you must! You can't work all day and night without something in your stomach,' Diedra said playfully.

'I suppose you're right, but I could get breakfast in the mess after I've attended to the office work… there's a lot to do, what with new arrivals coming in all the time and I'm still not sure what to do about the Tomlevski business.'

Coyly, Diedra replied, 'We never did finish that conversation last night, did we? What are your views now?'

'I'm still uncertain, but one thing I'm completely clear about is that I've got to talk to the Provost and ask him to do an unofficial investigation. After all, I've nothing other than a sixth sense on this one, no real evidence. Yes, I've decided. I'll ask for a favour, we can't go official.'

'I suppose you're right, dear. It seems a shame when they have been here for such a short time, but if you must, you must.'

Major Roche sat sternly behind his desk, his drained face indicating that what he considered to be the 'Judas' side of his job, had been done. The receiver was still being held tightly to his ear by his white-knuckled hand, the Provost's voice causing only the flicker of an eyelid.

'André, you must not worry. I can do a search and follow procedures which will cause little if any, inconvenience to my team, so please don't worry yourself. No one will know from this office, unless there is something to know.'

Provost Marshall Robin Cadwallader's reassurance eased the tension showing on André's face as he replied. 'Thank you, Robin, but will you promise me you'll let me know anything you find out and if needs be, you will tell me prior to any arrest?'

'Of course, André, but you don't have to be involved. I would just add to my final report that you were the originator of the investigation and that your vigilance in protecting the interests of the Corps is to be commended.'

'Words, my friend. Words which exonerate on the one hand but leave the vigilant man to live with his own betrayal!'

'André, you are a loyal and respected officer of Eurocorps, a unit which is the giver of life and hope to thousands... millions potentially. That is what you are protecting – peace, health and humanity for the whole world. Please don't put yourself down. You are worth far more than that, to yourself and, of course, to Diedra.'

'Possibly, Robin, but it isn't easy.'

'For me neither, and it's my job!'

'Go on with you. I always thought you loved your job.'

'I do, absolutely, but I only do it by obeying the standing orders for the Corps and by following our articles of inauguration to the letter. That, for me, is the only way. If they come within the scope of this office, they are just a number. If I allowed any personal feelings to get in the way, I could not function. Please don't worry too much, my friend, and I promise I will tell you anything that may transpire.'

'Thank you, Robin, it's always good talking to you. See you in the mess as usual.'

After the short conversation with Robin, André was restless. So strong was his need to get away that before he knew what was happening, he found himself standing on the edge of the parade ground, watching the pockets of activity and training taking place. His mind began to relax as he enjoyed the marching, arms drills and physical exercises taking place before him. Without realising it, he started walking in time with one of the squads passing nearby. As his chest began to fill with fresh air and his marching feet synchronised with the squad alongside him, he found his pride returning in full flood. The barracks gate got closer surprisingly swiftly. The command 'About... turn!' which was promptly obeyed by the squad, left him isolated, marching, arms swinging, with a good-humoured smile across his face; he marched smartly to the barracks' guard room. The Sergeant of the Guard sprang to attention and called out the guard, although not knowing what to expect, he knew from past experience that the guard would undoubtedly be inspected. Coming to a halt at the same moment that the last guard member arrived at his position in the ranks, the Sergeant stood like a ramrod to salute his Adjutant with, 'Guard fell in and ready for inspection, sir!'

Having had his bit of fun playing marching soldiers, André replied, 'Thank you, Sergeant, lead on.'

'Sir!' came the reply, then an about-turn and a step away to the front file of troops to be inspected.

André took great interest in the guard's turn-out as he walked between their ranks, and when he returned to the front, he announced to all assembled, 'Thank you, Sergeant, and men. A very good turn-out, very good. You may dismiss the men, Sergeant.'

André stood motionless as the guard were dismissed and waited to speak to the Sergeant, as was customary after a guard inspection. As the Sergeant approached him, André started the conversation with, 'Good, alert and smart guard, Sergeant. Keep up the good work.'

'It's been pretty easy so far, sir. They are all full of the "our new corps", "what we will do for Europe" gusto, sir. A bit different from the old days. It seems being a volunteered, multi-national force all starting off as new boys, seems to keep up their enthusiasm, sir.'

'Let's hope it continues once we are fully operational, Sergeant.'

'I'm sure it will, sir. There's a nice feeling about the Corps, sir. I'm sure you don't have to worry about a thing, sir.'

'I hope you are right about that.'

'Well, it all feels good, sir. I've been in at the formation of new companies, corps and brigades, but nothing before has had the enthusiasm and pride so early in its formation as this one. It's going to be a winner, sir, believe me!'

'Thank you, Sergeant. So, what's been happening lately, anything of interest?'

'Not really, sir. That old Mercedes is still parked over the road with a bloke in it. I can't move him on that road, not Military. I've told the local civvy police, who can't do anything because he's not illegally parked, but they want us to let them know if he does do anything wrong, so that they can do something.'

'How long has he been there and what is he waiting for?'

'He's been there two days, sir. Once I saw another guy talking to him, giving him some sandwiches, I believe. The guard finishes at 1600 hours, sir, and he's normally still there then, so I don't know who he waits for.'

'I see, Sergeant. Has your relief Guard Commander made any reports to anyone about this? Anything in the report book?'

'No, sir, I've looked. I don't know why I checked up on a colleague, but I did. In fact, he hasn't even mentioned it.'

'When does that car arrive, Sergeant?'

'He comes along at about 1500 hours, sir. I haven't logged the time exactly, but I'm sure it's about 1500 hours.'

'Sergeant, tonight, will you change guard as normal and stay on duty to check who comes to the car and if it's anyone of ours, let me know immediately. We will keep this just between ourselves for the moment, Sergeant.'

'Yes, sir! Anything you say. How will I contact you, sir?'

'Up until 1830, in the mess. From 1900 hours, my quarters. I will clear it with the switchboard to connect you.'

'That will be fine, sir. Do you want me to stay until the car leaves? It could be quite a while.'

'Please, Sergeant. I'll get the kitchens to get some rations over to you.'

'No need, sir. There'll be enough sent over for the guard and myself, sir, don't worry.'

'Right then, I'll leave you to sort it out. I'll look forward to your call… I hope he's just waiting for one of our lady cooks!'

'The poor guy must be desperate if he's waiting for any of the lady cooks that I've ever seen – begging your pardon, sir!'

'That's all right, Sergeant. Perhaps our new crop of ladies will be an improvement! Good evening to you for now.'

Chapter Twenty-One

The last words spoken by Yute Polenkovich to Lanov and Mogatin before he left for Russia were, *'Get home as quickly as you can. I will make all the arrangements for your accommodation and money, but I want you to go via Cordoba, Strasbourg, Baden-Baden, Luxembourg and Achern in France. You will learn anything you can about Eurocorps. This is an elite army for Europe. Just get the feel of things – messing, transport, communications, general organisation, the general area around the bases – places of work for us.'*

Lanov recalled that Mogatin broke into the flow of Yute's instructions with, *'We may have some nice work to do in our work-place then?'* Both men remembered the stinging reply.

'You will only act on my orders. What I am planning is very little, if any, personal contact with your subjects. The information you will receive from me will be all you need to persuade anyone.'

Lanov and Mogatin, almost at the end of their scheduled tour, decided they had not had a good night out since the day they had learnt about Tashimov's death. Mogatin was sitting on the end of the bed in yet another hotel room, this time in Achern. Turning his head, panning across the same distressed furniture, mottled mirror, curtains that let in too much light and didn't quite fit the windows. As Mogatin's gaze continued on around the room, his eyes stopped at the ill-fitting toilet door where his friend Lanov had been for the past few minutes. Suddenly and with a roar, his friend tore open the door.

'You need to be a bloody contortionist to use these bloody French bogs! No bloody room in them! And, of course, after you've finished, the paper's behind the cistern and to get yourself wiped, you bloody well have to stick your arm up your own arse!' Mogatin burst out laughing at his friend's remark. Lanov stopped abruptly in the doorway, about to tell his friend off for laughing at him when he realised that what he had just said was really quite funny and joined in the laughter, until, not wishing to let it continue any longer, he asked Mogatin, 'Do you think it's worth going out tonight? It's not much of a town – we could just go down to the so-called bar, if you like?'

'No, let's at least stretch our legs; we can always come back here later.'

'Okay, let's go then. I'm thirsty, hungry and if I'm lucky, I could be lustful.'

'You're getting a bit reckless, my friend! Is it the relief of finding out about Tashimov's death?'

'Probably. We've both been through hell, lately.'

'Yes, it was far from pleasant, but it seems that Yute has got things in place for us.'

'Yes, but I'll only be happy when I know exactly what we're going to do and of course, when we have some guarantee of our fees!'

'I'll be happier when we get back some of that lovely money we've already spent doing his bidding.'

'Are we running out of funds then?'

'No, we're flush enough, but I don't like being this low.'

'You always worry… something will turn up, or what usually happens is when you get back you'll find we've got some left over. Come on, my friend, let's go out now and tomorrow be damned.'

The narrow canyoned streets in Achern were the same as many other small towns throughout Europe – a pleasure to walk through in daylight with the high sun casting its diagonal line of light and shade, drawing the eyes to look through the contrast of light into the deep shadows, which was not in the least scary, except when there was full darkness covering the town. Then, in full darkness a menace seemed to prevail upon whoever ventured into the chasm. Lanov and Mogatin felt that menace waiting to engulf anyone who trespassed upon its secrets.

'Dimitri, do you feel a… tension in what you see before you?' asked Mogatin.

'Caution is what I feel, Mogatin… caution. The signs tell me to beware.'

'Do you remember the last time we both felt the same way about a town?'

'Yes, Hamburg.'

'I don't like this feeling I'm getting. Somehow, I feel it's a warning.'

'Don't be silly, my friend, how can you compare Hamburg to this?'

'It's a strong feeling!'

'There's no comparison, my friend.' Dimitri's voice was soft and consoling as he added, 'In Hamburg we were already committed to a scheme of things and as we were being forced to use unknown colleagues, our faculties were working overtime. This is different; we have no brief, we have only to perform a reconnaissance. We have no information that we can even suppose may be of any consequence to feed your imagination.'

'I know you're right, Dimitri, perhaps I'm getting a little tired and in need of a holiday.'

'Well, my friend, make the most of tonight. Tomorrow we leave for Mother Russia and as you know, she can be very demanding!'

'Okay, okay, let's forget everything for tonight and find the "Cockatoo Club" the concierge told us about!'

'It should be just around the bend ahead if he told us correctly.'

Playfully, Mogatin replied, 'Do they ever?'

The conversation ended as both men focused their eyes ahead, looking at the flashing green sign. The dimly-lit basement club was like so many others around the world; low-ceiling, low lighting, noisy music, noisy conversation in competition with the music, smoke-filled, tucked away alcoves almost in total darkness which fill up very early in the evening, allowing some relief from the morass of bodies around the bar. Lanov and Mogatin stood, allowing their eyes and ears to adjust to the human hell-hole sprawled out in front of them, until Lanov with a shrug of his shoulders, said, 'Well, my friend, we've come this far, let's have a drink!'

Mogatin shouted his reply, 'Another bloody dream factory!' and walked down the stairs. Lanov followed, knowing his friend hated too much noise, but loved the darkness where, if he should have to suffer any inconvenience from anyone, he did not have to move far to take his revenge. Mogatin liked to drink and be happy, but every so often when he was in this mood, some little man would pick a fight. Mogatin could never understand why, but it invariably happened.

Skirting their way around what passed for a dance floor, one alcove was noisier than the rest; high-pitched female laughter followed by the usual 'Stop it!' and 'Don't be silly!' and 'Not now! Wait!' Neither Lanov and Mogatin could resist looking in at whatever they could see. As if struck by a thunderbolt, neither of them could at first believe their eyes. Two fairly sober, but dishevelled friends from their past escapades in Africa rose up like phoenixes from the ashes, all heated and angry at being disturbed, but then, on recognising their friends, rose up with open arms.

'Lanov! Mogatin! Tovarich! where have you come from? Come, sit down. Vodka! Sit here… come, sit down, tell us everything!' The two voices were not yet synchronised, but they were both saying the same things.

Lanov and Mogatin both sat staring at their friends' startled faces. Lanov was the first to speak. 'We did get out of Hamburg, as you can see!'

Anton Zabiak replied, 'We heard rumours, but we also heard about Tashimov's threat, so Uri and I gave up hope of ever seeing you again!' he said, his tinny voice becoming quite shrill.

'We had a long tour around Europe, finishing up in Portugal, where Polenkovich told us the news that Tashimov had been killed by a female CIA agent. She apparently had some sort of vendetta against him. The story is not clear, other than that Tashimov is definitely dead,' said Mogatin.

'It's just as well for you! He was great and I am sure you and Lanov here respected his work, but he would have been relentless in pursuing you,' said Uri Melentkov, Anton Zabiak's partner.

'Absolutely, but Lanov and I had worked out a contingency plan. So many things were going wrong and we didn't want to be disloyal, so we saw it through to the end, but an escape plan seemed the only way out to us.'

'It really went wrong then?' the tinny voice of Anton Zabiak asked.

Lanov replied, 'It went really wrong. Too rushed, insufficient disciplined troops to support spineless, greedy local area bosses, not enough support from those above… brilliant idea, but a perfect scheme spoilt by greed.'

'We heard rumours that the plan was brilliant, but that it was Tashimov's fault that it failed?' questioned Uri Melentkov.

'I think we both agree that none of it was Tashimov's fault, other than he trusted the word of the Council.'

'Glasnost didn't help any of us in the early days,' Anton interjected.

'Bloody Glasnost! Screwed up a lot of things! It allowed too many people too quickly into the free market that we had been trading in for years. Too much too quickly, in the eyes of world trade. I suppose the Organisatiya had to flex its muscle to let the little fish know that they, as always, are the bosses!' Yuri said.

Mogatin, having got over the first reactions of meeting these two comrades again, cut into the conversation. 'You always were a good communist, Yuri. High dreams of grandeur and not a single courtesy in your whole body!' Mogatin stood up to his full height before adding playfully, 'You never think of offering anyone a drink!' Lanov's laughter followed by Anton's and Yuri's set the pace and style of the evening until the early hours of the morning. The girls had been used, brought back to the alcove, wined and dined, and used again. Now came going home time. The girls had been paid off and forgotten and just the four men remained in the alcove for one last drink.

Chapter Twenty-Two

Lanov was fidgeting about in their hotel room whilst Mogatin was trying to revive himself under the shower, attempting to sing now and again, but the croakiness of his voice told of the previous night's over-indulgence in food, drink and cigarettes. Lanov, having had a bad night's sleep, had risen early, walked the streets for a while, found an early morning café and had two huge cups of sweet black coffee. His fidgeting now was being caused by the memories of last evening. Refreshed after the coffee, most of the memories and the conversation were back inside his head. He would be uneasy until he could have a debrief with Mogatin. Time passed. Mogatin shuffled through the bathroom door into the bedroom and seeing Lanov already dressed, his eyes struggling against the sunlight from the now open curtains, he leant against the doorframe heavily and croaked, 'It's no good you talking to me, I need coffee and food and then we will talk.'

As he continued across the room, he threw himself down on the bed and added, 'I promise, I promise! For a drink I'd promise anything!'

The long process of revival slowly took over Mogatin's brain and body. The dehydration and nausea seemed to be leaving him after the dutiful attendance of Lanov, but the head and eyes were still taking their own time to unite with the now partially mobile part of his body.

'Mogatin!' Lanov barked, having finally lost his patience. 'We've got less than an hour to get out of this bloody town and get on our way, and there's still a few things to check on.'

'I'm sorry, Dimitri… why do I never know when to stop?'

'Come on, my friend. We haven't got time for your remorse. Let's just say you're like a child when you drink. You like what's happening and you always want one more.'

'Ha bloody ha! That doesn't help me one bit!'

'Sorry. Come on, let's get on!'

'Those two buggers last night, Anton and Yuri, they always were cocky little bastards! They got under my skin, that's why I drank too much.'

'Anton always did manage to wind you up.'

'He's a little shit! A vicious little shit – he likes to hurt people just for the hell of it!'

'Come on, Mogatin, don't let's go over that old ground, we haven't got time.'

'I suppose not, but the job he's on now seems to be making him happy, playing husband and wife off against one another, turning the screw to break them and then enjoying giving them physical pain after they have collapsed. That pig Anton never knows when to stop and that bloody Yuri is a sadist when it comes to women.'

'Stop it, Mogatin! I agree with you, they have been allowed to get away with their little fetishes in the past, but when we are out in the big wide world as now, you can't just leave bodies lying around, like Russia in the old days. Let's hope they've cleaned up their act, otherwise it's going to be bad for all of us.'

'Sure, Dimitri, but those two have been going over the top for so long, can they stop? Come on, Dimitri, we are going to be late.'

Picking up his hat, coat and suitcase, he left the room and Lanov stood there momentarily flabbergasted. Swiftly gathering up his own case and coat, he chased after his now almost normal friend.

Anton and Yuri sat bleary-eyed at the breakfast table at their hotel. No conversation had passed between them since their arrival. The only conversation had been purely through eye and head movements. The third cup of coffee for each had brought a little life back, but it would take a while longer yet.

'Yuri,' croaked Anton, after a little cough in the hope of moving away the boulder stuck in his throat. 'We didn't say anything out of order last night, did we?'

'No. We teasingly told them that we have a job we like doing, that we liked breaking people down and that they were fairly local to where we are, and that it looked as if the job could have a fairly long run.'

'We didn't mention any names, did we?'

'No, and strangely enough they didn't ask, either. In fact, they were bloody disinterested in anything we said and gave nothing away about their assignment, even when I raised the question once or twice during the evening. They were most evasive, come to think of it. They just said they were not allocated yet, but when they get back to Russia, an assignment will be waiting.'

'Don't you think, Yuri, that it's a very devious route back to Russia via Portugal, France, Spain and practically the whole of Europe?'

'Yes, they are working now, I'll bet you!'

'Are they going to be our minders, do you think?'

Anton's tired face tightened. 'God, I hope not! Those two are merciless!'

Yuri looked into Anton's face and read the anguish then asked, 'If they were our minders, they wouldn't have made contact with us, would they?'

'I hope you're right. Do you remember when we first met them in that alcove, they were genuinely surprised to see us. I'm convinced, thinking about it, it was one of those fluky coincidences!'

'I hope you're right, those two are a bloody crafty pair!'

'Yes, I know. Maybe we should operate a safety plan between us to watch each other's backs. We can't be too careful, can we?'

Yuri didn't answer, but the determination that showed on his face assured Anton that Yuri agreed.

Inspector Ernst Ulbrecht's office was silent. Silently waiting for reports, waiting for a reply to each of the hundreds of questions that had been asked of what was now hundreds of people involved throughout Russia, Europe and America. The occasional call came through, the ringing of the phone, causing each of them to look up and wait for the attitude of the person to indicate whether or not the office would spring into action. Meanwhile Ernst Ulbrecht's mind was in turmoil.

Come on please, someone come and tell us something! Mayer, your people seem to have dried up! My own people are tailing our Russians back across Europe. The bloody Portuguese haven't got their reports in yet, there may be something in those transcripts which could be important. Joc, my friend, the only one who seems to appreciate the possibility of stopping worldwide crime...

With a heavy sigh in his heart, his mind offered up a little prayer, asking for something to happen. Ernst paced around his desk, stretching his tired shoulders. In the distance of the long, open-plan office, he could see the unmistakable figure of Mayer coming in his direction.

'Something from Russia, please,' he whispered softly to himself. 'No! No. Don't turn away, surely you have something for me?' The dropping of his shoulders summed up his disappointment as she turned away to a colleague's desk. A distant phone rang.

'Ernst!' Willi's soft voice called. 'That Portuguese policeman, Vargas, is on line one. He wants you. I said you aren't here, but he's pulling rank and getting a bit heavy. Roth isn't around today either, so will you speak to him?'

'Sure, Willi, do you know what it's about?'

'He wouldn't say, he was just being belligerent talking to a pleb like me!'

'Put him through.' By the time Ernst had got back behind his desk and lifted the receiver, Chief Inspector of Police, Manuel Vargas was on the line.

'Chief Inspector, sir. Sorry to have kept you waiting.'

'It's not your fault, Inspector, you were not to know I was going to call you, but you see, Commander Roth is not there it seems, and I, knowing the urgency and importance of international policing, felt I had to tell someone in authority that my reports are being faxed to you as we speak.' The sarcasm and innuendo was not missed by Ernst.

'That is most kind of you and most prompt, sir. My office will give them immediate attention. When we have analysed the information, we will telephone your office to let you know of this fact, and of course, any other information we may require will be requested at the same time.'

'No, no, Inspector. You are to phone me directly yourself please, or Commander Roth. I am available at any time. Your Commander has all of my telephone numbers.'

'Thank you again, sir. I will do my best to obey your request.'

'I am sure you will, Inspector. Remember, you or Commander Roth may phone at any time.'

The sarcasm was cutting into Ernst's pride, but he had to be civil. He could not afford to upset the pompous ass at the other end of the line.

'I will tell him, sir. Thank you again. Goodbye.'

The speed at which Ernst put down the receiver, gave him no time to listen for a 'goodbye' from Chief of Police, Manuel Vargas.

Ernst called through to his secretary and asked that the fax from Vargas be brought to him on completion of its transmission. Waiting... the time seemed endless. Ernst's fingers tapped on his desk, entwined themselves into each other, making steeples, ran through his thinning hair, but then, seeing his secretary coming towards him, the expectation of reading the report suddenly broke a smile over his face.

Handing over the volume of papers, his secretary muttered, 'It's more like a book!'

Ernst thanked her and said, 'Is it any good?'

Looking down at Ernst's smiling face, she replied, 'There are an awful lot of "I's" and "my men and I's" – should be a good read as long as he hasn't forgotten the story line!'

With a heavy sigh, Ernst said, 'Well, I'd better get on with it, thanks again.'

Having fought his way through the report, Ernst rested back in his chair, his hand rubbing the back of his neck. He asked himself, 'There surely must be some valid information in these sixteen pages... at least one simple thing?' Stretching his arms and placing his forearms firmly each side of the report on his desk, he started to read again.

His head suddenly jerked up from the papers in front of him as he whispered to himself, 'Our "ringed-hand man" couldn't have stayed eighteen hours in his room without moving!' Ernst threw himself back in his chair while his mind took over. 'It's not Polenkovich's style! Let's check all of our men's reports – and, while we're at it, the Americans' too!' The phone was his lifeline, first dialling Willi and then Mayer, asking them to come into his room. Dialling swiftly again, he waited for the clicking of all of the numbers to end and ring, once, twice.

'Joc Latimer here…'

'Ulbrecht heir!'

'Wonderful to hear from you! How are things now you've got more or less everyone playing in your backyard?'

'Things are pretty good, Joc, but I would like to ask another favour of you. Could you read through what written stuff you might have. I know you were doing us a favour without official sanction from your bosses, but there is a gap in the Portuguese report of eighteen hours without any sighting of Yute Polenkovich. Vargas's report claims he spent eighteen hours in his hotel room on the twenty-first.'

'That seems out of character, Ernst. I'll phone around and see if maybe some of the boys have taken some notes.'

'Thanks, Joc, it would be most kind of you. I'll await your call as soon as possible – either way please.'

'Sure, Ernst, ASAP. Bye now.'

'And you, Joc, thanks again.'

Willi and Mayer entered through the ever-open doorway into Ernst's office exactly as the phone reached the cradle. Both Willi and Mayer said their hellos and Ernst told them of the possible flaw in the Portuguese report and how the missing eighteen hours without a sighting of Polenkovich worried him. Ernst expressed his fear that maybe Polenkovich had somehow got out of the hotel and made a connection with someone unknown. It could be in all their interests to know the answer to that question.

Willi asked, 'Should our boys in Portugal go behind Vargas's back and talk to the men on the street that they met?'

'Could be an idea. Vargas's report seems to be all one flow and could have been compiled entirely by him. He could have disregarded, or misunderstood the significance of such an absence of a key player, but don't let Vargas's men report back to him! Only talk to people we can trust.'

'Understood, Ernst. I'll get on to it now. Will that be all?'

'Yes thanks. Mayer will be matching our own reports to Vargas's. Will you liaise?' Both Willi and Mayer answered affirmatively and left Ernst to his ponderings.

The report on Major Roche's desk from the Provost, Major Robin Cadwallader, was disturbing. It was openly apparent from the report that Lieutenant Daniel Tomlevski had been meeting with other 'nationals' (origins unknown at present) which was against the unwritten protective agreement Eurocorps had placed upon itself as a security measure. Major Roche, as the originator of the worry about Lieutenant Tomlevski, would be informed of any further action necessary. After reading the report fully, he slapped the top of his desk hard in annoyance. Matters were now out of his hands.

Lanov and Mogatin arrived back in Moscow and as ordered, reported straight to Yute Polenkovich. Both Lanov and Mogatin were unhappy at the time it took to make contact by phone and disturbed by the fact that their telephone conversations were being listened to. The fact they were being followed even before they had officially been commissioned to start work by Yute, caused a dilemma. Was it Yute having them followed, or was it someone else?

Marshall Yute Polenkovich, in full dress uniform, in response from a call to the Council, arrived at the War Ministry, walking through the tall, arched corridor. His thoughts were hopeful that today was to be the day when he would be given the lists of names which he and Igor Tatlanovich had been exchanging over the past few weeks. After all, were not all of the people put forward to the Council selected carefully, with due care being taken in each individual case? All of them having more than one misdemeanour from their parents' past to force them into the web?

Yute's stride was strong as he approached the large double doors. The sentries came to attention and walked the large doors open to reveal the emptiness of the giant-sized room which lay beyond the long green baize table with the Council sitting in full uniform in silence, making the fifty paces from the doors to his position in front of the table seem like a journey into outer space. Halting exactly where he was expected to, his courtesies spoken and acknowledged by all of the Council members with a nod of their heads, Yute relaxed slightly, although still standing to attention.

The brief silence before the Chairman spoke did not appear too long, but his first words caused Yute's body to jump. He had mentally briefed himself that it would be a full minute after his entrance and halting at the long table. All of the Council members, barring the Chairman, gave a little grin at Yute's obvious discomfort. The Chairman continued, 'You have been granted your wish to commence the initiation of the personnel listed on this document and when you are satisfied you have control of these personnel, you will report back to us. At which stage we will sanction stage two and then when you have positioned stage two, you will return and we will approve the third and final stage, providing we are satisfied with your progress.' Missing the 'Yute Polenkovich, Marshall of the Army of Russia' bit on the front did not worry him now, nor the shock that had run through his body, giving the Council reason to grin. Yute only knew that he wanted to shout with joy. He had been granted the three stages he had requested, without a timescale. Stiffening his back and tightening his whole body to attention, he thanked the Council for the trust they had just extended to him, with a special 'thank you' to the Chairman for his tolerance during the enormous research required to enable his plan to get this far. The dismissal, the about-turn and the long walk back to the large double doors, Yute could not remember; he was on cloud nine. The marching through the doors, the marching in the long, empty corridor was all a haze, until instinctively knowing he was out of the Council's earshot, he hit the air with his fist and screamed, 'Yes!'

The sun was warm on Yute's face as he walked out into the quadrangle after the light and shade of the long, arched corridor. Inhaling his only breath of fresh air in the past hour, he decided a cigarette and a coffee and cognac would make his life rather happier than it had been for the first time since the Tashimov disaster. This was a good day, Yute thought. A very good day. His steps grew faster as he walked through the tall, unroofed columns on his approach to the stone steps down to the square below where he would sit for a little while, enjoying being around normal people whilst he smoked and savoured his coffee and cognac. His mind played as the rhythm in his feet made him think of himself as the greatest ballet dancer in all Russia, playing Romeo, or as a solo artist, centre stage, performing the greatest leaps. As his feet jarred to marching pace, his memory of the dreams he had dreamt as a young man were being forced out of his mind; the shudder of the constant jarring ran through his body from his feet to his head, leaving only the cold, military man he had since become.

Although Yute sat there in his full dress uniform, he was not particularly conspicuous. Over the years, many thousands of senior officers had sat on those café chairs, some full of pride, others bewildered they had not got the posting they had hoped for. The military were always welcomed in this little part of Russia as the largest employer and the largest spenders, but whether they were alone, or whether they came in a group, a welcome was all they got. The people had never learnt to give of themselves, the fear that drove Mother Russia reached the waiters and servants before it spread to the rest of the country. An area which should be light-hearted, lived in silence.

He sat alone. The service was impeccable, but the happiness in his heart soon became a burden when he realised that although there were dozens of people around him, he was slowly being ostracised and was as alone as he always had been throughout his life. His own laughter and joy was never heard. The coffee and cognac finished, Yute stood up, fighting away the melancholy rising within him. A phone booth was needed. He must speak to Lanov and Mogatin. It was time to ring. Yute's mind was now racing again. The 'job' must be started as quickly as possible without panic, but quickly. Snatching the handset, he dialled the numbers for the contact place for that day, the prompt answer and Mogatin's voice loudly answering, 'Fourteen!' (which was the number of calls made to date by Yute, since the arrival of Lanov and Mogatin back in Moscow).

'Correct,' replied Yute. 'Lanov is fifteen tomorrow.'

The identification was always completed by the same response, 'I will make certain he is told.'

'We should meet tomorrow at 1000 hours. It is important. We have been given approval.'

Mogatin held back a moment before asking, 'Everything is as you wanted?'

'Exactly so, no more, no less.'

'My friend and I are very pleased.'

'It will be my pleasure to work with you directly, as opposed to through a third party.'

'We prefer it that way.'

'Until tomorrow then. You know where.' Yute replaced the phone onto the hook, waited for the sound of his coin to drop and pensively walked away.

Daniel and Nicole were sitting silently in the unlit room which, since the visits from 'the bastard Russians', as Nicole insisted on calling them, they did every night. The days were not so bad as they both carried on with their lives as normally as possible, but what could they do at night? Their love and expectations had been mutilated by their own belligerent words, accusation after accusation about each other's parents was eventually destructive. Silent, because it was less destructive to be so, silence by agreement, silence whilst they waited for that inevitable phone call or meeting which would start them on a new road of breaking the trust they once had for each other. Tonight's silence was only broken by the occasional low sob.

Major Cadwallader's special investigations team had been briefed to observe and report. Before that, Major Cadwallader had put a team to work, thoroughly researching the family background of these two young people and up until two hours ago, it had seemed that Daniel and Nicole had led a blameless life. The past two hours, however, had sown a small seed of doubt. Nicole had been followed. Without doubt, her 'shadow' had been vigilant in avoiding being noticed by her, but he had been noticed by one of his watchers when he was playing games, getting as close to Nicole as he possibly could without being observed himself. Now Major Cadwallader had something to go on. A description provided by one of his own staff as a first step was good, a photograph would be better next time, fingerprints could be obtained, and then he and his team would be well on the way to something.

Lanov and Mogatin arrived separately at the museum because they felt Yute's phone might have been tapped and he might well have a tail on him. They had both agreed to take every precaution against being followed. They also agreed they would not make contact with Yute until they had made absolutely certain he had not been followed. To this end, and from separate positions in the museum, they observed the comings and goings for half an hour prior to the time arranged. Yute had arrived ten minutes early and positioned himself in the centre of the Great Room. Easy to observe and easy to watch, Lanov and Mogatin's approach was swift from either side of Yute. He saw them the moment they left their cover.

Walking around the galleries, the three men showed mock interest in all they saw. On the steps of the museum, they said their goodbyes as if the meeting had been pure chance. Mogatin, being the last to shake hands, whispered, 'Until the next time then, but beware, we think your phones are tapped and a new schedule of phone boxes must be implemented. Watch your back!'

Yute replied, 'I will. It was nice for me to have met you. Maybe tomorrow, same time, same place? I'll have the list and a place available for us to transfer to.' All three men left in separate directions, knowing that the same place a second time in two days was a little risky, but they had to reorganise their methods of contact in view of the suspected phone tap!

The ease with which Major Cadwallader's men achieved the getting of photographs and fingerprints surprised him, but never one to look a gift horse in the mouth, he started the wheels rolling to find out who and where the intruders came from and their reasons for trying to 'invade' Eurocorps.

Mayer tapped lightly on the side of Ulbrecht's office door. As Ernst lifted his head, she saw his customary smile and returned it with a smile of her own. 'Come in, Mayer. What can I do for you?

It will be nice to have a little chat for a moment or two and get my head out of these papers.'

'Well, sir, Lanov and Mogatin are back in Russia, hanging around Moscow. They met up with Yute Polenkovich who has been spotted wearing his uniform and attending the War Ministry. The meeting took place in the Gorky Museum. Luckily, Polenkovich was followed before and after the meeting.'

'Very good, Mayer. Your Russian friends are informative!'

'Yes, sir. They all want to come over to the West, so it's their way of scoring brownie points for when they make their applications for entry into Germany.'

'We must keep cultivating these people, Mayer, but maybe they would help the West better if they stayed where they were.'

'I believe they realise we would like to keep them in place there. I've never discussed it with them, but I do sense they could be more use to the West where they are. Some of them are very senior and know where a lot of bodies are buried. It's very interesting and useful, knowing them.'

Ulbrecht's head had returned to his paperwork as Mayer smiled at the top of her absent-minded boss's head.

Joc Latimer could not believe his ears. In response to Ernst's request, he had asked the boys in Portugal to ask favours of Vargas's investigators and now, Joe Lomax was on the phone telling the most amazing story. One of Vargas's men had let slip about the eighteen-hour gap in Vargas's report and that Vargas had only put one man on the outside of Polenkovich's hotel. 'This contact is saying that he could not believe Vargas's action in view of the seriousness of having Russians running around unchaperoned, so he and a colleague worked without orders or pay to take turns watching the back of the hotel and the interior lobby and bar et cetera,' Joe continued.

'Come on, Joe, don't hold out on me, give me the news!'

'Well, Joc, it seems both of these Vargas men reported that Polenkovich had had lunch with a very debonair young man. They don't think it was sexual, but here's the juicy bit… Vargas's wife visited the debonair young man in his hotel room! The report went in to Vargas, but no mention of it went into his report. Both men were acting without orders, so neither man has been reprimanded nor asked to follow up on the sightings.'

'Bloody hell, Joe, if we let this go, it could cause a lot of damage. I think Ernst in Hamburg ought to know straight away. Get the names of these two Portuguese investigators and any name for this "debonair young man"... Did they get any photographs?'

'Their names are coming, and yes, there are photos as well.'

'Thanks, Joe. Thank your boys for me too!'

'Sure, I will. I'll get back to you with the names ASAP.'

The phone went dead and Joc instantly reached out to get another line.

Ulbrecht felt the urgency surging into his office as the phone rang. Moving around his desk as fast as his cluttered office would allow, he snatched the phone.

'Ulbrecht heir!'

'Latimer here!'

'I have a feeling this call is an urgent one, Joc.'

'You are definitely not wrong, my friend!'

'Tell me then, please.'

'The missing eighteen hours in Vargas's report are turning out to be very interesting! Two of his investigators evidently could not believe that what they had reported was nowhere to be found in Vargas's report. They could not understand why, when Polenkovich was holed up in his hotel, only one man was ordered to watch from the outside. They decided that Vargas was wrong and worked the lobby and the back entrance between them. Polenkovich apparently had lunch with a debonair young man, and wait for it... the debonair young man then had a visit from Vargas's wife!'

'Good information! I suppose the investigator, on seeing Senora Vargas, couldn't help but follow her when he saw her enter the lift to go up?'

'Sure he did!'

'They have photographs, I hope!'

'Yes. The investigators' names, the photos and the debonair man's name, will, I hope, be with you in about an hour or so.'

'Thank you once again, Joc. I owe you.' The humility was clear in Ernst's voice.

'No thanks needed, my friend, on any account. We all want the same things; peace and no crime. You have made us wide awake to the fact that crime is worldwide. Thank you.'

Joc knew his emotional German friend would be lost for words, so the receiver was placed lightly back in the cradle.

On enquiry at the Police photo laboratory, the Portuguese investigator who had spotted Senora Vargas in the hotel, was relieved to hear his photographs weren't quite ready yet, but that they would be shortly. The lab technician said if he could wait, it would save him the job of addressing the envelopes anyway. Vargas's investigator was relieved and happy to get the prints out of the station where there was far less chance of them being found, or of him having to explain any of the pictures to his boss. 'After all,' he whispered to himself as he sat waiting, 'I've got enough problems in my life already without having Vargas breathing down my neck. I could even be put on assignment watching her and reporting back to him direct. Better that the prints don't get to him, a quieter life all round!'

The lab guy came out and as he handed over the prints, he jokingly said, 'That's one good-looking lady in those shots! If she's not done anything too bad and you're willing to give out her address or phone number, put me at the top of the list!'

'Joc, the names of the Portuguese cops are Demi Portaga and Manolo Dias. The photos haven't got out onto the circuit yet, but the debonair young man has no identity so far, although there is a feeling here that he's Swiss, maybe a banker of one sort or another.'

'What does "one sort or another" mean?' asked Joc bluntly.

'Don't jump down my throat, old buddy! I'm only reading from the report, the bits that are missing from the report Vargas sent you!'

'Sorry, Joe, I didn't mean it the way it sounded.'

'I know, Joc. Don't worry about it. Now, the word is the debonair guy has been seen around, always in good hotels, restaurants, et cetera. When he has meetings, he arrives in a rented limo, shops at Pierre Cardin, et cetera…'

'I've got the picture. Can you spare anyone to find out if he's real or a hustler?'

'Well, Paul Isaacs has offered to follow any loose ends through.'

'If you could let him loose, it would be good for me. He's a good guy.'

'Okay, he's yours for a week. I've got a rotation of leave after that and it'll leave me without cover on my real work!'

'Ha ha! You know you'd rather live in the real world than that stuffed shirt world you're in now!'

'You could be right, but I bet I eat better than you!'

A light tap on the frame of his office door told Ernst that Mayer was there even before he lifted his head up from the papers in front of him. 'Hello, Mayer,' he said, as he lifted his full face to hers.

'Good morning, sir.' Her soft voice had a little tremble in it. Ernst was always sympathetic to anyone's unease and said, 'I'm sorry if I surprised you, I've come to recognise your knock. Please come in and sit down.'

'Thank you, sir, but it won't take a minute. I'll stand.'

'As you please. What have you got for me?'

'My Russians are reporting a lot of movement around Polenkovich. It appears he has surveillance on him twenty-four hours a day. The surveillance is authorised from on high with no trace of any written orders. They say it's just like the old days when maybe as many as a dozen could supposedly all be secretly in the chain of command.'

'We know how bad their old system was, Mayer.' Ernst paused, letting his mind reflect upon the past misery of the 'old system' before he spoke again. 'If only someone in that system had asked questions of the system itself, it would have collapsed. It was only fear that held it together!' Ernst stopped as suddenly as he had started, then continued, 'I'm sorry, Mayer, you would not have come to see me unless there was something specific you wanted to tell me.'

'Yes, sir. My Russians feel the fear that drove the system before Glasnost is back in a big way. Polenkovich, who has been given wide powers at his level, also has a death warrant out on him in the event of failure!'

'My God, Mayer! Is this true?'

'My Russian contacts felt very confident of the fact before they told me. They suspect that when Polenkovich's plan was accepted by Council, his one condition was that the plan, whatever it is, must be allowed to become established very slowly to ensure its success, but other forces are moving in to speed the whole scheme up.'

'Do you realise what you are saying, Mayer?'

'Yes, sir, of course!' she replied, a little indignant.

'Well, which one of your Russians is leaking Council information?'

'My God, sir, do you really think it could be one of my friends?'

'I don't know yet, but if I'm right, we need to know, Mayer!'

'How, sir? I wouldn't know where to start that kind of enquiry with my friends. If I get it wrong, the whole source of information we are receiving would collapse.'

'Mayer, it would help considerably if we could find out, but we must keep all of your connections in Russia giving us information. It's imperative. We, on the other hand, will have to look at what we are being given through different eyes, in case your Russian, or Russians, may be giving us some information to benefit their cause.'

As the possible deception Ernst had just explained sank into Mayer's active brain, she replied, 'Sir, I'll do whatever I can, but I do hope my Russians are on our side!'

'So do I, Mayer, so do I!'

'May I go now, sir?'

'Yes, of course you may. You should have taken the seat I offered you – my ramblings sometimes take a while.'

Mayer left but was annoyed with herself for not anticipating the possibility of being fed false information.

Yute sat pondering over the papers set out before him. The two folders sat side by side. All the other papers scattered around on the desk were of no significance. The folders waiting to be opened, contained the final selection of the chosen few, names which would begin the infiltration of Eurocorps. Reflecting for a few moments before opening the folder's flap, he remembered Igor Tatlanovich; that nauseating civil servant, the hours spent down in that dungeon of an office, and as Yute thought of the social occasions that it had been necessary to endure, his body gave a little involuntary shudder. The torment at having to accept this spineless creature as a colleague sent another shudder through him. Turning both covers of the files open simultaneously, he read the large capitals typed at the top of each page: THE FOLLOWING ARE THE SELECTED PERSONNEL WHO WILL BE USED IN OPERATION TEMPKIN. The folder on Yute's left had one extra word centred and underlined, MEN. The one on his right, the word WOMEN.

Each name on each list had a little memory-jogging biography by its side, each name numbered. Flicking over the pages he could see the total selected on both lists, a total of ninety-six persons; seventy-nine men and seventeen women.

Yute flattened his hands on the desk on the folders and pushed his body and chair back from the desk, his anger contained for the moment. A moment passed. The muscles in his jaw tightened. Holding back his words, this was now a time for action.

Sitting back in his chair, his anger having been contained, his mind started the plotting of the protection of his original plan of the slow infiltration of Eurocorps and the disposal of Igor Tatlanovich who could have warned him earlier of the growing numbers on the lists. He had known of the huge numbers being vetted and had helped with the selection for his own requirements. There must have been a second list going direct to Council. The words passed coldly through his clenched teeth. 'Igor, you betrayed me! Your visit to my dacha will come sooner than you hoped for!'

'Joc? Joe here – it's a s h i t world we live in!' The letters were spelt out and the sadness in Joe's voice was obvious.

'It's been going that way for a long time, old buddy. What's wrong with it now?'

'Vargas's wife – she's nothing but a whore. She's on the bloody game regular, working through an agent with any visiting fireman who'll pay the price!'

'Christ, Joe! That's one for the book – doesn't the husband know?'

'It seems he probably didn't, but after he read the reports from Portaga and Dias, he is suspicious and that's the reason for losing the eighteen hours in the report he compiled.'

'The poor sod! Does he know we had some pictures?'

'No. Portaga and Dias have apparently admitted they shouldn't have continued the surveillance and that no photographs were taken. The photolab guys have been squared away with dollars that Dias "borrowed" from us.'

'I suppose Vargas is doing his own "tailing" now?'

'No, he's all of a sudden lost his air of self-importance and has become very reticent.'

'It affects people in different ways. You'd better keep an eye on him if you can. If he hits the bottle he could mouth off about the Russians in Portugal and it could upset things for Ulbrecht, set tongues wagging – you know what I mean!'

'Okay, Joc. Got to fly... It's sad, whatever the nationality of the cop involved, when you hear of something like this.'

'That's for sure, Joe. I wonder what sent her down that route?'

'If any of us knew the answer to that, the world would be a happier place.'

'Could be, but I haven't got time to ponder on that one. See you, Joe... and thanks, I'll let Ulbrecht know. Bye.'

Joc made the quick phone call to Ernst and told him the news about Vargas's wife. The sympathy in Ernst's voice for a fellow officer's misfortune was touching. Now that the phone was back in its cradle, his last words rang bells in Joc's head: 'Joc, your guys know Vargas – could he be the pimp and could he just be play acting for his men's sake?' It was a thought which had run through Joc's head while he discussed the matter with Joe, but he had dismissed it swiftly on hearing the sadness in Joe's voice. If Vargas was his wife's pimp, he could be vulnerable, blackmailed into all kinds of things and would be of no use whatsoever to a European police force. Joc knew he had to phone Joe back and ask what would sound like a very sick question…

Chapter Twenty-Three

The large, coldly-lit Records Office of the Hamburg Police Bureau looked saddening. The manual side of the thousands of files, indexing, typing, which had been done in the past by dozens of staff rotating on twenty-four-hour shifts, had gone. The slick computer database now set up, had left so much space that the atmosphere had disappeared, making it feel eerie.

Ulbrecht was standing beside Mayer, fidgeting as her fingers slid across the keyboard. He knew the technology contained within the database, and all of the support linkage it could draw on, would conduct the search quicker than he, and produce more than all of his staff working around the clock could possibly achieve on their own, but still he fidgeted.

He leant over Mayer's shoulder at the questions and answers appearing on the monitor screen, then more information, then a window bringing more information, and so on. He looked down at the photograph of the suave banker, having been given a name of Boris Parentov by the Portuguese police investigators who had searched hotel listings and found four entries which synchronised with the last one mentioned in Manolo Dias's report. When Ulbrecht had been given the fact by Mayer in his office less than half an hour ago, he had decided to come down to records with her, in the hope the search would be short and conclusive.

'Do you think our Boris is in there somewhere, Mayer?'

'It's worth a try, sir. With a name and a picture, we're in with a good chance.'

'I'm pleased, Mayer. I'm pleased that you're happy.'

'I will be happy, sir, if he's on our network and we don't have to start asking for more favours.'

'What chance have we got of finding him?'

'If he has had even a parking fine in Germany, that's East and West, as we've got most of their computer info alongside ours now, then we'll find him. If not, it's down to favours, sir.'

'Let's hope then, Mayer, that we can sort this one ourselves.'

Mayer's fingers kept finding information, then asking more and more questions of the wizardry before her. It seemed like magic to Ulbrecht, but he knew in his heart of hearts that the button pushers had taken over and his thoughts were of who was going to teach them to think – to anticipate the criminal's next move?

'Sir!' Mayer's voice cut into his private thoughts. 'Sir, we have got a match on the name. We're on "search" – shouldn't be long now.'

'Good, Mayer, good. What was his offence?'

'Drunk and disorderly, sir.'

'When and where?'

'Berlin, last year on his birthday.'

'It seems we have a real criminal then!'

'Well possibly not, but he holds a position with an American bank.'

'That's interesting, Mayer, very interesting.'

'Why is that, sir?'

'Well you see, I have a very good friend – a very good investigator who works for the CIA and he wants to keep crime out of America. He's a real thinker and would help us, I know.'

'That's good, sir. Hold on, the ID is coming up now...'

A rectangle started forming at the bottom of the screen and continued its way up until it settled itself in the centre of the screen.

'That's great, Mayer. Are we going to get a picture as well?'

'One of two things. Either he would not be photographed for a drunk charge unless he had resisted arrest and struck an officer, or, he has no other charge against him than this.'

'Going by the information from Portugal, is it the same man?'

'Most certainly, sir.'

'Can you get a copy of that ID card for me?'

'I'll print off a copy for you now, sir.' She struck the print key lightly and a clicking whirr commenced.

Ulbrecht waited until he saw the image appearing on the printer before he spoke again. 'You said, Mayer, that he worked for an American bank?'

'Yes, sir, that's what our information said.'

'On this ID it says 'Occupation: Banker. Employer: Deutsche Bank.'

'He must have changed jobs after this incident, sir.'

'Will you see who remembers him and, out of curiosity, why he left? We should be able to get the picture verified by someone, don't you think?'

'Most certainly. Do you want me to carry out the investigation myself, sir?'

'Please,' was Ulbrecht's reply as he wandered off through the large empty space towards the door.

Majors Roche and Cadwallader sat side by side in the bar's alcove. Both were in civvies, with a glass of beer in front of each of them. The words Roche had just heard from Cadwallader had stopped the usual, easy flow of conversation between them. Roche broke the silence.

'So you are saying, Robin, that both the Tomlevskis have been got at? Well, in my book, I think Tomlevski is a good officer. In fact, so good, if he stays where he is, he will have a staff job within a few years I'm sure, and I can't possibly agree with giving him the chop!'

'But what you're asking of me and my men just can't be done! We have spent many man hours, stacks of paper and a fair amount of expense – I can't just tear the report up!'

'I'm not asking for that and you know it. What should happen in your investigations? You have witnessed people who are invading the privacy of one of our people and his wife – turn the bloody investigation around and build your evidence against the invaders! You'll lose nothing. You've still got Tomlevski and his wife in your sights, so you can shoot them down at any time and you could be doing the military and police forces a big favour.'

'It doesn't work like that, André!'

'Well, bloody well make it, is what I say! We could let two people kill themselves if we don't do something!' André just stared at Robin – the silence, whilst both friends searched their hearts and their heads, trying to find a solution. Robin knew André would not give him any peace until they were working on the same side. André knew he was asking too much of his friend, but believed if Eurocorps was to survive and gain strength, it must have the good will of the people it was set up to protect and the support, when needed, of all the public services.

André spoke again. 'Please, Robin, turn it around. Get into the civilian police forces around here. Something may just tie in with your information. At least put your toe in the water for a little while at least, before you throw two lives away…'

'I believe in what you are trying to do, André. Okay, I'll give it a go, but you'll have to cover my back when I need it.'

'That goes without saying, Robin. Thank you. I know how exposed you'll be.'

'After this decision, I think we ought to have another drink… on you, I think!' Both men shook hands. The sincerity in their eyes glowed. André raised his hand to catch the waiter's eye and ordered more drinks.

The days had passed very slowly since Yute had received the final lists of selected candidates. The meeting he had requested with the Council had taken four days to arrange and when he arrived, he had been virtually immediately dismissed with, 'This Council commands that all personnel on these lists are used, and are placed within Eurocorps as soon as any opportunity arises. We will be watching the acceptance lists and will be following the postings with interest. We wish you to start an initial test run of goods through the organisation which you will be putting in place, within six months from today's date.'

The scraping of chairs on the marble floor as the whole Council stood up simultaneously was followed by the last words of the Chairman. 'You will not fail us. Russia needs a world market.'

Like gossamer, the Council faded away from Yute's view, his stunned mind slowly recovering from the shock the ultimatum had given him. Knowing that any redress of his grievance would not be permitted and that the severe timescale set now would jeopardise the whole scheme, Yute felt that the curse of Tashimov had been placed upon him. Left sitting in the Great Hall, Yute knew if Lanov and Mogatin were told of the Council's decision, they would not want to join him in opening up the Organisatiya to the world. He had promised them a well-organised, disciplined, unhurried operation, but how dare he try and cheat them by not telling them? That stupid thought, no sooner in his head, was pushed away. How could he deceive them when to fulfil the command of Council, he had to start now? The speed of his thoughts, the question and answer, question and answer, time after time, was beginning to tire him, but a resolve was forming in his mind. First though, he must meet Lanov and Mogatin with great secrecy. Looking at his watch, 11.40 a.m. registered. Twenty minutes to be at the phone booth at St Basil's Cathedral... he could just make it.

On the second ring, Lanov lifted the receiver, the code was gone through and Yute's message was acknowledged. Yute, conspicuous in his uniform, knew that having lost his tail, it would be no good going back to his apartment to change. Slipping into a clothes store, he had found a full-length raincoat which would cover most of his uniform, but the well-polished shoes would have to go. Looking at himself in the shop's full-length mirror, he was happy with the effect, but a final touch would be plastic bags; one in each hand to carry his briefcase, shoes and his uniform cap. Satisfied with himself, he left the shop with confidence, but cautiously. The crowded streets around the railway station gave a little help as he made his way to the venue prearranged with Lanov and Mogatin, but Yute knew his bosses would be going crazy for news of him; there would be many people searching for him. It had been two hours since he had left the ministry building and he was certain he had not been picked up by anyone. As he walked, he talked to himself. 'You're doing okay, Yute my boy! Two hours out in the clear! Those bastards don't deserve to ever see you again, do they? Ruining a damn good plan... wasn't it greed went wrong with the last operation? Yes, greed. The bastards are doing the same to me as they did to Tashimov, but we'll see, won't we? Hold back. Don't push to the front here. Wait for the lights to change. That's it, let the crowd push you along a little. There's the café, you're nearly there. An hour with Lanov and Mogatin, then back to the apartment.

"They" will be there… They will have given up on me until they see me there!'

He opened the door to the dimly-lit bar, allowing himself a few moments to adjust to the light after closing the door behind him. He moved between the aisles of booths to the very end where his two friends were waiting. Before sitting down, he excused himself and on the pretext of going to the toilet, surveyed for an alternative escape route, should the need arise. Having satisfied himself, he returned to Lanov and Mogatin.

'You chose this place well.'

Both men nodded their silent thanks as Yute continued, 'Not one, not two, but three ways out, if you include the bathroom window.'

'Just luck,' said Mogatin with a wry smile spreading across his face. Yute settled into his seat and asked the waiter who had appeared at his side for a coffee and cognac, before he bent across the table to shake hands warmly with both men. The three of them sat in silence until Yute's drinks had been brought over.

'I believe you should know that we have met the first bit of trouble. The first list of selected personnel is at least three times larger than planned, which makes for a lot more time required for the persuasion of our subjects; but we have been given a deadline for becoming active within six months.'

Mogatin shifted in his seat. 'So you have told them it can't be done?'

'It will be impossible to do that. They have decreed there is no appeal, no redress.'

'We're dead already then!' said Lanov.

'Could be, but I want to try for my own sake. At least until I get my revenge on one slimy civil servant who has been playing a double game with me.'

'Who is that?' asked Lanov.

'A clerk in the Records Office called Igor Tatlanovich. I'm sure the bastard withheld information from me and I'm also sure there are two lists of selected candidates.'

Quietly, Mogatin spoke up. 'It's not much good without us knowing what these lists are for and it would be nice if we knew what is expected of us!'

'The job you are both good at. After the selected few who I initially wanted to feed into Eurocorps, some people with a history of various matters which they would not want known in the West – even the sins of their fathers would be taken into account – would be persuaded to do as we require of them. After which, they would need delicate handling until we wanted a job activated.'

'Sounds like the sort of job we could handle with ease, but how many are on those lists you are on about?'

'Ninety-six.' The sharp, abrupt response caused silence. Yute waited, but he knew both men opposite him were shocked at the number to be managed. The main worry was the timescale. How do two men turn ninety-six people to believe in Mother Russia and to be active and placed within a single organisation within six months?

Lanov spoke first. 'This is unreal! The Council must be crazy. You might get some into place, but to start from scratch and be operational at the drop of a hat is totally impracticable!'

Mogatin cut in, 'You know the European tour you sent us on? Would we be operating in all those countries, or just around the Headquarters?'

'You would control whatever, wherever within the jurisdiction of the Corps. Why?'

'Just asking really, only when we were in Achern, Lanov and I ran into two nasty pieces of work who had worked with us in the past, when we were out having a few drinks one night. We got talking and drinking, and they intimated they were putting the shits up some people. I just thought as it's a large operation, we might have been working a separate area.'

Yute became instantly angry, his large left hand crashing into his ringed right hand.

'You bloody fools! Why haven't you told me of this meeting before? I want their names and I want to know their controller!'

'Hold on! Don't take your anger out on us! We only met Zabiak and Melentkov at the very end of last week and we didn't go into asking who they were working for, we just had some drinks together and they let a few things slip.' Mogatin's strong delivery of his reply brought Yute back to a more balanced state of mind.

'I'm sorry,' Yute said to both men. 'It took a long time to come up with this plan, a long time to get it approved by Council, a lot of living with "loss of face"; unknown and unaccepted by anyone and then you tell me that two friends of yours could be already working on my plan, before I had even gained full approval. It was a shock. I'm sorry.'

'We understand,' both men concurred.

Mogatin continued, 'What is our next move?'

Yute pondered for a moment. 'I think you should go back to Achern very quietly, visit your friends and find out exactly what they are doing. It is very necessary to get their controller's name. If you feel they are cutting across my plan, after getting as much information out of them as you can… get rid of them.'

'What if you are both working for the same bosses?' asked Lanov.

'My Chairman would get a rude awakening and I will have the control back to me with the plan reverted back to the original timescale. We may have one hell of a job selling it to his committee, but at least we would be back in control!'

Lanov thought for a moment before answering. 'If you are willing to go that far, I think Mogatin and I will support you.'

'Yes, you can count on me,' Mogatin cut in. 'You turn it back with your Chairman and I'll be happy.'

'Good,' replied Yute. 'Furthermore, I'm going to get time to see Igor Tatlanovich… a few words first… then the pleasure of watching him die!'

Mogatin looked at the hatred on Yute's face and he knew the death would be quick and without mercy. He asked Yute, 'If we have a little problem after talking to our men in Achern, I think we ought to despatch them too. Your Council doesn't know of us yet, and if we are kept under wraps it will give you a bit more leverage with which to change the Chairman's mind. At least he'll know you're in business and assume that it's caused some major trouble in breaking his direct connection with his field operatives.'

'My point exactly! So then, shall we meet again in five days time – same time, next rendezvous on your list?'

'Lanov will be happy now. He has an old score to settle with Uri Melentkov!'

'Don't make it a messy vengeance killing of either of them. Just take them out cleanly.'

Both Lanov and Mogatin stood up and silently shook hands with Yute. Lanov said, 'Five days then.' Nodding to Mogatin to leave by the back door, he left by the front. Yute sat and pondered the last hour and was pleased with the loyalty he knew he could expect from both men when he had turned the Chairman and Council back to his original outline. Sipping the remains of his coffee, he allowed himself a little smile as he ran through in his mind the little treat he was preparing for Igor Tatlanovich.

His phone call to Igor was answered swiftly. His proposal was that they met at a restaurant local to Igor's flat for an early meal before they drove out to the dacha for the weekend. Yute emphasised the need for Igor's total discretion and that it was not usual for civil servants to be invited by a high-ranking officer to his dacha. Igor responded exactly as Yute predicted.

The restaurant Yute had chosen was in a cosmopolitan part of Moscow. Like so many other international cities, once one foreign restaurant gets established, other nationalities follow and slowly a new atmosphere grows and success follows. The misshaped houses, the small alleyways and underlit streets, gave to the eye of the beholder what he or she wished to see; romance or homeliness. Restaurants clung together side by side, pushing their lights of many colours across the shadowy pavement, making many dark shadows in the place where Yute stood watching. The time passed and then, as expected, Igor arrived at the restaurant, exactly on time. Yute waited for the tell-tale sign he knew would soon show itself. *There it is – the tail. Igor's tail!* Sliding further back into his alleyway, crossing into a corridor of light and shade, he slowly crept out into the alleyway behind Igor's tail. Yute came quietly up behind the man, one hand to the mouth, pulling the head and body backwards, then lunged the blade swiftly into the kidneys. No sound. He helped the body to slide quietly down behind the rest of the garbage piled in the alleyway.

Yute burst into the restaurant, a little flustered and apologised profusely to Igor for his lateness whilst also thanking the manager for entertaining his 'dear friend' in his absence. Sitting down, the pretence of *joie de vivre* was still with him as he made his apologies yet again, giving his reasons in great detail about how his car was late arriving and that the driver had to explain that he was late delivering the car to him because when he had gone to collect the car from the motor pool, it had a flat tyre. Throwing himself back in his chair, he laughed and said to Igor, 'I've never known anything so tedious in all my life as being late!'

'Please, Yute, it was only a few minutes. Honestly.'

'Okay, it's forgotten as of now. After we leave here, I thought we could go straight to the dacha. Everything is there, good wine, good whisky, good food. It will take two hours or so to drive, so it is inevitable we will arrive late, but I thought perhaps a nightcap, and then as early as possible to bed, then tomorrow, we can picnic on the lake, and fish.'

'That sounds perfect to me!'

The conversation throughout dinner was small talk mostly, with Igor bleating on about his bad pay, bad apartment, bad office. Yute managed to keep smiling in the right places and he made sure all of his 'yeses' and 'nos' fell in the right place. The meal over, Yute excused himself on the pretext of making a quick phone call before he started the drive. Swiftly slipping out into the alley, Yute edged his way to the corner looking deeply into the shadows, searching for anyone or anything suspicious. The body obviously hadn't been found during their time in the restaurant, but had anyone decided to keep an eye on the car? It was important no one saw Igor leave the restaurant or saw him getting into his car. It had seemed an age since he left Igor, but looking down at his watch, it was actually only three minutes. Back inside the restaurant, coats on quickly, straight to the car, Igor's case inside, then away as quickly as possible, keeping alert for any followers.

The route out of town was easy; from this side of town there was the wide ring road, then several very long straights on different roads to the dacha.

'Make yourself comfortable during the drive, Igor. Sorry to rush you so soon after our meal, but leaving promptly tonight will make sure we will be well rested for an exciting day tomorrow.'

'I'm more than content, Yute, you do as you please.'

Yute looked across at the normally whining lump sitting by his side and thought, *There wouldn't be enough time in the world, Igor Tatlanovich, for you to grow up and play with the big boys!*

A silent car and a steady speed soon saw the outline of the forest filling the whole of the horizon, the rimmed edge of the moon placed a fringe of light across the tops of the trees. Taking a last look at the long straight they had just travelled for any flicker of lights or for anything that moved in the rear-view mirror, Yute was relieved that the windy paths through the forest would give him ample cover, should anyone start to follow them. Yute was more relaxed now as they neared the dacha; nearly time to start an hour's potential enjoyment before Igor's final demise.

'It wasn't too bad a journey, was it, Igor? We are almost there now.'

'Very nice, Yute. You drove well, and I think you picked the right time to leave town, just before the main rush home after the theatres and restaurants closed.' Pausing for a moment from his 'know-it-all' attitude and having checked his watch, he then added, 'You only took an hour and forty-five minutes.'

Yute smiled to himself in the knowledge that he was only minutes away from hearing the last irritating remark from this grabbing, conceited little man. The headlights twisted and turned as Yute floated the car through the dense wood. No matter which way the headlights pointed, never once did Igor see any sign of a house. The final right turn moved them into a corridor of heavy pines, a straight road outstretching the headlights' beams, then slowly a left turn, a slight rise in the ground, the car's beams danced around the tops of the trees, breaking over the brow of a hill and then the headlights shone across a hollow to the large, beautiful, heavily logged, dacha.

'It's beautiful, Yute, how many more are there like this?' Yute felt the avarice in his voice.

'There are dozens in this park alone. Maybe one day, this one could be yours.' The teasing tone in Yute's voice went unnoticed.

'Oh, I do hope so, but what will you do?'

Selfish, stupid idiot, was the only thought that went through Yute's mind. Their arrival at the front steps saved him from giving an answer. Yute unlocked the door. Standing aside after turning on the lights, he allowed Igor to have one last dream before the game began. Igor walked past Yute and took in the surprising vision of chandeliers and matching wall lights, the opulent leather armchairs and couches, the carpets, the pictures, the ornaments. Igor stopped at the top of the two steps from the hallway, looking down and across the enormous room stretched out before him. The door closed softly. Did Igor hear a slight swish before he was clubbed to the floor? His dreams had disappeared from his eyes before he hit the floor.

Yute sat silently waiting for the trussed-up body sitting directly in front of him to come back from the black tunnel he was in. Yute wanted to ask his questions, but he could afford to wait. He was not going to revive him with any kind of stimulant; he didn't want anything to cloud Igor's brain. Time was on Yute's side and he knew from past experience, if you didn't help the brain back to recovery but just let nature do her own thing, the brain would be more receptive to his questioning. The slower the recovery, the clearer his mind would be to work out the predicament he was now in.

Igor's eyes flickered, but he was still struggling for awareness of any kind. Yute smiled to himself as the thought, *You don't know your own strength*, ran through his mind. The waiting would have to continue a while longer.

Lanov and Mogatin's task was of no real consequence to them. They knew what they had to find out and they knew the ending. Both had decided the method should be friendly and sociable for the first part, in the hope they didn't have to exert themselves with beatings; if in their drunkenness Anton Zabiak and Uri Melentkov did give out the information they wanted to hear, the beatings could start before the final curtain for them both. Knowing they would not use the same bar night after night, they decided to take areas of the town and keep in touch with each other by mobile phone, only to be answered after the third ring. After Mogatin entered a bar, his normal procedure was to hang up his hat, take the longest route to the bar, check out the toilets on the way if possible, then order a coffee at the bar, taking a position so that the rest of the bar could be seen without him looking too conspicuous. But this time, before he had time to sit down, Mogatin heard Anton Zabiak's voice.

'Hello, are you on your own, my friend?'

'No, you bloody fool, I've got five chorus girls in my pockets!'

'So, you've enough girls of your own tonight, then?'

'Yes, my friend, I have enough to do tonight.' Mogatin turned, smiling, to shake the hand offered to him and shook it heartily.

'So, are you still working in the area, Anton?'

'Yes, Uri and I are both still here. It's quite boring really, six of us rotating around two people, sometimes four. We're off tomorrow to Paris and when we finish there, it looks like Africa again! But what about you? You're still paired with Lanov, are you?'

'Oh yes, we're like Siamese twins!'

'He's not with you tonight though?'

'No, he's paddling around somewhere…'

'Shame. We could have had a good night, all four of us. Uri's over there in the booth.'

'Well, I could try his mobile – if he's not fixed up. I know he'd enjoy it. He often talks about our last get-together.'

'Well try him then, get him to meet us here. It's as good a place as any we've found.'

Pulling his phone from his pocket, Mogatin answered, 'Yes, it looks all right, that's why I came in!'

One ring, two rings, three rings, four… Mogatin looked up. 'It's ringing, I bet the silly bugger's fallen asleep!' Five rings, then Lanov's answer came slowly as he acted out his part of the over-the-three-rings limit, 'Hello, Lanov here!'

'Dimitri… Mogatin. I was just out walking around, having a few beers and I bumped into both Anton and Uri. They've suggested we get together tonight. It's not a bad-looking bar and it's well equipped!'

Lanov, playing his part, replied, 'I don't know. I'm in my room looking at the TV and reading, that sort of thing.'

'Oh, come on out, you keep mentioning the good time we had with them!'

'I was thinking of an early night!'

'Come on, don't be such a wet blanket, Dimitri!'

'Oh, all right, but I'm not going to be out late. Where are you?'

Mogatin turned to Anton. 'He's coming – what's the name of this place and the address?'

'Café Sans Fleurs, Rue Designy.'

Repeating the address to Lanov, Mogatin continued, 'So you'll be along soon?'

'Give me at least half an hour.'

'Okay, we'll see you.' Mogatin knew his friend would be walking around the café and reconnoitring before he came in, to make sure of their escape route or if unsatisfactory, looking for an alternative venue. 'He said half an hour or thereabouts. Let me and you get started, Lanov will have to catch up!'

Both men left the bar, arms around each other's shoulders, and walked happily over to the booth to join Uri. It was nearly an hour before Lanov arrived, which immediately indicated to Mogatin that the venue was not good for their purpose, and that Lanov would most likely suggest a new venue later on in the proceedings. As he sat down in the booth with Uri and Anton, Lanov said, 'This is a nice surprise, I thought you'd both be long gone!'

'We both wish,' replied Uri. 'The bloody job we're on is a bloody bore. Six of us rotating around two people, sometimes four, is boring. Bloody boring!'

'Well, you seem to be making the most of your boredom by the looks of you!'

'You mean the booze? It's been a very long time since Anton and I have had the chance to booze, so we are definitely making the most of it, yes.'

'Good for you,' echoed Mogatin, starting to act out his role as the fool.

'Yes, good for us all!' joined in Lanov. 'When do I get a drink?'

The group shuffled the bottles around on the table and found some wine to offer to Lanov.

Igor's eyes were now wide open. Yute could see straight into them and could see the fear. Neither of them moved. Yute wanted to start the game, but first he had to mentally bear down on the *rubbish* in front of him. Yute wanted to see him collapse and beg without any further violence on his part, and make this excuse for a man feel his death inside before it actually happened, to make him have no doubt that he was going to die and that it was entirely up to him whether it was quick or slow, painful or painless. The silence was eventually broken by Yute, with one very pointed question.

'Who is your controller?'

The question was not preceded or followed by any threat. The surprise on Yuri's face could not be hidden and the reply came straight back. 'Comrade Gregori Alexei Androv.' Tears flooded into Igor's eyes as he realised that now he was going to die.

The small calibre bullet left a small hole in the centre of his forehead, with a single line of blood dripping down the bridge of his nose. Yute was completely relaxed now. The name was all he needed to know, and it confirmed what action he now had to take to protect his initial plan. However, first of all, he needed to dispose of the rubbish and get back to Moscow before anyone missed him.

The Café Sans Fleurs became fuller as the evening went on. Mogatin was playing his part as the sociable drunken fool, and Lanov the mother hen. Anton, as normal, became more morose and Uri just wanted to dance with everyone. It was Uri's dancing in and out of the groups around the bar area that started the fight which caused them to be thrown out and Lanov, having had time to reconnoitre prior to arriving at the café led the way with Mogatin playfully pushing Anton and Uri forward like a shepherd guiding his lambs to the slaughter.

The dark, narrow, echoless alleyways were plentiful. Lanov had selected a cul-de-sac. The block end wall was two and a half times a man's height. The factory windows on both sides were small metal industrial fan-light windows, one and a half times a man's height. Mogatin, knowing his partner well, knew instinctively that this was the place where Anton and Uri were going to tell and die. Taking his lead from Lanov, Mogatin took his time, continuing to play the fool. Lanov's first blow, when it came, would change the role he was playing in an instant. Lanov's hand struck the back of Anton's neck, pole-axing him to the ground. Uri, on seeing this, went forward to assist his friend, and Mogatin only put Uri off balance. It was enough to allow Lanov to turn and kick violently into Uri's body as it tumbled towards the ground.

Lanov and Mogatin stood over the bodies for a moment, then with great speed, both men were turning their victims' over onto their faces and cuffing their hands across their backs. Simultaneously, their feet were tied with a cord, cut from the knot carried as a standard accessory by each of them. When Anton and Uri came round, their bodies were placed in each corner of the cul-de-sac, their backs firmly placed into the right-angle, with their knees bent up in front of them and their arms running under their bent-up knees. The first words they heard from the men standing oven them were, 'Who is your controller?' Anton and Uri knew that the moment they gave the answer, they would both be dead. Both men were too experienced in the art of extracting information and were aware that the trussed-up position they were in, would make it difficult to get their bodies in any position to escape – the first blow shattering an ankle or a shin would make escape even more difficult. Lanov and Mogatin's history was legendary. They were both efficient during torture, but merciful at death – they were gentlemen! Both Uri and Anton realised that after the information was given, mercy would be handed out swiftly. Just one bullet to the head. The words simply flew out of Anton's mouth. 'Comrade Gregori Alexei Androv.' The name meant nothing to Lanov or Mogatin, but on impulse, Lanov asked one more question of Anton.

'What exactly are you doing here?'

'Scaring a husband and wife shitless.'

'You're what?' questioned Lanov further.

'The husband's in the military – Eurocorps – and we have been doing some arm bending. Letting them know they are working for us and Mother Russia now.'

'Mother Russia now' were the last words ever spoken by Anton Zabiak.

Mogatin whispered into Uri's ear, 'Before you say goodbye, you had better tell me this poor couple's name.'

'Nicole and Daniel Tomlevski…' uttered the trembling voice. Before he could close his eyes, the bullet entered his brain.

Chapter Twenty-Four

Ulbrecht's face lit up as Mayer sat down in front of his desk. She had asked for a meeting and, as always, she was on time, bright and efficient. After exchanging the normal pleasantries, Mayer explained her reasons for calling the meeting.

'Sir, my Russians (a phrase she used because she was the only one capable of speaking on a one to one basis) are not getting very much information for us. I have a feeling something is going on and they are a bit reluctant to talk at the moment.'

'Do you have any theories as to what this might be?' asked Ulbrecht.

'No, things are rather garbled. They all seem to be in a panic, some of my contacts have been moved off their usual tasks and placed on new projects without warning and, as it seems to them, without reason.'

'I see,' said Ulbrecht. 'Are there no ideas at all that might give us a clue?'

'None, sir, I only wish there were. The way my Russians are being moved around, we may finish up with no one willing to exchange information with us.'

'Stay with it, Mayer. Keep in touch with me at anytime you are worried.'

'Yes, sir.' As an afterthought, she added, 'I'll make contact later today and see if there is any change in the position.'

'You do that, Mayer.'

'I will. May I call back later?'

'As I've already said, feel free.'

'Sorry, sir, my mind's racing around. I'll be back, sir. Thank you!' No sooner were the words out of her mouth than she was gone.

The usually neat and tidy office of Major Robin Cadwallader was very active this morning, with investigators and policemen entering and leaving, some passing on verbal messages, some faxes, some papers. The activity was caused initially by an Inspector Gilbert Torneau, asking if anyone in Robin's army had got lost within the last twenty-four hours. The men had met when Robin first joined Eurocorps and they and their wives had become good friends over the past months. A little teasing between them was always part of their friendship. The phone call ran through Robin's head. 'No, Gilbert, I checked all of the boxes this morning. Why?'

'Well, I've got two that have fallen over rather badly and will not be getting up again!'

'What makes you think they are mine?'

'Oh, I don't necessarily, they have had all their identification removed, but their clothes were British labels, so I thought maybe they might have been tied up with your army.'

'Good thinking, but I don't think so. Are there any distinguishing marks that might help identify them along with their physical descriptions?'

'I'll send what I've got over.'

That was the start of the fast-paced activity now prevailing throughout Robin's office. After his conversation with Gilbert, Robin had immediately asked for a station check throughout Eurocorps command, for any missing personnel, AWOLs, or personnel who just hadn't been seen around for a day. Two people who normally hung around together and were both missing, was offered as another possible line of enquiry. Gilbert's report had arrived within the hour. Robin duly read the report, made some side notes and had it sent out with his comments and theories to his investigators in the field. There were several individuals who had not shown up for duty within the timescale given, but no pairs.

'The way it looks, all of our army is taking off!' His flippant remark was to a uniformed clerk, but he was rather surprised by the response he got in return.

'This one's a bit different I think, sir. If you would please take a look here, you'll notice the description is exactly the same as the descriptions we have logged for the Tomlevski case.'

'My God, you're right! Which two guys are these, out of the

six we know are active? Get me the files back as soon as you can. Did we ever get the names of our bogeymen?'

'I'll get the file up, sir.' The uniform walked out of the office.

'Thank you. As quick as you can, please,' was Robin's unnecessary reply.

Mayer entered Ernst Ulbrecht's office without waiting for her boss's usual invitation of 'Come in, Mayer,' after her usual tap on the doorframe. Coming straight up to his desk and without any formality, she announced, 'It seems a civil servant has gone missing, sir.'

'Do you have a name?'

'Yes. Igor Tatlanovich.'

'Do we know anything about him, Mayer?'

'Only that my people don't understand why there's such a flap on. It seems he's small fry. He's been passed over a few times for promotion, some of which he should have made on length of service alone!'

'It seems strange. Do we know who's pulling the strings?'

'I did ask, but it's being played like the old days evidently: directives landing on desks overnight, with the right stamps and marks, and an unreadable signature; but you can't question or disobey its message, as those that tried it in the past just suddenly disappeared. My people don't want to go along with it, but they are.'

'This is what you have been told, Mayer. Is any of it just conjecture?'

'Knowledge which has been collected over the past months, sir. We have often talked of the past.'

'Anyway, can your people come up with what this chap Igor was working on?'

'I did ask, but nothing's come through yet. I can't push too much.'

'I do understand, Mayer. Please stay with it... and keep me informed, please.'

Mayer looked at her boss as his mind left her and started to churn over the consequences of the information just received. Mayer left the office quietly.

Yute's telephone had hardly rung before he snatched it up. It was the call he had hoped for, he knew that by instinct. The confirmation came as he heard the voice ask his name.

'Yes,' was his one word reply.

'We must meet as soon as possible!'

'I don't think that will be necessary.'

'May I ask why?'

'You have been playing my plan wrongly.'

'What proof have you?'

'Igor Tatlanovich!'

'Who might that be?'

'Your man at Records. Your man with two lists... your man whom you were sweetening up to betray me and put Russia in disgrace having had yet another disastrous entry into the dollar market – vital for Russia's very existence – pushed along too fast just like Tashimov's original plan...' Yute paused for a moment, expecting some response, but as none came, he added sharply, 'Your man at Records is dead.'

'When?'

'Yesterday, Comrade Gregori Alexei Androv.'

'So, you have my name also! No matter, it is to no avail.'

'Your two help-mates in Achern gave me your name.'

'They are dead also, I presume?'

'Yesterday was my clean-up day.'

'What are you expecting me to do?'

'I want your lists and you will convince the Committee to slow the process down.'

'Is that all?'

'That's all, or else you are exposed.'

'You would have me in your power?'

'Yes, but it would be used only to keep you in check.'

'You believe in Russia so much?'

'You know that I believe she must get onto a dollar footing before she can trade competitively and I will go to any ends to see that it is achieved.'

'You will only use what you know of me in this way?'

'Yes. My reasons are simple. If you go, a new Chairman would be appointed, if not a whole new Committee, which will cause a long delay and I feel the time is right for Russia to make her first step into the twenty-first century.'

'Great words, but how do you know I will keep in line with your thinking?' I have not only got information on your dead playmates, I have many other things from Comrade Igor. His notes tell of dozens of your misdemeanours. Yes, he did have a file on you. The date of May the nineteenth should mean something to you. I found that in his files and many more. I could have you dangling for a very long time!'

'It seems I have no alternative but to comply.'

'I thought you would say that.'

'What assurances do you want from me?'

'None, other than your Committee runs the way of the original plan and when we ask for information from the system now in place in Russia, it is always open to us. After all, you will still be at the head of the Committee and when this great plan is working for all of us, you will still be at the head of the table, getting your head patted.'

'You have my word.'

'Fine. First I want the file you opened on Achern.'

'It's on its way now.'

'Unaltered?'

'As it is, now.'

'Good. Never forget, comrade, we know where the bodies are buried.' The delight on Yute's face lit up the whole room as he put the phone down.

The conversations Cadwallader had been having with some of his colleagues throughout the command automatically got out of the military arena. It was not long before the police forces locally to the camps were being asked direct questions by Cadwallader's investigators about any missing civilians they might know about.

Cadwallader's information about missing persons was coming from Southern France, Spain, Belgium and Germany. The military network was more responsive than Inspector Gilbert Torneau could have expected without opening his case to the Paris police – an 'evil' Inspector Torneau was trying to avoid. Cadwallader admired his Inspector friend and knew the dilemma it was causing, so Robin had resolved to help hold the case in the Inspector's own district.

For the past half hour or so, Cadwallader's office had been relatively quiet. The sudden ringing of the telephone brought him back into action. Picking up the phone immediately, he announced, 'Robin Cadwallader here,' into the mouthpiece.

'Aah, Robin! Gilbert here. Have you by chance any news for me?'

'Not yet, I'm afraid.'

'That's a pity. The local press have got on to it. I think Paris will take Achern, don't you?'

'It is possible, I suppose, but let us try and keep them away from you. In the military we can secure ourselves behind wire fences. Isn't there anywhere you could go to get out of the way for a day or so?'

'Non… impossible!'

Robin, feeling sorry for his friend, asked casually, 'What about jewellery?'

'Rubbish. Could have been picked up anywhere in Europe. Except for one crucifix on one of the bodies. That was obviously very expensive, but it could have been a confirmation present from the family.'

'Where did it come from? You should chase that up to find out the country of origin.'

'I am, but everything is so slow here!'

'Well my—' Before Cadwallader could finish his sentence, his friend's voice interrupted him.

'Mon Dieu! Sorry to interrupt, my friend, but I have just been given a memo. The jewellery is Russian. Most of it junk, but the crucifix is very expensive. I thought it was probably a family present, but now I'm sure.'

'Keep being sure, Gilbert. I'll do what I can from my contacts. I'll put out the information about the jewellery.'

'Merci, Robin. I will see you tonight?'

'Yes, we will be over around eight.'

'Till then. Thanks for listening and understanding.'

'Nothing to say thanks for! It's all good PR for Eurocorps. See you tonight.'

'Yes. Till then.'

No sooner was the phone placed in its cradle, than it was raised again to initiate the call telling his men about the jewellery.

Yute sat reading the file sent over by Gregori Alexei Androv, along with the list of further people who would be activated over the next two months. The under the breath utterances by Yute did not bear repeating, but the constant changing of the expressions on his face would have told anyone watching that he was getting angrier by the second. Looking at his watch, he saw it was another fifteen minutes before he should phone Lanov and Mogatin. Slowly placing everything neatly back into the file, he placed his hat on his head, put his overcoat on and left the room, preparing mentally for the game of hide and seek which was waiting to start the moment he left the front door.

It had taken only eight minutes to lose his followers and now it was a race to get to a phone box and dial out the number where Lanov should answer. The number was dialled, the passwords exchanged, and a brief, one line message was given. 'Location fourteen, six-thirty tonight. Be careful... we are active!'

Ernst Ulbrecht, having just returned from a station meeting with Chief Roth and other senior divisional heads, was satisfied with what extra financial support he had been able to obtain. His anxiety was, was he wrong to pursue such a slim chance of smashing another attempt to turn Europe into a cesspit of drugs, vice and gang-wars of such magnitude as a corrupt regime, with the weaponry to support them?

Ernst stood up and paced his office. The light tap on the doorframe calmed him, as he hoped it would be Mayer. He stood still for a moment to study her worried face, then kindly he asked her, 'What is it, Mayer? You look as if you have lost a Deutsch-mark and found a pfennig!'

'It is possibly the other way around, sir. It is uncorroborated at the moment, but Igor Tatlanovich appears to have been working with Yute Polenkovich – our ringed hand!'

'Wonderful, Mayer! Now we have some meat on the bones!'

'Yes, sir. I'll keep you informed on everything!'

'Please, Mayer. But please don't torment yourself trying to put the puzzle together too quickly. We need a few more clues yet before we can do that. We will get there!'

'I'm sure you will, sir!'

'No, we will, Mayer. Koslowski, Zimmer, Engelman – all of us together.'

'If you say so, sir. May I leave now please?'

'Yes, Mayer. Believe me – it's all of us together!'

Yute sat in the window seat watching night slowly closing in. The roadside café on the outside of town which was location fourteen, was one of his favourite dispersal points whenever he had to leave town in a hurry. The open terrain all around the straight road that passed by, made it very difficult for a tail to pick you up, or, in retrospect, if you arrived early for your meeting, should anyone want to get close to you unobserved, it was nigh on impossible.

Yute could see the car approaching and watched it slowly turn across the road onto the rough car parking area. The two men in the car were Lanov and Mogatin. Leaving the car, they walked into the café only acknowledging Yute once they were inside. Yute stayed where he was and waited for what he knew would be a subtle approach towards him. Yute watched and then it started. A map came out of Lanov's pocket. It was held up and a discussion was started about where they should turn off the road when they left the café. Moving over to get more light onto the map, Yute was jokingly brought into the conversation. The waitress walked over with the tea they had ordered and it was natural they should join Yute at his table.

'We have problems,' were Yute's first words after the waitress had left.

'They've found the bodies?' guessed Lanov.

'They have both of yours and one of mine,' replied Yute.

Keeping the tone of the conversation light, Mogatin injected the conversation with, 'Oh! You had a good day too?'

The other people in the café heard their laughter, but no one else was interested in what they assumed to be the obviously dirty stories of some kind of sales representatives.

Yute continued, 'You are both going back to Achern to survey and, I hope, salvage the situation. Your two friends were over-zealous in attaining the cooperation of Lieutenant Daniel Tomlevski and his wife, Nicole. No one should have been out in the field recruiting yet. I only had my final list a short while ago and Tomlevski's name was not on it. My illustrious Chairman, in conjunction with a civil servant named Igor Tatlanovich, worked their own list and started working on their candidates without my knowledge. That has now been stopped and I assure you, we are back in control of the game!'

'If you say so,' answered Lanov.

'I do and I assure you, we will not have any further interference.'

'Okay then, Achern it is. What are we going to do?' asked Mogatin.

'Firstly, I want full surveillance on the two victims to see if they are still under stress. What sort of a team have we been left with by Anton and Uri? Is there any suspicion from anyone about anything not quite the same as usual? I want reports from colleagues, family and friends – even the checkout girl at their supermarket.'

'The usual stuff, then. What kind of a fuss is being raised over Anton's and Uri's bodies?' asked Mogatin.

'French police are still trying to identify them,' Yute replied.

'No identification was left on them, just a bit of junk jewellery and the crucifix we left on Anton – you know, he'd always believed!' The sarcasm in Lanov's voice was not missed.

'I need to know what your opinion is of our Tomlevskis as soon as possible. When can you leave?'

'We're already packed. We'll be on our way by tonight. Have you got a new contact list for us?'

'Yes. All Moscow sequences and numbers, and two emergency numbers should you stay out of contact longer than twenty-four hours. Either of you can break the rotation of your call to me, but before the sequence of identity. You, Lanov, your prefix will be "bull", and you, Mogatin, your prefix will be "lamb". This of course, will only be operated if one of you is down.'

'Understood,' said Mogatin.

'When do we get on to your list of candidates. I prefer fresh work rather than taking over someone else's half-finished jobs,' suggested Lanov.

'I hope we will be on to my lists within two weeks,' came the reply.

'We'd best leave now then.'

'Yes!' Jovially, Yute added, 'Stay in touch,' as he handed over a brown envelope containing a copy of the Gregori Alexei Androv file, with all references to him and his Committee colleagues removed, not even permitting Lanov and Mogatin the names of their superiors.

Chapter Twenty-Five

Staring down into the street from his office on the seventh floor, Ernst Ulbrecht was not seeing anything of the scene below. If he had looked up, he would not have seen anything that rose to the skyline before him. His hand rubbed across the back of his head, telling all who knew him that their boss was in another world. The world of ifs, buts and maybes, which had made their boss a legend in his own lifetime. Any one of his many staff who had seen him over the past few days knew that his wrangling with the ifs, buts and maybes would eventually produce a logical solution which he would act on immediately. His old team of Willi Koslowski, Arnie Zimmer and Jon Engelman had been waiting on the decision for days, watching the build up going on in their boss's mind, all anxious to get on to the team.

The tiredness in Ernst's face was beginning to show, the dark rings around his eyes made him look older, but inside his head, his brain was as sharp as ever. He was, he knew within himself at this very point in time, clutching at straws but again, his hunch had told him there would be a piece of the puzzle that should fit and then the whole picture would take shape. The agitation as his right hand punched into his cupped left hand was a normal reaction for him, but this time his anger turned to prayer. 'My God, help me! I know there is something happening out there! Please, give me the facts and the ability to read them and I promise you with all my heart to help rid the world of torment and sin.' Ernst's voice as he spoke now turned conversational, all of the anguish lost. 'I'm sorry, Lord, that remark was presumptuous of me. Forgive me, but please help me to help You in any way I can.' The peace that shone through on his tired face as he turned at the soft knock of Mayer tapping on his door slowly changed to the look of a small boy who had just been caught out doing something secret.

'Sorry, Mayer… Come in, sit down… sign of old age, talking to myself again!' He stuttered the words out.

'I didn't hear you, sir.' Mayer sounded genuine and Ernst felt more comfortable now.

'Well, that's fine then. Have you got any more pieces of the puzzle, Mayer?'

'The Russians are definitely connecting Tatlanovich to Polenkovich. There are some others missing; it sounds as though they were in the field working, and someone upstairs is making a lot of my Russians unhappy.'

'But they will confirm Tatlanovich and our "ringed-hand man"?'

'Hopefully we will be faxed confirmation within the hour, sir.'

'Good, Mayer. I think I'll have to start deciding on an administrative team to help out soon!'

'There is quite a lot of paperwork, sir. I'm coping at the moment, but it's nice to know that you are thinking long term, sir.'

'It's part of my job, Mayer,' Ernst muttered. He was going back within himself – the permutations had to be worked out on the ifs, buts and maybes of the now-confirmed piece of the puzzle. Mayer whispered her goodbye and waved her long fingers as a goodbye, leaving her boss to ponder.

The oversized railway station at Achern was a dismal place, it seemed to Lanov and Mogatin as they stepped off the train. They stared all around them, taking in the grime of a past decade still hanging on to the lofty iron girders. The grime on the inset windows across the vast covered area, if cleaned would have increased the daylight spilling onto the well-trodden platforms by at least sixty per cent. Mogatin, turning to Lanov, said, 'I bet it looks romantic at night!' Both men were still laughing as they passed through the barriers onto the main concourse. The laughter continued with prompting from each of them in turn, until they got to the taxi rank and separated as each took a taxi of their own.

By prior arrangement at 1700 hours exactly, the phone in Lanov's room rang. Quickly getting around to the other side of the bed, he picked up the phone and said, 'Room twenty-one.'

'Room forty-six,' came the reply from Mogatin.

'A good hotel?' asked Lanov.

'Quite good,' replied Mogatin, who then asked, 'And yours?'

'A bit dog-eared, but okay.'

'Am I seeing you tomorrow?' asked Mogatin.

'As arranged, then we can talk about the day's work.'

'Fine. I'll be over. I've got your number!' he giggled.

'Don't you start giggling again, you fool!' Then Lanov added laughing, 'I've got your number, too!'

Ulbrecht's house was a tidy house, kept immaculately clean by his still handsome wife, whom he thought of as beautiful as the day he first met her all those years ago. When he was home at a respectable hour, he would walk with her around their immaculately-groomed garden, which stretched all around the house. He enjoyed her comments on the flowers and shrubs, not taking in one word of the Latin names, but Ingeborg liked to show off her knowledge, and as the names rolled off her lips one after another, Ernst had time to review his day. Inge knew he wasn't concentrating, but she accepted this precious time walking, sometimes hand in hand, talking, as a prelude for a pleasant evening when they sat down later side by side, being their natural selves. Tonight, she had felt Ernst was strung out from the first moment they had met at the door. She knew it would take a long time for his mood to change, but she could wait as she had many times before. Finishing their stroll, they entered the house through the French doors to the dining room, where the table was laid neatly for two and the sound of a distantly ringing telephone came through from another part of the house.

'You answer it, Ernst. It's probably for you anyway,' remarked Inge.

'I'll go for the one in the hall.'

'Don't be long, dinner's nearly ready now.'

'I won't,' Ernst called as he went through the now open door and along the passageway to the hall phone. 'Ulbrecht here, sorry to have kept you.'

'That's all right, Ernst. It's Franz here.'

'Oh… wonderful to hear from you! Are you in Hamburg?'

'No, Köln… sitting at home with a great attack of a guilty conscience about not phoning you.'

'It's wonderful to hear your voice. But why should you feel any guiltier than I do, I could have phoned you too!'

'Anyway, we're talking now. Any news for me?'

'No, nothing ever happens in Hamburg, Franz, you know that!'

'That means you don't live there any more then!'

'Well, sometimes we have a little excitement, Franz, but not too often, I'm pleased to say. What about your big city? Are you and your policemen still complaining about being overworked?' Ernst teased.

'We are, Ernst, you know we are… but your city fathers are better than our city fathers, so your boys get better cars, better offices, better canteens, better overtime pay, and you know that has always been my argument.'

'Yes, I know, Franz. But I can't help that I use it the best way I can to get the most for my men. I feel that it is an essential part of my job, but it still isn't easy. The money Roth allows me to have, he makes me beg for.'

'I know. I phoned for a family nag, I'm sorry I got up on my high horse.'

'That's okay. Anyhow, are things going better now Flora's out of hospital?'

'Yes. They say the hip replacement will make a new woman out of her and looking out of the window here, I can see she is clipping the bloody bushes as she's zimmer-framing around!'

'They're all the same, Franz, but I'm pleased to hear the operation has been successful. I'll tell Inge, maybe we can arrange to get down to see you both.'

'That would be great. Try and fix it up; maybe we could get a round of golf in!'

'Or a few beers! Anyhow, what else have you got going on down there?'

'The usual really. Got one murder – going through the process of bringing the blighter to trial, a couple of rapes, house burglaries by the score, the same as you, I expect… although there is one thing that's a little different. It appears over at Achern they've found two unidentified bodies. The local gendarmerie are asking the military if they have lost anyone and that young British provost chap you met with me last time, has sent out a memo requesting a search through missing persons.'

'Why does he seem to have such an interest, your British provost man?'

'I think he genuinely wants his Eurocorps to be accepted by all civil police around the area of his camps and it's good PR for the military to be accepted and work together with us, whenever it is possible.'

'I've heard nothing about his memos, Franz.'

'Hamburg isn't one of the towns his units are near to.'

'Oh I see,' said Ernst contemplatively.

'See, you boys in the super big towns don't get to know everything!' Franz teased.

'What other questions has he asked, Franz?'

'Come off it, Ernst, don't get one of your hunches just because there are some unclaimed bodies lying around!'

'Well, we have loose ends up here as well and there might be a connection.'

'Ernst, don't stretch your imagination too far, please!'

'Humour me, Franz. Well, what other things has your "Brit" asked, or told you?'

'Not a lot, really. Just have we got any missing persons? He gave me a very thorough description, then came back with some information about some jewellery being either cheap Russian stuff or cheap European stuff, and there was a crucifix, probably a present, which was very expensive and definitely Russian... I'd need to see the memos to refresh my memory.'

'That Russian bit might interest me a little. Is there any chance you could send me a faxed copy when you get back to the office?'

'If I must, I suppose I can.'

'Please, Franz, we have some Russians running around up here and our contacts inside Russia keep asking us questions. I may be able to help your friend.'

Knowing his friend as well as he did, Franz knew it would be pointless to refuse, and said, 'Whatever I've got, you'll have a copy tomorrow, Ernst.'

'Thank you, Franz. Now, I'll make certain the girls are in touch and arrange something. Thanks for your call, love to you both. Bless you.' Franz was not particularly surprised at the abrupt ending of their phone call. He knew his friend well, and with the piece of information he had just given him, Franz imagined that Ernst Ulbrecht would not rest until he had assured himself that the information either would, or would not, fit into his puzzle!

No sooner had the phone gone dead from the call he had just had with his friend, than Ernst was re-dialling. Inge looked on, waiting to hear the news from Ernst, but she knew now was not the time to ask. Perhaps when they were in bed later that night, he might get around to telling her about his conversation with Franz. The impatience on Ernst's face told her it would be a long time before the news would get to her, so with a wave of her hand, she left just as Ernst said, 'Ah! Mayer, you're there... our friends Mogatin and Lanov... where are they now?'

'Out of Russia, so my people think.' The surprise at the abruptness of the question did not show in her voice, but on her face you could read that her mind was already wondering what the next question would be.

'Do we know where?'

'No, sir.'

'Well, we need to know, Mayer.'

'Yes, sir.'

'We also need to know if Mogatin and Lanov have been any-where near Achern. Tomorrow we will receive descriptions of some Russian jewellery. Let your people have the information and ask where it was made, what part of Russia et cetera. Try and find out who bought it and for whom.'

'Is that all, sir?'

'Yes, thank you. As quickly as you can, please!'

'It's Sunday, sir. It will have to wait until tomorrow, sir!'

'It's Sunday? Oh, I'm sorry! I shouldn't have phoned you at home... I'm sorry, you must be cooking or something. I'm sorry... please excuse me!' The panic in Ernst's voice was obvious.

As Mayer listened to his apology, she could picture his

'naughty schoolboy' look as she replied, 'It's no bother, sir. It was a nice break from my housework!'

Lanov and Mogatin met as arranged in the late afternoon. Mogatin had arrived first and had been making notes in his notebook when Lanov arrived. Both men sat side by side in silence after exchanging handshakes. The casualness in which their meeting took place and the contentment at just being together without speaking made them look like one of the crowd in the working-men's bar which they intended to use as their meeting place. When they had made contact with the other members of Uri and Anton's team and the young lieutenant and his wife, there would be other places, but they had decided between them, that here they could sit in obscurity. Looking across at all of the others crowding into the bar, no one wanted to be recognised.

'What kind of a day have you had?' Lanov asked.

'I've met my two of Anton and Uri's team. They were no trouble to find or bring around to my way of thinking!'

'Good. My two bastards ran me ragged. They didn't spot me, but they split up and went separate ways, I followed one – he's a useless git – didn't know I was there and he visits whore houses like a bloody tourist! He eventually met up with his mate, who I assume was shadowing our lieutenant, his wife, or both!' said Lanov.

'Did you make your mark with them?' asked Mogatin.

'Sure, they know they will work as a pair, not one trying to cover for the other.'

'Did they have the Lieutenant and his wife in view?'

'Yes,' replied Lanov. 'Both. The excuse for only one following was that today is the day they always leave the base together and go shopping and have lunch together.'

'You explained to the idiots that they could have split up and we could have lost valuable visual information?'

'Yes, they won't go their separate ways again, other than if their targets split up.'

'Good. So, this shouldn't be too difficult an assignment?'

'Not unless we make it so.' The tone in Lanov's voice caused Mogatin to ask what was worrying his friend. 'I can't be happy when we are both doing the work of a bloody tea boy.'

'Don't be daft. The important bit will come when we twist our lady and her lieutenant into the mould we want them to fit.'

'I know, you're right, that's where our skills lie, but why do we have to watch four bloody amateurs making what could possibly be a total balls-up?' The sarcasm in Lanov's voice could be cut with a knife.

'Because Yute, our beloved Marshall, wants us to do it this way.'

'Yes, we both got his message, which sold us on going along with this scheme and what we were promised, with regards to only being answerable to him and no one else... that's the reason we're here, checking on plebs who have cocked up, making dead bodies, and we are still having to use the bloody plebs.' Lanov paused for a moment then added forcefully, 'We are starting a job in the middle again, just like bloody Hamburg, and it doesn't sit well with me.'

'Lanov, it did start wrongly, but our beloved Marshall, as you call him, has got it under control now, and this little jaunt down here will soon be over and we will be the stars of the future!' The jovial way in which Mogatin ended his reply did not please Lanov.

'Do you believe that, Mogatin?'

'Well, yes. I believe in Yute and you, and I see no reason for things not going according to the future plans Yute has in store for us.'

'I hope you're right, my friend, but we ought to think of an escape plan sometime and this time, it needs to be to the other side of the world!'

'Don't be a pessimist, Lanov! Let's just get this bit over and then we can start working on the big picture.'

'All right, but think about escape. I'd hate to leave without you.'

'Are you that serious?'

'I was right to suggest one for Hamburg, I've got the same gut feeling now...'

'Okay. We will think about a plan and then sit together and work it out, if that's what you want.'

'I do, for both our sakes. Now let's work out a pattern for

holding this little part of the scheme together.'

'Well. What I would like to do is to make contact with our lieutenant and his wife. They need to know that Anton and Uri are dead and that they now have two nice controllers like us. We needn't tell them we killed their nasty controllers until a later date, should they ever get out of line. But with our kindly ways, we shouldn't ever have to tell them, should we?'

'No, we shouldn't. Shall we call on them tomorrow evening, then?'

'Why not. Perhaps they will invite us in for coffee!'

'I think they just might, they seemed like nice people, well-mannered and kind!'

'And of course, trusting!'

Both men laughed at the sick humour they were enjoying. They then stood up and shook hands, the smiles still on their faces and each of them left the bar without being noticed, looking forward to their next meeting.

Robin Cadwallader sat quietly in his tidy office, agitation registering on his face. Investigations in connection with the dead bodies had come to a halt. Information was slow in coming back from the enquiries he and his men had been making over the past few days. He knew they could do no more than wait. In his mind, he felt sure the dead men were working together, possibly part of a team. The jewellery, being of Russian origin, worried him a little, but he had no answers in his head as to why. He only knew that several times over the past few hours, he felt that Russians were involved.

Ernst Ulbrecht had never been so pleased to see anyone as he was to see Mayer sitting in front of his desk. The news was exciting, but at the moment, the names of the people he had in front of him from her Russian friends meant nothing, but if Lanov or Mogatin had been within twenty kilometres of where the bodies were found, maybe Commander Roth would extend his team. Mayer was tired and since his conversation with her on Sunday, he knew she had probably come back into the office straightaway and had worked out her rotation chart for the order of her calls for Monday with a list of questions for each contact she would make, along with a few sheets of paper columned off to enter name, date, time and also the place where any name mentioned was supposed to be.

'This is good news indeed, Mayer!' Ernst broke the silence. 'If only we can connect Lanov and Mogatin to these names, it could lead somewhere.'

'I hope it does, sir.'

'Thank you. We really do need a connection, otherwise we are going to sit here with egg on our faces, having done all this overtime!'

'I'm sure your fairy godmother will come through, sir!' Then she added warmly, 'They know how much they all owe you and Commander Roth – your "godmother" will always fight for you.'

'You're right, but that doesn't make it any easier for me to keep going to friends with the begging bowl, does it?'

'I suppose not, sir, but you have known the system for a long time. Its mysteries are unfathomable as far as I am concerned, but I can see how a man of pride would have to go cap-in-hand.'

'You're learning, Mayer, aren't you? Maybe in years to come, policing throughout the world will be financed as it should be and when you get into a position of some power, you won't be plagued with being half policeman and half juggler of figures!'

'Should that day come, sir, I hope you're right!'

The phone rang sharply and cut into their philosophical discussion. 'Ulbrecht heir!' There was a slight pause then, 'Yes, she is here…' Handing the phone over to Mayer, Ernst stood up and offered his seat to her and indicated to the empty pad and pen, ready for her use.

'Hello, who is this, please?'

'Rudi.'

Excitedly, she signalled to Ernst to pick up the extension and listen, while she thanked Rudi for calling and stalled by asking about the weather as Ernst got himself ready to listen in.

'Where are you phoning from, Rudi?'

'A phone booth… I have plenty of coins.'

'I'll call you back if you like?'

'No, please… Lanov and Mogatin travelled through Portugal,

Spain, Germany, Switzerland, Italy, and northern and southern France on their way out and back to Russia. The French bit was definitely on the way back. Two associates from the past were met there: Anton Zabiak and Uri Melentkov. They are now missing, the ones who have caused us so many problems. I don't know what the assignment was that they were on, but I'm living through the wake of the waves that are washing through Moscow.

'You must be exhausted, Rudi. What do your bosses feel has happened to these men?'

'Well, they believe them now to be dead. It has gone quiet. Things usually go this way when they get the news they want, or don't want. The next thing is to wait and see where they will place the blame and who will pay!'

'Oh, Rudi, you sound so worried, what can you do?'

'Nothing. I am not high enough up the echelons to be of any real danger to them, nor have I been included in any of the collation of the information coming in. I have only been researching with a very small amount of menial investigation, but I know that someone somewhere will pay dearly for rocking the boat.'

'You take care of yourself, Rudi. We will speak again very soon.'

'I'll call again soon. Thank you for all of your help. Goodbye!'

The long warm goodbye did not show the excitement she felt about the news or the anxiousness which was charging through her, to speak to her boss. The soft, 'I'll wait for your call, please make it soon,' from Rudi was only just heard as Mayer's phone was placed lightly down. Ernst heard all the emotion of love in those lost words; the warmth and emotion made him happy for both of them. He understood the pain the man was feeling and how unaware Mayer was of her own feelings. Although the conversation was in Russian, he was anxious to know exactly what was said.

'Mayer, that man is in love with you!'

Mayer blushed. The flush ran across her cheeks like fire, and ran around the edge of her ears and burnt her ear lobes.

'Sir! We have never even met!'

'But you have spoken often and you both have an easy understanding of each other.'

'Sir, that means nothing. We haven't even exchanged photographs!'

Teasingly, like a father figure can, he said, 'But you have been talking about doing so, haven't you?'

'Well yes, but it was good PR for the department!'

'I wish you both well, Mayer. He sounds a nice, romantic man!'

The answer came quickly back. 'He is, sir.'

'Shall we get on? What exactly did he say?'

Mayer translated the conversation word for word. As she did so, she watched her boss get more and more excited as his mind put the pieces of the puzzle together in his head, and started to let in thoughts from the 'what if?' side of his mind.

'…Well that's the whole conversation, sir,' finished Mayer.

'Do you realise, Mayer, if we can link Lanov and Mogatin to these other two, we may have stumbled onto something.'

Joc Latimer was sitting in his office back at Langley, working on reports from Europe regarding computer crimes. It was interesting enough as a subject, but it was a struggle for him to keep up with the new directive that all government employees were to be computer literate; because of his workload, it had been impossible for him to attend every class of instruction, so armed with the basic skills learnt from the initial classes, he had decided he would make himself more adept by setting himself tasks, and played questions and answers with the new technology. Although his aptitude came slowly, he was beginning to understand how so many man hours could be saved and whatever he searched for, seemed to come up on his screen almost immediately. The depth and scope of the Langley computers was getting to the stage of amazing him and dragging him into new ways. Connecting into the European information spread at Langley gave Joc wide flashes of in-depth information, easy access whenever he wished, day or night. Information that as a trained investigator, he could not get from CNN or CBNC. His fingers pushed a key unintentionally and, after seconds, onto his screen moved a police report from

Hamburg, regarding an unidentified body being found at the bottom of a dry dock after it had been drained.

Lying back in his chair, he thought of his friend Ernst Ulbrecht and instinctively lifted his phone and dialled the number. One, two rings, the lifting of the receiver and then, 'Ulbrecht heir…'

'Latimer here!' the tease continued.

'Joc, you make me feel guilty. I should have rung you – all of the things you have done for me – I'm sorry.'

'Don't worry about it! You seem to be busy over there still… just saw you on my screen – something about a body in a dry dock?'

'A matrimonial. The best friend of the husband got caught playing around with his wife. The husband strangled him and dropped him in the dock. It's all wrapped up.'

'So, you do get some easy ones, then?'

'Oh sure, quite often. Local crime in a big port town is always with us, I'm sorry to say.'

'And that wall coming down didn't help you one bit, I'll bet.'

'You're right. We seem to be coping, but the first wave of crime that literally swamped us, scared us half to death!'

'Are you having any more problems from that direction?'

'Things are not too bad, we have learnt to watch and wait.'

'Anything on that I can help with?'

'No, that last lot of help on the "ringed-hand man" cleared up a lot of things for us. It's given us several leads and names and we have them under surveillance. All thanks to you and your friend, Joe Lomax.'

'Well, we're always here if you need us, I'll phone again soon. My regards and good luck!'

The phone went dead in Ernst's ear. He leant back in his well-worn chair and wished he had mentioned where they may be going with the 'ringed-hand man', Lanov and Mogatin, plus the two dead bodies found on military land.

It seemed only minutes since Mayer had left his office, but here she was again, sitting upright in the chair opposite. Ernst had beckoned her in and signalled for her to wait a moment while he finished off writing a report. The time seemed endless to Mayer as she held back the information she was bursting to pass on, but she had to wait.

No sooner had her boss lifted his pen from the paper and lifted his head towards her, that she spoke. 'They have criminal records, photographs of both Anton Zabiak and Uri Melentkov and medical records from the prison hospitals. They will be coming very soon, sir!'

'Well done, Mayer! Will you let me know the moment it all arrives?'

'Sir!' The abruptness of her response forced Ernst to lift his head up again from his paperwork. 'I'm sorry, Mayer, was there something else?'

'Yes, sir. Rudi, my Russian "boyfriend" as you call him, has started intimating about some kind of agreement between his office and ours. He wants to come over.'

'Why are you so upset, Mayer? You know this sort of thing goes on all the time.'

'I am surprised at Rudi. I thought it was a very personal thing between us, but he's trying to use me!'

'Mayer, we must keep our Russians cultivated. We can't afford to lose any single one of them. I know you may feel used, but remember you have said before that they want to get over to the West and you thought nothing of it until now. May I suggest you think again about your being used. We are using them – especially Rudi. He's in love with you, he wants to be with you. Even though you have never met, he's been dreaming of you night after night. Think of it that today was the day he decided he wants to be with you always!'

Mayer stood up in front of Ernst, a little tear appearing in the corner of her eye. With a sob in her voice, she replied, 'Do you really think it can be like that… sir?'

'I do, Mayer. I really do. Now let's get on with some work, shall we?'

The sniffing sigh was cut short as she responded, 'Yes, sir.'

Robin Cadwallader sat upright in his wooden armed office chair, aware of everything going on around him. Investigators passing through into the incident room which had been set up in the office next to his, which had been used for meetings, prior to today. It was disturbing his thoughts as he wrangled with the problems of two deaths on military ground. Although his friend, Inspector Torneau had asked if there were any soldiers gone AWOL, at first Robin thought the investigation of all his camps would last maybe a day or two at the most, but a nil result on any missing personnel, the junk Russian jewellery, a gold crucifix, plus finding no identification on either body, roused his interest enough to set a full investigation in tandem with the French police. His aim was to assist his friend Gilbert and keep the investigation local to the district, keeping the glory boys from Paris away. The search for missing persons in Germany, France, Spain and Belgium had shown up hundreds of people. In view of this, Robin had decided to make use of the meeting room, furnish it with incident boards and place a team of investigators to plot and cross-plot every occurrence.

Inspector Franz Gelder's office was quiet and still. It was stuffy, with no natural daylight which made it seem claustrophobic. Somehow today, it seemed there was no crime in Köln. His day so far, had consisted of one minor meeting of fifteen minutes, a second meeting with his detectives, then he had studied every memo circulated to him twice, and took three outside phone calls, one of which was from his wife. Like his old friend Ernst, he had to be doing something. He fidgeted like Ernst, he paced the room like Ernst, he rubbed the back of his neck like Ernst, but although he was a fine policeman and had had many successes, his world was smaller than Ernst's. He was a good investigator, but he needed the pieces to make the puzzle work. Unlike Ernst, who used his imagination and the 'if' factor, which always made the cases much larger and gave a bigger return to the Town Fathers of Hamburg, Franz had often wondered over the years, why he had never been blessed with the flair Ernst had, but he had reckoned that his life was better than Ernst's without the driving force his friend had. Franz was not jealous of his friend's success now, but there had been times when they were younger that Franz had cried out with frustration in the night, 'Why does he have to be so successful and not me?'

The phone rang once, twice, three times before Franz, immersed in his thoughts, finally heard it and picked up the receiver. 'Hello, Franz Gelder…'

'I thought you had gone home already, Franz!'

'Hello, Ernst! Strangely enough, I was just reminiscing about the old days. It took me a while to get my head back in gear!'

'I wish I could spend my days doing that!'

Franz's voice changed to a soft and gentle tone. 'You know you couldn't do that, Ernst. You're not made like that, you have to keep punching the bag, but we can't all be the same you know!'

'I suppose not, but it's too late to change now.'

'I suppose it is, Ernst, but you should slow up a bit. Anyway, my friend, have you got a date for when we can all meet up?'

Ernst's flustered reply told Franz that in all probability, he had forgotten to mention it to Inge yet.

'Oh well, I guess this is a surprise call then. What can I do for you, Ernst?'

'Your Brit… would you mind if I spoke to him? It seems he has your respect, so he must be good at his job and I want to ask him a few questions to get something off my mind that's been gnawing at me.'

'Another of your hunches, Ernst?'

'Well, yes, Franz. But it might help him and the French to clear up a portion of their mystery.'

'And then the circles get larger and larger from the stone you have thrown in the pond.'

'Yes, that could be, Franz, but it would all be for a better world.'

'I'd never doubt you, Ernst, never.'

'Thank you, Franz. Could you let me have his number then?'

Franz asked Ernst to hold the line a moment whilst he found it and then passed on Robin Cadwallader's direct line number.

'Thanks again, Franz. I'll let you know what happens after I've spoken to him and I will speak to Inge, I promise!'

Before Franz had the chance to say, 'Let the wives sort it out,' Ernst had rung off.

Chapter Twenty-Six

Robin Cadwallader's office was turning into a passageway. The idea of turning the meeting room into an office was a good idea, but a very inconvenient one. The two men sitting at the desk in front of him were scruffy and untidy, but their street credibility relied on it. Robin did not like exposing his men to undercover work, but in these modern times, he knew that there was little alternative but use to every alternative available to fight crime. The only thing Robin promised the few 'special men' as he called them, was that they would get full support from everyone in his office including himself. If things got too dicey, they would be called in to safety and everything handed over to the civilian authorities.

Robin's first question after having asked if they had any problems was, 'You're absolutely sure the men you reported on here are new to our couple?'

'Positive, sir. They are different, they're pros – well trained, no habits or twitchiness, they are as smooth as silk, they work well together. I can only emphasise the word "pro".'

'But you don't have any names for them?'

'No, not yet, but we will get them. The people they seem to be ordering around will let something slip and two of our lads drink in the same bar, so it shouldn't take too long.'

'Let me know as soon as you have anything to report and good work in picking these two up – keep your eyes on them, won't you?'

'Yes, sir, no problem. We'll get on then, sir?'

'Thank you, yes, there's nothing else I need that I can think of.'

The two men ambled out of the office, slipping into their street characters. The marching and stamping of feet seemed a long time ago in their clean-living past. The phone rang on Robin's desk. Lifting it to his ear, he answered it in his own way.

'Robin Cadwallader…'

'Hello, my name is Ernst Ulbrecht. I am Inspector of Police in Hamburg.'

'I have heard of you, sir. I've greatly admired your work since I have been in Germany.'

'Thank you, Major. If I may, I would like to have a little talk with you on the phone. When would it be convenient to call back? I will need your undivided attention.'

'Well, I was just going over to the mess for lunch, so now is a good time. The office is quiet. You know what the military is like, it runs on a timetable when it's in barracks!'

'Yes. Like so many things in civilian life now, everyone is… how do you say it? A clock-watcher?'

'There's only a few out of the mass of people in the world who understand the word "flexible"!'

The chuckle in Ernst's voice at the end of his sentence had warmed Robin to this man. 'Sir, instead of calling me "Major" would you call me Robin? It is my Christian name and it's far more friendly.'

'Thank you, Robin, my name is Ernst.'

'Ernst. Well then, shall we begin our little talk?'

'Please. You have been making enquiries about two unidentified dead bodies. The French have asked if you have anyone missing from the army and you are searching around for clues, I understand.'

'Basically, yes. There were a few bits of cheap jewellery and one expensive crucifix, all Russian made, but other than that, no identification whatsoever.'

'As I understood from your memos. I think I can give you the names of your two mystery men, well I hope so, anyway.'

'Please, Ernst, it would save a lot of time and make a French friend of mine very happy!'

'Why would it make your French friend happy?'

'He's an Inspector of Police local to here, and he is trying to solve the mystery before the big boys from Paris come swarming all over his district.'

'Oh, I see.'

'Yes, he deserves to be helped. He is a good investigator and should be left alone to solve his own district's crimes.'

'I agree with you, Robin. Now, have your bodies got any distinguishing marks?'

'Well yes, actually, they both have scars. The smaller one of the two has a long appendix scar, quite recent, possibly no more than two years ago. The larger man has an appendix scar also, but much smaller – possibly his operation took place in the West. The larger man also has a scar probably caused by a heavy blow to the head at some time in the past, and the smaller man had a broken little finger on his right hand.'

'I don't have the appendix scar recorded on the big man's health records, but the head scar is. Can you describe it for me?'

'Top of the cranium, starting inside the hairline about 10 cm in, I would say. A very jagged line for a further 10 cm across from left to right of the centre of his head, with what looks like a "tick" on the end of the main scar, pointing towards the crown, about 5 cm long.'

'Okay, your two names are Anton Zabiak and Uri Melentkov. Both unsavoury characters, both have worked for the KGB and since the wall came down, they have been freelancing a bit, but I would guess they had powerful masters in Russia.'

'How do you know all this, Ernst?'

'We've been working on something else. When the Russian contacts we were using started running around panicking like lunatics, we found out that two men had been gunned down and the man we were after had caused a lot of waves within top management and now there has been a coup in the top echelons. Two other men we have been keeping tabs on, have left Russia and are working in Germany at this moment. We are watching their every move, but we cannot work out what they are up to just yet.'

'How do my two dead bodies fit in?'

'I think they got in the way of a man we know. His full title is Marshall Yute Polenkovich. He masterminded the biggest drugs and arms trade-off in the world so far, along with another Russian, Gregor Tashimov…'

'In Hamburg…?' Robin interrupted.

'Yes, in Ham—'

Robin cut in again, 'You mean to tell me that you have been working on that case all this time?'

'Yes. We had some loose ends to tie up and slowly we are working it all out.'

'Would you let me have a copy of your medical reports so that I can send them to the French?'

'Certainly. It will be my pleasure, as it has been talking to you.'

'Well, thank you for talking to me. I would like to meet up with you some time, if we can arrange it?'

'I would like that also. Perhaps when my case is over, I can get together with you, another chap who has helped me no end, an American called Joc Latimer, a chap called Manuel Vargas, he's Portuguese, and your Frenchman. It would make for a nice evening, I think. Oh, and there's my friend, Franz Gelder, who gave me your number in the first place.'

'That's a great way to work, Ernst. That's what police work is all about, international cooperation – it's the only way forward these days.'

'The more cooperation the better, Robin. We must get better at it if we want to succeed. Some of the police forces in the European alliance are still protecting their information very jealously. When you reason it out overall, very little is exchanged between them, considering the vast amount of misdemeanours happening in any one day.'

'Yes, I fully agree with you, Ernst. That's why I stretch my limits as far as the army allows me to, with all the civilian forces and defence units that I can. In fact it's because of that we're talking now. I don't mean that in a cocky way, Ernst, but if Europe is to be protected, somehow we all must learn to speak to each other without prejudice to our nations.'

'I would hate to be young again with all the problems and speed with which you have to react, but, thank goodness there are people like you, Robin! My only problem is, are there enough of us to give ourselves a chance of winning this terrible battle?'

'We are getting better, I promise you, Ernst!'

'Good! What are you working on now – anything interesting?'

'I'm not sure really. It's mostly surveillance work, but the Adjutant here was a little worried about one of his new officers.

Evidently there was a sudden change in his attitude almost from the moment he arrived at his depot. There have been some approaches made to both himself and his wife by certain undesirables and we are asking the local civilian police for identity checks, but nothing seems to be forthcoming so far. We can't force the issue, so we sit and wait. I have put my own men out there to keep an eye on things, but that's unofficial. Tomlevski and his wife – I'm sorry, that's the name of the officer who has just joined the depot – although they have not been approached by any of the new watchers, we feel that something may happen, so we keep watching the watchers!'

'Tedious, very tedious! Have there been any changes in the techniques of the followers – is each follower working the same shift?'

'Identical day by day. Until four days ago, things were very haphazard. Come to think of it now, it was just after the two dead bodies turned up. My God! Why didn't I spot that before? I'm sorry to ramble on like this, Ernst, but what if they are connected?'

'Simple! We would be working very closely together!'

'That would be a great experience for me. Look, I'd better circulate your descriptions and pictures to my team to see if either of these men were ever on the Tomlevski surveillance team.'

'The response could be interesting!'

'I'll attend to it straightaway after you fax it all through. I'll let you know what happens.'

'Would you let me have descriptions of the new people watching your officer, Robin?'

'Of course, but they wouldn't be connected with the dead bodies if they've only just arrived, surely?'

'I suppose not, but all information is good information.'

'Very true, Ernst. Anything I can find out, I shall let you know.'

'Thank you, Robin. Until then.'

'Thank you, Ernst, on behalf of myself and my French Inspector friend – Gilbert Torneau.'

'We are exchanging a lot of names today, Robin – I hope we can always do this!'

'Me too, Ernst. It really is the only way forward!'

After finishing his conversation with Ernst, Robin made contact with all his investigators, asking them to come in when relieved of duty so he could get the identity of the two dead men corroborated as being part of the surveillance team put on to the Tomlevskis. The first team he spoke to, he had managed to catch before they left to relieve the team out in the field. Both investigators, on reading the medical reports and looking at the poor quality, faxed copies of the photographs of the dead men's faces were certain. It was definitely Anton Zabiak and Uri Melentkov. Robin's first instinct was to phone Ernst back straight away, but in his hurried attempt to glean favour, he suddenly remembered Ernst's words – 'All information is good information' and 'Has there been any change in the watchers' team?' The two investigators he had just seen had not noticed any change in the opposition's behaviour during yesterday's shift.

Sitting now waiting for his team to check in with him as he had ordered, the time dragged. His active mind trawled through the 'if' factors. He was also worried when his long-term thoughts took shape in his mind – the possible coercion of his soldiers by a criminal element whose aims and motives they had yet to discover. When his next team of investigators returned, they had worrying news. Why would they have brought in (whoever they were) two replacements for the two dead men? Why were the Tomlevskis so important to them?

Robin made a few pencilled notes before picking up the phone to speak to his new friend, Ernst. No sooner had the phone rang than it was answered briskly. 'Ulbrecht heir!'

'Sorry to trouble you so soon, Ernst, but it's information I thought you should have right away – oh, sorry, I should have said – it's Robin Cadwallader here!'

'I guessed that, Robin. What can you tell me?'

'My teams are certain that the identities of the dead men are the same as you have supplied us with. There is one more development we have picked up on… two new trackers, who are good, but they are now on our books. One is much larger than the other, both men are in dark-coloured suits. The larger man wears a black trilby hat, has a large gold-link bracelet loosely filling his left wrist, no visual facial scars, dark trimmed hair and is clean shaven. The face is square jawed, with high podgy cheekbones, sunken eyes, with a deep forehead. The smaller man has no hat, no visible jewellery except a plain gold wedding band, same square jaw, blue eyes, very alert and darting, a flattened nose, wide forehead. I need more time to get better descriptions, Ernst, but we are sure these two are the replacements for the dead men.'

'I was hoping for something like this, although it is going to make a lot of problems for you.'

'What do you mean, Ernst?'

'I am fairly certain I know the men you have described. They were here in Hamburg as organisers for the Organisatiya. They managed to get away from us after the last shindig, along with a "ring-handed man". He wears a very distinctive ring. We had a line on your two for several weeks until something disturbed the top brass in Moscow. We had very little knowledge of them, but it seems your two guys have been tied in with our "ringed-hand man", who is a full Marshall in the Russian Army and they have been meeting up in various parts of Europe as well as in Russia.'

'Christ, Ernst, this is getting serious!'

'Well, let's say your memo started my brain racing to see if they would tie in with anything we were doing up here, for which I thank you.'

'What are their names, do we know?'

'For sure we do. The bigger man is Mogatin. We haven't been able to get a Christian name for him, but the other one is Dimitri Lanov.'

'Would it be presumptuous of me to ask for a copy of the case notes and anything you may have on the two names you have just given me?'

'Certainly. There was an awful lot of paperwork – I'll send you the press coverage. I reckon you can work out what police work and organisation was needed to achieve it.'

'Thank you for your confidence. I'll do my best!'

'I know you will, Robin. Let's just hope we can get enough warning to see what they are planning, so we can capture all of them this time!'

'We have a slight advantage at the moment, Ernst – they don't know that we are watching them, and the fact that the Tomlevskis are new postings to us from a totally different army, is surely a good sign?'

'I hope you're right, Robin, but are there things going on in other areas that we don't know about? What is Tomlevski's connection with them? How was the connection made?'

You're right, Ernst, I think we ought to meet to outline some sort of strategy and, of course, we work differently in the military, so I'll probably have to take some leave so that wires don't get crossed.'

'It would help if we didn't have any confusion. When do you think you could get here?'

'It would take a few days to get my leave granted, tie up my loose ends and brief my men on what I want done while I'm away...'

'As quickly as you can, Robin...' Robin noticed the little pleading in Ernst's voice and decided he would bend the rules in any way he could to help his new friend.

The newspaper clippings and the identity reports on Mogatin and Lanov arrived within an hour of Robin finishing his conversation with Ernst. Having read through everything, he felt that there was a lot more he should know about Ernst Ulbrecht, Chief Inspector of Police in Hamburg. Reading the twenty-four clippings for a second time, he was searching for any reference to this man who had stopped a ten billion dollar heist. There were none, but one passage in one of the clippings intrigued him: 'Inspector Ulbrecht's attention to detail together with his crystal ball, brought this case to a close.'

Leaning back in his wooden-backed chair, Robin muttered to himself, 'Crystal ball be blowed! It's anticipation... read everything, remember everything and tie them together before anything can happen... *anticipation!*'

The phone rang. Robin reached to pick it up. 'Robin Cadwallader...' he answered.

The soft, cultured voice of Major Roche replied, 'Robin, your leave's approved. When would you like it to start?'

'From tomorrow, André, if that's all right?'

'Well, yes, but will you come and see me before you go?'

'Yes. Is there a problem?'

'No, not at all, just a bit of detail to sort out. Whenever you like, just drop in.'

'Right now would suit me, sir.'

'Okay, now then!'

During the few minutes it took to reach the Adjutant's office, Robin's mind raced through his memory bank and concluded that no Adjutant had ever previously asked to see him prior to his taking some leave, and the thin line about 'just a bit of detail' did not ring true somehow. The door of the Adjutant's office was in view. Ten more steps, knock, knock, and then the reply, 'Come in!'

The Adjutant stood up to shake hands. 'You were quick, Robin!'

'I didn't run, sir.'

'I'm sure you didn't!' Major Roche smiled, then asked Robin to sit down. 'Have you got any personal problems I should know about, Robin?'

The question caught Robin unawares for a fleeting second, but then Robin replied convincingly, 'No, sir!'

'Good, good. It's just that your request for leave was rather sudden, that's all. I thought there might be something wrong. Where can I get in touch with you should the need arise?'

Again, Robin was caught a little off-guard. 'Erm... Hamburg. I'm going to see a friend for a few days. I haven't got a contact point yet. I'll call you with a telephone number if you feel it's necessary.'

'Please. For such a small detachment, there seems to be an enormous amount of things going on in your section at the moment...'

Robin was well aware that André Roche knew everything that went on around his army and that he considered Robin, as his Provost, to be his first line of defence against all manner of intangibles, but surely, Robin thought, he hasn't got wind of what I'm actually doing?

'André, may I ask for your indulgence? I would be grateful for your trust in me, knowing I would do nothing to hinder the security of your army. My leave will be spent gaining information, with a view to making its position more secure in the tasks that it has undertaken in its charter.'

'Very well, thank you. Whatever it may be, will stay with me alone. Thank you for coming over… see you on your return.'

Robin stood up and leant over to shake his Adjutant's hand in thanks. Their strong hands met across the desk. 'André, I'll tell you everything when I get back. I'll keep nothing from you, I promise. In fact, I have a feeling I may have to ask you to compromise yourself on the Corps' behalf.'

'You make it sound most intriguing, Robin. I look forward to your return.'

Standing back from the Adjutant's desk, Robin stood to attention, saluted and said, 'Thank you, sir. Until my return then!'

Robin's walk back to his office was slower. His mind kept wondering. How much did the Adjutant really know about the deployment of his men which Robin had instigated recently?

The green and white police car stood waiting to take Robin to meet Ernst Ulbrecht. The driver stood tall outside of the car when he saw Robin approaching across the airport arrival lounge, escorted by the light beige-green uniformed policeman who had met him at the baggage carousel. He pulled himself to attention, his hand going to the passenger door to open it, to allow Robin to enter the car unimpeded. The journey into the city of Hamburg was pretty much the same as the journey into any major city from any airport, but the city itself, with the blending of the new and the few old remaining buildings left standing after the severe bombings during the war, showed the City Fathers' pride in its rebuilding programme and was a shop window for the commerciality of the city.

Pulling up in front of Police Headquarters, Robin was a little disappointed. He had expected an old building with a history, like Old Scotland Yard in London, but like Scotland Yard, all of the history was only in the memory of the men who had served there, doing their duty. Now, Robin looked up at the modern, flat, glass-fronted edifice rising skyward. The silent lift soon whisked him and his escort to the seventh floor. A large, open-plan office stretched out before him. The efficient, curved and moveable screens caught Robin's eye. He felt 'efficient' was the correct word, when he noticed a young policewoman move a screen effortlessly to block the hard shaft of sunlight from hitting the top of her desk. The glass-partitioned offices at the far end of the room, slowly came closer. He noticed that no door was closed – an idea that he liked, then suddenly there was Ernst Ulbrecht, the man who had laid a legend of crime prevention and crime beating quietly out before him for his peers to applaud. Robin's throat was dry and he felt that when he had to speak, it would, at best, be a croak that he would be able to manage. The round face smiled at him as he lifted his head in response to the escort's introduction. The face showed humour, respect and welcome, all at the same time. Robin's own face beamed happily back, as they shook hands over the desk. Robin's voice sprang back to life as he said, 'Wonderful to meet you, sir. Thank you for arranging my escort and the transport.'

'It was the least we could do, Robin. Oh, and please… call me Ernst. You did on the phone, so why not now?'

'Ernst it will be, from now on. As it was our first face to face meeting, I thought I should show a little extra respect, that's all.'

'Most courteous, Robin. Now you must want to wash up after your journey. May I suggest that I take you along there and when you are finished, you can come back here and we can get to know each other better for an hour or so before we go to lunch and return for a little meeting I have set up for three o'clock.'

'It sounds good to me, Ernst – you're in charge!'

Ernst did not quite understand what was meant by 'you're in charge', but he smiled at Robin affably, as they both left the office.

When they returned from lunch, both Ernst and Robin were animated with hand gestures and flowing conversation. The time was five to three. Walking side by side along the aisle between the desks, the staff could see this man was an accepted associate of their boss. The meeting Ernst had called, consisted of himself, Robin, Mayer, and Willi Koslowski, senior investigator and a permanent member of Ernst's team, having worked with Ernst for the past twelve years. The friendly gathering settled around the table, having been formally introduced by Ernst. Ernst abruptly opened the proceedings.

'We are here following a request for information on two men, believed to be soldiers, by the French police in Achern. Our friend here, notified all of the areas which have Eurocorps troops, in requesting missing persons. Franz Gelder, a friend of mine at Köln, mentioned the memo to me, Mayer obtained information of panic in the "mid-regions" of the civil service in Russia and eventually we came up with two names which have now been corroborated as being the two men from the French police enquiry, who have been notified and are happy. They have been replaced by two more known criminals, Lanov and Mogatin, who have been identified by Robin's British investigators for us. We have been chasing Lanov and Mogatin all over Europe and Russia. As Willi and Mayer here will know, during the Hamburg incident, we had some loose ends. Firstly, the "ringed-hand man", reported by Klaus Mennen, the Harbour Master in Hamburg and his boyfriend, Dieter, as the cold-blooded assassin of an American CIA operative. She has since been proven to have been on special assignment, but took her work too seriously when she found out that the mastermind of the Hamburg incident was none other than Tashimov, the man she claimed killed her mother and father. This CIA agent, Nadine Dashnikov, was subsequently taken in as an orphan and brought up by a Russian family already living in the USA. Her Russian language skills were encouraged by the family and she was eventually recruited by the CIA. She stalked Tashimov following the Hamburg incident and took her revenge for her family, killing him in front of Klaus and Dieter. She wanted to enjoy her revenge for as long as possible, trying to keep Tashimov alive long enough to make him suffer, but mostly she wanted to identify herself to Tashimov so that he knew why his suffering was going to be prolonged. But he died and then Nadine Dashnikov died at the hands of Marshall Yute Polenkovich – the "ringed-hand man".'

Ernst stopped his résumé for a minute, taking a sip of water before he continued. 'So, we are left with only questions as we sit here. What are Lanov and Mogatin up to? Polenkovich, being their controller and presumably returned to favour by his masters – is it his plan? Or is it a plan his bosses have dreamed up and he is simply a controller? Of what significance are the Tomlevskis, the couple under surveillance by a six-man team, controlled, we think, by Lanov and Mogatin? Are there any more military personnel being tailed? What are their jobs? What power do they have in their command structure? Are there any reports of any sudden behavioural changes or mood swings by any personnel, senior or not, throughout the army?'

Robin started his response by thanking Ernst and his staff for making him welcome and for all the good work they had done already, piecing together so many parts of an ambiguous jigsaw.

'For my part, I would like to transfer all of my investigators onto every query regarding any disloyalty of every Eurocorps personnel that may fit Ernst's last point, which would reveal where they fitted into the command structure, but this is above my head. My Adjutant, who is pretty sharp, is probably aware I am already stepping out of line, but he would do almost anything to protect the Corps, provided he were convinced something was really out of order across the board rather, than as it appears at the moment, an isolated incident.

'We can supply you with corroborated evidence that the two dead men and Lanov's, Mogatin's and Yute Polenkovich's paths have crossed in the past, plus the fact that the dates of Lanov and Mogatin's last visit to Achern were as close as one day before the bodies were found!' Mayer stated.

Willi was just about to contribute to the discussion when Mayer interrupted again. 'Excuse me, Willi, an important point – we know Lanov and Mogatin were in Russia on the same day the bodies were found, causing lots of ripples on the waters and that when the bodies were found, they had been dead for at least twelve hours. Although not conclusive proof, I think it's a good enough theory to go along with for the moment, for you to ask for all the help you can get from your Adjutant.'

On finishing her analysis, Mayer suddenly realised she was only a junior member of this group and before Willi could speak again, she said, 'Sir, excuse my forthright approach, I apologise for my rudeness.'

Willi, who was opening his mouth to speak once more, was cut out this time, by Robin.

'You have no need to apologise. Be assured my Adjutant will be duly approached and if you would like my opinion, I would hope he will allow me… us, to continue with our investigation, but I feel sure he will insist on a time limit.'

'Then it will be up to us to get some disturbing facts placed before him as soon as possible!' Ernst stated.

Willi finally managed to speak. 'Well, Robin has the first moves available to him… these Tomlevskis should be approached by his men and made aware that their dealings with these Russians have been known to the Provost's office for several weeks now and try and work them into becoming double-agents.'

Robin pondered a moment, pulling the writing pad towards him, pen in hand. He wrote: *No! Let them run*! He turned the pad around for all to see.

Ernst's eyes glinted at the thought and his hand automatically reached out to shake Robin's, saying, 'That's exactly what I would like to do, but in playing it, you realise all the pressure will be on you, what with the Adjutant breathing down your neck and possibly your whole force being used to check every little incident reported to your office, causing some areas of your command to complain they are not getting a fast enough response to their petty pilfering from stores! As it will all be happening on military designated area, we won't be able to help.'

'I realise that, Ernst,' replied Robin. 'But, if I go all out against the Tomlevskis and we succeed in turning them into double-agents, we could be weakening a much larger plan.'

'We will give you as much support as we can,' confirmed Ernst.

'I know that. It seems we are all agreed, then?' Robin asked.

Ernst, Mayer, and Willi each nodded their heads in agreement. Robin thanked them for their support, and with a smile on his face, said, 'Well, let's work out our plans for getting this show on the road, then on to my Adjutant, whose full cooperation is very much needed!'

The single table lamp spread a pale yellow light across the papers in front of Major Roche. Although not unusual for him to work later than most of his staff, tonight was different. All day long he had been a little tense. In fact, some of his junior officers had made remarks about how tetchy the 'old man' was today, after they had left his presence. His workload over the past few days had been attended to, but often not in the slick, efficient manner everyone had come to expect of him, causing discussions in the mess about whether the 'old man' was sickening for something. Major Roche himself knew what the trouble was; he had exceeded his authority in allowing Cadwallader a free hand. 'After all,' he said to himself as his right hand punched into his left, 'this is an army – a disciplined unit, that moves forwards at the command of its General, not a fluffy lot that floats around in all directions!' He sat back in his chair in silence, waiting for a knock on his door, or for the phone to ring, advising him Major Cadwallader was back in camp and his message had been passed on.

The time hung heavily as he sat in the semi-darkness. He had to find out what Cadwallader was planning. What was irritating him so much? He had an officer whom he trusted implicitly, but here he was, waiting for a friend to return from a short leave and he had left messages all over camp for him. 'Why am I doing this?' he asked himself. The only conclusion he could reluctantly come to, was that it boiled down to jealousy. The whiplash of this thought brought him bolt upright in his chair. 'Jealousy? My God, it can't be!… Get away from me, evil thoughts… let me get back to just running my army… impartially, but with no soul. Get away, you are wrong about me… get away!'

A vigorous knock on his office door brought him abruptly back into the real world. 'Come in, the door's open!' he called.

'You wanted to see me, sir?' Robin said as he popped his head around the door.

'Yes, Robin. Please, sit down. It won't take long – did you have a good leave period?'

'Quite good, André. I learnt an awful lot, the social side was good – early to bed, early to rise and all that stuff…'

'Would you say that I am a jealous man, Robin?'

Robin was rather taken aback by the question. His mind worked overtime before answering. 'No, you're the most level-headed, straightforward Adjutant I've ever worked with. Why do you ask?'

'It was a thought that went through my head as I sat here waiting for you and I just thought I would ask you the question.'

'Well, I'm quite sure you're not, André. Now, you wanted to see me…'

'Well, yes. To be blunt, what's going on?'

'I would like the opportunity to write up a report before I answer that, André; besides, why are you assuming there is something "going on"?'

'I know your men are being deployed into areas which I personally cannot see as an advantage to the security nor disciplinary support for this Corps.'

'I believe you're wrong on that first point and as for the second, no complaints have come to me so far.'

'Well they have come to me, Robin. Two COs on detachment – both have pilfering or civilian theft, and you have not responded.'

Robin thought for a moment. 'Sir, I have not seen those reports. I will investigate immediately and notify you of what action I will be taking.'

'Not so fast, Robin. Don't use a little foul-up as an excuse to get out of my office!'

'That was not my intention, sir!'

'Are you sure about that? It's always easier to run away rather than face hard facts.' André's voice was becoming hard and brittle.

Robin was feeling decidedly insecure… how could he avoid this unusual and unreasonable attack from his supposed friend? 'Sir, my office code is that evasion is not allowed in any situation, so please may I ignore your last remark?'

'No you may not. I give you free rein in your work, I allow you leave at very short notice, I give you full support and freedom to manage your own destiny, I cover for you in your absence and what do you do? You give me nothing when I ask, just "I would like the opportunity to write up a report"!'

'It would be my preference to commit everything to paper, sir. That way, nothing will be lost.'

'All right. When are you going to let me in on your little game?'

'Sir, it is not a game. Shall we say, tomorrow afternoon?'

'If that's the best you can do.'

'There is a lot of information, sir, and I would like to submit a full report. There is something that may be bigger than we in the military can handle alone. It will need all of your support and skill to get it through to top brass. It will have to be nursed like a baby and who better than you to coordinate it?'

André was about to interrupt, but Robin carried on forcefully. 'What I have heard here tonight, André, has worried me. We have always been open on everything, close friends until now. I've had to make a decision to give up my personal leave to attend an important meeting with the German police and you want to talk it through! No, André, you can't have it until it's written up. Even if that makes you a little more jealous of my "freedom" as you call it!'

The words hurt. Both men realised they had each tested the other and now it was time to leave. Neither would apologise just yet.

'Until tomorrow, then – 1600 hours?'

'Yes, sir.' Robin turned and left the office. The disgust he felt with himself would not show until he was outside in the dark corridor.

Promptly at 1600 hours the next day, Robin knocked loudly on Major Roche's office door. The command to come in was harsh and unfriendly.

'My report and operational strategy, sir, as ordered!' Robin saluted.

'You didn't have to bring it yourself, you could have sent it!'

'This is the only copy, sir, and parts of it, I feel, are sensitive. Without your authority, I would not open a "red file".'

'So, you feel your report is sensitive, Robin?'

The 'Robin' at the end of the sentence, was offered as a 'let's forget yesterday' but Robin decided it was too soon to break down the fence that had suddenly sprung up between them. 'Yes, I do, sir,' was his reply, then he added, 'I would like to sit here whilst you read it, sir, in case you need clarification on certain points.'

'As you wish.' Major Roche set his glasses and lifted the report into a reading position as he leant back in his chair. Robin sat silently, watching for any reaction to register. Robin knew his report was good and that the design of the preventative structure to sift out any would-be infiltrators into the Corps would cause minimal interference with the policing of all the other Corps units throughout the whole of the Eurocorps structure. Robin knew that the German and French intelligence services would have to be the largest contributors, but with the administration which Major Roche and Robin would initiate, they would be able to control all enquiries made of the military by any civilian police force that might become involved, simply by nominating both Roche and Cadwallader, plus one anchorman, to be the only ones to be contacted.

There was a rustle as the last page was turned. With the still-frozen face in front of him, Robin wanted to move, fidget, anything really, to try and get some reaction, but he continued to sit, motionless. The Adjutant finished reading and let the last page fall into place. Slowly, looking up at Robin, he asked, 'Do you seriously believe, as this Ulbrecht does, that we could be infiltrated and used by the Russian Mafia?'

'We both feel it could be a strong possibility, sir.'

'You have explained it hypothetically, but what is the immediate probability?'

'We are now sure the Tomlevskis are being blackmailed in readiness for some future assignment. As I have noted, a confidential "Company Commanders Only" memo would be initiated, ordering any fall-off in performance, sudden cases of drunkenness, argumentativeness, isolation, et cetera. The full list of things to look for will be in the appendix to this report, which was not quite finished being typed as I left my office, sir.'

'Good, good. I will not need to see that at this point, I'm sure.'

'As you wish.'

'I trust your analysis, and the possibility of infiltration by an outside force is something we cannot have happen. You obviously agree with that statement as you brought it to my notice. My dilemma is whether to support it and send it upstairs... and we both know how long that could take for a decision.'

The pause in Major Roche's summary, for no apparent reason, jarred Robin. What's the wily old fox going to pull now? immediately sprang into his mind.

'Robin…' the Adjutant spoke. The warmth in the way he said the name surely indicated he was sorry for yesterday. 'I understand the urgency. I will be pleased to assist in any way you think best. We are not going upstairs for a decision at the moment, we will see how your baby grows first, don't you think, Robin?'

'André.' Both of them accepted their relationship was back on an even keel, perhaps even stronger than before. 'You do realise the problems if we are caught without authority?'

'Oh, certainly I do, but let's get out there and score points for our team!'

'Thank you, André. Shall I start straight away, or would you like a few minutes to think again?'

'Don't be silly, the thinking I've just done is enough for one day; let's get on with it. I do think, however, we ought to have a quiet drink in the mess to seal our bond!'

'For sure. Let's get going now, I'm buying!'

With a twinkle in his eye, André replied, 'I never thought anything else, Robin!'

The drinks over, Robin went back to his own office and dialled Ernst Ulbrecht, hoping for a reply at that late hour, but not really expecting one. He was pleasantly surprised when what would soon become a familiar 'Ulbrecht heir!' entered his ear.

'Ernst! It's Robin… thank you for being there. I've some good news from this end. My Adjutant, Major Roche, has approved the whole scheme without going upstairs. He's taking a lot of responsibility on his shoulders, but he is willing to run with it until we have more corroboration.'

'Your Major sounds like a nice man!'

'He is, but had you been a fly on the wall of his office yesterday, you might have thought differently!'

'What happened?'

'Oh, Ernst, it's a long story… maybe I'll tell you one day, but it's of no consequence now.'

'I'm pleased about that!'

'Me too! Now, my plan is to put phase one into operation first thing tomorrow and hope for early results to enable civil and military forces to work together.'

'We will make a good team, Robin, you and me. Let's hope that what we have started will turn into nothing, but if it does, may we have caught the thing early enough not to have caused any lasting damage.'

'You're right, Ernst. I hope it won't be too long before we speak again. Goodbye for now.'

'Goodbye, Robin, and good luck!'

Yute Polenkovich, having forced a meeting with Gregori Alexei Androv, realised his initial plan of moving slowly with regards to the selection of the personnel to be infiltrated into positions throughout Eurocorps had been ignored. Androv's personal greed, with the help of Igor Tatlanovich, had found five people who were already being manipulated and primed, ready for positioning, quite apart from the Tomlevskis. The immediate problem for Yute, was to get a very fast appraisal of these five by Lanov and Mogatin and their reporting back with their opinion. Coupled with the reports from Androv's files, he would make a final decision on who, if any, would be suitable for his own needs. Those not suitable would be disposed of. The phone rang, pulling him out of his mental wrangling. 'Hello,' he answered. The usual procedure was solemnly gone through, identity being accepted by both parties.

'Is everything working out satisfactorily?'

Mogatin's reply was delivered in monotone. 'Fine. Our charges seem to be reconciled with their lot, no more threats or demands from them. It's quite peaceful.'

'Would one of you be able to go off and check out a few more mistakes?'

'Yes, we could split up. It is inconvenient for you, I suppose.'

'It could be, but with one of you checking on it, I'm sure things wouldn't get out of hand and could soon be pulled around.'

'And if we feel they can't be?'

'You would have to revert to the same arrangement,' said Yute.

'I understand you will be making the decision on who stays and who goes?' Mogatin asked.

'I think it really is my decision to make. I have all of the information here on file; with your report it should not take long to decide what action to take.'

'I'm sure you're right. You will get the names and addresses over to us in the usual way, I suppose?'

'Straight into your post box,' replied Yute.

'We are going to move fast then?'

'Definitely. We don't want anything we feel is not good enough to be included in our end product. At the same time, without your analysis, it will be impossible to tell. It would be good if all five were acceptable.'

'Five, you say?'

'Yes, they are all quite close to your area.'

'I suppose, but it's going to make an awful lot of activity in a small area. I'd much rather have distance between locations.'

'It's unfortunate, but I understand your problem.'

'I'm sure you do. Be in touch then?'

'Yes, by tomorrow I would think. Goodbye.'

The line went dead in Yute's ear. Feeling confident, having reflected that the apparently innocent conversation he had just finished with Mogatin was fully understood: as nebulous as it may have sounded, should anyone have listened in, they would have concluded it was just another boring conversation between a sales manager and his poor sales representative, who was going to have to do some extra legwork. Yute picked up the phone, dialled the number and on the third ring, the phone was lifted up. Yute spoke softly into the mouthpiece, 'Natasha, are you free tonight?'

Mogatin and Lanov sat in a dimly-lit restaurant, hidden from the street by a partition. Lanov, having been told of the conversation Mogatin had had with Yute, was not very happy and it had made his unhappiness even worse on hearing the news about the five additional people entering the arena, when Yute had promised a completely new game from the beginning. Mogatin had reconciled himself to the fact that they were not on a level playing field and said, 'Our decision is simple, Dimitri. We get out now,

264

and look over our shoulders for the rest of our lives, or we do as we are told, taking whatever we can as we go along.'

'You're right, I know you are, but ever since the bloody wall came down and some bloody idiot shouted "Glasnost!" we have turned into a pair of sanitary engineers, cleaning up other people's shit before we can see the nice clear water at the bottom of the bowl!'

Mogatin could only laugh at his friend. His analogy was so descriptive and he knew Lanov would soon start laughing with him and at himself. When the laughter died down, followed by a brief discussion on which one of them should go on the new assignment, Mogatin had said simply, 'I really don't mind going.'

Lanov responded simply, 'Okay, you do it!'

The reports coming into Robin Cadwallader's office had shown up very little of interest. 'Is it going to carry on this way?' he was asking one of his investigators.

'Sir, sometimes these damn things drive you mad if you let them. I find the secret is to pretend you are doing nothing. Think of your girlfriend or your wife. As soon as you get to the interesting bits, the bloody phone rings and all hell's let loose!' Within a few seconds, the phone rang, making both of them jump a little from the surprise. 'There you are, sir, as ordered, the phone that brings hell!' Lifting the receiver, the investigator answered it. 'Duty room!' There was a pause, then, 'Yes, Sergeant. It will be logged… You will phone and you will need back-up… understood, Sergeant… I'll tell him right away… Goodbye!'

'Sergeant Robinson, I suppose?'

'Yes, sir. He was at Achern railway station. Mr Mogatin is on the move. He's booked a ticket to Karlsruhe. He will phone in when the opportunity presents itself, but he says he will need some back-up. I am to log this conversation and you are to be told immediately, sir.'

'Thank you, Corporal. I am going to my office should I be needed. Will you tell your relief that if it is possible when Sergeant Robinson phones, to try to put the call through to me wherever I am?'

'Yes, sir!' Then cheekily, he added, 'I will log your instruction along with the Sergeant's message, sir!'

Chapter Twenty-Seven

Mayer was approaching Ernst Ulbrecht's office for the fifth time that day. Her steps were still springy, her body upright and firm, the only tell-tale sign of tiredness were the dark rings under her eyes. The light tap on the doorframe brought the usual response. 'Come in, Mayer, please sit down.' Normally she would prefer to stand, but as a result of the confused messages she had been receiving over the past few hours from Rudi Simusov, her leading Russian contact, she needed to sit. Her own analysis was that Rudi had been caught feeding information to outside sources and that he was in danger. Rudi's constant assurances that he was safe and secure did not reassure Mayer.

'Sir...' Mayer started as she sat down, 'I feel sure Rudi is in danger. He must be got out.'

'But we need him where he is for a little longer!'

'I just don't think he can stay there safely any longer. I feel sure he has been found out and that they will try to turn him into a double-agent. If they succeed and he starts giving us false information, we could be running around all over the place and he'd be useless to us!'

'I think we have to keep him in place and take that chance, Mayer.'

'Oh, you do, do you?... A man's life means nothing to...' Mayer didn't get to finish the sentence because tears flooded down her taut face. Through her thickening throat, the streaming nose and eyes, she blurted out, 'I'm sorry, sir, it's not your fault... he just sounds so lost when we talk. Never once has he said he's being watched and that things are difficult for him, but I know they are – he's so brave!' Her heaving sobs took over her body, her sobbing was uncontrollable.

'Mayer, he really could be so helpful to us. Right now, he is probably more important than ever before. What has he actually said to you?'

'Nothing…' the sobs were still heavy. 'Nothing, but his voice is like a tape recorder on slow speed and Rudi has always been so alive and often quite humorous.'

'I'm sure he was, Mayer, but what has he actually been saying?' Ernst noticed Mayer's face harden, then he added, 'Please?'

Mayer looked sternly at Ernst. 'Yute Polenkovich is being watched day and night. He can't find out who ordered it. It is very worrying, Rudi thinks, because the last time there was a situation like this, with the watchers being watched themselves, the tidal wave of Glasnost broke out and there was no control. Rudi feels there is going to be another revolution in Russia or something very close.'

'Mayer, Russia is being watched by the whole world – it is highly unlikely.'

'Rudi feels something tragic is imminent and it is following many things that happened last time…' Her sobs were deeper but calmer now that she was talking to someone she could trust.

'Mayer, do you see why we need your Rudi to stay where he is?'

'Of course I do but…' Mayer wanted to say, *'but I love him – don't you see how difficult it is for a woman in love?'* Instead, she continued, '…he feels that he is not contributing to making Russia strong anymore. He feels that the first flush of Glasnost gave Mother Russia a new vigour, but he is worried that a new revolution will fragment her and her many zones will be run by mobsters and the deceptions of the "Stalins" upon her people will start again.' Mayer's voice whilst fighting Rudi's corner was getting stronger with only the occasional sob now.

'You make your Rudi sound like a true patriot, Mayer!'

'He is, sir. Even if there is to be a revolution, I think he would want to stay and nurse its broken bones.' Mayer stopped suddenly, realising what she had said. She looked at Ernst. 'You are always right, aren't you? I suppose I will finish up a Russian?'

'You love him, so maybe that could be the end of your story, Mayer, but I don't think so. I think your Rudi wants to get into a world with less corruption.'

'That has always been one of his biggest objections about Russia – even after Glasnost, the corruption was still there.'

Ernst slowly leant across the desk and took her hands in his. 'Mayer, you have to ask him to stay a while longer!'

Mayer looked into her mentor's pleading eyes and knew she had to ask the question which might take her lovely Rudi away from her.

Mogatin checked into the station hotel on arrival at Karlsruhe. The bright light in the reception area had given a pleasant impression as he gazed in through the large, glass front door, but sitting in his crummy room, he realised why it was only rated one star. Mogatin, ever the optimist, sat on the edge of his bed, looking at the phone that hung just above the light switch by the side of the door into the room. How the bloody hell can you use the phone standing up? What are you supposed to write your notes on? The question he had asked himself he already decided long ago, had no answer. Only an idiot would lay out a room like this! Lifting himself off the slack, sprung mattress and aiming himself towards the phone, he grumbled to himself, 'It would cost no more to put the phone near the bed, would it?'

From the moment Mogatin had left the train, Sergeant Robinson of the SIB (Special Investigation Branch of the Military Police) had him under surveillance. Placing himself at the head of the train, on arrival at Karlsruhe, he had sprinted to the exit like a man racing into the arms of his lover, then play-acted out the 'Oh my God, how could she be so late?' routine. The agitation on Sergeant Robinson's face as he paced the forecourt, looking breathlessly down at his wristwatch, even brought a smile to Mogatin's face as he passed the poor distressed young man. Robinson was surprised when after only a minute, he entered the station hotel. He had thought that he would have had a 'traipse around' for a while. Having checked the hotel perimeter for exits, cul-de-sacs and the possibilities of a roof escape, he now sat in the bar opposite Mogatin's badly-lit room. The huge shadow that grew across the window as Mogatin stood up from the bed caused Robinson to mutter to himself. 'Damn! The bugger's coming out and I haven't phoned in yet!' As the shadow came back across the window and decreased in size as its owner sat down again,

Robinson let out a small sigh of relief. Now was the time to make his phone call to Cadwallader.

The abrupt entrance of Gregori Alexei Androv into Rudi's department caused a flap. Without ceremony, Androv had blustered into Rudi's superior's office and had attacked him verbally. It was impossible for Rudi to hear what was said between them through the glass panels of the office, but it was obvious to all the people sitting around in the open-plan office that Gregori Alexei Androv, who was unknown to Rudi or any of his colleagues, was certainly frightening his superior. Slowly, after the initial onslaught from Androv, Rudi's boss seemed to be snatching back the initiative and it appeared to all looking in at the silent play being acted out in front of them, that the man no one knew was now being stopped in his tracks. The play before them was coming to a close, the anger on Rudi's superior's face showed that he was not a man to trifle with. The gesture of his arm and the suddenness of his hand unclenching and his index finger pointing to the door, the unheard words being mouthed by his lips, 'Get out of my office!' brought the play to an end. Androv left as suddenly as he had arrived, then the phone on Rudi's desk rang, summoning him into his superior's office.

Sergeant Robinson's call to Major Cadwallader had produced swift results. He had arranged in Karlsruhe, a team of six investigators giving total blanket coverage of Mogatin. Robinson had been a little surprised when Mogatin didn't leave the hotel early the next morning. He had worried a little that being on his own on the first day would have made his job difficult, but during the night, investigators had been reporting in to him from all over France and Germany. The bar, with the aid of the local police, had remained open all night and from the street, it looked as if a private party was going on. Mogatin's first move from the hotel was at 10.30 a.m. As he stepped onto the pavement, the bar door opposite burst open and what appeared to be a drunk fell onto the pavement. The distraction was enough to allow two other men out onto the street, one turning left, and one turning right. Mogatin's eyes were on the stupid fool who had fallen down drunk! Having slept in one of the bar's alcoves, Robinson was refreshed. It was only four hours' sleep, but it was enough to bring him back to full alertness. There had been nothing to report to Robinson from members of his team covering Mogatin, so they had not attempted to wake him.

'Anything from anyone?' asked Robinson.

'Nothing, Sarge. Williams cut his finger when he fell over, if that counts!'

'Don't be a bloody ass!' Robinson said gruffly, then added, 'Has anyone got a brew on?'

'Coming up, Sarge!' said a voice from behind the bar.

The tea was wet and warm but that was all you could really say about it. The bloke who had made it had never heard of a good strong cuppa, that was for sure, but it did help to clear some of the soreness from Robinson's throat.

'Have you all got accommodation fixed?' Robinson asked. Everyone confirmed they had and that a room had also been booked for him at the Royale. Robinson just had time to thank them when the door opened and one of his investigators who had left that morning, walked in.

'Sergeant, it's been a doddle. We've just been around town, checked over three houses from the outside, no attempt to make an entry or talk to anyone at the houses or their neighbours.'

'Have you got all the addresses?'

'Yes, Sarge. They'll all be in the report. I left Jones and Harris tailing Mogatin. He wasn't coming back to the hotel, so maybe they might get a few more addresses before it gets too dark.'

'Hope so, Reynolds, the more the merrier. Anyway, get those addresses to Cadwallader now, then they can do some work instead of us!'

Jones, with his Welsh accent cut in. 'Now you mustn't make them work – it's not good for them!'

Cadwallader received the addresses from Reynolds by phone. After arranging with the civilian police to run a check on the people living at the given addresses, he was standing by the fax machine, waiting for Reynolds's full report to finish transmitting before he could start to analyse the information. The civilian police were getting behind the idea of working along with the military, although some of them objected to opening up their computer files, feeling that it was an invasion of privacy as it was an extension of information going into military computers. Cadwallader had anticipated this and through the Director of Military Law's office, had had drawn up an acceptable form for signature, stating that any names or information given would only be held until the case was proven, thence all civilian information gained during this particular investigation would be erased. Some had asked for a release, but the majority of people contacted, had not. The phone rang. The one word, 'Cadwallader,' answered it.

'Sir, all of these addresses you have given me are parents of military personnel. None of the families are connected with each other in any way, all the parents have been in the military, including one of the mothers. All the children are bi- or trilingual and committed Europeans.'

'Thank you, Sergeant. Have you found out what corps or regiment these people belong to yet?'

'I've just started that ball rolling, sir.'

'Thank you, Sergeant, we will get to the bottom of it. Get back to me, if you will – there may be a clue in the type of work they do in their regiments.'

'As soon as I know, sir.'

'Thank you, Sergeant.' Placing the phone down, Robin cupped his head in his hands and was just about to rub his tired eyes when the phone rang again.

'Cadwallader?' he replied after the second ring.

'Robinson here, sir.'

'Sergeant! How are things going for you?'

'Fine, sir. We are having to break up our team. Our friend has just got on a train heading back towards you. He's on the train to Mülheim.'

'Eurocorps country!'

'Yes, sir, very much so. Very "feet on the ground" worker bees, you might say, as opposed to us types!'

'I take your point, Sergeant. When you get where our man settles, let me know.'

'Certainly will. I'm sending the rest back to their units, sir. I'll stay here until I hear from Mülheim, then probably go there to set up a base.'

'I understand. If you need cover whilst you're travelling, centre on my office. The message will get to me in minutes.'

'Agreed, sir. Until the next time, bye for now.'

The phone clicked dead. Robin was uneasy that every contact made by Mogatin was around his army. A shudder of fear ran through his body before he picked up the telephone and punched in the numbers for Major Roche's office.

'Adjutant,' came the sharp reply.

'Robin here, sir. Have you got time to listen?'

'Yes, if you want to come over here, you can speak at will.'

'I'd rather not, André. I need to be here to take calls. It's easier when I've got all my bits and pieces to hand, should I need a quick reference or something.'

'I understand. What did you want to tell me?'

'Mogatin, one of our Russians, went to Karlsruhe. He reconnoitred three family homes which we have subsequently discovered each have either directly themselves, or through their children or marriage, military connections. Now, he's travelling to Mülheim – one of our bases.'

'He didn't make any contact with anyone? That's a little odd, isn't it?'

'Not if he is just reconnoitring for escape routes, prior to bringing in a team of controllers!'

'What do you think the reason is, Robin?'

'Before he brings a team in, is my guess.'

'Your guess, Robin?'

'Yes. We don't know that these people have been contacted yet. No one from the Karlsruhe or Mülheim areas have responded to my memo requesting information on personnel exhibiting any change in behaviour. Now we are onto them even though we don't know what their objectives are. I feel sure no approaches have been made, which puts us a little bit ahead of the game.'

'I hope you're right, Robin, I sincerely do!'

'Me too, André. May I contact you at any time?'

'I'll inform the switchboard that you are to be put through at any time of day or night.'

'Thank you, André, and thank you for your support. It shouldn't be much longer before I can give you full and corroborated proof that something is happening, even if we still don't know exactly what!'

'It would be a relief if I could share this load of responsibility with the Colonel or better still, the General, but don't you worry about me, it was my decision.'

'I respect the pressure you are under, André, thank you!'

André broke in light-heartedly, 'That's enough, Robin, forget it – besides it's for the Corps!'

Robin sat there listening to his friend's flippant way of trying to put him at ease, but what if things did go wrong?

As he placed the phone back in its cradle, he swore a silent oath to himself that nothing would endanger the Corps, or most of all, his good friend, André.

'Ulbrecht heir!'

'Robin here, Ernst. How are you?'

'Fine, Robin, fine. What news?'

'Lanov is staying put in Achern, but Mogatin is out and about seeing the countryside. He has just looked over three houses belonging to personnel posted to us in Karlsruhe. He made no contact with anyone, just surveyed the area. Now he's in Mülheim, another one of our areas. He is unaware of our tailing him. Perhaps in Mülheim he may make contact, or if not, wherever he may go next may be the turning point.'

'These houses he reconnoitred, you say he did not make contact with anyone. Doesn't that seem strange?' asked Ernst.

'We thought so too and decided we would research the family backgrounds of each one. It's a long drawn out process, but necessary. The company commanders of the serving officers have all been contacted in secret and they swear they have not noticed anything untoward!'

'What about Mülheim, Robin?'

'A little early, he is only just arriving about now, but no one has been reported to us as not functioning well at his job!'

'I wish we could get something moving, Robin!'

'Me too, Ernst! By the way, about the Tomlevskis, who we already know have been contacted by Melentkov and Zabiak – my

Adjutant is allowing them to run in the hope they will not be too forthcoming.'

'Your Adjutant must be an interesting man.'

'He is. He has really stuck his neck out on this one. I hope he doesn't get it chopped off.'

'We must see that that doesn't happen – good men are hard to find!'

'Absolutely, Ernst. I must get going now, I'll phone you later after the first reports from Mülheim come in.'

'Until then, Robin. I'll wait for your call.'

Mayer sat quietly at her desk, analysing every scrap of information for the third or possibly the fourth time. Had anything been missed, or was it just to keep her from going crazy while she waited for Rudi's next call? Over the past few days, her normal happy and efficient attitude to her work had dulled along with her radiance. The tell-tale sleepless nights were beginning to show on her face. So engrossed was she, that when the phone eventually rang, she almost jumped out of her skin. Snatching the phone, she asked warmly, 'Is that you, Rudi?'

'Yes, Mayer, it is,' came the reply. 'I have just come from a meeting with my superior. He wants to be got out of his entanglement with the regime and get placed in the West. He is willing to barter with many years' worth of records, plus many up-to-date affairs that are being planned around the world.' Rudi paused for breath for a moment. The excitement in his voice made him sound more boyish.

Oh, come with him, Mayer thought.

Her dream was snatched away as he carried on, 'I'm obliged to tell you this because he is forcing my hand. He knows of our conversations!'

'Oh, Rudi, I want you to come over now. You must, and soon! My boss will help you, he said he would; we have talked about it several times, but he wants you to stay there a little longer first.' She realised that her heart had led throughout the conversation. Mayer suddenly stopped, the declaration of her wishes left her mind in a whirl. What if Rudi didn't feel as she did? They had never spoken of anything as tender as love, he had only asked if they could exchange photographs. The panic rose within her.

'Mayer, dear Mayer. I love you and I want to be with you more than anything, but if that boss of yours, the one you think is so wonderful, wants me here for a little while longer, I suppose we can wait to meet each other a little while longer too.'

'You're so sensible, Rudi. We are young, and now your superior wants to defect and knows about the information you have been passing to me, with or without his permission. It's a catch-22 situation and you are now out of danger from betrayal by him! Wonderful news, Rudi. Your boss can't harm you now – you're almost as safe as being in the West!'

A little giggle of happiness touched Rudi's ear, then the tingle went through his body as Mayer said, 'Oh, Rudi, I love you!' The warmth in her voice, stopped their world for a moment. The silence held between them, and there was nothing left to be said.

Mogatin's journey to Mülheim was uneventful, apart from the two rather immature British soldiers who had plagued the train, playfully running up and down the corridor but were now thankfully fast asleep in the opposite corner of the same carriage. He knew when the train stopped at Mülheim they would be panicking to gather up their kit, scamper off the train and clear their heads before they reached their barracks. Hadn't he done the same often enough in the past? As the wheels of the train passed over the cross rails and junctions on its entry into the station, Mogatin mused, Shall I do them a favour and wake them now? He thought better of it. Just think if they woke up and started a fight. 'No,' Mogatin whispered to himself under his breath, 'I won't wake you, but I'll make enough noise to wake you and I'll even delay closing the train door.'

Having done his good deed, as he considered it, Mogatin watched the soldiers get into the back of the small truck which had been sent to meet them. He had not seen the team of three investigators, whom the soldiers had identified Mogatin to, fan out across the station.

The journey to the nearest hotel was easily accomplished by the new surveillance team. It took eight minutes' walking time. One of the investigators decided he would check into the same hotel, making it easier to obtain Mogatin's room number and get a complete layout of the rooms. The first thing Mogatin did when he reached his own room was to phone Lanov and tell him he had arrived safely, pass on the phone number and say he would be going to visit his 'friend' tonight.

The eerie shadows of night grew deeper as dusk pulled her bedclothes over her head and went to sleep. Mogatin stood in the doorway of the hotel watching, waiting for any tell-tale signs of movement. Satisfied there was nothing, he strode out, without hesitancy, further into the centre of town. Having asked directions at reception, he turned left onto the street he needed, his mind switched on: twelve houses in, before a crossroad passed along the bottom, making a T-junction. Walking to the end, the T-junction proved to be a 'no vehicle' exit, but an easy escape route through gardens and open fields beyond. Turning back and crossing the road, number eight's small driveway invited him in. The black, painted lantern came on as he moved towards the front door, the only other visible light was a chink stretching the length of the tall window, where the heavy curtains had not been fully closed. The house and garden had been well-tended. Walking into the tiny porch, the light on the bell-push shone through the tip of his finger as he pushed. The chimes echoed their tinny sounds around the large hallway. The chink of curtain opened, spreading light across the porch. Mogatin turned towards the light and lifted his hat. The curtain fell back into its original position. Fifteen seconds later, Mogatin heard the first bolt being drawn back on the heavy door. 'Good evening!' Mogatin said. 'I believe we have a mutual friend... his name was Anton Zabiak!'

The thirty-year-old man standing before him seemed to go into shock. The only action from him was a hand passing across his body, waving Mogatin to enter his house.

With the news that Mogatin had made contact in Mülheim, Robin's office had become exceedingly busy, firstly notifying Ernst Ulbrecht and André Roche, but the procedure now had to be set with all of his investigators. The man at number eight was to be allocated six investigators on a 'round-the-clock' basis. It was decided that all background research on the man and his family would be thoroughly carried out, as had been the case with the Tomlevskis. The fact that Mogatin had now left Mülheim and was on his way to Colmar, meant more investigators had to be assembled and briefed on the delicacy of the matter they would be working on. The Adjutant briskly entered Robin's office, having been told the news of Mogatin's contact. He felt a brief talk with Robin was in order.

'Robin, is it time for me to open this can of worms with the boys upstairs?'

'I'd rather you didn't quite yet, sir, we haven't got sufficient evidence. I'd like to wait on events in Colmar, then if we are right, we will be able to bring in all three people whom we know have been contacted.'

'What then, Robin?'

'Well, we try and turn them, with promises that no action will be taken against them, whatever their past. Failing that, we will have to remove them from the circuit by transferring them from unit to unit so they are not allowed to settle long enough anywhere.'

'Will that be all it takes, Robin?'

'It will be an irritant to whoever is giving the orders, but that's all. Our biggest problem is that we will be losing the slight advantage we have at the moment.'

'When will you start bringing them in to try and turn them?'

'We will have to start with the Tomlevskis. I think you ought to be in on that one, André – but we haven't got enough background on any of the others yet.'

'When do you plan to see Tomlevski, or do you want to see them both together?'

'Just him, I think. He's military and there are certain things we can threaten.'

'When then, Robin?'

'Let's say tomorrow, as informal as possible. I'll just drop in around 1600 hours, ostensibly for a drink?'

'Fine. Until then. Goodbye, Robin.'

The Adjutant left as swiftly as he had entered. Robin carried on with the pressure of work being unleashed by the information which had now started flooding in. The most startling piece of which, was that Mogatin had arrived in Colmar and had proceeded directly to his 'prey' at 'La Foret', Rue Kaiserburg, the home of a certain Colonel Keller, staff officer with Eurocorps GHQ in Strasbourg. The report from the team in Colmar was that Mogatin had not hesitated on his approach to the Colonel's house. He strode up to the door, rang the bell forcefully, and when the Colonel appeared at the door, there was a momentary verbal confrontation, but then Mogatin entered, pushing the Colonel aside as he did so.

Robin searched the notes in from Colmar swiftly, for the latest news. Mogatin hadn't left yet, he was still inside the Colonel's house. Robin phoned through to André and quickly informed him of the new developments. André wasn't happy, but he promised he would not go to GHQ Strasbourg just yet, adding that as this Colonel was a staff officer, it could well be his excuse for not informing his superiors! Robin warned him of the problems if things went wrong. André's reply had been, 'You go and have your fun – we'll worry about my little problem later!' Robin was still smiling to himself about his Adjutant's attitude as he punched in the numbers for Ernst Ulbrecht.

'Ulbrecht heir!'

'Ernst – Robin. We've had another little development here, Mogatin has made contact with one of our own Colonels, by the name of Keller. He is on general staff appointment in Strasbourg. One thing more – my Adjutant, in view of the Colonel being on staff, feels he is now fully justified in not reporting the suspicions we have.'

'You have a true friend there, Robin!'

'Well I know it! We'll be in touch again, Ernst, just as soon as there is any more information from this end.'

'Well, you seem to have things going your way for the moment. It's very quiet here. One little thing – our Russian contact has been found out by his boss and is being blackmailed by him. He wants out of Russia and an appointment in local government in the West!'

'That's a nasty blow; what's happening now?'

'Well, Officer Mayer is in love with our contact. They have never met, but it seems their "off the record" conversations have built up a fondness between them. She wants him to come over – she had already mentioned it to me that it would be nice to meet her Russian friend, Rudi. I had a tearful scene from her, but she understood how important it is for us to keep him in place. She is now walking in fear of what his boss might do, but she has asked Rudi to stay a little longer. We, in turn, are supplying her with stories in the meantime, to keep Rudi's boss at bay. Mayer is working practically normally and Rudi, we hope, without his boss dangling him on a string, will find it easier to get information and call it in.'

'So, the situation is stable at the moment?'

'We have done the best we can to make it so. Have you any more news for me?'

'Tomorrow, very informally at 1600 hours, we – that is, the Adjutant and I – are going to meet Tomlevski and see what he has to say for himself. If he turns to us for help, well, fine. If not, we post him away from here and continue to do so until we get to the bottom of this potential mess!'

'The more you move him around, the less chance the enemy has of finding him useful?'

'And we hope they won't get suspicious whilst we continue pursuing our other investigations.'

'I'll say "good luck" for tomorrow, Robin. I think it would help us all if Tomlevski and his wife came back to you.'

'The Adjutant and I think it proves that the systems of security work and it has taught him a lot about the selection stage.'

'I wish you well, Robin – and your Adjutant – for tomorrow. I hope it works the way you both want. You will keep me informed and let me know if there's anything I can do?'

'You'll be the first to know, Ernst, I assure you. I think we are going to need each other a great deal before long!'

'I hope so – the "ringed-hand man" has a lot to answer for in my book!'

'You'll get him, Ernst, I'm sure.'

'No, Robin, *we'll* get him, *all* of us. Now I'll say goodbye and let you get on, Robin.'

The phone went dead in Robin's ear. Robin knew his friend Ernst was not the type to point out that it was him who had started bringing the equation together and that without his alertness to detail, a possible devastating blow to European security might have gone by without even getting noticed. Robin had great respect for Ernst's modesty and as he placed the phone down, he murmured to himself, 'When I get as old as him, I hope I'm as good.'

Chapter Twenty-Eight

The last of the watery-looking sun was just about to leave André Roche's office, turning it into darkness. Standing looking out at the occasional headlight from somewhere going to somewhere – as vehicles passed along the parade ground perimeter, the occasionally bellowed instruction faintly managed to invade his office, easing his anxiety a little. The interview with Tomlevski was about to commence and these past minutes alone, with just military things happening around him, was one of the ways in which he relaxed at the end of his day. Turning away from the window he reached across his desk and switched on his desk lamp, just at the very same moment as Tomlevski knocked on his door.

'Oh, do come in, Lieutenant.' He felt he had pitched his voice just right: light and friendly.

As the door opened, Tomlevski entered the room with the customary, 'Thank you, sir.'

'Would you turn on the main light, it's just by the door there – it'll brighten the room up, don't you think?'

'Most certainly, sir.'

'Good, good. Come and sit down, make yourself comfortable. What I've called you in for won't take long. Drink?'

'No, thank you, sir, I'm playing badminton later.'

'I understand you're settling in quite well then?'

'Yes, sir. Sports-wise, both my wife and myself are, but we seem to shy away from the purely social scene.'

'I must admit that I had noticed you were not at the mess dance the other evening. Is there any reason why you don't enjoy mixing socially?'

'Since we have been here we seem to have vegetated in front of the TV after our evening meal!'

'Is there any particular reason for that?'

'Not really, sir.' The hesitancy in Daniel's voice before

answering was due to the sudden realisation that his Adjutant wanted to talk to him a little more seriously than just this idle chit-chat.

'Well, we don't want that to continue, Daniel! An attractive couple like yourselves should be on our social lists! I'm sure a lot of your subordinates must have invited you both out to dinner or something; besides, you have applied for the post of "Social Affairs Officer"!'

'That's true, sir, but as I say, we seem to vegetate in front of the TV.' The tiredness in Daniel's voice was noticed by André, as he watched Daniel take a deep breath and then continue, 'We always seem to be making excuses...'

André studied Daniel's face as he struggled for words. André was just about to blurt out, 'Is it because you sit in night after night waiting for your Russian friends to come and visit you?' but Daniel started to talk again.

'We enjoyed the social life very much – we organised many trips, picnics, barbecues, crèches and babysitters, dances – it was a full life in the past.'

'Well, why not now? One of my reasons for seeing you is that people have mentioned to me that our potential Social Affairs Officer isn't very sociable himself!'

'They can think what they bloody well like!' The outburst shielded Robin's light knock on the door and his subsequent entering the office.

'I'm terribly sorry, sir, I didn't realise you had someone with you. I just dropped in on the off-chance we could have a drink?'

Gathering his wits about him, André replied, 'Come in, this is purely social. You don't mind one of your fellow officers joining us, do you, Daniel?'

'Of course not, sir. It would be my pleasure.' Relieved that his little outburst appeared to have been ignored, Daniel rose from his chair and offered his hand in welcome. 'Lieutenant Daniel Tomlevski – been on station for only a few weeks, sir, so I haven't met everyone yet, but it's nice to meet another new face!' Daniel felt a little more comfortable with another officer in the room and hoped he would not have to answer any more questions about his boring social life!

'Robin Cadwallader, Eurocorps Strasbourg and Achern. Probably, I've been away while you've been here and vice versa, if you know what I mean!'

Playing the words for fun made Daniel happier. 'Yes, Major, I think I do!'

'Well done – I didn't understand the words myself, but I did know what I meant! By the way, Robin will do, and you're Daniel, right?'

'Yes, sir – sorry, Robin.'

'Forget it. That Tomlevski bit, were your parents Polish?'

'Father is, Mother is a dyed-in-the-wool Brit!'

'Interesting combination that, the adventurous, rowdy Polish mixing with the sweet, quiet English rose!'

'Mother is quiet and beautiful and by all accounts Father had led a full life, but he's changed now.'

'Who do you take after then?'

'Everyone would say my mother, I'm sure of that. I've always been serious and forward-thinking, not like my father who only lived for the moment and still would, I think, but for his age.'

'He can't be that old, you're still quite young?'

'He was in the last European war, sir – er, Robin, sorry. He escaped from Europe and served in London doing liaison work between the British and Polish forces.'

'That must have been a full-time job!'

'It certainly was, the way he tells it, Robin, although I think there were as many good times as bad ones. He had a sort of "roving commission" and a lot of freedom. He travelled extensively, escorting non-English-speaking Poles from pillar to post. Apparently they had to be escorted, otherwise as soon as they were issued with uniforms and rifles, they headed off to the coast looking for anything that floated to take them back to Europe to fight the Germans!'

'They must have been exciting times,' injected André.

'They were as my father tells it, sir; when he's had a little vodka, he goes on and on about the good bits!'

'Only the good bits, Daniel?'

'Yes, sir, only the good bits.' Daniel stopped suddenly.

'Surely he must have told you about the adversity as well,

when you were a lad? I mean, no father only tells his son just half a story!' remarked Robin.

'Well, my father did.' The anger rose in Daniel's voice.

'Did what, Daniel?' Robin kept on probing.

'Cheated and lied! He was not a good man to the Polish people, nor was he honest with the British government.' Tears welled up in his eyes. Both Robin and André instinctively turned away so as not to embarrass the man further. The tears were pulled back under control again by the time Daniel pulled his body upright in his chair and stared at the two men in front of him.

The hard silence was broken by Robin's soft voice. 'Do you want to tell us more, Daniel?'

The long intake of breath into Daniel's lungs gave Robin his answer. Daniel spoke for about twenty minutes without stopping, telling them of his meeting with both Anton Zabiak and Uri Melentkov, of the pain his wife Nicole had been forced to endure with the revelation about her father's wartime indiscretion, about the blackmail he and Nicole had been expecting from the Russians, the anguish they had both been enduring in silence because they both felt no one would listen. That they couldn't betray their families and each time they had decided to report to someone, a fresh piece of evidence would be forced upon them by the Russians. André and Robin listened attentively, having some of what they already knew corroborated, and making mental notes of their new information. Daniel paused for a moment then added softly, as if in prayer, 'Thank God that's over. Would you like me to turn myself in at the Guard Room on the way out?'

'I don't think that will be necessary, do you, Robin?'

'It could end that way, André, it depends on Daniel here…'

'Well, I suppose you're right, but what would you require of him?' André asked enquiringly.

Daniel's face had turned to watch as each one of them spoke in turn, his face showing its response to each remark until the final '…require of him?' had set his mind racing. He wanted to shout out loud and clear, 'Anything!'

But before he could, Robin carried on, '…full cooperation with us, he and Nicole will have to work for them and us. They will need to probe in an effort to find out what the Russians are planning to do. We want any names mentioned, Russian or otherwise, to be reported back to us, and at the end of it all, we will make every effort to further his career. His wife, as a civilian, will be immune from civil investigation for the duration of this case.'

Daniel, whose chin had been stuck on his chest, slowly lifted his head and looked Robin squarely in the eyes and said, 'I have no problem with that, and I'm sure my wife will agree to it also, but I must insist on having some protection for her!'

'That will be arranged, but there are a lot of people out there being followed. I will need a list of meetings in advance so that my operatives can protect her at your house and on arrival at any external destinations. We daren't risk putting any more "tails" out there!'

'May I have some time to talk to my wife before I say yes?'

'Yes, of course, but she can't say no!'

'I understand. May I go now, please?'

'Please do, but tomorrow morning is your deadline.'

'Thank you both. I will never forget the opportunity of this second chance you are offering me. I will be in touch with both of our approvals tomorrow, first thing, or I will go straight to the Guard Room.'

'Well, that would save us from coming to look for you!' Robin's voice had a threatening edge.

As he left the room, Daniel appreciated that both men had treated him fairly and the suggestions for Nicole's safety was the best he was going to get. For the first time in a week, as he walked along the corridor towards the exit out of the building, Daniel felt there was hope after all.

Robin and André sat in silence for a few minutes after Daniel had left. Robin was the first to speak. 'That was a lot easier than I thought it was going to be, I'm pleased to say!'

'He must have been terribly torn between right and wrong!'

'He wanted to be asked, "Are you being a naughty boy?"'

'I don't know how he has been carrying out his duties so well with all that guilt plus that of his wife!... It must have been horrendous, but thank goodness by tomorrow, if his wife agrees with our proposals for her safety...' André paused for a moment before adding, 'They are devoted to one another and they would have got my vote as being the happiest couple from the moment I first met them! Of course she will say yes.'

'You really are a romantic Frenchman, aren't you?'

'*Mais oui*! But of course, I only wear the uniform to get the girls. It is born into every Frenchman to know them and also what to do with them!'

'That's enough sweet talking for one day. It's talk like that we British have never understood and that in itself could cause a war!'

'A love war the French would win easily!'

André threw up his arms in playful rebuke at his friend's remark. Laughing, he put on his hat deliberately askew and imitated Maurice Chevalier as he left the office singing, 'Thank heaven for little girls!'.

The drive home for Daniel was as if his little car had wings – his favourite tune was playing on the tape deck, his entrance into the driveway, the parking of the car and his rapid exit from it, the short run up to the front door, the snatching up into his arms of Nicole the moment he saw her, was like it had been before their tormentors had come. Now, Daniel felt free from the torment; the solution for both of them had been provided.

'Just endure it for a little while longer, my darling, the army know all of our problems now, they will protect us both. Oh darling, isn't it wonderful? We can start thinking about our futures again, the European future we believe in. The army knows they want us to cooperate with them. Isn't it going to be wonderful for us again – just like it used to be!'

The tears of happiness, relief, love and exhaustion welled up into his eyes. His head searched for a hiding place for his tears and automatically his head slid gently next to Nicole's and his nose breathed in the freshness of her long, dark hair. Nicole's hand ran up the nape of his neck, pushing his head closer to her. When his ear was close to her mouth, she kissed it. Her breath was warm as she whispered, 'It's wonderful darling, but what if the Russians find out?' The tremble of fear that passed through their bodies was electric.

Daniel pulled Nicole closer to him as tight as breathing would allow. Through his sobs and clogged up nose, he whispered, 'Nicole, please let us worry about the Russians tomorrow!... Let tonight be for us alone!' The gentle pull of her tiny hand in the centre of his back told Daniel that for tonight at least, there would be no mental fear of Russians being under their bed... tonight their lives would recommence!

The early morning sunlight spread across the bed. The light breeze occasionally moved the patterned lace curtain which filled the window and made the shadowy patterns dance the elongated shadows across the walls. Nicole lifted her slender body onto her elbow and stared down at her beloved husband's face. Before kissing him awake, she whispered, 'Go and tell your army I agree with you, and I only hope they can protect us!' Her lips gently kissed his broad forehead, then she lowered her lips gently down upon his.

Yute Polenkovich had been restless over the past few days, not because of his inactivity, but because Lanov was placed in Achern and Mogatin was flitting around the countryside, not bothering to pass information on, firstly to Lanov and then to himself. When he had made contact as arranged with Lanov, all Yute had been hearing was, 'I'm sure he'll be in touch soon!' During his own early experiences in the field as an organiser, he had been willing to make excuses, knowing the difficulty in the old days of out of the way towns and villages, but nowadays there were mobile phones.

The phone rang in the other room of Yute's apartment. He quickly finished pushing his tie up to his collar and walked slowly to the phone, the ritual of identity having been gone through and the sales manager to salesman talk began. 'I understand your visit to Karlsruhe was very successful and you are preparing to return?' asked Yute.

'Successful indeed, it's an open market, no competition. In fact, we could control the market easily in three or four days; it will be necessary for two additional people to make it a one hundred per cent certainty.'

'I'll despatch them to you, to arrive no later than the day after tomorrow. You'll meet them there in the usual way.'

'Fine. In the afternoon would be better for me, we can start that evening.'

'Very good, they will be there. What about Colmar – an important client, I believe?'

'Yes. He's on the board. I had an appointment to see him at his home. He was not impressed by our other representatives and was, to say the least, opposed to our proposition, but after some hard bargaining, he has agreed that our terms were the best option!'

'Well done! When do you think the contract can start?'

'Immediately, but I think it ought to be given a little time to put the Karlsruhe people in place first, along with the nice new prospect the office asked me to follow up on, while I was in the area.'

'Oh yes, I remember. How did things go with her?'

'She was a little tetchy at first, but after an hour or so, she fully realised that what we were offering could not be beaten by anyone in her field.'

'So she is happy to do business with us?' asked Yute.

'Definitely a "yes" to that question, but I feel it will be necessary to keep up our promotional pressure from time to time.'

'At the moment, if I can arrange it, she could be put into our distribution system?'

'Yes, for sure, it's only in the future she would need reminding of our product services!'

'Good. I suggest you get Karlsruhe into place now – we will organise something small as a trial run, for, shall we say, ten days from now?'

'Yes, it feels right. Ten days then. I will phone after Karlsruhe.'

'Yes do and may I congratulate you on behalf of the company – very well done.' Mogatin decided that Yute's last words did not require a response, and hung up the phone.

A very excited Rudi came onto Mayer's phone. 'There is a tape on its way to you, to prove good faith from my boss. It's important. Yute Polenkovich and Lanov and Mogatin are all in touch. Something's going to happen soon. Rudi paused for breath and realised he hadn't said 'hello'. The apologies poured from his mouth. He asked to be forgiven and hoped the 'I love yous' he was now saying would make up for his mistake.

Mayer teasingly responded, 'Maybe…'

When the tape arrived by courier later that same day from Moscow, Ernst Ulbrecht immediately had a copy made and sent directly to Robin. The hours lost by Rudi's office not having transcription equipment could have been a serious loss of time. Ernst proceeded to his office to listen to the tape's contents, calling Willi Koslowski and Mayer from their desks as he strode across the main open-plan office.

Robin had invited André to come and listen to the tape with him and his team of investigators. André accepted without any hesitancy and sat listening without comment. The notes he and all the others in the room were taking as they listened would be debated after the tape finished.

'Well, gentlemen, we know one thing for sure, between now and ten days' time, if we are good enough, we should be able to work out what the bloody hell's going on!' The laughter from all in the room was spontaneous, which is what Robin wanted from his team. Happy and spontaneous approaches by his investigator had spelt out success in the past.

'Let us first make plans for the next Karlsruhe visit. I think Sergeant Robinson should finish what he has already started up there. The dossiers on the three houses are nearly complete, I understand, and the evidence proves that four people from the three houses are all military and two have a direct link with Eurocorps. The two remaining are connected to mechanical engineers who keep our transports moving. This may become an important point, a little further into our puzzle. Mogatin, as you will see in the report, visited Metz after Mülheim. We know who and where, but at the moment we will keep the house and any movement covered. I suggest Sergeant Hackett and three men of his choosing with extra support when needed. Is that all right with you, Sergeant Hackett?'

'Certainly, sir,' came the mumbled response.

'Activity in Mülheim at the moment, looks to be our heaviest concentration, so it will be our Sergeant MacKenzie who will have to cover this with what is left of the investigators, so he will have the support of the office staff to keep his reports up to the minute!' Robin paused, then added, 'It could mean they report in by phone and the poor clerks will have to do all the paperwork for them.'

The boos and hisses following Robin's tongue-in-cheek remark soon quietened down. Robin began to speak again. 'As you are all aware, we have a staff officer involved. After receiving Mogatin into his house, he has to be watched very thoroughly. Sergeant Donaldson plus two men will have to be very discreet on this one and will report back only to me or the Adjutant.' Robin took a sip of water from the glass he had brought with him. Raising his eyebrows playfully, he remarked, 'Only water, I assure you!' The joke taken, he continued. 'You will see a transcript of a telephone conversation commencing at the bottom of page five. I am suggesting that we take ten minutes to read it and afterwards, we will debate its meaning. The Adjutant and I think we have worked out its meaning ourselves, but your opinions are also vital.'

The ticking of a large, white-faced Roman-numeralled clock with a wide dark-brown wooden surround was the only thing to be heard. The first cough breaking the silence came from Sergeant Robinson, who contributed with, 'Sir, I think everything is spelt out in this transcript. It's a childish conversation, so that should their calls get intercepted, people would just think it was a pair of poxy salesmen discussing their business.'

'I think that part is true, Sergeant,' the Adjutant remarked, 'but is there anything to be gained from the body of the message that Robin, the Major here and I may have missed?' André looked over at Robin and apologised with his eyes, knowing it was not his place to ask questions of Robin's teams. Robin gave a forgiving nod as Sergeant Robinson spoke again.

'Well, it seems they've got the Colonel in Colmar by the short and curlies!' The whole group laughed.

'But what is he going to do and how does he fit in with the lower ranks in Mülheim? Are there any clues we have missed?' Robin's probing question brought sobriety back to the meeting with a bang. The discussion went on for another hour and after the acceptance of the findings by everyone, Robin dismissed the men to pursue their duties.

André and Robin stood outside of the administration building, looking across the parade ground. André asked searchingly, 'What do you really think is going to happen?'

'I wish I knew, André! My mind says we are being infiltrated for a purpose, but militarily, we have nothing of value like nuclear weapons or anything that is really dangerous. Yes, the Corps will be trained on nuclear and chemical weapons, but we will never have them on station at any of our depots.'

'True. We are a mobile force, floating in and out of wherever we are needed.'

'That's exactly what I mean. There has to be a reason, but what it is, is damn well beating me!'

'Don't get angry with yourself, Robin. You and your German and French policemen have done well so far, just keep gnawing away – you'll get there, I'm sure!'

'I hope you're right.'

'Just keep level-headed. Everything will work out. Haven't you got the first initiative? You are watching and now listening to them without anyone on their side knowing about it.'

'Yes, that really is our trump card, but it's finding out what else is in the pack that I'm afraid of!' Both men stood for a few moments before Robin broke the silence by saying, 'Well, André, I must get on to Hamburg and Achern to tell my policemen friends about our day so far. Will I see you in the mess later?'

'Possibly. I'll phone you later on.' As they parted, both men saluted each other.

Returning to the hurly-burly of his offices, Robin grinned and muttered to himself, 'I wish I'd stayed outside!' With a few acknowledgements and a few 'yes' and 'no' answers to questions, he passed along to his office door. The door closed behind him, holding back the constant noise from the outer offices. Reaching for the phone, he dialled Ernst's number and waited a few seconds to hear, 'Ulbrecht heir!'

'It's Robin, Ernst. How are you?'

'Fine, thank you. What happened with you today?'

'I've managed to allocate teams to cover Mülheim, Metz, Karlsruhe, Colmar and we're carrying on with the surveillance in Achern. Even though they have agreed to work with us, we have promised the Tomlevskis protection.'

'You have been busy!'

'Not too bad really, although if our surveillance has to be increased any more, I won't be able to sustain it. The system is working well at the moment though.'

'Good for you, Robin. What did your people make of the tape?'

'I think point by point is the easiest way of going through our thoughts and opinions, Ernst. One. Generally, we all feel we are containing the situation and with the additional manpower I have put into the field, we can cover every move they make. Two. We are also of the opinion that any major moves will either be made in Mülheim or Metz.' Realising that Ernst had no knowledge of Mogatin's visit to Metz, Robin added, 'May I come back to you on the subject of Metz, Ernst?'

The thoughtful 'Yes...' he received in reply made Robin realise that Ernst trusted this would make no difference to the summary being given.

'We also feel that with a staff officer from Eurocorps in the frame, we must place a separate team of investigators sworn to secrecy for the moment, reporting directly to the Adjutant or myself. Three. Karlsruhe. The teams which followed Mogatin's first run are fully surveying the area and the backgrounds of people who are connected with the houses looked at. The team will remain the same. Achern will be covered and Tomlevski and his wife are cooperating with us and, may I add, when he was brought in, he collapsed and was relieved that we knew. We have tightened up security at all bases. Colmar is going to be our trickiest situation, with the staff officer. The house he lives in is large, the grounds are large, the hedges are high and the roads are mostly empty when he travels into Strasbourg. That is an update of our workload. We have tossed around the possible reasons for all of this and the only one thing we can all agree on is that we are a fast-moving force. We would be given freedom of movement across borders with whatever equipment we felt necessary to complete the job in hand, possibly from all the compass points throughout Europe, but thank goodness we don't have conflicts everyday and as we are an instantaneous force, they would have little time to jump onto our merry-go-round. We think this aspect is what they are after, for some as yet obscure reason.'

'Robin, have you got many transport depots throughout Europe?'

'I haven't counted numbers, but I would have thought about twenty at least, why?'

'In Hamburg, on the last intrusion we had from our Russian friends, an awful lot of transport was involved.'

'My God, Ernst, do you know what I've just started thinking?'

'I think so. If you've got transport running throughout Europe day and night, keeping your units supplied, you have a ready made transport system.'

'Bloody hell, Ernst! They're infiltrating communications and transport commands!'

'I think you could be right!'

'It would be so simple to infiltrate; we have a lot of civilian workers involved and of course multi-nationals in that area!'

'You'll have to look into this area, Robin – if we and you can get your people in place, you at least would have a counter force that could upset their system.'

'I haven't got the manpower to be able to keep up the tails on inside workers. I'll have to go to GHQ with the Adjutant's permission, but we have a problem to work out in that direction. I mentioned that we had a staff officer connected to Mogatin, which means we may be infiltrated already, possibly by more than just one.'

'You're right, but surely there must be some way?'

'Not without concrete proof and then it's at Premier and Presidential level!'

'I'll give you all the support I can, Robin. My connections are pretty good in Germany and France; if you need any doors opened, I wouldn't hesitate to push!'

'I know, Ernst, thank you. But we'll have to run a bit longer as we currently are, I'm afraid!'

Ernst wanted to get off the subject of Robin's dilemma and

asked, 'What about Metz, Robin, you said you would come back to me on that subject?'

Robin raced to get his brain in gear and remember the salient points clearly, without causing too much of a delay before answering the question.

'Metz could be a problem. Mogatin visited the Mayor – a Lady Mayoress in fact, who has not been seen at her duties since. She is still alive, we know – her husband leaves for work every day, the housemaid comes and goes, we have even seen the husband kissing the Lady Mayoress goodbye in the mornings. It has been verified that it is definitely her, but she just hasn't left the house since Mogatin's visit. We have tried several times to get a clear photograph of her, but so far, we haven't succeeded. She is always wearing one of those large, floppy-brimmed hats. We are talking to the gardener and staff whenever we can, but they are very loyal to their mistress and just keep saying their mistress has "one of her migraines".' Robin stopped to draw breath before continuing, 'The staff are defensive to any questions. Even when one of our investigators asked whether the Mayoress had had an accident or such like, the reply fired back at him was "The Mayoress's damn condition was nothing to do with him!"'

'Robin, you need some photographic evidence – has a doctor called to the house?'

'Getting into the grounds is no problem, taking a photograph is no problem, but it's political. My friend in the civilian police won't gamble that any photographer getting closer to the house will not be seen by a member of the Mayoress's staff. He wants to take photographs at night through chinks in the curtains – we're doing it tonight, but success can't be assured.'

'You can only do your best, Robin.'

'For sure, but it's a long wait for success or failure.'

'It will work out, Robin, have faith.'

'I have, Ernst, it's just the bloody waiting that I hate!'

'If our friends have been playing around, it isn't only photographs you will be wanting, Robin. Why not start an investigation on your Mayoress and see what turns up? Maybe she has something tucked away in her past!'

'Ernst, thank you. I was getting too focused on photographs, wasn't I?'

'Maybe just a little, but it could be a good exercise for you and if there is something in her past, you would be slightly ahead of the game.'

'Thanks, Ernst, I'm sure I would have got around to thinking about her in the end... talking with you always helps, Ernst!'

'A necessary part of the job, Robin. Call on me whenever you wish, but remember I'm not always as much of a help!'

'I know, Ernst, no vanity... but thanks a million. You've set my mind working again as opposed to blaming everything that gets in my way.'

'Good. I'll hear from you soon, then?'

'As soon as anything breaks, Ernst.'

In Robin's haste to get on with the investigation into the Lady Mayoress, his last words were cut off by the speedy click of the receiver being slammed down in its cradle. Ernst looked at the now dead phone in his hand and murmured into it, 'Oh, to be young and enthusiastic again!'

Robin immediately snatched up his phone, dialling the four digits of his Adjutant's direct line.

'Sir, Robin here. May I ask your permission to have the Mayoress of Metz investigated, sir?'

'Robin, aren't you going a little too far?'

'Well, we're sure she is incapacitated in some way. We are going to have to wait until tonight to get any photographs of her and we'll be losing nearly a day... a day which, if there is something in her closet that shouldn't be, could give us something solid to work with and a head start... sir.'

Robin stopped abruptly. He wanted to carry on, but realised he had said enough.

'Robin, I can't sanction your investigating civilians, least of all foreign nationals, whose soil we walk with their permission. No, I can't sanction it. You will have to get your information from your French Inspector Torneau – see what he can do.'

'Thank you, sir. I was actually meaning to go through him as a special request. As you say, sir, it really is their province.'

'Sorry, Robin, of course you would do it correctly. Got a few problems this end and I snapped at what I thought was an over-zealous request!'

'Is there anything I can do to help, André?' Robin's tone had softened and he used the Adjutant's Christian name, offering true friendship.

'You may have to soon, Robin. I'm out of my depth in all this police work, but not at the moment, though.'

'Would you care to tell me whom or what it concerns, sir?'

'Our staff officer… Keller. He seems to be ruffling a few feathers over in Strasbourg.'

'We are watching him, sir, but we can't get inside HQ even if we would like to.'

'It may be nothing, maybe it will blow over… I'll let you know.'

'Please do, sir.' The formality in Robin's voice came back into the conversation. 'We in investigations are worried about some of his movements and contacts, but we have nothing specific, just hunches!'

'Keep him in your sights, Robin. He may be very harmful to the Corps!'

'We will watch him closely, sir.'

'I know you will, Robin. I know you will…'

Seconds later, Robin was patched through to his friend, Inspector Torneau. The courtesies over, Robin came straight out with his request. 'Would you carry out a background check on the Mayoress of Metz and her husband, Gilbert?'

'Mon Dieu, Robin, you are crazy!' was Gilbert's first reaction, but after hearing the story of Mogatin's visit and the lack of sightings of her since then, plus the cover-up by her staff and the lack of comment from her husband, Gilbert replied, 'On behalf of the people of France, you leave me no option. I will investigate, but I hope you are wrong, Robin.'

'Me too, Gilbert. I'm sorry to have to ask, but there really is no alternative. Will you keep me informed of anything you dig up, please?'

'Yes. Daily, I think.'

'That will be fine, say at 1600 hours each day – that gives us time to act instantly with at least some part of the day left.'

Gilbert responded, joking, 'It's good to be in the army when your day is so short!'

'Ha ha, Gilbert, ha bloody ha!'

The laughter between them faded as their respective phones were placed back in their cradles and both men primed their minds for the delicate tasks which they both needed to undertake.

The warmth generated by Daniel and Nicole's entwined bodies gave them both comfort. The torment of the past weeks had almost torn their love to shreds, but now they were allowing their bodies to fluctuate between clinging and caressing, intimately. The full fluid endurance which they had shared eagerly not so long ago would come back to them, but the uncertain times they were sharing would not yet allow their spirits to totally flood their minds and bodies. For the moment, they must both play their part in helping to bury the sins of their parents and return to the effort of the fight to secure the total unity of Europe.

Their heads side by side, lips nearly touching, was the position they awoke in each morning, their arms and legs entwined. Perfectly natural until they opened their eyes, then a little bit of the hate returned. The hate which had grown between them as they both attempted to defend their parents, trying to find excuses, then the silence and the acceptance of guilt. Then came the relief after their admission to Eurocorps and now today, what would it bring to their lives? The doorbell rang. The suddenness of it jolted both of their eyes open immediately, firstly with fear, then a showing of love, then with panic.

'Daniel, who is it?'

'I don't know, do I!'

'Well, look then!'

Getting disentangled from his wife and the bedclothes seemed to take forever and the second ring cut through the house as Daniel's feet touched the floor.

'All right, all right!... I'm coming!' he shouted at the walls. Fumbling for slippers and his dressing gown, then the door handle, he reached the top of the landing. The doorbell cut through the air again. 'Wait a minute, you fool! Have patience, I'm coming!' Daniel was still shouting his message as he opened the door. Pulling his dressing gown around him as he pulled the door open, he said, 'You should remember it's Sunday and it's only 7 a.m.!'

His eyes lifted to see an angry red face with a well-trimmed moustache, about to go into apoplexy, shouting back at him, 'I am Colonel Trevor Keller, let me pass, Lieutenant!' Without hesitating, the Colonel pushed past Daniel and walked straight into the lounge, and taking a seat in an armchair, he continued, 'You may have heard of me – GHQ staff.'

'Yes, sir, I have. May I see your papers, sir?'

'Unnecessary, I would have thought, but here you are.'

'Thank you, sir. All seems to be in order.' As he passed the document back, Daniel added, 'We cannot be too careful, sir.'

'Especially in your case, Lieutenant – especially in your case!'

'I don't understand, sir. What are you implying?'

'We will get to that in a short while. First, coffee, then your wife will attend our little chat!'

'My wife has nothing to do with the military, sir. I do not expect her to be ordered around by my own Corps Commander, yet alone some unknown Colonel off the street!'

'We'll see, Lieutenant. I'm sure when you mention a certain Russian encounter, she will be curious and wish to attend.'

'She knows no Russians!'

'Don't treat me like a fool! I know very well that you both know some Russians. Now, coffee – black, no sugar and when you have had a whisper or two with your wife, we will get on. Do please try and be quick. I know you will both enjoy what I have to tell you!' The sarcasm and torment promised by the Colonel's little speech did not go unnoticed by Daniel.

The coffee having been duly served and the whispering having taken place upstairs, Nicole and Daniel were now sitting stiffly upright on the small sofa with the Colonel still sitting in the armchair opposite. Daniel and Nicole had already come to the conclusion the Colonel was on an official visit from some military cloak and dagger outfit who had heard of their plight, but the paperwork hadn't circulated far enough for him to know they had agreed to work for both sides, their own military police as well as the Russians.

'You stupid children!' blurted out the Colonel. 'You fools! Why did you hold out so long against your persecutors?'

Almost instantly, Daniel answered, 'We didn't believe them at first. Checking with our families was the obvious thing to do...'

'But you admit you were wrong to cause such a delay?' Both Daniel and Nicole looked at each other, not understanding the question. They chose to remain silent. 'Well, I'll tell you why. You have been softened by easy living and no discipline!'

Daniel and Nicole looked quizzically at each other, trying to fathom where the Colonel was coming from. Both felt his abuse unnecessary and were becoming irritated. Daniel knew he did not have to take this abuse from anyone and that his right to reply to senior and junior officers was in the military law books, but they just sat in silence waiting for the reason for the Colonel's presence to become clearer. 'As your superior officer, I want you to tell me exactly what your commitment is at barracks?'

The question seemed reasonable to Daniel, so in the next few minutes, he explained that he had not been fully committed by the Adjutant yet, but was hoping to be fully occupied in communications at all levels within the Corps.

'When will you know of this commitment?' asked the Colonel brusquely.

'There is no way of my telling, sir. My request for the communications section has been well known since my application to join the Corps.'

'I know that, but give me some idea when you expect to be in that position!'

The tone of the Colonel's voice disturbed Daniel; his mind whirled like a tornado. This man is not quite what he seems to be, I'm sure, he thought. 'My Adjutant will be in charge of my posting, sir. May I respectfully suggest that you contact him?'

'You will tell me directly, the moment you know!'

'May I ask why, sir?'

'Because I will have orders for you!'

'May I ask on what authority, sir?'

'My authority!'

Both Daniel and Nicole immediately stiffened as they realised this man was the enemy – a staff officer of Eurocorps, being controlled by the Russian Organisatiya – the peril they were being given a chance to save themselves from, a chance to balance their lives, back to serving Europe.

'You have been sent by the Russians then?' Nicole's voice was barely audible.

'Yes, and willingly so. I am not frightened like you, I gave myself to communism years ago and have been waiting for my chance to act. That time is now and you will obey my orders!'

'Is there anyone else we should expect to be contacted by?' asked Daniel. He was surprised by his own coolness after the shock of the Colonel's revelation.

'Not immediately, no, but Lanov and Mogatin will be keeping an eye on you in the event you should attempt to deviate from my orders!' The Colonel stood up and leant over them. Through clenched teeth, he assured them both that he would be obeyed. No sooner were those threats out of his mouth, than he turned on his heel and left without saying goodbye.

Sergeant Donaldson held his position under the deep shadow of a large horse chestnut tree, having followed the Colonel. Whilst observing the front of the house, he had managed to discreetly use his mobile phone to report his position, unaware of the excitement he caused when his report and the location of his whereabouts reached Major Cadwallader's desk. For the moment, Sergeant Donaldson would doggedly pursue his quarry.

The crisp ring of the phone on the Adjutant's desk was responded to almost immediately. Before he had time to announce himself, Robin had asked, 'Hello André, is that you?'

André was slightly taken aback by his friend's abruptness, but answered calmly, 'On my direct line… were you expecting someone else?'

Robin flustered out an apology for his rudeness in not allowing André to speak first and then he said, 'Sir, our staff officer has made direct contact with the Tomlevskis!'

'We are moving into new fields very fast then, Robin! What are you thinking of doing next?' replied André.

'There really is no alternative. Ulbrecht must be told of this confirmed approach of Lanov and Mogatin and now of our

Colonel's direct approach to the Tomlevskis.'

'I can see problems, Robin.'

'There is no alternative, sir. In my opinion, we can't withhold information from our friends in all the national police forces.'

'I'm aware of that, Robin, but it means the Colonel of Eurocorps and our General will have to be informed now. I don't have the authority, and neither do you, to knit a civilian operation together alongside us.'

'I'm sorry, André, but you always knew there was a possibility of this happening.'

'True, but when we discussed this before, we didn't know a staff officer was going to be implicated!'

'Agreed, sir. May I suggest you go direct to the General?'

'The Corps Colonel should be involved. It's going to ruffle a few feathers when he finds out I've been going above his head!'

'Sir, the General must decide who he places into what will be his team for an operation like this. I'm sure he will put our Colonel in charge and when he does, you can apologise to him! He will be so chuffed with his new responsibilities, he will soon forgive and forget your indiscretion.'

'Robin, I think you are most probably right in your assumption, but what if the General doesn't pick our Colonel?'

'Once again, André, I'm sorry, but we don't have much choice.'

'You're right, of course. You'd better tell Ulbrecht right away. We will all need to meet and I mean all those involved, for a full briefing by the General… on neutral ground, of course.'

'Thank you, André. I feel sure we are doing the right thing. We have become involved in something, God knows what it is, but we both know that the threat is too great to ignore.'

'We are agreed on that, Robin. Let's get moving to stop this decay spreading!'

'On it now, sir!' Robin held the receiver for a few moments before adding, 'Thanks again, André.'

Ernst Ulbrecht looked over the messages on his desk. Only one really caught his eye: *Major Cadwallader called, he is unobtainable now, but will call you again at 1600 hours today.* Ernst automatically looked at his watch. It read 1610 hours. Rapidly checking that there had not been a second message in the pile, he sat down mumbling to himself, 'He said 1600 hours – it's ten past now!' The drumming of his fingers became even quicker. The natural light outside his office had begun to fade, and Ernst just sat waiting for the phone to ring. 1620 hours… 1630 hours… 1647 hours. Simultaneously as the phone rang, he switched on his desk light, saying, 'Ulbrecht heir!'

'Have you been waiting long, Ernst?'

'Well, I was expecting your call sooner!'

'I'm sorry, Ernst. My Adjutant has been in a flat spin all day and I have had to sit with him at HQ getting some things sorted out.'

'Don't worry. Your message said you would call, nothing about it being urgent.'

'I'm afraid it is urgent and I've lost some time, but what I was doing this afternoon was relevant, although the time lost may make things difficult for you.'

'Why don't you start at the beginning, Robin, and we shall see?'

Clearing his throat softly, Robin started. 'We have had a startling development. One of our Staff Colonels has been approached at his house by Mogatin, as you know from my report. Well, that very same Colonel has now approached the Tomlevskis insisting that he is their controller and that they will tell him every military move that they are instructed to fulfil. The Colonel does not know that they have been intercepted by us and are cooperating with us. That is the most important part, but we feel it confirms that Lanov and Mogatin are aware they are being followed, and so they have briefed the Colonel to break his cover.'

'That second part is very reassuring from all points of view! Are the Tomlevskis expecting instructions immediately from your army or this Colonel?'

'No. We are keeping normal surveillance on all of our suspects – I've checked all of Eurocorps' schedules and commitments, but nothing seems to be knitting together at the moment in any way.' The pause was not long, before Ernst spoke again.

'Your Adjutant has a problem now.'

'It has been reconciled, Ernst. He never wavered, just acknowledged he would have to go over the head of our Corps Colonel, straight to the General, which is where I've been today. The Adjutant and the General feel we should all meet up on neutral ground, secretly of course, possibly tomorrow?'

'By that, you mean everyone involved?'

'Well, we were hoping for everyone…'

'The Americans, Portuguese, French, et cetera?'

'If possible. We have good relationships with other armies, so we thought the Brits could give us a barracks somewhere for a day or so.'

'There's not much time, especially for the Americans, but let's try. You will organise your own. I'll beg, borrow or steal what monies I can for flights, et cetera. You'll owe me a beer when we get this organised – I suggest you set it up from tomorrow but cover it for forty-eight hours at least.'

'That's what I thought, Ernst. I'll try to help in any way I can, but with the cash – we don't have a facility for extracting it from the system.'

'It isn't easy here either, but let's go do it and cry afterwards!'

'I'll start straight away. Come back in an hour and we can compare notes on our positions.'

'Look forward to it!' With a little chuckle in his voice, Ernst added, 'This little exercise will keep the adrenalin going, Robin!'

The phone clicked down in both their offices, only to be picked up again and again over the next hour.

Having spoken to everyone necessary for the complete cover of all aspects of the operation so far, and a few more he had anticipated, Ernst noticed Mayer coming towards his office. Disappointed that she only acknowledged him and passed by his doorway, he couldn't believe himself when he called out her name when he had nothing to ask or to say to her. The thought, you stupid old fool, ran through his mind as she turned back and now stood in his doorway smiling.

'You called me, sir?'

Ernst's mind snapped to a decision. 'Mayer, we are setting up a meeting with the military and all of the police forces involved in our little drama so far. I thought you should join us and do you think Rudi could sneak away for forty-eight hours?'

Mayer stood there, dumbstruck. For the first time in her association with Ernst, she turned into a gibbering fool as she tried to say, 'When and where, sir?'

Ernst replied, father-like, 'He will have to leave Moscow now to get here in time to come with us!'

Mayer was still dazed as she answered while turning to leave, 'I'll get on to Rudi and ask him if he can go.'

When her back was turned, Ernst allowed himself a little smile and muttered under his breath, 'Isn't life wonderful!' He was still slightly dismayed at his impetuosity in asking Mayer and Rudi to the meeting, which delayed him in picking up the phone that had already rung three times. Finally clearing his head, he answered it, 'Mayer heir… sorry! Ulbrecht heir!'

'It's coming to something when you can't remember your own name, Ernst!' The American accent of Joc Latimer soon cleared his head completely.

'Sorry, Joc, I've just asked Mayer and her Rudi to join us, if he can get out of Russia quickly enough and she turned into a gibbering love-sick child before my very eyes – sorry, you don't know anything about them, do you? They have fallen in love over the phone and never met!'

'So you're playing cupid?'

'Well, I suppose so, but it's nice to see love blossoming in the world!'

'You're right. Anyway, I must push on, Ernst, I've got a plane to catch!'

'Great! Just you?'

'No, I've got Brian Fullerton of Foreign division, who has been very useful and Joe Lomax from Portugal. We are all meeting up at London Heathrow airport at about 1100 hours. Our London Embassy will be our contact point, we'll leave all information with security – we'll check in with them on landing. By the way, it is still on, isn't it?'

'France, Germany and Portugal are all confirmed, along with the British Army. It's moving along quite well!'

'Good. Look forward to meeting you in the flesh! Must press on now, bye... Oh, hold on, Ernst, one other thing – I've managed to get all of the American fares paid!'

'Joc, you really are a miracle worker! Thanks so much!'

'Good Old Uncle Sam! He's not a bad guy really. I'll see you tomorrow!'

Robin Cadwallader sat rechecking that all the 'fine-tuning' had been arranged and sent to each member of the teams who would be coming to London. Each car would have to be an unmarked car with driver, each would be as inconspicuous as possible, all arriving at London Heathrow airport within a three-hour time span, and all proceeding to Dorchester by as many varied routes as possible, all arriving in Dorchester within a five-hour time span. Accommodation plus meeting hall, chairs, tables, boards, pads and pencils for each individual, all organised, set up and all information to each individual sent by fax, informing them of each and every fact and arrangement. Robin reached for the phone and pushed the buzzer button. A second or two passed, then a female investigator entered his office.

'You rang, sir? Is this the finish?'

With a sigh, Robin answered, 'I hope so. I've checked and rechecked it until my eyes are ready to drop from my head!'

'Everything you have passed through has been sent, sir. I'm pleased this is the last, because you have exactly thirty minutes to get over to the airstrip with Major Roche and neither of you will want to keep the General waiting! May I suggest you leave the rest to us, sir? The communications people are having the time of their lives keyboard-tapping, things are buzzing and clacking then whirring as orders come out printed and sent! Now, come along, sir, your bag and your driver are waiting, and when you've gone, I can get on with the last transmission, sir!'

Robin looked at this unknown girl who had been transferred in for the emergency which had arisen since the Adjutant had said, 'Let's get moving to stop this decay spreading!'

Smiling, Robin politely thanked 'Miss No-Name' for all her efforts and asked that she say thank you and well done to everyone else. Before Robin was in the car, she had vanished to finish her job. Robin fell back into the leather upholstery, next to the Adjutant and whispered just loud enough for the Adjutant to hear, 'You have a very fine army, Mr Adjutant, very fine indeed…'

The contingency of four French, four British, four Germans, two Portuguese, four Americans and one Russian all slid into Britain unnoticed by any of the airport watchers. Robin sighed deeply as he sank back into the ministry car next to the General. 'Just you sit and enjoy the ride, Robin. I've got some papers to sort out… you just enjoy the view!'

The General's attitude, after the original spontaneity, became tedious to Robin throughout their journey. Robin felt the crafty old fool was angling for glory in this wild foray he had authorised to begin. The glory, Robin felt, should there ever be any, should be played very quietly and not publicised for the whole world to know. Robin relaxed further into his seat, his mind racing over details of movement of each and everyone as they all converged on Dorchester to the now unused Records Offices. Unused, but nevertheless, still maintained until the day every history of every soldier in its files would be locked into some computer in alphabetical order… a few moments of keyboard time, just essentials, name, rank, number and an assessment by the clerk entering the information in no more than fifty words of the soldier's entire military career… no paperwork, no keeping of the notes made by people he or she knew, along the way during their service… Robin's shudder at the thought of this heartless end good men had to endure, brought his thoughts back to the present.

'Sir…' The sudden sound in this whispering car sounded like gunfire. The General just raised an eyebrow over the top of his wire-rimmed glasses. 'Sir, when we've got to the end of this case, we really must not publicise our part in it. It will be better to pretend the military were not involved.'

'Explain your reasons for saying that, Robin.'

'Sir, we are relying on the auspices of our civilian police friends. If our army's part in this became known, it is my opinion that we would lose kudos and the security this outer shell of protection gives your Corps. My advice would be to take little praise, because it brings with it its own spotlight which would be a distraction from our aims as a Corps in the future.'

'Fine, Robin, I gave you permission to start this thing because it was and is, a necessary thing to do, but my worry was to protect my army from outside interference. In general terms, Robin, you have allayed my fears. Give me a clean army at the end of all this. Of course, I'm sure you will, no matter what it is we are heading into. Now, Robin, I must get on with these papers…'

Robin sat there dumbfounded. How had he got the General so wrong? The rest of the journey passed in silence with the General catching up on his paperwork and Robin mentally chastising himself for making his speech and for the evil thoughts which raced through his head about the General. Major Roche, who had sat next to the driver and had overheard Robin's conversation was convinced now that the General and Robin would work very well together. The satisfied, wry smile which passed over his face showed his contentment.

The beautiful countryside floated by outside, the dappled sunlight danced on the windscreen and cast a kaleidoscope of patterns throughout the car. More hedgerows, more gaps to admire, the rolling countryside, more bends, then suddenly a barred road and uniformed soldiers guarding the tall wire fence to keep people out and the secrets in. Well done, driver, Robin thought as the car came to a halt. An envelope with final directions to the prearranged quarters was handed over after the guard commander had verified each and every passenger and that the correct transport had carried them there.

Robin wound down his window and called the guard commander over asking, 'Are we the last to arrive, Lieutenant?'

'No, sir. A gentleman called Vargas and a Captain Tias are approximately fifteen minutes behind their estimated schedules.'

'Will you inform me, please, when all of your visitors have arrived?'

'Yes, sir. Immediately.'

As Robin said, 'Thank you,' the car slid away to drop off its passengers in order of rank and seniority. Robin looked at his watch and mumbled to himself, 'Only another forty-five minutes and I will have met Ernst again and Joc Latimer, his American that he speaks so highly of… What is Vargas up to? His plane landed on time!'

The meeting with Ernst Ulbrecht's group was very congenial with lots of banter about the exquisite accommodation the military had managed to find for them at such short notice, all of it given and taken in good humour. The American team were very content and Joc Latimer and Brian Fullerton both gave Robin a slap on the back for 'getting it on' so quickly and in true 'British style'. The French were arrogant as usual, but friendship between Robin and Inspector Torneau soon broke the ice and the Inspectors from Paris, Strasbourg and Colmar warmed to the whole group, becoming more and more friendly with each new handshake. Rudi Simusov and Mayer were inseparable wherever they went. Following Ernst, they were never more than inches apart, but both were serious regarding the business about to commence. Ulbrecht, playing the father-figure, expounded long explanations to everyone about the reasons for Rudi's presence and emphasised the good work he had been doing for his office in Hamburg by collaborating with his Russian-speaking colleague, Officer Mayer. The General, who was to be chairman of the committee, was passing amongst the group and conversing in French and German with ease. Sergeant MacKenzie also mingled and with his lilting Scottish accent, even made the German language sound romantic.

The pleasantries over, a Sergeant-Major called the mêlée to order and announced the arrival of Chief Inspector of Police, Manuel Vargas and Captain Maria Tias of the Lisbon police department. Until then, everyone had been admiring Officer Mayer. The silence which caught in the throats of everyone present at the sight of Maria Tias's long legs, hour-glass figure, full firm breasts, slender neck, full lips, high cheekbones, dark, sunken, tormenting eyes, and long dark hair draped softly over her shoulders, forcing their eyes downwards again to take in the apparition in front of them, was almost audible. She was encased in a plunging necklined dress of gold lamé, stopping above her knees with bare, bronzed legs stretching down to tiny feet, encased in finely strapped sandals. The trapped air held in all of the throats in the room made the largest wishful sigh ever heard in an army barracks anywhere in the world. Vargas, in full dress uniform, standing beside her, was very much overdressed. The rest of the group being in casual clothes, some military personnel in fatigues; Captain Tias still outshone her boss.

Vargas and Tias both stood proudly in the doorway showing no sign of embarrassment at being so overdressed. The General moved forward, received a salute from Vargas, followed by a handshake, then turning to his right, he took the offered hand of Captain Tias, shook it lightly and ushered her, followed by Vargas, into the well of the group; as he passed through, the group closed in to get a closer look at Tias. The General was heard to say, 'I'm terribly sorry, but there really was no time during the setting up of this gathering to have dress code instructions printed, which of course, now we have male and female personnel at all levels of our organisations these days, we should really think of!' Although the General's words were heard by many of the people there, Vargas still strutted like a peacock, showing no embarrassment whatever.

Allowing a settling-in time of half an hour and allowing for the lateness of Vargas and his friend, plus the shock of seeing such an apparition, the General considered he was running about fifteen minutes behind his estimated schedule. He nodded to the Sergeant-Major that the time was right to call the assembly to the more formal meeting room which had been set aside for them.

The meeting soon settled down to its work, the exchange of knowledge between them was rapid and given without any political overtones. They were policemen trying to help the military. Analysing the Russians' approach to military personnel, the hours taken in discussion about why they should try to infiltrate the military, had ranged from looking into a built-in communication system for their use, along with the transport system. Mainly the discussions had been along the line of what the army might have that the Russians would want. The arsenal for the Eurocorps, although it would grow in the future, was at that moment, very small. Its design was a fast-moving, peace-keeping, or a 'prevention of possible troubles' force within the European structure and also to supply an efficient mobile support group to any corps within the EEC. The military could offer no other thought other than communications and transport as an answer to the Americans, Germans, French, Portuguese and the one bemused Russian. The General stood up to stretch his legs and continued speaking...

'So you see, gentlemen and ladies, of course... we have nothing worth the stealing of our own, except communications and transport. Although we are self-reliant, we do and are, in the habit of coupling into member nations' armies, to keep our costs down. This is the fact of the matter, we have transports and depots, but nothing worth stealing! It's a puzzle, gentlemen – I declare a mystery that needs an answer!'

Ernst sat quietly next to Joc. Neither of them at all surprised at the General's remarks, both gave him full marks for his chairmanship and his summing up, but neither of them had the answer. Ernst subconsciously started to rub the back of his neck. Joc looked at his friend, having been told by Koslowski about his boss's habit. Ernst then stood up, his hand still cupping his neck. 'General, sir... what if we were to look at it another way... let's say they are not going to steal from you, but are going to give you things to move around for them.'

The surprise at the thought of such a premise stunned everyone in the room, most of all the General, whose pacing stopped and as if pole-axed, fell into his chair, uttering, 'My God, it could be possible, but what and why?'

Robin, who had been sitting behind Ernst and Joc, whispered to Ernst, 'Ernst, if you are right, our charter gives us freedom of movement at all times!'

Ernst replied, 'Robin, it's only a hunch, but perhaps the military should watch its supply lines!'

The general discussion continued for a few more hours, with everyone endorsing the fact that at that moment, it must remain a military matter, but should their anticipation be correct, it would have dramatic effects on Europe and the world. The meeting broke up just after midnight, everyone assuring each other of their vigilance and cooperation. The General stood up to make the closing address, suggesting they each take to their beds whilst his team work out ways to get them all back unobserved to their respective countries... 'May I wish you well and thank you for your assurances in the protection of my army... thank you.'

The group slowly moved away from the meeting room with the exception of Vargas and Tias, who just seemed to dissolve away as the last 'thank-you' was voiced… or was it before?

The personal goodbyes prior to being picked up by their respective drivers were brief, but each and every one was sincere and the promises made would be kept; the bond struck against international crime would be forced into their administration and extended into generations of police to come.

The resolve that each member of the group cogitated as they were whisked away back to their own hunting grounds, was that no one single enemy would become a world threat. Robin, after saying his farewells, returned to pause for just a brief moment as he saluted the last departing car, before getting into the car waiting to take his General and Adjutant back and to begin the plan of action which had been agreed by everyone during this short time they had been together.

Chapter Twenty-Nine

It was not as if there was nothing to say, but no conversation of consequence had taken place between the General, the Adjutant, Sergeant MacKenzie or Robin himself. Odd comments like, 'I wonder if Vargas and Tias caught their plane?... They were living in a different world to us – they probably got beamed up!' All of them were secretly jealous of Vargas, but they, nor anyone at the meeting would admit that Vargas was a very lucky man to have such accommodating staff. 'Ulbrecht was a very old-fashioned policeman!'... 'Rudi the Russian will have a great deal of problems if they find out what he was really doing in the West!'... 'Mayer is a very pretty, intelligent girl. Rudi and she look good together!'... 'Latimer and Fullerton seem to have been around in some tough spots!'... 'The French contingency look to be of the right type – old school, and won't let politics get into the job, even the Paris chap, when he realised what might be in store for Europe, if not the world, pledged his total support to his regional police inspectors!'

The staff car passed through the gates of GHQ Eurocorps having stopped for a few moments for a security check. There was a light cough from the General and it seemed apparent to everyone in the car that the General was about to speak. Even the light rattle in the door seemed to stop immediately after he opened his mouth to speak. 'Gentlemen, you have an enormous task. When you require any support and it is in my power, or I can attain it on your behalf, call on me.' Somehow the pause was expected by all of those who sat there, then the General continued, 'Your task is a demanding one, stay with it. Adjutant Roche, you will give me a weekly report – security report, say my office, 1500 hours every Friday.'

The car stopped, and the General was gone. Robin and Sergeant MacKenzie sat open-mouthed. The Adjutant spoke. 'Don't worry, gentlemen, the General always makes a timed exit.

He hates saying goodbye, but I promise you he will be thinking of you often during the days ahead. Now, I'll drop you over at your section and take the car on afterwards.'

Robin, now back in his office, could not believe that in just over forty-eight hours, his desk could have become so cluttered. It would take at least an hour to read and analyse all the reports laid out in front of him and he could possibly work deep into the night before all of the answers were available to him.

Sergeant MacKenzie knocked lightly on Robin's door, entering as soon as the command, 'Come in!' reached his ears.

'Sir, can you spare a few moments?'

'Certainly, George, come in!'

MacKenzie walked to the chair placed in front of Robin's desk, happy in the knowledge that, having been called 'George', the meeting would be informal and that his Major was not expecting any other visitors.

'The latest on the Tomlevskis, Robin, is that whilst we have been away, they have been approached by both Lanov and Mogatin, twice. A third man, unnamed at the moment, but has been connected for the past twelve hours with our Colonel Keller!'

'If he is connected to Keller, why the hell haven't we got an ID?'

'We are certain who he is but it needs to be verified, that's all.'

'Stuff the mystery, George, who the bloody hell do you think it is, then?'

'Our boss man himself, Marshall of the Army, Yute "bloody" Polenkovich!'

'I can see why you want to corroborate the fact, George. Have you thought about why he's here?'

'Something must be going to happen, all of the investigators are sure of that, but what exactly?'

'When the Colonel made contact with the Tomlevskis, you couldn't get any clues from that transcript?'

'We have all gone over that, but nothing jumps out. When you add it all up, the transcript reveals only that the Colonel made contact, threatened them a little, ordered them around and made certain the Tomlevskis knew he was in complete control of their lives, both in Eurocorps and on behalf of their newly found Russian friends, and that he would be issuing instructions later. Really, the whole meeting was a "power play" which the Tomlevskis could only accept!'

'I'm sure you're right, George, but let me have a copy of the transcript at some point, and I'll make my own opinion. Have you any other ideas?'

'Not really, Robin, we've just got to play "Mr Plod" and wait!'

'Boring but true, George, boring but true!'

'Yes, Robin, but at least we have quite a lot of irons in the fire, thanks to the Jerries, the Yanks and the Frogs!'

'Sergeant, they are Germans, Americans and French!'

'Just language, sir... Sorry.'

'Sorry, George, I know, things are getting on my nerves. We've got so much information and we're probably guessing correctly, in that we're likely to be used in the transportation and communication areas, but a bag full of probables doesn't make a very good springboard!'

'You're right, Robin. Lie back and rest while "Mr Plod" plays Batman.'

Robin's eyebrows arched at the remark from his subordinate, then looked at his dour Scots Sergeant and burst out laughing at his analogy, saying, 'Thanks, George, I needed that, I was getting a little tense!'

'Yes, Robin.' The teasing emphasis on the name 'Robin' caused more laughter between them both.

'I think you'd better coordinate the reports coming in on the Keller situation, George; it's a lot more load to put on you, but it's better centralised on you.'

'Possibly, Robin, but I'm really expected by the team over at Mülheim – it's quiet over there now, but my gut feeling is something is going to happen.'

'Well, let's play it my way for the time being, George. Ask your Mülheim people to do the best they can, please.'

'Okay, leave it to me for now. I'd best get on, if that's okay?'

'Yes, please do, George... and thanks.'

Robin watched as George left him alone to wrestle once again with his Corps problem.

Rudi spent the night alone with Mayer, walking the streets of vibrant Hamburg until it was time for the car to take him to the airport to catch the 0600 hours flight back to Moscow. A car ride that would always stay in his memory: the sweetest kiss, the gentle natural merging of their bodies, the tightness of that final pull of their arms. The pull that said, 'I love you – you will always be mine, oh yes, I will… I will never leave you – I want us to stay like this forever!' The whispers of 'I want you so much!' The dreaded moment as the car arrived at the terminal, the anguish of having to separate and come back to the real world – a place where only half their emotions would ever be expressed. They embraced before he passed through into the no-man's-land of airport security and into the vacuum of his old life, a life controlled by his boss, Gregori Alexei Androv, and his own all-consuming love of Katerina Mayer.

The long, underlit corridor leading to Rudi's desk seemed extra long, the heaviness in his heart seeming to turn his world into slow motion. His mind wanted this day to end quickly, he wanted to see his boss, he wanted to know the reaction to his leave of absence. Would he still be in favour and have the same amount of access to all departments? Sitting down at his desk, he was almost sure nothing had been moved. His papers were still neat, his in and out trays squared to each corner of the desk, even the pencil and pen remained where his memory told him he had placed them, even his Babushka doll.

An hour passed, no telephone call, no one even passed along the corridor. Rudi pushed himself out of his chair. His intention was to at least find his acquaintances. The so-called canteen seemed the most logical place. Striding into the corridor, he forced speed into his legs. The panic increased in him as he began to realise there was no one about in any of the corridors or offices! The murmuring noise Rudi seemed to be now racing towards was becoming louder with each step, words were becoming audible – there seemed to be a tinge of mutiny. He was forced to stop. The little corridor he normally passed through into the vast canteen area was blocked. Staring over the heads of the people in front of him, he stared into the crowded, smoke-filled room. Standing on a table right at the back was a fellow worker. Rudi did not know his name although he had seen him around the office before. He was normally a quiet chap, saying nothing to anyone, barely raising his eyes to acknowledge anyone he passed, but now he was in full voice… 'What we need to know is what is going to happen to us? We have, it appears, as of this moment, no boss! No boss to tell us what to do, nor to take the anger from further up the ladders of power.'

The fear of having no one in charge was contagious and by the 'Hmmms' and 'Ahhhs' and a few shouts of 'You're right,' he was clearly gaining support, but no one had asked what solution the man was offering.

Rudi recognised a colleague just ahead of him, squeezed through and asked him, 'What's brought all this on?'

'Oh it's you… well, it appears that over the past few weeks, the middle management has been whittled away and as you know, we were left with Comrade Androv, but it seems now he's gone as well!'

'How does anyone know this?'

'It seems the bloke speaking is a senior administrator and has had about eight different bosses over the past few weeks!'

'And?'

'Oh, today he had been to collect work lists for distribution and there was no one there. He evidently waited around for an hour and then was given a note to say Androv had left and he should carry on as best as he can.'

'Well, he can't just dream up things for us to do, things must go with the system or we all lose our jobs!'

'That's what he's saying, Rudi – wake up or you'll be left behind!'

'Sorry.' There was a little hesitation before Rudi added, 'I want to keep my job for a while at least – I've got a girlfriend now and we want to get married.'

Rudi knew it was only part of the reason, but his friend gave him a beaming smile and said, 'Congratulations! I hope her father's rich!'

Rudi just smiled. 'Tell me what happens will you… I'm just going to the toilet!' Hurrying away from the meeting which was becoming a little rowdy, Rudi went back to his office, threw himself into his rickety chair, his head clasped in his hands, and whispered to himself, 'What am I going to do now? Without Comrade Androv to protect me, I'm no use to Mayer!' The whisper seemed to echo from side to side in the room and go on forever. The day was long. Rudi tried very hard to concentrate but he knew he must not just leave the office and phone Mayer, he could be being watched. He could be wanted by someone and his absence might cause a hiatus. No. He must wait; a little research, that's what he could do, backgrounds on his comrades... find out more on Comrade Gregori Alexei Androv! Until his comrades started to leave at their normal times, he did not dare speak to Mayer.

Joc Latimer had just finished his report on the meeting with the Europeans. Louise, his secretary, was just about to leave the office when Joc asked her, 'What's your opinion about the report, Louise?'

'Fine, Joc, fine... although it would be better still if you knew exactly what the Russkies are attempting, but there's enough "meat" in your report to maybe get you permission to work officially on it.'

'That would be great, Louise! How would you like a few trips to Paris?'

'Fine, on my own and with the department paying – great!'

'Even with me tagging along?'

'You'd be the worst person to take – you'd be working all the time and I don't see any fun in that!'

'You know me too well, Louise!' Joc replied, laughing.

'You're darn right I do... Now I'll go and open a file for your next escapade!'

'Not really my show, Ernst and Robin were there first.'

'Well, no doubt you'll make certain that you and Brian Fullerton contribute some more!'

'Hope so, Louise – we'll phone Ernst tomorrow afternoon if we don't hear anything from him before then... will you remind me?'

'Sure, but don't you think you ought to become official first, before you start throwing Uncle Sam's money around?'

'Get out of here – you're too strict with the rules, you should relax them more!'

'Fine, but you'd soon be out of a job!'

'I can't win today, can I?'

'You never could, in fact, you've never had a chance!' As soon as she said the words, Louise was out of the door.

Joc fell back into his chair knowing both she, and his wife, Liz, were right – he never had a chance!

Joc's eyes were just about to close – a position he proclaimed to be his best 'thinking mode', when his direct line rang. Snatching the receiver, his normally courteous greeting seemed abrupt to Ernst's ears.

'Sorry, Joc, did I wake you?'

'Who's this?' Joc asked abruptly.

'Ulbrecht heir!'

'Oh sorry, Ernst, I've just finished my report on the trip and I wasn't expecting a direct line call. What have you got for me?'

'Young Rudi has arrived back at his office and now his boss Androv has gone missing!'

'Rudi got his permission from Androv before he left?' Joc asked, showing the surprise in his voice.

'Yes, why do you ask?'

'I've heard that name Androv from somewhere, just a prick waking up my subconscious…'

'Was it a Gregori Alexei Androv, or some similar name?' The question had an urgency about it.

'I can't remember, Ernst, but it will come to me, I'm sure! It's so long ago… Saudi, I think, but I need to ramble around in my head for a while. Why are you asking, anyway?' Both men were silently thinking the same thing.

'What if this Androv has been "communicating" with our Rudi?' Ernst's sharp question stunned Joc momentarily.

'You don't really think that, Ernst.'

'Yes, but we could be as you say… "led up the garden path"!'

'You mean if Rudi was being fed information to give to us?'

'Exactly that, Joc. It could be, although it doesn't appear so. Will all Robin's reports, corroborating all of the local Russians' moves, and your background on Polenkovich, keep criss-crossing to make it appear true? The possibility that this Androv is connected in any way to the ones we have in our sights – we may… just may, be on the wrong foot!'

'I hope you're wrong, Ernst! What's Rudi doing now?'

'He's staying in there and doing research on the instructions given by Androv.'

'He's keeping a low profile I suppose, but he is probably losing his usefulness to you!'

'Yes, but we've asked him to obtain a photograph of this Androv.'

'It could help to identify him if he turns up on our patch.'

'Yes, and it might just "prick" your memory too!'

'Ha ha, Ernst! I'm sending you a copy of my report for your files. It's the only way I can justify the expenses to Uncle Sam. Got to be on record, as you know.'

'Do you want me to read it and initial every page?'

'You've got the same system, then!'

'Yes, we Germans invented paperwork, don't you know!'

'Are you sure, Ernst? I thought it was the good old US of A!'

'Whoever, Joc. Send it direct, it will be kept confidential.'

'Thanks, my friend; when, if ever, my top brass realise that what is happening in Europe is already affecting the US, I become legitimate and you can publish it, but until then, confidential is what I am!'

'Why won't they let us human people run the world, Joc?'

'It's because we are stupid and don't listen to the crap our clean-shaven politicians keep dishing out – they are so full of their own importance spending too much time on their own personal vanities, they don't have any time to do their own jobs or listen to any advice!'

'Same over here, Joc, but you will think and let me know the result with Androv, won't you?'

'Sure, Ernst; once the grey matter has given up its secrets, you'll be the first to know!'

'Thanks. Give my regards to everyone, hope to see you again soon.'

'Me too, Ernst, to you and all the gang, especially Rudi – he could be out on a limb there!'

'Yes, Mayer is at sixes and sevens. I'm working on a plan to get him out, but I can't let her know.'

'I understand, Ernst. I must press on now, things to do. I'll be in touch as soon as Androv pops out of my mind!'

'Goodbye!'

The phone went dead immediately in Joc's ear. Looking at the receiver, he murmured to himself, 'Something is happening at your end, Ernst. The way you cut off is not like you at all. I'll start on Androv for you right now.' Lightly placing the receiver back, Joc picked up the phone again and punched out Brian Fullerton's number. Ring, ring, ring, silence.

'Fullerton, who's this?'

Joc went straight in. 'Me, Brian. I just had Ernst on, asking have I ever heard of an Androv? It stopped me in my tracks. Gregori Alexei Androv – do you remember the problems with him?'

'That bloody son of a bitch got away with murder plus a gratuity from the US. How does he fit into this case?'

'It seems that when Rudi got back to his office, his boss, Gregori "bloody" Alexei Androv, who had given Rudi permission to take some leave, had gone missing, along with the whole of the middle line of civil servants, and to date, no senior replacement has been put into place. Rudi is trying to get a photograph for positive ID, but the poor kid's out on a limb and Ernst is trying to get him out.'

'Poor guy. If this Androv is our one from Saudi, what are you going to do?'

'Well, he isn't going to get away with it this time, I'll swear to that!'

'Joc, ease up – he may still be in favour with our politicians and that would leave you vulnerable. It's only five more years for your pension, old buddy!'

'What that SOB did, and got away with, was wrong. I'll take him out quietly myself… and that's a promise!'

'Take it easy! You'll burst a blood vessel if you are not careful!'

'Not until that scumbag is out of the way!'

'Joc, it's a long time ago, ease up a bit for your own good.'

'Killing five Americans, two kids, one teenager and their mother and father whilst driving on an American base, drunk, then threatening to notify the Saudi government that he had been force-fed alcohol to obtain information about Russian and Saudi agreements, which was an insult to the Saudi Royal family, the US having been allowed to run bases on Saudi soil, just to get out of being prosecuted by us Americans!'

Joc's voice lost its anger and returned to its normal tone again. 'You remember, Brian, how the diplomatic boys, because of the possible shit that could have flown around, started talking to Androv, showed him a weak side, like, "Please don't tell the Saudis we did that," then he came back with, "I want a million dollars and you can be assured I will leave Saudi." The weak-willed bastards paid up! Androv walked away rich and we had one whole American family destroyed. This Androv, Rudi's boss – if he is the same one this time – he's dead. I promise myself that, if we have found him, we are not going to let him hide behind Mother Russia's skirts.'

'For Christ's sake, Joc, ease up… I believe you! When do you think you will get a picture?'

'Rudi's got to find one. I doubt if he'll have one on his desk ready to be snatched away!'

'I hope you get it soon, buddy. I'm with you on this, should you want some help.'

'Thanks, Brian.' Joc's attitude had quietened as fast as it had risen. 'Have the gals sorted out that dinner yet?'

'No, but I'll get Sandra on it, Joc, see you soon.'

'Thanks for listening, Brian.'

'No problem, bye.'

The phone went quiet. The room was quiet. The whole world seemed quiet. Joc rested his eyes as he leaned back in his chair.

Robin sat sorting his paperwork from one side of the desk to the other. The speed at which he read had always disturbed his parents and they had subjected him to many tests on his recall of what he had read, but were often surprised that his retention was over ninety per cent. His team of investigators had got very used to it and had all made jokes, like inserting 'Merry Christmas' or one word, 'Flash' and three lines later, 'Gordon'. Robin had always spotted their bit of fun, so the jokes eventually went away. Robin enjoyed his extra skill but found on occasions, such as on large crime cases like the one his team was employed on now, that his mind became very cluttered with unnecessary information, which would sometimes make him indecisive. Today had not been one of those days. His mind flowed over the pages, he made notations where he felt necessary, then a sudden stop. A report in from Metz. Sergeant Hackett's report of four days previously had reported that his normal quarry had been followed from 0630 hours until 1900 hours when he had returned home to entertain four guests to dinner, and that Sergeant Hackett would be back on duty at 0600 hours the following morning.

Under 'Remarks', Sergeant Hackett had written:

Boring long day, nothing unusual in routine, no additional contacts made. Tall hawkish man noticed three times. He was not observing me or my quarry, but looking for someone else. I would say he was five foot eleven, slim build, long aristocratic face, long thin nose, clean shaven, head covered by a trilby hat, but judging by the light dusting of grey in his sideburns, his hair would be dark and aged about forty-five to fifty-five years.

Passing the report across his desk after marking it with his initials, Robin placed it in his 'Out' tray.

Ernst and Mayer sat opposite each other in his office. Her tears could be held back no longer. The torrent exploded down her beautiful face, which would soon be a swollen, blotchy mess. Ernst quickly moved to her aid. His natural fatherliness seemed for a moment to hold back the deep sobs, but as he gently put his arm around her shoulders and went down on his knees, she threw her body into his arms and the torrent of tears leapt again from her now bloodshot eyes. Her blubbering words repeated over and over. 'Sir, I love him so much, he has no one to protect him – we must get him out!'

Ernst could not tell her what she wanted to hear – that he would set things in motion for Rudi to come over, but instead, patted her shoulder between sobs, saying, 'I know we must, I know.' Ernst hated to see his protégé in such distress. The distress he was forcing her into to protect his beloved Germany and the international community. It seemed an age that he had knelt there with Mayer's head resting on his shoulder before she quietened down, her sobs trembling less and less through her body. Ernst's light patting on her back was comforting, but they both knew Rudi being in Hamburg or at least in Germany was the only answer. Suddenly Mayer pulled herself away. Wiping the tears from her face she said, 'I'm sorry, sir, I shouldn't have done that.'

'Why, my dear… It's a problem that I have created, my stupid thoughts about a brave new world have once again started to involve people I love!'

'It's not you, sir, it's all the nasty people who think they are bigger than they are. You have the dreams and strength to fight them… they are the enemy!'

'You're right, Mayer.' Ernst had seen she was gathering her strength back and he brought the conversation from informality back to his normal form of address, 'Mayer'. 'We both realise as well as Rudi, that it is important for him to be there in his position of trust with his political bosses.'

'I agree he must stay, but my heart aches! He feels that without Androv there will be no one to give him any orders, nor to protect him.'

'It is difficult, Mayer, but with new people coming in to the West every day, we need him to check out anyone we are uncertain of.'

'I know. I just hope it will end very soon.'

Ernst had been watching Mayer prepare her face subconsciously as she had been talking, her pain being put back inside, in the hope it would never have a reason to resurface and bare her emotions to the world again. Gently and quietly. Ernst said, 'It would be beautiful if it could all end tomorrow but in the meantime, let's get back to work, and try to keep your fears at bay.'

'Thank you, sir, yes, I will.' Mayer stood to attention, straightened her hair and clothes, and left.

Brian Fullerton rang Joc's number to tell him the file on Gregori Alexei Androv was 'restricted' and his own security clearance was not sufficient to gain access to it. The phone rang continuously for a full three minutes, but there was no reply.

By devious means, Rudi had obtained the home address of Gregori Alexei Androv. It was in the old Latin Quarter of Moscow of the 1920s: big houses, big driveways, big rooms. Rudi was unsure what the neighbourhood was like, but had heard that it had been used by high-ranking party officials until Glasnost, when he understood there had pretty much been an exodus, the district being totally repossessed by the military. Rudi's plan was just to knock on the door and ask to speak to his boss. If he was in fact home he would, if he was allowed to speak to him, say he had come to report what a wonderful time he had had on leave and thank him very much. He thought he would mention he had met the sweetest girl in the world. Should Androv not be there, and it was house staff only, he would cap-in-hand ask for any kind of work in the hope he would be allowed inside. Both methods he hoped would enable him to procure a photograph of his boss. It was very fortunate that having rung the large ornate bell-pull, a handsome young lady called up to him from below the stairway he had just climbed. The girl was bright and talkative, stating that her master and mistress were away on vacation and although she did not know where they had gone, the butler would, and he would be back in about half an hour if he would like to come below stairs and wait. Rudi quickly accepted the invitation and was, within seconds, following the girl into the long corridor leading to the very large kitchen. Rudi talked to the girl about how she must have to work very hard in such a large house and that surely there must be more staff than just herself.

'Oh my goodness yes, there are four more girls like me. No one person could manage a house like this, especially with her ladyship never being satisfied with anything we do!'

'It must be a beautiful place…' Rudi asked enquiringly.

Cheekily the girl replied, 'Come on, let's start at the top – quickly, before the others get back. They'll have my guts for garters if they find out!'

Rudi could not believe his luck. With only quick glances into each room from the doorway however, there was no opportunity to steal the picture he needed, but the long hall on the ground floor was suddenly blocked by large double doors, which, when opened, showed a large comfortable sitting room, complete with grand piano. Rudi could not believe his eyes when he realised it was full of framed photographs of Androv and his family. His opportunity to steal one would come as they passed the piano. The smallest full-face picture of him... quick, where are you? he thought. It took seconds. He was through the room and the picture he had come for was not even noticeable as it sat snugly in his jacket pocket. The waiting continued. Would the butler never return? The girl was beginning to fidget. Rudi's good looks were disturbing her. She wanted to be embraced – after all, hadn't Glasnost made her free so that she could hope for better things? Her dreams and fantasies were beginning to make her blush, her blood giving a rich glow to her cheeks and neck. Rudi was getting anxious, his mind racing. Surely it would be better for him to leave now, before anyone returned? The tick, tock from the large kitchen clock was the only sound to be heard until, 'I will have to leave now – I'll come back tomorrow,' boomed out across the kitchen, shattering the girl's dreams.

She said curtly, 'Yes, perhaps that would be best,' and before Rudi realised what was happening to him, he was outside the house and walking down the drive.

The excitement in Rudi's voice as he talked to Mayer was contagious and for the first time in two days, Mayer felt relatively happy again. Her love was safe and speaking to her, saying all the things she wanted to hear, particularly that his work in the ministry so far, had just been allowed to continue without supervision. 'I must go, my love, you will receive the picture by courier.'

'Don't hang up yet – just a minute more to hear your voice – say anything. I just want to hear you speak. Please, my love, please!'

'I love you... love you always!' Then the soft click as Rudi placed the receiver in its cradle hurt them both but they both knew Rudi could not stand around in phone kiosks for too long in case it aroused suspicion.

Ernst looked at Mayer's happy face as she walked quickly up to his desk. 'I've heard from Rudi!' Ernst would never have guessed. 'He has got the photograph of Androv... it's coming by courier.'

'Thank you, it will be nice to see if he fits into our puzzle...' Before he could continue, the phone rang, and instinctively his hand reached for it. 'Ulbrecht heir! Hello, Joc, calling again so soon?'

'I owe you an apology. Androv is known to us, me especially. I'm trying to get the file, but it has a restriction order on it.' The fast, jerky speech with which Joc delivered his bombshell apology, made Ernst realise that his friend was ashamed of himself for not admitting he recognised the name when first mentioned and that he was probably breaking orders in telling him now.

'I felt something in your voice when you first heard that name, do you want to tell me about it?'

The outline of the story was swiftly told and Joc added at the end, '...I'm sorry, Ernst, to have not been fully open with you at the time.'

'You had to reconcile your problem your own way, Joc. I'm sure if it were my situation I would have found it necessary to think a while first. You are telling me unofficially?'

'Yes. Hopefully I'll get a release. A lot of people know that I'm working unofficially... I'm probably the best unkept secret in the whole of the CIA... the file may be opened to me!'

'I've got a picture coming over from Rudi, but I hope when it gets here, you won't tell me it's your shit Androv!' Ernst looked up, suddenly remembering Mayer was still in the room and whispered an apology for his swearing.

'I hope so too, but how many Gregori Alexei Androvs are there?'

'Who knows, Joc. I'll put a picture on line as soon as it arrives... I hope you get your file. I won't repeat anything you've told me until you give me the word.'

'Thanks, Ernst. I'll be in touch... soon, I hope!'

As Ernst placed the receiver down, Mayer asked, 'Joc knows Androv?'

'He thinks so. It's not confirmed. He's trying to get the file up as soon as possible.'

Mayer said more to herself than to Ernst, 'Rudi didn't know his boss could be known throughout the world!'

Ernst didn't answer but watched her get up from her seat and leave with just a nod of the head as a goodbye.

On receiving the portrait picture of Androv, Robin circulated it immediately to his men in the field. There had been no response from them, the French police nor Ernst's men. Robin had been told about Joc and Brian's problem: that they were tied up in politics, plus the fact they were three thousand miles or so away from the playing field, unlikely to contribute more than support, from the vast store of information from their computers, and vast network of agents throughout the world. Lifting the picture up again for the third or fourth time, he was sure he knew the man, or something about him. Putting it down to answer the phone, he became lost in thought. Where are you now?

'Hello, sir, Sergeant Hackett here.'

'Sergeant… My God! He's in your report! He's the "hawkish-faced" man! Where is he now?'

'Sorry, sir, I don't understand what you mean!'

'Haven't you seen the ID picture of Androv?'

'Nothing's come to me from your office, that's why I'm phoning – to see if I'm still working for you!'

'Your remarks about a hawkish, long-nosed fellow in your report of four days ago. Have you seen him again?'

'As a matter of fact, sir, yes, but not in connection with my man. He was at a railway station, local train going to Strasbourg only yesterday evening.'

'How do you know it was Strasbourg?'

'Local train and it terminates there. It's a line I use a lot and it's the only place it goes!'

'Thank you, Sergeant, don't move out of Metz – I want that man found again – don't do anything, just keep him in sight if he comes back. Keep me informed of anything you find. Thank you, Sergeant, goodbye!'

Placing the phone down momentarily, he then lifted it up again and dialled Ernst. 'Ulbrecht heir!'

'Ernst, Robin here. A report by one of my investigators of about four days ago, placed your Androv in Metz. He has been seen again joining a train to Strasbourg.'

'Wonderful, Robin! You have got someone watching in case he returns to Metz?'

'Yes, Ernst, plus an extra man will be instructed to get out there immediately.'

'Good. How quickly can you get reports from Strasbourg, assuming he's still there?'

'Everything will be put on top line everywhere possible. We'll get him in the net soon, Ernst, I promise.'

'I know you will, I will send some of my men down to you under Koslowski. I'll make certain he locks into you as soon as he arrives.'

'He'll be welcome, Ernst. I'm running a little short of players!'

'We'll manage, Robin. By the way, Robin, has Androv met up with Lanov or Mogatin?'

'No, Ernst, definitely not.'

'That's a pity.'

'Things aren't that simple, Ernst. If Androv, Lanov and Mogatin were running together, that would bring in Polenkovich, my Colonel, the Tomlevskis, et cetera. It could be the first time a crime has been solved without anyone knowing what the crime was exactly, at the point of arrest!'

'What a wonderful world that would be, Robin! Thank you for your information, I'll send everyone I can spare. Thanks again!'

As was quite often the case, the phone went dead abruptly. Robin put his receiver down and called for Sergeant Donaldson to be sent to see him ASAP and to arrange for someone to cover for him. The hour that it took for Sergeant Donaldson to arrive seemed eternal and when he did arrive, Robin was not pleased with what he heard. 'This picture I received via my replacement is the man who met the Colonel three days ago. Was it totally by accident, or was it prearranged? They are a pair of fine actors.'

'How and where did they meet?' Robin's voice echoed the stress raging through his mind.

'The playground at the town's municipal park, on the foot-bridge over the railway line – a train was passing, they were looking down onto the tracks and bumped into each other – apologies all around, less than ten seconds, it was all over and they went their separate ways.'

'Did anything pass between them, an envelope, a camera, anything?'

'It could have, I suppose, but I saw nothing. Both of their coats were open, it made it difficult to see if anything was passed between them.'

'I think we will have to put twenty-four-hour surveillance on the Colonel. You pick who you want and I'll authorise it.'

'Yes, sir. Will that be all?'

'Yes, Sergeant, for now. If our friend in the photograph turns up, we'll be very stretched to cover him until we get organised again, but please, if you make contact, keep him covered in preference to the Colonel.'

'Understood, sir. I'll be moving back straight after selecting the rest of my team.'

'Well done, Sergeant, and thank you.'

Robin's face seemed to become more relaxed as the real police work started.

Lieutenant Daniel Tomlevski was finding a natural rhythm to his work. During the past week he and Nicole had recaptured their previous relationship. Nicole woke up happier, worked out her day and quite often she met Daniel in the mess for lunch or sometimes for dinner. Through this contentment, Daniel had been performing his duties efficiently and commanding respect from his men and his fellow officers.

The intrigue since he had agreed to become a double-agent gave him no anxieties, he just carried on doing as he was asked or told, which he had found was the only way both he and Nicole could handle the situation. Having agreed they would inform on the Russians and also having agreed with Robin to organise the passing-on of any information to him or Major Roche, Daniel felt he had every reason to feel rather more content with his life than of late. His body gave a sudden shudder as a 'montage' of Nicole's suffering crossed through his mind. 'Those bastards!' appeared on the black and white placard in his mind. His telephone rang. He lightly picked it up and announced himself. 'Oh hello, sir. Any problems?'

'Not really, Daniel, I just wondered if you could spare me five minutes or so?' Robin Cadwallader's voice showed no anxiety.

'Of course, sir. Do you want me to come to you?'

'I think not. Perhaps the mess after duty?'

'Fine with me, sir, I'll let Nicole know I'll be a little late.'

'It really will take only a few minutes, it shouldn't turn into a heavy social!'

'All right then, sir, 1610 in the mess?'

'Fine. Look forward to seeing you!'

Placing the receiver back down, not one anxious thought entered Daniel's mind and, returning to his statistical task, he looked forward to meeting Major Robin Cadwallader of the Military Police.

Chief of Police Manuel Vargas shielded the harsh sunlight streaming through the curtained window, his other elbow embedded in the pillow supporting his head. His gaze was directed at the naked body of Captain Maria Tias and even though her hair was spread partially over her face, she looked ravishing. The rise and fall of her breasts as she breathed, the fullness of her lips, the deep darkness in her eyes, made her irresistible. Vargas spoke, gently. 'I promise you, my love, one day we will marry!'

'I doubt it. If you meant what you said all those years ago, you would be divorced and free by now!'

'You don't understand, Maria, my wife's family is an old traditional family, they would cut me off from my wife's money and then I could not afford the house, the school fees for the children…'

'You selfish, weak little shit! Now you've got an international police career and you've got your arse in gear, why don't you say "balls" to your bloody wife and kids – you never see them anyway… you see more of me than you do of them!'

'What if I get completely involved in this Ulbrecht case? They are still asking for my support, you know. They want me to find some other Russian called Gregori Alexei Androv!'

'When did they ask you to do that?'

'Yesterday morning.'

'And you haven't found him yet?' The venom in her voice cut Manuel to the quick.

'You stupid whore! What do you think I am… a miracle man?'

'You certainly aren't that! You're a lazy, good for nothing, disliked, unrespected, laughed-at, shit!'

'Is that all? What about you?'

'Me? I'm pretty stupid – just a pretty face and a body that I've learnt to use out of necessity, but I'm not a lazy, vain, strutting popinjay like you! Oh, and by the way, your Russian is staying at the Plaza. If you get over there right now, stark naked… it'll be easier to see right through you… it will probably be the only chance you've given anyone!'

'You cow! You conniving bitch! You money-grabbing tart! Your "anything for a dollar" attitude makes you no better than me!'

'You're right! Fuck me, we are the same animal, sniffing and fucking… let's be animal!' The words that had just passed between them meant nothing. The walls of their hotel room would tell you that that scene was enacted every time. From under the covers, Vargas's voice said contentedly, '…and then I fuck the Russian!'

Sergeant Donaldson and his team of investigators could not pick up Androv's trail; it seemed as though he had just vanished. No sign of him in Strasbourg, Metz, Colmar or Achern. Panic was beginning to set in after the railways, airports and car hires had all been exhausted.

'He can be only in the town, Sergeant, it's a road by road grid-search. It's going to take a week at least.'

'We may not have that amount of time. You had better set up your search pattern. Hold it a minute. France is full of small flying fields, have they been checked?'

'No, they're full of "pop-pop" aircraft, great for joy-riding but no good for going anywhere!'

'I bet they visit friends for lunch on Sundays a few villages away – he could hedge-hop. Let's do a run at it anyway.'

'Okay, Sergeant, with all the mountains around, he'd have to do a lot of zigzagging, take a bloody age to get anywhere!'

'Let's check it anyway. Circulate the picture, but don't give anyone any reasons as to why he's wanted!'

'Right, I'm off! Be in touch, Sergeant.'

'Thanks. See you soon.'

Vargas had left the delectable Maria in the hotel room to attend to her hair and make-up – the time they considered to be a discreet length of time between their reappearance back at Police HQ. Vargas hurried behind his desk and dialled out to Robin Cadwallader. Without waiting or announcing himself after Robin answered the phone, Vargas said, 'I've found your man... he's in Lisbon at the Plaza!'

Robin snapped back, 'Great.' Pausing for a moment, he then asked, 'Have you verified that it's definitely our man?'

Vargas's hesitant response, 'Well no... not me personally...' put up a warning light in Robin's head and he asked sharply, 'Who then?'

'Our normal police hotel checks had his name on the list.'

'Wonderful, Chief. Has he been verified as our Gregori Alexei Androv and is he still there and being watched?'

'It will take a while to get that arranged, but I will see that it is done.'

'Chief, this man could be everything or nothing to our investigations, but until we find out which, he is the most important man on your pitch!' Robin's insubordination towards Vargas was probably going to get him into trouble, but he had already made up his mind that Vargas was a dickhead and continued in the same tone. 'The report sent to you with the picture said specifically, make no contact but cover his every move and report everything. You tell me he's in the Plaza Hotel and you are trying to organise surveillance! You haven't read the report, have you?'

The wind completely taken out of his sails, Vargas fluffed a few lines. 'I can't do everything myself, I'm a very busy man... I shall attend to your requests right now and you will be phoned right back!'

The crashing sound in Robin's ear as the phone went dead nearly deafened him. Vargas waited for his blood pressure to go down, then he puffed himself up, opened his door and bellowed across the outer office, 'Get me Captain Tias, right now!'

Robin, having phoned all concerned, and reported the Androv sighting in Lisbon, continued to request all surveillance teams continue with their efforts to find him until verification came through that Androv was still in Lisbon.

Captain Tias walked smartly into Vargas's office. She stood flaunting herself, using her eyes and lips: a game she always played when her face could not be seen by anyone else but him. Vargas looked up at her animated face and spat out through his teeth, 'You whore, you've made me look a right arsehole! Why didn't you tell me Androv's circular was full of do's and don'ts, put him under surveillance straight away, et cetera? Why didn't you tell me the whole picture?'

'You had other things on your mind at the time, although I did notice you quickened your pace a little after I told you – so fucking much of a rush in fact, you didn't even have enough sense to read the circular before you got on the phone to tell the world how good a policeman you are!'

'You cow!'

'Don't call me names if you want to get out of the shit!'

'What the fuck are you going to do then?'

Looking Vargas coldly in the eyes, she leant across and snatched up the phone, punching in the numbers. Waiting for an answer, her cold eyes stared into her lover's face. 'Pedro? Maria here – anything happened over there?'

'Not really, Captain. He's been up and down in the lift a few times, paced across the lobby to the main doors, probably working out his escape routes in his mind. He's had one call through the switchboard, we are fairly sure it was from a man in a call box and there was one outside call he made himself. I'm still trying to trace that. He made it direct-dial from his room. The phone company is moving pretty fast... they know it's a call box at the Central Railway Station, but they can't seem to pinpoint the exact phone as yet.'

'Well done, Pedro, keep on it!'

'Yes, Captain!'

'Lover, here's what you need to try and rescue your ego!' And Maria proceeded to relate what Pedro had reported while Vargas sat deflated behind his desk.

Daniel ran up the stone steps of the baronial hall which had been converted into the Officers' Mess. As he entered the large hall, the grandfather clock struck the first stroke of four and automatically, Daniel's arm rose to check his own wristwatch. Exactly four o'clock. Craning his neck around the doorway into the bar area, he could not see Robin and he hesitated for just a second before he walked in.

Robin had been standing with the Adjutant at the top of the stairs and had noticed Daniel enter. He had not mentioned to the Adjutant that he had told Daniel of the Androv photograph and simply said, 'He's come to see me, André!'

'Good. It's good to see him in the mess.'

'I hope after he sees the photograph he won't go back into his shell again!'

'I don't think he will, Robin, they both seem to be relieved now they have you and the Corps on their side.'

'Yes, but I know the poor man is going to be stressed when I've told him, and of course even more so when he gets back home and tells Nicole!'

'They'll cope... mark my words, Robin.'

'It's one hell of a strain we're putting them under – I hope you're right!'

'Get along now and meet him. You'll be looking after them, won't you?'

'My best may not be good enough when this comes to a head!'

'You'll manage, Robin, I'm sure.'

'Thank you, André, but this web is getting bigger and bigger!'

'Get down there, Robin, and have a large gin, then you'll feel better!'

'That was my intention and after I send him home to his sweet wife Nicole, I may even have a second!'

André patted his friend on the back saying, 'Good for you!' and then left Robin to his task.

Slowly Robin entered the mess, saw Daniel immediately and crossed to the lounge chair which Daniel offered beside him.

'Good evening, Daniel,' Robin said, offering his hand in friendship before sitting down. 'Thanks for holding a chair for me!'

'No problem, sir. What can I get you? Gin and tonic?'

'That would be fine, Daniel, but put the drinks on my chit.'

'Thanks, sir.' The steward approached Daniel and the drinks were ordered.

Both men sat quietly for a few restful moments until Robin said carefully, 'Daniel, in order to protect both you and Nicole, I need to involve you more...'

'This sounds very serious, sir. What's happened now?'

'The trouble is, none of us knows yet, and we are working blind. In a moment, I am going to pass you a photograph which I want you to engrave on your mind and should this man ever pass your way, or Nicole's, you must swear to tell me or Major Roche immediately.'

Daniel shifted his feet and, leaning forward in his chair, asked, 'You seem very worried, sir. Nicole and I will cope, we are happy for the chance you are giving us to exonerate our parents and stay with the Corps.'

'I know, but our web of deceit is getting wider and if this man, whose picture I'm going to show you, is recognised immediately, or comes into your lives in the future, we'll have yet another Russian to worry about – a Russian who is already known to our American colleagues as an absolute shit!' The venom in this last word was cut off abruptly by his right hand. 'Now, I want you to study this photograph well, then when you get home, describe it to Nicole. I can't let you have a copy because if it's found on you... or her, it could be your death warrant!'

Daniel took the picture offered with some trepidation. Staring down at it, as it was held between his shaky finger and thumb, his head shook from side to side, assuring Robin that this man in the picture, whoever he was, meant nothing to him. 'His name is Gregori Alexei Androv. If ever you see him or hear his name it is important that I know about it ASAP.'

'It sounds as if this man is really important, sir?'

'We don't even know if he is... it may seem strange that we don't, but his name only came to us yesterday and so far, we can't lock him into any connection with our Russians, but he is the boss, or was the boss of one of our agents in Russia and all of a sudden our Mr Androv has disappeared out of Russia!'

'Where is he now?'

'Portugal... Lisbon, actually.'

'Lanov and Mogatin were both there, yes, and that other one, Petronovitch or something?'

'Polenkovich. Yes, you're right, but we haven't connected them, so don't worry, just keep your wits about you.'

'I will. Here's your photograph back. I'll finish up this drink if I may, and then run along to give Nicole the description... another drink, and I may not remember the details quite so clearly!'

'Very wise, Daniel. I've got to get on anyway, so leave when you're ready.'

'Joe?... Joc here. I'm in a call box... what do you think about Androv being in Portugal?'

'It's not confirmed that it is our Androv, I was expecting you to call the moment it was!'

'Ha bloody ha! Joe, I want us to find him. I want it confirmed. I want us to have the credit for catching up with that bastard!'

'You mean put some men on it, confirm Androv's identity, and then request that as you were case leader when the bastard killed those kids and their parents, and as you know what's going on in Europe, you should be transferred out here?'

'Come on, Joe, it's not a lot to ask... we work well together anyway...'

'True, old buddy, but a request is all I can make. I'm still getting cuffed around the ear by the Ambassador from the last time I helped!'

'You make the request, Joe, I'll ask for a transfer this end. I'll remind them of my age and that they owe me this one as a retirement present!'

'Good luck with that one, buddy, I'll request you when I confirm ID... the rest is up to you.'

'Thanks, Joe, thanks a million!'

Pedro had called Captain Tias to the Plaza Hotel. They were sitting at the small bar with a full view of the stairs, lifts and the wide, uncrowded lobby. Pedro was stunned when his Captain arrived, her firm body encased in the tailored, light-blue suit jacket and skirt, set off with a powder-blue blouse buttoned at the neck, gold-chained matching shoulder bag and simple court shoes in two-tone black and blue. Topped by her beautiful face and long stockinged legs, Pedro was finding it very difficult to concentrate.

'...but Captain, it is reassuring you are here. There are some very funny little things happening, some make sense, others – I don't know, because I can't keep getting into the lift to follow the people!'

'So you want more people to stake-out properly?'

'Yes, I suppose I do, but they would have to be special people.'

'I don't understand you, Pedro...'

'Well, look quick now, here he is – Androv! He will come across the hall, gaze out of the main door, turn, walk back to the bank of house phones, pick one up, speak briefly, walk back to the lift and push a different floor button each time. Within twenty seconds of placing the phone down, he's followed by an – always expensively dressed – man or woman. It could be coincidence but every time that man makes a move, he is followed by someone!' Pedro held his breath for a moment. '...Look, Captain – coming out of the dining room – let your eyes follow him!' Maria watched as the tall, suave, tailor-made-suited man quickened his pace to follow Androv. Within an instant, Maria slid gracefully from her stool and with an urgent pace, strode towards the lifts and what was now her quarry, two men. Pedro sat stunned by the spontaneity of his Captain's act, but decided to just sit and wait.

Both Androv and the suave man ushered his Captain into the lift, both men stunned by her beauty, although Pedro thought he saw a little hesitancy in the suave man's movements.

At the back of the lift, Maria stood looking disinterested with the two men standing each side of the doorway. Although she could not remember the suavely-dressed man's name, Maria knew he was mentioned in one of the reports which had passed between the police forces of Europe. It was obvious the two men wanted to talk or something. She must stay alert... first floor, second, third, fourth. The slight hand movement which passed the piece of paper into the suave man's hand gained no response from the attractive lady. Androv was certain that the lift's mirrors would have enabled him to detect some reaction. Fifth floor. The doors opened, Androv and Maria got out, and the suave man looked up at the floor indicator, waiting for the light to 'ping' and the doors to close.

When Androv stopped at his room, he could not hold back the licentious smirk which crossed his face as he followed Maria's undulating body floating along the long corridor.

Pedro sat anxiously at the bar for a while, then was surprised as the suave man exited the lift. Where was his Captain?... She must want this one tailed... Pedro had no difficulty in following his unwitting prey. There never seemed to be any attempt by him to hide, as he walked from one side of the street to the other, window shopping. Pedro began to wonder if he had done the right thing in following. Eventually at the railway station, Pedro followed him to a bank of telephones and snatched the telephone off its hook in the booth next to his quarry. Pretending to dial, he was most attentive to the conversation which had begun in the next booth.

'How are you?' The suave man's voice was cultured, assertive, but possibly a bit heavy for such a lightly built man. 'Oh, are you? I'm so pleased... I met a mutual friend of ours today... Androv has given me a message for you... No, I can't read it to you. His instructions were that it had to be handed to you personally... Lisbon at the moment, my flight to Paris is at six... Yes, I could by midnight... well, midnight it is, then.' The receiver was replaced, the suave man walked away purposefully, followed by Pedro, until Pedro turned off at the nearest point to the Plaza Hotel to meet up with Captain Tias.

The excitement in Joc's voice was contagious; even Louise, his steadfast secretary, had never, in all the years they had been together, seen him work so fluidly. His concise 'questions and answers' with his boss down in Washington was like the old days, both men fighting their corners, both men respecting each other. Louise had heard it all before, and to her mind, she could not see her man losing!

'Okay, Gerald, I'll put my application for transfer in right away, and you will look on it favourably?' At this time, Joc normally got frustrated and threw out some comment like, 'Don't let it sit on your desk for too long!' Joc's petulance was well known throughout Langley and unlike most of his colleagues, the petulance mostly got him his own way out of respect for his field work. Louise was stunned as the phone went down without further ado, and she simply placed the 'Application for Transfer' for Joc to sign on his desk.

'Thanks, Louise, you're great!'

'I know. I thought you'd need a roving commission, so I've stated European Community, Russia and her satellite states.'

'That should cover everything; if not, we'll just have to break a few rules!'

'Now listen to me, Joc, you're getting too old for trouble!'

Pedro was back on the same bar stool at the Plaza Hotel, sitting anxiously waiting for Captain Tias to reappear. He had phoned HQ and learnt that she had not gone back there, so Pedro assumed she must have got out on the same floor as Androv and was purely looking for an opportunity to escape past his door and return by the lift. As she approached him, a little flushed, from the general direction of the main doors, he guessed she had walked back by the fire escape. The expression on her face as she approached him told him his assumption was correct. She was fuming mad.

'Why are you still here, you silly arse! You should be following the suave guy; you've lost a golden chance!'

'He's going to be on the six o'clock flight tonight to Paris, and he's meeting someone at midnight.' Pedro proceeded to tell his Captain his story and then she was delighted with him, although now she would have to tell Vargas and give the credit away.

Nicole sat silently staring into Daniel's face. The news of yet another person intruding into their lives was becoming too much for her to accept, but words would not come out of her dry, tight throat. Slowly, one solitary tear welled up and held in the corner of her eye – one tear which said, 'Whoever you are, you will not break Daniel and me.' One tear of happiness which left nothing else to be said.

Joc stood in the doorway of his nice, suburban house with his arm loosely around Liz's shoulder. Today, after the pillow-talk of the night before, they stood a little closer and a little tighter together, knowing that the big embrace, the hard kiss, was not going to be long. The taxi would be the clue; when it turned the corner into view, they would come together and as they held each other, the taxi horn would sound as it drew to a halt. Joc would be gone at the sound. 'I'll write every day,' he would say. She knew he always meant to. The release as their bodies parted, no sighs, no more words, a cold snatch for the suitcase handle, the light touch from Joc's fingertips as they slid across her cheek, then he was gone.

Chief Inspector Vargas sat scornfully behind his desk, hating everyone under his command. His mind saw things only one way. They were the people he had spent time training, training that he alone could supervise and pass on because of his wealth of experience. The sharp blade of conscience cut swift and deep into his head. The puzzle of words rushing into his mind was unreal compared to the normal pompous, vain and unfair remarks he normally bullied his staff with. Lifting the phone, his scornful face seemed to show the acceptance of his conscience. His call to Robin Cadwallader was a brief, concise one, delivered manfully and without any mention of their previous conversation. Signing off from Robin, he wished his colleague well, and that he would have success with the information he had given him and the assurance that Androv's movements would be continuously monitored by his top operators and reported daily or sooner, if anything unexpected happened.

Robin, who had not on this occasion had to sort out the 'wheat from the chaff' was nicely surprised by Vargas's brevity and the conversation's fullness in content and was even more surprised when just before the call finished, Vargas had said, '...a full written report will be faxed within minutes; adios, Robin.'

Robin felt confident with the report made by Vargas. Without hesitating, he picked up his phone and dialled his friend, Inspector Gilbert Torneau. His direct line rang only twice before it was answered.

"Ello, Gilbert Torneau ici.'

'Gilbert, Robin here.'

'What can I do for you my friend?'

'Your Inspector of Police in Paris – the man who was at our meeting – would you phone him and lay on a stake-out and surveillance of someone who keeps walking through our picture?'

'Certainly. You have a name, photo and corroboration that he is definitely in Paris?'

'In his own words, he is coming to Paris on the 1800 hours flight from Lisbon, ETA Paris 1930 hours, but according to him he is travelling onwards somewhere!'

'How do you know this?'

'One of Vargas's men used some initiative and followed him from a hotel after he met Androv, who carelessly didn't spot his tail and Vargas's man overheard our man's conversation in full.'

'The Portuguese had some luck, mon ami!'

'A lot of luck! Will you speak to Paris if I send you the details – name, photo and transcript of the phone call?'

'Certainly, Robin, and thank you for speaking to me first and not going direct to Paris.'

'There was no other way, Gilbert.'

'Well, thank you anyway!'

'I'll put everything on line after I've read the transcript, with any comments I may have. Sergeant Donaldson has just walked in with it – Vargas seems to be on the ball!'

'It's about time he came up to speed, Robin. I'll phone back when everything is in place, just to confirm.'

'Thank you, Gilbert.'

The time was 1500 hours. Four and a half hours before Parentov was to come into play in Paris.

Chapter Thirty

Joc sat loosely strapped into his aircraft seat, knowing he wouldn't be there but for his getting a friend to request him to help out in the European theatre of operations. Joc knew in his heart he was flying in the wrong direction. Portugal was not where the action was going to be. True, his Bureau Chief, Joe Lomax, understood his quest, and as Androv for the moment was holding court in Lisbon, it seemed the natural place to be, but when push came to shove, would Joe be able to let him fly like a bird to Ernst or Robin? Joc nodded his head, expressing his problem to himself, but he knew in his heart that whatever Joe, his Ambassador, or even Langley itself, said, if it was time to chase Androv he'd be gone from Portugal. His first priority on arrival at the Embassy in Lisbon would be to state his case clearly to Joe and, if need be, the Ambassador for total freedom of movement. Joc was fairly content with himself and gradually relaxed his face and upper body tension and slowly let sleep overcome him, not knowing that at the approximate time of his touchdown with the advent of Boris Parentov's movements, the stage was already shifting to middle Europe.

The message to Robin from Inspector Torneau confirmed everything was in place to receive Parentov in Paris. Robin, who had earlier confirmed to Ernst in Hamburg, Parentov's movement to Paris, decided this last piece of information should be passed on to him. Picking up his phone, dialling the string of numbers, waiting for the burr-burr, burr-burr…

'Ulbrecht heir!'

'It's Robin, Ernst.'

'Nice to hear your voice, Robin. You have news for me?'

'Yes. Torneau has confirmed that Paris is in position and that they will let him run.'

'Good. It's ironic, Robin. It started in Portugal when two previous German victims spotted the "ringed-hand man".

Portugal is still very much in the frame and will be as long as Androv stays there. Joc Latimer wants Androv for a crime committed a long time ago. We have a lot of collaboration from past Russian enemies, all European police forces are cooperating. You have knitted your army into the web of civilian policing and we are all guessing at what we are chasing!'

'You know, there is something horrible, Ernst!'

'Yes, I believe there is. Knowing Polenkovich as I have come to, I'm convinced it's something rotten and with the story Joc tells me of Androv and your Colonel Keller plus Mogatin, Lanov and a few dead bodies along the way, I feel we should know what their plans are by now!'

'It would be nice if we did, Ernst, but look at it this way. If you hadn't kept your file on your first encounter open with the Russians, we would all be wallowing in a sense of false security. At least we know we have a European security problem and we are keeping an eye on the whole pattern!'

'You're right, of course. "Forewarned is forearmed" is one of your English sayings, I think?'

'Yes, Ernst, and a very true one it is.'

'It may be so, Robin. We don't know what to arm ourselves for or with!'

'Ernst, it will come and it will be thanks to you initially.'

'Possibly... but it will take all of us from now on.'

'Let's hope that we are clever, and strong enough to hold it together.'

'That's why we must learn to communicate with each other in every detail of every event.'

'It seems to be working well at the moment, between ourselves, but heaven forbid if they put up any type of committee to tie us together!'

'As you say, Robin, heaven forbid! I must get on now, it is time to contact Moscow. Bye, my friend!'

The word 'friend' rang in Robin's ear for what seemed a very long time.

Easily recognised as he travelled the escalators and walkways of Orly airport, Boris Parentov walked confidently. He stopped once in the toilet and then again to talk to an Air France steward, asking for advice on a forward booking to Strasbourg. He was advised it would be better to exit the secure area he was in, collecting his luggage and re-entering the main concourse of the airport which would make things easier for him. The collecting of his bag, his exiting of the arrival lounge and his re-entry to the main concourse was covered by his observers. Parentov's destination had been forwarded to Inspector Torneau of the Achern district, who now sat patiently in his office waiting for the confirmation that the plane had taken off and that Parentov was on it.

In the stillness of the night with only a green-shaded desk lamp lighting the room, Gilbert sat and waited.

Robin, having been told by Gilbert that Parentov was on his way to Strasbourg and having agreed on a plan of collaboration between the French police and his own men, was content with the arrangement. Having had a few minutes of conversation with Ernst in Hamburg (passing the information on) Robin now sat relaxed, waiting for the phone to ring.

At Strasbourg airport, it had started to rain, the nasty drizzle which always seemed to come when surveillance teams had to stand around outside, the drizzle which seemed to get everywhere around your body – neck, hands – at that crucial moment when you want to make a quick note of a license plate number and the pencil slips, the wet eyelids making vision more difficult. Sergeant Donaldson sat with Sergeant Robinson on a bench seat opposite the arrival lounge for internal flights. Both men were casually dressed, joking and teasing one another as they acted out their drunken role each time the frosted glass automatic doors opened, allowing passengers to exit from the airport's secure area.

Slowly the passengers trickled through; eventually Parentov passed through the door, looking as if he had just walked off the page of a fashion magazine, carrying his leather briefcase and a Gucci suitcase. Sergeant Donaldson recognised him immediately. Both he and Robinson started their charade again, but this time, rising up from the bench seat, gathering up their newspapers and plastic bags noisily, obviously a little worse for wear. Parentov took no notice of them as he strode across to the taxi rank with the sergeants following closely behind. Close enough to hear Parentov ask to be taken to Colmar.

Whilst the ready and waiting pursuit unit prepared to follow the taxi, both Donaldson and Robinson watched the taxi leave, ensuring Parentov didn't get out of the taxi before the tail car was in position to observe the taxi fully. As the tail lights of the pursuit car disappeared down the slip road, both sergeants turned to each other not believing their luck, before they raced to their car and phoned in what they had just heard – the destination was Colmar.

Robin had been sitting anxiously waiting, but the phone call now galvanised him into action, moving the few troops he had around the outskirts of Strasbourg, after the taxi had passed outside the town limits to proceed to the Colmar area and report when hidden and static. The pursuit car was changed at intervals, although Robin knew that when things got close to the by-roads around Colmar it would be difficult, but he trusted his men's skills. In a lull amidst the activity, Robin wrote on his note pad, COLONEL KELLER in large block capitals. To fill in time, Robin faxed a handwritten note to Ernst Ulbrecht, and Joe Lomax in Lisbon for information. Ernst knew Robin was in control and that no action was required of him at this time and that Robin would let him know whenever Yute Polenkovich entered the area. Ernst believed they would all come together: Androv, Mogatin and Lanov and the man he wanted for trying to corrupt his beautiful Hamburg… Yute Polenkovich, Marshall of the Russian Army. He must not escape this time.

Joe Lomax, on receipt of Robin's fax, woke his pal, Joc, who was sleeping at the Embassy.

'It looks as if you've got some movement, old buddy!'

'Where Joe? In bloody France, or Germany?'

'France?'

'Get me out of here, Joe!'

'The Ambassador won't agree to you just hopping about Europe, as you know. He knows full well you have an authorised freedom of movement order on your posting, but he hasn't been given a budget to support it.'

'I know, we've been through all this, but he also said it should only be a formality. It's been a day and a half... Come on, Joe, chase the old boy up. I've got to get up there!'

'You can't go above the Ambassador's head. Even if you pay your own way, you'd have political flack barring your way and no support from us.'

'Speak to him now, Joe, see if he's heard anything from the States.'

'You're out of your skull, it's 0130 hours, there's no way! Besides, it would be better to wait till the morning. I'll see him first thing, about 0800 hours... even planes and airports will be open then!'

'Do it, Joe!' The hardness in Joc's voice told Joe that if it was still a 'no', Joc would be going anyway.

Robin, on hearing from his pursuit unit that the taxi carrying Parentov was exiting Colmar on the road of Colonel Keller's house, was not surprised, but angry that one of his army looked to be personally involved. Contacting the unit assigned to watching the Colonel, he instructed them to close in tighter to the house and that it was important for him to know how Parentov was received by the Colonel.

Inspector Torneau had emphasised that at any time of day or night he was to be informed of any new people who came into his area, of any nationality, but more especially Russians, an order which had been laid down quite a while ago. Sitting in his office, looking through all of the daily reports which came in, nothing of earth-shattering proportions caught his eye, until he came across the report from Guillaume Truffait, a man whom Inspector Torneau knew to be patient and thorough in his reporting. The last paragraph jumped out of the page: ...*an increase of five landings over yesterday*. Calling Truffait to his office immediately, Torneau asked, 'Did anybody get off these flights other than the pilots?'

'No, Inspector, just the pilots who are known to me. They are all French. I'm sure they have been around for years.'

'You have not checked their identities?'

'No, Inspector, they have always been there!'

'Don't worry, Truffait, I want a list of every pilot who has used that field in the past month.'

'Everyone, Inspector?'

'Everyone, Truffait, and the sooner the better!'

'What exactly am I looking for?'

'Everything. Did they just go to the same place all the time? Did they deviate on any occasion? Did they meet anyone unusual at either end of their journeys? How many times have they made the same journey?'

'Inspector, it will take an age if I do it alone.'

'Agreed. I will assign five more men to you, but be quick with your results – I feel sure things are about to happen!'

'We will be thorough as well, sir, I promise. We will start as soon as you give me the men, sir!' There was no insubordination meant and none taken by Inspector Torneau; he knew it was just part of Truffait's manner.

Parentov alighted from the taxi outside Colonel Keller's front door, which opened immediately, the Colonel standing to attention to meet his guest. The step up to the porch level and the three paces to the front door took seconds, but seemed ages to the Colonel who had not had to show this amount of respect (or was it fear?) for a very long time.

'Good evening, Colonel,' Parentov said, offering his hand.

'Comrade! Welcome. Everything is waiting for you.'

Coldly, Parentov responded, 'I'm sure it is, Colonel. And our guest is rested?'

Stiffly, the Colonel closed the door and fell in side by side with Parentov before he replied, 'Yes, comrade, his journey was tedious, I understand, but he is ready to take your instructions, I'm sure.'

The slight echo of their conversation as they walked across the baronial-style hall, emphasised the sinister undertaking which would be planned that night. The Colonel moved ahead to open the heavy door, throwing a shaft of light on Parentov as he walked through the door to a beautiful sitting room, offering his hand to the man who walked towards him doing the same. Parentov took the strong hand offered to him and with one remark, took control of the situation.

'Marshall Polenkovich, may I thank you for coming to see me...' Staring straight into Yute's eyes, he added, 'Your journey was somewhat difficult, I am led to believe?'

'Your instructions to get here at all costs for this specific time and to be unobserved, made it so!'

'You were successful on both counts, I presume?'

'Yes, I am sure.' Yute wanted to say, 'Are you sure *you* were not followed?' but decided against upsetting this man, now comfortably sitting opposite him.

The Colonel offered drinks, but both men refused to partake. Parentov said to him coldly, 'That will be all, Colonel,' and as the Colonel closed the door behind him, a chill fell across the room.

'My principal has instructed me to make ten million dollars available to you.' Parentov slumped further back into his well-upholstered armchair.

Yute pushed his body forward, the anger reflex in his body took control for a split second. 'What do you mean, your principal? I am the principal, it is my plan, my concept, and my execution. There is no one other than the Council above me on this!'

The slow, calculated response from Parentov was succinct. 'If that is what you feel, I can leave, but there is someone giving me direct instructions who has the correct authorities which I have personally seen. My boss – and yours it seems – is the one we both will answer to!'

The anger inside Yute welled up again and his body wanted to grab this suave gentleman in front of him, to force the name of his boss from his lips, but Yute held back, letting his brain work instead. Finally, he simply asked, 'May I know the name of our boss?'

'You know that, without his authority, it is impossible for me to divulge that information!'

'He wishes for me to spend this money he has okayed on my plan... or has he a new one?'

'Marshall, I only do as I am told. My involvement with my

homeland was increased a hundredfold since the collapse of the wall, but I have learnt the rules very quickly... don't ask questions and do as you are told!'

'That's all very well for some, my plan will work and has Council approval, plus it has been agreed that my plan will work at my speed!'

'It appears to me that things have changed and there is a new engine driver!'

'We'll see about that!' The words were out of Yute's mouth as he leapt at Parentov, shouting, 'Tell me his name!' Yute's hands were tightly clenched around Parentov's throat, then the 'click' which he heard behind him was the cocking action of a hand gun. He couldn't see, but he felt the cold muzzle at the nape of his neck. Yute's body relaxed and he slowly stood up to see who his attacker was.

'Thank you, Marshall. My instructions were to protect Comrade Parentov, whom I can only assume is in command of our poor souls.' The Colonel's voice was firm and as Yute's anger subsided, the Colonel allowed the berretta, still in his hand, to fall to his side. Yute sank back into his chair, stunned by the revelation, but already his mind was active trying to find a way to fulfil his pledge to Lanov and Mogatin that he would be in charge.

Robin's men, along with the active team from Inspector Torneau's contingency, were making full use of the darkness around the house. One observer had found a slight chink in one of the sitting-room curtains and had watched all that had happened from the point of entry of Parentov and the Colonel; the last part, though, had been videoed. The observer was in a static position at the window and managed to signal one of his buddies for the video camera from the car. Although a few minutes were lost before the camera arrived, the recording would serve as evidence. When it was reported that there had been some video action, Robin sat excitedly in his office waiting for the duty driver to bring it in. Sergeant Donaldson's knock on his door brought forth an instant response.

'Come in!' Robin got up from his chair and walked to the TV

and video recorder which had been set up in his office in readiness.

'Thank you, Sergeant. What is this going to tell us, I wonder?'

'I've called the observer in, sir, he should be here shortly.'

'Well done. Well, it's set up, let's have a look.' Pushing the 'play' button, the tape started to roll. At first, nothing – other than a lot of snow – but yes, there it was: the narrow opening in the curtain made for a very small, narrow opening in the middle of the frame and very little advantage in moving the camera. Once a chair with someone sitting in it was found, there were some slight jerks as the camera stopped and focused, which was a torment to Robin and to Sergeant Donaldson.

'Come on, man, come on! Focus it! Focus it! The other way!… Good, good, hold it there!… That's bloody Marshall Yute, sodding Polenkovich! How the hell did he get there?… How the bloody hell did he get past us and into the house?'

'That's bloody serious, sir. We ain't doing our job right!'

'Too damn right we aren't! Let's see if we picked up any sound on the tape. Turn it up, we may be lucky.'

The Sergeant fiddled with the volume to find what sounded like nasal-like talking in a vacuum. 'It's the best we'll get here, sir. May I suggest the sound lab has a go? It should hopefully tell us a bit more.'

'Yes, Sergeant, do that. Put what pressure you can on them. Let's just see the tape through again. When we spotted Polenkovich I didn't concentrate on the rest of them!'

'Me neither… here goes.'

The viewing was interesting in that it would hold up in evidence that the three men on the tape knew each other and had met secretly at the Colonel's house. All three men were recognisable as they passed in front of the camera's narrow field of vision. Switching off the tape, Sergeant Donaldson said, 'I'll get it over to the boffins now and chivvy it along.'

'Please get them to do a full analysis… even if they can only make out a word or two, they could maybe write up a possible scenario using lip movements.'

'I'll get on, sir, then I'll find out how our bloody "Houdini" got in there!'

The Sergeant left quietly, leaving Robin to have his private curse and swear over the Yute Polenkovich situation. Picking up his phone, he dialled Sergeant George MacKenzie. As soon as the Sergeant answered, Robin shot his question at him. 'Where exactly is Polenkovich now, Sergeant?'

'We believe he left for Moscow, sir, as reported by our men in Berlin four days ago.'

'Faxed and phoned, or posted?'

'Phoned, sir, to your office and written up and faxed. I've seen the copy myself, sir.'

'Thank you, Sergeant. I hadn't caught up with that one. Sorry to have bothered you.'

'That's okay, sir, no problem. My gut feeling tells me he will be coming back to this area, though.'

'He is here, Sergeant. I've got a video film of him talking to one of our Colonels and a known banker, in our Colonel's home!'

'How did he get back here?'

'Exactly, Sergeant. It's important to know and if we don't lose him this end, you'll be the first to know where he is.'

The phone slammed down in the Sergeant's ear with a loud crash, almost deafening him. Robin hated losing his temper. Eyeball to eyeball was more his style, not hiding at the end of a phone. He whispered, 'I'm sorry, Sergeant!' then carried on with sorting the pile of reports on his desk.

Sergeant MacKenzie knew losing Polenkovich was serious. His boss was quite correct to admonish him, but it still stung.

The phone line between Ernst and Robin hummed as it did between Ernst and Joc. On hearing the news, Joc was even more determined to get into the middle of at least France, feeling that Lisbon was just a tad too far away. Leaning back in his chair, his methodical mind went through the cardex system in his head, the pieces not always fitting together, but it exercised his mind until such time as he became a player in what he felt would be a very big game. Joc understood the central European pattern of things; road, air, rail links. Portugal, although European, was not as fluid in these areas. What or why had all of the Russian group journeyed extensively there? 'We need to find a connection.

There's got to be something, or maybe we have missed something that has already taken place...' The words spoken to himself in his empty office sent a chill through his body. Grabbing for the phone, he dialled Police Chief Manuel Vargas on his direct line. One... two... three rings.

'Chief Inspector of Police Vargas here, who is calling?'

'Joc. Joc Latimer, US Embassy, Lisbon.'

'Joc, you want to speak to me?'

'Sure, for Christ's sake! I dialled your number, didn't I?'

'Yes, you did, Joc, and thank you for calling. Why you want to speak to me?'

The rhythm of the broken English spoken by Vargas became contagious and Joc replied, 'I want to speak you about your road and rail services, also maybe where you go by air, please?'

Vargas thought nothing of Joc's delivery of his question and replied, 'Our road are good when good, but when bad... lots of mountain roads in north, very twisty and no good. Good roads on coast and some in middle. Train okay, but not over all country. Very slow travelling, have to travel first class for air conditioning – very expensive, yes? But airplane flies all over sometimes, two times or more a week.'

'Anyway, you think you could cope with heavy – gigantic loads?'

'I not think so, we do sometimes have to move generators around, but we design the route so we get motorway as quick as possible. Trains go nowhere and no big flat top platforms or not many!'

'What about your rivers anyway; shall we say from Spain, that rivers would connect to the sea?'

'I don't think possible, I will find out and call you back, all right?'

'Yes, please do. I don't have a direct line though, I'm sorry.'

'Okay, I will call you around five!'

Robin's agitation was obvious to everyone who came into his office. The word had soon spread that Sergeant MacKenzie had got a bollocking and that he in turn was giving his team hell, which had not brought to light how, or where, Yute Polenkovich had got away from Sergeant Hackett's beady eyes in Metz. Every one of the team and each of their last sightings – hour and day – were spread out onto graphs and cross-checked and showed that he could not have been in Colmar. On hearing this news, Robin knew they had been duped, probably by the simple use of a double – same clothes, same build, leaving an apartment house or hotel at distance without constantly seeing the face; it happens. Robin picked up the phone and called MacKenzie into his office.

'This is pretty much of a disaster, George, you've got to cross-check all the groups everywhere that we know he's been, to see if and when he's returned to any of the old haunts.'

'I see what you're thinking, sir, but may I suggest with the network of civilian and military police, we should put out an "all-points", requesting any sightings of this man anywhere to be reported.'

'I'd need convincing before I authorised that. First we announce we had lost him, then put his picture up in every police station for him to see that we have been tailing him, lost him for a while, but now we're on his tail again!'

'It's not quite like that, it can be circulated to all commanders and civvy police, et cetera, on a "need-to-know" basis and request that the photo ID is not displayed. In doing it this way, we will have minimum risk, and if he has been seen out there, we have a much better chance of filling in the gaps.'

'You are probably right, but we shouldn't have lost him in the first place! Okay, go for it your way, but cover all countries he has been to nationally, and not just the areas that we know.'

'Good idea, sir. I'll get moving on it now.'

Teasingly, Robin asked, 'We do know where he is right now?'

Sergeant MacKenzie liked the humour and looked down at his watch. 'Yes, sir, it's about time for his ablutions!'

Robin laughed quietly and said, 'Thank you, Sergeant,' to MacKenzie's back.

Chapter Thirty-One

With the advent of his boss's absence and no one having been sent to take over the day-to-day running of the department and because of his willingness to succeed, Rudi was taking on more and more administrative duties. He knew he was capable enough but wanted to be recognised for his efforts. He had written to the personnel chief who was vaguely known to him, stating that his new function within his current position was far in excess of his grade three qualification and on the next wage review would it be possible for a small increase in his meagre salary? Today, on his arrival at his desk was one of the infamous brown envelopes which arrive during the night. Remembering his request for an increase in pay and not expecting to have a reply so quickly, fear automatically struck the thoughts tumbling through his head. Mayer will never forgive me losing my job – it will be unfair on her to just arrive – there's so little information for me to give even now and when I'm sacked there will be even less. Oh, Mayer, don't leave me – I will die without you. The panic having eventually subsided a little, he stared at the envelope now in his hand, for any distinguishing marks, anything which might tell him whether it was from the personnel chief, but no, nothing. Just a plain old brown envelope. Taking a pencil from his drawer, he placed the sharpened end under the sealed flap. Reaching inside for the thin single sheet of paper and having prepared himself for bad news, he began to read: *You will attend a meeting at 0915 hours this morning – Room A117.*

For a moment, the terror struck. A directive, a brown envelope, unsigned? He must have been found out! He didn't ought to go to that meeting, he really should escape from Moscow right now! Calm yourself, Rudi! his inner voice told him. Since Androv left, you have not been very active on behalf of your German friends. If there was anything to be found out, Androv would have – he would have reported you. *Yes, he would*, crashed into his brain, *yes, he would*! Rudi whispered to himself, 'I will go to Room A117 at 0915 and I will use whatever guile I have to, so as to remain here for Mayer's sake.' His voice rose from a whisper as he mentioned Mayer's name. Sitting down at his desk he looked at his watch. Only one hour to wait – no time or method to escape the office and call her about this letter; besides, if I told her now, she would worry unnecessarily and if I don't come back from the meeting? Rudi shook his head. I will come back from the meeting! I love you, Mayer, I love you! His strong whisper seemed to boom around his small office, bringing him back to the reality of the moment.

Vargas had phoned Joc back very quickly, stating that in his opinion, and that of his colleagues, it would be impossible to use Portuguese rivers as a mode of transport as not enough were connected to each other, the rivers Teto and Douro being the only real commercial rivers in Portugal. In the conversation, Vargas mentioned that when his men were ferreting around in Lamego they had been surprised by the number of Spanish people there from the coastal regions. Joc sat still in his uncomfortable chair, going over the conversation in his mind. His conversation with Vargas had been succinct at the beginning and then rambled on about the generalities of his country. They were without emotion – just ramblings, but had Vargas given him a clue? Spanish people from the coastal regions of Spain! Joc began to fidget. He must phone Vargas again and ask him if his colleagues saw at anytime any of our Russian friends talking to Spaniards.

0905 hours. Rudi washed his hands, checked his hair and tie and left the basement; ten minutes to get to the lifts, wait for the lift and get to the top floor and be on time for his appointment. 0912 hours, he was outside room A117, polishing his shoes on the back of his trouser legs, the last touch-up of hair and tie, then he gently but firmly knocked.

A woman's voice answered, 'Come.'

Entering, he noticed the office was as dingy as his own. 'Good morning, I have an appointment at 0915 hours. I'm here as directed.'

'You are early – you will have to wait.' The tone of her voice made Rudi angry, but he realised the poor woman was probably exerting authority over him, satisfying a frustration of her own inadequacies.

Pleasantly, Rudi asked, 'Who am I going to see?'

'You will find out when you are called, he will tell you if he wants you to know his name!'

'Sorry, I didn't mean to disturb you. It's just that my note was not signed…'

'I send out hundreds, and they never are.'

'Doesn't that seem strange to you?'

'No, my bosses have far more important things to do than sign every piece of paper!'

'Is that just an excuse to cover up their laziness, I wonder?'

'My bosses never stop working, ever…' The harsh buzz of the intercom at precisely 0915 hours, cut in and stopped her completing her sentence. 'You may enter now!'

'Thank you.' The abruptness disturbed him as he walked quickly to the large door. Entering the room, the first thing which caught Rudi's eye was the dimness for such a large room. He felt that a chandelier could do so much – the long table, the twelve matching armchairs, the heavily-framed, unseen pictures on the walls. The one solitary chair on the opposite side of the table – his chair, his instinct told him as he walked towards it.

'Sit down, Comrade Simusov, thank you for coming.' The voice was in the room with him, but where was the man?

Rudi sat down before answering. 'Thank you, sir.'

'You are welcome, but I expect you wonder why you are here?'

'I assume it's to do with my request for extra pay for my work in the absence of Comrade Androv, sir.'

'In a way, you are right.' Rudi was relieved. The heavy footsteps of his interviewer told Rudi that he was coming out of the shadows on his right. Rudi held his eyes forward, looking into the weak shaft of light coming from the tall window. The interviewer was a heavily-built man – his profile passed through the light – Rudi would have said handsome, moustachioed, over two metres tall, square shoulders. A fleeting glance was cast before he sat immediately in front of Rudi and became a silhouette.

'Comrade Androv was a good boss to you, Simusov?'

'He was demanding, but fair, sir.'

'How well did you know him?'

The alarm bells in Rudi's head started ringing. They know I have been informing to the West! 'Hardly at all, sir. Socially, he never came to our canteen on any occasion to my knowledge; sometimes I might see him in the corridors, he generally walked straight past and if I had any queries, he always granted me time within his own heavy schedule of work.'

'A favourable report... would you say your feelings are the feelings of the rest of the staff in general?'

'Yes, sir, I would.'

'You are very loyal to your boss!'

'He has never done anything to make me feel otherwise, sir.'

'Good, good. I like your honesty and openness with me. How would you like to take on some of his duties officially, with additional pay of course?'

'I don't know what his full duties were, sir. I know he attended a lot of meetings.'

'You will not be involved in the meetings immediately, possibly that will come, but we need a central point on the work floor where we know everything will be attended to efficiently and without question.'

'If you think I am worthy, sir, I'm certain that I will do my best not to let you down.'

'Good, good. I will put out instructions of your new authority which will become operative from tomorrow morning.'

'Thank you, sir. As you will be my new boss, may I know your name and your telephone extension number?'

'That will not be necessary, I will contact you in the same way as this morning.'

Rudi was about to say, 'Yes, sir,' when the voice dismissed him sharply with, 'You will leave now.'

Startled and confused, Rudi found himself outside the large door, with the secretary screaming at him, 'Come on, get out – you've had your moment of glory; now make room for the next one!'

He walked in silence out into the long corridor. He had got

the raise he wanted, the man had said so. He is going to get additional instructions and authority to carry them out. Rudi could only feel unhappiness. Shaking his head back to reality, he murmured to himself, 'What have I started?'

Joc Latimer was speaking to Manuel Vargas, asking if it were possible to go back over the past reports of his men when they were active in the Lamego district, to see if any of the meetings between the Russians and the Spaniards had turned into anything more than just 'mates' in a bar. Vargas, who was now talking like a real policeman, said, 'I don't hold out much hope, but I will get on it right away.' Like the last time, the phone went down before Joc could say 'thank you'.

Rudi continued working after his meeting; the time dragged terribly. At five minutes to five, his desk was clear and the silence of anticipation took over the whole building, waiting for five o'clock. Today seemed even slower for Rudi – all that had been on his mind was phoning Mayer. He had rehearsed his route a dozen times in his mind; get newspaper across the street, stop on the corner to read the sports page, turn left down the alley, turn right, stop just outside the alley exit, watch for anyone who might be following. When he felt his path was clear, he would run to the railway station, again watching the entrance from the bank of telephones he always used prior to making his call to Mayer.

The first ring took an age, the second seemed endless, on the third, thank God, she picked up the phone.

'My darling Mayer!'

'Rudi, my love!' The phones went quiet as they listened to each other's silence.

'Rudi, have you had a good day?'

The suddenness of Mayer's question brought a spontaneous, 'I've been promoted!' It came spurting out and sounded full of conceit. Immediately, Rudi started apologising. 'I didn't mean that the way it sounded...'

'I know, Rudi, quiet please!'

'Sorry, but I do feel different since I was told this morning.'

'It proves they know nothing of us, I think.'

'Me too, but I still take precautions.'

'You must, because I love you so much!'

'Me too! When will they let us run our own lives?'

'Soon, Rudi, soon. Ernst will do everything he can, I know he will as soon as the time is right.'

'May it be soon!'

'Don't be glum now, what will your promotion mean?'

'More money and a letter authorising me to supervise the staff in my group.'

'You've taken Androv's position, then?'

'That would be impossible. He went to meetings and often had foreigners to negotiate with. No, I will just be doing the administration I suppose, connected with day-to-day running and I'll write reports and send them somewhere… In fact, I don't really know what I will be doing until I get my first note of instruction tomorrow morning!'

'What do you mean, "a note"?'

'Oh, the interviewer told me there would be a note every day, that I did not need to know his name or telephone extension number, any reports would be collected… Oh my God, let me come to you now – please, Mayer, please! I will live like a refugee. I'm afraid, my love! I'm afraid!' The tears were welling up in his eyes. His throat became syrupy as he continued, 'It wouldn't be so bad if I really totally understood what I'm doing. The snippets of information I give you seem so disjointed to me, and inconsequential.'

'Oh, Rudi, no! Without you, Ernst would not be as confident that something is about to happen. Just think, Rudi, we would never have met and found true love!' Mayer stopped herself. She felt like some blackmailing whore. 'Forgive me, Rudi, that must have sounded awful to you. Believe me, it is you I want. It is you I have centred my life around. I would never hurt you, I love you, Rudi, I love you!' The tears started running from her eyes, and the swelling in her throat turned the last, 'I love you' into a whisper. 'You do understand, Rudi?'

'I understand completely, it is only my belief in you that keeps me going on!'

'I will always be true to you, Rudi, always and always!'

'Me too, I love you!' Rudi placed the phone down. He had to; he could not have held his own tears back any longer.

Mayer slowly walked to Ernst's office doorway. Seeing him cheered her up a little bit, but the tears were just below the surface.

'Come in, Mayer, you look a little down.'

'I have just spoken to Rudi. He has been promoted at work this morning, he will have more authority over his group. He won't be replacing Androv and going to meetings in his place, but he will receive his daily instructions by a note on his desk every morning. His interviewer would not give his name and withheld his phone number too.'

Ernst, seeing Mayer was unhappy, tried a little joke. 'Your Rudi works for funny people!'

Mayer's reaction flared; she was about to jump to Rudi's defence when she caught the glint in Ernst's eyes. 'Oh, you tease, sir!'

'Feel better now?'

Smiling, she replied, 'Yes, but when do you think this will all end? Rudi is very tired, and remember he is not a policeman – he's untrained and unprotected.'

'I know that as well as you, Mayer. Your burden is your love for him, mine is to try and cut the head off what could be another monstrous crime crippling Europe!'

'Sorry, sir.'

'Don't be, Mayer – keep reminding me of Rudi and love and romance and longing to be together and your dreams. It reminds me that the whole world is not a cesspit.'

'Sir…' Mayer couldn't manage any more words, the flood of tears suddenly broke as she ran out through the doorway.

Lanov and Mogatin had moved to their second contact point, having waited the maximum time at the first and it was nearly time they should leave to go to the third location. Just a few minutes more, both men were thinking, when the phone rang in the open domed kiosk. The relief showed on both of their faces as Lanov answered and gave the reference of the day to the caller who identified himself as 'Yute'.

'Correct. We will meet today at position fifteen on your list, at 1500 hours. Be careful!'

Mogatin had stood with his back to the phone, watching for any suspicious movement and had not seen any of Lanov's reactions to the call, but when their eyes met it was apparent that Lanov had been slightly worried by the change of venue.

'What has happened, my friend?' Mogatin looked forwards and showed no anxiety on his face.

'We are meeting at three this afternoon at position fifteen, which is an emergency position and the code "be careful" was used!'

Mogatin stopped as if pole-axed. 'Something has gone terribly wrong! Sorry to sound so stupid, Lanov, it's just with Tashimov in Hamburg things went wrong, we've already had one serious fright with Yute and now an emergency call… we'll never get back on our feet at this rate!'

'Or survive!' Lanov paused then continued, 'Do you realise we have less and less friends to call on in the event of trouble? We are clever enough to survive any situation short term, but long term, we should make plans for escape now.'

'Possibly – but let's wait until after we meet Yute.'

Mogatin nodded a silent approval, both men walking purposefully onwards. Lanov and Mogatin knew in a moment or two, they would split up from one another and execute well-planned and devious routes to keep clear of any detection.

Both the Military Police and French Gendarmes had observed everything which had taken place at the phone kiosk and were now in pursuit of their quarry, each knowing from Lanov and Mogatin's attitudes, that something was wrong and that they would split up any minute now and be very skilful in protecting their backs and must be extra vigilant in their surveillance.

'There they go!' The split had taken place and the whole of the districts of Achern, Colmar, Strasbourg, et cetera could become their playground.

Receiving the information at Military Police HQ, Robin decided Ernst should be informed of this movement and phoned him immediately. Having placed the receiver down, he pondered for a moment before dialling his Adjutant's office.

'Roche here…'

'Robin, sir. Just thought you'd like to know we have two running and by the reports coming in, they are both showing a little anguish!'

'Let's hope they start making mistakes, Robin. I know we have the General's blessing on this, but, without results, he is capable of pulling the plug!'

'I hope not, André – it's really getting interesting with this Androv in the picture!'

'Things have speeded up a bit since his arrival, it's a blasted shame we still don't know where we are speeding to!'

'Perhaps the young Russian we met – Rudi, I'm sure you remember him, sir?' Robin held back, expecting André's reply.

'Of course I do; he was mooning around after that German girl… he's got good taste, I remember thinking!'

'Well, he has been given extra duties and power within Androv's old department. Hopefully, we'll get faster and better information from now on!'

'Hope so, Robin. Anyway, must get on. Possibly see you in the mess around five?'

'I'll call if things delay me, sir, but I would like to see you.'

Both phones were put back into their cradles at the same time. No sooner did Robin's reach the cradle, than it rang again immediately.

'Cadwallader here.'

'Sir, Sergeant Donaldson speaking… that suave Russian, "Parentov" has just booked a flight to Baghdad for tomorrow, no visa needed!'

'Is this confirmed, Sergeant?'

'Yes, sir, in fact, he's had to upgrade from business class to first class to make sure he could get on that flight.'

'Sod it! Baghdad… we can't follow him there! Sergeant, make certain he gets on the plane and leaves. Check his arrival if you can… you're going to have to keep some of your crew watching for his return. I'll advise his exit to all concerned and plead for more help from our civvy friends to stand vigilant at all entry points to their countries!'

'It's a bugger having to ask for favours all the time, isn't it, sir?'

'No one minds the favour being asked, Sergeant, but they loathe the bloody "red tape" it causes in all languages!'

'That's progress – as they say, sir!' The cheeky humour in his monotone Scots voice did not go unnoticed.

Robin's conversation with Ernst in Hamburg, Gilbert in Achern, then Paris, Vargas in Portugal and Joc and his American network had received a 'You're asking a lot!' but each of them knew they were fully committed and had been from the start. Robin rubbed his eyes and lay back in his chair, knowing all he could do now was wait.

The brown envelope was waiting for Rudi as he arrived at his desk. Although he had been warned that his instructions for each day would arrive this way, he could not hold his body back from the shudder passing through him. His nerve gathered as he tore open the envelope, the feeling of panic and anxiety mixed together making his fingers clumsy. The three pages of instructions fell open onto his desk. Sitting down, his hand pushed the pages flat, then he read the first page, which reiterated his daily duties, which must be performed without fail. He turned the page. The heading, 'Transport' jumped from the page and his panic began again. He had never had anything to do with transport before. God, what am I going to do? Calming himself, his logic started taking over. Within his group there must be a transport specialist; where would he be?... In Androv's old office will be a list of names and functions – I must go there now!

Rudi entered Androv's old office with confidence. Why not? Didn't he now have the authority? He would keep his section lists in a cabinet, not a drawer, Rudi thought. A cabinet... Aaah! There it is... Grabbing for the top drawer handle, Rudi's surprise increased as the drawer slid open – it wasn't locked! Strange, Rudi thought, but in his anxiety to look, he dismissed the thought from his mind almost straight away. Running his fingers across the top of each file he read aloud each heading until finally, reaching the back of the metal cabinet, he found what he was looking for – 'Personnel'. The file jumped into his hand and he turned and sat audaciously at Androv's desk. The file opened, he turned the pages of the thick file very slowly, reading the hundreds of names laid out before him, each with a cross-reference for further personal information and job allocation neatly placed in appropriate columns. His finger followed the job allocation column, finding eight names allocated to 'Transport'. Taking a note of the information he required, he placed the file back in its place in the cabinet and left the office to return to his own. Whilst walking back he had decided to interview the eight people on his list and find out who would have been the strongest player on Androv's team. But first he must read and understand his instructions more fully. Throwing himself into his chair, Rudi snatched up the envelope and the three pages, tearing the envelope slightly more as he opened the letter to read:

TRANSPORT (The Snake)

You will ensure that the 'snake' is on schedule by Friday. This will enable extra supplies to be taken on, plus other units to join its body.

Again, Rudi read the message, then read it again, trying to figure out what the message meant. Rubbing his brow and rattling his pencil between his teeth, he swore in bewilderment before snatching the phone and calling the group of men he had listed, instructing them all to convene in his office at 10.45 a.m. that morning. Rudi sat watching as the group found themselves some space in his tiny office – watching for a leader although they all looked fairly nondescript, it seemed that seven of the men were all trying to leave one man at the front.

'Stop fidgeting, all of you!' The command in his voice surprised even Rudi himself. He hadn't shouted, just talked from the back of the throat. No sooner had they stopped moving than Rudi's index finger cut through the air, pointing straight at the man stranded at the front of the group. 'Your name?'

It was impossible for the man not to realise that he had been singled out and he replied dutifully, 'Dimitri Kernlikov, Comrade Simusov!'

'Thank you. You will be the spokesman for this group, it is apparently what they wish.'

'Comrade.'

'You know that I have been given some authority, I suppose?'

'Yes, comrade.'

'My review so far, tells me all of you are in transport. I have an instruction to carry out for what I can only believe to be a convoy of lorries or maybe a train, called the "Snake". You, Comrade Kernlikov, will tell me what this is, its route and its manifest.'

'That is impossible, Comrade Simusov.'

'What do you mean – you have orders not to tell me?' Rudi's temper rose at the thought that he was not in full control after all.

'Please, comrade, we have been moving this damn thing from Vladivostok across the whole of Russia. It is a road convoy of enormous proportion, travelling on lorries that keep breaking down – the distances for each day's travel were overestimated. The convoy is added to by the local commanders at will. We started out with a catering unit feeding fifty men, we are now feeding, at the last count, six hundred! It is sometimes days before we have the full picture and we never know where we are going to!'

'Please stop a minute, comrade – allow me to take what you have just said into my already tired brain!' Rudi paused for a moment, smiling at the bunch in front of him.

'Comrade Kernlikov, I am right in thinking the other men with you are of lesser seniority than yourself and that they are on your team on this project?'

'Yes, comrade, you would be right.'

'Good. May I suggest your team carries on with their duties and we carry on with trying to sort out our problem!'

The words 'we' and 'our' were not lost on Comrade Kernlikov and with just a nod of acknowledgement from him, the group faded away, back to their offices. Rudi stood up and offered his hand. 'My name is Rudi…'

'Mine is Dimitri. Nice to have met you, but as far as sorting out the problems of the "Snake", when you have heard the full story, you may wish you had never even heard of it!'

'Things are that bad?'

'We think so. We also believe that this is the biggest heist the Russian people have ever suffered!'

'You are being very open, Dimitri!'

'I'm trusting you, Rudi, with my true feelings and I can assure you they are the feelings of my men and many others.'

'Mine too, but until now, I've never had any power… although I am uncertain of what power or control I may have. Every day will now begin with a brown envelope.

'Mine too! Is yours unsigned?'

'Yes. Did you go to the top floor and meet that harridan of a secretary and enter "the room of shadows"?'

'Yes! Yesterday. My warning was that someone will contact me with instructions when it was necessary, so I knew that there was someone above me. You calling this meeting makes you my boss!'

'Don't look at it that way, can't we work together?'

'I'd like that, Rudi. I'm a little scared of my position. I'm really just a training civil servant with logic; and transport is not my first love… I wouldn't know the difference between a Merc and a Trabant!'

Rudi joked, 'That's why I'm senior – I could if they were side by side!'

Dimitri's laugh was contagious and Rudi could not hold back. 'We'll work well together, Rudi, I know we will…' Dimitri stuttered through his laughter.

Rudi answered him, 'Well, let's get on with it then!' Both men looked at each other and the laughter began again.

'Sir, Sergeant Donaldson here… our suave Russian is on his way to Baghdad – I had a mate follow him on.'

'You have friends everywhere, Sergeant!'

'It's a steward on the flight. He took a fancy to my sister when she was visiting me and we sometimes get together for a drink… he waved his hankie to me from the cockpit!'

'Are you sure it's your sister he fancies?'

'I'm not going to answer that, sir, it might incriminate me!'

'Thank you, Sergeant – I'll see you when you get back.'

Robin was about to phone the circuit of police and notify 'need-to-know' personnel in the military, when his phone rang.

'Cadwallader.'

'Ernst here, Robin…'

'I was about to phone you to tell you our suave Russian is airborne!'

'Good! We must keep our eyes open for his return. I feel he could become an important player.'

'Will you keep me posted, Ernst?'

'Definitely. I see Lanov and Mogatin are still in your area!'

'Yes, they are becoming boring – they just follow the Colonel and the Tomlevskis. They look, but they don't touch.'

'I feel sure they will become more active fairly soon.'

'I agree, Ernst. I just hope we have everything in place for when they do!'

'You will, Robin, everyone will. It will be a great coup when we Europeans start marching against world crime and with the far-thinking Americans on board, we have a good chance of success.'

'I'm sure you're right. I just wish I knew exactly how we will be drawn into the net. None of my players have become active yet…'

'It will happen soon enough, my friend. I feel it getting nearer, then what – heaven knows!'

'Let it be sooner rather than later, Ernst. There are so many watchers and those who are being watched – we are very vulnerable.'

'Keep your fingers crossed, is what I think you would say now, Robin?'

'And our legs too, I think!'

'And your legs… I suppose that is so the ball will not go through… from your game of cricket, yes?'

'Yes, Ernst, our stupid game of cricket… but what we are playing is not a game!'

'No it isn't, Robin, but we are prepared, so let's be thankful for small mercies!'

'You're right, Ernst. If you'll excuse me, I must get on with passing this information forward. I will phone you with anything new.'

'Me too.' Both men placed their phones down and snatched a few moments of rest before continuing the fight.

After Dimitri had left, Rudi read the third page from the brown envelope. The heading was, 'Loyalty to Mother Russia'. At first, Rudi put it down on the desk, thinking that he had already, in his short life, read every bit of political propaganda in the whole of Russia; he did not wish to read more after what had happened so far today. He started to work on other things, but the third page kept drawing his attention. Irritatedly, Rudi finally snatched the page from the desk.

LOYALTY TO MOTHER RUSSIA

Loyalty is rewarded. You will be judged by your mentor throughout your life from this moment on. Your success or failure is in your own hands. Failure is punishable by death.

Rudi shuddered and for the rest of the day wrestled with his conscience. Dare he ever phone Mayer again? The day dragged on – his longest day. Dimitri whistled softly as he walked along the corridor on his way to Rudi's office and seeing the door open, he took his position in the centre of the doorway, whistling through his teeth as he came to a halt.

Rudi was not very amused. The shrillness of the whistle seemed to touch every part of his brain. 'You bloody fool, Dimitri! Happiness is great to have, but a stupid mind like yours should never have learnt to whistle!'

'Sorry, Rudi, just mucking about – what's the problem with you anyway?' Rudi handed him page three of the memo. Dimitri read it and said, 'Surely everyone gets one of these? You know, to boost maximum effort, you're going to rise through the ranks and your rewards will be there for the taking... do you think they will kill you if you fail?'

Rudi's sullen face looked into Dimitri's and saw real friendship there. He blurted out, 'I've been talking to a girl in Hamburg for weeks... we've met up. Androv gave me some leave... someone else must know, surely? Some day, Dimitri, one piece of paper will catch up with another piece of paper and I'm dead. I love her so much. I can't speak to her again, I can't take that risk... she's so beautiful, Dimitri, so alive, so true... why me?'

Rudi's eyes filled with tears but he managed manfully, to hold them back. Dimitri, having had a true love in his life – a burning passion of devouring proportions – understood Rudi's despair.

'Rudi, go for love – get out now before the job devours you and the perks start arriving!'

That advice was exactly what Rudi wanted to hear, but how could he let Mayer down? She with the beautiful face, sparkling eyes, luscious lips, the body of Venus, working for the police trying to save Europe, wanting this information for her nice boss. Is she right? Is Russia full of gangsters? Is it? Is it? Rudi's mind stopped racing and he calmed down and said, 'Dimitri, it's not that simple, I promise you. Would it be possible for us to have a drink together on the way home?'

'It sounds important – why not?' Dimitri whispered as he offered his hand to his friend. The first day of his new appointment dragged. Rudi functioned well, but the witching hour of five o'clock could not come quick enough.

The bar Dimitri had chosen for their drink was a warm, homely place, just enough of everything – natural light, stools at the bar, round tables with chairs in the centre of the long room. The alcoves of varying sizes were enticing for small groups of rowdy drinking, lovers, or people who just wanted to talk to each other quietly. Dimitri had found one such quiet alcove in the furthest corner of the room. When Rudi arrived, he saw Dimitri's excited wave to attract his attention and, smiling, Rudi walked briskly over to Dimitri and they embraced each other like long-lost brothers. It was obvious to Rudi that Dimitri was well known and liked by everyone around them; some of Dimitri's friends even acknowledged Rudi with a wink of welcome and a wave with a tankard-filled hand.

'You are well known here, Dimitri...'

'I was born here, strangely enough – almost at the very spot you are now sitting at!'

'You're teasing me!'

'No, my friend, absolutely true. Everyone here knows me, most of the young ones went to school with me, the older ones went to school with my parents. My family have had a bar here for over one hundred and fifty years. Slowly we've expanded and my parents live above the bar, but I live across the street.'

'It must be marvellous for you, everyone and everything all around you. I've been on my own now for a very long time; even my sister is lost and I can hardly remember her.'

'You poor chap, is there no one at all?'

'No, only Mayer and it seems I will lose her too!'

'Is there any reason you should lose her?'

'Very definitely, yes!'

'Tell me, Rudi, I'm a good listener.'

'You would have to be, but if I told you, you would be incriminated if you joined me and I would be living in fear of you telling on me!'

'Rudi, I do not let my friends down, nor do I tell tales. You are, I realise, on the Russian upward spiral, but you always have a friend in me, if or when you want to talk things over.'

'I'd like to, Dimitri, but I don't know what I'm actually doing for our bosses, but I know what Mayer has asked of me so far and it seems to me, using her eyes, that there is an awful lot of corruption in Russia and that the West is trying to protect itself.'

'The core of corruption in Russia is real, Rudi, you must surely have realised that?'

'Not really, I just lived day-to-day, when one day I was authorised to answer some enquiries from Hamburg police and...' Realising he had started his story, he stopped.

'Why have you stopped? I've told you I'm here to listen in friendship.'

'It would involve you...'

'Maybe I would like to be involved! For God's sake, Rudi, I'm here, the time is now! Tell me... we could work well together... and who knows, your beloved Mayer could be the prize at the end, but if you lose the fight in Russia, at least you would have fought for your ideals!'

'You're saying what I want to hear, but I don't know if I have the strength to go through with it.' Rudi paused to think for a moment, then asked, 'Dimitri, you are a romantic, you must have been hurt terribly?' After he had asked the question, Rudi felt it was too direct and added, 'Would you like to talk about it?'

'It was a long time ago, Rudi, and I'm settled in my mind now; everything is sorted out.'

'It concerned a girl, Dimitri. You speak with warmth, the warmth that can only be spoken by someone who has been hurt by an all-consuming love. Tell me that it was a girl, at least!'

'Yes, Rudi, but that is all you need to know; now let us see how we can help each other. Tell me your problem.'

Rudi quietly unfolded his story and his dilemma about how his love would only survive if Mayer kept receiving information from him to help her boss's wish to make Western Europe a bastion of peace and tranquillity succeed.

'You are not being honest with yourself, Rudi. You know Russia is corrupt and that disturbing things have happened to keep its people under the thumb of the few. I would not mind betting with you it was the very reason you started cooperating with the Germans in the first place.'

'For goodness sake, Dimitri, are you always so blastedly logical?'

'If that's what it is, I call it a code for living!'

'You are making a heavy load to carry for yourself, Dimitri.'

'It's better than no load at all!'

The alcove became silent as both men sat making appraisals of each other before the inevitable bond of commitment to what would be their common cause. Rudi liked his new friend who had changed from a brusque oaf, into a thinking, romantic with a cause before his eyes. They sat in silence as they finished their drinks, until Rudi broke the silence with a question, 'Will you work with me in finding this "snake"?'

'It will be difficult until it gets a lot nearer to Moscow. I'm certain someone is trying to make it difficult for us and our invisible master to keep track of it. Rudi, I also believe no matter how many threats the invisible man makes, unless he kills us all, he will have difficulty finding the "snake" for himself!'

'Why would he have to kill us all?'

'We, including Androv, have been tracking and servicing its needs since the very beginning. We know as much as anyone does!'

'A good point, but it is me who has been threatened.'

'True, but I know Androv received many such threats before

he eventually left us. It's my theory, that it is Androv who has taken control!'

'That's wild! What reasons do you have?'

'None, Rudi – none at all, but I have worked around Androv for a very long time and he is a survivor.'

'That's only a hunch.'

'But in those very corridors, not too long ago, the KGB were almost at his office door with a warrant of arrest, but he escaped them and, using the system which he knows very well, turned up in charge of another department, shortly before the "snake" started to move!'

'You can prove this?'

'No, but we could get everything I'm saying corroborated by all members of the team.'

'But would they all tell the truth?'

'Yes, I've spoken to them all and none of them like all this secrecy that has increased since Glasnost!'

'I'll let the Germans know – I feel it is all I can do in view of what you're saying.'

'I would, Rudi. If you love her, you must stay on the path you've already been walking. Your heart was in it then when you were alone, now you have a friend.'

'Thank you, Dimitri, that is very comforting – it was lonely.'

'I know; now get off and make your call and make sure you are not followed!'

'I'll make sure. Is there a back way out of here?'

'Yes, my friend there is, but use the front. If they did see you come in, they will be extra vigilant in the future if they don't see you go out again.'

'Thank you... for everything.'

Dimitri offered his strong hand in silence. There was no more need for words – yet.

Chapter Thirty-Two

'Be careful!' still rang in both Lanov's and Mogatin's ears as they each made their way individually to 'rendezvous fifteen'. They knew what it meant: they must be extra careful, they must not even be seen by the birds in the sky. Rendezvous fifteen was a derelict building isolated on the edge of a disused warehouse area outside Strasbourg. Lanov and Mogatin had not queried the position of the site until now. They had both taken separate routes there, but they had both found great difficulty in arriving unseen. Yute had already arrived and could not understand their obvious anxiety as they approached him. Mogatin was the first to speak.

'The whole bloody place is swarming with watchers... we've been rumbled!'

'The whole of France looks like it's alive with watchers. I agree with Mogatin!'

'There was no activity when I came through. If you're not being paranoid about this, it must be to do with the "big-wig" visiting from Spain!'

'What bloody "big-wig"?'

'Some General from Burgos taking up a Eurocorps appointment and there's a big parade for him later.'

'Well, it made it bloody hard work getting here!' said Mogatin.

'I just hope you're bloody right! We'll soon know when we leave.'

'I am, and don't give it another thought until you leave... there are more important things to worry about!'

Lanov, with his lethargic-sounding voice, asked, 'What's gone wrong this time?'

'We have a visitor on board. I don't know who it is, but he's going to cause problems if we don't find out and dispose of him. I want you two to keep on making yourselves "visible" to our "clients" and keep them ready to become mobile at your instructions. I'm going back to Moscow to get some answers.'

'This is the second interruption you've had to sort out so far!' Lanov pointed out.

'True, but I did sort it. This is too big an operation for the Council to interfere with; it's got to be a single maverick operative. My discussions with the Council lead me to believe I'm right, but no one is very talkative on the phone, so I'm going to show myself around personally.'

'Will that do the trick?' said Mogatin.

'The Council is still in support of this scheme, I've no real doubts, but I think now is the time to protect all of our interests.'

'How long?' asked Lanov.

'Three or four days, no longer.'

'And we just carry on "doing our thing"?' asked Mogatin.

'No reason why not,' replied Yute.

'Good, but when will we have some real work to do? This fiddling about is boring!'

'I promised you action and wealth… it will take time to position ourselves. Time is the most important thing for us… we do a lot of organising, a lot of consolidating and we will reap big rewards!'

'You're right. When are you leaving?' asked Mogatin.

'Today. It's important I find out who may be encroaching on my domain. If there's no one and it's just a bureaucratic hitch, it will be sorted very quickly.'

'Good.' Both Lanov and Mogatin answered in unison.

'We'll meet at location five in town on my return. I'll phone and set it up with you. Now, get a move on, and don't get caught!' No sooner were the words out of his mouth, than Yute had turned on his heels and was gone. Lanov and Mogatin held on a while longer watching for any movement around them before they left to follow the instructions and carry on with their injections of fear to their clients.

The reports fed back to their respective headquarters by Robin's, and Gilbert Torneau's men were informative; Lanov visiting the Tomlevskis, Mogatin returning to Metz to re-establish contact with his list of victims; Polenkovich left to catch the service from

Strasbourg to Paris, where arrangements would be made to enable his departure from French soil.

Rudi walked the unfamiliar streets near Dimitri's home, looking for a telephone box; they seemed few and far between. The tedium of constantly checking his back for a stalker was dragging it out. It had been fifteen minutes so far, fifteen minutes which had kept him away from hearing the dulcet tones of Katerina Mayer. His pace quickened at the thought of her, but nowhere could a telephone box be seen. A wide road with bright lights could be seen at the end of the street he was walking down. Thank God, a tram to the railway station, thought Rudi. He heard the whirr of metal on metal and the electricity conductor drawing its power from the overhead cables. Rudi ran hard, hoping the tram would be going back into the town centre. At the corner, Rudi was relieved to see the tram and automatically waved at the driver to stop. It slowed, Rudi ran, jumped, caught the handrail and pulled himself aboard.

The tram was an excellent solution to Rudi's dilemma and when he began to recognise some of the shops and streets he knew he would not be kept much longer from hearing Mayer's voice.

The railway station stood towering above him as he approached the wide marbled steps. The telephone box which he always tried to get, the one at the end of the bank of phones in the corner, the one where he could blow kisses down the phone to his beloved, the one in the corner where he could keep his hand in his trouser pocket as he spoke. The marbled steps floated two at a time under his speeding feet.

'Mayer, I love you!' were his first words.

'Me too!' came the warm, low response.

'You are not alone?'

'Not quite, but they are looking my way!'

'I see. I want to hold you…'

'That's impossible, now don't be silly… I'll blush!'

'I want to kiss you… squeeze you!'

Fidgeting on her hard chair, Mayer replied, 'Have you been drinking?'

'Yes, Dimitri and I!'

'Who's Dimitri?'

'He works for me. His views are the same as mine. He is a romantic like me. He says I must stay in love with you and help to save the world. He wants to help me. It's wonderful to have found a friend, someone to help with the double game I'm playing.'

'You are not forced to do anything, Rudi, you know that.'

'When we made the arrangement all those phone calls ago, I wasn't in love with you… but now I am and I have a friend who believes Russia has been corrupt for a very long time. It's a whole new way of thinking for me to understand. Before, I just went to work, did my job and went home. Glasnost came and I'm allowed to talk to a world that is alien to me, but my nature has always been to do my best. You ask me to help, I fall in love! My dreams have always been of freedom, even when I was a little boy without knowing what freedom really meant; I knew if there was truly a thing called freedom, I wanted it and now I want to shape it with you!'

'Oh, Rudi, we will share everything, I promise you that!'

'It's the condition that I play a double role?'

'No, no, it isn't now!' The sob in Mayer's throat stopped her speaking for a moment. 'Yes, it was all mechanical and we were using you in the beginning, but not now!'

'Please, my love, don't let it be. I want to marry you. I want just you forever!'

'Rudi, it will be so. When we discussed the East and West, we never said I will come East nor you to come West. We did agree my boss would try to help you across, but that is not what it's all about now. I love you and will until there are no stars left in the sky. Rudi, I love you forever!'

Rudi fell even further in love at that moment, stunned into silence by the emotion in Mayer's voice.

'I think we are looking for a "snake". A very, very long convoy of lorries from Vladivostok, wiggling its way across the whole of Russia.'

'Are you still drunk, Rudi? What are you trying to say?'

'I'm drunk with love… a burning, devouring love. Not drunk,

Mayer, happy. Dimitri has helped me to see that love is all and is the altar to make every sacrifice at!'

'Rudi, we must believe in wonderful things like that, but we must also live in the real world.'

'My world is real now, Mayer. It was not before, I know what I want and am willing to do anything to achieve it for us. Darling, I love you. The "snake" is a convoy and my orders are to find it by Friday, under dire threat. It seems to have more than one controller and keeps getting diverted, which Dimitri thinks is Androv's doing. All of my team endorse how slippery Androv is; he even escaped arrest from the KGB a while ago before he got the job as my boss. Dimitri feels Androv is up to some private enterprise.' There was a sudden 'burr' as Rudi's money ran out.

The 'I love you,' squeezed from Mayer's sobbing throat was only partially heard by Rudi, but his mind completed for him the message he wanted to hear. Mayer's fingers wiped the tears from her very flushed cheeks as she stood up from her chair. She walked slowly towards Ernst's office, pausing only to blow her nose prior to entering.

When he saw her puffy face and the mixture of sorrow and happiness in her eyes, Ernst raced to her as she stopped in his doorway.

'Mayer, Mayer, you poor, poor thing. What has happened?'

As Ernst's arm went around her shoulders, her sobbing began again. When she had calmed herself sufficiently, with Ernst patiently waiting until she could speak, she finally said, 'Rudi is safe. He's been ordered to find a "snake"… but he's found a true friend.' Her emotions could be held back no longer and the words came tumbling out. 'I hate what I'm doing to him! I'm so happy he now has a friend to talk to… I want to be with him… he should never be on his own!'

The tightening of Ernst's arm around her body forced the hate out and the sobbing racked her body. She turned her head into Ernst's shoulder and allowed all the sourness to explode from her body.

Ernst remained quiet, only allowing a little tightening of his arm when her heavy sighs brought her body closer to his. Slowly, she quietened down, her body began to relax and her mental turmoil eased.

'Inspector…' Her voice was muffled against his chest. 'May I talk to you like this, then when I've finished, run quickly away?'

'Of course, my dear!'

'Well, Rudi has a new friend. His name is Dimitri and he has also been working for Androv. He has been following a very large convoy – they call it the "snake" – from Vladivostok and they keep losing it. It changes its route. Dimitri thinks it is Androv's doing.'

'Can he explain his theory?'

'No, not really. But all of Rudi's team are willing to endorse how slippery Androv is. He escaped the KGB in his own offices, then returned in the new position above Rudi, then he disappeared. Dimitri thinks Androv is up to some private enterprise!' Mayer fell silent.

Ernst could not believe his ears. Could it be possible that Androv was the key… could they have stumbled on to something as big as this, starting with Hans and Dieter seeing the 'ringed-hand man' when on holiday in Portugal… the twists and turns with Robin, Joc and so many others. Was it drawing them to yet another transit of illegal goods through Europe?

'Mayer, are you feeling better now?'

Lifting her head from his shoulder and automatically rubbing the remaining tears away with the back of her hand, she croaked, 'Yes, thank you, sir.'

Ernst smiled. 'I think just a little make-up would make you feel even better, Mayer!'

'Sir, thank you. I must look a mess!'

'Oh no.'

Mayer knew very well her boss was gently teasing her. 'Well, I'll take your advice anyway!' She bowed her head down and was gone.

Ernst stood numb for a brief while, not quite believing that the transfer of arms for money could potentially happen again. Where are all of the elements? was the first question he asked himself as he sat down at his desk. Can it be this simple? Ernst asked himself, as he reached for the phone.

Androv's highly secret return to Moscow took the people he contacted by surprise. They had all felt without exception, that he had always walked the thin line between obeying his masters or going his own way. Since his rise to the echelons of power, his natural flair always caused his brain to work overtime to expand on what in recent months he called 'underdeveloped' schemes, some of which he had expanded without Council permission. Now following his 'silent' exit from the corridors of power, Gregori Alexei Androv was back amongst the controllers... he had not been exterminated as most had thought, he had come back with what seemed to be more power and a greater independence.

Gregori Alexei Androv was winning his power struggle in his home town. He was recruiting from the underworld, a large number of enforcers who must swear allegiance to him and him alone, before he would employ them. He never questioned that they were only doing it for the money and not out of respect for him, as they had done previously. This time the word was out that he had upset the apple-cart but no one was willing to explain how.

The twenty-four hours which he had allowed himself to recruit the hard men and heavy-duty lorry drivers had taken forty-eight hours, but he was happy that the men he had picked would be loyal. When he called on them to act, they would all react as one and obey without question. To make sure of their loyalty, he had paid them half their fee up front.

'Robin, Ernst here...'

'Nice to hear from you, Ernst! How are things with you?'

'I don't know, Robin, things have happened, things which cannot logically be true, but yet my instincts tell me it is so simple and many more pieces of the puzzle will in fact, fit.'

'Tell me, Ernst!'

'We are being raped by a snake!'

'Ernst, it's unlike you to fool around; now come on, tell me how your puzzle fits together.'

'Okay. Rudi has been ordered to find a large convoy of lorries they call the "snake". We only know that it left Vladivostok some weeks ago and that it has been mislaid at the moment. My theory is that it's carrying surplus Navy and Air Force weaponry. The route into Moscow from there is littered with military installations and is within range of the "poppy fields"!'

'Hold up, Ernst. Are you saying it has the same MO as your Hamburg caper?'

'I don't see the logic and I can't explain my hunch, nor can I guess where it's going to, but I know, my friend, that I am frightened of my thoughts and am dreading the consequences if we do nothing!'

'Where does Rudi think this "snake's" journey will take it before it comes within our jurisdiction?'

'It seems this "snake" has two controllers who are working against each other. Dimitri, Rudi's new friend in the team, reckons that Androv could be one controller.'

'And Androv is in Moscow now?'

'He is indeed; we have few police in Moscow that we can manipulate, but we will try our best. Rudi is getting back to us when they have found the "snake" but my guess is, it will be coming to Moscow for some reason.'

'Mine too, Ernst. Is there any kind of manifest for this convoy and can we get any idea of its size?'

'Requests have gone out to Rudi but we'll have to wait a while before we get any more information, I suspect.'

'Ernst, I'd be interested as soon as you know. By the by, would Joc be able to re-route a spy plane to find it?'

'Good idea. Joc would like to become more involved, but his Ambassador isn't giving him much rope. He might have to go above the Ambassador's head, but knowing Joc, if that's what it takes, that's what it will take!'

'If they are coming to Moscow, why are we so active in the south of Europe? Geographically, the line runs across the top end of Europe.'

'We will have to look into that, Robin. If it's lorries and ships, logic demands North. We'll keep an eye on things up here.'

'I know you will. It's great news if we've got the guessing right on the "snake" and her contents… I'll wait anxiously for your call when you've found it, Ernst.'

'You'll be the first to know, Robin. Bye for now!'

Immediately after he came off the phone, Robin notified his

good friend, Inspector Torneau, and all of his own men, emphasising that all of the Russians and known contacts must not be 'lost' and that any new ones were to be fully investigated, plus the principal players, Androv, Polenkovich and Colonel Keller, must be given special attention.

Yute Polenkovich sat upright in the rickety old military truck, staring out of the windscreen onto the broken asphalt road stretching endlessly before him. The driver had been instructed to drive from here to there over the past few days. He liked sitting behind the wheel high off the ground, pretending he was the master of all he surveyed, but now he was no longer a driver; since this passenger got into his cab, he had become a chauffeur. No one had told him he would have to take a passenger with him and go about a hundred miles further than he needed to. No one had told him he wouldn't be allowed to whistle or sing as he normally did when driving. He knew he was just a farm boy, but when these driving jobs came his way, he enjoyed being a 'king of the road'. The irritation of having this 'invader' in his cab had got to him. He had to be told who was boss.

'I don't know your name, comrade, and I don't care, but this cab is my cab and I like to sing, whistle or even talk to myself when I'm driving and now I'm going to sing!' Yute's eyes stared in front of him neither answering the driver, nor giving him any acknowledgement.

The driver's off-key notes floated around the tinny cab. When he whistled, the shrillness not only hurt the ears, but the eyes and the frontal lobe. Yute did not change his posture, just sat staring into the distance. The driver nudged Yute's shoulder. Yute did not respond in an 'attack mode' but just listened to this stupid irritating fool telling him that very shortly they would have to stop to put petrol in the tank and that this would be the last time he would have to fill the tank from the 'bloody' cans he was carrying in the back. 'It's bloody hard work, man, I can tell you!'

The off-key singing started again. The first push on the foot-brake had no effect on the truck's momentum. Release and push again, release and push again then the lorry slowly came to a halt under the branches of trees spreading out from a small copse which had come into view on the flat horizon a full ten minutes earlier. 'Right! Out you get and have a pee. If you're shy, go in the bushes, I won't look!' The loud belly laugh which followed the inane remarks received no response from Yute who just stepped down from the cab and walked into the copse.

'You could give me a hand to fill her up, if you like!' the driver shouted over his shoulder in the general direction of the copse. Quietness fell as the driver concentrated on his task. Yute was happy to have this silence, but then the voice bellowed again, 'It's all right, comrade, you can come out now, this is the last drop going in – all the work's done, you won t have to do any—'

Yute's blade cut straight through the windpipe. The silence was so enjoyable, and the rest of his journey to Kanak would be enjoyed even more.

The Kanak Flying Club signs had started giving their instructions twenty kilometres from its entrance, the only signs along the straight, flat, boring road. Yute, riding out what he thought to be the twenty kilometre distance, was surprised that the flying field hadn't yet come into sight. It will soon, he thought. Let's face it, I can't miss it, there is nothing else out here, according to the map. Yute allowed himself a wry smile, then there was the wind sock with just a little flutter, the perimeter fence, then entrance, the reception, the introduction to his pilot. The jet would soon get him to Orekhova's small flying field.

Rudi and Dimitri had decided they would meet every day in different places sprinkled throughout Moscow. At each meeting they would nominate the meeting place for the next day, always out in the open with other people and traffic around. They would try to make it appear that they kept meeting by accident, although they were both aware of the naïvety of their efforts, but neither of them wanted to risk talking in offices they felt sure could be bugged. Dimitri's smiling, whistling face was walking towards Rudi. Today, they had chosen a small square of grass and trees which were a joy on sweltering summer days. The square had a narrow street entering at each corner which allowed what breeze there was to cool what air there might be. The trees with their heavy boughs loaded with their millions of leaves in summer made it a paradise, but today was chilly, cold enough for a coat, hat and scarf, Rudi felt, but here was his friend Dimitri, striding towards him in just a jacket and trousers, making only one concession to the chill – his hands were stuffed into his trouser pockets.

'Rudi, you old son-of-a-gun, what are you doing here of all places!' Dimitri had said they should meet and show surprise each time they met, but Rudi felt Dimitri was being a little overzealous, especially when he stood back, arms open wide and almost shouted at the top of his voice, 'You look good, you haven't changed a bit!' having only seen him the previous evening.

'You're overplaying it, Dimitri!' Rudi responded as they shook hands.

Dimitri grinned from ear to ear and just whispered, 'Shall we walk or just stand here like lemons?'

Rudi responded, taking on the mood, 'Only if you hold my hand!'

Dimitri's response was, 'Now my friend does jest!' Both of them laughed and started to walk back under the trees.

'Rudi, I've found the "snake". Well, I think so, anyway!'

'What do you mean you think so?'

'Well, it was at Ulan Ude for sure, I think Irkut after that, but then it seems to have disappeared.'

'Don't be a fool, please, Dimitri. How can something that big just disappear?'

'Well, it has!'

'The requisitions for food and fuel will tell you where it's going, surely?'

'That's just it! There have been no requisitions!'

'You can't mean that, Dimitri?'

'I'm afraid so. Everything has been double-checked and it's just gone!'

'Dimitri, there must be an explanation – it's impossible!'

'I agree with you, but no requisitions, no cash movement to any towns past Irkut – that's why I'm saying possibly Irkut!'

'You are checking if the money…?'

'I haven't had a reply yet as to whether any was transferred from the Treasury people.'

'Push them as hard as you dare… don't raise any suspicions… something that big has got to turn up!'

'I'll go back to the office now and check. Are you going to phone your friends?'

'Not yet.' As an afterthought he then added, 'When I leave this evening.'

'Okay. See you later if I've got any news!'

'Fine, Dimitri. Hope you will have some news by then.'

Later that afternoon, Rudi looked at his watch. 1635 hours. His thoughts were of Mayer. He knew he was going to phone her even if Dimitri had no further information. The waiting for five o'clock, plus the time taken in getting to the phone booth was going to seem endless. Dimitri suddenly appeared at the office door. No whistling, just a scuffling of feet.

'Rudi, our "snake" has turned into three trains!'

'Three trains?' The disbelief in Rudi's voice was unmistakable but then his initial surprise cleared. 'It's logical. Whoever is controlling the train has to keep it on schedule… what better way than booking your own train or trains through a very underused goods train service. It's brilliant! It will give him time to pick up the schedule he has lost, give him greater control and pockets of time into the bargain which would also enhance his schedules!'

'Rudi, who is in charge of the train?'

'What do you mean? Well, we felt there were two or more people wrestling for control of the lorries. We knew there was someone in our offices after Androv left who was pulling strings, and some departments whom we knew were also involved, enabling us to cross-check on certain other things—'

Dimitri cut sharply into Rudi's train of thought. 'There's a man… the Yard Manager who's done a runner with a whole lot of money stashed in a suitcase. Buggered off without paying the crew he'd had working day and night unloading lorries and loading trains. A lot of people in Irkut are not happy. The local police were paid off. It appears he bunked off in one of the last lorries which have all disappeared into the sunset!'

After a short pause, Dimitri added, 'Rudi, at least we know the goods are on trains going west.'

'Going west with what? Can't we get a manifest at least?'

'We're pushing all the buttons, Rudi, there's nothing more we can do for the moment. We're working on the Army, Navy and Air Force over there but these types are always so protective about their doings as we know only too well.'

'We need to know before this train goes much further. By the way, did it get onto schedule and did it pick up any more loads?'

'The yard man did say he had never seen so much military stuff since World War Two and the Yard Manager had to find an additional five flat-bed rolling stock.'

'We know it's military and it's connecting up with bases as it passes through Russia. My God! It's got dozens of military establishments before it gets to Moscow!'

'Our "snake" is going to have one very full belly!' Dimitri's attempt at trying to break through his friend's serious mood fell on deaf ears.

Daniel and Nicole Tomlevski had slept in each other's arms the whole night. Their caress had not broken. Their contentment these past weeks had been complete in every way. The strange silence in their bedroom disturbed them and fear momentarily jumped into their eyes. As suddenly as the fear had shown, it left them, turning to defiance as Daniel sat up in bed and reached for the light.

'Don't put the light on, you know who I am!'

'Mogatin!' remarked Daniel. 'Taken to hiding in decent people's bedrooms now? One day you will have to come out of the shadows!'

Like a tiger, Mogatin leapt across the room and swiftly had his hands around Daniel's neck. 'Don't try to ridicule me! My orders are to tell you that in one week you will become operational. Next time you hear my voice you will do whatever you are instructed to do. Your instructions will last for three days and along with the northern and southern commands of your European toy army, which will act for us for the same reasons as your dear wife and yourself... the sins of the father—'

Daniel cut off Mogatin's words. 'You mean blackmail through fear!' he croaked, as the hands tightened around his throat.

Mogatin steadied himself. 'No, I won't strangle you now, but it is something to think about... or even something better still, if you let us down!'

Daniel didn't need to hear the threats hanging over him any more and shouted, 'Do it now! You need me to perform for you... what would your masters do to you if you harmed my wife or me?' The crack on his jaw as Mogatin's fist struck him was unseen by Daniel in the darkened room. It was so sudden that the darkness of unconsciousness enveloped him without a fight.

Mogatin snarled at Daniel's still body. Turning to Nicole, he whispered menacingly, 'Tell him that your fate could be worse if he fails us. Both my friend and I, as we have told you before, like playing with women!'

Nicole pulled Daniel's limp body closer to her and before she could shout or scream, Mogatin was gone.

'Rudi, I've been longing to hear your voice!'

'Me too! It's been an age since yesterday. I miss you every second!'

'Me too, Rudi. The feelings I have for you won't let me do my job properly. All the time you are here in my mind.'

'The longing consumes me, Katerina, even when I sleep, you take over my dreams.'

'I hope they are nice dreams, Rudi.'

'Mostly they are wonderful, but sometimes you seem to be a long way in front of me. I chase you and chase you, but I can't always catch you.'

'That's because I ask you to find out so much for Ernst. It's your inner fear of losing me, Rudi. I know you will never lose me, you will always be mine. I love you always.'

The silence between them lasted only seconds but mentally they had given their all to each other.

'Rudi, my love...' Mayer was the first to speak. 'There will never be anyone else for me ever!'

'Please, Mayer, wait for me, I will come to you soon and stay forever and you will never run away in my dreams unless I always catch you!'

'That will be wonderful, Rudi. When I'm in your dreams next

time, I won't run so fast, I promise. You'll catch me every time!'

'Please may it be so!'

'All your dreams will come true, Rudi, I'll make sure of that.'

'May it be soon, Katerina!' Rudi expected a response from Mayer but all he heard was a stifled sob. 'The "snake" is coming West!' Rudi whispered into the phone.

The sobs stopped mid-breath as she replied, 'Please, Rudi, don't take my dreams away!'

'I am sorry, my love, but it is difficult to phone. Each time I feel sure I'm being watched, even though I take every possible precaution. I don't know... but I do feel sometimes that I am... please don't cry, tell Ernst that the "snake" of lorries has transferred itself onto three trains at Irkut. The lorries went empty in all directions, but the train is heading west. More goods joined the train before they left. We can't find a record of the manifest but Dimitri and I feel fairly sure it could be arms or drugs as there are dozens of military establishments and free access to vast quantities of drugs in the areas the convoy has passed through. I must leave now. I love you, I love you, I give you my heart and kisses. Bye, I love you...' Rudi just managed to gently place the phone back in its cradle before the tears welled up in his eyes.

Mayer's saddened body trudged its way to Ernst's office. Her usual sprightly walk and happy disposition were nowhere to be seen. The hardness showing in her face echoed her determination to get her Rudi out of Russia. As she stood in the doorway of Ernst's office she could not contain herself. Her words were sharp, like a woman protecting her child. 'He must be gotten out... he's doing things he knows nothing about... he can't protect himself. He's walking around in constant fear!' Ernst looked up for a second irritatedly at being spoken to in that manner, but the distress on Mayer's face quickly changed that and he reverted to his 'father-figure' role.

'We'll get him out safely, but not just yet.' His voice was level and quiet.

'He is risking everything and we all know it!'

'Yes, Mayer, but you are acting a little like a love-sick child. You are a grown woman working in a world full of corruption and violence and I know both you and Rudi would not want to bring your children into a world like this without putting up a fight to make your own space!'

'He has been pushed around enough! First by his own and now by us… we are turning him into a liar, a traitor to his own people. He's leading a double life… he can't protect himself… he's going to die!'

'Mayer! Listen to me! He won't die if you don't keep distracting him. When you speak to him, comfort him but don't constantly whine your lovelorn platitudes at him. You are only drawing out his self-pity for not being with you already. He needs your strength, Mayer, not your constant pronouncement of love for him. He does, and you do too, but the time is not right until we finish this job.'

Mayer's eyes were aflame. 'You bastard! How can you say such a thing. You who thinks of Hamburg before you think of your wife!'

'If you think that is true, then you must—' Ernst managed to stop in mid-sentence to save any more hurting.

'Of course it's true – all of you men put your job first… fight the good fight, the crusade against oppression, the protection of the almighty Deutschmark. Our gun is bigger than your gun so don't get out of line like little children, you play the game for reward and supremacy! Rudi has never had that opportunity. All he knows is that he has been lied to and cheated, along with his fellow Russians, for years and years. That until Glasnost they were all oppressed and used. Now it is the "good times" and he is being used again by me! I'm as big a bastard as you!' The words Mayer was expecting from Ernst didn't come. Instead, the pleasant face before her just stared at her over the rim of his glasses. He stared and waited for her torment to float away and for Mayer to become herself again and then she would get to her own answer.

The soft voice croaked as Mayer began to speak but it did not change anything. 'Rudi wants to do it… all of the rotten bloody mess… the being watched… the fear… the hate for the system when he sees his fellow men being used… the greed… the dishonesty… the corruption… oppression… lies and deceit. Rudi's heart wants to do it. Rudi is a normal human being, like most people in the world he has a good heart – he believes in freedom. He wants to do it, he's made up his mind, we're not forcing another life on him, he's asking for another one. I'm so stupid… he's already chosen his new path! Is he using me and not the other way around?'

'Nonsense. Grow up, he adores you. If you believe what you have just said, you will give up contacting him right now!'

'I'm sorry, sir, I'm so frightened for him. He was almost in tears a few minutes ago as he put down the phone.'

'What did he have to say?' Ernst's voice was purposely soft and rhythmic to ease Mayer's anguish.

'The "snake" now has three heads. It seems that at Irkut all of the lorries were emptied and put onto three trains, all heading west. It looks highly likely they are carrying weaponry and hundreds of wooden packing cases. One man seemed to be in charge and was in fact the paymaster, but we have no identity for him yet. The Yard Manager and the police were paid off and it seems have disappeared out of the district.'

'Your Rudi and his friend have done a good job so far, Mayer. Do you think they will continue now?' Ernst's soft voice drew the exact response he wanted from Mayer.

'I think they will, sir, but for different reasons. Rudi because of me, and Dimitri because he's an idealist.'

'Both reasons are out of love and fervour!'

Mayer waited for a moment, thinking out her reply before answering. 'Doing the dangerous things they are doing for freedom and of their own free will, will need all of the love they can give and all of the love and support we can give.'

'We will do everything in our power, Mayer. Will you please keep me informed of all information you may receive?'

'Yes, sir!' Knowing she was being dismissed, Mayer came to attention and left the office a lot happier than when she had first entered it. Nothing had been resolved, how could it be, when you are so desperately in love?

No sooner had Mayer left than Ernst reached for the phone and dialled Robin's number. The dialling tone turned into 'pip-pip-pip' as each digit of the number was tapped in, the ringing tone cut in harshly… one… two… three times.

'Hello, Cadwallader here…'

'Ernst heir, Robin!' The familiar pattern of courtesy followed, then Ernst followed up in every detail with the information from Russia as relayed by Mayer.

Robin's first question was, 'We will be in difficulty if we have to try and arrest three trains all at the same time, Ernst, don't you think?'

Realising the visual humour of trying to physically arrest three trains, Robin could not hold back a little chuckle but Ernst, not understanding this British sense of humour went straight to his answer. 'We will need hundreds of men to make the raids on each one of the trains and goodness knows how many more for all of the field operatives we know of at the moment, but I feel there are many more to be accounted for.'

'You're right, Ernst, it'll be a job for an army!'

'Ha, ha, Robin.' Pausing for a few seconds, Ernst then added, 'And I suppose you know where you can get one?'

Both men laughed at the weak joke before continuing their conversation. 'We need Joc to pull a few tricks with the satellite boys. I would say we need daily observation at this point in time at least.'

'I agree with you, Robin. Shall I speak to Joc or will you?'

'It doesn't really matter, Ernst, but it's your case, your hunch and Joc is your friend so, please, you do it.'

'Okay, if it's at all possible, I know he will achieve it, but to keep ourselves informed in the meantime, I think we must watch every rail line coming west into Moscow. What troops can you spare?'

'I'll have to clear it with the Adjutant, but I could possibly spare around fifty – undercover, of course. The Adjutant will give me permission I'm sure, but we will not be acknowledged by the army if we are caught.'

'I couldn't match that number, possibly twenty, twenty-five.'

'Well, that should get us started; maybe when we know where we're going we can get the French to join in. Tonight at 1600 hours I'll be with the Adjutant and I could be actively "train-spotting" in Russia by tomorrow morning. Will you let me have the latest sighting of any of the "snakes" that may come in?'

'Ernst, I don't want to involve any friendly Russians at this point, it will hamper us – besides, the more Russians we're exposed to the more it could weaken our operation.'

'Agreed, Robin. You can be active from tomorrow morning!'

'Yes, Ernst. It's great playing soldiers, you just get permission from someone senior to yourself first, then you can throw your weight around!'

'You have to have the right men, whom you chose in the very beginning, I think.'

'The system does most of the work, Ernst, it's only the loyalty of the people you choose that keeps the whole thing going.'

'It must be more than that, I'm sure.'

'Maybe, but we don't harp on about the fact, I'll see the Adjutant and be in touch with good or bad news by 1900 hours!'

'I'll wait in the office, Robin; bye for now.'

'Bye, Ernst, till then…'

The soft knock on Major Cadwallader's door broke his concentration from the complicated cross-plotting of the agents he would be using on 'train-spotting' duty in Russia. Thirty-two agents had been allocated since his conversation with Ernst, all with a cover story of just being tourists. Stretching his back and shoulders as he lifted his chest from leaning over the desk, he called, 'Come in!'

Daniel Tomlevski entered and Robin instinctively felt his day was going to become even busier than it had been already. Raising himself out of his chair, he offered Daniel his hand after returning Daniel's salute. 'Is there anything I can help you with, Daniel?'

Rather solemnly, Daniel replied, 'We had a visit during the night – in our bedroom. Our Mr Mogatin with heavy threats and warnings about a "stand by" time being a week away and intimating that more people will be brought into play who I will have to control.'

'My God, what a fright that must have been for you! How is Nicole?'

'Scared stiff, like me. I was knocked out for being insolent and she was alone with him – this time it was only a message he gave her. "Tell him your fate could be worse if he fails us. Both me and my friend as we told you before, like playing with women!"'

'They really are bastards, Daniel, real bloody bastards!'

'Both Nicole and I know and are glad you are giving us the opportunity to prove ourselves to the Corps and to help make the world a better place to live in!'

'What else did he come for?'

'Oh sorry, the important bit, Robin, to quote, "In one week you will become operational. Next time you hear my voice you will do whatever you are instructed to do by me, on time. Your instructions will last for three days and along with the northern and southern commands of your European 'toy army' which will act for us for the same reasons as your dear wife and yourself... the sins of the father."'

Robin whistled. 'In one week! Whatever is going to happen isn't going to be long in starting or finishing. Let me know day or night when you are contacted. Would you like us to put a watch on your house?'

'No, sir. It's better this way; we have come this far without it, so I think it's better as we are. If he sees any activity around the house, he won't go through with it and it will probably mean certain death for us anyway.'

'As you wish. I'm sure you're right!'

'Me too, more's the pity. I just hope I don't let anyone down, even the Russians in this instance – without them there would be no game to play, would there, sir?' The tremor in Daniel's voice showed signs of his fear that he would not be able to complete the tasks he would be asked to perform.

'You'll be all right, Daniel. Worry all you want, but I know you'll be fine and remember, everything will be okay!'

'I hope so, sir! Nicole deserves a life... it would be nice if we could share it together!'

'Stop talking like that. Now I'm going to be rude and throw you out... goodbye for now, Lieutenant. Love to your wife!'

Whilst Robin had been saying goodbye, he had got up from his chair, walked around his desk and ushered Daniel to his office door. Daniel reached for the door handle, opened the door and said, 'Goodbye Major, sir,' and found himself alone in the chilly corridor. Robin hastened back to the phone to pass on this decisive new information to Ernst, Joc, Gilbert Torneau and his

Adjutant – in that order. He suggested they should all meet with their teams, excluding the Russians, Rudi and Dimitri, whose absence from their respective duties would prevent Mayer from receiving any information and for fear of exposing the only two known people with any knowledge of the train and its possible whereabouts. Both Ernst and Robin discussed their hunch that Paris would come into play during this game of cat and mouse which was just about to begin. Robin asked his friend Gilbert to alert his people of the train's possible convergence on that city.

Chapter Thirty-Three

Joc's carefully played strategy of being just a plain old-fashioned tourist paid off on the second night of his stay in Lamego. His daytime and early evening meanderings had been around the hub of the town, but at night he frequented the bars and restaurants along the shores of the River Douro, the short taxi ride always helping his rich American tourist image when he had the taxi stop outside the most classy-looking places in the hope he would get noticed. He always made a point of having a drink in a classy bar before he began his wanderings. The well-dressed, handsome, dark-skinned man sat alone at the bar, his head bowed over his drink, fingers playing with a beer mat. Joc reckoned he had either been stood up or was a tout waiting for suckers who could be parted from their money at a casino he just happened to know. Joc felt sure that although the man was expensively dressed, he would certainly know about the seedy side of the area.

'What will you have, Señor?' the smiling podgy-faced barman asked.

'Scotch and water on the side, please.' The certainty in Joc's voice left the barman in no doubt Joc was a regular drinker and knew his own mind.

'Coming up, Señor!'

'The best drink in the world!' The well-dressed, handsome man said into his half-empty glass which he had been staring into for an age.

Joc took the bait willingly. 'Always drink the same poison myself. Would you have a drink?'

'That's kind. Just a beer for me please, I'm waiting for some-one...'

Joc thought, yes, someone like me! You're a tout for sure, but he replied, 'That's okay. When she arrives I'll push on. Don't worry, I wouldn't cramp anyone's style.'

'It's not a she, it's a he. A business partner. We've just finished negotiating a good deal. A fair price for about three weeks' work.'

'Sounds good. Congratulations.'

'Thanks. If it goes as well as we expect, we will live well for the next few years.'

'Well, if you tread carefully and wisely it could give you a good foundation for your next venture.' Joc raised his glass to have a sip and changed the subject swiftly. 'I say good luck to you again, but tonight business doesn't interest me. I've got a bloody mouldy long weekend off from my boss. I've done the architecture bit and tonight I'm going to live a little!'

'Wish I could go with you, but my partner, you know.'

'No worries. How long are you going to hang on for him?'

'I've been here over half an hour already. I'll give him another half hour, then sod him!'

Joc sat silently for a few minutes. His thoughts raced… Yes, he had made contact with the seedier side, he was sure. Was he only a pimp? No, he was more intelligent than that… his English was colloquial. He's German or Dutch!

'Your English is very good. You're not Portuguese, are you?'

'Yes. Well, English mother, Portuguese father. There are lots of us around with dual nationality. We are famous here for our port but we are also as famous for our English educations. We joke amongst ourselves that when we are in a group we are the only ones who know exactly who we are!'

'Yes, I've just remembered, of course, your trade with the Brits has been going on for hundreds of years. Stupid of me… I thought you were a well-educated German or Dutchman!'

'Our parents' generation would take offence at that, but not us modern free-thinking generation… we talk to everyone in the whole world; we are not an insular breed anymore!'

'Hey man! You're getting too philosophical for me and we haven't even introduced ourselves!' The phoney southern drawl sounded as phoney as he had intended and it fooled no one but raised the smile on the Portuguese's face. Joc continued, 'My name's Joc Latimer, Washington DC. I'm in electronics.'

'Pedro Matros. Home town Oporto, but I live in Lamego. I'm in import and exports.' Joc's handshake was firm and Pedro tried to prove his grip.

Both men almost simultaneously said, 'Nice to meet you.'

It was not long before the conversation between them became quite mundane. Marriage... children... schooling... the price of booze... the whole gambit of past recollections. Joc was beginning to feel the strain of the boring conversation and wondered when Pedro was going to get around to saying, 'My partner seems to have found something more important to do than coming to see me! Let me get you one for the road before I go. What will you have, the same?'

When Joc had first arrived in the bar he had instinctively felt Pedro Matros had another side to his character and now, after talking to him for fifteen or twenty minutes, Joc was convinced.

'Well, I was thinking of moving on, it's my normal pattern of events!'

Quickly, Pedro responded, 'Well, if you're on your own and you feel my company is acceptable, why don't we mooch around together?'

Joc mentally said to himself, 'Gotcha!' but he replied, 'Could be good, Pedro, you must know where the good food and the "action" is.'

'Food yes, good local cooking, but after that it's only bars!'

'What about the river men, they must hang out somewhere?'

'True, but it can get a bit rough. If you'd risk it, I think you'd find it interesting. Some great old characters mixed in with young characters, mixed in with many other nations. In fact, we have even got a couple of resident Russians!'

'What do bloody Russians want here?'

Pedro immediately changed the subject on the pretext of acknowledging one of the barmen at the other end of the bar. 'Sorry about that, Joc, had to give him a wave. Shall we move on then?'

'Why not. You lead, I'll follow,' Joc said, jovially.

They walked silently side by side, Pedro thinking, I've got a right mug here! and Joc thinking, Why is this guy so obvious? Turning west at the river's edge, the hot red glow of the setting sun reflected upwards from the wide river to the tops of the surrounding hills, the sun showing off its strength by turning the view into a burning fire. Joc stopped in his tracks.

'My God, that's beautiful, looking at that view is an honour!'

Pedro looked through the eyes of a man who'd seen it hundreds of times and it had lost its wonder. It was just something that happened. 'Yes, it's nice. We need to turn up here.'

Joc could find nothing to say and fell into step alongside Pedro.

The sun's warm light shone and shimmered over the faded green paintwork of the unnamed bar that appeared to be jutting out of the hillside without any visible means of support. The deep shadow of the setting sun painted its magic of black.

'Here we are, Joc. Hope there is enough local colour here for you.'

'The view alone was worth the walk. I could go back now and be more than satisfied!'

'Don't do that, Joc, I've still got to buy you that drink!' Pedro had become more congenial the closer he got to the bar. It was obvious Pedro was a regular, there were lots of acknowledgements from people both sitting and standing, but Pedro was guiding them both towards the bar stools at the far end of the bar. The people seemed to melt away from that area, the closer they got to it. The weather-beaten faces of the older men stared into their drinks as Pedro passed by, only the younger men and women were affable towards Pedro and his new friend. It was obvious the corner seats at the very end of the bar were where everything happened, and in addition, any comings or goings could be watched. Joc felt like aiming himself at the commanding position, but thought it would be better not to try. He fully realised he would be disadvantaged with his back to the door, but for the moment, he felt sure Pedro would protect him from any villainy, should any occur. Joc decided to play it as the American tourist, working for a bastard of a boss, living on the minimum overseas allowance, liking to travel around and see the country.

'Will you have whisky, Joc?' Pedro's voice bought Joc swiftly back to his present predicament.

'Yes please, a little water, no ice. The characters in here could be interesting to talk to, and I'd love to photograph some of their faces!'

'Stop being a tourist, Joc. I doubt if there's a man here who hasn't or doesn't live looking over their shoulders for the law to come. It's a shame really; most of these blokes ran their own boats at one time. They took the barrels of port down to the coast. It was a hard life, but now the bosses at the vineyards take orders from the distributors to get it to the coast quicker, so a lot goes by road. Half of these poor old men were left without a pot to piss in practically overnight!'

'Surely the government did something for them?'

'You'll find that governments don't stretch as far as the hills and they have to fend for themselves.'

'That makes it tough. How do they live?'

'Well, my partner and I do what we can!'

'How do you use them?'

Joc felt the question come out a bit sharp but it didn't seem to disturb Pedro, who continued, 'Sometimes we have cargo to go down or we use them as couriers. They know their way around the waterfront in Oporto probably better than the Harbour Masters themselves!'

'Good for you, old buddy! This looks a good place to spend my hard-earned money, so let's have another drink!'

'I'm all for that, Joc, let's get on with it!'

Pedro seemed to relax and become more talkative. He had made up his mind that this stupid-arsed American really was a tourist. The food at the bar was good and the wine was a delight, but now was the time to leave.

'Pedro, it's time for me to hit the road. Could your friend the barman call me a cab, please? By the way, let me have your number… I promise next time I'm up this way I'll call. We got on well, didn't we, for a first meeting?' Joc had run everything in together. He wanted to say thank you, goodbye, it's been great and I'll keep in touch. Tonight was over and this poor tipsy Yank had spent his daily allowance! Sitting in the taxi on his way back to Lamego, he ran the night's events through his mind and was even more convinced Pedro Matros was someone to have watched.

The hour was late when Joc arrived back at the hotel. He was excited. It had been years since the feeling of the 'hunt' had coursed through his body. He still felt his assessment of Pedro was correct… he was a double-dealer and he spread fear not goodwill. Gut feeling told Joc his import/export business was just a front and he felt sure his partner was probably watching him all the time he was with him at the bar. Walking around his small room he was convinced that had he not been a 'poor American tourist' and gone along with him, he would probably be lying in some gutter with a broken head right now. It wouldn't have been worth their while; he had mentioned that he never had enough money, in his own opinion, to use credit cards and could only afford nights out drinking once in a while. The truth did not matter to anyone he had wanted to meet but everything that could be used in any way to make him recognisable to the world was in the hotel safe. Had anyone come snooping after him or just his name, the Bureau's computers would know. He wanted to speak to Ernst. It was even later now – why hadn't he phoned immediately after he had got back? Ernst wouldn't mind... you SOB... you know it could wait. It's only a gut feeling, leave it until tomorrow! Joc fell back on the bed, rubbing his eyes. Must phone Ernst! Instinctively his hand went to the phone and his fingers were dancing across the buttons, dialling out.

'Ulbrecht heir!' It was answered immediately, the voice a little more guttural.

'It's Joc, Ernst. I'm sorry to call you, it was sort of automatic!'

'Don't worry, Joc, I was half-awake anyway.'

'Good. I'm up in Lamego...' Joc told the story in every detail and finished up with '...it's a long shot, I know. There is an undercurrent of fear in the bar. Pedro was only accepted because on occasions he shells out money. What if Pedro and his pal are Russians?'

'You feel that, Joc?'

'Yes. I'll be brief and let you get back to sleep. I don't want to get involved here in Portugal. I feel the action is going to be north of here... but Joe, who has a working arrangement with Vargas, could approach him to put some men to keep an eye on Pedro and his partner, do a little fishing around. If it turns out to be nothing, it's Vargas's wasted man-hours and not yours!'

'Any more, Joc?'

'Only that the original lead came from this town, and Mogatin and Lanov, and in all probability, Polenkovich!'

'I hadn't forgotten that, Joc. Let Joe approach Vargas and I'll square it away with my boss. Robin and the French ought to be informed. I'll talk to Robin and he can liaise with the French.'

'Thanks, Ernst. You won't be telling Rudi or any of the Russians, I suppose?'

'Too risky for the moment.'

'I agree, Ernst. I'm travelling back to Lisbon tomorrow. I'll be back there around lunchtime. Sorry to have called you so late!'

'Forget it, I'll probably do it to you one day! Bye now; get some sleep, Joc, well done!'

Before Joc could answer, the phone went dead.

'Come on, Joe, answer the bloody phone!' Joc sat on the edge of the unrumpled bed, still in the same clothes. He had allowed himself to undo the top button of his shirt and loosen his tie. The sun shone into the room and onto his unshaven face. 'Come on please, Joe, I want to leave and get on my way back... I've got a feeling I'll need the airport fairly soon!' His mutterings into the mouthpiece were for himself really, it was only ten past eight. Joc was about to put down the phone and shouted, 'You lazy SOB!' as the phone was lifted.

'Thank you, Joc, you've started my day well for me!'

'Sorry, old buddy. I'm going to be out of contact for a while. I'll be in Lisbon by lunch and want you to cover for me with the old man if I'm a bit late back.'

'No problem, Joc. It will cost you a drink later... anything else?'

'A favour from your chum Vargas...' Joc told Joe the whole story from last night and finished off by saying, 'I think Ernst feels I'm a bit wild with my "hunches" but he did say, "Well done," at the end!'

'A bit bloody wild in my book, but you were wild in Columbia and even I didn't believe you, let alone that you'd pull it off!'

'You'll speak to Vargas then?'

'Consider it done. See you later then.'

'Yes, and thanks a million.'

Ernst had not managed to get back to sleep after Joc's phone call.

The remainder of the night seemed to fight the dawn's entrance. Now Ernst could get out of bed, shower and get to the office. There was so much Ernst wanted to know. Where was the train now... why hadn't Rudi phoned back yesterday... what if Joc could not get aerial surveillance... when it is time to strike, where are all of the personnel coming from? Sure it was okay the last time, it was in the port – close the exits and they're trapped... what if it spreads itself all over Russia and Europe? The turmoil of the questions as he journeyed to his office had helped bring him back to life after his lack of sleep.

'Koslowski, good morning! Can we talk in a bit? Plus Mayer and any of the team who are in the office? Shall we say, ten minutes, in my office?'

'Sure, Ernst!' was all of the reply necessary. After all the years he had worked with Ernst, he knew it was not the right time for questioning.

Ernst sat at his desk, scanning the pile of paperwork which he swore grew overnight. Seeing Mayer approaching, he didn't have his normal under-the-breath curse of, 'How the bloody hell is anyone expected to do any real work?'

'Good morning, Mayer.' His voice sounded happy and fatherly.

'Good morning, sir. May I speak to you now?'

'Would it not be better to wait for the others?'

'What others, sir?'

Realising she must not have yet been told about the group meeting, Ernst replied, 'It doesn't matter, you're here now. I had asked Koslowski to set up a meeting with as many of the team as he could find.'

'I didn't know, sir, but you may not want this news to become general knowledge immediately.'

'That sounds intriguing, Mayer. Fire away!'

'Rudi phoned again. They have acquired some manifests for the train's cargo. He is willing to swear the manifests are nowhere full enough to cover the total of what the train is now carrying, nor detailed enough to give an assured assessment. He feels someone should maybe get on to the trains and verify the contents or wait and see if later on in its journey the paperwork begins to talk to us.'

'How is Rudi now, Mayer?'

Her spontaneous answer, 'Oh, he's fine, sir!' told Ernst she and Rudi had reconciled themselves to the situation since he had spoken to her when her heart was breaking.

'Has he worked out where the train is heading for?'

'Sorry. He and Dimitri are both agreed that if the train continues west, it will have to go through Moscow. Moscow junction would be the only one large enough to handle such sized trains. He also feels the many military establishments east of Moscow could become very interesting. He has picked up information that the weaponry protecting Moscow is the latest in Russia's arsenal.'

'So he thinks it's arms then, Mayer?'

'He always has, sir, but he can't corroborate it for you. The paperwork is always delayed till the last minute of the train's departure, adding to the chaos that a train of these proportions causes. One thing both Rudi and Dimitri are convinced of is that the papers only appear when the train's ready to travel on!'

'Well done, Mayer. You will give a big thank you to them both.'

Before Mayer could respond, Koslowski's voice broke in, 'Ah! There you are, Mayer! I've been looking for you to tell you about this meeting with Ernst. Are you free now?' he said sarcastically.

'Yes. Sorry to have caused you the trouble of looking for me!'

'Willi.' Ernst broke into the conversation to stop it going any further. 'Mayer has just delivered a message from Rudi which we will come to shortly. We have more immediate problems. Joc Latimer has come up with a rather wild idea... which if it comes out positive, will make my hunches seem like fairy tales!' Ernst related the whole story to explain Joc's wild hunch of the Russian connection in Portugal and his own theory that they could be planning an escape route into the open sea as opposed to an enclosed seaway.

'Willi, I think we better start pulling some favours and make a start on getting a team together. Don't make them active yet, but warm them up to the possibility.'

'Shall do. Can I have Mayer?'

'Mayer, do you want to be involved or just stay liaising on the phone with Rudi?'

'That's not fair, sir, I want to do both, but—'

'But you can't!' cut in Ernst. 'This time I think you will be better used in answering Rudi's calls. As a trained policewoman you will be able to see his problems as they arise and answer any problems he will be going to have…' Ernst's voice broke in mid-sentence. The light cough to clear his throat made his voice warmer, more gentle. 'Besides, he will need all the love you can give him. He will be in a maelstrom, which will require both of your strengths pulling together to survive.' The room went quiet. Mayer knew Ernst was right; Rudi would need her so badly.

'Robin, Ernst heir!' Ernst had picked up the phone to speak to Robin as soon as his team had left his office, having accepted their assignments.

'Nice to hear your voice, Ernst, even if it's before I've had my morning's intake of coffee!'

'Sorry, I thought you would have started early being in the British Army!'

'That was in the old days, Ernst. Now we are given time to think in the mornings!'

'Well, I hope your brains are fully awake now. First of all, we have every reason to believe the trains are heading for Moscow. Also, it is felt the best weaponry is around the eastern side of Moscow, and the trains will stop there. The manifests are manipulated at the last moment before departure from each stop. Someone is playing with the systems, who must have a vast knowledge of how the system works and enough power to make it work. Rudi feels we should get someone onto the trains to confirm the theory that it's arms and the guess that it must be drugs.' Ernst paused for a moment, but continued before Robin could interrupt. 'There is Joc's theory coming into play at the same time. It seems he got a few days' leave and went up to Lamego, where Klaus and Deiter first saw Polenkovich. It is his belief that there are Russians there, operating a fear and obedience campaign on the locals. The man Joc met purports to be in import/exports with English colonial parents, vineyard owners, old stock, et cetera. He's having him put under surveillance by Vargas.'

'Blimey, Ernst, Joc's on a flyer, don't you think?'

'Yes I do, but I love the audacity of it!'

'If he's right, Ernst, how do we get this train through to Portugal?'

'I've looked at a rail map of Europe and I would say with great difficulty, but it will not detract our forces from the northern area if Vargas will take it on and keep us informed.'

'I agree, Ernst. His reports have been improving; let's hope he does well this time!'

'Time will tell, and the way this train is moving he will have a long time to search for the information!'

'Vargas will have to be reminded from time to time that too much of it can be an enemy!'

'Joc will remind him, I'm sure!'

'Ernst, looking at the disposition of this funny European Army, we have in Burgos, Spain a brigade of soldiers… maybe my General would let us use them if we needed to.'

'I hope we don't have to use them, Robin, but it's nice to know there's a "maybe".'

'I'll sound things out, Ernst. You've given me enough to think about now, so with your permission, I'll get on.'

'Please keep in touch, Robin, I feel the pace of our lives is going to speed up very soon. Bye, Robin.'

'Bye, Ernst.'

Yute Polenkovich stood outside the heavy Kremlin walls. From his vantage point, he could view the comparatively small entrance the workers used to enter and leave the building. Yute was looking for one man, Rudi Simusov, a name ferreted out for him with a description, by one of his trusted contacts within the dark, satanic walls. Tall, handsome, blond-haired, wide-shouldered, athletic-figured young man, was the description he was given for his search. One distinguishing feature, although a weak one, was that he had just given up smoking and sucked away on one of those fake cigarettes continuously.

Yute had not realised how many people worked in the labyrinth below the Kremlin and had only allowed himself half an hour for his first observation, but the ants had been entering for nearly all of that time now... he must leave, he must not be late for his next meeting. Just three more minutes left. There he is! It must be him. Where is the phoney cigarette? Rudi Simusov prove yourself to me... where's your bloody fag? There it is, you bloody play actor, using it as a real cigarette! Right, now I know you by sight, tonight we will meet. Now for more urgent things.

Chief Inspector Vargas and Captain Maria Tias sat across Vargas's large imperial desk. Their conversation had been quiet and official but Maria expected the pleb of a man she loved to say more. Eventually she could not wait any longer. Leaning across the desk, stretching her hands out to reach him across the other side, she asked lovingly in her sensual voice, 'What is the matter with my little boy today? Have you been naughty, done something Mamma should know about and can't find the strength to tell me?'

'No, Maria. This European involvement we have is becoming a very big issue. It seems we have people in Lamego who are undesirable and one of our American associates is asking if we can do a favour and put some people discreetly in the field to see what can be attributed to a certain Pedro Matros and his partner.'

'What a silly thing for my little boy to worry about! You have lots of people under your control – you could soon get a team together!'

'It's not the team that worries me, it is who is going to head it up. You know this could be my big break into the full European network of Police!'

'Yes I know, my beautiful baby wants all the nice things in life, but Mamma doesn't understand baby's problem.'

'I can't go myself, I've too many things to keep under control here and I can't be in two places at once and I can't trust anyone else but you to head up the team!' Maria gripped his hands and removed them, then automatically gripped them again. The shock-horror and surprise of his remark passed from her.

Her strong voice answered, 'I can handle all that and give you all of the credit. It doesn't sit well, but I'll do it!'

'I knew you would and you are more than capable, but we have no in-depth policing in those hills. You would be in terrible danger, from what our American friends are implying. I can't lose my best officer. Besides, I love you and I would never be able to sleep again if anything ever happened to you!'

Maria's hand tightened on Manuel's hands again. The pleasure of his words tingling through her body, the electricity throbbing through her fingertips, saying without words, I love you too and don't be afraid for me, our love is forever! The swiftness of Manuel's hands as they tightened around her wrists and pulled her from her seat into an embrace across the wide desk; his strength as he pulled her further towards him caused her tip-toed stance to give way and she fell across the desk. Her lithe body turning, offering her lips, wanting the kiss, wanting... her moist lips whispered, 'Why have you never told me before?'

Rudi left his office with Dimitri at approximately five fifteen. The day had been busy but neither of them had been able to confirm the train's journey. It seemed it had disappeared! They were frustrated but persistent in their efforts in the search. Dimitri had reminded Rudi of the possible consequences of the lack of information; for whoever it was that left the instructions for him in the depth of night, could become very irritated.

Rudi's attitude was, 'If I can't find it, I can't. I'm experienced at my job and he or they know that I can't do more than my best!' From the tremor in Rudi's voice, Dimitri knew his friend was afraid of failure. He was deeply in love and wanted only one thing – to be with his beloved Mayer. The weak sunlight cut into their eyes as they blinked into focus then walked out onto the street. 'Do you ever feel you are being watched, Dimitri?' Rudi asked quietly as they started to walk.

'Somehow, Rudi, I've had that feeling all my life. First, it was the attitude that if they have got my name from someone, then it was definite they were following, then the paranoia, then I started hiding from them, then I said, "Sod them!" I don't care if they do follow me. If you feel you are being watched, I suggest you and I split up and I'll watch your back... we should be able to tell fairly quickly, I suppose!'

'Would you do that for me, Dimitri?'

'Sure. It's not a game that I've played before, but I think I could pull it off!'

'I'd like to know, and I'd feel a lot safer with you there. When shall we start?'

'What about now. You turn left at the crossroads, take any route you like. We'll meet at the pub in half an hour. Bye now, Rudi!' His voice became louder and his waving gesture seemed exaggerated, but then he was gone. Rudi waved a slow goodbye and watched a few moments as his friend threaded his way through the pedestrians on the pavement.

Rudi was alone. What should he do now? Walk naturally. Come on, ignore what's behind you. Dimitri is there, trust him, he's your friend. Just walk, Rudi, maybe look in that shop window over there... cross the road, now stop on that traffic island. Let the car coming go past. Go now, the time is now! I'm sure there's no one there. I couldn't even see Dimitri. Ah well, perhaps I'm worried for nothing, but it's better to be safe than sorry!

The commanding voice stopped Rudi in his tracks just as it had ordered. Who was this who had called his name? He must stay calm!

'You called my name... do you know me? How can I help?'

The man walked forward menacingly; his body forced Rudi back against a wall. The once handsome face locked onto the frightened young face of Rudi and snarled, 'You don't know me. I am Marshall of the Army, Yute Polenkovich. You are now Senior Comrade Clerk Rudi Simusov. You get your orders in the night. Orders that instruct and orders which require information. You are involved in a convoy of lorries originating in Vladivostok. That convoy was mine. The Council made it mine. Now the Council tell me that you have lost my convoy. I want it back!'

'Your information is correct, although it surprises me. I have never had any contact with the Ministry of Defence and why a Marshall of the Army is talking to me now, I have no idea!'

'How did you get in this position of authority?'

'I have no authority, sir. As you said, I answer messages left on my desk during the night.'

'Is there anything else you should tell me?'

'I don't see how or why I need to tell you anything, sir!'

There was a glint from the blade as the pressure of its tip was pressed under his ribs. The surprise on Rudi's face turned into animated panic as his jabbering told the whole story.

'There was Comrade Gregori Alexei Androv who was my boss, then all of a sudden he went missing. I got my first letter and am told to report to Room A117. I was told I was to take over the duties of Comrade Androv. The lorries were already there, codenamed the "snake". They are now a train, three trains in fact. They are in the middle of Russia, of that we are reasonably sure, but we can't get an exact position. The lorries scattered in every direction. The "snake" seems to have changed masters. Whoever it may be, he is playing the game on his own. My bosses are very disturbed.' Rudi's breath just lasted long enough to finish the sentence.

'You're right, I am disturbed. They were my lorries. Where is Androv now?'

'Sir, I have no idea. When I find out, and you have the right credentials, I see no problem in giving such information to you!' Rudi's voice remained firm, but his stomach was churning over. Here he was, never having even spoken to a Lieutenant before, conversing with a Marshall of the Army!

'Young man, I am the authority, it can be your little memos on your desk or it can be direct instructions given to you by me, face to face... but just think you will know that it will cause me irritation having to find you every time.' The menace in Yute's voice was unmistakable, but Rudi didn't wince from the situation. Yute continued in a quieter, more menacing voice. 'You will meet my instructions which will arrive on your desk tomorrow. You will not under any circumstances mention my name, this meeting, or this conversation.'

The words were finished, the light touch of Yute's index finger on his lips left Rudi in no doubt he was in a very large game. A game he must play to the very end. Yute's eyes bore into Rudi's but Yute's stare was stronger and Rudi's lids fell heavily over his eyes as they dropped towards the ground. One more blink of Rudi's eyes and Yute was gone.

Having witnessed the scene from a distance, Dimitri made his way forward to his friend's side, only to be rebuked for his efforts. They must not be seen together outside the office or their secret bar until this was all over. Dimitri's normally calm attitude was knocked out of kilter until he realised that Rudi was trying to protect him. Rudi felt suddenly all alone with the turmoil of his love for Mayer, and now this new threat to his life. Alone in a crowded city.

Under Yute's instructions, Mogatin and Lanov had left a lengthy trail of contacts for Robin's Military Police investigators to keep under surveillance. He was going to need help, despite Inspector Gilbert Torneau's frequent comment, 'The great thing in the military is you never seem to run out of soldiers!'

'Well, he's wrong!' The sound of Robin's own voice brought him out of his reverie. 'Goodness me! I must be going mad, I'm talking to myself now!' Well, okay then, talk it through, his mind answered him. There's only one solution and you know it. Yes, of course I do! Well then, get on the phone and be quick about it! Robin's hand lifted the receiver and punched in the numbers for his Adjutant's direct line.

'Major Roche.'

'Robin here, sir. Is there a chance of your fitting me in? I've got a logistical problem and it needs a better head than mine to solve it!'

'How about now? I've got an hour before the old man arrives.'

'Thanks, sir. I'm on my way.'

The five minutes it should have taken to get to the Adjutant's office actually stretched into ten minutes, with Robin being delayed by questions from his personnel as he passed through the Orderly Room and the passageway. Robin's knock on the door was answered immediately.

'Come in, Robin! What took you so long?'

'The very thing I've come to see you about, André!'

'Well, tell me all about your problem.'

'I simply haven't got enough trained investigators. With all of

411

Mogatin and Lanov's contacts within our depots across Europe having to be watched, plus Mogatin and Lanov themselves; the internal investigations of possible disloyalty within our own personnel, the necessary doubling up of army police working alongside some sections of German, French, Russian and Spanish units, I can't make the numbers work!'

'A problem indeed, Robin. How many more people do you think you will need?'

'It's really inestimable, André. A lot depends on how long this whole caper will go on for, but I could use a hundred good investigators right now!'

André whistled out loud. 'That's impossible, Robin. Have you got a more precise idea of the minimum you would need to solve the problem before it becomes a mess?'

'The problem is, we are an army, André, and we have been invaded. When Eurocorps was formed it was never anticipated that our own constitution, stating that all ranks must be bilingual, would prevent us poaching from the British Army. My contacts at police training depot would, I'm sure, help in supplying manpower – but not bilingual.'

'Have you got any better ideas then?'

Robin hesitated for a moment. The answer might be in the audacious idea which had not yet been fully thought out; it had literally only jumped into his brain as he knocked on the Adjutant's door, but now was as good a time as any.

'Would, or could it be possible for military trained police to temporarily "join" our army?'

Major Roche sank further back in his chair. 'That's outrageous, Robin! Our code for operating in Europe would be broken, we could upset many a national chain of command if we were found out!'

'It could work, sir. We would have to make certain that any civilian police had previously had some military training... after all, you have often said one army's training is much like another! All I am aware of, sir, is I need skilled investigators and if we don't get them we will become just another load of boys in brown uniforms who talk a lot of "bullshit" about European security and helping to stabilise the world!' The passion in his pleading moved the Adjutant, who sat silently, thinking.

'Robin, see how quickly it could be set up. Don't infiltrate anyone in behind my back, though... put it down on paper and I'll give you a quick decision. I think you had better leave now to allow me a few minutes to think over what I've just said before the General arrives!'

Robin stood upright, placed his hat squarely on his head and saluted. He managed to 'about-turn' before the relief welled up in his eyes. He was a very lucky man to have an Adjutant like André who offered him so much support.

Rudi walked for a while. His whole body seemed to be malfunctioning. His shoulders dropped, he kept losing his concentration, his feet had no spring in them, his mind kept sliding into self-pity. As he neared the telephone box at the railway station, he stopped and checked all around, searching into the deep shadows for any movement. Satisfied he had evaded anyone possibly following him, he swung the door of the end box open and his fingers automatically dialled Mayer's home number.

'Hello, is that you, Rudi?' Her sweet voice warmed him.

'My love, I'm sorry I am late calling you. I have been walking and walking. I needed time to think.'

'About what, Rudi? Not about us, surely?' Her voice sounded a little nervous.

'No, not about us, my love. I've had a visit from an old friend and I'm now working for two bosses in Russia and one in Germany. My visitor was Yute Polenkovich.'

'Rudi! What is going to happen to us... if I lost you I'd kill myself!'

'My love, my love! Then I would have nothing.' Rudi's voice had warmth and was getting stronger. The few words they had exchanged were slowly bringing life back to his earlier, dejected mood.

'Rudi, what can I do? I will speak to Ernst again and see if he can bring you west earlier than planned.'

'Darling, no. Don't you see? Although it's a strain for us to bear, with me getting two secret memos each night, we must be able to grasp both ends of the "snake" and possibly a lot more information!'

'But you will be in even more danger!'

'Well, they can only kill me once!' Rudi's intention of being flippant fell well short of the mark and Mayer's response cut into his heart.

'You fool! Allowing yourself to be used by everyone!'

'Even your precious Ernst!' Rudi's swift reply distressed him as soon as he had said it.

'This is not about Ernst, it's about you bloody corrupt Russians!'

'Us corrupt Russians? You German usurpers is more to the point!'

'If that's the way you feel, at least you have an option with us to walk away… and why don't you if that's all you think of us!' The words were coming out the wrong way – she loved him, longed for him – how could she say those things?

'Mayer, I think we should stop talking now. Tell Ernst, Yute is in Moscow and giving me instructions. We'll talk tomorrow.' The phone went dead abruptly. Mayer cried in the loneliness of her bedroom, and Rudi walked into the first bar he came to.

The thick huskiness in Mayer's throat caused by her almost continual crying since Rudi had hung up on her was noticeably apparent to Ernst, who during the conversation, had gone from the initial surprise at receiving a call from Mayer direct to his home, to one of extreme interest at the information offered, to one of sadness at having to put someone he liked and respected through such daily torture. 'Mayer…' His gentle voice reached her ear. 'You know we must keep Rudi on our side. It is going to be even more important now he has two strings pulling at him.'

'I know, sir, but we had such a row – we were horrible to each other!'

'Your first row is always the worst. I promise you, he will phone on time, if not earlier, and just think, Mayer, maybe he will have information for us which will mean he will have to phone the office in the morning. Now, I suggest you get some sleep now and dream of only good things. Promise me you will try.'

'Yes, sir, I will try. See you tomorrow.'

The phone clicked softly as it was placed into the cradle too soon for Mayer to hear Ernst saying, 'Tomorrow will be a lovely day for you, Mayer.' Ernst's wife looked at him, knowing by the tone of his voice that he was playing the father-figure role again. She just smiled smugly over the top of her spectacles.

The phone calls to both Robin and Joc from Ernst's home were succinct, informing them that Yute Polenkovich was in Moscow and had threatened Rudi and that information would be gotten to Rudi's desk during the night for action the next day. Both Joc and Robin agreed there had to be another insider Council member, if not two, who would be arranging the memos for Rudi. How great it would be if this information could be obtained.

Dimitri knocked on Rudi's door the morning after Rudi's encounter with Yute, not knowing what kind of reception he would receive, but the information he had just had, had to be passed on to his nominated superior.

'Good morning, Comrade Simusov!'

'Good morning, Dimitri. I'm sorry.'

'I realised why you sent me away.'

'We must be so very careful. I must not get people involved, I must filter the information alone. You should not be seen with me outside of these offices. When this is—'

Dimitri cut in, 'All over, then we can be friends again. A fat lot of good that will be! You need a friend now!'

Rudi stood up, offering his hand and said, 'It will be impossible without your help, Dimitri. Thank you.' They shook hands and embraced to seal their pact to help Mother Russia.

'Now, Dimitri. What news have you for distribution?'

'Are we going public? A word like distribution covers a lot of ground!' The flippancy was back in Dimitri's manner.

'It feels like it, with two envelopes appearing every morning, plus my other duties, collating it and passing it on!' The words 'collating' and 'passing it on' were emphasised just a little to let Dimitri know he had not forgotten his western friends.

'We have a big discovery regarding the "snakes". They are all going around Moscow on old World War Two rail tracks that the vast majority of railway workers had forgotten existed. It is confirmed that hundreds of maintenance men are repairing tracks and replacing sections as required. It appears that no expense is being spared from district funds and that all work has to be completed within a week!'

'Hell, Dimitri! They are going to be here in one week!'

'The instructions are that all tracks and signal gear are to be ready in one week!'

'The district controllers are agreeing to this?'

'It seems they are gleefully doing so. My guess is, Rudi, that a lot of money is passing into a lot of people's pockets.'

'Make the district pay, then take a large "thank you" from the shadows in the dark!'

'A bit like us, Rudi. The "shadows in the dark" bit, anyway.'

'Dimitri, I hope we still have a clean conscience when this is all over. You would never take money, would you?'

'No, Rudi. I will do anything to make Mother Russia strong again, but I would never make her bleed!'

'Me neither, Dimitri. Although between you and me, I wonder what our controllers are really up to.'

'You mustn't think too much. Remember, curiosity killed the cat. One little bit of information that needs special attention is that there are two railway cuttings and one rail tunnel where the lines are closest to the city. All precautions must be taken!' Dimitri stopped talking. Rudi expected more to be said, but Dimitri remained silent.

'Why do you think our bosses have insisted on that?'

'What I fear is that it's arms and drugs in vast quantities. They are afraid of bombs going off in built-up areas or worried the "snakes" will be vulnerable to ambush.'

'Your imagination is a bit ahead of itself, Dimitri.'

'Well, a bit of guesswork maybe, but why renew the tracks on the old World War Two route when the rail system we have through the centre of Moscow is efficient and large enough to handle the "snakes"? It would be much slower and cause quite a few shuntings. On two occasions the trains would have to be shortened and reconnected because they are far too big for some of the change stations. My theory is they're nuclear weapons and if they exploded they would not only blow up half of Moscow, but result in the largest nuclear cloud full of heroin, making the whole of Europe and most of Russia totally addicted to the sniffing habit!'

Rudi laughed along with Dimitri, both men seeing the humour in Dimitri's vivid imagination, but it was not long before they were wondering whether what they were laughing at could actually ever become fact.

'Where's the "snake" now, Dimitri?'

'It is nearing Kazan. All three sections have had diversions onto military lines and are now converging on Kazan, at Kaska junction. Our contacts are predicting the trains will undergo running repairs out of necessity.'

'Only seven days then?'

'Afraid so.'

'Let me pass on the information as ordered without the guesswork.'

'We can't stop now. Maybe the guesswork could be useful to someone.'

Rudi liked Dimitri very much, but his constant play on words and 'cocking his snoot' at the system, worried him. Dimitri chuckled at Rudi's discomfort, raising his hand to his mouth in an imaginary drinking motion. Rudi just gave a slight nod of the head, knowing Dimitri meant them to meet up later at his bar.

Rudi left the office at lunchtime. It was unusual for him to do so, but he had to speak to Mayer. He paraded himself at the side entrance of the ministry. He saw no movement in any of the shadowy corners, or on his journey to the familiar telephone box at the railway station. His vigilance was maintained the whole time and he was absolutely sure he had not been followed.

'Mayer.' The stern voice cut into Mayer's ear. No tenderness, only the hurt in his voice. Her weak reply disturbed him. She sounded half-dead... distant... a little afraid.

'We have found the "snakes". They are converging on Kazan as we speak. The only junction large enough to take rolling stock of this magnitude will be Kaska Junction. Without the manifests we cannot confirm the cargo, but Dimitri and I guess that it's arms and drugs. A vast amount of work and restructuring is being done to the old World War Two rail track around Moscow, which has to be completed within the next seven days. The danger points are two railway cuttings and one rail tunnel. Dimitri and I both think it could be noted as dangerous for the city, from possible explosions or potential hijackings. You must excuse me now, I have work to do.'

'Please don't go, Rudi. Nothing has changed my feelings for you. Please talk a little longer, please…'

Rudi's heart hurt. He wanted to say 'I love you, I love you' a thousand times but he had been hurt so much, he felt cruel, but he had to make his point that he wanted to give his love, to live their dreams together, but without conditions. 'Perhaps tomorrow,' was Rudi's reply. The quiet placing of the receiver back in its cradle cut even deeper into both their souls.

The pace quickened noticeably in the offices of Hamburg Police HQ after Mayer's report and assessment. The contact procedures for Eurocorps, French, Spanish and Portuguese police forces were quickly followed.

Captain Maria Tias walked into the foyer of the hotel in Lamego, her well-tailored suit clung to her shapely figure. The pale lemon blouse contrasted well against the silver-grey suit, her stockings moulded her legs in see-through grey silk, her feet were elegantly encased in simple shiny patent-leather court shoes, the hat she carried at her side was a wide-brimmed summer straw hat in a matching shade of lemon and the hat band was silver-grey. Her hair, with just a little curl, fell from a centre parting to encircle her face, falling across her shoulders and halfway down her back. Maria had made her entrance and captured her audience in one pass through the revolving doors. Her passage to the reception desk was timed elegance (this was the part she had always wanted to play – a lady!). The few people occupying the foyer all floated from her path.

'I have a reservation, I am Maria Tias.'

'Your room is ready for you, Miss!' He waited for any

correction on his addressing of her, but none was forthcoming, Maria was single and in the game she was about to commence, being single would be less of an encumbrance.

'Would you like to be shown to your room now?'

'Yes please, and bring my luggage up too, if you will.'

Maria watched the reception clerk ritually call over the hall porter, who in turn made a play-act out of obtaining the bellboy and giving him instructions on seeing Maria to her room. Having taken note of all the facilities the hotel offered, Maria followed the poor boy carrying her bags. Her only thought was to freshen-up and return to the bar as soon as dignity would allow, in the hope she could begin the work she had come for.

Robin's office was becoming very stuffy. Inspector Torneau and Ernst Ulbrecht had promised some personnel with some military service; but they had arrived rather quicker than Robin had expected. In a few minutes, when the trucks and cars arrived, the open windows would be able to do their job and let in some fresh air. Robin was very impressed after meeting each of the men. Everyone present was excited following their first general meeting which had just finished. The questions were intelligent and plentiful and it seemed all of the men sent by Ernst and Gilbert were all loyal countrymen committed to ridding the whole of Europe from evil. With the help of the Adjutant, Robin had worked out placements for the new intake of men, mostly around Achern, Strasbourg and Paris, where accommodation on regular army bases could be absorbed without creating any obvious inconvenience or attention. It was both André's and Robin's hope that all of the new placements would become 'invisible' in their new surroundings.

Maria Tias sat on the hotel bar stool furthest from the entrance of the foyer, giving her a view of each and everyone entering. She had noted from Joc's report that Pedro Matros had mentioned this hotel bar as being one of his favourite places in town, so after journeying from Lisbon, why shouldn't she have a restful evening and go to bed early? Tomorrow would be soon enough to start! With her beauty, Maria knew it would not be long before the 'barflies' started gathering. That was the part of the evening she always hated, but it had generally occurred only on the rare occasions she had arrived too early to meet her Manuel. Tonight she would be pleasant; should anyone approach her, she would be mysterious – evasive to any direct questions but polite. She would stand her ground until that bastard Pedro Matros appeared. You can't call him a 'bastard', you're here to investigate him, you can't assume him to be guilty before you've even met him, she thought. Now, steady yourself, girl – don't let this position of power go to your head. You know you're basically a 'home and fireside' type, in fact you're still surprised that you're even here! You can't believe your luck! You... Christ! Get yourself together! That's him in the doorway... Christ! He's coming straight over here!

The movement of the bar-keeper from behind the bar gave her the opportunity to break her stare which had been locked onto Pedro's smiling face. He came closer, closer, finally sitting two stools away, sitting down heavily, play-acting his 'very hard day at the office' routine. Maria sat and waited until his drink arrived. The words came from his mouth after the first sip, 'I've really earned that one today!' Maria knew it would be addressed to the bar in general, searching for someone to answer him. This time, he hoped it would be her. Maria chose not to. It seemed the rest of the bar felt the same way, so Pedro just sat there silently, fingering the rim of his glass. Maria would sit and wait for the direct question, 'Would you like a drink?' which would inevitably come when he ordered another one for himself.

The silence held. It seemed an age, but then it came. 'Would you like a drink?'

Maria smiling back, said, 'Yes please,' while her mind said to her, Let's go to work!

'The three "snakes" are coiling around Moscow rail yards!' The words were whispered into Dimitri's ear through the telephone.

'Are they nesting, or going straight through?'

'They will be in the yards for around forty-eight hours. They will be shunted around to organise each train to carry the same goods. I know one train will be at least three times the size of the other two... they've got to go west from here!'

'Do you know where, and have you found the manifests yet?'

'My guess is Paris or it could be Berlin. It's the shortest route to the Atlantic ports and it would need a marshalling yard the size of Paris to break the big "snake" into smaller pieces! No manifests.'

'How long will it take travelling to Paris?'

'Travelling direct, with no stops… she won't be a greyhound!'

'Let me know when she leaves, or any other important information that may crop up before then.'

'Sure. Must go now, see you sometime!' The phone went dead and Dimitri immediately left his office and rushed along the corridor to tell Rudi.

Although there was a chilliness between himself and Mayer, Rudi could hardly wait for the end of the day to come so he could hear her voice, give her the information she wanted to hear, fulfilling her wishes, weakening his own position, becoming her 'lap-dog'. What am I saying? I love her. Why am I angry with her? Why do I do it? We are both fighting in our small way for a free world; gathering information, passing it on for others to use as they will. When you hear her voice, shout out loud, 'I love you!'

In his daydream he had dialled out the numbers for Mayer on his office phone. Her voice was sweet and clear. He shouted his, 'I love you!' and threw the phone down immediately he realised he was still in his office. The panic set in his body. Do they listen to his calls? An international call is bad enough on the office phone, but an international call to a direct line in Hamburg Police Headquarters! My God, what have I done! When will they come for me? I must make an excuse to leave the office now, to warn her of the stupid mistake I've made! Dimitri would cover for him and he would explain the stupidity he had committed when they met in the pub later on.

Rudi left the office and made his way to the railway station telephone box, dialled the numbers, his fingers barely strong enough to dial the old-fashioned spring-loaded dial. Panic was taking over. He must not let Mayer know he was 'hyper' because of his own stupidity. How could she love a man as stupid as he was? he thought.

'I love you, Rudi, thanks for calling back so soon – what went wrong?'

'I love you too. I was daydreaming... I phoned you from my office. I wanted to talk to you more than anything and I automatically dialled your number. If I'm not being monitored, it will be all right because I know the switchboard is not fully automated. I'm sorry!'

'My darling, why are you sorry when it is us that's putting you through all this torment? You poor love, you must be feeling pretty desolate.'

'I am, but...' Rudi wanted to continue with '...everything would be wonderful if we were together...' but it would sound as though he was begging her to approach her bosses to get him out of Russia.

Instead, Rudi continued with, 'We have some important information. Dimitri has spoken to his train-spotter...' Rudi related all the details he had been given by Dimitri. Mayer was stunned with the magnitude of the problem and the estimated time span which would make every second count from now on.

'Rudi, I must get this information to Ernst. It is imperative!'

'I know,' Rudi replied as he placed the receiver down. Walking dejectedly across the station concourse, the question in his mind was, why couldn't she have said, 'I love you darling, I'll let Ernst know now!' Why wasn't he for once, the important one? His mood became oppressive. It was not his nature, he was normally a happy-go-lucky, playful joker. Is this love? he thought.

Ernst telephoned Robin as soon as he received the news from Mayer. They agreed between themselves they would each take on responsibility of their separate contacts; Robin the French and his military, and Ernst the Americans, Portuguese and his own police force.

'Robin, do you think it would be a good idea if we all met up again?'

'I think it is the only way forward, Ernst. I'll get the Adjutant to speak to the General if you are thinking of a UK venue again?'

'It would be good for us all.'

'I'll come back to you ASAP. Shall I try for this weekend?'

'The sooner the better. When the "snake" gets into our own

territories it will be much more difficult for any of us to get any leave!'

'Agreed. I'll get onto it right away. Be in touch with answers. Bye now, Ernst. Will Rudi come?'

'Allow for him, but I think it unlikely. Our "snake" is very slippery and by the sound of things, he is having trouble keeping his hands on it!'

'You've made a "funny", Ernst! I'll be in touch. Bye now.'

Robin telephoned the Adjutant, asking if he would approach the General and if possible this time, could he arrange for the RAF to lay on transport for the French? Robin knew that now the Parisians were involved, Inspector Torneau would not be invited and Robin felt it was necessary and only right he should be at the meeting.

'I'll do my best, Robin. I suppose your request is immediate?'

'We would hope for Friday afternoon to convene, Sunday afternoon to disperse, sir.'

'Not much time to set things up, Robin!'

'No, sir!' was the reply. The phone went dead. The Adjutant was already doing what Adjutants do – making an army get its fingers out!

Maria was becoming a little stressed. Pedro had played a mellow hand at first, but now after several drinks he had gradually become a little aggressive and was making demands about when they were to meet up next.

'You will have another drink… you're a stuck-up cow!'

Maria wished she could break cover and arrest this little shit but she daren't… not yet. She thought to herself that maybe when they left to go to this great bar he kept on about, he might accidentally fall down some steps! 'Come on, we're going.' His brusque, drunken manner irritated Maria and her fire rose within her.

'We will go when I'm ready and not before!'

'We're going now!' The speed at which his hand shot out and grabbed her wrist shocked her, but as his grip tightened and her hand bent steeply back against the joint, she found herself standing up and leaving with him, her arm being forced behind her back. She wanted to kick out but she mustn't yet... her time would come.

'I told you, we're going now!' His putrid breath passed under her nose as the command was whispered threateningly into her ear. As if by magic a taxi drew up outside and Maria knew she was not going to enjoy the journey – his hands would be everywhere, trying to touch her bare skin, to kiss her mouth, to kiss... Maria hoped it would be a short journey.

Surprise took over from threats when Pedro, although slurring his words, said, 'I think we could be good together. My partner is only good for the heavy work, like making sure people do as we tell them. He hasn't realised that to succeed in crime now, you have to have intelligence as well.'

Naïvely, Maria asked, 'What do you mean?' adding a soft 'Pedro' after the pause.

'I've got a partner. I think you would make a much better one. You're beautiful, he's ugly, you're soft and gentle, he's a brute!'

'What are you saying to me, Pedro?' The soft approach seemed to be working, she thought.

'I'm a quiet countryman at heart. Years ago things were tough for me. When I met my partner, who was a crook – a successful one, but nevertheless a crook – he persuaded me to leave the land and work with him. It was good for a while, then Glasnost seemed to break down the traditional structure of the underworld for a short while. We left Russia for Portugal and set up this import/export company which is quite successful, so I was happy. Then some of our old friends found us and now I am not so happy anymore, but I will still do my job properly.'

His head slowly rolled onto Maria's shoulder, his hand resting gently on top of hers. Maria sat quietly, knowing she would have to remind herself of his story later and start to prod further.

★

Memo: Security Grade 1.
From: Commanding General Eurocorps.
To: Adjutant, Achern and personnel listed below only.

Meeting set, commencing 1600 hours Friday, following receipt of memo. RAF liaison: Wing Commander F Johnstone (use directory). 180 accommodations arranged to cover five nations as previously, minus possibly one person. Return on completion Sunday. Recommend same procedures as before for all transfers to your previous destination. Good luck.

Robin read through his copy and understood the reason for its ambiguity but was cock-a-hoop at the speed at which the authority was achieved by the General.

As the cars and trucks kept passing the guard room gate, the Sergeant of the Guard remarked to his Corporal, 'There's a bloody lot of them this time! I remember some of their faces from when they were here before, but this lot look more foreign... if they were in my army they'd have had their bloody hair cut by now!'

'Do you know what they're up to, Sergeant?'

'No, Corporal, but I bloody well hope they do or you and me will be up to our necks in it if they don't!'

'Well, let's hope they do, Sergeant, don't you think?'

'Yes, I certainly do!'

As the next staff car approached, the Sergeant curtailed his words of wisdom and clawed himself back to things he really knew about. 'Turn out the guard!' The loud, crystal-clear tone cut through the air. In a lower voice, he turned to the Corporal. 'A lot of flags on this one, check it out thoroughly – show 'em we know what we're doing!' The Sergeant went back inside the guard room quicker than lightning, to avoid any hassle.

Robin, who had arrived very early, stood in front of the large window, staring across the well-trimmed lawns spread out before him. This time, being a weekend, his General had managed to procure the mansion house, which had been converted into the Training Centre many years before. In its wisdom, the army had managed to maintain it. The view was tranquil. To Robin, it appeared the army always needed large, well-maintained houses to teach war in. The noise coming from the faceless voices in the 'baronial hall' brought Robin back from his thoughts. Turning from the window, he was thinking that the mixed contingency of German, French and Portuguese investigators seemed to be integrating well. It would not be long before Ernst, Joc, Gilbert and Manuel arrived, along with André, who would be orchestrating this group of hardened investigators towards success.

★

The signal boxes at every junction and intersection were busy. Each and every signalman had received an envelope with the Kremlin's stamp embossed on it, with instructions that on no account must the 'special' trains be impeded on their journey from Kazan to Moscow. On no account must it be allowed to stop until they arrived in Minsk. Dimitri had been told about this instruction and after quite a while negotiating with one of his contacts, he managed to be staring at the original memos. He had read them several times, searching for any clues about the 'snake's' eventual destination. There was nothing! The only directive was that the trains were not to stop in Moscow. Was it because someone writing these memos loved Moscow so much and wanted to pass the variously routed trains through quickly with the unstable cargo of weapons? Or was it because the cobweb of rail lines throughout the suburbs would, on numerous occasions, bring the trains running side by side and very prone to hijacking? Dimitri was convinced it was the latter, two people in charge of the trains with different objectives. Dimitri was convinced of his own assessment of the 'snake's' disposition and rushed into Rudi's office to expound his theory, adding that if, on home ground, someone was scared of a hijacking, it would become more and more of a fear for him or her the further west the 'snakes' got. Having expounded his theory to Rudi, he asked, 'Well, what do you think?'

'It's a great theory, and I'll pass it on again to Mayer. Do you know anyone with a fax who would send a copy of the memo, no questions asked?'

'I'll find one. Why do you want to send it?'

'I'd like them in Hamburg to at least have something to look at. They are used to this kind of work, we are amateurs and it may help them in some way.'

'Okay, I'll take it with me when we leave here tonight. You'd better warn Mayer there's a fax on its way.'

'I will, on our way home tonight. I'll see you in the bar about eight?'

'Look forward to it. See you then!'

Maria had sat for what seemed an age with Pedro's snoring, snorting hulk next to her. The longer he slept, the better the chance he would wake up feeling remorseful. Maria watched the agitation of the taxi driver building up. First, the quick furtive glances in the rear-view mirror, the shifting of his body weight, scratching his head.

Eventually, it came. 'You going to get out or what?'

'I can't move him!'

'What a pretty lady sees in a bloody lump like him always baffles me. I suppose I'd better help you if you're going in there with him.'

'I don't know what good I'm doing here, but I suppose I'd better!' Her voice was forlorn. She knew the night would probably be a waste of time, but she had a job to do.

'Here we go then, push! Put his head over this way... I can get his shoulders and drag him the first bit of the way, if you get out and come round this side. Perhaps you can lift his feet out and then we can stand him up.'

'Okay, I'm game. What if we can't stand him up and get him inside the bar?'

'Well, we'll prop him up against that tree and I'll take you back to your hotel!'

'I'd like that, it will maybe teach the bastard a lesson!'

'You'd be right about that! Well, the tree it is then!'

'Thanks.'

In his drunkenness, Pedro could hear voices, but was so tired he could not physically revive himself enough to carry on and enjoy his evening. Whoever this pair were, they were not hurting him. That's good, they've put me down, he thought. His swimming, out-of-focus mind went back to darkness.

'He'll be all right there. People will be in and out of this place all night long. They can wake him if they want to, or he'll sleep it off. No harm done either way!'

'I hope not,' replied Maria.

'Don't worry. I'll take you back now and then come back and watch out for him. I'm the local police captain. Chief Inspector Vargas told me what you are doing and I knew you would be needing a taxi at some point.'

'For my exclusive use?'

'Yes and a direct line for you to contact me. I'll give you the number now. Call me whenever you need me.'

The combined meeting of European investigators was going well. As it was taking place on military grounds, Robin was nominated (as he was last time) as chairman of all group meetings and also of the British contingency. The Adjutant had graciously bowed out from the position, declaring that his not being in the middle like a relay station would make for swifter decisions and greater continuity, if everyone dealt directly with Robin and only brought him into the equation if there were any complaints about the food!

It had been decided Joc would attend all Eurocorps meetings as it looked unlikely that the 'snakes' were going to the USA and that his great contribution in finding the 'ringed-hand man' gave him the natural right for a position where the centre of the action was expected to be. All other groups would discuss all the information as it arrived and work out their own counter plans, bearing in mind the limited information on the 'snake's' route to date. But a plan of preparedness was to be agreed by each nation and the whole group. The belief of all nations involved in the 'snakes' pursuit because of the Lamego/Oporto possible connection still under investigation made all groups aware that another sea and land operation was possible, but not desirable. It was easily agreed that wherever the final showdown was to occur, it would be an international force which would confront the 'snake'.

Yute's position of chasing the train had made it difficult to keep in control of Lanov and Mogatin. He had always arrived at a telephone booth late to make the designated calls, but today was the day that after missing two chances, both men would walk away from the project. He would have failed before the train and its cargo had reached its destination. Yute stood, leaning back against the windbreak of the telephone booth, his eyes following the second hand of his watch as it pulled the minute hand closer to three o'clock. It seemed an age to Yute, but when the time arrived for him to dial and Lanov's voice would answer, he must not show any anxiety in his voice. He must not reveal in any way that he was not solely in control. The hands on his watch converged. It was three o'clock. His finger swiftly dialled the assigned number. One ring... two rings... three rings... pause as Yute mentally heard the answer – Lanov's voice. Exchanging identities as before, Yute apologised for not having made contact and asked if Lanov and Mogatin had anything to report. Having received a negative answer, he proceeded with his instructions.

'You will visit the Colonel. He must be brought into play three days earlier. His final instructions will still be activated on the same date. I repeat, his final instructions will still be activated on the same date – only his advance tasks will be brought forward.'

'It will be done. I'm less than twenty kilometres from the house now. I'll see him this evening. Is there anything I should know if he asks me why?'

'No. He knows only too well what his position is. By bringing him into the action sooner, it will upset no other instructions he may be thinking of taking!'

'So you are still having problems?'

'Not for much longer!' Hearing that sinister response, Lanov knew his boss would not be more forthcoming.

'Same time tomorrow?'

'Same time.' The phones were simultaneously placed back in their cradles.

Yute strode from the telephone box. A talk with this clerk, Rudi Simusov, was his next task. Making sure he was not being followed, he eventually arrived at his observation point across from the side door of the Kremlin. His watch told him he would not have long to wait before the 'below-stairs plebs' started to leave. Missing the initial crush, Rudi would not be many minutes behind. Walking casually across the street, Yute hoped to synchronise with Rudi exiting the tight little doorway. Yute recognised Rudi just behind three flat, uninteresting faces. Yute placed himself to the right-hand side of the doorway. Sliding his arm into Rudi's as he passed, they walked silently side by side. Rudi knew he had no option, Yute knew he had control. The short walk to the small tree-filled square where the 'plebs' normally sat to eat their sandwiches in the spring and summer months was silent. At this time of day, the square was empty. Yute manoeuvred Rudi to a bench at the bottom end of the square where he could see both the central entrance gates.

'Your idea about who you think is sending you the other brown envelopes?' Rudi felt the voice was gentle and warm.

'Ideas I have, but no proof!'

'I didn't ask for proof, tell me your theories!' Yute's voice was angry, annoyed that this civil servant whose help he needed had the cheek to be cocky with him.

'My view is the other envelopes come from Androv – Gregori Alexei Androv, my former boss.'

'How do you come to that conclusion?'

'He disappeared like so many other people from our department. There are rumours he escaped being killed, but they are still looking for him.'

'Who are they?'

'I don't know. I was called to Room A117, told to take over Androv's position and report daily to an unknown face. In fact, an unseen face. He walked about in shadows during my so-called interview for this promotion!' Rudi was just waffling. He felt a tension between Yute and himself but he was tired of these secret little intrigues.

'What did this interviewer act like?'

'Military, upright, tall, slim-figured, walked a little foppishly, had authority in his voice.'

Yute sucked air into his lungs and forced out one word through his teeth, 'Parentov!'

'Who?' asked Rudi.

'Never you mind, my lad. You just listen to me. I want all the memos you have had and those you will receive each lunchtime. Sit here, I will come or someone will use the password "Tsar Nicholas". Pass the memos over to him or her. Do you under-stand?'

The threat in Yute's voice prompted an immediate reaction. 'Yes I do.'

Rudi was about to stutter out some further response but again, Yute vanished as quickly and silently as gossamer on the breeze.

Alone in his room, Yute thought through his conversation with Rudi. His mind was still buzzing from the description Rudi had given him. Was it really Boris Parentov, ex-Battalion-Major of the Infantry, whose previous battle orders included the defence of Moscow during World War Two? A Battalion-Major who refused promotion and instead, took up international banking for what was announced as a family wish of Boris Parentov – joining his family's old established bank. It was the wish of his father that his eldest son should be trained to take over his role as Chief Executive Officer before his father's retirement from that office five years later. Yute remembered the newspaper announcement and the jibes he and his fellow officers had made at the time. 'Little rich boy running home to Papa!' 'Getting out quick before we invade Afghanistan!' 'Nasty guns, they go bang, bang! They might frighten Daddy's little boy!'

Yute stretched out in his armchair and thought out loud, 'It seems that Daddy's little boy is playing a double game!'

The reports of Lanov and Mogatin's movements and those of the rest of their subordinates were rushing into the small command unit which Robin had set up at the British barracks and which enabled him to update every facet of information on a regular basis every three hours. Lanov and Mogatin were constantly changing addresses and their daily sequences. The French pursuit teams had them sighted twenty-four hours a day. This was true of their contacts, with the exception of Yute Polenkovich, who seemed to pop up at will, cause some activity amongst his team, then disappear without trace. Sergeant Hackett, aware of the frequent use of local airports, had noticed three entries from

Colmar to Budapest with one of his passengers. The pilot waits sometimes up to three days and returns with the same passenger. Sergeant Hackett emphasised in his report that as Yute Polenkovich had been sighted by Rudi Simusov, on one occasion coinciding with his exit dates from France, could it be surmised that his destination was in fact Moscow, on all of his disappearances from French soil?

Robin discussed the point with Ernst, Gilbert, Manuel and Joc, all of them agreeing both Budapest and Moscow should be covered if possible, but by members of the existing group. Everyone felt sure Hungary and Moscow would cooperate, but to extend the operation by bringing in two more police forces could cause delays in communications or, worse still, a leak!

Yute sat pondering over the description Rudi had given him of his interviewer in Room A117. Yute was confident it was Boris Parentov whom Rudi was describing but how did he get back into favour? How is it he is still walking the corridors of power? His father was in banking; has he now followed in his father's footsteps? With Boris Parantov in a position of being the owner of a bank and with Glasnost opening up opportunities of money transfers worldwide, Boris could be very useful to the Council! Yute suddenly sat bolt upright in his chair as it dawned on him that the Council owned the bank. It was their money and Boris was just a pawn in the game! A shudder passed through Yute's body as he realised how protective the Council would be with each of their personal fortunes invested.

'Oh, I swear they are not going to take my credit!' The words quietly left his lips. His thoughtful mind raced to review the events which had led him to the decision of going to war against the Organisatiya. First, he must speak with his man on the inside of the Kremlin.

432

Chapter Thirty-Four

Pedro sat up painfully in his very rumpled bed. The alcohol he had consumed lay heavily in his throat and on his tongue. The dehydration had exhausted his mind and body. The sliver of light breaking through the side of the heavy curtains forced his eyes closed. Why won't my brain work?... Where was I?... How did I get back here? His head lowered, he was going back to sleep. It seemed it was the only thing he was capable of doing. The noises from the corridor which ran outside his hotel bedroom kept floating in and out of his brain. Why aren't you more aware, you bloody fool? The noises outside could be someone seeking revenge! Suddenly he was fully awake, sitting bolt upright. 'My God!' he whispered. 'What did I do with that beautiful woman?' His distress held him still for a few moments as his mind caught up and went into replay. He must see her and apologise. Although his body fumbled a little as he showered and dressed, he knew the coffee in the coffee shop when he got downstairs to the hotel lobby, would make him feel human again. As the lift doors opened, he felt more human already. First coffee, then beautiful flowers for a beautiful lady.

Entering the open-plan coffee shop, he instinctively looked for a window seat as he walked forward. 'God, just my bloody luck! There she is... she's seen me.' His soft mutterings were not heard by anyone as he passed by. 'Good morning, Maria, how are you today, may I ask?' The strain of being flamboyant must have been noticed by her, he thought to himself.

'Probably a little better than you feel. Come sit down and have some coffee!'

'Thank you. Lots of coffee for me I think!'

'I'd only have a little coffee, but a big breakfast.'

'I will do as you advise...' He stopped and looked into her eyes. There was a sincere, apologetic pleading in his voice as he asked, 'Did we?'

'Maria's soft, 'No,' made him a little happier.

'I'm sorry, I started drinking too early. My partner reckons we are being taken for a ride on this contract and we had a few drinks without any food to soak it up.'

'Don't worry, I know how it goes. I am a career lady, don't forget.'

'Again, thank you. Would you take lunch with me? It's almost time now, and it will save me having breakfast.'

'Yes, all right. Lunch on the terrace would be nice. I'll find a shady spot for you!' The naughty boy look turned into a smile as he realised she was teasing him. The time before lunch, although short, had made Maria and Pedro cosy with each other. A warm brother–sister feeling, rather than that of the male predator and victim, although both knew they could be comfortable with that, it was nicer having this period of non-confrontation.

The light lunch had been enjoyed and the conversation had not waned throughout. Maria could wait no longer to make her play for information. 'You were damned annoyed at your partner last night, why?'

'He's a bloody great ox. He has no brain, just brawn and nasty gangster contacts. Okay, it makes a good living for the two of us, but sometimes I know my partner is flirting with danger.

'How do you mean, danger? Your import/export business surely can't be dangerous? Sorry Pedro, if that's too direct a question, it's probably unfair to ask.'

'No, not really. I know he has meetings at all hours around the docks in Lisbon, boats coming and going, cigarettes, watches, computer gear. He's no need to play with this small profit gear now. We expanded into ships brokerage, renting, leasing long and short term. Although our very first assignment was cancelled yesterday, we have two further packages being put together, each of which will give us twice the profit we each made last year, with half the work and, if you remember, I said already we made a good living!'

'Why did you lose your first assignment?'

'Russians are a law unto themselves!'

'What do you mean, exactly?'

'They had us charging around all over the globe looking for

very special ships, which we found – did sea-worthiness trials on some of them too. Big consignment of thousands of tons of cargo to be exported on arrival in Oporto to Cape Town, Akaba, Panama – all to leave at exactly the same time on the same day, which was to be advised later. It was all set up, then it was cancelled.'

'What a shame for you. Did they pay your expenses?'

'They paid expenses plus ten per cent so that was not so bad, but, after all the trouble, they pulled their schedule forward; because of the complicated rail services across Europe they had to change the port for export.'

'Poor you. Which port are they going to use? Can't you get your ships to it?'

'Very logical of you. No, we couldn't use our ships. We were all deep-draft vessels and they claim they wanted shallow draft. It seems the trains bringing the freight to Coruña had its schedule cut by two weeks, so my guess is it will be some of the small harbours around the Cherbourg peninsula. It's only a guess, but there were so many phone calls, faxes and e-mails, I doubt if they know themselves. Too many chiefs and not enough Indians syndrome, it seemed to me!'

'Sounds just like the company I work for; they really do drive me mad as well!' Maria interjected.

'I tell you what, Maria, why don't we have dinner tonight? A quiet dinner and we can pull your company to pieces. I can cry in my beer a little and tell you what a really hard upbringing I had in Russia!'

'Are you Russian?'

'Yes, by birth and upbringing. I left when I was twenty the first time, then went back after two years. Why, where did you think I came from, Mars?' Pedro's light, infectious laugh broke out, reflecting his naturalness and the happiness he found in her company.

'I thought you were one of our Brits!'

'That's what I sell, but it's not quite true. Maybe when we meet tonight, we can talk some more. I feel I've said enough already and it's time I try to find my office and at least say "hello" to it.' Again, his even more relaxed laughter bonded them together.

'See you tonight at eight then, Pedro.' She offered her hand which he took and kissed lightly.

On entering her room, Maria leant back against the door. Her body surged with excitement. She recounted her luck that she had found out valuable information for her dear Manuel. Allowing a smile to cross her radiant face, she whispered cheekily to herself, 'You wait until I get home, Manuel Vargas... all of this excitement is going to cost you dearly!'

Shaking her head to bring her back from her thoughts, she kissed the air. 'Just one for now, Manuel.' Softly, the words crept out from her moist lips. 'Now to report to you officially!' The phone placed by the window got nearer as she paced across the room towards destiny. The touch keypad swiftly responded to her fingers, one ring and his voice was there. Her Manuel would be so pleased with her... she would be efficient, concise with her report. The words tumbled out of her ruby lips, 'I love you so much, Manuel!' Her voice faltered whilst her brain caught up. 'I do... I've said it. Now, officially, from the import/export company, I heard less than ten minutes ago that a change of plan forces the cargo they thought was going to leave from Oporto – something to do with draughts of ships – will now be shifted to Cher—'

Maria never saw the hole in the glass, nor felt the bullet enter her forehead. Nobody heard the 'phuut' of the silenced rifle shot.

'Maria! Maria!' The voice of Manuel bellowed down the phone. 'Maria! Please speak, please!' He sat still as if frozen. He knew Maria was dead. His fingers pushed down the button to get another line and dialled the 'taxi-driver's' direct line.

★

The short phone call Yute had made to Nikolai Curentov had brought back many memories. He had been a dashing young captain when Yute joined his company of cavalry all those years ago. An excellent officer, but he would not move with the times, wishing to stay with the old traditions of soldiering, as his father and grandfather before him had done, back in the past – the dark days of the last Tsar. Yute felt sorry for Nikolai now. He knew from the moment they had met that Nikolai would not survive in the new Russian Army and in their private talks had often suggested his friend should leave the military as it would be impossible for him to get any advancement – even if he deserved it, it would not come. After many years of being passed over for promotion, Nikolai resigned his commission and joined the thousands of other civil servants in the Kremlin. Nikolai was, by then, very discontent at having left the army and became a bit of a rebel. Drank too much, arrived late for work, but then he met Natasha and it was she who changed him back to being a more reasonable human being again.

Nikolai had been happy in his little office in the Kremlin for many years now, swearing that Yute had given him the best possible advice all those years ago, and his beautiful Natasha had made his life rich and contented. In his twilight years, Nikolai had jumped at the offer of a little subterfuge on Yute's behalf.

Yute had arranged to meet at the Officers' Club. Nikolai liked to go there and Yute thought that to meet in an obvious place would be less suspicious than trying to find a corner to skulk into. Wasn't he still a serving Russian officer and wasn't it common knowledge that Nikolai Curentov was a friend of his from all those years ago? Wasn't Nikolai that poor flat man who worked somewhere in the Kremlin and who was of no consequence to anyone? Yute saw his friend walking upright – his military bearing had not disappeared over the years, except that the use of a walking stick had become necessary. Raising himself from the well-upholstered leather chair, he smiled at the beaming, friendly face coming towards him, his hand extended, waiting for his friend's grasp, the squeeze, the forthright stare into each other's eyes, the bear hug and heavy slap on each other's back.

Standing back from each other, Nikolai was the first to speak. 'All of the wear and tear you have been through over the years hasn't told on you very much, Yute!'

'The wrapping, my old friend, still looks good on the outside, but sometimes it takes a while in the morning to get the engine started.'

'The same here; this bloody stick started out as an affectation, but now it's a necessity!'

'You look well, Nikolai. A little less colour than in the old days, but you've got an inside job now!'

'You don't have to remind me of that, but I will say thanks to you, I have a full life now, not too much pressure, regular hours, home each evening to my vodka before my home-cooked dinner and my beautiful wife… all is content with me now.'

'Even with me coming back into your life?'

'A little excitement does an old man good!'

'I must say I'm pleased you're at the Kremlin, but exciting?'

'The fear of someone just coming and taking me away at any moment, the stealth and silence with which they will arrive if I get discovered, the challenge of my getting the information you want from a system which never sleeps – all of these things, my dear Yute, contribute to one thing for me – excitement!'

'You're still a romantic, even though a system which would never let you rise in its military and because of your education, could only find you an office job of little significance. You must feel you are worthy of better things?'

'Not really, I've liaised with all ranks in the military and political echelons, putting the schemes their conniving little minds dream up, down on paper for them before they run off to get permission to put their little plan into action. A lot of plans don't get through because of me; perhaps I express myself too dynamically on the poor little fools' behalf! Now and again one gets through something to help Mother Russia. Unfortunately, there are not enough of these schemes, and like your plan, Yute, most of them will do her great harm!'

'That is not true, Nikolai.' Yute knew his friend was right. The original plan was designed to get American dollars flowing through the Russian economy. Yute knew he had set in his mind his own advancement with complementary rewards, but wasn't the original idea of dollars flowing through Russia's economy still in place?

'You know it's true, Yute. Why defend your position with such a weak defence? I don't blame you for your greed, but I can only see failure.'

'Explain yourself, please.'

'It is very apparent to me that many unexpected facets have appeared over the past weeks which are upsetting your operation. It seems to me there are three principal players pushing lorries and trains around Russia, but each one of you is issuing different orders, which makes for very untidy management of what was supposed to be basically a very simple organisation.'

'You are quite right, of course, Nikolai. The reason I asked you to come here is exactly that. I want you to get me proof that Gregori Alexei Androv is my adversary.

The surprise on hearing Androv's name could not be more obvious from the expression on Nikolai's face. 'But he's thought to be dead!'

'Have you any proof you can offer me, Nikolai?'

'No, none. The story is in the corridors of whispers that he, like so many others before him, just disappeared in the night.'

'He planned his disappearance. I have confirmation of his being in Portugal only last week. What position does Boris Parentov have in all this?'

Nikolai managed to hide his surprise on hearing that name and he calmly replied, 'The poofter banker's son has always been a mystery to me. It seems absurd he would be a big enough fish to fit in with the enormity of your overall plan! He has no basic skills, he could not control a platoon of men when he was a serving officer.'

'What was he good at?'

'Fiddling the mess funds, money-lending. With him, it was always money, always money!'

'Do you think that Boris, with his father's bank as backing, would be enough to finance this whole operation?'

'No, would be my immediate reaction. The bank is secure, but it has never ventured into the real world, speculated or invested… the sort of things without which there is no way the bank would have built any reserves; it takes years and years!'

Yute watched his friend's face, expecting him to carry on speaking for a few more seconds, but now it was Yute's turn to be surprised. A moment passed, with each of them expecting the other to speak. Yute leant forward in his chair, and taking

Nikolai's hands in his own, he said, 'My very dear friend. I respect your judgements greatly, as you know. What answer would you give if I asked you this? Could Parentov have been placed to handle the Organisatiya's money?'

Yute saw the sweat break out on Nikolai's forehead, then felt the tightening of his grip around his own hands. The words tumbled from Nikolai's mouth. 'Do you think it's a serious possibility?'

'I don't know for sure, but it would give Parentov limitless resources and power!'

'And certain death if he fails!'

'Damage to Russia would be the biggest disaster. The economy would never survive. The "management" would be looking for new reserves of money to replace their losses.'

There was a moment of silence before Nikolai continued, 'Yute, the Russian people need to have a voice. With Glasnost, they have a chance, but they need help from strong men like you. It's a duty you must fulfil. They need honest leaders, fair in judgement, open-hearted.' Nikolai's hands gently wrapped around Yute's hands in friendship before he continued to speak. 'I will find out all I can for you and despatch my findings as instructed. I just hope you remember the Russian people. I must leave now, we have been together too long and if we have been seen, we have probably shown a little too much friendship.'

'My friend, I will remember your words. Any information you can get for me is urgent, and I need confirmation, not rumour.'

'I will do my best, my dear friend. Goodbye.'

Yute watched as his military friend walked stiffly away, aided by his walking stick.

Pedro Matros's mutilated body lay in the morgue in the Coroner's office in Lamego. Chief Inspector Manuel Vargas stood staring down at the rag doll effect of the partially severed hands, which had been expertly cut, leaving them dangling on sinew and skin alone. Pedro had suffered very little; although his body was cut from head to toe, most of the wounds had been inflicted after death.

Police Captain Juan Pirez had never seen anything like it.

Although his view of the body was partially obscured by Manuel Vargas, he sensed the evil which must be within the being who perpetrated such a dire act on another human being.

'You are sure this is the man who was in your taxi with Captain Tias?'

'Yes, sir. The flashy gold watch, the initials on his shirt pocket, the crocodile shoes. I'm sure if we reconstructed his face, it is Pedro Matros.'

'You're sure?'

'Yes, sir, positive!'

'Why was he murdered, and why like this?'

'My theory is he was seen with Maria Tias and someone got wise to him… his partner, for instance! When his partner tackled our Pedro here, there was a falling out. Pedro may have hinted he thought Maria was an undercover agent, or it may have been the partner had suspicions… either way, Pedro was silenced and dumped in the woods where we found his body. Captain Tias was silenced because the partner didn't have enough time to pussy-foot around to see if Pedro had given anything of importance away to her!'

'My views exactly. Where is this partner now?'

'On the river, on his way out to sea.'

'Is that corroborated?'

'Yes, sir. We are following discreetly by air and a reception committee is waiting.'

'Get him, Captain. I want this man. I have a personal score to settle with him on behalf of one of my officers!' Vargas turned away from the body with his back to Captain Pirez. The stern expression on his face softened as the single tear ran down his cheek. The silence in the morgue was oppressive until Vargas's voice cut into the vacuum. 'Captain Pirez, he will not get away with it. He will be caught. I know he has killed his own partner… I know thieves fall out, but to kill my beautiful Captain Maria Lopez Tias… Pirez, he will be caught alive. I want this cold, murdering bastard to suffer. Do you understand me, Pirez?'

Pirez's startled reply was a firm, 'Yes, sir.'

Vargas acknowledged the reply with a nod of his head, leaving Captain Pirez with an enormous task. Vargas resolved that the

441

information about Matros and his beloved Maria must be passed on to Ernst in Hamburg immediately, then he would go to church and pray for the Lord to accept Maria into Heaven even though he selfishly had never made an honest woman of her.

Ernst felt pity in his heart on hearing the cold, unemotional voice of Manuel Vargas relating the details of losing a police officer, but the moment he put the phone down, Ernst, nevertheless, dialled Robin's direct line. 'Cadwallader,' came the sharp announcement in Ernst's ear.

'Robin, it's Ernst. I have just had Vargas on the phone. He has reported the finding of the mutilated body of one of the Russians they were watching and Maria Tias, his *aide-de-camp*, has been killed by a sniper's bullet.'

'My God!' was Robin's shocked response.

Ernst continued, 'It is terribly sad, but she did find out that this Pedro Matros and his partner had lost the contract. She was on the phone to Vargas when she was shot, but she has corroborated that the draught of the ships procured for the operation were too deep for the new venue. She was saying "Cher—" when she was shot, which I am assuming to be Cherbourg.' Ernst waited for Robin's response.

'It brings it into a more controllable area, Ernst. I never liked having to deploy our men to Spain and Portugal. It will tighten up our lines of communication.'

'You're right, of course, but we still don't know whereabouts exactly, the Cherbourg peninsula is a large area to cover if you ignore the town's name!'

'Yes, I know, but I do feel a little less exposed to the threat, the closer it comes to northern Europe.'

'Yes quite, but our "snake" is only just in Moscow by now. Maybe when it gets to the borders we will be able to determine where it is really going.'

'Perhaps, if we could corroborate the manifest we could attack it in Moscow, Ernst!'

Ernst sucked in his breath at that thought and his immediate feeling was, 'What if?'. His thoughts quickly focused and he replied, 'Robin, it's a great idea, but who the hell would you trust to coordinate any such adventure?'

'I was hoping it could be you? With such close borders and the wall coming down, it would have given you some heavyweight, honest Russian policemen who could authorise a cross-border action?'

'No such luck, Robin. Lots of groundwork policemen, but no real commanding generals, I'm afraid!'

Robin's reply sounded very dejected when it very slowly came. 'Ernst, it seems to me only right that if it's a Russian train, moving towards northern Europe, which both you and I personally feel, it should be stopped on Russian soil, letting Russia take the financial loss and damage which will be caused.'

'Agreed, Robin, but we haven't got that kind of liaison with our Russians.'

'Well, we will just have to carry on as we are, Ernst, and bite the bullet a while longer.'

'You're right, Robin. Sad but true. I'll speak to Joc in the meantime and see if he can come up with a connection for us... but...' Ernst never finished his sentence, and cut back into his own conversation with, 'Will you excuse me, Robin, Mayer is coming into my office and it seems there is a panic. I'll phone you back.' There was a light click as Ernst put down the phone.

Chapter Thirty-Five

Robin sat thinking about his spontaneous remark. Perhaps if we could corroborate its manifest we could attack it in Moscow. He sat mulling over the idea. It would save thousands of man-hours shadowing the slow and dangerous train which could possibly explode at any time. Why should this almost certainly perilous load be allowed into Western Europe... her seaports, endangering innocent lives? Robin grabbed at the phone, punched in the numbers, one ring, two...

'Roche here.'

'Sir. Sorry to bother you, but it's necessary. Our train is approaching Moscow terminal. We are certain it's coming our way, possibly to somewhere on the Cherbourg peninsula. Our latest direct report from Russia is that it will be taking on more cargo and circumnavigating the yards over three days. We ought to take the "snake" out there!'

'You must be mad, Robin!'

'No, sir, not mad, bloody afraid of the consequences if this train runs its course!' Robin paused for effect then continued with less pace in his voice. 'Sir, I know it's going to be a political decision. Our General was in Berlin as a staff officer in the British zone; he must know someone he could trust to act against these criminals and murderers.'

'Robin, calm yourself. Your idea is very worthy of you, but the Corps are not policemen. Our aim is to be a spearhead force, quelling possible disturbances throughout the world.'

'I know that, sir, but prevention is better than cure. The world will need a lot of curing if what we are all guessing really is the true cargo on board our "snake".'

'You feel strongly about this, don't you, Robin? I'll try and bring it up casually when I next see the General.'

'The time is now, sir. Our information gives us a three-day window at most.' The cold pleading in Robin's voice prevented the Adjutant from calling him an audacious son of a bitch. His reply came softly to Robin's ears.

'I'll see the General as soon as possible, Robin. You had better make yourself available at all times for a meeting.' The phone went dead.

Robin felt happier now, although again, it seemed he was putting his friend in a very difficult situation. Robin's phone rang. He answered swiftly, 'Cadwallader.'

'Ernst here. Mayer's conversation with Rudi confirms the "snake" will enter Moscow's marshalling yards tomorrow and be under supervision from each and every one of their yard officers who have all been put on forty-eight-hour standby for the next week. Stories abound around the rail yards; some people are saying this one train is causing more headaches than anything handled during World War Two!' After Ernst had finished and having expected a spontaneous reply, he added, 'I'm pleased my news has got you so excited, Robin.'

'I'm sorry, Ernst. I've put the cat amongst the pigeons again. I've just told my Adjutant to speak to the General, who was stationed in Berlin for a long time, and find out if he has anyone he knows who would help us… I also said now would be better than tomorrow!'

'My God, Robin, but sometimes a good idea can only be put into practice by stating the facts along with your honest opinion.'

'I hope you're right, Ernst. Again, I've stretched my Adjutant's good will to the limit. He knows there is no chance to obtain political approval and I have taken the liberty of suggesting our General may have an old buddy in high places who can be trusted and believes in what we believe in.'

'Moscow would be the best place to stop the monster. It would be great, it would send shock waves throughout the criminal communities of the world that Europe will not put up with their violations. God, what a message it would send out, Robin! What a wonderful message!'

'Ernst, don't hold your breath. It's a chance possibly, but no more as yet. Besides, there is no army in the world who would know how to tie up the kind of paperwork a jamboree like this would cause. Permission would have to be granted to you at least, possibly Joc and Joe, Manuel, Gilbert... it has been a united European operation so far, so why not bring all concerned in?'

'Don't forget Rudi, Mayer and Dimitri!'

'You're right, Ernst. The more the merrier!' Jokingly, Robin added, 'I'll just have to tell mon General!'

'Rather you than me, Robin. Call me with any news?'

'For sure, Ernst... even bad news!'

Both of them gave a little chuckle at the end of their childish conversation. They both knew the consequences if the 'snake' disappeared across Europe, and that Moscow was the obvious place for the intercept. Quietly, almost with reverence, their phones were placed back in their cradles, ready for the next call. Instantly Robin's phone rang. There was a snatched announcement of 'Cadwallader here!' then silence. Robin's face tightened and his anxious reply automatically left his lips, 'Thank you. In fifteen minutes then, General!'

André Roche was waiting in the anteroom of the General's office as Robin entered.

'André... thank you for fixing this. I phoned your office and obviously I got no reply. I guessed you would be here... he gave me so little time.'

'Robin, calm yourself down. This meeting is important to you and the Corps. You must be concise in your proposal and everything must be unembellished – facts, facts and more facts!'

'We haven't got many of those, André, mostly theories!'

'Tell it just as you told me. I'm sure he will help where he can.'

'Hope so.'

The buzzer on the secretary's desk gave one note. Promptly, she rose from her seat, and moving towards the large door to the General's office, she said, 'The General will see you now. This way.'

As the door closed behind them the General did not move. He just sat, studying the many papers stacked up on his desk. Both men stood in silence, waiting for the General to speak.

'Major Cadwallader, don't you think we are getting too involved in civilian policing?' Robin was expecting a greeting for

André and himself, not a question requiring a careful answer.

'No, sir, I don't. We are certain this train is carrying arms and possibly nuclear warheads which are not civilian toys, sir!'

'Don't be facetious with me, Major!'

'Sir, that was not my intention. Will you accept that it was nerves, along with my apology?'

'Very well. We in the military have a duty to protect, I grant you, but our political masters weave a web of mystery around policies which we know very little about and to move without their permission would cause embarrassment.'

'I understand your dilemma very well, sir,' Robin said, then continued. 'The train – we call it the "snake" – is entering Moscow's goods yards. My question is, do you, having served on the four national zones in Berlin after the Second World War, know anyone in Russia senior enough and with the same belief in the world as everyone connected with this whole investigation? In four words, sir, "a crime-free world". A crime is being committed which Eurocorps has become very much involved in and I personally believe that, on the premise that prevention is better than cure, I must ask for your help again!'

'And if I did have such a man tucked up my sleeve, how would he be used?'

'He could have total control of the Russian operation but he would have to be monitored by us. We would have to synchronise collecting in all of our military "bad eggs" and our civilian police would want to be sure of collecting in everyone under surveillance.'

'If this could be arranged, who would you send to do this synchronisation?'

'The first man would be Ernst Ulbrecht, sir.'

'He could not manage on his own, it's too big a task!'

'Yes, you're right of course, sir. Breaking all bounds, sir, the whole of the international team, Ulbrecht, Latimer and Lomax from the USA, Torneau from France, Vargas from Portugal and may I offer myself as well, sir.' Robin added, 'We have all been working well together, sir!'

'Who would be left here in central Europe to clear up all of the villains?'

'Ulbrecht has a very trusted crew, as have all of the other European police forces. The Americans really have no use other than offering satellite facilities and access to vast computers. Obviously when we have gathered all our bandits, Latimer in particular will want to follow up anything that may cause harm to the USA.'

'You have a good case, Major. You will place yourself at my disposal for the next few hours. I will see what I can do... I don't promise anything. Have you got your translators sorted out. You will definitely need them!'

'Ulbrecht has a trained officer who has been on the case since it started, I have no Russian speakers on my staff. I will look into it further, sir.'

The General stood up, declaring the meeting over. Offering his hand to Robin, he said, 'I hope you get your wish. I will do what I can without causing an international incident. Thank goodness this is planned to work in Moscow. The distance gives us a chance of not being found out, plus the Russians, if they cooperate, will want a blackout from all the press and media.' The pause was long enough for the General to clear his throat then he added, 'My Russian is fluent, if it helps.' Before that fact could sink into either André or Robin's minds, they were outside the office in the anteroom.

André whispered to Robin, '"My Russian is fluent, if it helps!" The crafty old devil! He doesn't only want to control an army, he wants to be Mr Plod!' Neither of them could allow their laughter to spill over until they had walked down the steps leading from Headquarters. Saluting each other as they separated, the Adjutant commented, 'The old man is bloody marvellous, Robin. Whether he pulls it off or not, he's really got balls!'

'I'm glad it's his decision rather than mine, sir. I'd better get to an office where I can be found. With the pace the General moves, I could be wanted by now!'

Robin had sat in his office for an hour already, but nothing had been heard from the General. Strangely, no one had phoned. No one at all. As he realised this fact, a sense of panic possessed him. Surely he should be doing something – phone Ernst, Joc, someone, but who? The whole operation was waiting to be kick-started by him, as soon as his General gave the word. How could he handle the responsibility? It was Ernst's case really despite all of them who had helped so far. Was he going to be a political animal and have to turn on his friends if his Eurocorps General wanted the kudos for himself or his Corps! God, what a mess! I'm like a ping-pong ball being pushed from pillar to post. I won't let them push me into any situation without the team. It would end in disaster. There are too many elements to be controlled, for one man to do it. Besides, if our team was not complete, it could reflect badly on my General if I fail. The thought of possible failure jolted Robin back to the real world. He muttered to himself, 'Come on, General, come on. The whole team is ready now!'

Ernst was sitting impatiently at his desk. Mayer had just left him with the news that Rudi and Dimitri could now confirm that the whole of the 'snake' would be contained within Moscow's goods yard as from 1000 hours tomorrow morning. Ernst had automatically asked how long the 'snake' would stay there, but Mayer had told him Rudi had not been able to say for sure. The original three-day instruction for the train to be reassembled and cleared through the yards had not been changed. Ernst's impatience was warranted, but he knew Robin's would be more so. Ernst's hand went to the back of his head and gave it a long, hard rub.

Yute stood motionless watching the side door of the Kremlin, waiting for Rudi. Yute had made his decision; he was going to take full control of the 'snake' before very long and Rudi was the only one with any kind of accurate information on the 'snake's' whereabouts. Yute's own routing for the train had not been followed. He decided Rudi had better tell him that or he would lose his friend Dimitri.

Boris Parentov sat in an ornate chair, his hands tightened on the carved end of the armrests, his knuckles were white. Above him stood Androv. Gregori Alexei Androv, the man no one could find.

He was staring down into Boris's soul. The fear in Boris would not permit his body to move an inch. Gregori's words kept pumping into his brain. 'You will free the promised monies which have been made available to you into the Swiss bank accounts I have designated by tomorrow at noon. You will do nothing else. The train is totally under my control. Your efforts on my behalf will be rewarded when my transactions with my buyers are completed.' The pause gave no respite to Boris. The eyes staring down into his face, kept the fear of instant death permeating through his body. Even the feeble reply, 'Yes...' to Gregori's question was an assurance that he, Boris Parentov, the puffed-up popinjay, was totally under Gregori Alexei Androv's control.

The scene that greeted him came as a complete surprise. As Rudi entered his own room, there he was, Yute Polenkovich, sitting in his chair, with his face in shadow. But Rudi knew this visit would not be his death knell. He realised Yute needed information so his quick mind could unravel the 'snake's' journey before it got too far out of his control. Yute's calm voice spoke. 'You took a long time getting here. I saw you leave your office and yet I got here first and had to wait for you. You stopped and had a drink with your friend Dimitri, I suppose.'

'Not at all!' Rudi's throat was dry and his voice cracked a little.

'You don't need to be afraid of me, Rudi. You have information about the 'snake' as you call it. I want that information. You will tell me everything you know, every day, here and at the same time. Should you fail to do so, I will have to entertain your friend Dimitri. You understand what I mean?'

'Yes. I'm too valuable for you to "entertain" me, as you put it.'

'Very good, Rudi. You learn very quickly. Now what is the position?' The coldness in Yute's voice left no doubts in Rudi's mind that he was not dreaming this part of his life. His reply was almost spontaneous.

'The "snake" is entering the marshalling yards here in Moscow as we speak. We are sure that all of the "snake" as we know it, will be in the yard's handling by tomorrow. Huge numbers of staff have been taken on in the shunting yards. We are assuming the "snake" is being cut up and reformed. We hear grumbles from the railway staff that they are not to be allowed home for three days, when the task will be complete.'

'I want copies of the manifests now!'

'We have nothing. We ask, we even at one point said, "No manifest, no entry into the Moscow system," but it made no difference. We can do nothing to stop it.'

'You will know when it is reformed?'

'Not officially, I don't think. We will find out from gossip and our intuition – nothing official.'

'You will tell me everything, Rudi, everything you know!' The menace was back in Yute's voice.

'Do I have any alternative?' Rudi heard himself say in reply.

Yute rose silently from the chair like a panther and with the speed of light was standing in front of Rudi, nose to nose. Yute's snarling voice whispered, 'This time tomorrow, then!' And then he was gone.

The twenty minutes which Yute had to wait after leaving Rudi's apartment before he could contact Mogatin at the next prearranged box, were annoying, but in his mind, Yute knew Mogatin would not arrive early and stand around the box waiting. He would time it to the exact minute. It seemed like an age. Tick, tock, the second hand swept past the six on the dial of his watch. He snatched up the handset and dialled. Mogatin's voice was loud and clear and the recognition code between them was exchanged. Yute spoke first.

'It will be necessary for you to activate some of your sales staff. I think the Tomlevskis and Keller should be advised that there is a lot of work for them.'

'Can I give them an exact start date?'

'Not yet, motivation is what's called for!'

'Difficult without a start date, but I'll do my best. May I ask, are we going into Portugal again?'

'No, it seems our representative there has decided to go it alone. In fact, his partner has dropped completely out of the picture.'

'Shame. You will tell us in good time where you want the exchange made?'

'Yes, I feel it will be a big sales conference in Paris.'

'Fine. Dimitri will be around tomorrow.'

'Good. Until then, goodbye.'

The telephone was ringing in the empty underlit office of Hamburg's Police HQ. Rudi had tried the direct line for Mayer but had got no reply. Now, he waited. Surely someone must be there.' Another five rings and then I'll give up, his mind was saying to him as it had done for the last five rings as well as the five rings before that.

'Ulbrecht heir!'

Taken aback at the announcement in his ear, it took a few seconds before Rudi answered. 'Sir, it's Rudi. May I possibly speak to Mayer?'

'I will get her to the phone right away. Do you understand me?'

'Yes, I do a little, but better with Mayer.'

'Your number, Rudi?'

'Mayer knows. Please hurry!'

The phone went dead in Ernst's ear as Rudi hung up. The few minutes it took to locate Mayer seemed an age to Rudi as he waited in the shadows of the partially concealed telephone box at the railway station. The ringing sounded like music to him, snatching the phone before he answered, 'I love you! I love you!'

'Me too, Rudi, so much. I'm sorry you had trouble finding me, I was chatting to a girl friend in her office. I'm so sorry I wasn't there for your call.'

'That's all right, Mayer. I had a visit from Polenkovich tonight. He was right there in my flat! He has threatened to harm Dimitri if I don't get him a complete update of the "snake's" whereabouts and potential movement each day. He's going to come to my flat each day at 1900 hours. I now have two Russian bosses, one secretly telling me what is to be done, the other threateningly acquiring for himself the information he wants!'

'Then there is us. Ernst, Joc, Robin, et cetera, and me pestering you all the time!'

'Yes, Mayer, then there is all of you, but that is the nice side of the story for me. You are what I want, always!'

'I want you too, Rudi. It won't be long now. I feel something is going to happen very soon and we will be together always and always.'

'I want you so much, I want to see you every day. I want... Oh, Mayer, when will we be together? Polenkovich was in my flat threatening Dimitri's life unless I tell him everything about the train. It seems to me he is trying to either gain, or maybe regain control. I don't know how, but he is getting some information, plus he is aware of Dimitri and me, now. Androv is my guess as the one who is stealing the train from Polenkovich if that's the way it's happening, but with the information Yute is getting, there is someone else in the corridors, feeding out information. There must be, Mayer, how else is Polenkovich managing to claw his way through this quagmire of corruption?'

'There are probably quite a few others, Rudi, but until they come out of the woodwork, we must work with what we have. I'll tell Ernst about your theory that there is someone else; after all, two heads are better than one!'

'I feel it strongly, Mayer, there must be someone else!'

'I'm sure you are right, Rudi, but please don't worry, we will find them all this time.'

'I hope so, Mayer, I hope so...'

Rudi and Mayer talked a little longer, the whisperings of lovers, the dozens of 'I love yous', the thrown kisses reaching each other down the telephone line – the emotional turmoil which they had caused each other had now passed. Mayer was now striding towards Ernst's desk.

'You spoke to Rudi, Mayer?' Ernst enquired.

'Yes, sir,' the memory of the last 'I want you' still burning in her heart. Ernst waited patiently until Mayer came back from the dream world of lovers. The moments passed. 'Sorry, sir! I spoke to Rudi. He is being threatened by Yute Polenkovich. Polenkovich is saying that Rudi's friend, Dimitri, will be harmed if Rudi does not supply all the information he knows about the "snake". He thinks Polenkovich is trying to gain control over Androv if he is correct in thinking that Androv is the one leaving the instructions for him in the brown envelopes. But, Rudi also thinks Polenkovich must be getting information from another source in the Kremlin, but who, he has no idea. Rudi feels there is a race between at least three people, all wanting to get control of the "snake", all of whom seem to have the authority to get his information, but none of them actually is in control of the train! Rudi is following the instructions but is terribly worried about Dimitri!'

'I understand, Mayer. I feel it will not be too much longer before we have to take the head from the "snake". We will protect Rudi and Dimitri for you, I promise, but I'm afraid we will have to wait a little longer.'

Robin sat impatiently in his office, his whole being wishing the phone would ring. The time was dragging. Robin had started something with his General which must curtail him from talking to anyone. He must wait for the General's response. He must remain stagnant in this pool of sleaze which seemed to be oozing over Western Europe in the guise of a train. He must wait for what he hopes will be an opening, directly into Russia.

'Cadwallader here!' His usual reply was a little croaky.

'André, Robin. We need to meet now. The General has approved the scheme and has got someone in place for you! Shall we say five minutes? No telephones other than secure lines, I think.'

'Yes, André, and thanks. I'm on my way over!'

In his excitement, Robin did not hear André say, 'I'll see you in a few minutes then.'

The phone rang just once. Lanov gave his identity for that day and received the correct reply from Yute, then the unembellished message. 'Make the Tomlevskis and that Colonel active as from 0800 hours the day after tomorrow. All other potential clients will be activated twenty-four hours after that.'

'Are we in a rush or a panic?' Lanov's laconic question did not amuse.

'We are bringing our sales effort forward!'

'Everything else remains in place as organised, then?'

'Correct. Just an opportunity to increase sales figures in mid-term. It will benefit us all later in the year. Will speak to Mogatin as arranged.'

The phone went dead. Lanov felt there was a tinge of panic and uncertainty in Yute's voice. He must speak to Mogatin as soon as possible.

The Adjutant's door was wide open. The Adjutant sat listening to Robin's footsteps as he approached along the long corridor. When Robin came into view, André with just a little more voice, said, 'Come straight in, Robin.'

'Thank you, André. I wanted to run to get here quicker, but I thought better of it.'

'Never run blindly in, Robin!'

'That's a bit profound, André, even for you!'

'It's just a warning, Robin. We are rushing in, we are blind. Remember our eyes are a lovelorn junior official who is being manipulated by at least two people, his friend and a few people like the banker floating around the edges whose position or purpose we really can't clarify, and a maverick Staff Colonel. Our General has opened up a new area which is going to place you, Ernst and everyone from here to Timbuktu into great danger. On this flimsy evidence you are going into Russia?'

Robin was astonished by his Adjutant's news, but the stunning blow to Robin's system soon left him and he answered for the whole group. 'It is a risk all of the civilians are more than willing to take. With regard to myself, I have a duty to protect Europe.' Robin paused, then added, 'It doesn't worry me that this time our arms of protection are stretching into Russia itself. I rather like the idea of going out and slaying our enemies on their own ground!'

'With local permission granted.'

'Oh yes, André, we don't want a "political" situation to arise.'

'When you go into Russia, get it all done with no deaths caused, have written statements from all of the criminals owning up to the crime, all of the manifests confirming the cargo to be what we suspect it to be – arms, drugs, uranium, all of the monetary transactions corroborated. Anything less would be a political mess, but we would have beaten a very audacious plan, and sent out an enormous warning to all the criminal elements around the world, that we are not asleep!'

'We had better be right, Robin. I'm not going to envy your

trip. First you and your selected team will silently enter Berlin at twelve noon tomorrow. Room 124, Hotel Berlin, you will meet Asslomov. He will have two staff with him. Asslomov's identity will be verified with a photograph of Asslomov and our General together, with a message on the back from our General. Can you make this meeting with everyone tomorrow?'

'We have to, sir. It's imperative!'

'Then I'll confirm it, Robin. You had best get on. You have a lot to do.'

'Yes, sir. Thank you and thank the General for me?'

'You can thank us when you come back successfully. In fact the General could be thanking you with all the glory you could bring his Corps if you are successful!'

'Not necessary, sir. It's just a job of work, really.'

With that last remark, he left without saluting or a goodbye, his thoughts locked onto the adventure ahead.

Robin knew now that his General had done a fine job with the initial introduction to this Russian, Asslomov, but what if German, American, French, in fact all of the politicians forbid their respective crime officers to participate?

'Christ!' Robin shouted as he entered his office. 'I'd be on my own. I'd have to do it, it would make the General bloody mad if I didn't!' The sudden shock of his realisations stole his happiness. His fingers moved like lightning across the phone keypad. He didn't hear the phone ring, just the 'Ulbrecht heir!'

'Ernst, Robin. Can you be in Berlin tomorrow at noon to meet someone?'

Ernst was a little taken aback, but agreed before asking, 'Who are we meeting?'

'It's a surprise, Ernst. It would be nice if we could have all the family there... everyone.'

Ernst realised Robin was speaking on an open line and could say no more. He asked, 'Does the invitation include Rudi?'

'I would think not, bearing in mind his family may not approve and could cause him problems later!'

Ernst thought for a moment, before coming to the conclusion that Robin's use of the words 'his family' must mean another Russian, then he quickly realised Robin was trying to give Rudi some protection until an accurate assessment had been made. 'I think you're right, Robin.' Then he added, 'With all of us away, someone has to mind the shop.'

'Absolutely, Ernst. Will you contact Joc and Joe and Manuel? I'll do the rest of them. I don't think initially that we will need secretaries, just heads of departments.'

'Yes, I think that will be enough of an exodus from the team at this point. You will be sending me a schedule?'

'Yes, and will you confirm your personnel?'

'In minutes, I hope.'

'Thanks. Until then, Ernst.'

The sight of Lanov and Mogatin in the rear-view mirror sent a chill down Daniel's spine. He forced the words out of the side of his mouth; they were barely heard. 'They are back and this time it looks urgent.' He reached across for Nicole's trembling hand to caress it and give her courage for what he was sure in his mind would be the last ordeal inflicted on them by these terrible men. Her hand had given him strength too and he opened his door before Lanov and Mogatin reached the car. His expression was flat, but defiance was in his heart.

The arrangements made and movement orders circulated by fax, Robin had only one thing to do prior to his leaving. The day so far had been hectic, to say the least. The worst decision was having to leave all of his team behind, with the news that Lanov and Mogatin had contacted the Tomlevskis and two other contacts had reached Colonel Keller. When he knew what facility Asslomov would be extending, that would be the time to draw in his troops and, hopefully, the men they were watching, along with them. Only then would he have the luxury of calling his own troops to him, wherever he might be. His hand lifted the phone, the direct line of his Adjutant was swiftly answered. Robin spoke as soon as the handset was lifted. 'Sir, everything is set. I'm off now, Sergeant MacKenzie will hold up this end and should be your contact point.'

'Well done, Robin. Have a good trip.'

'I'm sure I will, sir. By the way, I owe you a salute!'

Robin's group had all filtered into Berlin unnoticed. As hoped, all of them had arrived on time and had mustered in Robin's room at the Hotel Berlin. The courtesies were brief as it was 1130 hours and to be late for Asslomov could be held against them if he was so inclined. Robin had suggested that Ernst should be the spokesman for the group. Ernst was very moved to be chosen by everyone. Ernst made a little speech rejecting the offer.

'My reason for not accepting the responsibility is simple. It is obvious to me that the outcome of this meeting with Asslomov is highly critical and since Asslomov has a military background, I think we need someone from the military as our spokesman, so I feel Robin is the natural choice. It isn't a matter of seniority or the fact that it was originally my case. We are all working for the same thing – to rid Europe of the incessant threats from the East.' The whole group agreed Ernst was more than likely correct in his analysis and Robin insisted nothing would change in their working arrangements, and confirmed his acceptance of the post.

The identification and introductions were soon over in Room 124. Patiently, Robin introduced Ernst, Joc, Joe, Manuel, Gilbert and Katerina Mayer. Robin had given Asslomov a very brief verbal résumé of each person as they were introduced. Asslomov's alert eyes acknowledged each of them as he shook their hands, his eyes boring into each of them as they stood in front of his erect, well-honed body.

'My name, as you know, is Asslomov, Josef Asslomov, ex-Marshall of the Russian Army, turned diplomat because my view with military policy and its very corrupt and disloyal senior staff officers who totally lost control against the known Organisatiya regime which had been kept reasonably under control until Perestroika. Since the sacking of the Czar, the military has always had officers placed in positions of power by some friendly ministry in Moscow; these were not career soldiers who believed in the preservation of Russia and its people, but were scavengers working for some corrupt official in Moscow… many cases were proven against the corruption which was creeping into the system.

We managed to keep the theft of the military weapons and vehicles down to a reasonable level, never quite stamping it out altogether. From what I have heard so far, your case may be the *coup de grace* for what I and my friends see as the thorn in the side of the West which stops Russians walking proudly into a world of opportunity.'

The emotion in Asslomov's voice left them with no doubt. If there was any justice for the Russian people, and provided he believed their story, he would move heaven and earth to help them. Robin thanked Asslomov for being so open about his beliefs and assured him that everyone in the room shared his views about their own countries and saw the problem from the East as a global one. The niceties over, and now they were all working to the same end, Asslomov asked Robin directly, 'What do you know and what do you expect of me?'

'We are convinced a gigantic freight train is coming west from Vladivostok, collecting weapons, drugs, uranium possibly. We know the cargo it carries is well guarded and that it has at least two people vying for control of the train. We think one escape route will be via Cherbourg, depending on which of the protagonists wins the battle for the train. This same group have infiltrated Eurocorps. We feel all the connections Yute Polenkovich's team has made outside Russia are covered by operatives sharing the responsibility in France, Germany, Portugal and USA, whom you see here. Our plan is not to wait for the train which we all refer to as the "snake" to cross the borders out of Russia, but with support from whomever it takes, to strike where we feel an attack would be least expected and thereby cut down the risk of uranium leakage across Europe.'

'You have an awful lot of "ifs" in your plan... where is your proof that this wild scheme is actually happening at all?'

Robin could hardly contain his agitation. 'Sir, we would not jeopardise our jobs on a whim. We know we have no manifest for the cargo on board, we know the train exists, we know and can prove the activating of what your KGB used to call "sleepers" across military, and in some cases, civilian establishments throughout Europe. We know of at least five murders and can corroborate two factions of known Organisatiya in conflict trying to gain control of the train; there is a possible third faction also trying. They are all Russian and your problem is a Russian one, so why not let it be sorted out in Russia by Russians!'

Asslomov thumped his fist down on the desk. 'Who are these Russians – I want names!'

Robin held his ground and stared back into Asslomov's face. 'Yute Polenkovich, Marshall of the Russian Army, and Gregori Alexei Androv, ex-military and now a heavy player in the corridors of power. He was recently believed dead, but is very much alive. Boris Parentov, a military reject, through his father's bank and a free Russian enterprise system – he is moving letters of credit around as if he owned a post office!'

'You are absolutely sure of the names?'

'Yes. We have lots of photos to prove their identities also.'

'With you?'

'Of course!' No sooner were the words out of his mouth, than Ernst placed a file of photographs into Robin's hands. Robin acknowledged Ernst's quick reaction in providing the photograph file with a wry smile. Asslomov snatched the file and quickly flicked through the pictures, his eyes absorbing every detail.

Closing the file slowly, he stood up from his chair, pulled himself to his full height, then one hand passed across his mouth and chin, giving the chin a little rub before he spoke, 'Polenkovich, Androv, Parentov. There must be others… Lanov, Mogatin perhaps. Tashimov is long gone, killed in Hamburg I believe, Inspector Ulbrecht. Baldin and Lechenkov also met their end there, I believe.' The pause was brief, but with a dramatic change in his voice, he continued, 'Unsavoury people, all of them, and many more are hiding away in the corridors of power. It is only when they poke their heads up – like your "snake" I suppose – that we get the opportunity to cut it off! Well, gentlemen, and lady, we must now get to work on our task!'

There was a huge sigh of relief from everyone in the room and a few spontaneous whistles and a spattering of hand claps. Robin was the first to regain his composure and thanked Asslomov with great reverence and sincerity. As the words came tumbling out, the whole gathering broke out into a gaggle of excitement and relief.

Later, Ernst and Robin sat opposite each other at dinner. Both men looked very content, but the stress of the day, along with meeting all of the Russian controllers, organised by Asslomov, the discussion and the planning, and the talking and more talking, showed in their faces.

Mayer seemed to be holding ten conversations at once in Russian, German and English. She must be exhausted, Ernst thought, his eyelids falling fast, stopping the glare from the overlit room entering his eyes any more.

'I'll just rest my eyes a moment, Robin,' he muttered. Robin did not hear his friend.

Chapter Thirty-Six

Asslomov liked all of the people he had met, the only doubt in his mind was the Portuguese peacock. Having left the group, he took the lift two floors up to Room 324 where his own travelling communications unit and personnel were waiting to be brought to life. Each one of his staff welcomed him with anticipation of another assignment to intrigue them. Asslomov sat heavily behind his desk and called for his senior staff to circle around him for a briefing. He related the story he had been told only a few moments ago and of his decision to help.

'Gentlemen, we go to war! We are going to cut off, in a literal sense, the head of a snake!' His wry smile spread across his face and then he continued more seriously. 'Within the next twelve hours, we must have my brigade of soldiers, transports, communications, and my specialist group placed, unnoticed, into Moscow's railway yards.'

The jaws of the people around him dropped. They had heard a lot of impossible things from their boss, but what was his reason for the short timescale and, once they got there, what was the assignment? Asslomov sat patiently answering each and every question, building the belief that his plan was going to work, and work on time. Questions over, the meeting was about to break up when Asslomov calmly added, 'We will also have a party of civilian police from Germany, France, Portugal and America plus a British military policeman.

One of his staff nonchalantly asked, 'Are they going to make their own way there and what is their purpose?'

Asslomov answered swiftly, 'They will come in with us, under control of the Brit. They have all done a lot of work investigating all over Europe and they have proved to me that the principal rogues are known to be in Moscow. They want them for crimes perpetrated in their countries, plus they believe the train to be full of arms, nuclear weapons and drugs, so they and I would much rather stop the train in the Moscow railroad network!'

'What are your personal views, sir?'

'These people who are obviously in positions of power are robbing Russia of her resources and her honour by constantly stealing from her larder. The men from the West do not want these things in their backyards. They want nothing else than to have the train stopped and the freedom to pursue the perpetrators in the confines of the rail yards.'

'Are we guaranteeing their safety, sir?'

'If we can help, we will. We have an interest... Yute Polenkovich and Gregori Alexei Androv along with that weasel Parentov, all of whom we have our own scores to settle with from Afghanistan!'

'When we brief the men, sir, do we mention these shitheads as an incentive?'

'If you feel it would help, but don't forget the prime objective is to stop and immobilise the train.'

'I think it will help, sir. We still have enough old soldiers who remember being cut off with no air support because those bastards had spent the petrol money!'

'It was a lot deeper than that, Captain, but we get your drift, I'm sure.'

'I have called for all maps and plans of the rail yards including all the "ins" and "outs" within a twelve-mile radius and they will be arriving any minute. Will you be attending our planning meeting, sir?'

'No, but I shall want to approve them... plus it's important our civilians know exactly what we are doing at all times.'

'We will be ready for them in about an hour. Will you advise them we will be in conference room number one on the ground floor. It's not totally secure as a venue, but if we rotate the staff, we feel we can keep prying eyes and ears away until we get out of Berlin and back to our own pitch.'

'Well done, Captain. We will all be with you in an hour then.'

'We will be ready, sir. You might like to tell your civilians that we will be leaving for Moscow within an hour of your approval of the plans, sir.' The Captain noticed the raised eyebrow at the speed in which he had anticipated his boss's moves. As he stood to attention and saluted Asslomov, he cheekily added, 'After all, sir, we do have a train to catch!'

Mayer had not been able to contact Rudi prior to leaving Hamburg but her friend and mentor, Willi Koslowski, had promised to listen out for Rudi's call and let her know if there were any messages. Willi had been waiting the better part of the day but to no avail. He put down the phone after checking around the department in case Rudi had phoned and he had not been told. 'Nothing,' Willi whispered to himself, then he mumbled, 'Some people have all the luck, dining in Berlin, paid for by the department... luxury hotels... frothy glasses full of Berlin beer... Eisebein Berliner!' With the taste of Berlin still on his lips, he picked up the phone on its second ring.

'Koslowski!'

Rudi's quiet voice asked for Mayer.

'Rudi, is that you?'

'Yes. Mayer please... I'm in a call box.'

'She isn't here, Rudi. She left a message that she loves you very, very much. She is in Berlin and if you leave a message with me, she will phone you back within minutes of me getting the message to her.'

'Why can't I phone her direct?'

'Ernst and everyone are worried about security. There is something going to happen very soon.'

'What?'

'I don't know really, something about an "away fixture" getting mixed up. Evidently someone has mixed up the timetable, but everything is going to be all right. Will you give me your number?'

'Tell her it's the number she already has. I'll wait as long as I remain unnoticed. Should I be, I will be back here every half hour.'

'I understand. I'll start to find her now – it should only be a matter of minutes, Rudi. Be patient.'

Rudi stood in the box with the receiver held to his ear, his finger resting on the cradle. To him, it had seemed an age but it only took minutes for Koslowski to contact Mayer and a few more for her to excuse herself from Ernst and Robin.

'Rudi!' she almost shouted.

'Mayer!' he shouted back excitedly.

'I love you, Rudi, sorry to make you worry; we have a little hold-up here in the schedule, but everything is going fine for us. In an hour or so the schedule will be sorted out, I'm sure.'

'I hope so, Mayer, I had another visit from the other team today. They are in a very strong position, it seems. In fact, there was no request through the usual brown envelope last night. Dimitri feels the teams have been playing too many games and, without the right training, are losing their grip in the league!'

'Well, I hope they have a good enough team to give us a good game when we arrive – after all, we have been planning this for over six months now. They have an evil reputation in the league.

'Very true, Mayer. I'm sure they will give you a good game.'

'I'll invite you and Dimitri to the first match, when I arrive. When can you perhaps give me an update on how the teams are playing?'

'For sure, Mayer. Anything for you. Everything you want to know!'

'Thank you, Rudi; soon then. I love you!'

'Me too. Keep getting that ball in the basket!'

'I will, Rudi, I will, I promise you.'

Mayer placed the receiver down gently. She had had no embarrassment about declaring her love openly, overheard by Robin and Ernst, but the plan of trying to hide the true nature of the call in a basketball disguise in case any lines had been tapped had caused her a little hesitancy in her conversation. Both men felt that, as usual, Mayer had performed her task well.

'It was a shame we couldn't get an exact position for the "snake", but at least we know it's still there and that there is some kind of discord in their ranks which could work in our favour,' Ernst remarked.

Robin responded, 'It would be great to get the manifest before we go in. Drugs and weapons can be handled, but if there really are potential bombs with supposed uranium and some bloody lunatic with a timing device… let's just say it would be nice to know which carriages to watch out for so we can run the other way!'

Both Ernst and Mayer were a little shocked by Robin's suggestion initially but when they noticed Robin's wide smile they realised it was his cranky British humour and eventually laughed along with him. The abrupt knock on the door quickly put an end to the laughter, however.

'Come in, it's open,' called Robin.

One of Asslomov's staff entered and stood to attention for a moment before he spoke. 'Sirs, and mademoiselle, Comrade Asslomov requests your team to join him in fifteen minutes in conference room one, please. Will you please be discreet about the way you enter the room. Thank you.'

Robin got up from his chair before answering. 'We will be there, thank you.' With a slight dip of his head in acknowledgement, Asslomov's orderly was gone.

The fifteen minutes passed quickly. After phoning Joc, Joe and the rest of the team, the three of them sat quietly with their thoughts. The ringing of the telephone startled them, but quickly gaining his momentum, Robin answered it. 'Hello…' He gave no name.

'Please, Mayer, please!'

Robin didn't answer but covered the mouthpiece and called to Mayer, 'It's for you, Mayer, I think it's Rudi.'

Mayer took the phone hurriedly from Robin. Ernst and Robin became very attentive, sitting on the edge of their seats listening to Mayer's conversation.

'This is Mayer, can I help you?'

'It's me, Rudi! I have just phoned Dimitri, who said the game would have to be played before the night after next. It is moving west at 2300 hours. I'm phoning you from the same phone box, so I must go now before I'm seen. I love you!' Before Mayer could respond, the phone went dead, Mayer stared anxiously into the mouthpiece of the telephone… Did he hang up or was he cut off?

'Good news?' Ernst tentatively asked.

Pulling herself back from her anxiety, Mayer replied, 'Yes, sir, if knowing the "snake" is due to leave Moscow at 2300 hours the night after next is good news.'

'Well, at least we know when our deadline is. Let's inform

Asslomov when we get downstairs. We ought to leave now or we will be late for our meeting!'

As each member of the team entered the conference room, they were amazed at the hive of industry going on. There were huge maps of Russia on the walls and in particular, a countrywide plan of Russia's railway system plus a more detailed survey map of Moscow's railway infrastructure. A war room – a complete communications centre. Asslomov proudly moved towards Robin, Ernst and Mayer, welcoming them into his command post, his hand outstretched to grab Robin's hand first, pumping it like an excited schoolboy.

'Not bad, eh? Of course, I had to use your name, Ernst, to put this equipment in here. At first the management went mad when I started organising all this, but your fame has preceded you. Thank you! Now, all of your group has been introduced to my senior ranks and are already observing our planning and communication methods. Can I suggest for the next few minutes, you just mingle? In a few more minutes we should have our first proposals for you to scrutinise. Now, my Captain here will introduce you. If you'll excuse me for a short while?'

The introduction to the Captain never actually happened, there was a half-hearted hand gesture from Asslomov, then he was gone, fading into the morass of activity which seemed to be all around them.

Ernst said, 'Sorry, Robin, I didn't mean to get brownie points!'

'No, I'm pleased – you have won every brownie point with honour and I still feel you should be in charge anyway!'

'You will be better with all these soldiers than me – besides, our friend Asslomov here seems to like his own methods of working, as I do, and possibly the two of us would clash. You poor thing – as a soldier of lower rank you will have to knuckle under!'

Robin recognised Ernst's teasing and decided not to respond with a British quip, but he had secretly thought that Asslomov was well organised although a little of a prima donna in his attitude.

It seemed only minutes before Asslomov called the whole assembly to order. With a baton in his hand, he pointed to each and every part of the railway junction map, giving his opinions for the success of the operation and all salient information obtainable, including points which could possibly cause their failure. Overall, considering the short time factor, Asslomov's team had amassed a great deal of information and documentation. Asslomov stood in front of his audience, lightly tapping his baton into the palm of his left hand. The pregnant pause... Without consulting his own team, Robin said, 'Sir, your plans look very thorough and things look well covered from all aspects, except one.'

'Which is that... Robin?'

The way in which his name had been added almost as an afterthought seemed a little snide; a challenge even, but Robin held himself in control before replying, 'Well, sir, I am only guessing that the distances in the yards are vast, shall we say, even as much as ten kilometres?'

'A fair assumption, Major. Your point is?'

'The distance may not matter, sir, for catching trains, but we want the people! You see, sir, the acreage we would have to cover is far too great for our own manpower to cover. Would it be possible to build into your plan, once we know which lines are being taken by the "snake", that we can slowly send our own "snakes" in behind and in front of the "snake" so we can squeeze it into as small an area as possible?'

Asslomov coughed. 'Good point, Major. If you approve our initial plan, I'm sure we will have no problem in trying to accommodate your thoughts. Now, may I suggest in view of your latest information from Russia, our "snake" leaves the night after next!'

'Sir, may I ask when we can bring in our own teams?'

'All arranged – I assure you that you will have until tomorrow morning to submit your lists – you will make your own calls and give authority to your personnel. We have allotted in our planning that they will all come to Berlin as inconspicuously as possible by noon tomorrow. We will then have them for you to start work mid-afternoon, giving a possible thirty hours prior to the event for you to get organised.'

'Thank you, sir. You are suggesting Berlin Tergel as our departure point?'

'Correct, Major... our own transport leaves in two hours, so I feel we ought to get going.' No sooner were the words out of

Asslomov's mouth, than he was preoccupied with his team once more.

When he got back to his own room, Joc locked in with his boss at Langley and briefly outlined everything which had taken place over the last few days. His news was received as routine, but nonetheless the warning, 'You're on your own, Joc... you're on leave or something if things go wrong, and don't forget to tell Joe the same thing!' was made very clear. His boss did, however, finish by quietly adding, 'Good luck to both of you,' which he meant sincerely.

Ernst checked with Willi Koslowski in Hamburg and explained what he anticipated would be a rough chronology of events. Ernst's final words were, 'Keep alert, Willi. It looks as if none of the villains we have been looking for are in our territory, in fact the French and Russian police should be having a field day when we strike, but Lanov and Mogatin know Hamburg very well and they may decide to go to ground.' Willi asked if he could come on the jaunt but Ernst saw him as indispensable in running the operation from Berlin and that he, Arnie Zimmer and Jon Engelman be in Berlin before noon tomorrow. The 'good luck' Willi wished Ernst was meant with all heart but he could not hide the disappointment in his voice.

Vargas let his office know what his movements would be over the next few days and ordered Captain Pirez to join him via Tergel airport in Berlin as soon as possible. Now that his darling Maria Tias was no longer with him, he felt he needed someone who had been close to her in death – a romantic gesture but he must have someone, his rank demanded it!

Joc phoned Joe on the house phone and told him he had phoned in to Langley, given them an update and had logged a movement order for the next few days. He also mentioned the warning which had been meant for both of them. Joe gave his thanks for the message, then asked, 'What do you really think of this Asslomov, Joc?'

'What do you mean?'

'A bit of a prima donna, don't you think?'

'Yes I do, but he's certainly got this operation in good shape in a very short time.'

'Exactly my point, it's all come together too quick and too well!'

'Robin's boss put this guy in the picture – let's keep aware, but let's not rock the cradle.'

'Agreed, Joc.'

'Fine. See you downstairs.'

Mayer phoned Rudi in his office. 'I'll be with you, I will be able to see you, touch you, kiss you, make love to you!' was what she wanted to say, but instead, she said only, 'We'll be in Moscow, don't know where, later today. I will make contact.' The phone was placed silently back into its cradle and a solitary tear ran down her cheek.

Ernst dabbed the tear away with his handkerchief as he said, 'I'm sorry, Mayer, but you had to be ambiguous and keep the message short for security reasons.' Ernst pulled her head onto his shoulder for a second or two of comfort, but the tears in her heart didn't stop.

Lanov and Mogatin had visited Daniel and Nicole and had told them in no uncertain terms that they would become active very soon and should they fail in their task, woe betide them and their families – although neither Daniel nor Nicole had been given any actual duties to carry out. When they reported to Major Roche at Eurocorps, they had no doubt they would, without any contradiction, have a duty to fulfil. Lanov and Mogatin had proceeded over to Colmar to Colonel Keller's house and from observation, the Colonel was becoming very agitated with the lack of information he was being given, also with Lanov and Mogatin's lack of respect. It was felt by the surveillance teams when their daily analysis reports were collated, that the Colonel had lost heart for the game going on around him. His short-tempered attitude had now taken over from his 'hail fellow, well met' style from only a few short weeks ago, and was deteriorating into aggression day by day. Lanov and Mogatin, together or separately, had visited all of their victims. Now was the time all factors and personnel were in place, ready to spring into action. Now the waiting began…

Robin phoned André and gave a full report of the excellent contact which the General had made with the introduction of Asslomov. Robin told André that they were going on a journey rapidly and that there should be good news for him and the General very soon. André said 'thanks' on behalf of himself and the General and proceeded to tell him of Lanov and Mogatin's visits, adding, 'Don't worry too much, Robin. That ferret of a man MacKenzie seems very much in control. Should you want any strings pulled, I'm sure he would leave no loose ends!'

Robin thanked his Adjutant most sincerely, and the confidence that he had in his men, then said, 'André, thank you for being my friend!'

'The pleasure has been all mine. Now you had better get on and play soldiers!' The quiet respect they each felt for each other seemed to hang in the ether.

The rain fell heavily onto the ground, the night mist mixed with the spray from the wheels of the planes as they touched down, giving the impression of a magician's illusion as the grey cylinder floated across the airfield, suspended level and sleek, until the tail plane suddenly bit into the ground, raising the nose skyward. Silence. The spray finished, the illusion became reality as the activity of the ground crews emptied the passengers and cargo into waiting cars and lorries. The landing area which Asslomov had chosen was approximately fifteen kilometres north of Moscow's town centre but only six kilometres from the commencement of the in-runs of the railway network, and only eight kilometres away from the exit of this vast criss-crossing of rails to the west.

Ernst, Joc, Joe, Gilbert, Manuel and Robin had knitted well into a team and as Asslomov, along with his troops, would only be interested with the capture of the train, his men, although intelligent, hadn't the time to do the investigative work necessary in trying to capture Yute Polenkovich, Androv and Parentov along with anyone else which the investigation might draw into the frame. It was decided between them that as Ernst had the greatest interest in Polenkovich, with the outstanding murder in Hamburg, that he and his team should keep the villains under surveillance, with the added incentive agreed by Asslomov that if Polenkovich was captured, he could be whisked away immediately for trial in Germany. Robin, because of his military training, and the assumption that all armies have the same basic structure, should remain as coordinator with Asslomov and his network of investigators in the field in France and Germany. As the ringmaster, he was ideally placed to pull all of the strings together when the climax came. Joc, Joe, Gilbert and Manuel were to stay with the military, filtering all information from Asslomov and his men's infiltration of the train and the assessment of its cargo.

Yute Polenkovich waited patiently for Rudi to leave his office. He knew that today, or early tomorrow, the whole train would be stationary in the railway complex, but why? His plan was to pass his train as quickly as possible through the rail complex and split the train into three sections as it left Germany at Hannover, then direct to the Atlantic coast of Europe. At the sight of Rudi leaving the building, Yute became immediately alert. He must speak to him, but he must not be seen. Rudi strode on, unaware he was being followed or that his 'brown envelope in the night' man, was following both him and Yute. Tonight, it seemed to Rudi there were more people on the pavements; the constant swerving to avoid bumping shoulders, the stopping and starting of his walking was beginning to irritate him.

Rudi was aware of some problem in the crowd behind him, but took little notice. He wanted only to be home to wait, dreaming of the caresses which he longed for, to come to him. His key was entering the keyhole when Yute's sudden unseen hand gripped his wrist.

'Get inside quick!' The ferocity in Yute's voice brought fear into Rudi's heart. Tonight Mayer may be coming. She must never be seen by this evil man! Rudi's other hand swung to place an armlock around Yute's neck, but Yute was too fast for Rudi's untrained opposition. Rudi found himself, in seconds, pinned against his own doorway, one arm locked up the middle of his back and Yute's other hand at his throat. 'Now, let's stop playing games and get inside!' The force with which he was pushed took him reeling backwards through the unlocked door into the one and only armchair in the room. Yute was upon him again, this time with a gun which was held rock steady, pointing to his forehead.

'Don't ever think about attacking me again! You will always lose!'

Rudi nodded his head in acceptance, but added by way of defence, 'You only had to say hello. Isn't it quite normal to defend oneself if attacked?'

'You're right. I apologise.' The gun disappeared inside Yute's jacket.

'That's better,' said Rudi, his flat voice giving nothing away, then he asked, 'Why are you here in my house at this time?'

'I know the trains are in the rail complex. I want to know exactly where they are placed and I want copies of the manifests as well as when they are leaving.'

'They are all in the complex, placed alongside each other at junction sixteen, east, sidings eleven, twelve and thirteen.'

Yute interrupted, 'You're doing well, you're learning. Go on...'

'There are no manifests and they all go the night after next.'

'Are you sure about this?'

'My instructions were to make certain that all exits west out of the complex must be free for the "snake" from 2100 hours.'

'What else?'

'Nothing!' Rudi cheekily added, 'Not even a thank you!'

Yute sprang forward again, like a leopard, a hand locked around Rudi's throat. 'You will not joke with me! But you will contact me the moment you get the manifests – have no doubt in your ability!' Yute's hand tightened still further around Rudi's throat. Rudi could not answer. He felt the release of Yute's hand and sucked air rapidly into his lungs. Yute prowled around the room, making decisions in his mind. He stopped his prowling and looked out of the window down into the street.

'Rudi, I killed a man who was following you a few minutes ago. I think your "brown envelope man" will expose himself to you and it will be your old boss, Gregori Alexei Androv. You will say nothing to him of your meetings with me... you will even deny you know my name.' Yute walked over from the window and placed his face full into Rudi's.

'But you will not forget me, nor will you forget that I control you!' The coldness in his voice frightened Rudi more than at any time previously. But before he could give any reply, Yute had disappeared after making a gesture that the paper he was placing on the table contained the telephone number Rudi was to call. Rudi sat stiffly in his chair. Was the problem in the crowd behind him that he had only briefly been aware of, an actual murder to protect him, or a cold-blooded act to make Gregori Alexei Androv come out into the open? What will Mayer think when she gets here?

'Please come soon, my love, please.' Rudi's whisper disappeared into the silence of the room.

Asslomov's recce into the marshalling yards had proven successful. They had given all their statistics back to the new, freshly made command post at the airfield. The large control building which was already standing was proving more than adequate along with the one small hangar which automatically became the supply 'tent' for all their needs.

Asslomov's plan, now that he knew the trains were stationary, was first to have the carriages which contained nuclear weapons and arms, marked. The drugs could soon be set ablaze and would cause little damage. Weapons and warheads would have to be captured and then isolated from any possible fight which might be put up by the perpetrators. The pleasure could be seen on Asslomov's face as all the information was put onto each carriage or wagon model which had been laid out around the perimeter of the room; each wagon identified would then be placed in position on the plan which now occupied a prominent place on the large planning table. Joe and Joc were impressed with the cold efficiency going on all around them, the teamwork inside the hut, and Joc commented to Joe, 'The boys on the ground at the train must be efficient, Joe.'

'Jealous, Joc?'

'For sure. I'd like to be able to join in! I know I can't for all sorts of reasons, but maybe when the game has progressed a little further?'

'You know what Langley said. We can look but we can't touch!'

'True, my dear friend, but if something came our way which we could do, you'd like to join in, wouldn't you?'

'You know I always obey orders and you are senior to me!'

Joc knew the teasing game that Joe would play; he also knew that if given the opportunity, Joe would jump in without his 'orders' and take the consequences later. Joc answered him, 'And you'd expect me to cover up for you as well!'

'For sure, Pappy, you're the big boy with the big desk in Langley, me – I'm just a peasant from the sticks!'

Both men enjoyed their little banter and after slapping each other on the back, their minds were soon back and very attentive to the swiftly changing scene around them.

Ernst stood at the far end of the room in a corner, the window to one side of him spread light onto his worried face, his hand kept rubbing the back of his head, his own small team from Hamburg knew not to disturb him when he was wrestling with a problem. The only thing they could do was leave him alone and wait for his brain to finish with its questions and answers, then they would be put to work.

'Mayer!' Ernst called softly.

'Sir,' Mayer said, coming to attention, showing the utmost respect for her boss in front of all the Russians.

'Please come over here.'

'Yes, sir,' Mayer's voice automatically said, unaware that every Russian in the room was looking at her smart non-subservient approach. Why couldn't Russian women be more like that?

'Mayer, I want you to see Rudi. It's important that we know that we have a spontaneous answer unclouded by Rudi's emotions. I'm sure he is telling you everything, but sometimes the news is hours late. I want you to live with him, be with him. I need to know that whenever he gets his messages, I'll get the information immediately. For the success of this operation we must know where our three star players are – the two that seem to be pestering Rudi and Parentov. With luck, Parentov may show his hand or at least contact Yute or Androv in Rudi's presence, or Rudi will mention his name. We must know that all of them are still active here in Moscow.'

Mayer was delighted that she would be with her love, even though Rudi was still being used by Ernst. 'Why are you constantly using him! He has done no harm but to fall in love with me, now even I am being used to nurture your plans. The West hasn't got a democracy, it's run by the manipulative few! It's a sham!' Mayer stopped herself. 'I'm sorry, sir.' Her downfallen eyes allowed no tears of emotion to fall. She stood and waited for Ernst's response.

'You may be right, Mayer, but this democracy is all we have. Maybe my fight has been to try and stop the bad guys from corrupting the good guys we voted in. We perhaps aren't doing as well as we should, but like everyone else in this room, we will fight – even for an imperfect system. Rudi has chosen and is square with his position and what he has committed himself to, and you want to protect him out of sympathy for the position he is in. Motivated by your love for him and his for you, you feel used and dirty. I know that, but better you suffer a little shame now, than just sit back and watch this democracy sink further in the West. You know your remark was from your heart – like a mother, you protect your child!'

'But…' Mayer's words wouldn't come. Her thoughts were in turmoil. The man before her was honest to himself, she believed in him and his brilliance, so why was she so upset about the position she was being placed in by Ernst? Do I love Rudi that much…? I do, but he must be protected. She was a trained policewoman, she must keep him alive for herself! Her rushing thoughts dried up as the selfish thoughts about herself came into her mind.

'I must be allowed to be armed and have support from Asslomov and yourself if I have to use my gun.'

'I don't see that as a problem from either of us.'

Mayer saw Asslomov's nod of the head in approval out of the

corner of her eye. 'Thank you, sirs. When do you want me to become a spy?'

'Thank you, Mayer. As soon as we get a cover story for you. It will only be a thin cover because we have very little time.'

'Gentlemen,' Asslomov announced, 'and ladies, of course. We can now verify nuclear arms of many varieties and drugs. This train is worth billions of potential capital – inestimable probably!'

Although there had been speculation that the 'snake' was totally illegal in every sense, the stark corroboration of the news by Asslomov still took everyone by surprise.

Joc looked at Ernst's worried face. He felt sorry for him. It was his anticipation which had brought them all this far, but because of 'political' situations, Ernst couldn't be in charge of the whole affair. Instead, the military would have to clear up everything concerning the train and its contents, Ernst would be left with capturing the 'rats' as they ran!

'Ernst, my friend, I know how you must feel. Use Joe and me to drag in these murderers and thieves!' The sympathy in Joc's voice comforted Ernst.

'For me, the murderers are as important as everything else, Joc, but I feel so insecure having to rely on so many others, especially as I'm looking for five, possibly six people!'

'I know, when they come running out of their hiding places you will not have much warning from Asslomov.'

'I'm hoping Robin will anticipate our needs, Joc. He is a good policeman. I'm sure he will see things happening that Asslomov will not.'

'Vargas, Gilbert, Joe and I are all here for you, your own group too will know that they will possibly get the information late and will need to be extra vigilant.'

'You're right, of course, Joc, but I'm a worrier.'

'It will be fine, Ernst. Just fine. We had better go over to Asslomov, he's beckoning.'

The two men walked side by side across the wide room, calling the European contingency to join them as they centred on Asslomov for a briefing.

'Well, everyone,' Asslomov said as the group mustered around him, 'Robin will be joining us in a few moments. He has been with one of my patrol groups and will verify the positions of the different segments of our "snake", but let me paint in some background whilst we wait. The train has had very little protection on its journey here, it has only been moved by railway personnel and not the military. Of the three men we have taken from the train, no one can tell us more than that the yard and line masters gave them instructions every morning, such as: you will be here by 1400 hours, two more goods wagons will join you, they will take a specific position within the train. The precision suggests military control, in my opinion. It may be that your source in Moscow can try and find your "brown envelope in the night" man and corroborate that he is who you think he is, then ask yourselves, has he got enough tactical knowledge to control this "snake" or is he working for another group? Personally, I must emphasise my belief is that he is getting his instructions from another group, but is trying to pull off a big double-cross. I knew Yute Polenkovich some time ago. He has the capabilities of a great planner and probably sold it to the Council. I hear that he was out of favour for a while and Council gave him a second chance. He's a planner for the Organisatiya, a thinker who doesn't rush but will fight to the death to defend one of his ideas. At all times, Polenkovich is dangerous, but when he's on the defence, he is lethal.'

'You never told us you knew Polenkovich in the past! Did you also know Androv?'

Ernst's probing question stunned Asslomov for a moment, but quickly gathering his thoughts, he replied, 'Yes, this man is evil and selfish. He has absconded a few times in his chequered career but somehow has always managed to get back into favour. Rumour has it that he married very well, to the daughter of one of Russia's top Generals, who was a Council Chairman of the Organisatiya – a rumour maybe, but one which has prevailed over the years.'

'Sir, I must ask,' Ernst stopped for a moment to watch for any sign of fear on Asslomov's face in anticipation of the question, but Ernst saw nothing and sharply finished his question. 'Have you any part in any activities of this Council?'

'No, nothing. I live on my pay only, my bank accounts would only prove my financial hardship!'

'Thank you, sir. Your surprise of knowing both of our prime suspects forced the question.'

'You must know your friends, Chief Inspector. I hope I will prove an honourable one!'

Speaking on behalf of the group, Ernst responded, 'We are sure you will be, sir. Please accept our apologies.'

Before Asslomov could reply, Robin entered the room with two of Asslomov's officers. He smiled acknowledgements to all around, finishing with Asslomov. 'Robin, you came... good! How did you enjoy the recce?'

'Sir, your troops were good.'

'Shall we get on with the brief to let everyone know what has and possibly will happen?'

'Please, sir. Shall I make any points as you go along, or shall I take notes and raise them after?'

'Interrupt me, I think, it's more spontaneous and everyone should be thinking on the point as it is made, it will be a better debate.'

'Thank you, sir.' Robin stood back and found an edge of a table to sit upon. Asslomov straightened his notes and began.

'Gentlemen, and lady. Today so far, we have located the "snake", we have entered a vast majority of the wagons and we know the disposition of the cargo. We have some danger should anyone try to booby trap our nuclear wagons, but we have placed men inside and out to observe and ensure that any possible plan of destroying this arsenal in the close proximity of Moscow will be stopped.' Asslomov's flat hand hit the top of the table. His jaw was set square in defiance of anyone even considering opposing him. His spontaneous anger passed, he continued, 'With regards to the drugs and sundry weaponry, that will not be allowed to move. We shall cause a gridlock of traffic by sending trains from each side of them on any line the "snake" may try to escape on. We will squeeze them back into a circle.' He stopped for a moment, then added, 'This movement is courtesy of the British!' A ring of laughter rang around the room. Robin looked embarrassed, but was soon over it when he saw the thumb-up sign from Ernst, Joc,

Joe, Gilbert and Manuel. When Asslomov had finished his briefing, he asked whether there were any questions, but there were none forthcoming. 'Shall we all get on with our duties? We shall reconvene in two hours, thank you, everyone.'

Mayer stood in the shadows of the corridor leading to Rudi's apartment. She was sure she had managed to get where she was without being seen, but where was Rudi? It was eight in the evening. He said that even if he had a drink on his way home, he was always back by seven. Mayer had to stay. She must make contact with Rudi. Her whisper sounded like a cannon going off. 'I want to make contact, Rudi, I want to devour you... hurry!'

Yute stood over Rudi as he sat in the chair. Yute had arranged for the meeting by phone, in the seedy Hotel Tosca. Rudi went with trepidation in his heart, but Yute made it very plain that if he didn't obey, his friend Dimitri would lose part of his anatomy! The stale air in the room and Yute's stale, pungent breath so close to his face was making him dizzy. The two hours since leaving the office had been the longest of his life. 'Now!' Yute continued, 'You will have for me, by seven o'clock tomorrow morning, the exact positioning of each wagon, carriage and engine. I will be taking men in to protect my interests and your friend Dimitri will die a horrible death if you fail!'

'Why Dimitri and not me?' squeezed its way out of Rudi's tight throat.

'You have some use until your brown envelopes stop, then you will be of no use to me but sometimes I am a grateful man.' Yute's unseen fist struck Rudi's temple and it went dark.

Rudi woke up, his head pounding. He must get to his office... speak to Dimitri... speak to the secretary in Room A117, to make an appointment with the 'brown envelope' man... speak to Mayer. No, go home and clean up first. As he lifted himself from the chair, his legs buckled but he held on to the table and didn't tumble. Quickly, I must move on. The ten minutes that it took to get to his front door were a struggle. The blow to his head had been delivered with considerable force and it was affecting his thinking and his vision. His key entered the door lock more by instinct, with the lack of focus in his eyes making it difficult. A small shuffling of feet nearby frightened him. Who was going to attack him this time? His eyes strained to see who was coming towards him… who?… who?… an angel, 'Mayer!… Mayer!… an angel!… Am I dying?' He slowly fell to the floor.

Ernst waited in the Command Centre for any news which would tell him where his villains were. The phone at his side rang. 'Ulbrecht heir!'

'It's Mayer, sir. I have contacted Rudi, he has been beaten-up by Yute who wants a complete displacement by seven o'clock in the morning. He is going to take men into the rail yards to protect his train.'

'Where are you now?'

'A phone booth. I'm going back to Rudi, he needs help.'

'Be careful, Mayer, keep in touch.' The call ended as quickly as it had begun. Now Ernst had information which might lead to the apprehension of one of the villains, at least. The smile of relief on his face did not go unnoticed by his companions.

Joc asked, 'Good news, Ernst?'

Ernst told them of Mayer's message, and then his thoughts wandered on. 'If Yute is moving in, would it be likely that Androv will confront him in the rail yards? Would the paymaster, Parentov, also be there? He surely would want to know who the winner of any confrontation would be… he could possibly make a better deal and make a much larger profit.'

'That's logical, Ernst, but who is going to let us crash around the yards picking up criminals from our shopping list when there could be a gang war going on with the Russian Army fighting both of them?' Joc knew Ernst had already thought out the possibility but wondered if he had a solution to prevent failure from a civilian standpoint and asked, 'What would be your solution, Ernst?'

Ernst hesitated before speaking. 'My guess is all the operatives Yute has out in the field, the Mogatins, Lanovs, et cetera, will have to be drawn in from their positions. We must know if they are coming! We must cover every single contact Yute's field agents have made. We must know what instructions they are to follow.

Robin and Gilbert will be very busy. Manuel, we must have any information your men in Portugal can obtain. I don't think Portugal will be very prominent now, but our first leads came from there and there must be agents out in the field there that we need to apprehend. When we get closer to the time, lots of loose ends will need to be gathered in, so Manuel, if any of your big criminals intend to leave Portugal, we need to know.

'With regards your question, we need to be with Asslomov's men, perhaps not in the front line, but closer to the action than we are now. He must allow us a command post of our own. We must be locked into his communications system so that we know every move of the game. Without it, we could lose. Robin, you must get this for us please!'

Robin saw Ernst's overall worry very clearly and the possible, terrible consequences should any of the long-outstanding adversaries slip through the net. 'Ernst,' Robin replied, 'it may be difficult, but rest assured I'll do the best I can with Asslomov.'

'You must succeed, Robin. If you don't, I think we will have many cancers upon the society of every nation represented here, left to just grow and grow, and we will all be fighting this fight into the twenty-second century!'

Robin agreed with Ernst, replying lightly, 'I assure you I'll do my best bit of military two-stepping!'

Joc, Joe, Gilbert and even Manuel understood the joke and laughed. Poor Ernst had to have the British sense of humour explained to him.

Rudi's head lay against Mayer's breasts, caressed by her gentle fingers. She had stopped whispering to him an hour ago. Now, after the excess of love, the words she had whispered, the hatred of Yute Polenkovich, she was the mother healing her child, wishing all the pain away. Her mind started to revolt at the new thoughts which were popping into her head. Rudi, you must wake up now, you must go and get the brown envelope and its latest information. You must get Dimitri's information, any information which might help stop the 'snake'! Damn you, Ernst! He's mine, and you keep pulling him deeper and deeper into your case. You use people, you manipulate people to protect your beloved

Germany, now you're trying to save the world. Have you ever thought that it doesn't want to be saved, it wants to wallow in filth and degradation!

There was a movement of Rudi's head as he tilted it upwards, searching for his whereabouts, as he mumbled, 'No, no, it wants to be saved...' The words faded as he tried to go back to sleep.

'Rudi, Rudi, my love, you're awake! Please talk to me, let me look into your eyes, please help me!' The torment within her and her split emotions made her feel very uncomfortable. Her hands tightened around Rudi's head as she tried to pull him inside her body.

'Mayer, we must stop them!' came the muffled cry. His hot breath on her breasts was driving her to distraction. She wanted to give herself now. Her logic was failing her; how could she think like that? He must be made better.

'Rudi, you're right, we must stop them. I'm being selfish, I only want you!'

'Me too, so much, but help me to get to my office please, then hopefully we can be together always.'

'We will my love, we will.' Her head dropped to kiss the top of his beautiful head.

The taxi pulled into the deepest shadows opposite the Kremlin's walls. Rudi, silent in the back seat, waiting for a few moments to see if anyone was around before he left to enter through the little side door. The short walk through the door, the security check, the walk along the corridor to his office, was like moving through a mist. His office door was open, the dim security light was just bright enough to guide him to his desk where he could turn on his green-shaded desk lamp. 'Sit down, Rudi,' he mumbled to himself. 'You're tired and bruised, just do as the envelope says.' Now the light was on he could see there was no envelope. 'I'm too early,' he whispered to himself. A slight, almost silent swish as his office door closed brought fear into his eyes, his thoughts racing. Surely I'm not going to be beaten-up again!

It took a moment for the figure from behind the door to walk into the pool of light surrounding Rudi's desk. 'My God! Gregori Alexei Androv! You're supposed to be dead!'

'That is what I wanted everyone to think, but now is the time to come alive again! There is not much time left and I believe many people will by now have worked out in their minds that my disappearance was planned. So here I am and I promise I will not disappoint any of you. You will see a master plan unfold before your very eyes. By tomorrow, everything will have a new manifest, officially stamped and will be moving across borders, carrying its deadly cargo quite legally. And you, my friend, will obey my every word.'

Rudi was becoming dizzy again from his earlier beating, but fought hard mentally to memorise every word. Mayer will want it for Ernst! 'Gregori Alexei Androv, you will be obeyed.' The words just tumbled out of Rudi's mouth.

'Good! Your task for tonight will be to reverse the train until it can be assembled into one long train, then green light it straight through Moscow at high speed. I will be there with my men watching you. Should you fail, you're dead!'

The words slowly sank into Rudi's mind; his broken body would not lift from his chair to oppose Androv, he must show him he was a man... 'Should you fail, you're dead!' Androv's last words finally gave Rudi the strength to rise. Unsteadily, he stood, his words forming in his mind, the words he would say. When his eyes had finally focused, there was no one there to speak to – Androv had gone. Rudi had to speak to Mayer again. Ernst must know that Androv and his men will be there, plus the fact that the train is to become one again!

Sergeant MacKenzie's conversation with Robin had been very long, but carried salient information for immediate action, that had left Robin very worried that all of his investigators were each having to take on two observations. One: the Russians were running to Moscow. Two: watch the sleepers, still local. He must request more support from Gilbert! But why was Colonel Keller not running and why hadn't his Russian watchdogs left him?

Robin requested a full group meeting with Asslomov's permission at the earliest possible moment. The room was full of smoke. Robin had brought everyone up to date with the happenings across France and Germany with regard to his field teams and his endorsement of Sergeant MacKenzie that all of Yute Polenkovich's enforcers were heading for Moscow at great speed. His worry about Colonel Keller's Russian watchdogs had not been depleted. Ernst then told all assembled about Rudi's encounter with both Yute and Androv. 'I will, of course, tell everyone everything as it happens. Mayer is established as Rudi's girlfriend.' Ernst paused a moment before carrying on. 'Exposing her like this is not my happiest of career decisions, but it has to be. Let's hope with no cover story, she doesn't get found out.'

Asslomov had sat taking all of the information in. After each of the other civilian team leaders, he spoke. 'Gentlemen, we seem to be building a stadium around our contesters, with my troops making the walls, Polenkovich bringing his gladiators who have been dragged from the sewers and now face good military authority, Androv has acquired two platoons of men from one of our Moscow garrisons, from yet another corrupt military commander who hires his men out as mercenaries. May I say it is my intention to allow all of the contestants to enter the arena, then close all the doors.'

For a moment or two, the room fell silent under the haze of smoke, then slowly, led by Joc, clapping began. Joc then said, for all to hear, 'Well done, sir. I take my hat off to you. It seems to me your plan is excellent and with your splendid troops, we could be going home by morning!'

'But first, Joc, we must get them all into the trap then not lose any when we do. That's why I am suggesting now that all of you civilian police form an outer perimeter outside my troops as additional security... I'm sure you all want more participation in all this... and of course, I will turn a "blind eye", I think is what you say, to your activity outside of my defence line.'

Ernst and everyone were surprised by the amount of freedom Asslomov was allowing them to have on Russian soil. Joc was very quick to realise, should anything go wrong with the plan, how politically vulnerable Asslomov would be and he jokingly quipped, 'We will keep your exposure under our hats and thank you for your trust.' Asslomov left the room a little embarrassed at the acclaim when Joc's play on words caused a little laughter.

At the breaking up of the meeting the civilian contingency had a strategy meeting along with Robin to work out lines of communication, should any of the gladiators escape Asslomov's troops.

Rudi fell into his apartment more from bewilderment than any other reason. He was getting used to the tightness in his jaw and limbs but the constant mental battle was tiring him more than anything. Why was he not allowed to be with Mayer? All I want is Mayer! The noise of Rudi's approach outside the apartment alerted Mayer. She was listening with fear in her heart, thinking that the noise was the police coming for her. She dashed forward after she had recognised that the 'intruder' was Rudi and managed to catch his head just before it hit the ground.

'Rudi, my love! What have they done to you?'

'Nothing, just threats… always more threats. I'm tired, Mayer. Let me go to sleep in your arms.

'You will, my love, I promise, when this is all over, I promise I will hold you to my breast forever!'

'Forever and ever, Mayer?' The tiredness in Rudi's voice was very noticeable.

'You mustn't go to sleep, Rudi. First, you must tell me about your instructions in the brown envelope.' She hated herself for asking the question. 'I am sorry, Rudi, but everyone is waiting for your information. My God, Rudi, I love you so much, I could never hurt you.'

Rudi knew she did love him and that he could not live without her as he started slowly to speak. 'Gregori Alexei Androv is in Moscow…'

Mayer's phone report to Ernst was cold and precise, by a woman who felt she was being used. Ernst listened, as did the others, with sympathy in knowing her torment and the split loyalties she was suffering. Mayer had just finished telling them how Rudi had collapsed into the flat, that he was exhausted and that he was anxious about the future she had promised him they would have together. Mayer felt justified in reminding Ernst of his promise to help Rudi into the West. Mayer stopped and stared into the faces around her. After a little cough to clear her throat, she continued,

'Rudi has confirmed the "brown envelope" man is Gregori Alexei Androv. He's alive and in Moscow. He has demanded that plans be made to draw the train together into one long train and to stand by to await further orders, then speed it on its way on his given signal to the yard marshal, straight out of Moscow.

'Once out of Moscow, which way is it going?' Asked Ernst.

'Rudi brought back no other information on that, just to get the train through Moscow quickly.'

'Ernst, does Androv know that Yute Polenkovich is in Moscow and is drawing his men in from all over?'

'I think he probably does, Robin.'

'They will fight each other for control. It could be very messy, Ernst. It's good we have Asslomov on our side!'

'Yes, Robin, very good, but let's be prepared with our outer ring of defence. We can rely on Asslomov's troops to do battle, I'm sure, but if everyone gets killed, we will never know if we have all the leaders and whether this monster will rise from the ashes again, under some other power-crazy scheme.'

'We will be okay, Ernst. I'm sure all the police forces represented here are all alerted and that a lot of favours have been asked of friends in the Benelux countries.' The confidence in Robin's voice was felt by all, but as Ernst rightly pointed out, true corroborative evidence was the only way to slay the monster.

The meeting between Yute, Lanov and Mogatin in the drab Moscow hotel was full of questions such as, 'You promised you would have total control – no one was ever going to usurp your position – you had the Council's agreement!' Yute had argued his position on these and many other points and slowly he was winning them back on to his side.

'You men have been through hell and back with me in the past, I have never failed you and I will not fail you now! So Gregori Alexei Androv has military troops to support his raid on our train – troops who are young and not baptised in fighting; each one of you is worth ten of them. Twelve of us here – I see it as no contest for the poor devils!'

Mogatin glanced around at Lanov and the rest of the men present. The cold nod of approval to support Yute's plea was in all of their eyes. His deep, level voice answered for all of them. 'Marshall Polenkovich, all of us here await your command, but do not fail us!' The threat did not go unnoticed by Yute, but now was not the time for another confrontation.

'Gentlemen, may I thank you all for your support. Now let us review the situation as it stands at the moment and make our plans for success!'

The instructions flooding into the railway marshalling yards office were somewhat confusing for the staff working there. The instructions changed so frequently that before they put any order into practice, another was issued to countermand it. The rail marshal and his men, out of sheer confusion, decided that each order, as received, would be carried out anyway, extending the confusion.

Robin sat waiting for news of the Yute Polenkovich meeting with his team. Sergeant Hackett had been called in from Metz to coordinate the policemen following Lanov and Mogatin. Robin knew he could trust Sergeant Hackett entirely. Over the years Robin had known him, he had proven to be a good, solid investigator, earning Robin's respect, but the anxiety was now showing on Robin's face as he waited. The phone had barely finished its first ring when Robin grabbed it from his cradle. 'Cadwallader here.' His staccato voice cut into Sergeant Hackett's ear.

'Hackett, sir. Sorry I took so long in phoning; the meeting finished about twenty minutes ago but a lot more people came out than my people had counted going in. It took a while to organise ourselves to cover our principal suspects and as many of the others as possible. We have identified a few of the new arrivals. All of our suspects are filtering into the rail yards.'

'Thank you, Sergeant. How many?'

'I can verify twenty-four, sir, with two others floating around in the background like they are spying on the others.'

'That sounds interesting, Sergeant. It would be great if we can link those two to a group even if it turns out to be the group they are following!'

'I don't think it's that way, sir. I think they belong to Androv's mob!'

'Don't lose them, Sergeant. Good work – thank everyone for me. Keep in touch!' Sergeant Hackett just managed to reply 'Sir!' before the phone went dead in his ear.

Ernst was talking to Asslomov's *aide-de-camp* as Robin arrived. Both of them could see the excitement on Robin's face and immediately stopped talking between themselves as Robin spoke. 'Yute and his men, Lanov and Mogatin, et cetera, are mustering in the rail yards. This has been confirmed, Ernst.'

Robin had not been introduced to the ADC and added, 'Sir,' with a nod of acknowledgement.

'Good, Robin, things seem to be going well for us at the moment. We know Androv has got troops, Yute has trained mercenaries. Our friend, Asslomov has his whole command surrounding the yards, ready to move should any of the train start to move. We look pretty well set.'

The ADC, like Robin, had got used to Ernst's rambling style of speech and both felt Ernst had more to say, so waited patiently. It didn't take long. With a little cough, Ernst cleared his throat. 'Where is Parentov, do we know?'

'We know he is in Moscow, Ernst. I'll ask the teams right away,' Robin replied. As he left the two men, Robin cursed himself, 'Where the hell is Parentov? You've cocked up, Robin!'

Joc and Gilbert approached Ernst and the ADC as Robin was leaving. They both called out Robin's name, but Robin didn't respond. Joc was the first to speak. 'Some information, Ernst, which we feel Robin should know about as soon as possible. One of Asslomov's officers over at the mobile response unit has just told us that some of his men have found a heliport, complete with helicopter and crew on top of building three – here on your map!'

'Who do we think may own it?'

'The officer had no idea, but his men discovered it about an hour ago and because of the radio silence he hasn't reported it to anyone but us!'

'Is it an escape helicopter or a heavy load?' asked Ernst.

'It's like a small bee sitting up on the roof, according to the soldier who found it.'

'Thank God for that, at least we won't have nuclear weapons flitting around in the sky. Can we get one of our team to watch it? It needs us to cover it, Joc, soldiers look at things differently to us.'

'Joe and I seem to be doing very little; we could take it on.'

'If you're sure, Joc. Great! I'll let Robin know. Good luck to you both!' said Ernst. Then he added as an afterthought, 'Don't forget to take a flask of coffee with you, it gets cold at night!'

Dimitri had met Rudi at Mayer's request, at Rudi's flat. She had felt, along with Dimitri, that Rudi needed to be in his office during the operation now that Androv and Yute had both made themselves known to Rudi. Mayer was adamant Rudi was in some way crucial to the success of the mammoth task before them. She had even persuaded Ernst that she could, should it be possible to get herself into the Kremlin, protect her beloved Rudi. It was to this end that they were stealthily observing the patrols and security checks in the hope of finding a possible way to get Mayer in. Dimitri had made the decision that Mayer would need to be disguised to hide her attractiveness and that he would have to steal someone else's identity papers.

In the command post, all of the TV sets came on simultaneously to a loud ovation. Ernst grabbed a telephone to tell Robin that the TV monitoring was going to be great and would he join him to test out all of the individual camera positions and the direct communication with the camera operators.

Dimitri knew the cleaning staff at the Kremlin worked from 0600 until 0900 hours, so he would go to the office early, steal a pass from one of their handbags, come out, collect Mayer, go back with her after disguising her, put her in Rudi's office and then put the pass back into the cleaner's handbag, then leave again to help Rudi's broken body through the long corridors to his own office and Mayer. He knew his entering and re-entering the building might be noticed, but it was the only way he could think of.

Mayer had no doubts in her mind. Rudi opposed dragging Mayer into the drama any further, an opposition which both Mayer and Dimitri knew would be broken. He had to be in his office to even have a chance of fulfilling Yute's demands.

Asslomov strode across the office towards Ernst and Robin, just as Joc and Joe were about to leave. They had all agreed the helicopter would play a part in the heist which was about to unfold. Joc explained their intentions to Asslomov.

Asslomov thought for a few brief moments then agreed their idea was a good one and wished them the best of luck. Robin stood to attention whilst Ernst explained which positions his men and Robin's investigators had taken outside his cordon of troops, emphasising that Chief of Police Vargas would have a roving commission with his few men and fill any gaps which might appear in the trap. He went on to explain that the French, German and the British were fully integrated with each other and not sectioned off.

'Thank you for briefing me, Ernst. Well done, it all looks under control. I'll be with one of the mobile units if I'm needed. By the way, Robin, why don't you stand at ease?' There was no vindictiveness in his last remark, just pure absent-mindedness.

Both Robin and Ernst shook their heads in understanding Asslomov's remark. Robin whispered to Ernst, 'I thought we had all the eccentric ones in our army?'

Silently, Mayer stood deep in shadow behind Rudi's chair. His head was resting on her breasts, her hand lightly brushed through his hair. Having angled Rudi's desk so it was possible to see the length of the corridor, their eyes never stopped watching. Mayer's hand tightened into Rudi's scalp, then she slowly released her fingers and floated across the shadows in the room to the position between the opened door and the four-drawer filing cabinet. They had both heard the light, approaching footsteps. The game was now going to be played again, the game of fear, her beloved Rudi being used again. Would she be silent enough? Would she be able to endure not taking action to protect her love?

Colonel Keller sat nervously in the large padded armchair, his eyes twitching a little as each sound in the old house caught his ears. He knew Parentov's and Androv's men were out there in the darkness waiting, he suspected, for an instruction to kill him or to force him into betraying the military which had housed and protected him all these years. Why had Androv visited him all those months ago, reminding him that he belonged to Russia and always had. His sin had been to have had a sexual experience with a junior officer. One single experiment, one distasteful experience and now his career was about to blossom, his rewards of a staff appointment in a very democratic society would not happen because of that stupid adventure all those years ago. The crack of the gun as it exploded from the muzzle into his temple startled the observers around the house. The unexpected suicide must be reported at once to their respective team leaders. Each surveillance team knew of each other's existence, but each of them broke cover stealthily to report back.

Yute entered Rudi's office. To Rudi, he looked bigger this time than last. With his anger rising, Rudi spoke first. 'You can tear me limb from limb, but the information you want is not here yet… so you are invited to wait,' Rudi was quite proud of the invitation bit.

'You fool, you facetious fool! Get the information now!'

'I'm waiting.' Rudi knew his voice was weakening.

'You will chase your department… now!' Yute's large fist struck the desk loudly. Rudi didn't cringe, he just sat and stared into Yute's thunderous face. Silence returned again to the tiny office. Both men sat motionless, staring at each other across the uncluttered desk. The distant, faint whistle was heard by both of them at the same instant. Progressively it got louder as Dimitri got closer, until he filled the doorway. He saw Rudi sitting there and the back of Yute was towards him. I could hit him now, crossed his mind, but a slight movement from Rudi's eyes told him 'no'. Dimitri tapped softly on the door and entered smiling.

'This is the most up-to-date information we have from your enquiry,' he said, handing the paper to Rudi. Dimitri stood back and waited to be asked questions, or be given further instructions. Rudi deliberated over the paper and passed it over to Yute.

Dimitri's surprise did not show on his face. Rudi's voice cut into the air.

'You have your information now, may I suggest you leave!'

'Don't bandy words with me, I want one more thing from you now!'

Coolly, Rudi replied, 'If it is possible and you lift your conditions, your threats on my staff, we will do as you ask.' He looked into Dimitri's face, who supported Rudi with an assuring nod of the head.

'You're getting very, very cocky, young man. Why don't I kill you both now?' Yute's voice had lost its anger and was now cold and menacing.

Rudi wanted to taunt him a little longer but decided now was not the right time to die and Mayer's position must not be exposed. 'Dimitri, will you listen to this gentleman's request and give him an approximate time when he could expect to have this information?' Rudi did not allow Dimitri to answer, but prompted Yute with, 'Your question, sir?'

The words came quickly from Yute. 'What are your instructions for moving the train?'

Dimitri's eyes were blank, giving nothing away but Rudi, rather than prolong the agony, snapped the answer back immediately, 'We are told to be ready tonight.'

'By whom?'

'My "brown envelope" man!'

'Do you know his identity?'

'Yes… my ex-boss, Gregori Alexei Androv.'

'Then it is confirmed then – my own thoughts and that of two of my men are confirmed. Should he contact you again, tell him that I will move the train and not him!'

There was nothing more to be told from either side of the conversation, but Yute felt he had to conclude the meeting.

'Your information on this paper is pretty accurate of each carriage, but by now, my men will be in control and you will find things are changing as we speak. It is all right for you to know this because what is going to happen is unstoppable now!'

Side by side in the shadow of the 'snake's' long body, Mogatin and

Lanov's operation of supervising the placement of his men along the 'snake's' length was going smoothly. Occasionally, a sound could be heard from the other end of the track, which would freeze them for a second or two. Mogatin's whispered instructions were crisply spoken and as they approached the middle of the train, his voice became more urgent, inspiring his men to move more quickly.

As Yute had said, 'Comrade Androv has been in control of the train until it gets into Moscow's marshalling yards and he will feel safe. We will strike hard and fast where he feels safe then move out as soon as we have control.' Mogatin and Lanov were sceptical at first, but now they had control of half of the 'snake', it was so easy. Androv had let his guard down… the train was surely theirs.

The 'phutt' of the silenced bullet was not heard by any in the group surrounding Mogatin, but the hot sting as the bullet cut into the man's shoulder and the unmistakable sucking-in of air by the wounded man instinctively alerted the group. Each of them, as if they were one, hit the ground and spread out without losing contact.

'Did you see anything, Lanov?' Mogatin whispered.

'Not for sure, left, about eleven o'clock possibly?'

'We'll wait a moment.'

'I'll go!'

'Be careful my friend!' Lanov was gone into the darkness.

Androv heard from his Commander that one of the advance groups who were taking over the train had fired and were believed to have wounded a suspicious character and that the remainder of the group had gone to ground at the centre of the 'snake.' Androv's anger at being discovered by anyone was going to advance his plans. He must get control of the total length of the 'snake'!

'Commander!' Androv's voice left no doubt that what he was about to say would be followed explicitly. 'You will remove these people from my railway and my train right now!'

'Is that wise—' the Commander began to speak.

'I said now, Commander, *now!*' The field phone went dead in the Commander's ear.

Androv fell back into his chair. 'You bastard, Polenkovich! It's you out there! You can't win, you have been out-manoeuvred all along. Now you're dead!' Androv's face contorted into a sneer.

Parentov was waiting in his hotel room for the phone call which would bring him to Androv's side where they would become successful business partners in the greatest heist in history. He will have great respect when the capital which would be made was in his bank – the bank his father owned and never really achieved its full potential, but he would. He, Boris Parentov, failed soldier, failed lover, failed small-time crook, will not fail this time. His work will be completed soon when he makes two phone calls. The first, to his client, saying that all the goods he required are in his possession and the second, within ten minutes, to learn the money is in his bank – a shrewd and very clever piece of brokering. He could not help but let the smug smile stretch across his face. The last thing would be Androv's signature on the true manifest as corroboration that the goods were his. The cheque for two billion dollars, drawn on his bank and signed by him, would be handed over. His daydreaming was about to become reality, when suddenly, the phone finally rang.

'Parentov, where exactly?'

'We have a delay.'

'Why?'

'Yute Polenkovich is here. I can't see him holding us up for long against my company of troops, but it will take a short while.'

'The bankers will be leaving in an hour and I want that money in my bank. Without it you don't get paid. It's a bloody typical military mess. Don't you know how long it takes to put a deal like this together? The wrangling, the constant talk, talk, bloody talk. Everything finally gets set into place and the bloody military balls it up!' Parentov's ranting and ravings were making Androv angry.

As Parentov finished speaking, Androv said, 'I will phone you again, be ready. I'm just going to do what the military does, start shooting and get shot at to protect money-grabbing little shits like you!' Androv threw the phone down before any reply could have come from Parentov.

Asslomov's command had been closing the cordon around both Polenkovich's and Androv's parties as they progressed along the train. The shooting of one of Mogatin's men had been observed by one of Asslomov's men. The report Asslomov found was possibly a mistake by one of the soldiers under Androv's command as the two groups approaching each other were still a little too far apart for them to fight each other for the moment, so he took this quiet time to phone Robin and Ernst to notify them of the shooting incident.

'Robin, pick up the party-line,' shouted Ernst.

'Hello?' Robin said to the unannounced caller.

'Asslomov. We have just had a shooting here. One of Polenkovich's men – don't know if it was fatal – I think they will fight Androv's men very rapidly now. Both sides will be reconnoitring each other, then fireworks. My men will contain them and force them into a tight circle just outside the communication control room, so you should be able to witness some action!'

'Thank you, sir, most kind of you!'

Ernst again didn't see the silly British humour in Robin's reply. How could he when slowly he would be in the firing line? Confused, Ernst also replied, 'Yes, most kind of you!'

Lanov returned to Mogatin. His face told the story of their group's plight but the words were still said. 'There's a bloody army out there! At least three or four of them are over twenty years of age. Apart from the fact that we haven't got enough men we would win anything we start, but my question is, who is connected well enough to get regular troops working for them?'

'It's got to be Androv, but where does he fit into the puzzle? Yute knew nothing of him until a few weeks ago, I'm sure!' said Mogatin.

'Unless he hasn't told us the whole truth!'

'He wouldn't dare not to have told us the whole truth, but if our opposition is Androv, he is pulling more strings than Yute is capable of!' replied Mogatin. 'We need to find out where we stand in this. We were sold out in Hamburg – it could happen here too!'

'Not likely; this time we will take out whoever gets in our way and I'll work out something for our escape.'

'Moscow is such a sprawling place I'd look for a chopper!'

'You could be right, I'll see you soon. Have an enjoyable day, my friend!' With a flick of his fingers and a lifting of his forelock, Lanov was gone.

Yute realised things were not going well for him or his men. The railway crane which was his observation platform gave only a true picture of events on one side of the train, but it looked that Androv was winning. His eyes strained searching for Androv, his mind clouded with one thought. If I don't succeed, I swear you will die! The purr of the headset in his ear alerted him. Mogatin's voice was cold. 'Have we been sold out?'

'Not by me!' Yute replied adamantly.

'Androv?'

'Yes,' was the only reply to the situation; they were all in it now and now was not the time to explain his views on the matter. Now was the time to kill Androv and take control. Yute continued, 'We must find him and kill him. We gain control and I have all of the escape routes for the train and for us.'

'You go for Androv and I will secure what I can of the train!' said Mogatin. 'I'll get Androv... until I call you, carry on as planned!' The set was switched off.

Rudi and Mayer sat silently holding hands and wishing for each other. Rudi needed Mayer's strength to help him collate the information Dimitri was constantly bringing to him. Information which Androv had demanded and was constantly phoning for the review. Rudi was feeling better but his head ached beyond belief. He knew in his heart everything was going to be wonderful with his beautiful Mayer. He knew that together they could conquer the world. He squeezed her hands gently, raised his eyes to hers and smiled the smile of 'thanks for being you'.

Ernst and Robin analysed the reports coming in from Asslomov and his troops. They could see his troops were moving closer and closer in, the precision of their advance upon both Androv's and

Yute's troops was engaging to follow, but Robin knew Ernst was worried. Up until now, no clues had come in as to the whereabouts of his three special 'subjects', Yute, Lanov and Mogatin. Ernst wanted those three men in particular, then he would worry less about European security. Ernst's own plight did not distract him from worrying about Robin's terrible problems to come. Facts which Robin was also well aware of; even after the action taking place all around them, Robin would have a whole army – the whole of Eurocorps – to investigate and eradicate the infiltration of the personnel duped by the promise of riches or more likely the weight of fear. Ernst allowed himself moments to think of his protégé, Mayer, stuck somewhere in the Kremlin consoling and protecting Rudi – a part of the drama where he felt at least she would be safe.

Yute spiralled down the railway crane's jib, arriving safely at ground level, stopping for a few moments to listen for his enemy and allow his eyes to acclimatise in the deep shadows all around him. Stealthily, he moved off, with his mind focused on Gregori Alexei Androv.

Lanov's survey of the rail yard area told him that a helicopter would be difficult to land in the yard itself but he felt certain that somewhere in this vast area, there had to be a heli-pad. His experience told him it must be on the roof of the main administrative building, that was why he was up in the air above the killing game happening below him. Where is this bloody heli-pad? I want to get to ground level and enjoy myself! That's got to be it – on that big flat roof, the tall flat wall towering at the back of the large flat area stopped him from seeing the small helicopter in its dark shadow towering above it from further away.

Joc and Joe felt the presence of someone, but who? They silently observed the helicopter forty yards across the rooftop spreading out slightly below them. Both of them knew instinctively that now was the time to be most vigilant, the seconds before the enemy came into view.

Lanov opened his radio. 'Mogatin! Helicopter on the roof of the admin building, below the high flat wall. Will cover... no activity at the moment.' The snarl on Mogatin's face as he received the message showed his anger, but more than that, his desire for revenge. His whispered words to Yute were short and sweet. 'You're dead! Your talk drew us along with your ideas, you lost control but blindly led us all on. You betrayed us! You will die!'

Androv's troops were losing the battle against Yute's mercenaries. Their silent killing skills had left dozens dead since the fight had begun, when he had tried to bring in more troops. It was then that Androv found he had been surrounded by Asslomov's troops and he knew he had to escape. Lifting his radio to his mouth, he called, 'Parentov! We are losing, save yourself... I am!'

Parentov's face became ghostly white. He had received Androv's message but still the colour had not returned to his once delicate face. 'Androv mustn't lose, he mustn't lose!' The desperate mumble seemed to hang on his lips as he sat stunned, realising he had lost everything.

Joc was the first to see the movement behind the helicopter. He touched Joe's shoulder and pointed – they were watching the single figure scouting the area. They both admired the skill of the man, but it would take a while to find out which side he was on.

Back at the command post, Ernst and Robin knew Asslomov's troops were tightening their grip around the conflicting troops within their grasp. It would soon be their turn to become active and stop the rot from spreading from the rail yards into Moscow and beyond.

'Yes, Comrade Polenkovich, your train has the green light to exit the yards at speed. You will be clear to the German border where, as you arranged, your own personnel will take charge.' Rudi's voice had just the lightest touch of fear in it, and there was a clamminess to his hand on the telephone receiver, but he felt that he had done reasonably well. Mayer was standing behind his chair and pulled his head to her breasts and tousled his hair.

Yute said, 'Thank you,' and promised rewards to follow, but Rudi was now at least content that Mayer would be in his life forever. A noise in a faraway corner of the Kremlin brought a tightness to their bodies. They listened intently. There it was again. Instinctively, Mayer left Rudi and crept back to the dark position between the filing cabinet and the open door. She stood still, her lithe body ready to pounce to protect her love. The noise came again, closer this time. Rudi's hands were laid palm-down on the desk, his face locked straight ahead to watch for any movement in the corridor stretching out before him. Another noise and a moment later, the index finger on Rudi's hand rose up. Mayer's attentive eyes saw the prearranged signal immediately. The next time the finger was raised would be just as the intruder was about to enter the room. The wait seemed interminable but now the finger moved as Parentov charged through the door. Rudi had not seen the gun in Parentov's hand so the prearranged signal for an armed assailant had not been given and now it was too late as Mayer's view was blocked by the body just about to stop at the desk.

Parentov shrieked out at Rudi, 'You have not heeded your masters, you pitiful servant of the state... You who are about to die for the stupidity you have shown in helping the wrong side! The "brown envelope" messages would have been your saviour, but because of a little beating around the head and a few threats, you decided to be disloyal and for that you must die!'

The words had just left his mouth when Mayer's karate chop cut him down to the floor. The binding and gagging took just a few minutes and then the eerie silence returned to the dark corridors as Rudi and Mayer waited to be released along with their prisoner.

Yute was circling wide as quickly as he possibly could. His intention was to ignore the battle going on between his men and Androv's, to get in behind Androv himself, and kill him. Yute wanted the death to be long and painful. He could see the suffering he would like to inflict in his mind, but in the cold reality of battle, he knew that whatever opportunity came along, he would take it. The command of the train was all that mattered to him. Standing still for a moment, getting his body and mind into a state of calm, his senses had told him Androv was nearby. His eyes pierced deep into every shadow. There... that must be him... steady now, Yute, you must make certain... use your skill, follow and observe... follow and kill.

Androv showed no signs of caution, his only interest was to push his men forward to take control of the train. Yute was aware that the more of his men whom he identified as dead, the more Androv was becoming haphazard in his self-preservation. Androv knew he was losing and Yute knew that within minutes he would have killed the man who was trying to steal his plan and make a success in the Council's eyes. It was his success, his begging and pleading, his planning, his hope of a true comfort from his efforts and a 'loyalty bonus' in his old age. Respect would be nice, but not necessary. He knew, with the magnitude of the operation and the opening of a continuous market in the West, that he would not need to have respect. His power would be so great, his every wish would be fulfilled without question. He must find Mogatin and Lanov and organise the movement of the train out across Europe. Yute knew in his mind that Androv was on his way to the helicopter. He knew Lanov and Mogatin would also be there – he must get there to stop Lanov and Mogatin from killing Androv. That pleasure would be his and his alone.

Ernst was beginning to worry about everyone. He could not see Joc and Joe who were stuck up on a roof, according to their last report. Manuel Vargas had decided, as he put it, to make things personal after what they had done to his beautiful Maria. Ernst had asked him to stay in the command post but Manuel's insistence that he could be of use surveying and reporting back on the action, could be nothing but good for the capture of the villains. Ernst had reluctantly allowed him to go, but had heard nothing from him. Mayer, Rudi and now Dimitri, stuck in the bowels of the Kremlin, must be got out without turning the whole affair into a red-alert situation. Rudi, Dimitri and the new prisoner had passes, but not Mayer. He must speak to Asslomov about Mayer's release.

The phone rang its persistent, purring ring – it was snatched from its cradle by Robin.

'Cadwallader!' he answered.

'Donaldson, sir. The whole bunch of us are encircled by the Asslomov chappie!' The dour Scottish voice sounded light and humorous to Robin's ears but he knew there was never a more efficient investigator in his command and waited for the few moments it would take to start reporting again.

'All around us, sir, but he's been tumbled now Polenkovich has become aware of the full situation and is chasing after this Androv fellow. When they meet up there will be one hell of a set-to, I'm sure.'

'Thanks, Sergeant,' Robin cut in. 'Where are they heading?'

'I'd say there's only one way out, and that's to sprout wings, sir!'

'Keep them under surveillance, Sergeant. Close your men in around those two. Don't lose them!'

'We'll do our best, sir!' Donaldson said chirpily, then the phone went dead.

Robin crossed over to Ernst and relayed what Donaldson had said. Ernst thanked Robin and said, 'The two of them must be making for the helicopter and Lanov's already there!'

'What's worrying you, Ernst? Joc and Joe are there as well!'

'Where's the pilot? Do both of them – Yute and Androv, I mean – both fly helicopters? We should have found out, Robin. We ought to see what can be found out about that from your military source. It may be important!'

'I'll get on it right away, Ernst. Don't worry, we won't lose them. You've kept abreast of everything so far!'

'Except for whether there is a pilot or not?'

'I'm on it now, Ernst. I'll contact Joc and Joe, then Asslomov.'

Joc was the first one to see the movement off to his right. Silently, he drew Joe's attention to it. They studied the new arrival as he worked his way along the lower of the two roof lines, using the shadows to his advantage. Joe had been scanning behind the new arrival and had discovered a second man. Joe had pointed out his find and now they were following every move, waiting for a little extra light to penetrate the shadows so they could get a definite identification. The night-vision goggles were held steady up to their eyes, knowing the fraction of extra light would come.

Androv's pace quickened instinctively as he felt Yute's presence closing in behind him. He needed more time. Where was that stupid pilot? He should be there starting the engine ready for his escape. 'The bloody fool's asleep, I suppose!' The words were barely out of his mouth when he tripped and fell onto a body. Although stunned by his fall, he did not make a sound; turning to try and lift his body up on his arms, his hand became clammy and warm. With his dry hand, he searched his pocket for his pencil torch. Swiftly turning the torch on the pool of blood, which had spread out from the pilot's throat, gave it a wet, fluorescent look. Examining the pilot's face, he confirmed his identity by his badges, but what was that stretched over his chest? Androv's mind was racing – what flag was that? His mind raced through all the flags he had seen in his life. Why was it taking him so long to identify this one? It was obviously left by the killer for a reason. What nationality was it?

Manuel Vargas stared down from his rooftop position, his face relaxed with a little smile at the ends of his lips. He whispered to himself, 'Vengeance for you, my darling Maria Tias, Captain of Portuguese Police!' With a moist tear in his eye, he lifted his head to the heavens and blew a kiss.

Robin studied all of the reports coming in to him from his men and the whole group. He knew there was no way now that they were going to lose the fight. Even Ernst was beginning to relax a little more, his face showing the grin of a Cheshire cat all of the time, but something was worrying Robin. He could not work out what, but he had a niggling worry in his mind which would not seem to reveal itself.

The speed of Yute's attack on Androv was quick. One shot from out of the darkness into the centre of the forehead. Yute wanted more time to torment his victim, but the speed of the events happening all around told him to get out and save himself. Live to fight another day. Androv is out of the way, I will denounce him before the Council – my plan was good... they will accept Androv's greed was the cause of the chaos that he, the planner of the biggest heist the world, had to endure. Wasn't my motive just to get a few more crumbs from the table to make my life more comfortable? To open a system for moving drugs, germ warfare technology, nuclear weapons and arms throughout the world? The vermin like Androv did not love Russia, they believed in private enterprise but at the expense of the state!

Yute faded away to regain his equilibrium before he came back to take control of his train.

Joc and Joe witnessed all of the events which had taken place and Joc was on the handset reporting to Ernst when Joe pointed out Mogatin working his way through the shadows to join Lanov.

Parentov sat tied up and silenced by the tape across his mouth. With his eyes and his nasal gruntings he was pleading to have the tape removed. The pleading had been going on ever since he had regained consciousness but neither Rudi nor Mayer wanted to listen to the whinings of a criminal in their charge. Dimitri, on the other hand, thought it could be interesting to hear the wild promises of a privateer! Tearing the tape away without any finesse whatsoever, he watched as the tears came into Parentov's eyes.

'Set me free now and my bank will give you a million roubles... you can come with me and collect the money... I don't deserve to be begging for your help but I am, in the interests of Mother Russia. If I do not get to my offices, the whole monetary transaction will break down. I am the only one with the key and the plan to all the moves in the chain of events which must be synchronised to make Mother Russia rich. This is what we have all been working for, comrade, a rich and acceptably stable country, enabling it to play on the world stage!'

The words were barely out of his mouth when the tape was angrily stretched back over his mouth. Dimitri said with all the disgust he could muster, 'You double-dealing vermin, shut up!' Dimitri's first blow struck Parentov on the jaw and, immediately,

Mayer jumped forward to prevent any more blows striking her prisoner.

Both Joc and Joe had witnessed the suddenness of Yute's attack on Androv. They had both only marginally identified the man before Yute struck. Within the second or two it took them to recover from what they had witnessed through their night-vision goggles, Yute had disappeared.

After taking Androv out of the game, Yute needed time to think. Escape was uppermost in his mind. The helicopter was the obvious choice, but the military commander, or whoever he was, had won the ground battle and he would not leave a hole in the sky for a helicopter to get through. He could fly the damn thing, it would be no problem, but his ground skills were better. I can elude them… It was an automatic reaction which took over his body. Yute's hand felt across the flat dashboard of the helicopter but could not feel the starter motor key in its usual position. Turning to the stiffening body of the pilot, his hands raced through the pilot's pockets. Finding the key, he rose up to be confronted by Lanov who stood silently, knife in hand, ready for the attack. Yute pulled himself up to his full height, his hands stretching behind his neck, a fleeting moment away from the handle of the throwing knife concealed in his collar. Mogatin's voice hissed through the night.

'Don't even think of trying it… you're covered from behind. Let's talk!'

The chill of death went through Yute's body at Mogatin's words, for he knew he had failed them both and the helicopter key in his hands was all the evidence they needed to prove he was ready to desert them.

'Yes, let's talk.'

Joc had phoned in his report about the death of Androv. Ernst and Robin were both happy with the news, but when Joc came back with the news that Mogatin and Lanov were in a stand-off situation with Yute, a worry crossed Ernst's already furrowed brow.

'Joc...' The word sounded urgent but also a little pleading. 'Can you save Yute?'

'It would be difficult without sniper rifles, why?'

'Yute will have all the answers as to why... why we are here... why he has caused so much death and misery, why he is failing and who caused the failure!'

'It will be difficult, Ernst, but we are on our way. We'll be in touch.'

Mayer was nursing Rudi's head against her breasts; the pain in his head was getting worse. He really needed an X-ray – he ought to be lying down in a snow-white bed in a clean hospital resting and receiving care, not sitting like a prisoner here in this cold draughty office, held there by his own courage.

'My love, it can't be much longer before they come and take us out through the security. Hold on, my love,' she whispered in his ear.

Asslomov entered the command centre, his happiness apparent from the wide grin across his face. Approaching Ernst and Robin, he punched his clenched right fist into his open left hand.

'We've got them! They are all boxed in. Those who are not dead are most certainly captured. A final sweep is being undertaken by my troops right now – they will all be accounted for in a few minutes. I think a well-done for all of us, don't you agree?'

Ernst was embarrassed at all the *joie de vivre* exuding from Asslomov when he still had a crucial situation to resolve. The last thing he wanted was Asslomov's exuberant troops rushing around noisily over rooftops where the possible ending to his and Robin's story was unfolding. Robin understood Ernst's plight: he couldn't be impolite to Asslomov, after all he had done, but there are things which still had to be revealed by Yute Polenkovich.

'May I offer you a coffee, sir?' Robin asked.

'What? Yes, of course. That is kind of you. One sugar, please, fairly strong.' As both Robin and Asslomov walked away together, Robin couldn't help noticing the furtive glances over his shoulder from Ernst. Robin promised to inform the ebullient soldier beside him of Ernst's true dilemma of trying to keep the last three players not in captivity, alive.

Dimitri was aware of Mayer's predicament of not being able to leave the Kremlin without the correct passes plus the condition of Rudi to contend with. Mayer obviously didn't want to be left, but eventually Dimitri won his argument on the grounds that Rudi needed help as quickly as possible. Touching Mayer's hand gently as he left, he whispered, 'Look after him, Mayer, he loves you. I'll get Ernst and his Russians here soon!' Dimitri's gentle squeeze of her hand told Mayer he would not fail them.

Joc and Joe were approaching Mogatin and Lanov's position from each side. Joc had taken the longest curve of the approach circle and they had both agreed they should position themselves so that Mogatin and Lanov would be between them. They hoped each of their field skills would get them close enough to eavesdrop on any conversation they may be having on the total surprise when they came out with that corny line, 'Get your hands up – you're under arrest!'

Even though he had stalked a further distance than Joe, Joc had managed to get into a position where he could almost hear Mogatin and Lanov breathing. Through his night-glasses he could see that Joc was almost in position and would nod his head as arranged, so Joc kept his glasses locked on to Joe and waited. Mogatin and Lanov were arguing, it was obvious to Joc. Lanov, the shorter of the two men, kept prodding Mogatin in the chest, much to Mogatin's annoyance. Mogatin was trying to play the appeaser, Lanov continued with his anger and would not let go, it seemed, on any point Lanov made. Eventually, Lanov turned away from Mogatin who pleadingly walked up behind Lanov. The word 'comrade' kept coming up in the conversation and 'friend'. Suddenly Lanov turned, the silenced hand-gun was ripped from inside his jacket and the gun exploded in Lanov's hand, propelling its lethal discharge into Mogatin's body. Joc knew instantly that Lanov must be stopped. His gunsight was following Lanov's every twitch as he bent down remorsefully to help his partner and friend of many years. Joc squeezed the trigger and the world went dark for Lanov.

Joe, who had witnessed Joc's action, covered the ground between him and the fallen men like lightning, kicking Lanov's fallen gun away out of reach, before he searched Mogatin. Turning Mogatin's twisted body onto its back to enable him to check the coat for weapons, Joe was surprised to realise Mogatin was still hanging on to life.

On receiving the news of Joc and Joe's escapade, Ernst was anxious to try and get Mogatin into hospital for treatment and then questioning. Ernst was getting frustrated with himself. His mind was active and anticipating the forward moves very well for bringing about the success of the operation, but he couldn't control his own destiny without the autonomy that his position as Hamburg's Chief of Police allowed him.

'Robin, for goodness' sake, can I order my men to help Joc and Joe to bring out Mogatin's body for medical attention? He's stuck on a roof in the middle of Asslomov's circle and I have no authority to go in myself nor order anyone to bring Mogatin out – it's bloody infuriating!'

Knowing the autonomy and automatic freedom Ernst would have in Hamburg was just not possible here, especially dealing with foreign army command and civilian administrations, Robin felt that a stern answer was needed.

'Ernst, Asslomov has worked bloody miracles – you're civilian police, yet alone my own men have fulfilled every task efficiently and on time, within record time. I will ask Asslomov how he can help!'

Ernst was stung by the rebuke and knew within himself Robin was right in every respect and replied, 'You're right, Robin. I apologise to everyone. Please see what you can do. I feel the way the Russians are killing themselves off and with Joc's contribution too, we will have no one to talk to, to try and piece the whole story together! Where has bloody Yute Polenkovich gone?'

Robin knew the reasons why, but replied a little sharply, 'We understand, Ernst, we really do!'

'Sorry, Robin, do what you can; Joc and Joe were the last to see Polenkovich.' The information now pouring into the command post left no more time to dwell on the little *contretemps* which had just occurred. The pace was driving them all on to a successful climax.

Manuel Vargas sat high above the helicopter. Killing the pilot at such close range had exhilarated him at the time, but now feeling rather melancholy after the event, he gazed down upon the scene with Lanov, Mogatin and Yute. He saw Yute move away from his colleagues into the deep shadow of the wall. He stood there waiting for his colleagues to join him, or so it looked. When Lanov's bullet hit Mogatin, Vargas's body twitched. Why did Lanov kill his closest friend? was the first thought through his mind. Then there was a second shot and Lanov fell like a log. He turned to look at Yute's position quickly – he seemed to be frozen to the spot. He had not fired, so who had?

Now Yute moved quickly through the shadows. He was trying to escape! Manuel knew his Maria deserved the death of the two men in the instant Yute moved. Manuel would wait for his prey to come to him. He clutched his silver gun and moved stealthily forward and stopped, covering the assessed line of Yute's retreat. The wait was short as Yute lifted himself over the edge of the wall. Vargas ran forward with his gun repeatedly firing into the unprotected body of Yute Polenkovich, Marshall of the Russian Army. Yute fell backward down to the helicopter site without a sound.

Vargas peered down into the darkness at the twisted body which lay below him. A tear rolled down his cheek as he remembered his beautiful Maria.

Dimitri's persistence at Russian Police HQ eventually got him escorted to Ernst's command post. Ernst welcomed him warmly, as he had heard his name mentioned often by Mayer and knew he was Rudi's best friend. 'You say Mayer managed to get into the Kremlin and has arrested Parentov?'

'That's right. She's very worried that she won't be able to get out again without identity papers, possibly until tomorrow morning when the cleaners arrive again and I can borrow one of their identity papers like I did to get her in. She won't leave without Rudi and he needs medical treatment, I think, plus of course there's the prisoner.'

Ernst looked a little forlorn, but he knew he would have to approach Robin and his 'military' again. 'Robin, can I see you for a few moments?'

Without any bad feeling, Robin answered, 'Of course, Ernst,' and strode over to discuss whatever points or action the unknown man sitting with Ernst might require.

'Robin, this is Dimitri Kernlikov, Rudi's friend and colleague at the Kremlin.'

'Nice to meet you. My name is Robin Cadwallader, Eurocorps. How can I help?' The last part of the sentence was addressed to both of them.

Ernst took the initiative and told the whole story. Robin whistled through his teeth again and said to Ernst, 'It's another job for Asslomov, I think, Ernst!'

'You're right, of course, Robin, there is no alternative. I just hope Asslomov is still in a good mood!'

The low drone of the helicopter was heard by Joc and Joe at the same moment. Their eyes searched the sky for its lights. 'There it is, Joc!' Joe said, pointing. 'It's a small one.'

'We'll go together, Joc, even if I have to sit on your lap!'

'Don't be silly, it won't lift all of the weight, Joe. You go, I'll follow on ASAP. Ernst wants this guy quick.'

'Listen!' Joe said. 'I hear another one – he's flying on the tail without lights! It doesn't make sense, Joc. Why? Plus it's bloody dangerous!'

'The two pilots must be working as a team – they're damn good!' said Joe. He continued after he observed the now clearly visible helicopters. 'The one with lights is coming in first... he knows he must get Mogatin out, so he's going to come in, lift off and light the second chopper down. He's worked it out that the cargo is more important!'

'You go in the first one, Joc, with Mogatin. As soon as you see the second land, I'll jump aboard and flashlight you when I'm on board. You clear away and I'll spot your tail wherever you're going.'

'Okay, I can't argue with you any more, I'll go first,' said Joc.

As they stood silently with Mogatin supported between them, waiting to run as quickly as possible to the helicopter on landing, Joe looked up at the helicopter circling above and saw the reason for there being no lights. They had been shot out and there was a streak of hydraulic fluid being drawn towards the tail of the fuselage. Joc did not see the problem Joe had seen. Swiftly, they manhandled Mogatin in, Joc quickly followed and the chopper lifted sweetly away.

The unlit chopper, with great skill, seemed to just float down the beam of the now stationary chopper suspended above it. Joc saw Joe throw himself into the body of the chopper, which lifted immediately and floated in slow motion out to starboard from the beam. It was now floating over the chasm between the buildings. Joc whispered to himself, 'Come on, lift or land!' Horror raced across his face as he saw the chopper lurch and then drop like a stone, turning into a fireball as it struck the ground five floors below.

★

Joc's report to Ernst and Robin was concise in every detail and allowed only one passage about his and Joe's personal friendship. 'He was a great guy with everything to live for.'

Ernst stared at the paper for a minute, then across the desk to Joc. Words were not said, but each knew the torment their hearts were feeling and that it would be a very long time before the mind would rest and stop asking why.

Asslomov's troops had finished the mopping up operation around the train area and the noose had finally been tightened. He sat happy but tired behind his makeshift desk in his mobile command post. He really wanted to get out of the situation for which he had felt, as a stalwart defender of the Russian peoples' rights, the deployment of his troops was justified. But now, the request from Robin that he should rescue three people from the Kremlin basement, disturbed him. To take armed troops into his own seat of government didn't sit too well... he was not going to start a revolution, he couldn't! He could work towards a better understanding between the now elected representatives of the people, but to take armed troops into the Kremlin was not the way, but how? It must be done! Rudi, a Russian national, must be protected from the corruption which has grown up all around him. How could a German policewoman be explained? Plus Parentov! His mind was racing, but one thing was sure, no armed troops of his would enter the Kremlin.

Snatching the phone from its cradle, he dialled his numbers and waited.

'Primrose. We must meet!' The words were terse and although 'Primrose' was not an easy word to say, as his codename it seemed too pretty, but he smiled when he remembered the person's codename he was speaking to... Violet!

Violet's reply was, 'Where and when?'

'Here and now!'

Knowing these phone calls were never made lightly, Violet replied, 'Four hours, where?'

'Moscow military airport – bring your own staff car.'

'What the bloody hell is going—'

'We are going to have some fun!' No sooner had he said the words than Asslomov hung up.

The British General smiled, remembering how he and his old consort from all those years ago, when they were staff officers, used to meet secretly without their politicos knowing in all sorts of places – smuggling cigarettes, cognac and the like, but a staff car – wasn't that a bit much?

Ernst talked to Mogatin. His words had been going on and on for what seemed like an age to those around the bed, watching the large man's shallow breathing and the non-responsive, unconscious face. Still Ernst spoke quietly, telling him all he knew about this episode of Mogatin's, Lanov's and Polenkovich's and how he had been looking for them, piecing all of the clues together. How a little observation of one of the victims had started the ball rolling for him after he had noticed the spectacular ring on

Yute's hand when he and his partner had been holidaying in Portugal. How, since then, dozens of people had become involved from many nations throughout the world. The occasional question had been asked during Ernst's discourse: was this a purely private enterprise? Was Yute Polenkovich the controller? Who was Androv? What parts were all the people held and blackmailed going to play in the long term? Why Portugal? Why military involvement? The questions went into Mogatin's head. The soft, intelligent-sounding voice droning on gave Mogatin's whole body peace.

The peace of his youth before they discovered him, before they exploited his particular talents, before they turned him into a mental robot working on command after command. They robbed him of the life he wanted; a wife to love, children to cherish and protect. They had forced him to abandon his beloved Natasha because to have got married at the time would have inconvenienced their plans, so, as he had chosen to further his career and postpone the wedding, Natasha, beautiful Natasha, had left him. Left him with a broken heart... which still hurt him and the thought of it made his body ache all over. *This man talking to me seems a nice man, straightforward. All of these questions he has been asking... I can't answer them truthfully. I wish I could. Come on, nice man, whoever you are, ask me a question I can answer.* The comfortable warmth engulfing Mogatin's body had started growing in his feet, then his legs seemed to grow numb. The warmth caressing his upper body was soothing away all his old torments with himself. *Ask me a question now... one that I can answer!*

Ernst knew time was running out for this man lying in the bed in front of him. 'Who was in control of this operation?'

Ernst's question was answered in three words. 'Council of Organisatiya.' Mogatin's face relaxed as he spoke his last words and a peace came upon him.

Ernst was quick to his feet. 'We at least know it was the Russian Mafia... will we ever know how the puzzle will totally fit together or will there always be a piece missing?' Ernst felt sad for Mogatin, stretched out in the bed, and gently pulled the sheet up to cover the face. 'Thank you, my friend. We have to get to Parentov now; maybe he's further up the chain than you are!'

Chapter Thirty-Seven

Asslomov was returning to his mobile command post having completed a survey of what his men had achieved. He was proud of them and realised his idea of a rapid response team, all those years ago, was the right way forward. The only thing was, the last two episodes performed by his team had been Russians fighting Russians which was not what he had designed this talented force for. He had wanted to know for a very long time now whether the military was polluted at command level... and, with the proof that he and his men now had of this corruption and how they handled the situation, Asslomov stood proud and assured.

Asslomov's ADC stood up as he entered and handed him a written message. It read:

> Mogatin dead. Believe his last words – 'Council of Organisatiya' to be confirmation of Mafia involvement. Need to speak to Parentov who could be the key to knowing if military command involved.

Four lines further down the page there was another message:

> Violet arriving early. Have brought my own carriage to sit under Moscow skies.

Asslomov smiled at the last quip and then he asked of his ADO whether his car was ready with all of his insignia in place.

The ADC replied positively, 'Yes, sir!'

'Well, let's go. We have fifteen minutes to get to the airport and before our guests arrive, we have things to do!'

Robin sat in his temporary office at the rail yard, knowing that all the possible escape routes had been covered by Asslomov and all of the other nations involved, but nothing was coming in from any of the tormented people who had either been beaten or blackmailed into submission to work on command for a boss they had never met nor would ever meet. Why hadn't his field men phoned or faxed? He must check the incoming files for messages which might have been missed, remembering his briefing speech and the emphasis he had placed on not letting these slaves to a system get away from the view of his investigators. The file he was checking on showed no signs of any report.

'Why?' Robin asked himself, then quickly he dialled Gilbert Torneau. 'Gilbert,' the word sounded anxious as he continued, 'has there been no movement on any of our citizens?'

'No, Robin, all are at home. The Tomlevskis haven't moved for two days. Do you want me to run through the list we have under surveillance?'

'It won't be necessary, Gilbert, thank you for all your help. It couldn't have been an easy ride for you with Paris getting involved. Let's hope we can do it again if we get some Easterners running amok!'

The clatter outside the office was loud and a lot of blaspheming was blurted out. It was unlike Ernst to use such words, so Robin rushed out to see what his dear friend had done to himself.

'How did you get down there, Ernst?' Robin stared down at Ernst who was kneeling on one knee and rubbing the other vigorously.

Making a joke of his mishap he answered, 'Getting old! My mind still works quicker than the rest of my body but my feet can't seem to keep up!'

'What were you rushing for, Ernst? We seem to be getting everything under control.'

'That's true, Robin, but Mayer, Rudi, with his potentially fractured skull, and this banker Parentov are all in the Kremlin. Mayer can't get out through security, Rudi's too badly hurt to think of an escape plan and Parentov thinks the longer he stays there the safer it is for him!'

Ernst became more serious with a last rub of his shin and a few twists and stamps of the leg to get the circulation going. 'Have you been in touch with your Commanding General, Robin?'

'No, Ernst, why?'

'Some Russians were predicting that Asslomov and your General are going to break into the Kremlin! Christ! It will cause an international incident! We had better get over there and see what we can find out!'

'I'm game, Ernst. I'd like to know what they are going to pull off!'

'Let's go then, Robin. It's military – at least you've got a chance to mingle!'

'Could be, Ernst, but I would think that Asslomov and our Corps General will have a plan worked out by now.'

The screeching siren sped through the gates of the Kremlin. The armed guard, just getting out in front of the cavalcade of cars speeding towards him, raised his automatic weapon to fire point-blank into the first oncoming car. The focus of his weapon sight, before being lined up accurately on the driver, had passed over the fixed rank flag of the occupant of the car and the much publicised one (within the officer class for recruits) of the rapid response team. 'No firing!' he screamed as he jumped clear.

'That officer deserved a medal!' said Asslomov. 'Go faster, main entrance!' The confusion that was expected at the main arch was complete when two columns of motorcycle escorts passed through, presumably escorting a General's insignia on a British staff car, two cars with civilians in, followed by more motorcycles. Screaming to a halt at the main doorway, all of the cars emptied – the occupants raced up the steps, Asslomov taking the lead as he entered the sweeping hallway. He must keep the pace up. 'You there, Captain! Are you the duty officer?' There was a little hesitancy and the captain was not spontaneous enough. 'You are now! Do as this young man instructs you. Jump to it, man, this is a matter of life and death!'

Dimitri was pushed forward. Asslomov shouted out, 'Comrade Kernlikov, lead this man quickly to where your friends are!' In a gentler voice he said, 'You can make him run if you like!' The twinkle in Asslomov's eyes was not missed on Dimitri as he started to run.

In English now, Asslomov said to his friend, 'This is easier than Berlin, don't you think?'

'You're a bloody mad Russian! I think if we had had the rank in those days the battle would have been over in an hour, straight through to Hitler's bunker, bluffed the black uniforms, saying old Adolf had invited us to tea as he had something to discuss with us, like… "How do I get out of this mess?"'

Both men laughed at their own stupidity and kept running. They were obviously in the basement but every corridor looked the same. The compass in Asslomov's hand read due east, but as he quipped when he closed the compass, 'Due east could be anywhere!' The humour was not lost on either of them, but the shortness of breath prevented their laughter.

Parentov was the first to hear the sounds of soldiers' running feet. In his mind, he knew they were coming for him. Androv had turned the rail yard battle into success, now he has found me. Dear Gregori Alexei Androv, I knew you would not let me down, the excitement in his mind causing him to shout out, 'You stupid people, can't you hear those soldiers coming for me, because I'm valuable to the Organisatiya's world finance structure? They, through me, will be able to accumulate vast cash reserves throughout the world. They will rebuild arms factories, sell our biological war technology to whoever wants it. Uranium, plutonium will be sold by us and it will advance the countries with nuclear weapons to buy raw materials off the shelf so they haven't got to invest in manufacturing – they will jump years ahead!'

The excitement in Parentov's voice was turning almost into hysteria when a look of sheer disbelief ran across Mayer's face. Then a beautiful smile brightened her face, lighting up the whole room. She pulled Rudi's head to her breasts so tightly, saying, 'My darling! Everything will be all right now… just a little longer!'

Parentov saw the guns pointed at him and knew this would be the end for him. Soon, someone would say, 'Guilty. You will serve a minimum of fifty years for crimes against the new constitution of democratic Russia.'

The raiding party, plus Rudi, Mayer and Parentov, left the Kremlin corridors as quickly as they had arrived in them, despite carrying Rudi out on a stretcher. At the main hall, the duty officer peeled off from the main column as they broke through to the steps. Asslomov saluted the duty officer – a bit more play-acting with a promise to the poor man that he would be highly commended for the assistance he had extended to his mobile force. As they drove through the archway they had turned out the guard and a traffic policeman held up the traffic for them as they entered Red Square. The chase was on now to get every single foreigner out of Russia – Asslomov and the General concurred that if there was no one around when the enquiry began on the break in (and out) of the Kremlin, without any of Ernst and Robin's entourage, he would have less to answer for.

Robin and Ernst recognised Asslomov and the General plus Mayer in one of the cars speeding through the gate of the Kremlin.

'Robin.' The quiet voice calling his name was too soft for Robin to recognise.

'Speaking,' he replied.

'It's me. André.'

'Sir!' André Roche, his great friend and without his support no one on this historic journey would have ever achieved the success which everyone and especially himself had had in stopping the invasion of the criminal classes from the East into larger arenas in the West.

Robin caught his thoughts and called them to a halt. 'Thank you, sir.' Robin continued, 'I think everyone here feels we have had a successful day!'

'I don't doubt you have, Robin, but now we have no more than thirty minutes to get all of your team out of Russia, including Rudi, Joc, Joe, Vargas and Torneau – everyone. You must get to the military airbase outside Moscow. Transports will be there. You're going direct to Hamburg.'

'Where are you, sir?'

'At the airbase. It's imperative everyone gets here and catches the flight. Asslomov has stuck his neck out and made out clearance orders for everyone. Pick them up at the gate.'

'Look forward to seeing you, sir.'

'And you, Robin. Over and out!'

Mayer was all smiles now. They were out of the hateful Kremlin and racing to freedom, both of them together, Rudi and she. The kisses gently touching his forehead from her moist, soft lips kept the pain away as the car drove over the cobbled streets of Moscow. Mayer's whispering in his ear every few minutes made him certain he was the luckiest man in the world and his love for her hurt more than his wound.

Joc stood at the exit of the rail yards looking at his watch. The time they had allowed themselves had almost run out. The night watchman had been watching them and was just about to approach, when the screeching wheels of a military lorry turning onto the exit road at speed stopped the watchman's approach and forced him to jump clear as the driver hit the horn in a prolonged blast. Manuel Vargas recognised Joc. Shouting to make himself heard, one word, 'Halt!' the truck seemed to put its bonnet into the ground, the rear wheels rising from the road a little and settled back with a violent metallic bump.

'Joc… you want a lift?' Manuel asked unhurriedly in his slow, Mediterranean bedroom voice.

'Please, Manuel,' he replied as he climbed into the cab.

'We had a good night, my friends! It is a shame we can't stay here longer to do some real police work. What do you think?'

'Manuel, I think you ought to tell your driver to get moving to the airport!'

'Of course. You Americans, you must always keep moving!' Turning to his driver, he said, 'Olga, ma chère, Airporte Militaire! Vite, vite, si vous plais!'

As Olga turned to acknowledge Manuel's instructions, Joc saw a beautiful woman, almost an exact replica of Maria. Manuel smiled his warm smile at them both. Quietly in English, he whispered, 'It would be nice to stay, gentlemen, but maybe one day she will come to Portugal.' Olga gazed for a moment at Manuel.

André Roche was fidgeting with paperwork attached to his clipboard. Around him were men placed to escort the expected two vehicles. The large, twin-cabin truck speeding round the perimeter road relieved some of his anxiety. The deadline for take-off was closing in and he needed Vargas, Joc.

'Olga, ma chère, stop the truck gently, please!' The words were no sooner out of his mouth, than the large cumbersome truck glided the last few yards and stopped, with the cabin of the truck level with André and his clipboard.

'Thank God you've made it, Manuel!' André was a little self-conscious about using 'Manuel', but in view of what they had all been through together, he felt Christian names were appropriate now.

Manuel surprised André even further when he answered, 'My dear friend André, thank you for your good wishes!' At that moment, Joc's face appeared in the smaller windows of the cab. André quickly gathered his equilibrium.

'Thank God, you too! Let's get on, if you would care to follow me and my driver, we can all leave courtesy of British Military Airways!'

Handing them their clearances and authorities to board, André slid into his car rather sprightly and beckoned them to follow.

The engines were already running when they got to the air-craft. André watched Joc board and be warmly welcomed by the others already aboard, but Vargas seemed to be delayed with his new love Olga. The gentle kiss between them held as their bodies moved closer and closer together.

'Manuel! Please get on board, you're delaying our take-off!'

'André, for a Frenchman, you do not have any respect for love, but I will come although it breaks my heart!' Olga's and Manuel's lips touched briefly one more time before he stepped onto the steps to board the plane. 'Olga, ma chère!' he shouted from the top of the steps and the kiss he blew towards her was only for her.

Ernst, Robin, André along with Joc, Gilbert and Manuel had all started writing up their reports which would go into the files of their respective administrative agencies. Knowing that should another plan be thought up by any organisation against this newly formed 'United Europe', there was some definite bonding which was going to build in strength and fight to protect the innocent from exploitation. This time they had been lucky, but the lessons they had learned would make them all vigilant for the sake of the generations to follow.

All the countries involved had decided there would be no press conferences but just a short review of the case, without mentioning the colossal amount of money involved nor the potential dangers had the germ-warfare technology and nuclear weapons been tampered with in their countries. The lunatic, fanatical element of any kind could have caused untold and possible reversible damage for many years to come. Ernst knew that the Mayers of this world, along with the Rudis, would have to fight the good fight but at least they now have a scenario which might help for future reference instead of making it up as they went along. It will be put down on disk and reviewed as standard procedure and its multi-faceted attack on the new democracy of Europe should keep everyone prepared for the future.

Mayer stood on the steps of Hamburg's Central Hospital. The sun shone brilliantly down on them. Today was the day that she would take the fit and well Rudi home to her flat. Knowing that today they would become one, they would marry in a private ceremony at the town hall. Ernst and his wife, Joc who was stealing time in Hamburg on the pretence of waiting for some confirmation from Asslomov before finishing his report, Robin, André, Gilbert and Manuel and their partners were invited, along with anyone who had been connected with the operation. Mayer could feel the new-born strength as Rudi put his arm around her waist, the tingle as he moved his fingers across her firm hips, pleased her. She put her hand over his long fingers, gently telling him that she wanted to be held tighter. She whispered lovingly, 'I won't break!'

The days leading up to this moment had been hectic. The worry about Rudi's X-ray when it showed a fractured skull, plus the meeting they both had to attend to get a work and resident's permit which they both felt, without Ernst's endorsement, they would have had even greater difficulty in obtaining. The entry of East Germans, let alone Russians was becoming increasingly difficult, but today they had all of the papers. Thanks to Ernst, thanks to everyone, today would be their day… then together they would work together to save the world!

Joc had been ordered back to their offices but had squeezed in a few extra hours to attend the wedding – although now they were getting anxious, trying to find everyone to say goodbye to was becoming difficult. Joc was finding it very emotional, he was more aware of the enormity of the problem which had just been lived through by the people gathered together at the wedding.

How lucky they were to get such a result, but like Ernst, he knew that now was a dangerous time. If Europe let down its guard for a moment, who knows what could affect them? The Organisatiya had been dealt a hefty blow, but what if the Triads started to make a move… what if they started making moves simultaneously – an organised two-pronged attack? Joc knew Ernst was aware of the possibility, but how long could Europe alone sustain the apparent upper hand of this moment? Joc knew, at that moment, he was going to submit at his debriefing session that if it truly is to be a fight against crime, it must be a fully organised one, with every police force and crime prevention agency worldwide drawn into working together to that end – a position in which the USA must play a leading role, alongside Europe.

The one goodbye which Joc never wanted to say was walking towards him now with two glasses in his hands, his warm, jovial face smiling as he approached. Joc stepped forward to take the glass which Ernst offered and they silently raised their glasses to each other. No 'prost!' or 'cheers!' – their eyes said all the 'thank yous' and showed the respect which had grown between them. The second raise of their glasses was to toast the happiness of Mayer and Rudi, again in silence. Their hands pushed forwards and held tightly, an emotional flooding of their eyes. Neither had any intention of following the stiff upper lip routine; the goodbye was sad. Sadder with the loss of Joe, a memory which would stay with both men forever.

The Eurocorps General entered the festivities with a swagger, followed by hotel staff loaded with packages for the bride and groom. 'Just thought, my dears, that these few bits and pieces might help to make your new life more comfortable!' Rudi and Mayer were stunned into silence by the General's generosity. 'Now, my dears, I have another surprise for you!' As if it had been rehearsed, the doors swung open and a troop of Cossack dancers followed by Asslomov, burst into dance, accompanied by balalaikas and violins. Putting his arms around both Rudi's and Mayer's shoulders, he whispered to them both, 'Sorry about the noise, but I just had to bring him after what he made me do in Moscow... parading like some film star playing the part of a General! Had to get my own back – besides, he likes to dance!' The good-humoured rhetoric, plus the twinkle in the General's eye, caused them both to laugh and their faces lit up the room.

Ernst stepped forward, hand outstretched to the General in welcome. Loud enough for Mayer to hear, he asked, 'Sir, when the General finishes could be the right time for Hamburg Police HQ to spring our little surprise.'

'My dear Ernst! You must, he won't dance for long, he's getting too old now. In the old days it was dance, dance, dance!'

Ernst, Rudi, Mayer and the General watched and enjoyed the antics of Asslomov and the other dancers stamping their feet, clapping their hands and swaying their bodies in time to the music.

Abruptly the music stopped for a moment. The whole room was in suspended animation before it erupted into spontaneous applause, whistles and calls for 'More!... More!...More!'

Marshall Asslomov was saved the embarrassment on continuing his reckless dancing by a loud fanfare of trumpets somewhere outside in the corridors leading to the reception room. Everyone became silent as they waited for the General's surprise to arrive. Manuel Vargas broke through the swing doors, wearing full dress uniform, carrying a black-framed, black-ribboned photograph of Captain Maria Tias. Solemnly, he walked to the happy couple whose wedding was being enjoyed up to this point in the proceedings. He stood before Mayer and Rudi, clearing his throat before speaking.

'Today, you declared your love for each other. I would like you to accept this picture of Captain Maria Tias to remind you to say to each other every day, "I love you"... words I should have said to my beautiful Maria much more often. I declare to both of you, who know the true strong bond of love, that I will say, "I love you, Maria" every day, for the rest of my life and I sincerely hope you will tell each other that you love one another. Maria wanted all the world to be happy… please be in love and be happy for Maria… I beg you!'

The whole room was stunned. Rudi and Mayer stared into Manuel Vargas's sincere face, until a natural reaction occurred, to reach out and gather him tightly to them, their smiling faces showing everyone that theirs was a day for lovers… the sincere in heart.

The Eurocorps General stood watching the crowded room as all the faces glowed with smiles and with tears on their cheeks, including the General.

Chapter Thirty-Eight

Ernst was now back in his Hamburg office as were the many people involved with the recent past attempt of flooding Europe with deceit and corruption. The press had been saying,

> We feel it is necessary to have a unified policing system throughout the world before the villains become too strong for us to contain. We must strike hard and deep now, unless we want to be driven into anarchy as has happened in Columbia and Panama.

Ernst had read the lines in an editorial that morning over breakfast. He agreed with the article but felt it lacking in one important area, the people of each country must want their police to win the battles every time.

Major Roche had called Daniel Tomlevski, with his wife, for an after-hours drink and general chat. The atmosphere was cordial, although they still did not have the results from the military enquiry carried out on Daniel and Nicole and their families' background. Were the sins of the father to be levied on the son?

'Wonderful to see you both again. I thought you ought to have the decision of the committee who have had the task of appraisal on the reports supplied by all of us. Daniel and Nicole looked pleadingly towards André, hoping – no – praying the committee's decision would be in their favour with Daniel being allowed to stay in the army and Nicole could rest easy, knowing that the baby she carried within her would have the assured future they both wished so terribly hard for.

André saw the anxiety rising in their faces and he averted his eyes from theirs down to the file in front of him. Opening the stiff cover quickly, he read, 'We the undersigned, serving as authorised representatives of the Combined Commissioners of Eurocorps...'

André stopped for a moment. 'Daniel, Nicole, there's approximately another twenty lines of formality, but they exonerate you completely and wish you success in everything you do.'

The excitement on their faces shone, turning to a little giggle of relief from the tension of waiting. The kiss they snatched from each other added to Nicole's excitement as she asked, 'André, would you accept the job of being Godfather to our child?'

'It would be a wonderful experience for me, thank you! May I suggest a celebratory drink?'

Robin and Gilbert were finalising the local report on Colonel Keller, a report on a man who had gone against his own country for money – not political belief. Both men were made to feel sick at the discovery the enquiry into his suicide had revealed. The Russians had turned him into working for them through a weakness they had found out about. He was a child molester and headed up a European organisation of pornography. Both Robin and Gilbert could not accept the level of depravity that children of both sexes were put to and vowed they would become ever more vigilant. They both bent over the report they had compiled for the umpteenth time, wherein the words of the Colonel's judgement on his death read:

> Suicide by his own hand through fear of others. A non-political player. Sold his services for money always claiming he had more power within his military life and a greater number of influential friends than he actually had. A 'Walter Mitty' character.

Both Robin and Gilbert signed above their typed names at the bottom of the page.

Ernst knocked on the newly painted door of Klaus and Dieter's home. Since they had made their life together, many changes had taken place within the interior of the old Hamburgian terraced house. The style of Dieter's design for the interior and the skilful hands of Klaus had made a pleasant apartment into a modern love-nest.

Dieter opened the door in response to Ernst's knocking and

was surprised to find Ernst on the doorstep. Normally, he telephoned before his visits to see them. Why has he arrived unannounced? My God, something has happened to Klaus! Those Russians have got to him... hurt him... killed him!

'Chief Inspector, you didn't phone, what is the matter, is Klaus all right?' The whole sentence was delivered as if it were one single word.

'Dieter, Dieter, shuush! It's nothing! I was just passing and thought I would drop in for a cup of your delicious coffee.'

'Come in, come in do. You are always welcome. Klaus is not back from work yet. I expect him any minute, though. Won't you stay for supper?'

'No, thank you. I must get home, my supper is being cooked already.'

'Here's Klaus now!' Ernst had not heard Klaus turn the key in the lock but there he was, standing at the entrance to the kitchen.

'What a nice surprise to see you, Chief Inspector!'

'Sorry to drop in unexpectedly, I was just passing.'

'You are always welcome! Is Dieter doing coffee or would you like something stronger?'

'Coffee, I think – I'm driving. Dieter has already asked me.'

'Good. To what do we owe the pleasure?'

'A little piece of news for you both!'

'Dieter, come over here please, the Inspector wants to tell us something.'

'Just a moment, Klaus. Coffee is just about ready.'

Ernst and Klaus sat down without answering Dieter. They made themselves comfortable in the actual few moments that it took Dieter to arrive with the hot coffee. He passed the coffees out and sat on the arm of Klaus's chair, placing his arm warmly around his partner's shoulders.

'Now,' Dieter said happily, 'tell us your news, Inspector.'

'It's good news for both of you and another thank you from me. Your observations in Lamego proved to be right and since then we have tracked him down, countered a gigantic infiltration into the European economy and your "ringed-hand man" is confirmed dead.'

The news brought tears to both Klaus and Dieter's eyes. Their embrace was spontaneous, their friend Ernst would not mind their kissing. They were now free from the ringed-hand's threat of death, both of them.

Ernst left quietly before their embrace came to an end – back to his office and maybe just sit and reread Parentov's confession one more time before he went home to Inge.

Nikolai Curentov walked down the marble steps leading to the mezzanine hall of the Kremlin. His footsteps were firm and regular as they carried his still agile military body to meet his President. The polished walking stick in his hand was pushed jauntily forward, touching each marble step lightly. His smiling President stood waiting to meet his friend Nikolai.